"I hear you have a warning for the king," he said boldly. "You may speak it to me."

"My orders are to speak only to the king himself," Miranda said. "It is a matter of some delicacy."

"I am Oban, Master of Security. You'll speak it to me, or not at all," he huffed.

Miranda looked at Gin, who flicked his ear in the ghosthound equivalent of a shrug. "I suppose we have wasted enough time," she said. "I am here on behalf of the Spirit Court by order of the Rector Spiritualis, Etmon Banage. Yesterday morning we received a tip that the known fugitive wizard and wanted criminal Eli Monpress has been sighted within your kingdom. It is our belief that he is after an old wizard artifact held in your treasury. I am here to offer my assistance to keep him from stealing it."

There was a long pause, and Miranda got the horrible, sinking feeling that she had missed something important.

"Lady," the Master of Security said, shaking his head, "if you're here to warn the king about Eli, then you're a little late."

Miranda scowled. "You mean he's already stolen the artifact?"

"No." The Master of Security sighed. "He's stolen the king."

By Rachel Aaron

The Legend of Eli Monpress

The Spirit Thief

The Spirit Rebellion

The Spirit Eater

Sprit War

Spirit's End

The Legend of Eli Monpress:
Volumes I, II & III (omnibus edition)

CONTENTS

VOLUME 1

The Spirit Thief

For Travis.

All the really good ideas are his.

CHAPTER 1

In the prison under the castle Allaze, in the dark, moldy cells where the greatest criminals in Mellinor spent the remainder of their lives counting rocks to stave off madness, Eli Monpress was trying to wake up a door.

It was a heavy oak door with an iron frame, created centuries ago by an overzealous carpenter to have, perhaps, more corners than it should. The edges were carefully fitted to lie flush against the stained, stone walls, and the heavy boards were nailed together so tightly that not even the flickering torch light could wedge between them. In all, the effect was so overdone, the construction so inhumanly strong, that the whole black affair had transcended simple confinement and become a monument to the absolute hopelessness of the prisoner's situation. Eli decided to focus on the wood; the iron would have taken forever.

He ran his hands over it, long fingers gently tapping in a way living trees find desperately annoying, but dead wood finds soothing, like a scratch behind the ears. At last, the boards gave a little shudder and said, in a dusty, splintery voice, "What do you want?"

"My dear friend," Eli said, never letting up on his tapping, "the real question here is, what do *you* want?"

"Pardon?" the door rattled, thoroughly confused. It wasn't used to having questions asked of it.

"Well, doesn't it strike you as unfair?" Eli said. "From your grain, anyone can see you were once a great tree. Yet, here you are, locked up through no fault of your own, shut off from the sun by cruel stones with no concern at all for your comfort or continued health."

The door rattled again, knocking the dust from its hinges. Something about the man's voice was off. It was too clear for a normal human's, and the certainty in his words stirred up strange memories that made the door decidedly uncomfortable.

"Wait," it grumbled suspiciously. "You're not a wizard, are you?"

"Me?" Eli clutched his chest. "I, one of those confidence tricksters, manipulators of spirits? Why, the very thought offends me! I am but a wanderer, moving from place to place, listening to the spirits' sorrows and doing what little I can to make them more comfortable." He resumed the pleasant tapping, and the door relaxed against his fingers.

"Well"—it leaned forward a fraction, lowering its creak conspiratorially—"if that's the case, then I don't mind telling you the nails do poke a bit." It rattled, and the nails stood out for a second before returning to their position flush against the wood. The door sighed. "I don't mind the dark so much, or the damp. It's just that people are always slamming me, and that just drives the sharp ends deeper. It hurts something awful, but no one seems to care."

"Let me have a look," Eli said, his voice soft with concern. He made a great show of poring over the door and running his fingers along the joints. The door waited impatiently, creaking every time Eli's hands brushed over a spot where the nails rubbed. Finally, when he had finished his inspection, Eli leaned back and tucked his fist under his chin, obviously deep in thought. When he didn't say anything for a few minutes, the door began to grow impatient, which is a very uncomfortable feeling for a door.

"Well?" it croaked.

"I've found the answer," Eli said, crouching down on the doorstep. "Those nails, which give you so much trouble, are there to pin you to the iron frame. However"—Eli held up one finger in a sage gesture—"they don't stay in of their own accord. They're not glued in; there's no hook. In fact, they seem to be held in place only by the pressure of the wood around them. So"—he arched an eyebrow—"the reason they stay in at all, the only reason, is because you're holding on to them."

"Of course!" the door rumbled. "How else would I stay upright?"

"Who said you had to stay upright?" Eli said, throwing out his arms in a grand gesture. "You're your own spirit, aren't you? If those nails hurt you, why, there's no law that you have to put up with it. If you stay in this situation, you're making yourself a victim."

"But..." The door shuddered uncertainly.

"The first step is admitting you have a problem." Eli gave the wood a reassuring pat. "And that's enough for now. However"—his voice dropped to a whisper—"if you're ever going to live your life, *really* live it, then you need to let go of the roles others have forced on you. You need to let go of those nails."

"But, I don't know..." The door shifted back and forth.

"Indecision is the bane of all hardwoods." Eli shook his head. "Come on, it doesn't have to be forever. Just give it a try."

The door clanged softly against its frame, gathering its resolve as Eli made encouraging gestures. Then, with a loud bang, the nails popped like corks, and the boards clattered to the ground with a long, relieved sigh.

Eli stepped over the planks and through the now-empty iron doorframe. The narrow hall outside was dark and empty. Eli looked one way, then the other, and shook his head.

"First rule of dungeons," he said with a wry grin, "don't pin all your hopes on a gullible door."

With that, he stepped over the sprawled boards, now mumbling happily in peaceful, nail-free slumber, and jogged off down the hall toward the rendezvous point.

In the sun-drenched rose garden of the castle Allaze, King Henrith of Mellinor was spending money he hadn't received yet.

"Twenty thousand gold standards!" He shook his teacup at his Master of the Exchequer. "What does that come out to in mellinos?"

The exchequer, who had answered this question five times already, responded immediately. "Thirty-one thousand five hundred at the current rate, my lord, or approximately half Mellinor's yearly tax income."

"Not bad for a windfall, eh?" The king punched him in the shoulder good-naturedly. "And the Council of Thrones is actually going to pay all that for one thief? What did the bastard do?"

The Master of the Exchequer smiled tightly and rubbed his shoulder. "Eli Monpress"—he picked up the wanted poster that was lying on the table, where the roughly sketched face of a handsome man with dark, shaggy hair grinned boyishly up at them—"bounty, paid dead or alive, twenty thousand Council Gold Standard Weights. Wanted on a hundred and fifty-seven counts of grand larceny against a noble person, three counts of fraud, one charge of counterfeiting, and treason against the Rector Spiritualis." He squinted at the small print along the bottom of the page. "There's a separate bounty of five thousand gold standards from the Spiritualists for that last count, which has to be claimed independently."

"Figures." The king slurped his tea. "The Council can't even ink a wanted poster without the wizards butting their noses in. But"—he grinned broadly—"money's money, eh? Someone get the Master Builder up here. It looks like we'll have that new arena after all."

The order, however, was never given, for at that moment, the Master Jailer came running through the garden gate, his plumed helmet gripped between his white-knuckled hands.

"Your Majesty." He bowed.

"Ah, Master Jailer." The king nodded. "How is our money bag liking his cell?"

The jailer's face, already pale from a job that required him to spend his daylight hours deep underground, turned ghostly. "Well, you see, sir, the prisoner, that is to say"—he looked around for help, but the other officials were already backing away—"he's not in his cell."

"What?" The king leaped out of his seat, face scarlet. "If he's not in his cell, then where is he?"

"We're working on that right now, Majesty!" the jailer said in a rush. "I have the whole guard out looking for him. He won't get out of the palace!"

"See that he doesn't," the king growled. "Because if he's not back in his cell within the hour..."

He didn't need to finish the threat. The jailer saluted and ran out of the garden as fast as his boots would carry him. The officials stayed frozen where they were, each waiting for the others to move first as the king began to stalk around the garden, sipping his tea with murderous intent.

"Your Majesty," squeaked a minor official, who was safely hidden behind the crowd. "This Eli seems a dangerous character. Shouldn't you move to safer quarters?"

"Yes!" The Master of Security grabbed the idea and ran with

it. "If that thief could get out of his cell, he can certainly get into the castle!" He seized the king's arm. "We must get you to a safer location, Your Majesty!"

This was followed by a chorus of cries from the other officials.

"Of course!"

"His majesty's safety is of utmost importance!"

"We must preserve the monarchy at all costs!"

Any objections the king may have had were overridden as a surge of officials swept down and half carried, half dragged him into the castle.

"Put me down, you idiots!" the king bellowed, but the officials were good and scared now. Each saw only the precipitous fall that awaited him personally if there were a regime change, and fear gave them courage as they pushed their protesting monarch into the castle, down the arching hallways, and into the throne room.

"Don't worry, Your Majesty," the Master of Security said, organizing two teams to shut the great, golden doors. "That thief won't get in."

The king, who had given up fighting somewhere during the last hundred feet, just harrumphed and stomped up the dais stairs to his throne to wait it out. Meanwhile, the officials dashed back and forth across the marble—locking the parlor doors, overturning the elegant end tables, peeking behind the busts of former kings—checking for every possible, or impossible, security vulnerability. Henrith did his best to ignore the nonsense. Being royalty meant enduring people's endless fussing over your safety, but when the councilors started talking about boarding over the stained-glass windows, the king decided that enough was enough. He stood from his throne and took a breath in preparation for a good bellow when a tug on his robes stopped him short. The king looked down incredulously to see who would dare, and found two royal guards in full armor standing at attention beside the royal dais.

"Sir!" The shorter guard saluted. "The Master of Security has assigned us to move you to a safer location."

"I thought this *was* a safer location." The king sighed.

"Sir!" The soldier saluted again. "With all due respect, the throne room is the first place the enemy would look, and with this ruckus, he could easily get through."

"You're right about that," the king said, glowering at the seething mass of panicked officials. "Let's get out of here."

He stomped down the steps from the high marble dais and let the guards lead him to the back wall of the throne room. The shorter soldier went straight to an older tapestry hanging forgotten in one corner and pushed it aside, revealing, much to the king's amazement, a small door set flush with the stonework.

"I never knew this was here," the king said, genuinely astonished.

"Doors like these are standard in most castles this age," the guard said, running his gloved hand over the stones to the right of the door. "You just have to know where to look." His fingers closed in the crack between two stones. Something clicked deep in the wall, and the door swung open with a soft scrape.

"This way, sir," the soldier said, ducking through.

The secret passage was only a few feet long. This was good, because it was only a few inches wide, and the king was getting very claustrophobic sliding along sideways between the dusty stone walls, especially when the second soldier closed the door behind them, plunging the passage into darkness. A few steps later, they emerged into the back of another large tapestry. The soldier pushed the heavy cloth aside, and the king was amazed to find himself in his own drawing room.

"Why did no one tell me about this?" he said, exasperated, watching as the second soldier draped the tapestry back into place. "It will be fantastically useful the next time I want to get out of an audience."

"Over here, sir," the shorter guard said, waving toward the wide balcony that overlooked the castle garden. The king didn't see how a balcony was much safer than a throne room, but the guard seemed to know what he was doing, so the king followed quietly. Perhaps there was another secret passage. The king frowned, regretting all those times he'd chosen to go hunting rather than let the Master Builder take him on that tour of the castle the man was always so keen on. Well, the king thought, if the Master Builder had put more emphasis on secret passages rather than appreciation of the flying buttresses, perhaps he would have been more inclined to come along.

The balcony jutted out from the drawing room in a large semicircle of pale golden marble. His mother had had it built so she could watch the birds up close, and the handrails brushed right up against the leafy branches of the linden trees. The king was about to comment on how peaceful it was compared to the nonsense in the throne room, but the shorter of the two soldiers spoke first.

"I'm really sorry about this."

The king looked at him quizzically. "Sorry about wha—" His question was answered by a blinding pain at the back of his head. The trees and the balcony swirled together, and then he was on the ground with no notion of how he'd gotten there.

"Did you have to hit him that hard?" The soldier's voice floated above him.

"Yes," answered a voice he hadn't heard before, which his poor, aching brain assigned to the tall soldier who hadn't spoken while they were escorting him. "That is, if you want him to stay quiet."

The shorter soldier took off his helmet, revealing a young man with a head of dark, shaggy hair. "If you say so," he said, tucking the helmet under his arm.

The shorter soldier trotted to the edge of the balcony, where the trees were thickest. Spots danced across the king's vision, but he was sure he saw what happened next. One of the trees moved to meet the soldier. The king blinked, but the tree was still moving. It leaned over as far as it could, stretching out a thick branch to make a nice little step up off the railing. So great was his astonishment, the king barely felt the bigger soldier heft him over his shoulder like an oat sack. Then they were up on the tree branch, and the tree was bending over to set them gently on the ground.

"Thank you," said the shorter soldier as they stepped onto the grass.

And the king, though his ears were ringing horribly, could have sworn he heard the leaves whisper, "Anytime, Eli."

That thought was too much for him, and he dove into unconsciousness.

CHAPTER 2

The ghosthound appeared at the gates of the royal city of Allaze without warning. One moment, the guards were standing beside the gatehouse playing divel shanks and speculating on what all the noise in the palace was about, the next they were on their backs, staring up at an animal that only lived in stories. From the way it was showing its teeth, the guards would rather it had stayed there. Twice the size of a horse and built like a racing dog, it had to swivel its head down to look them over. The great orange eyes, each the size of a dinner plate, twinkled with amusement, or perhaps hunger. But most horrifying of all was the way the white patterns on the animal's silver fur moved like night clouds in a high wind, forming terrifying, shifting shapes above its dagger-sharp teeth.

"Excuse me," said a voice, "but I need you to open the gates. I have an urgent message for King Henrith."

The guards cowered on the sandy ground. "Great powers," the left one muttered. "I never knew they could talk."

There was a long sigh, and the beast lay down in a fluid motion, bringing the woman on its back into view. She was very well dressed in a handsome green riding suit with a crisp white shirt and tall boots. Red hair hung in a cascade of curls around her pretty, girlish face. Overall, she had a very striking look that was entirely out of place for a woman who rode a monster.

When she was sure she had their attention, the woman said, very slowly and with a charming smile, "My name is Miranda Lyonette, and I am here on behalf of the Spirit Court with a warning for your king. Now, I'm on a very tight deadline, so I would appreciate it very much if you would open the gate and let me on my way."

It was the older guard who gathered his wits first. "Um, lady," he said, picking himself up off the ground, "we'd like to help, but we can't open the gate without the Master Gatekeeper, and he's been called off to the castle."

"Well," she said, "then you'd better run and get him."

The men looked at each other, then back at the woman. She made a little shooing motion, and the guards ran off, falling over each other as they rushed the tiny gatehouse door.

When they were gone, Miranda slid down the hound's back and began to stretch the last few days out of her joints.

"I could have just jumped it," the hound growled. It eyed the two-story wall and snorted dismissively. "Saved us some time. I *thought* you said we were in a hurry."

"We *are* in a hurry," Miranda said, shaking the road dust out of her hair as best she could. "But we're also trying to make a good impression, Gin. Mellinor has a reputation for not liking wizards."

"Good impressions are wasted on this lot." Gin shook himself vigorously, raising a small cloud of grit from his ever-shifting coat. "We should have just jumped and saved the act for the king."

"Next time I'll just leave the negotiating to you, then." Miranda stepped clear of the hound's dust cloud. "Why don't you worry less about the schedule and more about keeping your nose sharp? He has to be skulking around here somewhere."

Gin gave her a withering look. "My nose is always sharp." His long ears twitched, then swiveled forward. "The guards are coming back, and they brought a lot of other clanky metal types with them." He flopped down, resting his chin on his paws. "So much for doing things the quick way."

Miranda ignored him and put on a dazzling smile as the two guards, and a small squad of spearmen, marched through the gatehouse.

The gate guards had had no trouble finding the Master Gatekeeper. He was in the throne room, standing in a rough clump around the empty throne with every other official in Allaze.

"Sir," the older guard said, tapping him on the shoulder. "We have a situation outside."

"I'm a bit busy," the Master Gatekeeper snapped.

"But, sir," the guard said, clutching his metal cap, "it's really something I think you should—"

"There's a wizard at the east gate!" the younger guard burst out, and then shrank back as the older guard and the Master Gatekeeper both snapped their heads around to glare at him. "It has to be a wizard," he said sheepishly. "Ain't no one else can ride a monster like that."

"Did you say wizard?" The Master of Security pushed his way over to them. "Was it a dark-haired man? Young looking?"

"No, sir." The young guard saluted. "It was a lady wizard, sir. Redheaded. Said she had a warning for the king."

The Master Gatekeeper and the Master of Security put their heads together and began arguing quietly. Whatever it was they argued about, the Master of Security must have won because he was the one who started barking orders. Three minutes later, the two gate guards were back at their post, only now with a squad of royal guard and the Master of Security between them and the monster, which lay with its long chin rested on its paws, watching.

The woman appeared completely unruffled by the sudden arrival of a large number of spears pointed in her direction. If there were any remaining doubts about her being a wizard, the large, ostentatiously jeweled rings covering her fingers put those to rest. She watched patiently, gently tapping her nails against the large ruby on her thumb, which was beginning to glow like an ember in the bright sun. Several of the men started to ease back toward the gatehouse, their spears wobbling, and the Master of Security decided it was time to take control of the situation.

"I hear you have a warning for the king," he said boldly. "You may speak it to me."

"My orders are to speak only to the king himself," Miranda said. "It is a matter of some delicacy."

"I am Oban, Master of Security. You'll speak it to me, or not at all," he huffed.

Miranda looked at Gin, who flicked his ear in the ghosthound equivalent of a shrug. "I suppose we have wasted enough time," she said. "I am here on behalf of the Spirit Court by order of the Rector Spiritualis, Etmon Banage. Yesterday morning we received a tip that the known fugitive wizard and wanted criminal Eli Monpress has been sighted within your kingdom. It is our belief that he is after an old wizard artifact held in your treasury. I am here to offer my assistance to keep him from stealing it."

There was a long pause, and Miranda got the horrible, sinking feeling that she had missed something important.

"Lady," the Master of Security said, shaking his head, "if you're here to warn the king about Eli, then you're a little late."

Miranda scowled. "You mean he's already stolen the artifact?"

"No." The Master of Security sighed. "He's stolen the king."

Three hours later, Miranda was seated at the foot of a small table in a cramped office in the lower part of the castle. Oban, Master of Security, the Master of the Exchequer, and the Master of the Courts were crammed together at the other end of the table, as far from her as possible. Other than Oban, none of them had told her their names, and they all looked equally displeased at being cornered in a small room with a wizard. Still, this was a step forward. An hour ago, she'd been sitting in the throne room with all forty masters of Mellinor, whom she guessed were the local equivalent of the standard governing body of lords and appointees that most kingdoms this size seemed to favor, staring daggers at her. It was only after much official argument that these three had stepped forward to speak for the whole, but from the way they were glaring at her, Miranda didn't think she'd gotten off any easier. In fact, she was beginning to regret telling Gin to wait at the gate. Miranda knew from experience that a large set of teeth on one's side tended to make these bureaucratic talks much easier.

Still, for all their pomp, the men across from her seemed to be in no hurry to get things started. After several minutes of waiting, compounded by the hours already wasted while the Mellinor officials decided who was going to deal with her, Miranda came to the conclusion that civility could get one only so far in life, and she cut straight to the point.

"Gentlemen," she said. "This would be much easier if you just told me the whole story."

The two nameless officials sneered, but Oban, at least, had the decency to look embarrassed. "There's not much to tell," he said. "We caught Eli this morning trying to get the king's prized stallion out of the stables. The horse made a racket and the Master of the Stables caught him red-handed. The thief gave up immediately, and as soon as he told us his name was Eli Monpress… Well," Oban said and shrugged, "who hasn't heard of him? I was called in and we locked him up in our strongest cell. Now, of course, we're sure the horse business was only a ploy to get inside the castle proper, because no sooner had we put him in the cell than he was gone, and shortly after that, so was our king."

"If you knew he was a wizard," Miranda said slowly, "why did you leave him alone?"

"Well," Oban said, wiping his bald head with a handkerchief, "as I said, it was our strongest cell. We took everything off him that looked magical. He didn't have any rings or gems, nothing like that." He shrugged his shoulders. "Of course, as soon as we knew the thief was out, we tried to get the king to safety. His Majesty was with us all the way to the throne room, and then he vanished. We searched all the secret passages, all the hidden stairs. By that point, the grounds were crawling with soldiers and every exit was watched. No one saw a thing."

"This is our only clue," said the small man to his left, the Master of the Exchequer. He took a small white card from his pocket and slid it across the polished table. "We found it in the rose garden shortly after the king vanished."

Miranda picked up the card, holding it delicately between her thumb and forefinger. It was cut from a heavy white stock, like a calling card, and at the center, engraved in gold ink, was an extravagant, cursive *M.* Miranda scowled and flipped the card over. On the back, someone had written *Forty thousand.*

That was it, no instructions, no threats, just the number written out in small, neat capitals across the lower left corner. Miranda scowled and slid the card back across the table. "I assume he means forty thousand in council gold standards." She smiled. "A king's ransom, indeed."

"We can't pay it," the Master of the Exchequer groaned, clutching his bony hands together. "That's an entire year's revenue for a small country like ours. We don't even have that much cash on hand in our own currency, let alone Council standards."

"But we must have our king back, whatever the cost," Oban said, landing his fist on the table. "King Henrith is young. He has yet to take a wife or produce an heir, and he's the last son of House Allaze. We've never had any kings other than House Allaze. There's not even a protocol for this sort of thing. If he vanished, our country would fall into chaos, and that would cost us far more than forty thousand standards."

Miranda tapped her finger against the polished arm of her chair. "A difficult problem," she said, "and one that could have been easily avoided. It seems that Mellinor is paying the price for its long unfriendliness toward wizards."

"It is the law," said the solemn old man to Oban's right, the Master of the Courts. "The oldest law in Mellinor, decreed by our first king, a law that we are breaking, I might add, by talking to you."

"But your first king was a wizard, wasn't he?" Miranda leaned forward, enjoying the pinched look on their faces. Ruffling stuffy politicians was one of the best perks of her job. "Come now, gentlemen, you can hardly expect an agent of the Spirit Court not to be up on her magical history."

"If you know that much," the Master of the Courts growled,

"then you already know why he closed Mellinor to your kind. King Gregorn was disgusted by the misuse of power he witnessed at the hands of greedy, arrogant wizards, and he sought to create a country where people could live without fear, where no wizard would threaten us. For that purpose, he led his family and followers to the edge of what was then a great inland sea. In a tremendous act of magic, King Gregorn banished the sea and created a new land, made by magic, yet free of wizardly corruption. This act of selfless bravery took his life. That is why, for four hundred years, we have honored his sacrifice by upholding his law." The old man closed his eyes. "For Gregorn's direct descendant to be held for ransom by some wizard thief"—he took a shuddering breath—"it's only slightly worse than enlisting a wizard to rescue him." He lifted his chin to face Miranda, glaring snowstorms at her from under his bushy eyebrows. "Rest assured, young lady, were we not in such dire straits, you would never have made it into this castle."

"Had I been in this castle," Miranda said dryly, "you wouldn't *be* in such dire straits."

All three men glowered, and she gave them a scalding look. "I think you'll find that wizards have changed in the years since your country was founded. The Spirit Court exists to maintain a balance between the power of man and spirit, and to prevent wizards from abusing their gifts. So, as you see, the Spiritualist's purpose and your Gregorn's dream are dissimilar in method but not in substance. We both want to keep the world safe from people like Eli."

The overdressed men shifted uncomfortably, and Miranda saw her chance. "Here's my offer," she said. "I will get your king back for you, and, in exchange, you will let me work unhindered. When I return your monarch, you must promise me that he will allow envoys from the Spirit Court and consider welcoming our Spiritualists into his kingdom."

The officials put their heads together for a moment, and then the Master of the Courts nodded. "You drive a hard bargain, Miss Lyonette, but we do not have the luxury of time. Your terms are acceptable. We must have our king."

Miranda stood up with a triumphant smile. "In that case, gentlemen, let's get to work."

An hour later, when Miranda had wrung almost every provision she wanted out of the old men, they adjourned. After being shown to her room, she threw down her pack, grabbed a handful of bread off the dinner tray, and went to find Gin. This proved an easy task, for he was lounging in the afternoon sun right where she'd left him, surrounded by a gawking circle of stable boys at the main entrance to the castle.

Miranda approached with a grin, scattering the boys like sparrows. "Time to work, mutt."

Gin sat up slowly, stretching his paws. "You're in a good mood."

"There may be hope for this country yet." She smiled.

The dog snorted. "What about that artifact thing Banage made us rush down here for? Find out anything about that?"

"The bureaucrats didn't mention it, so I felt no need to bring it up," she said. "Gregorn's Pillar is only dangerous to wizards, and the only one of those we have to worry about is off having a slumber party with the king. Besides, I don't think I could have spoken ill of their honored founder and lived to tell about it. Though, mind you, I could tell them a few things about their precious *Gregorn* that would set their hair on end."

"So why didn't you?" Gin yawned, showing all of his teeth.

"Telling people what they don't want to hear gets us nowhere," Miranda said. "My duty is to catch Eli before he can mess things up more than he already has, not force old men to change their prejudices. *That's* the unhappy job of whichever poor sap Master

Banage promotes to Tower Keeper of Mellinor when we're done." She flopped down on the marble step with a sigh. "So long as Eli isn't interested in Gregorn's Pillar, I'm not either. There's no point in trying to convince a panicked kingdom to let us poke around in their treasury if we don't need to. Besides, if we play our cards right, Mellinor will be crawling with Spiritualists by year's end. We'll have a Tower and a court envoy with plenty of time to talk the king into giving the Spirit Court all the pillars and artifacts and whatever else Gregorn left lying around. Right now, we focus on catching Monpress, and speaking of which"—she leaned forward—"what did you find?"

"His smell is everywhere." Gin's nostrils flared. "He was probably scouting the palace for days before he let himself get caught. The smells are all knotted together, though, so I can't tell where he made his final exit."

"So much for doing things the easy way," Miranda said and sighed, running her hand through her curly hair. "All right, we'll do this by the book. I'll start with the throne room and work my way down. You check the grounds and try not to scare anyone too badly."

"Shouldn't you get some rest?" Gin said, eyeing the sinking sun. "I can take two days of hard travel, but we don't want you flopping over like last time."

"That was an isolated incident." Miranda said, bristling. "No breaks. We're finally in the same country as that thief, possibly the same city. I'm not going to risk letting him slip away again, not when we're this close."

"You're the boss," Gin said, trotting across the courtyard. "Don't get carried away."

"That's my line," Miranda called after him, but the enormous hound was already slinking away behind the stables, sniffing the ground. Miranda shook her head and fanned out her fingers, nudging her rings awake.

"Time to get to work," she muttered, smiling as the stones began to glow. With a final look at the setting sun, she turned and tromped up the castle stairs. With any luck, she'd have Eli by the time it rose again.

CHAPTER 3

Down below the stable yard, quivering away from the ghosthound's fearsome scent, a rat darted through a narrow crack in the castle's foundation and made a break for the wall. It bounded through the ornamental gardens as if all the cats in Mellinor were on its tail, though nothing followed it in the dim evening light. What terrified the rat was not behind it, but inside it, pressed like a knife against its brain. It hit the castle battlements at full speed and began to climb the rough white stone, running vertically as easily as it had run along the ground. The knot of guards at the castle gate didn't notice as the rat crested the wall behind them and, without so much as pausing for balance, launched itself into the air. For a terrifying moment, the rat scrambled in free fall, then, with a clang that made the guards jump, landed on a drainpipe. The rat clung to the pipe, stunned for a moment, and then the pressure was back, the inescapable voice pressing down on its poor, fright-addled mind, and it had to go on. The rat scurried down the drainpipe to the cobbled street. Keeping to the gutters and dark places people forget to sweep, it made its way through the tangled streets of Allaze, following the sewer ditches away from the castle, down and west toward the river, into the darker parts of the city.

Scooting between the tilting wooden buildings, the rat threaded its way through the blind turns and back alleys to a ramshackle three-story nestled at the end of a row of identical ramshackle three-stories. Without missing a beat, the rat jumped on a gutter pipe and, quick as it had climbed the castle wall, scaled the pipe-fitting to the building's third floor. The window had been left open for it, and the rat tumbled inside, squeaking in relief that the horrible journey was almost over. It landed on the floor with a scrambling thud, but the momentary triumph was pushed from its mind by a wave of pressure that thickened the air to syrup. The attic room it had landed in was scarcely bigger than a closet, and the slanted ceiling made it smaller still. Broken furniture and discarded rags were stacked in dusty piles, but the rat's attention was on the figure sitting in the far corner, the source of the pressure.

The man sat slumped against the wall, rolling a black ball in a circle on his left palm. It was the size of a large marble, black and shiny like a wet river stone. He was thin and long, with matted blond hair that hung around his face in a dirty curtain. For a moment, the man didn't move, and then, slowly, lovingly, he slid the black sphere into his pocket and beckoned the rat closer. The pressure spiked, and the rat obeyed, crawling on its belly until it was an inch from the man's bare foot.

"Now," the man said, his whisper humming through the room, resonating against the pressure that threatened to crush the rat's mind. "Tell me what you saw."

The rat had no choice. It told him everything.

Crouched on the floor in the hall with his eye pressed against a crack in the baseboard, the boy had to cover his mouth to keep from shouting. The blond man who rented the spare room had always made him nervous, which was why the boy took it upon himself to spy on him. He'd told his father over and over that their renter wasn't right in the head. He'd seen him talking to the walls, the floor, even the junk in the room as though they could answer back. Every time, his father had told him to lay off and leave the renter be. The blond man had come with the house when they'd moved in last year, and his money kept the family in shoes and off the street when times were hard. But this time was different. This time, the boy had actually seen the blond man open the window for a rat. His father was a butcher who kept his shop on the first floor. Once he told him the renter was letting vermin into the house, his father would have to throw the crazy man out, money or no. Grinning fit to break his face, the boy got to his feet and started to tiptoe toward the stairs. Before he took two steps, a strange sound stopped him. It was coming from the rented room, and it took the boy a moment to realize that the renter was laughing.

The door to the renter's room burst open, and the blond man was on him before he could run. Still laughing, the man grabbed the boy by his patched collar and dragged him up with surprising force.

"Young man," he said in a smooth voice, and something cold and heavy slid into the boy's shaking hand. "Take this. Find whatever passes for a tailor in this pit and bring him here. If you're quick, I'll give you another."

He dropped the boy as suddenly as he'd grabbed him. The boy landed on his feet and immediately looked at the object in his hand. It was a gold standard. His eyes went as wide as eggs, and, for a moment, he forgot that he disliked the strange blond man. "Yes, sir!"

"Tell your mother to bring some hot water up as well," the renter called as the boy tumbled down the stairs.

The child began to bellow for his mother, and the blond man stepped back into his rented room. The rat lay twitching in the corner where he had left it, and he kicked it aside with his foot. Such weak spirits were only useful once. He'd need something else. He turned his attention to the dusty wall beside him and grinned as the timbers creaked in fear.

"Find me another spy."

A fine cloud of grit fell from the ceiling as the wall shuddered its response. "Yes, Master Renaud." The room began to buzz as the order spread through the building, asking for a new rat.

Renaud slumped against the dusty piles of junk and stared out the open window at the last glow of the setting sun as it lit up the tall towers of castle Allaze, just as white and beautiful as he remembered from his childhood. Now, finally, after eight years of shame and banishment, eight years of watching for a chance, *any* chance, fate, it seemed, had paid out in spades.

He began to chuckle, and it was all thanks to a simple wizard thief.

His chuckle became a full-fledged cackle, and Renaud doubled over, his shoulders shaking. He laughed like that until the butcher wife's timid knock interrupted him.

There was much coming and going at the butcher's house that night, enough to attract the neighborhood's attention. Contrary to his usual nature, the butcher wasn't talking, and that just made the whole thing more interesting. Down the road in the raucous Merrymont Tavern, men with missing teeth made wagers about what was going on. Some put money on a murder; others said it had to do with the ruckus up at the castle. One man was blaming wizards, though he was a bit unclear about what exactly he was blaming them for. This led to more betting and speculation and, in their excitement, no one noticed the swordsman sitting at the corner table quietly nursing the same drink he'd been on for hours.

On a less interesting night, a swordsman would have been a fine topic of conversation. Especially this one, with the wicked scar he bore over the left side of his face, but with the mystery at the butcher's and rumors of a wizardess riding up to the castle on a dog the size of a house, the people had no breath left to spare for a swordsman. For his part, the swordsman didn't seem to mind the lack of attention. He simply sat in his corner, swirling his drink and listening. As the night dragged on, the talk began to go in circles. Finally, after the same theory was brought up three times in a quarter hour, the swordsman stood, laid his coins on the table, and, carefully tucking his wrapped sword into his belt, slipped out into the night.

He walked north for several blocks, ducking in and out of buildings almost at random. Only when he was sure no one was following him did he turn around and begin walking purposefully toward the butcher's house.

Renaud was fastening the starched cuffs of his new jacket when he heard it, an icy, blood-thirsty whine that grated against his thoughts. He froze. The butcher's wife stood in the corner, her eyes roving, looking at everything except him, just as they had for the last four hours. She gave no sign she heard anything.

"Get out," Renaud said.

The woman jumped and hastily obeyed, closing the door behind her. Renaud resumed working on the small buttons at his wrists. Outside his tiny window, the night was drifting toward morning, and in the faint gray light he saw the man's shadow seconds before he heard the window scrape.

"If you're going to sneak up on someone," Renaud said coldly, turning to face the man who was now crouched on the windowsill, "learn how to keep your sword quiet."

The man smiled, but the scar across his cheek warped the expression into a leer as he sat down on the window ledge and laid his gloved palm against his sword's wrapped hilt. The wailing stopped, and Renaud let out a relieved sigh.

The man's smile widened. "So it's true," he said. "There *is* a wizard in Mellinor."

Renaud did not move, but somehow his slouched posture shifted from bored to threatening. "Who are you? What do you want?"

"First answer"—the man leaned back against the window's bowed frame—"my name is Coriano, and I'm a bounty hunter. Second answer, I was curious. You've caused quite a stir."

"A bounty hunter?" Renaud laughed. "I'm afraid you've found the wrong wizard. The one you want has already struck and gone."

Coriano's good eye narrowed. "On the contrary, you're exactly the wizard I wanted to find, Renaud of Allaze."

Renaud's hand slipped into his pocket and gripped the glassy black sphere that lay hidden at the bottom. "How do you know that name?"

"It's my business to know," Coriano said dryly. "But don't worry, I'm not here to threaten you. In fact, I'd like to make you an offer."

Renaud's fingers eased their grip. "And what could you offer me?"

"Something that will help you reach your goals."

Renaud arched an eyebrow. "What would you know of my goals?"

"I told you," Coriano said. "It's my business to know."

"All right," Renaud took his hand from his pocket and folded his arms over his chest. "I'm listening."

Coriano, grinning, hopped down from the windowsill. Renaud gave the sooty, warped glass a warning look, and the window slammed itself shut with a terrified squeal, locking the men's words away from the brightening sky.

CHAPTER 4

When King Henrith opened his eyes, he knew he was dead. A few blinks later, the certainty hadn't changed, but he was starting to feel a little upset about it. However, what happened next put all of that out of his head, for the great nothingness he had been staring into, the endless void that lies beyond human experience, stood up and began stirring the fire. As his eyes adjusted to the sudden light, he saw it was a girl. Or, at least, that was his best guess. All he could see at this angle was a tangle of short, black hair and a bit of pale forehead. The rest of her was lost inside an enormous coal-black coat that, he now realized, had been the void covering his head.

The sudden knowledge that he was, indeed, not dead was further underscored by the extreme discomfort of his position. He was lying on his side on a dirt floor, his hands and feet tied behind him so that he was bent belly out. The fire the girl tended was far too large for the small stone hovel they were in, and the heat pressed down on him as tightly as the ropes.

Finished poking at the fire, the girl walked over to the woodpile, pushed up her sleeves, and, despite the suffocating heat, began tossing more logs on. The fire accepted them reluctantly, shrinking away from her thin, pale hands. In the flickering light, Henrith caught the dull gleam of silver at her wrists, and he leaned his head slowly to the side for a better look. They weren't bracelets.

The dull, thick metal was badly scuffed, and it was wrapped tightly around her bony wrist, like a manacle. His hopes began to rise. If she was a prisoner as well, maybe she could help him escape.

But before he could get her attention, the rickety wooden door burst open, flooding the small hut with blinding sunlight as two men stomped in. The first, medium height and gangly, was carrying a huge stack of wood. "Nico!" he shouted, craning his neck over the logs. "Are you trying to burn us to crisps?"

The girl shrugged and then turned and glared at the fire. The flames shuddered, and the fire shrank to half the size it had been only seconds before. A cold terror ran up the king's spine, but the man carrying the wood only sighed and started adding his armload to the woodpile. The second man, a towering figure with cropped sandy hair, carried two rabbits over one broad shoulder and what looked to be a sharpened six-foot-long iron bar over the other. The rest of him, from shoulders to calves, was covered in blades. He wore two swords at his waist, another sideways across his lower back, and knives of every size poking out of his belt, boots, and sleeves. Two long braces of throwing knives were strapped across his chest, with two more around his thighs. Anywhere he could strap a sheath, he had one, until it was difficult to tell what color his clothing actually was beneath the maze of leather sheaths.

The king cringed, terrified, as the swordsman walked past, but the man didn't even glance the king's way. He stepped nonchalantly over the scorched dirt the bonfire had vacated moments before and sauntered over to the small table set against the far wall, where he began to skin the rabbits. He kept all of his blades belted on as he did this, paying them as little mind as another man would pay to his jacket. The sword-shaped iron bar he leaned against the table beside him, keeping it close, like a trusted friend.

Not wanting to draw the attention of anyone so fond of sharp objects, the king focused his efforts on lying as still as possible. However, the girl looked at him, watching him with her head tilted to the side as the men worked. A few moments later, she announced, "The king's awake."

"Is he?" the man at the woodpile said and whirled around. "Wonderful!" The next moment, he was crouching beside King Henrith, a huge grin on his face. "Hello, Your Majesty! How have you enjoyed your kidnapping so far?"

The king looked up at him, noting the shaggy dark hair, thin build, and boyish grin that, in any other circumstance, would have been infectious. He looked just like his wanted poster. "Eli Monpress."

The grin grew wider. "You've heard of me! I'm flattered!"

At that, the king's fear was overwhelmed by indignation. "Of course I've heard of you!" the king blustered, blowing the dirt out of his beard. "We caught you trying to steal my horses this morning!"

"Yesterday morning, actually." Eli looked sideways across the fire at the knife-covered man. "I'm afraid Josef may have hit you a little too hard."

"I hit him perfectly," Josef said, not looking up from his rabbits. "He's not in pain, is he?"

Eli looked down at the king. "Are you?"

Henrith paused, considering. His head didn't hurt. He remembered being hit and the shooting pain on the balcony, but now he felt nothing, just uncomfortable from the ropes and the strange position. He looked up at Eli, who was still waiting for his answer, and shook his head.

"See?" Josef said. "Perfect."

Eli sighed dramatically. "Well, after that display, I suppose I'd better introduce my associates." He reached down and took the king's head in his hands, turning him toward the tall man with the blades. "That man of perfection you see mutilating the bunnies for our supper is our swordsman, Josef Liechten, and this little bundle"—he turned the king's head to the left, toward the girl, who was back to poking the fire—"is Nico."

That was apparently enough for introductions, for Eli let the king's head go and plopped down in the dirt beside him, leaning on his elbow so his eyes were level with the king's.

"Why are you doing this?" the king whispered, wavering between rage and genuine bewilderment.

"I'm a thief." Eli shrugged. "I steal valuable things. What could be more valuable than a king to his country?"

"Why me, then?" Henrith wiggled himself semi-upright. "If money is what you're after, why not go after a larger country, or a richer one?"

"Trade secret," Eli said. "But since you're being such a good sport about all this, I will tell you that we're not working for anyone. There's no great scheme, no big plot. Just pay our price and we can all go home happy."

Henrith supposed that was a relief. "What's your price, then?"

"Forty thousand gold standards," Eli said calmly.

The king nearly choked. "Are you mad? We can't pay that!"

"Then I guess you'll just have to lie here forever." Eli gave him a little pat on the shoulder, and then stood up and walked over to where Nico was poking the fire, leaving the king to wiggle futilely in the dirt.

"Of course," he added, almost as an afterthought, "you wouldn't have to pay it all at once."

"What," the king scoffed, "set up an installment plan? Would you leave a forwarding address, or should I just send a company of armed men every month?"

"Nothing so complicated." Eli walked over and kneeled down again. "How about this? You write a letter to your Master of the Money, or whatever you call him, and tell him to put aside a mere five thousand gold standards. Surely even Mellinor can gather such a small sum without too much difficulty. We'll make a switch"—he waggled his long finger at the king—"you for the money, and the rest of the debt can be pledged to my council bounty."

Henrith's face went blank. "Pledged to what?"

Eli gawked down at him. "The Council of Thrones' bounty account." He leaned down, looking incredulous. "Do you even know how bounties work?"

The king started to answer, but Eli rolled right over him. "Of course not, you're a king. I doubt you've even been to a council meeting. You've probably never even left your kingdom." He sat down again, muttering under his breath, "Council of Thrones, pah. More like Council of Junior-Adjuncts-No-One-in-Their-Own-Kingdom-Wanted-Around.

"All right," Eli said when he was settled. "So you know the Council of Thrones takes care of things no single kingdom can handle—large-scale trade disputes, peace negotiations, and offering bounties on criminals wanted for crimes in more than one kingdom." Eli reached into the pocket of his faded blue jacket and pulled out a folded square of paper, which he shook out proudly. It was his wanted poster, the same one the king had seen in the rose garden back when Eli had been his prisoner, and not the other way around.

Eli held the poster up. "Only the biggest criminals, those considered to be a danger to every member kingdom of the Council, are listed on the Council wanted board, and that means the bounties have to be in amounts that can get the attention of whole kingdoms, not just small-time bounty hunters.

"As you see," he said, tapping the numbers under his portrait, "my head, dead or alive, is currently worth twenty thousand gold standards. This price is guaranteed by five countries, each of which pledged a little of its hard-earned money to entice men like yourself to try and catch me. Since you've made such a fuss over how you can't pay the whole amount of your ransom at the moment, I'm going to cut you a deal. All you have to do to buy your freedom is top what those countries have offered by pledging your ransom to my bounty. Minus, of course, the five thousand in cash we'll be taking with us. Still, that means the kingdom of Mellinor will be responsible for the remaining thirty-five thousand only in the unlikely event of my capture. Now," he said, folding the poster back into a square, "I think that's more than fair. What do you say, Mr. King?"

The king didn't have much to say to that, actually. This was either the worst kidnapping in history or the best Council fundraiser he'd ever seen.

"So," he said slowly, "Mellinor pledges the thirty-five thousand to your bounty, we give you five thousand in cash, and you let me go. But," he said and paused, desperately trying to find some sense in what was happening, "that will bring your bounty to fifty-five thousand gold standards. It doesn't make sense at all. You're a thief! Won't having a higher bounty make stealing things more difficult?"

"Any thief worth the name can *steal*," Eli snorted. "I, however, am not just any thief." He straightened up. "I'm Eli Monpress, the greatest thief in the world. I'm worth more gold dead than most people will see in two lifetimes, and this is only the beginning." He leaned down, bringing his eyes level with Henrith's. "A bounty of fifty-five thousand puts me in the top ten percent of all criminals wanted by the council, but so far as I'm concerned, that's nothing. Child's play. One day," he said, smiling, "I'll be worth one million gold standards."

He said it with such gravity that the king couldn't help himself, he burst out laughing. He laughed until the ropes cut into his skin and his throat was thick with grit from the dirt floor. Eli just watched him convulse, a calm smile on his face.

At last, the king's laughter receded into gasps and hiccups, and he slumped to the floor with a sigh. "One *million*?" he said, chuckling. "Impossible. You could buy the Council itself for that much. You'd have to kidnap every king in the world!"

"If they're all as easily gotten as you were," Eli said with a grin, "that won't be a problem." He gave the king a pat on the head, like he was a royal puppy, and stood up. He stepped over the sprawled king and crouched down behind him, where the king's hands were tied.

The king wiggled, trying to get a look at what Eli was doing. But the thief put his boot on the king's side, keeping him still while he reached down and brushed his fingers over the rope at the king's hands and ankles. "Thank you very much," Eli said. "You've been most helpful. I think he's got the point, though, so you can let him go now."

Henrith was about to ask who he thought he was talking to when the rope at his hands wiggled like a snake. He jumped as the rope untied itself and fell into a neat coil at his side. Eli reached down and picked the rope up, leaving the king slack-jawed on the floor.

"Good-natured rope," the thief cooed, holding the coils up. "It's always such a pleasure to work with."

He left the king gaping in the dirt and went over to a corner where a small pile of leather packs leaned against the wall, well away from the fire. He tucked the rope carefully into the pack on the top and began to dig through the others, looking for something.

Henrith sat up gingerly, squeezing his hands to get the feeling back and trying not to think too hard about what had just happened. By the time he got the blood flowing in his fingers again, Eli was back, this time shoving a pen nib, ink pot, and a sheaf of slightly dirty paper into the king's hands.

"All right, Your Majesty," he said, grinning. "If you would write a letter detailing what we talked about, I'll make sure it gets sent to whoever deals with this sort of thing. Be sure to stipulate that you will not be returned until I see my new wanted poster—that part is key. With any luck, this will all be over in a few days and we'll never have to see each other again."

He clapped the king on the shoulder one last time and stood up. "Nico," he said. "I'm going to find someone who wants to carry a letter. Would you mind watching our guest? I want to make sure he doesn't get any ideas that might come to a sad conclusion."

The girl nodded absently, never looking up from the fire. Eli gave the king a final wink before opening the cabin door and walking out into the sunlight. The swordsman, who had long finished skinning his rabbits, picked up his iron sword and followed, leaving the king alone in the small, dark hut with the girl.

Her back was to him, and King Henrith flexed his newly freed hands again. The door was only a few feet away.

"Whatever you're thinking, I wouldn't suggest it."

The sudden edge in her voice nearly made him jump backward. He froze as she turned to look at him. When her brown eyes locked with his, the feeling of oblivion came roaring back. Suddenly, it was very hard to breathe.

"Write your letter," she said, and turned back to the fire.

He took a shuddering breath and spread the paper out on his knee. With one last look at the girl's back, he leaned over and began to write his ransom note.

"That was stupid," Josef said, closing the rickety door behind him.

"Why do you say that?" Eli asked, scanning the treetops. They were standing in the small clearing outside of the forester's hut that Eli had "repurposed" for this operation. High overhead, sunlight streamed through the treetops while hidden birds called to one another from their branches. Eli whistled back.

Josef scowled, leaning against the small trees that shielded their hut from view. "Why did you put that part in about seeing the poster? This job has dragged on long enough already. We'll be here forever if we have to wait on Council politics."

"You'd be surprised how sprightly they can be when there's a lot of money involved," Eli said, and whistled again. "The Council gets a percent fee on capture for every bounty posted, and fifty-five thousand is a lot of money, even for them."

"It wouldn't be so bad if there was something to do," Josef said, stabbing his iron sword into the patchy grass at their feet. The battered black blade slid easily into the dirt, as though the hard, rocky ground were loose sand. "There's no challenge in this country. The city guards were a joke. The palace had no swordsmen, no wizards. I don't understand why we even bothered to sneak in."

"A job finally goes smoothly," Eli said, "and you're complaining? All we have to do is lounge around for a few days, collect the money, get my new bounty, and we can be on our way."

"Smooth jobs are boring," the swordsman grumbled, "and you're the only one who enjoys lounging."

"You might like if you tried it," Eli said.

Josef shook his head and Eli turned back to the leafy canopy, whistling a third time. This time something whistled in answer, and a small falcon swooped down to land on the moss beside him.

"You needed a break anyway," Eli said, kneeling down. "You're too tense these days."

"I'm not tense," Josef said, pushing himself off the trees with a grunt. "Just bored."

He yanked his sword out of the ground and walked off into the forest, tossing the enormous blade between his hands as though it were made of paper. Eli watched him leave with a mixed expression, and then, shrugging, he turned back to the falcon and began talking it into taking a message to the castle.

CHAPTER 5

Miranda stood at the center of the empty prison cell, her bare feet resting on a springy bed of new moss that spread out from the moss agate ring lying in the middle of the floor. The heavy door to the cell was open, though it would have been useless even if closed, owing to the gaping hole in the middle where the wooden boards should have been. The boards themselves lay in disgrace a few feet away, piled against the far wall of the cell.

She could feel the moss humming under her toes as it crept across the stone, feeling for slight changes in the dust. "He's very light-footed; I'll give him that," the moss said. "It feels like he spent most of his time by the door, but"—Miranda got the strange sensation that the moss was frowning—"every spirit here is dead asleep, mistress. If he used any spirits, he was uncommonly quiet about it."

Miranda nodded thoughtfully. "What about the door?"

"That's the strangest bit." The moss crept over the pile of boards, poking them with thousands of tiny rootlings. "The door is sleeping soundest of all."

"Thief nothing," Miranda said, rubbing her palms against her temples. "That man is a ghost."

The cell was only the latest in a long line of failures as night turned to morning. "Well," she said, "Eli's not a Spiritualist. Maybe he used something else."

"Enslavement, you mean?" The moss wiggled with displeasure. "Impossible, mistress. Enslavements happen when the wizard's will completely dominates the spirit's until it has no choice but to obey. It's *not* a subtle thing. Why, even a momentary enslavement just to open the door would spook every spirit within earshot. They'd be moaning about it forever. But this room is so relaxed even I'm feeling sleepy. If you hadn't told me otherwise, I would have guessed these idiots hadn't so much as smelled a wizard in a hundred years."

"Why do you say that?" Miranda sat down on her heels. "If he didn't do anything flashy or dangerous, like enslavement, I doubt these rocks would notice a wizard standing right on top of them. Most spirits won't even wake up enough to talk to a wizard unless we stand around making a racket for a few hours. Remember how long it took me to get *your* attention, Alliana?"

Alliana ruffled her green fuzz. "Spirits might not always respond, but we always notice a wizard. You're very distracting."

"You mean we're loud and obnoxious," Miranda said. "But then why did no one notice Eli?"

"Sometimes, spirits choose not to notice," the moss said wistfully. "There are some wizards it's better not to look at."

"What do you mean?" Miranda leaned closer to the moss's fluffy green surface. "Is Eli one of those?"

"I wouldn't know," Alliana said with a huff. "I've never seen him."

"Then what—"

"It's no use asking any more questions, mistress," the moss said. "I can't say it any clearer. It really is too bad you humans are spirit blind. It's so hard to explain things like this when you can't see what I'm talking about."

Miranda blew the hair out of her face with an exasperated huff. Spirits were eternally complaining about the human inability to see the spirit world, as if humans chose to be blind out of sheer stubbornness. As always, she tried to remind herself that it was very hard on spirits. All humans had the innate ability to control the spirits around them, though only born wizards could actually hear the spirits' voices, and thus actually use their power. But this power came with a price, for, wizard or not, no human could see as the spirits saw. It was as if the whole race lacked a vital sense, and this lack was a source of endless frustration for both sides. It wasn't that Miranda didn't appreciate the difficulty. She did, really. For Alliana to explain how a wizard was distracting would be like Miranda trying to describe the color red to a blind person. Even so, it was impossibly frustrating when, every time she got a little closer to finally understanding, the spirit would pull the whole "Well, you can't see, so I can't explain" cop-out. Her spirits might serve her willingly, but sometimes she got the feeling she didn't really understand them at all.

"Let's move on," she said. "Go ahead and wake up the door. You said Eli spent all his time beside it. If he's as powerful as Master Banage seems to think he is, the wood should have noticed something."

The wood was not cooperative. First, it took thirty minutes of Alliana's poking to wake it up. Then, as soon as the wood recognized the moss as a wizard-bound spirit, it shut itself down in protest. Even after some direct threats from Miranda herself, the most she could get out of it was that Eli had been a nice and helpful human, with a strong implication that she was not. After that, the door buried itself in a sound sleep and nothing Alliana did could wake it.

Miranda threw herself down on the cell's narrow bench with a frustrated sigh and began to tug her socks back on. She still didn't know how Eli had escaped, but at least the door had mentioned him. Her attempts in the throne room had been a disaster. The officials had trailed her every step, muttering suspiciously, while the spirits remained sleepy, distant, and decidedly unhelpful. Ten hours wasted, altogether, and nothing but frustration and an attack on her personality to show for it. It was enough to make her spit.

She called Alliana and the circle of bright green moss began to shrink, returning to the moss agate ring that lay on the floor. When the moss was completely gone, Miranda bent down and picked the ring up. She ran her fingertips lovingly over the smooth stone, soothing the moss spirit into a light sleep. When Alliana was quiet, Miranda slipped the ring back onto its home on her right pinky finger.

"What are you doing now?" a perky voice behind her asked. "Did you find anything?"

Miranda's smile vanished. She'd almost forgotten about the girl.

Of course, Mellinor, a country that had built a long and proud tradition out of hating wizards, wasn't about to let one roam around alone. When it became clear they couldn't follow her all night, the masters of Mellinor had insisted on providing a "guide" who stayed with her at all times "for her convenience." Unfortunately, because of that long and proud tradition of hating wizards, volunteers for the position of wizard watcher had been scarce. Finally, the masters had given the job to the only person who actually seemed to want it, an overly inquisitive junior librarian named Marion.

Marion peered through the doorway, her round face beaming. "Are you done growing moss?"

"In a manner, yes." Miranda leaned back against the cool stone.

The girl poked around the cell, growing more excited by the moment. "Amazing! The moss is gone! Was that a spell?"

Miranda rolled her eyes. A spell? No one had talked about magic in terms of spells since before the first Spirit Court. "The moss was my servant spirit," she said, and she held up her hand, waggling her fingers so the rings glittered in the torchlight. "She was very helpful, but, unfortunately, we're no closer to finding where Eli took the king. I'd like to try—"

"Did the spirit cast a spell?" The girl looked hopeful.

Miranda pressed her palm hard against her forehead. "Marion, this would go more smoothly if you wouldn't ask questions."

The girl's face fell, and Miranda immediately felt awful. *Fabulous effort at making a good impression*, she thought. *The one person in the whole kingdom who doesn't think you're the living incarnation of all that's wrong in the world, and you yell at her.*

"Look, Marion," Miranda said gently, "how much do you know about wizards?"

"Not much, really," Marion said sheepishly, tugging at her long, formless tunic dress, which Miranda had come to recognize as the Mellinorian librarian uniform. "All the books about wizards were destroyed generations ago." She reached furtively into one of her cavernous side pockets and pulled out a slim leather book. "This was all I could find. I've practically memorized it."

The book looked ancient. Its leather cover was cracked and worn and missing chunks in several places. Miranda took it gently and stifled a groan when she read the title, Morticime Kant's *A Wizarde's Travels*. Of course, the one book the Mellinorian purge missed would be the most ostentatious, misinformed plague on wizardry that had ever stained a page. If you wanted someone to get the wrong idea about magic, this was the book you would give them.

Out of morbid curiosity, she flipped it open to a random page and started reading a section labeled "On the Dress and Manner of Wizardes."

"A wizarde is easily separated from his fellow men owing to the Presence of his Person. Often he will carry the Fragrance of Old Magic, gained from his years over the cauldron brewing his fearsome Magical Potions. If you do not wish to step close enough to determine his odor (for doing so may put you in his thrall, beware!) you may determine his demeanor from a safe distance, for all wizardes wear, by oath, the marks of their Station, namely the ever present flowing Robes of State, the flashing Rings of Enchantment, and the long-pointed, elegant cap of a Master of Magicks. Further more—"

Miranda snapped the book shut in disgust. Whoever had purged the library had probably left it on purpose.

"Well," she said, handing the book back, "that explains much."

The girl cringed at the scorn her voice, and lowered her head until the thick woolen veil that covered her blonde hair slid down to hide her face as well. "I did not mean to offend, lady wizard."

"Spiritualist," Miranda corrected gently. The girl peeked at her quizzically, and Miranda tried again. "Let me explain. Wizards don't do magic—at least, not like the book describes it. What Kant calls 'magicks' are actually spirits. The world we live in is made of spirits. Mountains, trees, water, even the stones in the wall or the bench I'm sitting on"—she rapped the wood with her knuckles—"they each have their own souls, just as humans do. The word 'wizard' is just a catchall name for a person who can hear those spirits' voices. Now, it's possible for anyone to hear the spirits if they are seriously injured or dying. Death brings us as close as humans can get to the spirit world. What makes a wizard different is that wizards hear spirits all the time, even if they don't want to. But a wizard's real power is not just hearing the spirits, it's control. Wizards can exert their will over the spirits around them and, if the wizard's will is strong enough, control them. Though, of course, this control must always be used responsibly and only with the spirit's consent."

She looked at Marion to make sure this wasn't more explanation than the girl was willing to listen to, but the librarian was practically leaning on Miranda's shoulder in rapt attention, so the Spiritualist continued.

"Not all spirits are the same, of course. There are Great Spirits, a mountain, for example, and small spirits, like a pebble. The larger the spirit, the greater its power, and the stronger a wizard's will has to be to control it, or even just get its attention. Almost any wizard can wake up a small, stupid spirit, like a pebble, or that door you saw me yelling at earlier, but it's how they treat the spirit once they've woken it that determines what kind of wizard they are."

Miranda pointed at her rings. "I am a Spiritualist. Like all wizards, I have the power to dominate spirits and force them to do my bidding, but I don't. The Spirit Court does not believe in forcing the world to do our will. Instead, we make contracts. Each of these rings contains a spirit who has willingly entered my service." She wiggled her fingers. "In return for their work and obedience, I share my energy with them and provide a safe haven. That's the way a Spiritualist works, give and take. Often, it's a good deal for both wizard and spirit. Born wizards often have large and powerful souls, and spirits love to share that power that is often greater than their own. In return, the wizard gets a powerful ally, so it works out both ways. Still, service is always by choice. We never force a spirit to serve us against its will. Any wizard who does is not a Spiritualist, and thus not someone you want around." She pointed at the only ring on her hand without a jewel, a thick gold signet on her left ring finger stamped with a perfect circle. "This is the mark of the Spirit Court. The only legitimate wizards are ones who show this ring proudly. It is a sign of the vows Spiritualists make to never abuse that power, or the spirits who depend on us."

"I see," Marion said, her blue eyes widening until her wispy eyebrows were lost under her square bangs. "But there are wizards who aren't Spiritualists, right? Who can dominate any spirits? Could those wizards dominate another person?"

"No," Miranda said. "A wizard can move mountains if her will is strong enough, but no wizardry can touch another human's soul. Brush it, maybe, press upon it, certainly, if the other soul is sensitive to spirits, but no power I have could force you to act against your wishes. I could make trees dance and rocks sing, but I couldn't even make you bow your head if you wanted it straight. Does that make sense?"

Marion frowned thoughtfully. "I think so, but—"

"Good." Miranda stood up with a smile. "Then today hasn't been a complete waste." She looked dolefully around the small cell. "I don't think there's much more I can do here. We need a change of scenery." She took a small leather folder out of her bag and began to flip through a neat stack of papers.

Marion looked quizzical. "Scenery?"

"Ah-ha," Miranda said and smiled triumphantly, holding up a small, tattered note. "Looks like we're going for a walk to the west side of town."

A horrified look spread over Marion's face. "Why?"

"I'm getting nowhere around here." Miranda stuck the folder back in her bag and slung it over her shoulder. "Either Eli is a much more powerful wizard than I anticipated, which is unlikely, or he's got some trick that lets him march around unnoticed. Either way, I need to learn more about him, so we're going to see an expert."

Marion's look of horror deepened. "An expert? But what kind of—lady!" She had to scramble to keep up as Miranda swept out of the room, past the prison guards, and up the narrow stairs. "Lady wiz...Spiritualist! Lady Miranda! Wait!" She chased her through the maze of narrow passageways and caught up just as Miranda pushed open the outer door, where the prison let out below the stable yard. With a gasp, she threw herself in front of the Spiritualist. "Wait!" she said, panting. "The west side of the city isn't exactly, that is, I have to alert the guards. You'll need a security squad and—"

"Security squad?" Miranda pushed past her with a grin. "Gin!"

He must have been waiting for this, because the ghosthound appeared with a speed that surprised even Miranda. Gin slid to a halt right in front of them, grinning toothily, while the misty patterns flew over his coat in a way that meant he was feeling extraordinarily pleased with himself. Miranda shook her head and turned to the librarian. Marion was almost sitting on the ground in her scramble to get away from the monster that had not been there a second before. It was all Miranda could do not to reach down and shut the girl's gaping jaw for her.

"I don't think a security squad will be needed," Miranda said, vaulting onto Gin's back. "Coming?"

The girl had barely nodded before Gin swept her up with his paw and tossed her on his back. The stable dogs howled as the ghosthound loped across the castle grounds, fast as an icy gale. He took the castle gate in two leaps and hit the city street running, sending the well-dressed townsfolk screaming in all directions.

"Did you find anything?" Miranda asked.

"Of course not." Gin sighed. "So, do we have a destination, or are we just putting on a show?"

"West side of the city, and slow it down a little." She glanced over her shoulder at Marion, who was clinging to the ghosthound's short coat with everything she had. "We have a delicate flower with us."

The ghosthound slowed just a fraction as he took a narrow alley westward, downhill toward the river.

CHAPTER 6

If looked at from the sky, Allaze, the capital and only walled city of Mellinor, was a thing of beauty. It lay like a sun-bleached sand dollar on the grassy banks of the river Aze, circular and white with the spires of the castle as the star at its center. Low, undulating hills, spotted with split wood fences and fat cattle, rose around it, so that the city was a bump at the lowest point of a soft, green bowl.

Along the city's northern wall, the bushy edge of the king's deer park met the city in a mash of green oaks and tall pines. Only a thin strip of grass and the taller than usual northern parapets kept the trees out of the city proper. Within the walls, a charming, if confusing, knot of streets twisted outward and downward from the castle hill. Following the king's example, the citizens had also arranged themselves vertically, starting at the top with impressive, stone mansions pressed right against the castle's outer perimeter and moving down to the sprawling ring of flat-roofed timber houses leaning against Allaze's edge, where the white stone outer wall ran in a nearly perfect circle around the city. Nearly perfect, but for one slight flaw.

In a fit of architectural rebellion, a small section of the city's western edge deviated to form an unsightly bulge. It was as if the stones in that part of the wall had tried to make a break for the river, only to fail halfway and rejoin the circle a quarter mile later in sullen resignation. If this building irregularity had a purpose, it was long forgotten, and the western bulge was now a pile of ramshackle buildings on top of what had been a swamp, but was now home to some of the least reputable businesses in Mellinor.

Gin trotted to a stop in front of one such establishment, a ramshackle building with the words MERRYMONT TAVERN painted in fading, uneven block letters across the shuttered upper story.

"This looks like the place," Miranda said, sliding off Gin's back. Marion followed timidly, wincing as her nice court slippers hit the muddy road with a wet slap. The wooden buildings here tilted in every direction, leaning on each other like drunks until it was difficult to tell where one ended and the next began. The smell of stagnant water and unwashed bodies hung in a haze over the narrow streets, but there was no one to be seen. Every window was dark and empty, projecting gloom and decay until even the noon sunlight seemed dimmer. Miranda surveyed the empty streets, her face set in her best imitation of the Rector Spiritualis at a Council meeting, equal parts nonchalant superiority and honed indifference to the opinions of others. If growing up in the enormous city of Zarin had taught her anything, it was that empty streets hid the most ears of all.

"Gin," she said loudly, "if anyone gives you trouble, don't bother asking permission, just eat them."

Gin responded by lazily stretching his forelegs out in front of him and yawning, revealing a mouth of yellow, glistening teeth as his ears swiveled for any hint of sound.

Satisfied that no one would bother them after that little display, Miranda marched up the rickety stairs of the Merrymont and pushed aside the muddy blanket that served as a door. The barroom was narrow, dark, and stank of the river. It was also just as empty as the street outside, though the mugs scattered on the warped tables told her it hadn't been that way a few moments ago.

Large, stained barrels took up most of the room, their taps dripping something that smelled faintly of rotting bread and vinegar. The only windows were papered over with advertisements and notices, including a large, peeling poster featuring a pair of girls wearing outfits that made Miranda blush. Looking away, she selected a cleanish table near the center of the room and sat down so that she was facing the main entrance. Marion, white as new cheese and twice as wobbly, took a seat beside her.

The librarian eyed the empty tables and the trash scattered across the warped floor boards. "I don't think your expert is here," she whispered.

"He will be," Miranda said, setting her bag in the chair beside her. "The Spirit Court pays its informants very well, and bounty hunters thrive in trash heaps like this."

"Such words of praise," a deep voice purred behind them. "You'll make me blush, little wizardess."

Marion fell out of her chair with a series of squeaks, but Miranda stayed perfectly still.

"Well met, Mr. Coriano," she said calmly. "You seem to be living up to your reputation." Without turning, she motioned to the chair on the other side of the table. "Since you have time to sneak around and scare young women, surely you can spare a few moments."

She felt more than heard him stalk around the table. As he came into her line of vision, Miranda did not waste her first look at the infamous Gerard Coriano. He was shorter than she'd expected, with black hair that he wore tied in a ponytail. His clothes were plain, brown cloth and leather, and his face had a sharp, hawkish handsomeness to it that was pleasant enough save for the long, thin scar running down the left side. It started at his temple, split his eyebrow, and ran down his cheek and over his lips, stopping just above his jaw. His left eye was discolored and murky where the scar crossed it, but it followed her movements just as well as his right, which was cold and flat gray-blue. He wore a sword low on his hip, but the guard and hilt were wrapped in thick felt that only hinted at their shape. Judging from the way he took his seat, however, Miranda harbored no illusions that the wrapping would slow his draw.

Coriano leaned on the table, gloved hands steepled in front of him and a small smile tugging at the edge of his thin mouth. "That was quite a display you put on outside. Normally, I prefer a note left at the bar, but I should know better by now than to expect subtlety from a Spiritualist."

"I would have contacted you more discreetly if I had time to wait in seedy taverns," Miranda said. "We Spiritualists lack the copious amounts of leisure time you bounty hunters seem to enjoy, Mr. Coriano."

His smile broadened, and he leaned back in his chair. "How may I help you?"

"You've been tracking the wizard thief Eli Monpress for months." Miranda leaned forward. "Both of our last tips came from you. I want to know how you do it."

Coriano glanced pointedly down at her rings. "What, can't root him out with your little menagerie? I thought that was one of the Spiritualist's specialties."

Miranda didn't bother to hide her annoyance. "With any other rogue wizard, yes, but Eli hides his tracks very well. You, however, always seem to be right on his heels." She reached into her bag and pulled out a heavy sack that jingled invitingly when she laid it on the table. "That's double the normal payment. It's yours if you tell me how to find him. More, if you lead me there."

Coriano glanced at the money, then back at her. "If I knew how to find Eli and his companions, do you really think I'd be wasting my time here?"

"Maybe, if you're as smart as the rumors say." Miranda moved her hand slightly, maneuvering her rings to catch the dim light. "You might be a great swordsman, but you can't take Eli on your own. You need a wizard to fight a wizard, or why else would you endanger your prize by tipping off the Spiritualists?"

"How do you know we're after the same prize?" Coriano said, tapping his fingers on the table.

"Because Eli is the prize everyone is after," she said sweetly. "Even us. If I catch Eli, his Council bounty belongs to the Spirit Court. Twenty thousand standards would be quite a boon to our budget. However"—Miranda leaned forward and lowered her voice—"there are things we value far more than money. If you help me, perhaps we can come to an arrangement. I have the authority to be very generous in this affair, Mr. Coriano."

Coriano leaned forward to match her. "Banage must be desperate indeed if he's stooped to making deals."

Miranda jerked back. "The Rector Spiritualis does what is best for the harmony of the Spirit Court," she said coldly. "Eli Monpress's rising notoriety threatens the good reputation we've spent the last several hundred years building."

"More valuable than gold indeed." Coriano smirked. "Can't have Monpress playing the wolf when the good Rector Spiritualis is busy trying to convince the world he's leading a flock of sheep."

"You will not find me a docile lamb," Miranda said flatly. "Will you help us, or am I wasting my breath?"

"Oh, you're not wasting anything," Coriano said. "This has been quite a charming chat. Sadly, I'm afraid I can't offer you my services this time around. I have a prior engagement. Besides," he smiled, "I don't think our methods would mesh."

"What kind of prior engagement is worth jeopardizing your good standing with the Spirit Court?" Miranda scoffed. "Master Banage has spoken so highly of your services, he would be most disappointed if you didn't help me now."

"How dreadful," Coriano said and arched his scarred eyebrow. "In that case, let me give you some advice, as one professional to another." He leaned in close, lowering his voice to an almost inaudible whisper. "Don't underestimate Monpress. He's a wizard, true, but not as you are, and he's been doing this for a long time. That twenty thousand bounty he carries isn't an exaggeration. Monpress has stolen enough gold from the Council Kingdoms to live like a king for five lifetimes, but the only records we have of him spending it are on setups for ever-larger thefts. Some of the world's best bounty hunters have chased him for months and caught nothing but stories, others simply vanished. This has led some experienced hunters to dismiss him as a wild chase, but that is because they have failed to understand Monpress's only constant: his pride in his vocation. Eli Monpress is a true thief. He steals for the joy of it. He doesn't make a show unless he wants you to see, and he never runs before he's gotten what he came for. He may act the charming fool, but he has a goal to everything he does. Find out what he really wants, and then position yourself so that he has to go through you to get it. Make him come to you. That's the only way you'll catch him.

"Now," he said, holding up the bag of money, which Miranda hadn't seen him take, "I've told you how to find him, so I'll be taking the payment as agreed."

He stood up in one smooth motion and bowed courteously, slipping the bulging coin purse into his pocket. "Forgive me, ladies, I must hurry to my next appointment. I'm sure we'll meet again."

He left the way he had come, disappearing as quietly as a cat behind the empty bar. Miranda gave him to the count of twenty before pushing her chair back with a clatter and stomping out of the decrepit tavern.

"Complete waste of time," she muttered, shoving the dirty

blanket out of her way. "For all the information he gave us, I might as well have interrogated the door a few more times."

Marion followed meekly, eyes on the dusty corners in case any other mysterious swordsmen were waiting to make an entrance. "What did he mean 'a wizard not as you are'?"

"How should I know?" Miranda said, marching down the creaking stairs. "I don't think he understands what comes out of his mouth any more than we do. We'll just have to expand the search. There's got to be something I'm missing. Whatever Coriano says about Eli's skill, Monpress can't do what he's doing without a spirit's help, and he can't use spirits without leaving some trace. He's been lucky so far, but as soon as I can figure out his gimmick, I'll wring his—" She stopped short.

The street outside was just as empty as it had been when they'd arrived. Gin was where they had left him, slouched on the ground. His large head rested on his paws, one of which had something squirmy pinned in the mud beneath it.

"You have a visitor," he said, tail twitching. "He didn't want to wait until you were done with your meeting, but I convinced him otherwise."

"Gin," Miranda said through gritted teeth. "Let him up."

The ghosthound lifted his paw, and Miranda hurried to help the man. Even covered in mud, the royal messenger's livery was recognizable. He wobbled a bit, like his knees wouldn't support him, and Miranda had to position herself between him and Gin before he could get his message out.

"T-the Master of Security s-sent me to f-find you, lady," he stuttered. "A letter just arrived from the king."

Miranda's face lit up. "A letter from the king? How long ago?"

"Master Oban sent me as soon as it came," he said, keeping his distance from the Spiritualist and her monster. "Ten minutes maybe? Twenty?"

That was all Miranda needed. She hooked her arm over Gin's nose and he lifted her up onto his waiting back.

"Lady!" Marion cried. "Where are you going?"

"To the castle, of course!" Miranda shouted. "Eli's made his move, and I'm not about to let him get away so easily this time."

Marion opened her mouth to say something else, but the ghosthound dashed behind her and Miranda swept the girl up onto his back. Gin whirled, patterns flashing wildly over his fur, and dashed up the hill, pouncing in silent bounds toward the castle.

The moment the ghosthound was out of sight, the neighborhood started pouring out of its hiding places. Men, women, and grubby children flooded the muddy street, and the royal messenger found himself surrounded by gawking, dirty people. One look at the knives some of the men wore in their boots and the messenger decided it was time to return as well, and he followed the ghosthound up the hill toward the castle at a dead run.

CHAPTER 7

Oban, the Master of Security, was waiting for them at the castle gate with a roll of parchment in his hand.

"Lady Miranda!" he shouted, running toward them as Gin slid to a stop.

"Is that the letter?" Miranda hopped down.

"Yes." He shoved the parchment into her hand. "Read it quickly."

She shook the paper open and read, muttering along as she went. "*King is safe... Send riders to the Council... Mellinor shall pledge an additional thirty-five thousand to Monpress's bounty*"—her eyebrows shot up—"*and five thousand in cash*—these demands are ridiculous!" She shook her head as she finished reading. "'*Raise a white flag from the second tower when you receive the new bounty notice from the Council and await further instructions.*' Why that greedy little thief, what is he playing at?" She thrust the note back at Oban. "You said the king wrote this?"

"Yes," Oban said, "under much duress, we fear."

Miranda gave him a flat look. "He has very good handwriting for a king under duress."

"Oh, this isn't the original." The Master of Security ran a nervous hand over his bald head. "It's a scribe copy."

"Well, that won't do." Miranda put her hands on her hips. "Where is the original? I need it now." Time was precious. If she got it soon enough, the faint, weak spirits in the ink might still remember the ink pot they'd lived in. That would give her a direction at least, maybe even a relative distance, but only if she got to them before they fell asleep completely and forgot that they'd ever been anything except words on a page.

The Master of Security blanched. "I'm afraid I can't get it, lady. The situation's, um"—he clutched his hands—"changed."

"Changed how?" Miranda's eyes narrowed.

"Go to the throne room, and you'll see." He sighed. "They don't know I let you see the note, lady, but I couldn't let you go in there without some information at least. Good luck." He bowed slightly, then whirled around and disappeared into the stables.

"He stinks of fear," Gin said, his orange eyes on Oban's retreating back.

"Do you know what this is about?" Miranda asked Marion, who was still working her way down off the ghosthound. The girl shook her head.

Miranda stared up at the white castle, which looked much more forbidding than usual. "Ears open, mutt," she muttered. "Be ready if I call you."

"Always am," Gin huffed, sitting down in the middle of the stable yard.

Miranda nodded and hurried up the castle steps, Marion keeping close behind her.

The entrance hall was quiet and empty. Miranda frowned, glancing around for the usual clusters of servants and officials, but there was no sign of them. She quickened her pace, trotting across the polished marble to the arched doorway that led to the throne room. As she rounded the corner, what she saw stopped her dead in her tracks. The entire servant population of castle Allaze, from the stable boys to the chambermaids, was crammed into the great hall that led to the throne room. They were crowded in, shoulder to shoulder, filling the hall to bursting.

Miranda stared bewildered at the wall of backs blocking their way. "All right," she sighed, slumping against the wall, "I give up. What is going on?"

Marion hurried forward, tapping the shoulder of a man at the back of the crowd wearing a blacksmith's leather apron to ask what was happening.

"Didn't ya hear?" the man said. "Lord Renaud's back."

Marion's face went white as cheese. She thanked the man and hurried back to Miranda. "Lord Renaud is back," she whispered.

"So I heard," Miranda said. "But let's assume for the moment that I know nothing about this country. Who is Lord Renaud?"

"King Henrith's older brother."

"*Older* brother?" Miranda frowned in confusion. "Is he a bastard or something?"

"Of course not!" Marion looked mortified.

"Then why did Henrith become king, and not him?" None of the research she'd done on Mellinor had mentioned any variance in the normal lines of succession. Of course, she hadn't had time to do much research in her rush to beat Eli.

"Lord Renaud was first in line for the throne, but then there were, um"—she glanced pointedly at Miranda's rings—"problems."

"I see," Miranda said quietly, following her gaze. "You know, in most countries, having a wizard in the royal family is considered a blessing." Marion winced at the coldness in her voice. "He was banished as a child, then?"

Marion shook her head. "That's usually the way, but not this time. You see, no one knew he was a wizard until a few days after the prince's sixteenth birthday. The old king was furious when he found out, of course, and he banished Lord Renaud to the desert on the southern edge of Mellinor."

"Sixteen is far too old for a manifestation," Miranda said, drumming her fingers against the stone doorway. "A wizard child can hear spirits from birth. It's obvious by the time they can talk that something is off. A prince, especially an heir to the throne, is hardly raised in obscurity. How did no one know?"

"The queen covered up for him," Marion said sadly. "It was no secret that she loved him the most. She wouldn't let the servants near him. She took care of him herself, dressed him and mended his clothes, prepared his meals, and so forth. We assumed it was because Renaud was the crown prince, since she never did any of that for Henrith. Now, of course, we know the real reason."

Miranda arched an eyebrow. "So how did it come to light?"

"The queen had a weak heart," Marion said sadly. "It got worse as she grew older, and finally there was nothing the doctors could do. She died on Renaud's birthday. They say the prince went mad with grief after that, his mother had been his whole world, and with him going on like that, there was no hiding what he was. He was banished before the week was out, and Henrith was made crown prince in his place." Marion leaned on the wall beside Miranda. "Of course, this all happened years ago, well before I came to the palace. I've seen Lord Renaud only once, when the king drove him out of the city."

Miranda eyed the packed crowd. "The return of a banished prince, no wonder everyone's making such a fuss. Well," she said and straightened up, "strange goings on or no, I need to get my spirits on that note or we'll be right back where we started. Follow me."

She walked up to the wall of backs and, without fanfare, began to elbow her way through. Marion wiggled along behind her, apologizing profusely to the angry people in their wake.

"I could have asked them to move," she huffed, squeezing between two guardsmen. "Despite the circumstances, you *are* a guest of the masters."

Miranda shook her head. "From what I've seen of Mellinor, announcing I'm a Spiritualist would be the same as shouting 'fire.' I don't want to cause a stampede."

As they neared the throne room doors, the press of people grew even tighter, and Miranda's and Marion's progress slowed to an agonizing crawl.

"This is ridiculous," Marion gasped, pressed against Miranda's shoulder by a pack of guardsmen. "We'll never get through."

Miranda pursed her lips, thinking, and then her eyes lit up. "Let me try something."

She closed her eyes and slumped forward slightly, letting her body relax. With practiced ease she retreated to the deepest part of her mind, the well of power her spirits sipped from, the well that was usually kept tightly shut. She breathed deeply, relaxing her hold just a fraction. The effect was immediate.

The crowd around them shivered and stepped away. It was

only a step, but it left just enough room for her and Marion to push through all the way to the golden doors. As soon as they reached the throne room's threshold, Miranda clamped down again. The small knot of people behind them gave a slight shiver and pressed in again as if nothing had happened.

Marion looked over her shoulder with wide eyes. "What did you do?"

"I opened my spirit," Miranda said.

"Opened your..." If possible, her eyes got wider.

That was all Miranda had meant to say, but, after that awed display, she couldn't help showing off just a little. "Opening the spirit reveals the strength of a wizard's power," she whispered. "Remember when I told you that a wizard's true power is control? That's because all wizards are born with more spirit, more energy than normal people. However, that energy is generally locked away shortly after birth by the child's own self-defense mechanisms. Having your spirit wide open all the time makes you vulnerable. Spirits are attracted to power, you see, and not all of them always mean you well. With training, wizards can learn to open their spirits, sometimes a little, sometimes all the way, depending on how much power you need to display. This is a vital part of getting a spirit's attention when you start really working with them."

"But," Marion said and frowned, thoroughly confused, "I thought you said you couldn't control people?"

"Well," Miranda smiled smugly, "what I just did is more of a trick on my part than any kind of real magic. Normal people can't feel a wizard's spirit even if it's open full blast—not consciously, anyway. However, I've found that with just the right feather touch even the most spirit deaf will feel a slight pressure without knowing they feel it, and step away."

"So," Marion shivered, "that feeling just now, like someone was stepping on my grave, that was you?"

"Yes," Miranda said, nodding. "A bit unconventional, but dreadfully handy."

"Must be," Marion said. "What would happen if you opened it all the way?"

"Let's say it would be very uncomfortable for everyone involved." Miranda smiled. "Come"—she grabbed the librarian's hand and pushed through the last line of people separating them from the throne room—"let's do what we came here to do. We've wasted too much time as it is." She tallied the time inwardly and winced. The note was probably dead asleep by now. Still, any clue, anything at all, and this would all be worth it.

Though the crowd was better dressed, the throne room was every bit as packed as the hall outside, and buzzing just as intently. Miranda stood on tiptoe, looking around for the Master of the Courts or anyone who could help her, when she heard the solemn sound of metal on stone. It must have been a signal, for all at once the whispers died out and the crowd fell silent. All attention was now on the tall, slim figure climbing the steps of the dais. When he was one step from the empty throne, he stopped and turned to face the crowd. As his face came into view, Miranda caught her breath.

After Marion's story, she wasn't sure what she was expecting. A bitter, weather-worn exile, perhaps, or a smug, spoiled prince enjoying his triumphant return. Whatever she'd expected, the man standing on the dais was nothing like it. He was, however, undoubtedly a prince. Tall and handsomely dressed in a dark-blue coat, he projected the confidence of someone used to being obeyed. A waterfall of golden hair hung down his back, swaying gently as he bowed low to the crowd. His fine-featured face was almost feminine in its beauty, and Miranda swallowed despite herself. He certainly didn't look like someone who'd spent the last ten years exiled in the desert.

The golden prince looked out over the sea of people, a benevolent and humble expression on his lovely face. He held up his hands in a welcoming gesture. Miranda could almost feel the crowd leaning forward to drink him in as he began to speak.

"Citizens of Mellinor!" His voice rang out through the enraptured room. "I come before you as a criminal and an exile. Many have asked me how, seeing this, I come to stand before you today, and so, first, before you all, I must confess. Eleven years ago, I was banished for being born a wizard, in accordance with the ancient law. Yet, despite this, and because of the deep love I bear this country, for the past eight years I have disobeyed my father's order and lived among you. For Mellinor's sake, I have lived nameless, a pauper among paupers. I was here four years ago when my younger brother, Henrith, took the throne, and I cheered him in the streets alongside you, without jealousy or malice. Until yesterday, I was content to live forgetting the duty I was born to and denying the curse that took my crown if that was what was needed to stay here, in my home. But yesterday, when I heard of the atrocious crime that had been committed, not just against the throne of Mellinor, but against my own flesh and blood, I could stay silent no more."

Renaud leaned forward, his ringing voice heavy with contempt. "You have heard by now that the wizard thief Monpress, wanted throughout the Council Kingdoms for a list of crimes too long to read here, has kidnapped our king. This crime must not go unanswered."

A great cry rose up at this, and Renaud leaned into it, letting it grow. When the noise reached a fevered pitch, Renaud threw out his arms, and silence fell like a knife.

When he spoke again, his words were choked with sorrow. "My friends, I come to you with no expectations, no pleas, nothing but the offer of my service. It was my wizardry that forced this burden upon my younger brother. Let it be my wizardry that ends it. As I was once your prince, I beg you now, let me face this criminal and help save my brother, the only family I have left. Let me serve him as I could not serve you, and I swear to you, I swear on my life that Mellinor will have her king again!"

He threw his fists in the air, and the crowd erupted. The nobles around Miranda clapped and cheered, but their polite noise was drowned out by the crowd in the hall, who hadn't seen such drama in years, if ever. Even the somberly dressed masters were milling about looking impressed despite themselves, and some of the younger ones were cheering just as loudly as the servants.

Marion bounced up and down on her toes. "Oh, isn't it exciting?"

"Quite." Miranda scowled. Something about Renaud's smile as he shook the waiting masters' hands didn't sit well with her. Marion gave her a quizzical look, but Miranda had already begun elbowing her way through the well-dressed crowd.

She ran to catch up. "Lady! Where are you going?"

"To hold him to his words," Miranda said, pushing past a pair of old ladies waving their lacy handkerchiefs at the prince. "He says he wants to help, so I'm going to make him give me that note."

Marion shrank from the nasty looks they were getting, but before she could start apologizing, a boy in page's livery popped out of the crowd right beside Miranda.

"Lady Spiritualist," he said, bowing nervously. "Lord Renaud wishes to meet you right away."

"Well," Miranda said. "That saves some trouble. Lead on."

The page turned and led them away from the crowd to a small door just off the back half of the main throne room. This opened into a small, richly decorated parlor. As soon as they were inside, the page vanished back into the crowd, letting the door close softly behind him.

"Well," Miranda said, dropping into one of the silk couches, "that was all very neat. We were swept up and tucked away before we could cause trouble." She glanced at Marion, who was still standing by the door, looking slightly dazed. "Your Renaud seems to have gained quite a bit of influence in a very short time for a banished wizard prince. His speech wasn't *that* good."

"Prince is the key word there, I think." Marion sighed, padding across the carpet to take a seat on one of the straight-backed, carved wooden chairs under the window. "With the king gone, Mellinor's been headless. Since our founding, we've never been without a king for more than a day. There's no precedent at all, so it's no wonder the masters are in a panic. I shouldn't say this, but they'd probably follow the king's dog at this point if it could prove a royal lineage." She glanced at the door. "Lord Renaud sure picked the right time to come back. Only in a situation like this could his status as a prince outweigh his stigma as a wizard."

"How very convenient for him," Miranda said thoughtfully.

Marion paled. "Please don't take offense, lady. Stigma's the wrong word. I—"

"It's fine." Miranda smiled. "Don't apologize. You've given me a lot to think about."

"It's just…" Marion pulled at her dress. "I've never had to think about things from a wizard's—Spiritualist! Spiritualist's point of view, and—"

She stopped midbabble and sprang out of her chair. Miranda looked at her, confused, but Marion shook her head fiercely and pointed at the door before dropping into a low curtsy.

A second later, Prince Renaud himself swept into the room.

CHAPTER 8

He was alone, which struck Miranda as unusual, and he bowed as graciously as any servant as the door drifted shut behind him.

"Lady Spiritualist," he said, "I've very much looked forward to meeting you."

Miranda stood up and bowed as well, hoping Mellinor had no special deviations from common court etiquette. "Lord Renaud, I appreciate your taking the time to see me. There are several things—"

"Shouldn't you be resting?" Renaud said, rolling right over her. "The masters told me you've been up since you got here."

Miranda stiffened. "I appreciate your concern, but time is of the essence. If we are to save your brother, I must have access to the king's original ransom note."

"Oh, it's far too late to question the spirits, if that's what you're after." Renaud smiled sweetly.

"I'll make my own decision on that," Miranda said flatly. "The spirits in that note are our only connection to Eli. If you will not give it to me, then tell me where to find it and I will fetch the note myself, but do not waste my time, or your brother's, with assumptions about my methods."

Renaud's smile did not waver. "I'm afraid that simply won't be possible."

"Excuse me?" Miranda's glare seemed to lower the temperature in the room. Lord Renaud continued as if nothing had happened.

"The court of Mellinor was in a panic when you arrived, and the officials you bullied into permitting your free reign of this kingdom had no right to grant you the freedoms they did. Now that I have restored order, I'm afraid your assistance in this matter is no longer needed."

"Forgive me, prince," Miranda said, "but it is not your place to decide my duties. Panic or no, my aid was requested by officials acting on the king's behalf. My duty lies with Henrith now, and only his rescue or death can relieve me of it."

"Your dedication is admirable," Renaud said. "But Mellinor will deal with Mellinor's problems."

"A bold statement." Miranda eyed him. "But how will you go about it? A wizard dangerous enough for a twenty thousand gold bounty is not one to be taken lightly. No matter what boasts you make, you are going to need my help if you plan to face him."

Renaud paused and flicked his eyes pointedly to Marion. The girl, who was trying to make herself as small as possible, froze. He made a slight shooing motion with one finger, and Marion, palace trained as she was, leaped to obey. After a series of overly polite curtsies, she hurried past him and out of the room. Only when the door was shut completely did Renaud continue.

"That's better." Renaud smiled. "As I was saying, your statement might be true, *if* we intended to fight him. The masters and I went over the ransom note as soon as it arrived, and we found Eli's demands to be quite reasonable."

Miranda stared blankly at him. "You're joking."

"I can assure you I am not," Renaud said, meeting her gaze levelly.

"Five thousand in cash and thirty-five in bounty pledges? In what world is that reasonable?"

"Is my brother not worth five times as much?" Renaud's glare sharpened.

"You can't just give that, that *thief* what he wants!" Miranda sputtered.

Renaud sighed. "You see, this is precisely why we cannot accept your help. How could we trust our king's life to someone who values it so cheaply?"

Miranda flinched, getting a firm grip on her rage. "It's not about the money," she said, calmly now. "Don't you see this is exactly what he wants? Think about it: by demanding you pledge thirty-five thousand to his bounty, Eli ensures that Mellinor has a hefty stake in keeping him uncaught. He's using this country as a safety net. If you just give in like this, think about what kind of signal you'll be sending other would-be thieves. Eli is an innovator, but he's not the only wizard thief. If he is successful, others will surely follow his lead. Doing this could make Mellinor a target for years to come, and your policy against wizards leaves you helpless."

"But you forget," Renaud said, folding his hands behind his back, "Mellinor has its own wizard now."

"Being born a wizard doesn't mean you have the skills to fight one. What if Eli double-crosses you? Did you think about that? If he decides to take the money and not return your king, do you really think you could stop him?"

"Your concern for our well-being is touching," Renaud said, "but such matters are no longer yours to worry about." He walked casually to the door and held it open. "You'll find whatever provisions you need in the kitchens. If that dog of yours is half of what they say, you should be able to make it over the border by nightfall." His smile didn't reach his eyes. "I sincerely suggest you make all haste. I might not feel so generous tomorrow, should you be caught on our lands."

Miranda stood her ground. "I am not one to be dismissed so easily."

"But you are a member of the Spirit Court," Renaud said, "and you are bound by your oaths not to interfere in internal kingdom affairs. You could be stripped of your position if you push this much further." His smile turned cruel. "Isn't that so, lady Spiritualist?"

It was all Miranda could do not to strangle the smug lordling with his own flowing hair. Her spirits picked up her tension and began to murmur in their gems. For a wild moment, she was on the edge of opening up and showing him the difference between a Court-trained Spiritualist and a self-taught brat. Slowly, methodically, she clamped down on the impulse. She turned and walked out of the room, but when she reached Renaud, she stopped and whispered in a low, cutting voice, "This isn't over."

"No," Renaud whispered back. "I believe it is."

Miranda stomped past him and into the still-crowded throne room, boot heels clicking angrily against the marble. The waiting masters scrambled to get out of her way, which made her feel a hair better, until she heard Renaud politely call after her: "Good day, Spiritualist."

She didn't give him the satisfaction of looking back.

Renaud waited until the Spiritualist was completely out of sight before he shut the door. "Are you sure that was wise?" asked an amused voice from the corner.

Renaud jumped before he could stop himself. "Must you do that?"

Coriano was already sitting on the silk couch when the prince turned, his boots propped up on the low table and his wrapped sword laid across his knees. He gave Renaud a smile and waved at the chair across from him. "Sit."

Renaud remained standing. "You were saying?"

Coriano shrugged and put his hands behind his head. "I was just asking if you didn't come across a little too brash with the whole 'I might not feel so generous tomorrow' bit. I gave you all the information you'd need to trap her with her own vows. There was no need to push her further. Old man Banage taught her how to put up a cold front, but anyone can see she's got a mean temper inside. After that display, I wouldn't be surprised if she really did leave tonight, just to spite you."

"She won't," Renaud said. "One thing I do know about Spiritualists is that they all share the same debilitating sense of duty. If she's been sent here to do a job, she won't leave until it's done." He eyed the man cautiously. "Why do you care? I thought all you wanted was Eli's swordsman."

"Yes." Coriano's bored voice hid a dangerous edge. "But that will be hard if you flub your part sporting with something as volatile as Spiritualist pride." The swordsman's gloved fingers drifted gently along the wrapped hilt of his sword and he gave the prince a sideways look. "You're not the only one who's been waiting for his chance, wizard. If you play games with this, we will gut you before you see us coming."

"Everything is on schedule," the prince said, the words grinding through his gritted teeth. "You mind your end and I'll mind mine."

"Fair enough." Coriano stood up. "We're about to have company, so I'll take my leave. I'll be back when the flag flies, so have my fee ready. Double rate, of course, but considering you'll be the one collecting Eli's bounty when this is over, it hardly matters."

"What are you talking about?" Renaud said. "You told me Josef Liechten had a ten thousand gold bounty of his own."

"He does," Coriano said, walking toward the servant's door, his boots quiet as cat feet on the stone. "But that's only if he's brought in alive." He gave Renaud a feral grin. "Some things are worth more than money, prince."

"There, at least, we agree," Renaud said, straightening his cuffs. When he looked up again, the swordsman was gone, the servant's small door swinging shut behind him. A second later, a soft knock sounded on the door connecting the parlor to the throne room.

Renaud gathered his patience and opened it before the second knock landed. When he faced the waiting crowd of masters, his smile was the picture of sad sincerity.

"Gentlemen," he said, "forgive me for making you wait. I had a lot to consider. I am sad to report that, for reasons of her own, the Lady Miranda has declined to aid us further."

"You must be mistaken!" Master Oban elbowed his way to the front of the group. "She promised to help us!"

"The Spirit Court is a single-minded organization," Renaud said gravely. "They care only for their laws and those who break them, not for the victims left behind. Honestly, we should have expected no less."

"But," the Master of the Exchequer clutched his ledger, "what are we to do?"

"There is only one solution," Renaud said, "in order to save my brother, I will meet Eli and make the exchange without her."

A swell of conversation erupted as everyone turned to his neighbor to remark at the selfless nobility of this gesture.

The Master of the Courts alone remained calm. "And, my lord, should the thief betray you?" He glanced at the Master of the Exchequer. "The bounty request has already been sent, and Council law says we cannot change it for any reason once our pledge has been entered in the official records. Your bold claim is noble, but Mellinor can hardly afford to lose our king, our prince, and forty thousand standards in one swoop."

"That will not happen," Renaud said, glaring at the old master. "The Spirit Court may be willing to gamble a country's safety to catch a thief, but I am not one of their pet wizards. Though I was banished, I am a prince still, and my goal is the preservation of Mellinor. That is why, in all the world, I am the only wizard you can trust."

A cheer erupted at this, and the old Master of the Courts was overwhelmed by the waving hands of the younger masters, who thought this was all very grand. Master Oban caught the eye of the Master of Courts and the two of them quietly retreated to a corner of the throne room.

"The tide in Mellinor is shifting," the Master of the Courts said with a sigh when they were safely away. "I wonder if we shall like where it takes us."

"Wizard or no, he's a prince of House Allaze." The Master of Security shrugged. "In four hundred years, they've never led us wrong. It'll work out in the end, old friend," he said. "You'll see."

The Master of the Courts stroked his gray beard thoughtfully. "I pray you are right." He turned his eyes to the empty throne, standing high and alone on the marble dais. "We must all pray."

CHAPTER 9

Miranda stormed into the stable yard, scattering the crowd of boys who had gathered to watch Gin eat the pig he had helped himself to from the swine pen.

"We're leaving," she said. "*Now.*"

Gin looked sadly at the pig, then pulled away with a sigh, licking his mouth clean as he trotted over. Miranda stuffed the bag of traveling food that she'd frightened out of the kitchen staff into her rucksack and slung it into position over Gin's neck. Gin lay down with uncharacteristic meekness as Miranda clambered into her riding position.

"Get us out of here."

The hound rose swiftly, but before he could spring forward a familiar voice called out: "Lady Miranda!"

Miranda looked up in surprise as Marion jumped down the castle steps and hit the stable yard at a dead run. She didn't stop until she reached Gin, slamming into his foreleg rather than taking the time to slow down.

"Here," she gasped, and thrust her hand out. Miranda reached down and plucked the creased slip of paper from her fingers. As she unfolded it, her face lit up. "How did you get this?"

Marion grinned from ear to ear. "All important papers go to the library for storage. Sometimes being a junior librarian does have its advantages."

"Won't you get in trouble?" Miranda frowned. "You know I probably won't be able to get this back to you before they notice it's gone."

Marion shook her head violently. "So long as the king comes back, I don't think they would care if I raided the whole treasury."

Miranda smiled. "Thank you," she said. "I won't forget this."

Marion waved and pushed off the ghosthound's leg.

Waving back, Miranda gave Gin the go-ahead. The ghosthound sprang forward, leaving the boys gawking as he disappeared over the gates in a cloud of dust.

"How convincing should I be?" Gin said as they jumped the final gate of the city.

Miranda glared darkly at the rolling countryside as it streaked by. "And what makes you think we're not actually leaving?"

She could feel Gin's chuckle through his fur. "You don't normally lose this gracefully. The castle isn't on fire, so far as I can see."

"Smart aleck mutt." Miranda smacked him good-naturedly. "You're right, we're not leaving. I'll give up my rings before I let that jerk have his way."

"What jerk?" Gin panted.

Miranda gave him the short version of her meeting with Renaud. When she finished, Gin growled thoughtfully. "Politics and gold are human vices, so maybe there's something here I don't understand, but I have trouble believing that an exiled prince like Renaud is really that concerned over the recovery of the little brother who took his throne."

"My thoughts exactly." Miranda leaned over to scratch his ears.

"What are we going to do, then?"

"That part is simple. We're going to find Eli first." She pointed to the left, where a thick line of shaggy conifers separated two fields. "Duck into that copse."

Gin picked up the pace, and a few seconds later they were hidden behind the small stand of pines. Miranda jumped down and, after checking the area for any stray watchers, pressed her thumb against the fat, smooth sapphire on her right index finger. "Allinu, wake up, I need you."

A moment later, a small, white spout of pure water bubbled happily out of the ring, forming a small pool in Miranda's cupped hand. When the water was up to her thumb, Miranda shoved the ransom note in. "Find this ink's source."

"Yes, mistress," the water whispered, and began to churn.

Miranda kept her fingers pressed as tightly as she could, though she knew it was not needed. Allinu was a mountain mist. She could stay together in a sieve if she needed to. Still, it made

Miranda feel better when the water was splashing in all directions like it was now.

A few moments later, the note floated to the top, perfectly dry.

"I'm sorry, mistress," the water said. "The ink's been dry too long. It doesn't remember anything."

"I figured as much," Miranda said, shifting the water to one cupped hand and plucking the note out. She looked at it once more before stuffing it into her pocket. So much for that.

"The paper was a bit more helpful," the water added, almost as an afterthought.

Miranda's head jerked up. "The what?"

"The paper," Allinu said again. "I noticed a few rips on one side, so I asked it what had happened. Once it realized I wasn't going to drown it into pulp, it told me about the bird. Apparently, your thief had the note delivered by falcon. In the falcon's talons, actually, which the paper did not appreciate. Claws are very hard on paper, and—"

"Yes, of course," Miranda said. "Did the paper say anything else?"

"I was getting to that," Allinu sloshed, insulted. "It said, 'At least the trip was short.'"

"How short?"

"Two, three minutes from when the falcon grabbed him until the falcon dropped it on some guards," Allinu bubbled.

"That's more like it." Miranda grinned. "Thank you, Allinu."

The water rose in a white mist, swirling and then vanishing back into the sapphire, leaving Miranda's fingers damp and cold.

"Two minutes," Gin said. "That's a pretty big area."

"Not everything's as fast as you are," Miranda said, wiping her hand on her trousers. "Coriano did say Eli wouldn't run far. Besides, if he wasn't close by, how could he see the signal when they meet his demands? He specifically told them to fly it from the second tower, which is barely visible above the wall." She smiled at the castle rising over the city, less than a mile behind them. "Look, you can hardly see it even at this distance. He must be close, and when they give the signal, he'll need to send another note to set up the trade and deliver the king. When he does that, we'll be ready."

She reached into the neck of her shirt and pulled out a silver pendant of delicate spirals wrapped around a large, white pearl. It was a lovely piece of work. She'd had it made especially for the spirit she kept inside, before she caught him, which wasn't the normal order of things, but Eril had been worth it. The number of Spiritualists who kept wind spirits could be counted on one hand. Wind spirits were almost impossible to catch, and nearly as impossible to control if you did catch one. That was why she'd chosen a pendant to house him. It kept him close. A Spiritualist never forced her spirits to serve, but some spirits required more supervision than others.

"Eril," she said, holding the pendant out. "I need you."

At first, nothing happened. Miranda stood stone still, eyes on the pendant, until a soft breeze tangled the wispy hair around her ears. "You called?"

Miranda grimaced inwardly. Talking to a wind spirit was uncomfortably like talking to thin air. Eril, of course, took full advantage of this.

"I need you to keep an eye on the castle and all surrounding land for the next few days," she said, careful to keep her face in the determined but slightly bored expression that worked best with flighty spirits. "You're watching for a white flag from the second tower. The moment it flies, you'll be looking for a bird, likely a falcon, but it could be anything, with a note in its claws. I'll want to know where it came from, where it goes once the note is delivered, plus anything else of interest you might see."

"Bird watching?" Eril said and sighed dramatically, blowing Miranda's hair into her eyes. "That sounds so *boring.* Can't I do something else?"

"No," Miranda said firmly. "Don't forget to keep an eye on *all* the surrounding territory—the city, the countryside, and the forest to the north where the king keeps his deer. I'll want reports on everything."

"All right, all right, I heard you the first time," he huffed. "Never get to have any fun," Miranda heard him mutter as the wind began to die down.

Miranda stayed frozen even after the air was still, a scowl etched on her face.

"He's gone," Gin said.

"Good," Miranda said, giving herself a little shake. "He likes to hang around sometimes, just to see what I say about him. Gives me the jeebies."

The hound snorted sympathetically. "How did you catch him in the first place if you couldn't see him?"

"I used smoke," Miranda said, untying Gin's pack and dropping it on the ground. "But even when I could see, it took me a solid month before I managed to catch hold of a wind spirit long enough to convince him to join me."

Gin shook his massive head. "I will never understand how you humans manage to get through your short lives being spirit blind. That's probably why the Powers gave your kind the ability to command spirits. It's a survival mechanism."

"We get by well enough." Miranda pushed aside the thick branches for a better look at the castle. "It might have been a little much, sending him so early. The riders won't even reach the Council city until late tomorrow, and that's if they ride through the night. Then there's the wait while the bounty is approved."

"So what?" Gin flopped down on the thick carpet of pine needles. "I could use a break."

"Lazy mutt." Miranda grinned. Still, he was right. Ever since they'd gotten Coriano's tip that Eli was in Mellinor, they'd been constantly on the move. She hadn't had more than three hours of sleep in one stretch since she'd left the Spirit Court.

"All right," she said, slumping down next to him, "you win. But since you got to sleep while I was searching the castle, you get first watch."

Gin snorted, sending pine straw everywhere, but he moved to the edge of the clearing where he could lounge and watch the road at the same time. When he was settled, Miranda lay back, looking up at the deep blue sky through the tree tops. Eventually, they'd need to find a better hiding place, but this would do for now. Anyway, the sun was warm here. She closed her eyes. When Eli made his move, they would be ready. The thought made her smile, and with that, she fell asleep.

CHAPTER 10

Josef glared at his opponent, watching for an opening. The smallest twitch could show the weakness that would turn his defeat into victory. A few feet away, Eli lounged in the sunlight, leaning against the branches that hid their tumbledown stone shack and grinning like an idiot.

The thief's eyes flicked down, and Josef saw his opening.

"Match and raise," he growled, tossing two gold standards on the grass in front of him.

Eli's grin faltered a fraction, and he picked up a pair of oblong coins from his own stack. "You're showing a knight," he said, pointing at the face-up card by Josef's foot. "That's five points at least. Maybe you're confused, but in Daggerback, it's the *lowest* hand that wins." He paused, twirling the coins between his long fingers, seemingly oblivious to the danger of taunting a man whose daily dress included over fifty pounds of edged weaponry. "You can take the bet back, if you want," he said, his voice positively dripping with generosity. "I won't mind."

"No." Josef crouched behind his cards. "You're not getting me with that again."

"Have it your way," Eli said, tossing his coins into the pot. "Let's see who was right."

Josef threw his hand down, adding a bearded man with a staff and an old geezer with a crown to his gallant knight in the grass. "Bachelor party: wizard, king, knight. That's ten points," he said, grinning.

Eli smirked and deftly flipped his cards like a fan. "Wizard, king, and my lovely lady." He scooped up the queen card he'd laid face-up in the grass after the first round of bets, and his smirk became intolerable. "Nine points."

Josef glowered murderously as Eli rubbed his hands together and reached out to gather his winnings.

"Grand sweep," Nico said quietly, and the two men froze. "Hunter, weaver, shepherdess." She named each card as she laid it in the grass. "Three points."

Eli sighed and shoved the pile of gold toward Nico. Now it was Josef's turn to grin. "Too bad, Eli," he said, leaning back against one of the mossy trees that ringed their tiny clearing. "Next time, you should worry less about bluffing me and more about not losing your shirt."

"I don't mind losing to Nico," Eli said, tossing her the last of the coins. "She's a much better winner than you are."

Josef grunted and nodded over his shoulder in the direction of the castle, where the spires were barely visible through the thick trees. "Speaking of winning, have those idiots gotten back to us? We've been sitting here for almost a week, and if I have to spend another day playing Daggerback with you lot, the name might start to sound like a good suggestion."

"Actually, the flag went up fifteen minutes ago," Eli said casually. "I just wanted to see if I could win the rest of your gold before telling you."

Josef jumped to his feet. Sure enough, a large flag dangled from the top of the second tower, its white folds lying limp against the slate shingles, twitching in the breeze.

Eli winked at Josef's murderous glare and walked whistling into the hut.

The king was lying on the dirt floor, looking miserable as always. Eli had left him under the watchful flicker of the fire, which, in exchange for Eli keeping Nico outside for most of the day, was willing to make sure their royal prisoner didn't escape. Eli skirted the edge of the hearth and poked the king's shoulder with the toe of his boot.

"Almost done, your royalness."

The king sat up stiffly, and Eli handed him a tiny pot of ink and a pen nib attached to a stick, which he produced from somewhere in his pockets. "All you have to do now is write exactly what I say, and we'll take you home."

The king looked defiant for a half second and then he nodded glumly and began to copy Eli's demands word for word.

Josef was gone when Eli emerged ten minutes later, the king's letter rolled in a tight tube and ready to go. Nico, however, was where he had left her, arranging her newly acquired gold in shining patterns across the scrubby grass.

"Don't worry," she said without looking up. "He's just gone to scout the meeting place."

"Why?" Eli said, laughing. "We haven't even told them where it is yet."

Nico shrugged. "He said you would say that, and he said to tell you that you can't make assumptions about anything." She paused thoughtfully. "He also said to tell you that if he does find any traps he's going to make sure you stand on them."

"Marvelous." Eli sighed. Why did swordsmen have to be so competitive about *everything*? "The good king was kind enough to write another note for us," he said, twirling the roll of paper in his hands. "I'm setting the trade-off for this evening, an hour before sunset. That should give them plenty of time to prepare, and us plenty of leeway should things go off course."

Nico turned back to her coins. "Do you expect things to go off course?"

Eli shrugged. "Does anything we do ever go as planned?"

Nico looked up at him and shrugged back.

"Anyway," Eli continued, holding up the note, "I'm going to find a bird to take this to the palace. If Josef gets back before I do, make sure to tell him that if his trap finding is as good as his card playing I'll gladly stand anywhere he tells me."

Nico's mouth twitched, and if Eli hadn't known better, he would have said she had just suppressed a laugh. Shoving his hands in his pockets, he turned and walked into the forest, whistling a falcon call.

An hour before the appointed time, Josef made everyone move out.

"You can't be serious," Eli said from his comfy spot in the grass.

Josef just shook his head and strapped another bandolier of throwing knives on top of his already impressive personal arsenal. "Last to a fight, first in the dirt," he said, hooking his short swords into place, one on each hip. When those were set, he grabbed his enormous iron sword from the log beside him and slung it over his shoulder. "Let's go."

He turned and walked out of the clearing, his heavy boots surprisingly quiet on the leaf-littered ground. Nico followed just behind him, moving over the fallen logs like a shadow. Eli lounged for a moment longer. Then, with a long sigh, he heaved himself up and went into the hut to get the king.

They walked single file through the forest. Josef went first, stalking through the tree shadows like a knife-covered jungle cat. Eli strolled a good distance behind him, leading the king by his rope like a puppy. Nico trailed at the back, her enormous coat pulled tight around her despite the warm afternoon, and her eyes glued to the thick undergrowth.

"You'll never get away with this, you know," King Henrith said, trying to keep some of his dignity as he stumbled after Eli. "As soon as I'm back with my own men, I'll put my entire army after you. You won't even reach the border."

"Splendid!" Eli said, ducking under a low branch. "At least things won't be boring. After this last week, an army on our heels sounds like a welcome vacation."

"Don't you understand?" the king sputtered, shaking his bound fists at the thief's back. "I'll have you drawn and quartered! I'll hang your innards up in the city square for birds to pick at, and what's left, I'll throw in the river for the fish!"

"That doesn't sound very sanitary." Eli pressed his finger to his lips thoughtfully. "Still, it's the thought that counts." He looked over his shoulder, a heartfelt sunbeam of a smile lighting up his face. "I'm so happy we got to know each other like this. That's the best part about this business: You meet so many interesting people!"

The king turned purple with rage, but before he could think of a proper comeback, Eli came to an abrupt halt, causing the king to run face first into his back. A few feet ahead, Josef had stopped and was watching the trees, one hand hovering over the short sword at his hip.

They were at the edge of a small gap in the trees, not really a meadow but a rare sunny space where bushes and wildflowers had taken root. The forest around them looked just like every other bit they'd spent the last twenty minutes walking through, a mix of midsized hardwoods and thick undergrowth. The only sounds were the cries of far-off birds and the wind rustling the leaves high above them.

"What is it?" Eli whispered, creeping toward the swordsman.

Josef stayed perfectly still, with his hands on his swords. "We're being followed."

As soon as he said it, a monster launched itself out of the undergrowth. It moved like mist over water, gray and cold and canine, with enormous teeth, which Josef managed to dodge barely a second before they would have sunk into his leg. He landed hard on his knees beside Eli, rolling to his feet as soon as he touched the ground, his short sword flashing. Eli pulled the king and Nico close behind him, backing them into the center of the small clearing to give the swordsman room to maneuver. Josef crouched low beside them, both short swords out now, and readied himself for the creature's next charge.

However, the charge never came. As soon as they were all bunched together, the trap sprang.

CHAPTER 11

The ground erupted at their feet, sprouting four enormous walls that grew ten feet before they could react. At first, the walls appeared to be made of dirt, but as soon as they reached their full height, the dirt shifted and became solid, slick stone, caging them in on all sides save for a tiny, open square of sky at the very top. Then, as suddenly as the walls had grown, they stopped, leaving the king and his kidnappers squashed together like fish in a square, stone barrel.

"Eli," Josef whispered. "Please tell me this is one of your spirits."

"No such luck," came a voice from above. A shadow fell over them, and the captives looked up to see a red-headed woman smirking down through the opening.

"Eli Monpress," she said, "I am Spiritualist Miranda Lyonette. You are hereby under arrest by order of the Rector Spiritualis, Etmon Banage, for the improper use of spirits, treason against the Spirit Court, and, most recently, the kidnapping of King Henrith of Mellinor. You will surrender your spirits and come quietly."

"Now wait a minute," Eli yelled up at her. "Treason against the Spirit Court? Don't you have to be a member of something to commit treason against it? I don't recall ever joining your little social club."

The woman arched her eyebrow. "The Spirit Court preserves the balance between human and spirit. When you used your abilities to ruin the reputation of all wizards by turning to a flamboyant life of crime, you committed treason against all spirits and the humans who care for them. Does that answer your question?"

"Not really," Eli said.

"Well, we'll have plenty of time to talk about it later," Miranda said, smirking. "Will you surrender the king and come quietly, or must I ask Durn here to march you all the way to the Spirit Court's door?"

The stone prison jerked several feet to the left, knocking its occupants in a pile on the dusty ground.

"You make a strong argument, Lady Miranda," Eli said, untangling himself from the king. "But I'm afraid there's a slight problem."

"Oh?" Miranda leaned forward.

"You see, we already had his royal dustiness here order his people to write a letter pledging thirty-five thousand gold toward my bounty. You know how the Council is; they never go back on something once it's been through the system, so you must agree it would be frightfully rude of me to just go off with you and forfeit all of Mellinor's money to the Spirit Court, especially considering the country's general aversion to practitioners of the magical arts."

"I fail to see how that is my concern, Mr. Monpress." Miranda waved her hand dismissively. "Why don't we wait and ask the Rector Spiritualis what he thinks?"

"Ah," Eli said. "That sounds lovely. Unfortunately, I must refuse. You see, I have a pressing prior obligation to take his highness home and pick up a rather disgusting amount of money."

"You might find that difficult, considering the circumstances," Miranda said, patting the wall below her. "I don't know how you charm your spirits, sir, but Durn here only answers to me, and he says you're coming with us."

"Really?" Eli rapped his knuckles against the hard stone. "Let's see if he won't have a change of heart. Nico, if you would?"

Nico nodded and stretched out her hand, pressing her long fingers delicately against the stone wall. For a moment, nothing happened. Then her eyes flashed under the shadow of her hat, and the wall beneath her fingers began to vanish. Not pull back, not crumble, but vanish, as if it had never been there to begin with.

After that, things happened very quickly. The stone walls of the prison collapsed with a thundering scream, falling over in an avalanche of rubble, including the wall Miranda had been so confidently perched on only seconds before. Suddenly without purchase, the female Spiritualist fell tumbling to the ground with a sickening thud.

The giant hound sprang forward with a terrifying roar, landing in a protective crouch above his motionless mistress. "Monster!" he roared, his patterns whirling through the thick cloud of dust and grit. "What did you do?"

"I'm sure we don't know what you're talking about," Eli said, dusting himself off. "We were the ones attacked by a mon—"

Gin didn't give the thief a chance to finish. He leaped forward, almost too fast to see, his claws going straight for Nico's throat. He would have struck true if Josef's blade hadn't been there. The swordsman parried the hound's swipe at the last second, but the impact took them both to the ground. Josef rolled and came up sword first. The hound pushed off the grass in a shower of dirt and wheeled around, narrowly dodging the swordsman's counter-swipe with a well-timed leap.

"Stand aside, human," Gin snarled, his hackles bristling as he circled for another charge. "It's not you I want now. Rest assured, I'll eat you later for what you did to my mistress."

"Growl all you want, pup." Josef flipped his swords with a toothy grin, and pointed both tips at the ghosthound's nose. "I'm no wizard, so if you have something to tell me, you'll have to say it in a language I understand."

The ghosthound clawed the ground and launched forward, teeth snapping in readiness to crush the swordsman's skull, but before he had gone more than a few feet, something extraordinary happened. On either side of the charging hound, enormous roots burst out of the ground. They flew like spears, shooting out of the dirt and over the ghosthound in a tall arc. Then, with a whip crack, they slammed down hard, pinning the dog beneath them. Howling, Gin clawed and tore at the ground, foam flicking from his mouth as he fought to get free, but it was no use. The roots were young and strong, and, as much as he struggled, they would not let him go.

Josef stared in confusion for a moment and then glanced over at Eli, who looked to be in deep conversation with the stand of oaks on the far side of the clearing, and his face fell.

"Powers, Eli, did you have to?" He slammed his swords back into their sheaths. "Things were finally getting interesting."

Eli finished thanking the trees and turned to scowl at his companion. "Don't worry, I'm sure he'll still want to kill you later, but we don't have time for this right now. You were the one who said we should be early."

Josef grunted and turned away. "Nico," he called, "grab the king."

Nico nodded and reached down. The king shied away from her with a terrified squeak. On her next grab, she didn't give him the chance to dodge. She took hold of his collar and dragged him up. Then, as easily as a thresher lifts a bag of chaff, she roped her arm around his middle and hoisted him onto her shoulders. She looked at Josef, who nodded, and they began to walk slowly in the direction they had been going before the disturbance.

Eli didn't follow immediately. Instead, he walked over to the struggling ghosthound and knelt just out of claw range, so that he was eye to enormous eye with the beast.

"I asked the trees to hold you until nightfall," he said, watching in amusement as the hound tried to snap at him. "You're no servant spirit, are you? I've never heard of a Spiritualist keeping a ghosthound in a ring, and no member of the Spirit Court would enslave a spirit against its will. So, I'm curious, why do you follow her? Did she save your life? Pull a thorn out of your paw?"

"Come a little closer," the hound growled, "and I'll tell you."

"Maybe later." Eli stood, brushing the dirt off his knees. "I'm sure you'll be able to find us easily enough when you do get out, but I would suggest you look to your mistress first." He glanced over at the Spiritualist's crumpled body. "We humans are so fragile."

"Miranda is no weakling," Gin snapped. "She would not forgive me if I let you escape, especially now that we've seen the company you keep."

"Nico? Don't worry about her. We've got things well in hand on that count. Besides," he said, grinning, "she's our companion, as I suspect that Spiritualist is for you. Companions don't leave each other in the lurch."

He turned and started to jog after the others. "Think on what I said," he called over his shoulder.

Gin growled and snapped at the wizard's retreating back until he disappeared into the brush. When Eli was well out of sight, the hound flopped against the dirt, panting. The roots snickered above him, and he snarled menacingly, which just made them snicker harder. Gin laid his ears back and flicked an eye over at Miranda. She was still lying where she had fallen, crumpled on her stomach, face down in the dirt. She wasn't moving, but her shoulders rose and fell slightly, and that gave him hope. Gin watched her for a moment more and then, with a sigh, he began the long process of digging himself out.

* * *

Miranda woke up slowly, one muscle at a time. Everything hurt. There was dirt in her eyes and, she grimaced, her mouth. She coughed experimentally and immediately regretted it as the bruised muscles along her rib cage seized up in protest. She lay still for a moment, with her eyes clenched shut, concentrating on breathing without pain. The world was strangely still around her. She heard nothing except the normal sounds of the forest, crickets and frogs croaking in warm air and the evening wind in the trees high overhead. Gritting her teeth, she raised her hand and began wiping away the dirt. When she had cleaned as much as she could hope to, she cautiously opened her eyes.

Gin's face filled her vision and she jumped in surprise, waking a whole new round of aches. The ghosthound's eyes widened at her string of mumbled expletives, and he bent closer, his hot breath blowing more dirt into her face. She coughed again, wincing. Gin gave a low whimper and, to her great surprise, gently licked her face. Miranda couldn't stop her grimace as his wet tongue slipped over her cheek, but it helped with the caked-on dirt and she knew better than to complain over a rare show of affection.

"Thanks," she muttered.

The ghosthound flicked his ear and nudged his nose under her, helping her up.

"Thanks again," she said, sitting up slowly. Then she got her first good look at her companion, and her eyes went wide. "Powers, what happened to you?"

Gin was filthy. His front paws, muzzle, and stomach were black with dirt, and the rest of him was so covered with dust and debris she could barely see his patterns moving.

"The wizard trapped me," he said simply, "and I got out."

Miranda looked confused. "Trapped..."

Gin shifted to one side, and Miranda stared in amazement at

what had been their neat, quiet, ambush-friendly clearing. It looked like a tree had exploded. Roots stuck out of the ground in every direction, some torn wide open, others in large knots. At the center was a deep ditch where the ground was furrowed with long claw marks. A Gin-sized pile of dirt rested against the trees to her left, and Miranda began to put the picture together.

"No wonder we both look like a dirt spirit decided to give us a hug," she said. "You never could learn to dig cleanly."

"Ghosthounds aren't made for digging," Gin growled.

Miranda shook her head and dug her fingers into the dirty fur at his neck, pulling herself slowly to her feet. "Any idea where the king is?"

"West somewhat." Gin flicked an ear in that direction. "They're waiting for something."

Using Gin as a prop, Miranda bent over with a wince and picked up a piece of her stone spirit off the ground. "I'm surprised Durn hasn't reformed himself," she said, clutching the stone to her chest. "That girl must have given him quite a scare."

"You know what she is, then?" Gin asked, surprised.

Miranda nodded. "What kind of Spiritualist would I be if I didn't know a demonseed when I saw one? Especially after it tried to eat one of my servants. This might be my first time actually meeting one, but Master Banage made absolutely sure we knew what to do if we did."

Gin crinkled his dirty nose. "And what is that?"

"Nothing," Miranda said, stepping away.

"What!" Gin roared. "I don't know what kind of demonseeds he's talking about, but the kind I know, the kind that just took a chunk out of Durn, those eat spirits like I eat pigs. 'Nothing,'" he snorted. "The next time I see her..." He snapped his teeth.

"Don't even think about it, mutt," Miranda said, hobbling slowly around the clearing, picking up Durn's broken pieces.

"Demonseeds are League business. If we want to stay in the Spirit Court, we don't interfere with the League of Storms. Besides," she said smiling sadly, "it's not like a Spiritualist could do much against her. Like you said, demonseeds gain their strength by eating spirits. If I did decide to fight her, the only weapon I have is you lot, and I'm not risking my spirits like that."

"You think so little of us—"

"Quite the opposite," Miranda said, shaking her head. "I'm sure that, if you put your mind to it, you could make her fight full force to defend herself, but look at it this way: If the girl can still maintain her human form, the demonseed inside her must still be small. However, if we offered it the chance to devour a larger spirit, say, a certain hot-headed dog, it might be enough to awaken her demon, and then where would we be?"

Gin bared his teeth. "Say what you want, but if I see a chance, I'm taking it. Any demonseed, no matter how small, is a danger to all spirits. Even the sleepiest, stupidest of us will try to kill one when we see it. I'm surprised Eli can talk to spirits if they know she's around. You'd think they'd want nothing to do with him."

"He must be hiding her somehow." Miranda frowned, piling the last bits of Durn in a circle on the ground. "You didn't sense her until she took a bite out of Durn, and your nose is sharper than most." She shook her head. "A wizard thief who uses only small-time spirits to kidnap kings, but travels with a hidden demonseed strong enough to damage my spirits and a master swordsman fast enough to counter your bite. This whole mission is one big knot of curiosities." She stood and dusted off her hands. "But it doesn't really matter. Next time I find that thief, I'm not going to take chances. I'm just going to fry him from behind. We'll see how he wiggles out of that."

Point made, she spread her hands over the collected pile of rubble that had been one of her most powerful spirits and closed her eyes. Durn's ring, a square of dark, cloudy emerald set in a yellow-gold band that took up the whole bottom joint of her left thumb, began to glow dully as she forced her own spirit energy through the stone. The energy flowed freely through the orderly pattern of the gem, calling gently to Durn's core. She felt his answer, weak and frightened, but there. Miranda sent a wave of power in response, the pulses repeating the pledge she'd made when she first bonded him—the exchange of power for service, strength for obedience, the sacred promise between spirit and Spiritualist that neither would ever abuse the other. With each pulse, the ring vibrated gently and began to glow. The rocks at her feet shook in answer, and then, at last, rolled together, matching their cracked edges and reforming until Durn himself sat crouched in front of her, his black, shiny surface dented but whole, and looking as ashamed as stone allowed.

"Forgive me, mistress," he rattled. "I failed you."

"There is nothing to forgive," Miranda said gently, running her fingers over his jagged edges. "I sent you into danger neither of us could have foreseen. You did well in the job I assigned you. Now it's time to come home."

Durn sighed against her skin, and then, with a sound like slag falling down a cliff, began to disintegrate. He broke first into small boulders, then gravel, and then dust that glowed silver in the afternoon sun as it drifted up into Miranda's open hands. She gathered him bit by bit into his ring, using her own spirit as a guide to fold him into the gem. When the last tendril of dust vanished, the emerald flashed faintly before dying out altogether as Miranda pushed him into a deep sleep.

"He'll recover," she said and sighed, twisting the ring over so the dark stone was against her palm. "But it'll be weeks before he's fit for anything except sleeping."

"It could have been worse," Gin offered, but she cut him off with a raised hand.

"I don't want to think about it. Let's focus on doing our job. Which way did they go?"

"This way." Gin stood up and turned with a swish of his tail, hopping over the remains of Eli's root trap.

Miranda hobbled after him, gritting her teeth against the pain in her bruised legs and side. "How far?"

"Less than a mile," Gin said, looking over his shoulder.

Miranda grabbed a broken root and, leaning her weight on it, hobbled faster. "I'm surprised you're not stalking them if they're that close. I could have caught up."

He gave her a long look as she limped forward pathetically. Then, with a sigh, he jumped back over the roots and flopped on the ground beside her. "Get on already, you're making me hurt just watching you."

Miranda grinned and tossed her improvised crutch aside, climbing up his back as fast as her aching muscles allowed.

"Anyway"—Gin lowered his head to his paws, which suddenly required his immediate attention—"I preferred to wait."

Miranda hid her smile in his fur as she made her way to her usual seat behind his ears. When she was settled, she nudged him with her boot. Gin rose and, together, they slunk westward through the trees.

In another world, a door opened in a white room. Or, rather, that was incorrect, for to say a door opened implies that a door existed. Nothing here existed if she did not will it, and she was not expecting the door. Still, it opened just the same, and a tall, angry man stepped into the perfect white nothing she lounged in, watching her sphere.

Her white eyes flicked over him, and a delicate sneer appeared on her flawless white face.

Why do you come when you are not summoned?

The angry man did not answer. He crossed the blankness with long strides and stood beside her, arms folded over his chest.

"He's doing it again." His voice was like distant thunder. "You have to put a stop to this."

What should you care?

The man's face grew even angrier, and his long fingers gripped the blue-wrapped sword at his hip. She smiled coyly. It was times like these, when his rages got the better of his sense, that she remembered why she treasured him still, despite his presumptions.

"With respect," he growled, "you created me to care. I spared your favorite's companion when he took in the demonseed. I even turned a blind eye when he gave her that triple-damned coat, but this is too far. The whole League just felt her attack a stone spirit, and yet you give no order to attack." His voice rose with each word, and small tongues of lightning began to crackle from the hand that gripped his sword hilt. "How am I to fulfill my purpose if you block me at every turn for the sake of your pet thief!"

He had barely finished when the empty whiteness pressed in around him, grabbing him in a vise of air and lead. The woman's coy smile never faded, but her anger thrilled through the emptiness until he felt the light itself burning his skin. Even then, he did not move, and his scowl did not change.

Eli is mine. The words were glass shards grinding through his mind. *You are not to go near him.*

"And should the demonseed awake?" he said, choking against the unrelenting pressure. "Am I to watch her devour the world and your precious Eli with it?!"

I have spoken!

The man staggered under her anger, dropping to one knee. Her white face softened, and she reached out to lay a snowy hand on his dark hair.

There, there, she cooed. *It will not come to that.* She slid her hand down his cheek and tilted his head up, her sharp nails digging into the tender flesh of his throat. *Have faith in me, my Lord of Storms.*

The dark-haired man shivered as his silver eyes locked with her white ones, unable to look away. Slowly, she leaned across the emptiness and laid a kiss sharp as broken ice on his trembling lips.

Now go. She pushed him away. *And do not return until summoned.*

Released from her grip, the Lord of Storms struggled to his feet, but the white woman's attention had already strayed back to the sphere that floated in front of her. It hung in the white nothingness like a rain drop frozen in the moment before it lands, and inside, a tiny, flat map of greens and blues, snowy mountains and glinting seas, revolved in absolute perfection under a cloud-strewn evening sky.

"As you ask," the dark-haired man said, bowing low, "Benehime." With those words he vanished from the white, empty world, leaving the lady to her delights as the door that was not a door closed behind him without a sound.

In the inmost chamber of a great stone fortress that stood alone on a sea cliff hundreds of miles from the nearest city of men, a thin, white line appeared on the soot-blackened wall, drowning the sputtering light of the oil lamps with snowblind brilliance. The man waiting there sprang to his feet, his long black coat falling around him like wings as the Lord of Storms stepped through the cut in reality and into his office.

The unworldly light had barely faded before he grabbed the sword from his side and flung it as hard as he could against the iron armor chest on the far wall.

"Damn that woman's moods!" he roared, and whirled to face the man who had been waiting for him. "Do you believe it, Alric? A blatant attack on a spirit and she still refuses to let me go anywhere near that thief and his damned demon!"

"But the seed has already eaten her down to skin and bone," Alric said, crossing the room to retrieve his master's cast-off sword. "With food like that, and unlimited time to consume it, the seed could reach full maturity before awakening. If that happens, we might not have the numbers to stop it, and it will be the Dead Mountain fiasco all over again."

"It won't come to that," the Lord of Storms said and began to pace the tiny room. "Have the League put up a watch for a hundred miles around the area where we felt the girl attack. Even if that blasted coat hides her when she's passive, it can't hide her when she uses the demon."

"You think she'll use it again in so short a period?" Alric handed him his sword. "Monpress has been very careful about that."

"It doesn't matter what the thief does." The Lord of Storms sat down on his desk and laid his sword across his knees. "No matter how careful he tries to be, the truth doesn't change. If he keeps letting the girl use her demon powers, then, sooner or later, the balance will tip. Once the awakening starts, nothing can stop it. Eventually, the demonseed will turn on him, and that infatuated woman will have no choice but to give the order."

"You say that," Alric said, frowning, "but a fully awakened demon is no small matter. We'll have to be extremely thorough if we want to keep the seed from regressing and switching hosts. What of the thief or his swordsman should they get in the way? They seem very attached to the demon's human shell."

The Lord of Storms unsheathed his sword with a ring of steel. "Killing the demon is all that matters," he said, admiring the blue silver blade with a bloodthirsty smile. "Everything else can burn to ash."

"Everything?" Alric arched an eyebrow.

The Lord of Storms swung his sword, his silver eyes lightning bright as he watched the air spirits flee before the blade. "Despite her whims, there are some rules even the Shepherdess can't afford to break, and the lady always finds a new favorite in time."

Alric bowed low. "We shall be ready. The League of Storms moves at your command."

The Lord of Storms nodded, and Alric slipped quietly out of the room. Closing the door behind him, he set off down the narrow hall to ready the League for the hunt.

CHAPTER 12

Josef leaned against the tall boulder that marked the outer ring of the clearing that he'd chosen as their trade-off point, sharpening his dagger. It didn't need the sharpening, but it was a good way to kill the time, and he had plenty of time to kill. Nico and the king were a few feet away, Nico looking thoughtful, the king looking terrified, standing at the very end of his tether. Eli was around the other side of the boulder, as he had been for the past half hour, talking to it animatedly. Josef ignored him when he could, focusing on the sound of the blade as it slid over the stone. Finally, the boulder rumbled gently, and Eli came around to Josef's side, looking very pleased with himself.

"Are you done gossiping with the scenery?" Josef said, holding his knife out in front of him to check the edge.

Eli rubbed his hands together. "For your information, I've just created a foolproof escape."

"From what?" Josef said sullenly. "There's nothing here. Are you sure your bird even made it?"

"Of course," Eli said, leaning on the rock face next to him. "The falcon told me he dropped it straight into a guard's dinner. They're just late. I'm sure the ransom will be showing up any moment now. In the meanwhile," he reached into his jacket pocket, "who's for a nice, friendly game of—"

"No." Josef's dagger landed with a thunk in the dirt less than an inch from Eli's boot. Eli glanced at the dagger, still quivering from the impact, and then back at the swordsman.

"You're oversharpening those."

Josef bent down to retrieve his knife. "I don't tell you how to wizard, so don't tell me how to fight."

Eli's eyebrows shot up. "I don't think you can use 'wizard' as a verb like that."

"And I don't see how your little tea party with a rock is going to cover our escape," Josef said, slamming the dagger back into his boot. "I guess we'll just have to trust each other."

Eli took a deep breath, preparing to point out all the ways that grammar and wizardry were different, but a look at Josef's expression told him it could be a bloody argument, mostly his blood, and he decided to leave it at that. Thankfully, that was the moment the riders appeared at the opposite edge of the clearing.

"Nico," Josef said, tightening the iron sword on his back as he and Eli took the forward positions. "Make sure his highness doesn't get any ideas."

Nico nodded and yanked the rope, knocking the king to his knees.

As Eli had the king specify in his instructions, there were only five riders. Three of them rode in a point formation while the other two hung back, riding as a pair, with an iron-bound, triple-locked chest slung between their horses. Eli's grin widened. When they reached the clearing's edge, one of the forward riders, a thickset balding man in polished armor, stood up in his saddle.

"Majesty!" he shouted. "Are you hurt?"

The king sprang up, jerking his tether. "Oban!"

Nico gave him a hard tug, and the king quickly sat down again. "I'm fine! Just don't do anything stupid."

"We had no intention to, Henrith," the man at the point of the formation said flatly, removing his helmet to let his blond braid swing freely down his back. "This situation's idiotic enough as it is."

The king stopped straining against Nico's hold. "Renaud?" he whispered. All at once, he lunged forward, fighting against the rope. "Renaud!" Nico slapped him hard behind the knees, and he tumbled to the ground, but his eyes were still on the blond rider. "What are you doing here, brother?"

Eli glanced back. "I didn't know you had a brother."

"Not many outsiders do," Renaud said. He sat back on his skittish horse, looking them over. "You must be Eli, the thief."

"The very same." Eli smiled courteously, nodding toward the reinforced chest. "And unless you're planning on setting up house in the woods, *that* must be my gold."

Renaud raised his hand. At his signal, the soldiers dismounted and began unlocking the chest. It took a full minute to undo the locks and the three chains before the soldiers threw back the lid and stepped aside. Eli licked his lips. The chest was filled to the brim with sparkling, oblong, golden coins.

"Five thousand council standards," Renaud said flatly. "As agreed."

"Ah," Eli said smiling. "And the other part of our bargain?"

Renaud took a tightly rolled scroll out of his saddlebag. "It arrived by special courier this morning," he said, unfurling the paper. "The first one, straight from the Council's copy rooms."

Stretched between his hands was a bounty notice bearing an

enormous likeness of Eli's face at its center and his name in block capitals across the top. Best of all, however, was the number stenciled across the bottom in thick black blocks: fifty-five thousand gold standards. Eli let out a low whistle.

Renaud rolled the notice back into a tube and tossed it casually on top of the piled gold. "Everything you wanted, exactly as promised. Now give me my brother."

"Gold first," Eli said, putting his hand on the king's rope.

Renaud nodded, and the third rider, a dark-haired swordsman with a scar across one side of his face, dismounted. He took the reins of the chest carriers and led them out to the center of the clearing, twenty feet from either party. There, he cut the straps, and the chest fell with a thud onto the dusty grass. He led the horses back to their riders and took his place again beside Renaud.

When he stopped completely, Eli nodded to Nico, and she released her death grip on the king's tether. Eli picked up the slack and twisted the rope around his arm until it was tight. Then he put his hand on the king's shoulder and, tied together, they started the slow, silent walk to the center of the circular field.

Five feet from the gold, Eli stopped. "All right," he said slowly, "I'm going to let him walk forward. Any funny moves on your part, and"—he tugged the rope, nearly taking the king off his feet—"Got it?"

Renaud nodded, and Eli unclamped his hand from the king's shoulder. The king walked forward. As soon as he passed the gold, Eli reached for the chest.

He heard the spirit almost too late, and he jumped back just in time as a bolt of blue lightning shrieked inches from his face. He fell backward, tugging hard on the rope. The king came flailing after him, and they landed in a heap a few feet from the chest.

"That's enough," said a cold voice. The thick brush at the edge of the clearing rustled, and the enormous ghosthound stepped into view, Miranda sitting high on his back. They were dirty, and Miranda looked like she was having trouble staying mounted, but the hand she pointed at Eli was steady as a stone, and the blue lightning arcing from the large aquamarine on her right middle finger was nothing to be flippant about.

Gin padded silently across the open ground. "I don't know how you dodged Skarest," Miranda said, and the lightning on her arm crackled angrily, "but the next shot will kill you before the girl can move." She shot Nico a glare before turning it on Eli. "Step away from the king and put your hands out where I can see them."

"What do you think you are doing, Miss Lyonette?" Renaud said, reining in his nervous horse.

"The Spirit Court is done playing politics, Renaud," she said. "My orders were to placate the local officials only if it did not interfere with my primary mission." She gave him a cold look. "Mellinor is free to deal with Mellinor's problems, prince, but this thief will answer to us. Now," she continued and turned her glare back to Eli, and the lightning arced high above her head, "release your hostage and put out your hands, Mr. Monpress."

Eli got to his feet, smiling cockily. "And if I don't?"

"My orders are to apprehend you and bring you to the Rector Spiritualis." She smiled right back at him. "But they didn't specify what condition you had to be in when you got there."

Eli opened his mouth to reply, but Miranda never got to hear it, for at that moment, her lightning spirit discharged.

It happened instantly, as if some giant hand had plucked the lightning off her finger and hurled it across the clearing. The world became very still, and she could do nothing but watch in horror as Skarest arced through the air with an ear-ripping crack and struck the center of the king's chest. King Henrith convulsed and toppled to the ground, a thin wisp of smoke rising from his open mouth. Lightning sparked on her fingers as Skarest returned to his ring, and the spirit's fear racing through their connection made her blood run thin.

"Mistress!" he crackled. "He was too strong, mistress. I couldn't fight him!"

"Who?" Miranda shouted, but the spirit had buried himself in his ring.

The Mellinor group was frozen in shock, and even Eli was gaping at her. Only the prince kept his composure, turning on her with a look of triumphant hate.

"Foul murder!" Renaud shouted, breaking the stunned silence. "The Spiritualist has killed our king! She'll stop at nothing! Soldiers, attack! We won't let her sacrifice our king to catch her mark!"

His words were like a match in a hayloft, and they were barely out his mouth before a wave of spearmen wearing House Allaze blue poured out of the brush behind him and charged the center of the clearing.

Master Oban started to ride with the charge toward his fallen king, but Renaud grabbed his horse's reins. "No, Oban! I'll handle this! Get back to the castle and tell the others!"

Oban shouted curses, but he turned his horse and rode madly back into the woods, parting the line of archers that was forming up on the clearing's edge.

"Kill them all!" Renaud shouted, waving the soldiers forward. "Avenge our king!"

The first volley of arrows launched with a ringing twang, and Miranda ducked low on her hound's back. "Gin!" she shouted. "Get to the king!"

"You sure?" he panted, launching forward as the arrows sailed over their heads. "I don't think it will do any good."

"Henrith's our only hope of salvaging this situation," she said, and her hand shot to her throat, clutching the pendant through her shirt. "Eril! Give us some cover!"

Even a wind spirit understands a real emergency, and Eril set to work with no backtalk, raising a thick dust storm in a matter of moments.

As soon as the lightning struck, Eli knew he had to get the money. He rolled the fallen king over and felt his throat. There was a pulse, erratic but strong, and he decided that was good enough. He stepped over the king and made a dash for the chest, reaching it just as the first wave of soldiers crashed into the clearing.

"Nico!" he shouted, ducking under the arrow that whizzed by his head. "Josef! Get to the boulder!"

He dropped to his knees and grabbed the chest, but as soon as he touched it, his stomach sank. The iron-bound chest was heavy, but not nearly heavy enough. He popped the three locks and flung it open, plunging his hand inside. His fingers barely made it past the top layer of coins before they hit the wooden false bottom. For a moment, he just sat there, staring, as the soldiers charged forward. Then, while more arrows struck the ground beside him, Eli carefully folded the bounty notice and put it in his pocket. When that was done, he slammed the trunk's lid and sprang forward, running toward where he'd last seen Renaud as an enormous, spirit-driven dust storm covered everything.

"Eli!" Josef shouted, squinting into the swirling dust. Get to the boulder? At this point he'd be lucky to find it. Voices shouted all around him, and he could hear the arrows whizzing overhead, but everywhere he looked, all he saw was dust. He didn't have to be a wizard to know the cloud wasn't natural. He just wished he knew which wizard it belonged to.

He felt someone behind him and whirled around, drawing his blade as he spun, only to find himself facing Nico. She pressed her pale lips together, cocking her head to peer quizzically at the sword point hovering beside her unguarded throat. "Jumpy?"

Josef sighed and lowered his sword. "How many times do I have to tell you not to do that? One day I might not stop in time, you know."

"I trust you," she said.

"Glad to hear it, but that doesn't change"—he chopped an arrow out of the air just before it struck her shoulder—"the situation."

A soldier loomed out of the dust behind her, his sword already falling. Without looking, Nico dropped to the ground, letting his overbalanced swing tip him forward. When he was halfway down, she shot up again, plunging her elbow into his unguarded stomach. The blow caught him right under his ribs, and he fell wheezing to the ground at Josef's feet.

"This is getting ridiculous," Josef said, kicking the fallen soldier's hands out from under him when he tried to get up. "Eli's probably already got the money. Let's just find him and—"

He froze. Nico looked up, confused. "And?"

With a whisper of steel, Josef drew his second sword. "Nico," he said quietly, "go find Eli. I'll catch up."

He caught her dark eyes and held them until she nodded and stepped away, disappearing instantly into the dust. He brought his swords up and turned to face the person he knew was standing there.

"Good guess," a voice said, floating on the swirling dust.

"Guess nothing," Josef said, stepping into a defensive stance. "I could follow a killing intent like yours blindfolded. Something you pick up when you live your life on the sword."

The swordsman with the scar across his face stepped out of the swirling dust. "I should have expected nothing less from *the* Josef Liechten." He laid his hand on the wrapped sword at his hip. "My name is Gerard Coriano," he said casually, as if they were meeting in a tavern rather than a battlefield, "and this"—he unhooked the wrapped sword, sheath and all, from his belt—"is Dunea. We are here to kill you."

"Is that so?" Josef said. "Why bother telling me your name then?"

"A final courtesy." Coriano smiled. "A true swordsman would want to die knowing the name of the man who killed him. Remember it well, Josef Liechten."

Josef's face broke into a feral grin. "I only remember things that deserve to be remembered. So, if you want me to remember your name, you'll have to make it worth my while."

Coriano held his wrapped sword out before him, the blade still in its wooden sheath. "When you're ready."

Gin led them straight through the dust to the fallen king. Miranda jumped down, gritting her teeth as the impact's force shot up her spine. The king was on his back, caked in yellow-brown dust. She kneeled beside him, pressing her fingers against his throat.

"He's alive," she said, her voice hoarse with relief. She slid her arms under his shoulders. "Help me get him up."

Gin lowered his head, and she rolled the king onto his long nose. When he was balanced, Gin lifted the unconscious man and, with Miranda's help, laid the king gently across his back.

She was getting ready to climb up herself when Gin growled low in his throat. He caught her eye, and she knew why.

"Lord Renaud," she said, turning around. "You're faster than expected."

Renaud stepped out of the swirling dust, a cocky smile on his handsome face. "Look at it from my perspective, lady. I see my brother's murderer stealing his body, is it so surprising I should hurry to stop her?"

"No, but not for the reasons you give." She brushed her fingers over her rings, calling her spirits awake. "Your brother is still alive, but I imagine you knew that, seeing how you were the one who flung Skarest at him."

"Skarest?" Renault folded his hands behind him. "Was that the little lightning bolt's name?"

Miranda's eyes widened. "You don't deny it?"

"Why should I?" Renault shrugged. "I am a wizard, controlling spirits is my right."

Miranda clenched her fists. "What you call your right we call enslavement, and it is an abomination. No spirit, human or otherwise, has the right to dominate another! Even if you hadn't tried to kill your brother, what you did to Skarest is crime enough to bring the whole Spirit Court down on your head!"

"Enslavement?" Renaud chuckled. "You Spiritualists were always very fond of giving things names, anything to set yourselves apart, to label your magic as right and everything else as wrong."

"Considering enslavement destroys the soul of the spirit it commands, I'd say it's a pretty clear-cut division."

"And what do I care for their souls?"

Miranda took a step back at the disgust in his voice, but Renaud stepped closer, ignoring Gin's warning growl as the prince closed the distance between them.

"We have our own souls to think of," he whispered, almost in her ear, and the cold hatred in his voice made her shiver. "In nature, it is the strong who dominate the weak, the strong who survive."

"Those rules don't apply to us, Renaud," Miranda said. "We're not animals! Only humans have the power to dominate another spirit. We have to—"

"It was the spirits who dominated me for most of my life!" Renaud snapped, eyes flashing. "It's because I was born with their voices talking in my ears that I lost everything to that idiot," he said and pointed to Henrith's smoking body sprawled on Gin's back.

"That's different."

"No!" Renaud roared. "No difference! I will take back tenfold what was taken from me. A hundredfold! It was the world that decided to make my will a weapon, Spiritualist, and I will use it bluntly, as it was intended. No rings, no pretensions, only my strength against the spirit's, my boot on its neck until it cries for mercy." He stepped closer still, clenching his fists beneath her chin. "I will take Mellinor from its weakling king," he growled. "I will take my inheritance with these hands, and then I will take dominion of the spirits from your weakling Court. I will return the world to its natural balance, with the wizard on top and the spirits below, and you"—he looked at Miranda with disgust—"you, with your hobbled power and your foolish pledge, will go down with the trash you've tied yourself to. A fitting end for a wizard who would not take her power."

Miranda jerked back, eyes flashing, but when she spoke, her voice was cold and sharp. "Bold words, enslaver," she said, holding up her right thumb, which was wearing a knuckle-sized ruby that was glowing like an ember. "But it will take more than the raving of a jilted prince to make me forget the truth of the vows I serve." She thrust out her hand, and the ruby began to smoke on her finger. "Perhaps you'd like to try your speech on another of my spirits? You'll have to speak quickly, though, because I don't think he'll listen as patiently as I did. Will you, Kirik?"

When she spoke the name, the wind around them died out completely. A flame winked to life above Miranda's fist. It hovered there for a split second, sputtering like a candle, and then, with a deafening roar, it exploded upward, growing into an enormous column of fire that reached the sky. Any dust it touched vanished, burned to cinders in an instant. The column surrounded Miranda on all sides, the heat pouring off it in waves until even Renaud was forced to step back and put up his hands to shield his face.

"What's the matter, enslaver?" Miranda crowed from behind the wall of flame. "Weren't you going to put your boot on his neck?"

If Renaud answered, it was lost in Kirik's crackling laughter. Grinning triumphantly, Miranda raised her voice to command the attack.

Just before she spoke the words, the prince fell to his knees. Miranda squinted against Kirik's bright light. No, Renaud hadn't fallen; he'd sunk up to his thighs in the sandy ground. As she watched, more sand poured up his chest, pinning his arms and pulling him toward the ground. He struggled frantically, but for every handful of sand he tossed away, five more took its place. Within seconds he was buried up to his shoulders, completely trapped in the shifting, buzzing ground.

"So sorry," said a smug voice.

Miranda whirled around, her eyes wide and astonished as a gangly, dark-haired figure stepped out of the dust. "Can't have any of that." He snapped his fingers and a torrent of water shot up from the ground at his feet.

Miranda had no time to react, no time to do anything except stare stupidly as the water arched through the air and struck her fire spirit full on. Kirik roared and steamed, but there was nothing he could do against the endless deluge. The column of flame shrank to an ember in the space of a breath, and Miranda barely managed to pull him back into his ring before the water extinguished him altogether.

For the next few moments, Miranda was so furious she couldn't do more than sputter and clutch the dimly glowing ruby on her thumb. When she did find her voice, however, she made up for lost time.

"What do you think you are doing?!" she roared so violently that even Gin flinched back.

Eli raised his hands. "Easy, Lady Spiritualist, I couldn't let you bake him just yet. You see"—he glared down at Renaud, still pinned by the dirt—"this man still owes me some money."

If possible, Miranda looked even angrier. "He tried to kill his brother, enslaved my spirit, threatened the entire spirit world, and you're worried about *money*?"

"Of course." Eli looked at her innocently. "I'm a thief. What else is there for me to worry about?"

"You could start worrying about your hide," she growled, "because I'm about to flay it off you."

"Charming!" Eli said, grinning. "But give me two seconds first. I need to make a point." He crouched down in the dirt beside Renaud. "Hello, Lord Whoever-You-Are. I don't know if you've heard of me, but I'm Eli Monpress, the greatest thief in the world."

Eli put his arm around Renaud's sand-covered shoulder. "I'm going to let you in on a secret. I didn't get to be the greatest thief in the world by letting hack wizards like you cheat me out of my hard-earned money. However, I'm a generous man, so I'm going to offer you a choice: Either you give me my money or I take it from you. Now, while five thousand may seem like a hefty sum, please take my word on this"—he smiled sweetly—"you don't want me in your treasury."

Renaud's eyes widened. "Aren't *you* the pair?" he said, spitting the sand out of his mouth. "The thief and the officer of the Spirit Court working together."

"We're not together!" Miranda shouted. "Enough of this nonsense! Gin, bite the thief's head off."

Gin charged forward, but all he got was a mouthful of sand as the ground in front of Eli sprang up to protect him.

"An impressive spirit, Mr. Monpress," Miranda said as Gin coughed up dirt.

"Oh, it's not mine," Eli said, grinning. "This particular stretch of ground was getting frustrated that a certain Spiritualist's wind spirit was whipping bits of it up into the air. I simply offered to help it stop the wind if it helped me."

Miranda stared at him in disbelief. "You offered? What, you mean you just had a chat with the ground, without opening your spirit or having a servant spirit to mediate, and it listened, just like that?"

Eli shrugged. "More or less."

"Don't be stupid," she scoffed. "You can't just sit down and talk to the ground."

"Some of us don't need slaves or servants to get things done," he said.

Miranda sputtered, but Renaud burst out laughing. Miranda and Eli both turned to stare at him, but the prince paid no mind, laughing until he was nearly choking on the sandy dirt.

"That's it?" he said when he could speak again. "*That's* the famous Eli's great secret that every bounty hunter is after? You just asked?"

Eli arched an eyebrow at him. "I don't see how it's so hard to believe. Most spirits are very obliging when you're not trying to crush them into submission. But you wouldn't know much about that, from what I hear." He straightened up. "Now, are you going to play nicely, or do I need to ask the dirt for another favor?"

The ground around Renaud began to snicker, but the smile on the prince's face did not change. "As grateful as I am to you for the opportunities you've given me, I'm afraid my thanks are all you're going to get, Mr. Monpress."

"Oh?" Eli crossed his arms over his chest. "Does that mean you choose the 'Eli takes the money from you' option?"

Renaud's smile widened. "Let me show you how a true wizard works."

Still chuckling, he closed his eyes and, for a moment, nothing happened. Then Renaud opened his spirit, and everything changed.

This wasn't the controlled opening Miranda had done earlier. Renaud threw his spirit wide for the world to see, and the strength of it was wholly unexpected. Miranda barely had time to register what was happening before it hit her. She fell to her knees, gasping for breath as the full pressure of Renaud's soul landed on her. Her rings cut into her fingers as her spirits writhed under the weight. Behind her, she heard Gin whimpering as he fought it, but even the ghosthound was forced to the ground in the end. Miranda gritted her teeth and focused on dampening the panic shooting up the link she shared with her spirits, but they were already beaten down. Another wave of pressure hit, and she gasped as it slammed her into the ground.

Spitting out dirt, she forced her head to turn, and she caught something out of the corner of her eye. Eli was still standing beside her, arms crossed just like before, as if nothing was happening, but the cocky smile on his face had vanished.

The sand trapping Renaud burst outward, the grains cutting Miranda's skin. The prince stepped calmly out of the crater he had made and looked over to where Gin lay pinned with the king's body still slung over the arch of his back. His hand went to his pocket, and when he spoke, his words pulsed through his opened spirit, battering over Miranda like iron waves.

"I've been saving this since I left the desert and returned to Allaze. I was waiting to use it on my brother, if I ever got the chance." He grinned at Eli. "Now that you have made me king, I won't be needing it anymore. Such a pity." His mad grin grew deadly. "I will miss collecting your bounty."

Eli glared at him. "And why's that?"

"Because once I'm done cleaning this clearing, there won't be enough of you left to turn in."

"Sounds like a stupid waste of fifty-five thousand standards to me," Eli said. "And if that false-bottomed chest was any indication, you could use the gold."

"Yes," Renaud cackled, "but as another of your kind once told me, there are some things that are worth more than money."

His eyes flicked away from Eli's incredulous expression and came to rest on Miranda, who was still fighting to raise her head. "Watch and learn, Spiritualist," he whispered, holding out his clenched fist. "*This* is how you master a spirit."

He opened his fist and a small, dark, glittering sphere dropped from his fingers. At first, Miranda thought it was a kind of black pearl, like the pearl she kept Eril in, but as it fell, the ball began to disintegrate, and as it broke apart, the sphere began to scream.

CHAPTER 13

Josef struck hard and fast, bringing his twin blades down one after the other so that there was no pause between strikes. Coriano blocked each blow on his sheathed sword, his scarred face bored and impassive. Josef tried striking low, high, and both sides at once, testing for weaknesses, but every blow was knocked aside with the same easy indifference, no matter how fast he struck. Finally, Josef tried a wild attack, striking high and low simultaneously while leaving his middle deliberately unguarded. The other swordsman ducked the high blow, slid the low off his wooden sheath, and ignored the easy opening all together. After that, Josef lowered his swords and stepped back.

"I'm sorry," he said, wiping the sweaty dust out of his eyes with the back of his hand, "but if we're going to fight, you have to do more than block. It also helps if you draw your sword, I'm told."

Coriano planted his sheathed blade in the dirt and leaned on it. "I'll draw my sword when you draw yours."

"I don't get what you mean," Josef said, swinging his twin blades in a whistling arc.

"Well," Coriano said, straightening up. "If that's the case, I'm going to have to start breaking your toys until you do."

Josef opened his mouth to say something rude, but before he had taken a breath, Coriano was there, his sheathed sword pressed deep into Josef's stomach. Josef went sprawling in the dirt, and only years of training brought his swords up in time to block the next blow before it landed on his head. If Coriano's blocks had been fast before, his blows were in another category altogether. The next one fell before Josef realized the scarred man had lifted his blade, and the force slammed Josef into the ground. A cloud of dust shot up at the impact, and a long crack appeared in the wooden sheath of Coriano's sword. Sprawled on his back, Josef brought both swords in a cross over his chest, blocking the next blow on both blades, inches from his face. Coriano's cracked sheath shattered on impact, sending wood flying in every direction, and Josef found himself staring down the blade of the most beautiful sword he had ever seen.

It was pure white from tip to guard, unembellished, except for a slight wavering shimmer along the sharpened edge that glittered like new snow in the dusty light. The hilt was wrapped in blood-red silk, but the bright color paled beneath the sword's cold, dancing light.

"River of White Snow," Coriano whispered. "Dunea."

He pushed down, and the shimmering white edge cut through Josef's crossed blades like paper to bury itself in the swordsman's chest. Pain exploded where the blade bit down, darkening his vision, and Josef gasped, forcing his lungs to work. Coriano only smiled and pushed his blade farther, clearly intending to pin Josef to the dirt like a butterfly on a board. With a desperate heave, Josef flung the hilt of his broken blade at the swordsman's face, aiming for his scarred eye. Coriano jumped back, and Josef scrambled to his feet, clutching his chest with one hand and the remaining broken blade with the other.

It was still hard to see, and every breath hurt like another stab, but Josef forced himself to be calm. The cut was small but deep, sticking right below the sternum. It hadn't hit his heart, and it hadn't hit his lungs, but it was bleeding in a torrent down his shirt.

Coriano looked him over casually, the white sword balanced perfectly in his hands. "No time for licking wounds," he said, and lunged.

Josef tossed his ruined sword on the ground and drew a short blade from his belt just in time to parry. However, his parry turned into a rolling dodge as Coriano's white sword snapped the knife neatly in two without losing speed or direction. The white edge simply cut through the metal like it was not there.

Josef rolled to his feet again and shakily drew another blade from his boot. Coriano gave him a scornful look.

"Come now," he said. "Surely you don't intend to keep insulting us with your dull blades?" He whirled his sword, and Josef could almost hear the snowy blade singing as it cut the air. "You must have realized what she is by now. Why do you not draw your sword?"

Josef's hand went to the hilt of the great iron sword on his back. Coriano's grin grew delighted, and he brought Dunea back to her ready position as Josef's hand gripped the wrapped handle. As he began to lift the iron blade, his fingers turned deftly and his hand flew out, flashing silver. Coriano sliced the first knife out of the air, but he was a hair too slow for the second. The throwing knife grazed his shoulder as he dodged, leaving a long, bloody gash.

Josef straightened up with an enormous grin on his face and three more knives fanned between his fingers. "Not yet," he said, tossing a knife and catching it in his free hand. "I'm not out of things to throw at you."

Coriano gritted his teeth, but as he leaned forward for another lunge, his posture changed. Just before kicking off, he stopped and shivered like a cat dipped in cold water. Josef lowered his knives a fraction and watched in confusion as the other swordsman clutched his sword to his chest like it was a frightened child. The wizard wind driving the storm around them died as suddenly as it had begun, and the dust fell to the ground with unnatural speed, as if something was pressing it down.

"That idiot," Coriano whispered, clutching his sword as the white light flew in wild patterns across the blade. "That short-sighted, power-drunk fool."

Josef shifted his weight, easing the knives between his fingers, waiting to see what kind of ruse this was, but the scarred swordsman lowered his sword and gave a little bow. "We'll have to finish this another time, Mr. Liechten," he said with annoyance. "Things are about to become very unpleasant. If your Eli has an escape set up, I suggest you use it."

"You can't be serious," Josef said. "You can't run now; we were just getting started!"

Coriano smiled back at him. "I have tracked you for a very long time, too long to waste my one chance on a wizard's stupidity. Don't worry, we'll meet again very soon. Then, Mr. Liechten, I promise, I will make you draw the Heart of War."

"Wait," Josef called out, but Coriano was walking away

through the falling dust. Josef hurled his knife into the dirt a finger's width from the scarred man's feet. "I said wait!"

But Coriano kept walking, disappearing like a shadow into the trees at the clearing's edge. Josef ran after him for a few steps, but the pain was too much. Clutching his burning chest, he reached into his pocket with a grimace and pulled out one of the long strips of cloth he kept for occasions like this. He wrapped it around his chest, binding the wound as tight as he could. The angle was awkward, but it stemmed the bleeding for now. He could have Nico redo it later, if there was a later. The wound was quickly dropping down his list of priorities. There was a ringing growing in his ears, a high-pitched wail just out of his hearing. It reminded him of the dull buzzing he heard in Eli's voice whenever the wizard talked to rocks or trees or whatever he wasted his time with—only this was more frantic, and it was getting louder.

As the dust cleared completely, he could see Nico on the other side of the circular clearing standing over a pile of groaning soldiers. She was looking away from him, watching something. He followed her gaze and saw Eli. Their thief was standing over the downed Spiritualist and her dog, who looked to be out of the fight, but Eli's attention was on the tall, blond leader of the Mellinor troops, who was the only other person besides themselves still standing as the dust settled. The man was saying something, but all Josef could hear was that high-pitched whine, more like a pressure than a sound. Then the man opened his fist and everything went to hell.

The scream shot through her, driving everything else from Miranda's mind. Only the sharp pain of her bruises and the feel of grit in her mouth told her she was writhing in the dirt. Still, her eyes were open, and she watched in horror as the screaming sphere broke apart completely, becoming a black cloud of glittering particles. A cloud that was growing.

"Miranda," Eli said, his voice cutting cleanly through the panic. She barely felt his hands as he grabbed her shoulders and dragged her to her feet, but his voice was clear and commanding. Somewhere in her garbled mind, she realized that he was speaking to her like she was a spirit. "Leave right now."

He let her go, and she nearly toppled over. Only Gin's cold nose pressed into her back kept her from falling.

"He's right," the hound whined, ears flat. "That thing is insane. We leave now."

Miranda opened her mouth to protest, but Gin didn't give her a chance. He ran for the forest with Miranda clutched like a pup between his teeth and the still-unconscious king bouncing on his back. Miranda was screaming something about Eli, but the hound didn't stop, and he never once looked back.

As soon as the ghosthound disappeared into the woods, Eli turned and ran as hard as he could in the other direction, nearly colliding with Josef and Nico.

"What are you doing?" Eli yelled, grabbing them both. "I told you to get to the boulder!" He did a double take when he saw the bloodstain across most of Josef's shirt. "What happened to you?"

"Never mind that!" Josef shouted. "Where's the gold?"

"I'll explain later!" Eli shouted back, yanking them both toward the rock at the clearing's edge. "Just run!"

Josef nodded and started running. If the situation was serious enough for Eli to abandon cash, then this was not the time to argue. They tore across the clearing, ignoring the growing roar behind them. Even Josef could hear it now, a high-pitched screaming that rubbed his nerves raw. It was like an injured child's scream, but there was nothing human in this sound and it did not stop for breath. Josef shuddered and kept running.

Eli was shouting at the rock even before they reached the

clearing's edge. However, the rock didn't seem to be answering, because Eli slid to a halt just in front of it and started to gesture frantically as a dark shadow fell across them.

Josef whirled around, grabbing one of his remaining knives just so he didn't have to face whatever it was empty-handed. But even a blade in his hand didn't make him feel better when he saw what was behind them. Across the clearing, an enormous tower of black cloud loomed over the blasted ground where Renaud had been standing only moments ago. Billows of dark dust, black and glistening like volcanic glass, spun impossibly fast in the windless sky, rising in great swirls that blotted out the sun. As if it had been waiting for him to turn around, the cloud's wailing reached a frantic pitch, and it began to move forward.

"Eli," Josef said over his shoulder, "whatever you're doing, could you do it a little faster?"

Eli gave him a biting look before turning back to the boulder. Josef backed up a step, pressing Nico into the stone. The cloud was not heading at them directly. Instead, it skirted the edge of the clearing, keeping close to the forest. The trees leaned back when the billowing black dust came near, lifting their branches high in the air, as if they were trying to get out of its way. Then the screaming storm touched a tree that had the misfortune of growing too far out, and Josef saw why. As soon as the spinning black gusts connected with the branches, they disintegrated. The cyclone passed over the tree as if it were not there, reducing it to sawdust without effort or notice, and without slowing its progress toward the huddled group by the boulder.

"Eli," Josef said again, "now would be good."

"Got it!" Eli shouted. "All right, *go*!"

"Go where?!" Josef yelled frantically. The cloud was almost on top of them, filling his vision from ground to sky. That was the last thing he saw before the rock swallowed him.

CHAPTER 14

Miranda didn't realize she had passed out until she woke up sore, stiff, dirty, and uncomfortably damp. She was propped on Gin's paw, and as soon as she moved, his long snout filled her vision.

"How are you feeling?"

Miranda thought about it, and winced. "Like someone's beaten me, eaten me, and thrown me up again."

She ignored his disgusted look and pulled herself up by his fur. "That went well," she muttered, cleaning the grit out of her mouth with a less dirty corner of her riding coat. "Somehow, I'm not surprised Coriano was there. I'd love to know what that enslaver's paying him to make him toss out his good reputation with the Spirit Court."

"I don't think it's always about money with that one," Gin said thoughtfully. "He smells more of blood than gold to me."

Miranda grimaced. "Well, that's a problem for later," on top of the mountain of problems they already faced. "Right now, we've got to figure out what we're going to do about Renaud."

Gin laid his ears back. "Men like that don't deserve to be wizards. Sandstorms may be stupid, but no spirit deserves what he did. It's even worse than being eaten by a demon. At least then you're just dead rather than jabbering insane and balled up in some maniac's pocket."

Miranda looked up. "Is it still around?"

"I can't hear it, but that's no guarantee he didn't put it back in his pocket."

Miranda groaned and rubbed her temples. "An enslaver with an ax to grind and a throne to grind it on, it doesn't get much worse than that."

"Wait," Gin said. "What about that Banage thing? The thing he sent us here to stop Eli from getting?"

Miranda blanched. "Gregorn's Pillar…" She put her knuckles to her mouth, thinking madly. "No," she said at last. "I don't think he knows about it. Gregorn's Pillar is a pretty obscure piece of wizarding history. Banage wasn't even sure Eli knew about it, but it was the only thing he could think of that Monpress would want from Mellinor. Anyway, Renaud was a jilted wizard in the castle for sixteen years. If he knew about the Pillar, he would have enslaved his way to it years ago, wouldn't he?"

"I'd think so," Gin said. "But can we count on that? I mean, I'm pretty good against enslavers usually, but Renaud had me down in the dust before I knew what was happening. He's got a strong soul, and he's not afraid to use it full tilt. Now, that's bad enough, but if that pillar is half of what Banage made it out to be, Renaud really will be able to put the spirit world under his boot if he gets his hands on it."

"That may be true," Miranda said and nodded, pulling herself up by his fur. "But Renaud getting the pillar is not a possibility we can handle, so there's no point in dwelling on it. Let's just focus on getting him off the throne quickly before he figures out what's in his treasury."

"It should be simple enough," Gin said. "Jump the gates, eat the prince, and get out." He snapped his teeth. "An enslaver is only human, after all."

"Out of the question." Miranda shook her head. "We'd just get flattened again if we tried a direct attack."

Gin snorted, and Miranda ignored him, pacing little nervous circles around the hound's paws. "What we need is help," she said. "But there's no time to send to the Spirit Court for backup, and with all of Mellinor thinking I murdered their king, we'll get no aid from—" She stopped suddenly, looking around. "Wait a minute, where *is* the king?"

"He's here," Gin said. "He's actually been awake for some time. I didn't want to bother you, so I asked him to wait."

Miranda stared, confused. "You asked him to wait?"

"Yes." The hound grinned, showing all of his teeth. "Nicely."

Miranda put her aching head in her hands. "Gin, let him up."

Gin feigned innocence for a few more seconds and then lifted his back rear paw, allowing the king, who at this point looked more like a pig farmer with a good tailor than royalty, to wiggle his way to freedom.

"Honestly," Miranda said and sighed, giving her companion a final glare before running to help the dirt-caked monarch. "As if things weren't bad enough."

Gin lowered his head and began cleaning the mud off his paws, completely unconcerned.

The king's clothes were nearly black with dirt, and if he'd had a jacket, he'd lost it somewhere, leaving him with nothing but the thin, dirty remains of a white linen shirt that had a large burn mark down the center where Skarest had hit him. Miranda winced at that, and at the marked resemblance between him and his brother. There hadn't been time to get a good look at him in the clearing, but now that the king was crouched in front of her, the family connection was painfully obvious. The two men had the same long build and blond hair, though Henrith's was nearly brown with dirt at this point. Also, the king's face was much rounder than the prince's, a trait that was emphasized by the dusty, overgrown beard that covered nearly all of his lower face after a week away from the royal barber. When he looked up to see who was helping him, his eyes were the same as Renaud's. The fear that shone in them, however, was new.

As soon as he recognized her face, he bolted for the trees.

"Wait!" Miranda shouted, jumping to block his way.

The king made a break in the other direction, but Gin stuck his leg out at the last moment, sending the king sprawling into the dirt yet again. Miranda ran to help him up.

"Your Majesty," she pleaded, helping him turn over. "I am Miranda Lyonette of the Spirit Court. I'm here to help!"

"Help?" the king sputtered, smacking her hands away. "*Help*!? You shot me!"

Miranda winced, but held her position, standing so that the king was stuck between her and Gin. "I know how this sounds, but you must believe me when I say that that was not my lightning bolt."

"Really?" the king shouted, pointing at his singed chest. "It felt real enough to me!"

"Just listen," Miranda said, crouching down to a less threatening height. "That was my lightning spirit, but he wasn't acting on my command. Your brother, Renaud, is an enslaver, a kind of wizard who uses the raw strength of his soul to force weaker spirits to do his bidding. He took my lightning spirit to make it look like I tried to kill you and he is now using the situation to usurp your throne."

The king looked at her blankly. "An ensla-what?"

"An enslaver," Miranda repeated. When comprehension failed to dawn on the king's face, she added, "A bad wizard."

Gin chuckled at the simplification, and the king, assuming the noise was aimed at him, went scarlet. "And I suppose it was Renaud who told your dog to sit on me," he said, pointing accusingly at Gin's nose.

"Unfortunately, that was his own idea," Miranda growled. "But it was for your own protection!" she added quickly.

The king crouched in the dirt, eyeing her suspiciously. Carefully, Miranda sat down across from him, trying to look as meek and harmless as she could.

"I know you don't have much cause to like wizards right now," she said gently, "but I will swear any oath you like that I am on your side."

"My side?" the king snapped. "You wizards ruined everything! How can you expect me to believe that you could possibly be on my side?"

Miranda answered honestly. "Because in this situation the fact that I'm a wizard makes me your greatest ally." She held up her dirty hands where her rings still glittered dully. "I'm a member of the Spirit Court. That means I took an oath to preserve the balance between spirit and man, and to do all I could to prevent the abuse of either. Without the Spirit Court's rules to guide him, your brother has turned to enslavement, forcing his will on the world and doing permanent damage to the spirits he abuses. By my oaths, by my life, I cannot let him continue."

She finished, looking as earnest as possible, and the king scratched his dirty beard thoughtfully. "It's that serious, is it?"

"Let me put it this way." Miranda leaned a little closer. "I was sent here on express orders to stop Eli before he did anything to ruin the reputation of wizards any more than he already has. But if it came down to bringing Renaud in to stand trial or catching Eli red-handed, I'd take Renaud in a heartbeat. I would be stripped of my spirits if I didn't."

The king eyed her suspiciously. "I'm still not convinced, but let's just say I don't find your story of Renaud's betrayal all that unbelievable."

Miranda bit her lip. "I understand it is difficult for you to hear these things of your brother—"

"Not so difficult as you might imagine." The king sighed, plopping down in the dirt. "You forget, I grew up with the bastard. He was Mother's favorite, no question, and he knew it. Father had nothing to do with us before we were old enough to hunt, so Renaud ran things for most of my childhood. It's safe to say I don't find it hard to believe that he misuses his magic."

Miranda's eyes widened. "You knew he was a wizard?"

"Oh no, not in the beginning," Henrith said, waving dismissively. "But when it came out, I wasn't surprised. He was always going on about his birthright and his inheritance and the proper way of things, but he never seemed very interested in the business of being king. Father didn't quite know what to do with him. Frankly, I think my brother scared him a little. It's always been my suspicion that he was secretly relieved when Renaud turned out to be a wizard and gave him a chance to reorder the succession." The king gave her a long wink. "I was always Father's favorite."

Miranda suppressed the urge to roll her eyes.

"Anyway, I'm not surprised that he was so quick to come in and take command, either," the king continued. "Ever since Father died, I've been hearing rumors that Renaud was hiding somewhere in Allaze. It's been my theory for years that he would appear the moment he saw a chance."

"And Eli handed him that chance on a plate," Miranda said hotly. "You may be more right than you realize. Renaud was in the palace the day after you were taken. That's suspiciously fast, even for an ambitious opportunist. I'll bet Eli was in on this from the beginning."

"No," the king said, vehemently shaking his head. "Renaud and Monpress are not the kind who would work together."

"But how can you know?"

"Believe me," the king answered. "I spent twelve years as brother to one and a week as prisoner to the other. Both stints were plenty long enough for me to know that much at least."

Miranda sighed. "If that's true, then Eli's actions are almost worse. If he was working for someone, that would at least show some forethought, but to just charge recklessly into a country and overturn the balance of power like this, with no attention to the consequences..." She shook her head. "He's lucky Master Banage wants him alive, or I'd kill him myself."

The king nodded approvingly at that sentiment. "Well, if you are on my side, what do we do now?"

Miranda tapped her fingers against her chin thoughtfully. "Let's look at our situation. I saw Oban get out, so I think we can safely assume that everyone at the palace thinks you're dead, and that I killed you. Your brother's control of the castle depends on them continuing to think that. That screaming black cloud was his way of erasing the evidence, but I'd bet Eli's bounty that he's taken steps to make sure there's a plausible story in place, just in case you did survive."

"That'd be easy enough," the king said. "All of Mellinor's heard the same stories about wizards. They'd never believe I wasn't a phantom you conjured if we tried to gather allies."

"A phantom?" Miranda frowned. "Where did you get *that* idea?"

"It was in a book," Henrith said. "It's banned, but everyone's read it. *Morticime's Travels* or something."

Miranda suddenly had a splitting headache. "Morticime Kant's *A Wizarde's Travels*?"

"Yes," Henrith said, laughing, "that's the one! Oban's son and I used to sneak it around under our armor and read it when our tutors thought we were studying. I haven't thought about it in years."

Miranda didn't have the energy for the rage she could feel building, so she put the whole affair out of her mind and focused instead on her spirits. Eril had come racing back the moment Renaud had opened his spirit, but he was curled up in his pearl in a deep sleep and traumatized beyond usefulness. Skarest had locked himself away, Durn was still recovering, and Kirik was little better than an ember. Her resources were looking grim indeed.

"You have no idea how much I hate to say this," she said slowly, "but I think we need some outside help."

The king frowned. "You mean send a message to an ally country? Get your spirit-whatever to send more wizards? But that will—"

"Take too long, I know." Miranda stood up. "That's not the kind of outside help I had in mind." She looked over at her companion. "Gin?"

The ghosthound glanced up from his grooming. "If you're asking what I think you're asking, the answer is yes, back the way we came."

"Good." She walked over and began pulling herself onto his back. "Let's be quick about it, then. We've wasted too much time already." She settled herself on his neck and patted the fur behind her. "Climb up, Your Majesty, time is wasting."

The king looked at the hound in horror. "Climb?"

The word was barely out of his mouth before the ghosthound lurched into action. Gin moved like lightning, plucking the king off the ground with a long claw and tossing him in the air. He landed in a heap on the hound's back, and Miranda righted him just in time as Gin set off through the woods at a full run. The king clung to the shifting fur, yelping in terror as the trees flew by, too busy trying not to fall off to ask where they were going. That suited Miranda just fine. As hard as this was for her, it was going to be ten times worse for him. Better to explain it when they arrived and he couldn't get out of it. She grimaced and gripped Gin's fur tightly. No matter how she sliced it, this was going to be some bitter bread to swallow indeed.

* * *

The sun had dropped to the horizon by the time the rock spit Eli, Josef, and Nico in a tumble on the dusty ground. Nico landed gracefully. Eli landed on top of Josef.

"I don't believe it," Josef grunted, shoving Eli off. "*That* was your great escape plan? Hide inside a rock?"

"It worked, didn't it?" Eli snapped back. "Besides, do you have any idea how hard it was to convince that boulder to hide Nico in the first place? *Before* the other nonsense sent it into a panic?"

"Maybe if it wasn't such a stupid idea to begin with, you wouldn't have had so much trouble pulling it—*ow*." Josef snatched back the fist he'd been hammering on the ground to make his point. "What the—?"

Nico took his hand before he could mangle it further and deftly pulled a long, glass splinter out of his palm.

"Where did that come from?" He glared at the glass, then at Nico. Nico just shrugged and nodded over his shoulder. Josef turned, and his eyes went wide. The forest, the piebald grass of the clearing, the injured soldiers, the broken weapons, the arrows—they were all gone. The three of them were at the center of a smooth, black dust bowl that bore no resemblance at all to the clearing they had left just a few hours earlier. The dust lay in undulating patterns, ground so fine that the slightest breeze stirred up a miniature tornado. Other than their rock, nothing else remained, not even the natural slope of the ground.

A hundred feet back from its original position, the forest started again, but the new tree line was unnaturally straight. Some trees were missing limbs; others had entire sections of their trunks ripped away. The damage was surgically clean, as if some giant had taken a razor and simply cut away a circle of the forest using their rock as a center mark.

"I take it back," Josef muttered. "The rock was a great idea. How did you know it would be the only survivor?"

"I didn't," Eli said, leaning in to examine the stone's face.

The boulder itself looked worse for wear. Long, sharp-edged gashes pitted the stone's surface. When Eli brushed his hand over them, a shower of glass dislodged and toppled to the ground, raising a sparkling cloud that sent them all into painful coughing fits.

When he could speak again, Josef asked, "What was that thing, anyway?"

"A sandstorm spirit," Eli wheezed.

"I've never seen a sandstorm that could do this."

"Normally, it couldn't," Eli said, covering his mouth with his hand. "But this one wasn't in its right mind. Did you see that Ronald guy drop the sphere?"

"Renaud," Nico corrected, casually pulling glass splinters out of her coat.

"Whatever," Eli said. "That ball wasn't a gem or anything you normally store a spirit in. It *was* the spirit. He used his will to overpower the sandstorm, like a bully crushing ants together. He forced it to press itself down into that tiny ball, and what do you get when you put sand under high pressure?"

Nico held up one of the dark glass shards.

"Exactly," Eli said and nodded. "Compressing it into a size he could carry around completely altered the spirit's form. Considering the color, he's probably had it like that for a very long time." He frowned, and his next words were uncharacteristically gentle. "It must have been very painful for the storm."

"Well, if it hurt so much, why didn't the spirit just escape?" Josef said, leaning over to knock the glass dust out of his hair. "I've never been clear on all this wizard talk, but a sandstorm's a lot bigger than he is. Couldn't it have just up and run?"

"It's not that simple," Eli said. "A sandstorm isn't a whole spirit to start with, not like other spirits. A rock, for example, has been a rock for a long time. It may have been part of a mountain in the past, but it's always been stone. The rock's spirit has a strong sense of identity. It's fully developed. Sandstorms are different. They're born when air spirits and sand spirits rub each other the wrong way, kind of like a spirit brawl. As the sand is thrown up into the air, both spirits merge into one violent storm. Eventually, they blow their anger out and the sand falls back down, separating the spirits again, but while they're fighting, the sand and air spirits together are a sandstorm spirit. Believe me, neither side is very happy about it. Storms like that are impossible to talk to.

"Unfortunately," Eli continued, "storms like that are also very stupid. Both spirits are battling for control of the storm, so there's a lot of raw spirit power, but no control. That's probably why Renaud was able to dominate it so completely. It didn't have the presence of mind to resist."

"So where is the storm now?" Josef said. "Did he roll it back into a ball and take it with him?"

"No," Eli said, shaking his head. "If there's anything left, we're standing on it." He nudged the sand gently with his foot, stirring up a small cloud of glitter. "Once a spirit degrades that far, it's only good for one last blow. Renaud knew that, so he used the last of its self-control as a leash to sic it on us, and then left it to blow itself out, taking all the evidence of his double cross with it." Eli ran his finger delicately over one of the long scars on the rock face. "It would have worked too, if not for my brilliant plan."

"Very brilliant," Josef said stiffly, pressing his injured chest. "Where's Renaud now, then?"

"Back at the palace, I'd say." Eli nodded toward the spires that poked above the treetops, dark and flat against the evening sky. "Princes who have just overthrown their brothers probably have better things to do than wait around for the likes of us. Maybe we should—"

He stopped as a strong wind blew across the clearing, swirling the loose glass dust into a biting whirlwind. Eli, Josef, and Nico huddled in the lee of the stone, trying not to breathe.

"Well, I think that does it," Eli wheezed when the wind finally died down. "Cowering in a glass dust bath with no gold, no king, and no easy way to get either. This is, officially, our worst job ever."

"It was your idea," Josef said. He dug out one of his spare bandages and tied it over his mouth. "Here," he said and handed one to Nico and another to Eli. "Let's go."

They secured the cloth over their faces and began their trek out of the dustbowl. It took much longer than it should have, for the dust was knee deep in places and so fine it got under their improvised masks within minutes, caking anywhere there was moisture. The bloody front of Josef's shirt was black with it, and even Nico grimaced when it got in her nose. The dusty circle was deathly silent. In the forest ahead, crickets chirped and evening birds called out, but inside the clearing the only sound was the shuffle of their feet sliding through the dust and the wheezing of their own labored breathing.

"Faster," Eli mumbled, trying to speak without opening his mouth. They picked up the pace, and by the time they reached the forest's edge, they were almost running.

As soon as they reached the trees, they tore off their masks and collapsed panting on the ground.

"There should be a stream or something around here," Eli said, spitting the dust out of his mouth. "If I don't get this mess off me soon, I'll be Eli jerky."

A leather canteen flew through the darkness and landed with a wet slap as his feet. Eli jumped back with a sound that was half obscenity, half squeal. Josef whirled in the direction the canteen had come from, blades out. In the last dim light, a pair of amused orange eyes flashed down from the shadows.

Eli recovered in the blink of an eye, slouching into a carefully nonchalant pose. "How long were you waiting?"

"Long enough," Miranda said, not fooled for a moment by his sudden cool attitude. Below her, Gin choked back a laugh. "You can call off your pet swordsman. My intentions are peaceful for the moment."

Josef looked nonplussed at his new title, but he put the knives away. Eli just grinned. "Such assurances!" He waved at the king sitting behind her. "Hello, Your Majesty! Couldn't live without us, could you?"

The king went scarlet and opened his mouth to protest, but Miranda cut him off. "You will refrain from harassing King Henrith any further, Mr. Monpress." Her voice would have frozen a boiling pot.

Eli gave her a wink and reached for the canteen. "So, Miss Spiritualist, to what do we owe the honor of this peaceful chat?"

Miranda folded her arms over her chest. "I want to know what your plans are for fixing this mess you've made."

"I'm afraid I don't know what you are talking about," Eli said, and took a long drink. "I'm just a thief."

"Just a thief?" Miranda gave him an incredulous look. "You kidnapped the king of a council kingdom."

"I was going to give him back," Eli said, splashing a handful of water on his face. He took another swig and then passed the canteen to Josef. "Actually, that makes me better than a thief, since they don't normally return what they steal." He grinned. "I guess I'm moving up in the world."

"I don't care what you were *going* to do. I care about what you *did*." Miranda leaned forward, resting her elbow on Gin's forehead. "Did it not cross your mind, even for a second, what kidnapping a king might do to his country?"

"For your information, I chose Henrith very carefully. How was I supposed to know he had a crazy wizard brother?"

"If you used half the time you spend talking on research, you would have known Mellinor's entire family tree," Miranda snapped. "Now, because of your shameful incompetence, that 'crazy wizard brother,' who also happens to be an enslaver and an attempted murderer, is in spitting distance of the throne, and it's All. Your. Fault."

"Now hold on," Eli said. "You can't blame all that on me."

"By the Powers, I can!" Henrith yelled. "Everything was fine before you came! Even Renaud stayed in line. Then you appear and turn things upside down and expect us to let you walk away?"

Josef finished his swig and handed the canteen to Nico. "I understand Dusty's concern." He nodded to the king, who fumed. "But I don't understand why you're involved." He fixed his eyes on Miranda. "You were sent here to catch Eli, right? So why aren't you attacking us and leaving the king to fend for himself? Mellinor doesn't even like wizards. Why should the Spirit Court care who's on the throne?"

"Because an enslaver king is bad for everyone," Miranda said. "He cannot be allowed to secure his power."

"Seems to me like you've already got the answer to that." Josef looked at the king.

"It's not that simple," Miranda said. "Renaud wouldn't take a chance on this brother surviving without some kind of cover. Henrith tells me that Renaud has probably already convinced the masters that anyone resembling Henrith who approaches the castle is a phantom I've summoned to trick them."

"A phantom?" Eli cackled. "Where did they get *that* idea?"

"Don't ask," Miranda grumbled. "Anyway, suffice it to say the direct approach is out of the question, but the Spirit Court cannot allow an enslaver access to a kingdom's power. We learned that lesson with Gregorn. Master Banage would back Henrith's claim, but the people of Mellinor would never believe it wasn't a Spiritualist trick. Whatever way we go, Mellinor will be thrown into conflict either with the Spiritualists, the Council forces, or itself. War is bad enough, but war with an enslaver involved?" She shuddered. "Imagine rivers used as soldiers, armies of trees, an infantry of bonfires, and all of them left mad at the end, no matter which way the fighting went. That mad sandstorm was nothing compared to what Renaud could do if he had the reason. We can't let that happen."

"Well, that sounds dreadful," Eli said. "I'm still failing to see what this has to do with us."

"It has everything to do with you!" Miranda shouted. "Who do you think started all of this? Everything in Mellinor was perfectly fine for four hundred years. Four hundred! That's four centuries without a coup, a rebellion, or any problems bigger than a trade dispute, until you three showed up."

"That's a bit unfair," Eli said and frowned. "We only—"

"I don't care!" Miranda rolled right over him. "I don't care what you wanted or how it was supposed to turn out. No matter what spin you put on it, this whole country is about to go to hell because of *you* and *your* stupid plan to bilk forty thousand gold standards by destabilizing a peaceful kingdom. So, what I want to know, Mr. Greatest-Thief-In-The-World, is what do you mean to do about it?"

Eli looked from the fuming Spiritualist to the king and back again. He turned to Josef, who shrugged, then Nico, who was trying to get the last drops of water out of the canteen, and his shoulders slumped.

"All right," he said. "I admit that things might not have gone exactly as I would have liked, but perhaps we can come to an arrangement." His smile was back as he looked up at Miranda.

"Say I agree to help you, what exactly would you be asking us to do?"

"Our primary objective is to apprehend Renaud," Miranda said, nodding toward the castle, which was now lost in the evening gloom. "After that, returning Henrith to his throne will be easy."

"And you'd want our help on the apprehending part," Eli said, tapping his finger against his belt idly. "That's a tall order. Renaud's pretty strong."

"Strong, yes," Miranda said, "but surely a man with a fifty-five-thousand-gold bounty on his head is plenty strong in his own right."

"Such flattery is dangerous for a humble man like myself." Eli grinned, and Josef rolled his eyes. "But I'm a thief, Miss Spiritualist, not an assassin. Robbing him blind is one thing, but confronting him outright?" He shook his head. "I'm afraid you'll have to sweeten the deal."

"How do you mean?"

Eli put on his best innocent look. "I do feel somewhat responsible for the current state of affairs in Mellinor, and I am a man who takes his responsibilities very seriously. That's why I'm going to offer you our services at a very reasonable rate."

Miranda's eyes narrowed. "I'm not going to pay you to do what you should be doing in the first place."

"Oh, not money." Eli waved his hand. "Nothing like that. Just a small trade of favors. I help you, you help me."

"If you want me to talk to the Council about your bounty—"

"Powers, no!" Eli laughed. "You couldn't change a thing even if I did want it. My favor is much, much simpler. You see, right now I'm wanted by both the Spirit Court and the Council of Thrones for different infractions. Two posters, two listings in the bounty roster, two payouts. It's all very impractical. All I want you to do is convince the Spirit Court to combine its reward of five thousand standards with the Council's. No extra money needed, just a tiny administrative change."

Miranda kept her eye on him as she went over the words in her head, looking for the catch. "But that would raise your bounty to..."

"Sixty thousand." Eli reached in his pocket and pulled out his new wanted poster. "It's really too bad," he sighed, unfolding it. "They just copied out all these new ones. I think it's their best likeness of me yet."

He tried to hand the poster to Miranda, but she held up her hand. "Stop. You're up to something."

Eli blinked innocently, but Miranda leaned forward on Gin's head, keeping her eyes pinned on his. "Asking Mellinor to pledge money, I can understand. That gives them a thirty-five-thousand-gold stake in making sure you don't get caught. But the Spirit Council won't stop chasing you no matter what it costs. You know this, so why raise your bounty? Don't you realize that every gold standard draws another ten bounty hunters out of the woodwork? Sixty thousand is enough money to bankroll a small war. Your own mother would turn you in for half as much."

"I don't doubt she would." Eli's grin grew wicked. "But you're missing the point, Lady Spiritualist. It's not about the bounty hunters or extorting countries. It's about the bounty. It's about a little boy's dream!" He threw out his arms. "Sixty thousand is nothing. Chump change! My goal is to be worth one million gold."

Miranda's eyes widened. "One million? Are you crazy? There's not that much money in the world! The Council's war with the Immortal Empress didn't cost half so much, and they're still paying it off. Even if you kidnapped a king a week, you'd die of old age before you got your bounty that high."

"Well," Eli said, "if that's how you feel, how can you object to a trifle like moving the Spirit Court's five thousand?"

Miranda hunched over Gin's head, glaring suspiciously at the grinning thief. "Why a million?"

Eli shrugged. "Seemed like a good number. No one's ever had a million-gold bounty."

Miranda gave him a scathing look. "It can't be that simple."

"I never said it was, but you're free to make up your own reasons if it'll make you feel better." He shoved his hands in his pockets and looked up at her, his face unbearably smug. "Time's ticking, Miss Spiritualist. Do we have a deal or not?"

Miranda knotted her hands in Gin's fur, thinking. Henrith shifted uneasily behind her while the hound kept a close eye on Nico, who hadn't done anything except sit on the ground and watch the show. Finally, the Spiritualist gave a long sigh.

"All right," she said. "I'm sure I'll regret this, but you have a deal, Mr. Monpress. If you help apprehend Renaud *and* put Henrith safely back on his throne, I will talk to the Rector Spiritualis about transferring our bounty on you to the Council. However"—she stabbed her index finger at him—"even though, at the moment, I'm looking the other way for the sake of the greater good, my orders to bring you in have not changed. When we are done here, I'm not going to stop chasing you."

Eli smiled graciously. "I expected nothing less."

Miranda blinked, thrown off balance by his sudden sincerity. "Well, that's settled then."

Josef pushed himself off the tree. "If you two are done chatting, we'd better get moving. Sitting out in the dark on the edge of the clearing where we were almost killed isn't a good place to talk strategy. Besides"—he slapped his neck—"I'm being eaten alive out here."

Now that he mentioned it, Miranda could feel them too. "Lead on," she mumbled, slapping one of the biting midges off her hand.

When she looked up, the swordsman was already stalking

off through the trees. The demonseed girl followed a few steps behind, silent as a shadow. Eli strolled along at his own pace with his hands in his pockets, whistling something off key.

Miranda exchanged glances with the king. At last he gave a resigned nod, and she nudged Gin with her toe. The ghosthound rose soundlessly. Quiet as his namesake, he slipped through the trees, keeping abreast with the swordsman but well away from the girl who followed him. High overhead, the moon was beginning its climb through the black sky, illuminating their winding path through the rocky hills and steep gullies of the deer park with her clear, white light.

CHAPTER 15

"*This* is where you were hiding?" Miranda gaped, sliding off Gin's back. The moonlight that filtered through the treetops was just enough for her to be able to make out the tumbledown walls and gaping roof of the small hunting shack. "You could barely spend a night in this."

"It's a bit run down," Eli admitted, "but"—he leaned over and pointed through a gap in the surrounding trees—"you can't beat the location."

Looking where he pointed, she could just spot the white walls of the city glowing silver through the trees, barely half a mile away.

"I don't believe it," Miranda said.

"First rule of thievery," Eli said, grinning, "only run if you're not coming back." He thumped his heels on the hard ground. "The last place a man looks is under his feet."

"All this time you've been hiding in the king's deer park?" She was almost laughing now. "You're putting me on. I had Eril search this area days ago."

"Spirits don't see everything," Eli said. "Besides, I had some excellent camouflage." He tilted his head back. "Ladies?"

The pleasant purr of his spirit voice reverberated through her. High overhead, a chorus of sighs answered, "Eli!"

Miranda took a step back as the trees behind the cabin, a clump of young hardwoods taking advantage of the tiny clearing's sunlight, shook themselves to life. They bent down, giggling like geese, and surrounded Eli in a nest of branches. He said something low, and they giggled harder before lifting away and settling lightly over the ruined roof. They rustled madly, fluffing their broad leaves over the gaping holes and forming a sort of net over the fire hole to diffuse the smoke. When they stopped moving at last, Miranda's eyes widened. The young trees covered the hut perfectly. In fact, had she not seen them move, she would have sworn that the hovel was just another rocky outcropping, and that the trees had always been that way.

"Welcome," Eli said, slipping between the branches with practiced ease and opening the rickety wooden door. Josef followed him, clutching his injured chest and grumbling under his breath the whole way. Nico went into the hut last, pulling her coat tight around her and her hat down over her eyes as she squeezed between the branches. Only when they were all inside and she saw the first sparks of a fire being struck did Miranda begin to untie her own bag from Gin's back.

King Henrith had just made it to the ground. He looked at the hut with no small amount of panic in his eyes. "What should I do?"

"For now, go in," Miranda said, struggling with the leather straps. "We have a deal, and I don't think he'll go back on it. After all, you're no profit to him now."

The king grimaced. "That's supposed to be comforting?"

"With a thief like him, it's the most comforting thing you'll hear. Go in, I'll follow in a moment."

The king hovered a moment longer and then timidly made his way into the hut.

"Can't really blame him," Miranda said as the king's shadow joined the others' around the infant fire. "It's not exactly a place of pleasant memories, considering what he's been through."

Gin snorted, sending a wave of dead leaves scurrying across the grass. "What kind of wizard starts a fire with rocks?"

"The same kind who flirts with trees, apparently." Miranda worked the pack free at last and set it on the ground beside her. "No wonder he was so hard to track. Half the spirits in this clearing are in love with him. It's like that stupid door all over again."

Gin rolled his eyes, but stayed oddly silent. Miranda walked over to his head and began to scratch his ears. "How does he do it?" she murmured. "How does he get them to just, I don't know"—she shrugged—"do what he says?"

"There's something about him," the ghosthound said quietly. "He's got a sort of brightness."

Miranda kept scratching, listening carefully. Spirits, even talkative ones like Gin, almost never talked about the spirit world. She'd tried to cajole information out of him on uncountable occasions, but every time he refused, saying it would be too difficult, like trying to describe the color red to a blind child. Some things, he would growl, you just had to see for yourself.

When he didn't continue on his own, she tried a delicate prompt. "Brightness? Like sunlight?"

"No," Gin said, "not like light through the eyes. Bright, like something beautiful." He shook himself and stood up. "Leave off, I'm no good at this. He's just got a light around him, all right? And spirits are attracted to light. Interpret as you will. I'm going to get some food. Be back in a few hours."

Then he was gone. It happened so quickly, she barely felt his fur slip between her fingers before he vanished into the night. Miranda stood for a long while where he had left her, looking up at the full moon with her eyes closed tightly, trying to imagine what light not like light through the eyes looked like. Only when Eli yelled something about dinner did she finally go into the cabin.

"All right," Eli said, rubbing his hands together. "What's the plan?"

They were seated in two factions on either side of the fire, Miranda and the king against one wall, Eli against the other. Josef was lying flat on his back in the far corner, gripping the hilt of his iron sword while Nico hovered over him, treating the nasty gash in his chest. She had finished cleaning the glass sand out of it by the time Miranda entered and was now stitching the skin back together. From Josef's bored expression, she might as well have been doing needlepoint next to him rather than *in* him, and Miranda was impressed in spite of herself.

Eli's question seemed aimed at no one in particular, but when no one answered, Miranda took it upon herself. "A frontal assault is out of the question," she said. "Renaud will be on high alert. He also has a master swordsman, as we saw, so there's that to think about." She nodded slightly at Josef, who either didn't notice or didn't care. "I just wish we knew what other enslaved spirits he had."

Eli shrugged. "Well, he can't have too many enormous, mad spirits just lying around."

"We can't count on that," Josef said. "I'm not a wizard, but even I can tell the man's obviously powerful. I mean, no offense,

Miss Spiritualist, but he had you squirming in the sand the minute he got serious."

Miranda blushed scarlet. "Do not postulate where you do not understand, swordsman," she snapped.

Josef looked at Eli, who was doing his best not to laugh. "Don't be prickly, Miranda," Eli said. "He didn't mean anything by it. Do you want to tell him, or should I?"

Miranda looked away, fuming. "I don't see why it needs to be explained at all. He won't understand it."

Josef's glare matched her own. "Try me."

Miranda tugged a hand through her hair. "Fine," she growled. "It's not exactly a secret." She held up her hand so that her rings glittered in the shaky firelight. "Wizards can impose their will over spirits. That's one of the basic principles behind magic. The other, of course, is that our control does not extend over other human souls. That's why most people feel only a slightly uncomfortable pressure when a wizard opens their spirit, no matter how strong the wizard is. Spiritualists, however, are different, because we maintain a constant bond through our rings with our servant spirits. Each of my spirits siphons off a small, steady stream of energy from my soul as per our agreement when they became my servants."

"Power for service," Eli said, with mock seriousness. "Strength for obedience."

Miranda ignored him. "Most of the time, this connection is one-way. But sometimes, for example, when a powerful wizard opens his spirit full tilt right in front of them, my servant spirits are affected like any other spirit, and that can cause feedback through our connection."

"So what does that mean?" Josef said.

Eli beat Miranda to it. "It means normal humans may feel a bit queasy when a wizard's open soul is pressing against them, but it can't hurt us, so we don't go all weak at the knees about it. Spiritualists, however, are tied into their pet spirits waking and sleeping, and when those spirits are squashed under a strong wizard's will, like Renaud's, the Spiritualist," he said and made a squishing motion with his hands, "goes right down with them."

Miranda shook her head, but Josef nodded. "Hell of a weakness. How does the Spirit Court fight an enslaver, then?"

"A strong, loyal fire spirit is usually enough," Miranda said. "They're so chaotic that most enslavers can't get control before they're burned. My Kirik would have been perfect had *someone*"—she glared murderously at Eli—"not doused him."

"How was I supposed to know he'd go out so quickly?"

Josef shook his head. "Well, that's out. Is there any other way around the problem?"

"No," said Miranda.

"Yes," said Eli.

She whirled to face him. "What do you mean?"

Eli shrugged. "Your rings are what give you trouble, right? So take them off. Seems simple to me."

"*Take them off?*" Miranda looked incredulous. "I can't just take them off!"

"Well, how else do you think you're going to be able to come into the castle with us?" Eli said.

"Maybe you can get by sweet-talking trees and doors," she huffed, "but I'm not leaving my spirits. I'll be defenseless!"

"Can't be worse than what happened before," Josef said. "I'm sure your wiggling on the ground really intimidated Renaud. Might and majesty of the Spirit Court and all that."

"There's no other way, Miranda," Eli cut in. "We need your help in this, and we can't go in if we can't count on you not to fall over when things get sticky."

Miranda looked at the king, who looked thoroughly lost in all this spirit talk. When he saw her looking, he smiled trustingly, and she heaved a long sigh. With great difficulty, she reached down and pulled off her rings one by one, laying them gently on the ground in front of her. She pulled Eril's pendant over her head and added him to the pile. Lastly, she slipped the Spirit Court signet off her left ring finger and laid it reverently beside the others, the heavy gold glowing warmly in the firelight.

Next, she dug around in her knapsack for the doeskin bag all Spiritualists kept for just this purpose. Her fingers felt uncomfortably light and naked as she dropped her rings one at a time into the soft leather pouch. It was a tight fit—no Spiritualist expects to have to remove all of their rings at once—but after a few tries she managed to wedge everything in and knot the bag closed with a red silk cord. Out of the glittering pile of rings, she'd kept only one. A small opal band, almost like a child's promise ring, remained on her left pinky. Her glare dared anyone to comment as she tucked the bulging doeskin bag back into her knapsack.

"Okay," Eli said, rubbing his hands together as Miranda settled back into her spot by the fire. "Now that we're serious, here's the real plan."

CHAPTER 16

The throne room of castle Allaze was as dark and forbidding as its prisons. The sun had set hours ago, but the lamps were still not lit. No one had let the servants in to light them. At the base of the dais stairs, below the empty throne, the masters of Mellinor stood in a loose circle around a balding man whose dust-streaked armor matched his tear-stained face.

"Friends," Master Oban said, his strong voice wavering, "as many times as you have me tell it, the story won't change. I saw with my own two eyes the Spiritualist's lightning strike our king. I watched him fall!"

"I thought the lightning was pointed at the thief?" an official in the back called out, sparking a new torrent of comments.

"Impossible!"

"Master Oban, are you sure you saw—"

"The real issue here—"

"—waited far too long—"

"—always said it was a trap—"

"—greatest tragedy of our times, that's what they'll say, and on our watch—"

"Enough," said the old Master of the Courts. "Leave Master Oban be."

The masters' chatter stopped immediately, and the dark room fell silent as the elderly master motioned for Oban to step aside. The Master of Security made way immediately, and the Master of the Courts took his place at the center of the circle. "We can't deny it any longer," the Master of the Courts said. "We have to accept that the Spiritualist used us. Perhaps it is as Lord Renaud theorized and she was in league with the thief from the very beginning, or perhaps not. Whatever the circumstances, we are to blame."

"It was awful convenient, her showing up not an hour after the king's disappearance," said a young, minor official, elbowing his way forward. "I for one always believed she was up to something. Why would a wizard come to Mellinor, except to cause trouble?" He glared at the old men. "The only wizard we can trust is Lord Renaud. Even banished, he tried his best to save his brother!"

"But where is the body?" another official shouted back. "Where is our king?"

This raised a new round of shouting, and it was several minutes before the Master of the Courts regained control. "Silence," he growled, staring down the younger members who were still miming punches at each other. He looked pointedly at Master Oban, who nodded, then at Master Litell, the thin Master of the Exchequer, who looked away. Satisfied, he spoke the words they'd all been waiting for. "In the four hundred years since her founding, Mellinor's succession has never once been compromised. After hearing your opinions, divided as they may be, I think we can all agree on one point: If tradition must change, it will not be with us."

The masters began to murmur again, but the Master of the Courts silenced them with a wave of his hand. "The discussion is over, send him in."

A young official broke from the circle and ran to the side parlor. His knuckles had barely touched the wooden door before Renaud flung it open. He was already clothed from chin to toes in mourning black, and his pale face seemed to float through the darkened hall of its own accord. The circle opened up as he approached, until only the Master of the Courts stood between him and the empty throne.

The Master of the Courts watched Renaud warily. For a moment, he seemed on the verge of sending the prince away again, but in the end, the Master bowed his head.

"Prince Renaud," he said, "it is with a heavy heart that we call you here, but in times of uncertainty the kingdom must not be even one day without its ruler. Therefore, it is the agreement of this emergency council that the crown should pass from father to son, brother to brother, as it has always been."

Renaud bowed solemnly, but there was a twinkle of delight

hidden in his blue eyes. When he stepped forward, however, the Master of the Courts held up his hand.

"Yet," the master said, and Renaud's eyes darkened, "in the absence of King Henrith's body, you must understand our predicament. Should, by some miracle, King Henrith be found alive, all titles will revert immediately to him, as is his right."

"I would expect nothing more," Renaud said, laying his hand gently on the old man's shoulder. "Henrith was my brother and my king as well, as dear to me as my own flesh, even in my exile. Still"—his eyes moved gravely across the circle of faces—"we must not let false hope take root. Miranda Lyonette is a powerful Spiritualist, and the Spirit Court is not an organization to leave such things to chance. I have long speculated that her initial goal was to kill King Henrith in the hopes of bringing me to the throne. She, no doubt, believed that a fellow wizard would be more sympathetic to the Spirit Court's demands. Only when I rebuked her for the cruel murder of my kinsman did she realize her mistake. Now, I fear she may try to conjure up a phantom of my brother to trick you and turn us against each other, throwing Mellinor into confusion so that the Spirit Court's agents can sneak in."

Master Oban went pale. "You mean, it's not a story? Wizards can really do that? Create apparitions?"

Renaud nodded gravely. "False images, but real enough to touch." He grabbed the Master of Security's shoulder with his other hand, and the older man shrank away, shivering. "Our only defense is watchfulness," he continued, looking each master in the eyes in turn. "I have sent word to the outposts, but I am sure she will try to strike at the castle, where she's had success before. If you or any of the people below you see anyone resembling the late king, he must be brought to me immediately. The Spiritualist must not be allowed to spread fear and uncertainty among us."

The officials mumbled to each other, sometimes agreement,

sometimes displeasure, but no one dared speak up. Renaud silenced them with a look. "We begin the seven days of mourning at sunrise. Go and make your preparations."

The circle scattered, but as they walked away, Renaud added. "Master Litell, another moment, if you please."

The elderly Master of the Exchequer froze and looked timidly over his shoulder. Renaud beckoned, and Litell returned without further protest. A few of the younger officials hung back, trying for a few words with their new king, but he waved them away, and they left the throne room like rejected puppies. When the last one shuffled through the great, golden doors, Renaud turned and gave the Master of the Exchequer his most pleasant smile.

"I need you to let me into the treasury."

"Now?" Litell rubbed his hands together nervously. "If my lord wishes to review the books, I have the country's balances in my office. I can wake my assistant—"

"I trust your accounts," Renaud said. "But what I need to see can be found only in the treasury. You have the key, do you not?"

"Entrusted to me by your father," Litell said, clutching the heavy chain at his neck. "But I'll have to call someone to help with the doors..."

"Do it," Renaud said. "There is something I need to confirm as soon as possible."

Master Litell jumped at his sudden sharpness, but did as he was told. Renaud followed him out of the throne room and down the steep stairs that led to the oldest part of the castle. Neither man noticed the shadow that followed silently behind them.

It took half an hour and twenty guardsmen to get the treasury open. Master Litell spent the entire time apologizing.

"I am so dreadfully sorry for the delay," he puffed, standing back as the soldiers heaved again. "That door hasn't been opened in thirty years at least, not since your mother's dower was added. Your father and brother never cared much for the historical pieces."

They were standing in a long hall deep beneath what was now the prison, but once, hundreds of years ago, had been the heart of the palace Allaze, built by Gregorn himself. The smoke-stained walls were still covered in undulating mosaics that, in the unsteady light of the guards' lamps, seemed to rise and swell like black waves on an underground sea. Renaud, however, saw nothing except the solid slab of iron as wide as the hall itself, set flush against the bare stone. The great treasury door was triple barred, each man-sized lock marked with the deep graven seal of Mellinor.

At last, with a bone-crunching scrape, the team of guards twisted the last great lock open. Unbound, the door swung slowly inward, picking up momentum as its weight dragged it into the blackness of the long-sealed room. Master Litell sprang forward, taking a torch from the guard captain and holding it aloft at the gaping entry. The glitter of gold bounced back to meet him.

"Everything looks to be in order." Master Litell handed the torch back to the guard and walked over to Renaud, taking a large stack of papers from a waiting page. "Your Majesty will of course want to see the inventory. Now, everything in the treasury is sorted by date, but you'll need this list..."

His voice faded as Renaud marched past him.

"That won't be necessary, Master Litell." The new king seized a torch of his own from one of the guards. "I know what I'm looking for. Wait here."

With that he turned and walked into treasury, leaving Master Litell and the guards to watch from the threshold as Renaud's torch bobbed out of sight behind the maze of ancient trunks and dusty gold.

* * *

Coriano sat in the shadows for a long time, pondering what to do. Following Renaud to the treasury had been easy enough, so had slipping past the guards gawking at the entrance. But now Renaud, after walking past cabinets stuffed with silks, chests of gold, and racks of ancient weapons, had stopped in front of what was perhaps the least interesting part of the whole affair, and he had been staring at it for the last twenty minutes. They were at the center of the treasury where the shelves opened up to make room for what looked to be a support pillar. The pillar, however, failed in that regard, for it stopped ten feet short of the cavernous ceiling. Its knobby, uneven surface glittered dully where Renaud's torchlight landed. Otherwise, it was completely unexceptional, rising without fanfare from the undecorated stone floor.

Patient as he was, Coriano was growing bored. Also, there was something in the air here. Maybe it was being so deep in the earth, close to the great, sleeping spirits on which the world rested, but the room felt thick with dormant energy. It made him uncomfortable, and the sooner he got out to cleaner, younger air, the better he would feel. After another minute of watching Renaud watch the pillar, Coriano decided it was time to make himself known.

He stepped forward, deliberately scraping his boots against the smooth, dusty floor. Renaud stiffened and whirled around, holding his torch aloft. When he saw Coriano, his eyes narrowed. "You."

Coriano leaned against a heavy trunk that skirted the edge of the empty space around the pillar and gave the new king a dry smile. "Me."

Renaud's scowl grew more menacing. "How did you get in here? Why have you come back?"

"How I got here isn't important, because I could do it twenty times again, each time a different way." Coriano's voice was dry as the air. He picked up a small gold lion from the case beside him and examined it with bored interest. "As for the why, I wasn't aware our bargain was complete. You got what you wanted, but I seem to have come up short."

"You must be mistaken." Renaud smiled politely. "I paid you before we left."

"The money is incidental," Coriano said, putting the lion down again. "I mean our real bargain."

"Our agreement was that you would take care of the swordsman if I prevented Eli's interference, which I did," Renaud said. "If anything, I should be the one complaining. I gave you Josef Liechten on a platter. You were the one who decided to run away."

"I would hardly call a three-minute fight in a dust storm followed by the release of a mad spirit 'on a platter,'" Coriano said, sneering. "But I wasn't the only one who let his quarry escape, was I?"

Renaud stiffened. "If you're talking about my brother—"

"Your brother?" Coriano shook his head. "No, no, I'm sure you've got that quite under control. I'm talking about Eli."

"Eli?" Renaud started to laugh. "You think I'm worried about that hack thief? The one who trades favors with dirt spirits? For all his posturing, he ran at the first sign of trouble. I'm only sorry I bothered to put any gold in the chest at all."

Coriano wasn't laughing. "You've been planning this for a long time, Renaud. You watched for weakness and jumped with both feet when you saw your chance. I respect that, so let me give you some advice. Eli didn't get to where he is now by being a fool, and he didn't get there by letting ambitious idiots like you cheat him."

Renaud's face grew murderous in the torchlight. "Such praise." He spat the words, "If I didn't know better, I would think he was your real target, not the swordsman."

"Eli is the one who makes Josef Liechten difficult to pin," Coriano said, laying his hand on his sword. "Only a stupid man doesn't respect his opponent's strengths, and if there's one thing Eli is good at, it's never showing up when you want him and always showing up when you don't."

"Sounds like someone else I know," Renaud said.

"Really?" Coriano's mouth twitched. "Then consider what I'm about to say very carefully. I was able to sneak into the castle, past all your guards, right into your treasury, where I waited twenty minutes for you to notice me. Had I struck at any point, you would have been dead before you felt the blow, and all this treasure would be mine." He slammed his hand down on the cabinet beside him and the resounding crack echoed through the cavern. "If I could do all this," he said in the silence that followed, "Eli could do it. Only he could do it faster, quieter, and with more backup. So think very hard before you dismiss either of us, Your Majesty. Because in this entire kingdom, I'm the only one who can protect you from what you started the moment you decided to cheat Eli Monpress."

"You," Renaud said, scowling, "protect me? What would you do, sneak up behind him and make a speech? That seems to be your only real talent—"

The last *t* of "talent" had barely left his lips before something sharp and unbearably cold crushed into his neck. Renaud hadn't even seen the swordsman move, but all at once Coriano was right on top of him, pressing the bare white blade of his sword against the king's throat. The torch clattered to the ground as Renaud gasped for air. He flung open his spirit and desperately swung his will against the blade's edge, trying to overpower the metal's spirit, but the sword was like a glacier against his throat, and no matter how hard he fought, it would not move.

"Your tricks may work on dull, unsuspecting spirits," Coriano whispered, inches from Renaud's ear, "but an awakened sword is different. Now"—the swordsman's voice scraped against Renaud's opened soul like a razor—"listen, and listen well. I don't care why you took this kingdom, and I don't care if you keep it. I don't care what kind of wizard you are or what you're planning here in the dark. I am here for the Heart of War, nothing else. Now, if you do exactly as I say and help me corner Josef Liechten, I can give you victory. You might even live to reap the benefits of all your years of plotting. Do we have a deal?"

Eyes bulging, Renaud held out a moment longer before nodding frantically. As fast as he'd lunged, Coriano stepped back, and Renaud sank to his knees, gasping and clutching his bruised throat.

"All right," Coriano said, sheathing his white sword as he kept his good eye on the king. "The original bargain still stands. I will fight Josef Liechten without interference."

Renaud glowered from the floor, still rubbing his neck. "And what would my part entail?"

"You will arrange your forces exactly as I tell you," Coriano said, "and then we wait. Without Josef, the girl will leave and Eli will be vulnerable. You should have no trouble dealing with him then. In any event, after I have defeated the Heart of War, you'll never have to hear from me again."

"That would be a relief." Renaud rubbed his throat one last time and pushed himself up, turning back to the pillar. Almost at once, his sour glare faded, and his face relaxed into a warm smile. He reached out to touch the pillar's dull surface with his bare hands, and when his fingers brushed the stone, Coriano felt a tremor through his boots.

"How long would this plan take?"

Coriano eyed him warily. "That depends on Eli. Probably not more than a day, maybe two. Monpress moves quickly when he needs to."

"More than enough time," Renaud said, reluctantly withdrawing his hand from the pillar. "Follow me."

He whirled and marched out of the treasury, shouting for his guards. Coriano shot one last glance at the strange pillar before following the king into the hall. Whatever Renaud was planning down here, Coriano had a feeling it was larger than Mellinor. He would need to keep his wits about him if he was going to face Josef before it happened. After that, Coriano smiled, Renaud could bring the whole world crashing down for all it mattered to him. Dunea sang in agreement, and Coriano gripped her hilt.

Somewhere in the darkness behind them, the pillar quaked in response.

CHAPTER 17

The morning mists hovered thick and wet over the forest. Deer, the king's own stock, had come out to feed on the delicate new leaves sprouting in the scattered open spaces, but they shied away from the tiny clearing by the stone hut, and for good reason.

Gin lay by the door with his head on his paws, his orange eyes half open. The door to the hut creaked and a growl rumbled up from deep in the ghosthound's chest as Josef stepped out into the gray morning with Nico close behind him.

The swordsman was shirtless, but the wide swath of bandages wrapped around his chest kept the mist off him. For the first time Gin had seen, he was unarmed save for the enormous iron sword that he held in one hand.

The swordsman and the girl walked a short distance through the forest, stopping at a spot where the trees were farther apart, not quite a clearing, but room enough for their purposes. Nico took a seat on a fallen log while Josef took up position at a wide spot between two young poplars. When he judged he had enough space, he held out his arms and, very carefully, raised his black blade. He brought it up in a slow arc until it was over his head. His shoulders tensed as the barely healed cut under his bandages stretched, but his face remained calm and serious as he brought the blade down again.

When he had lowered the point all the way to the leaf litter, Nico spoke. "Will it do?"

Josef let out a pained breath. "The stitches held," he said. "That'll have to be enough. It's not like we have time to lie around."

Nico stood up and went around to his back, adjusting the bandages to sit higher. As she reached up to get his shoulders, the wide sleeves of her enormous black coat fell away from her scrawny arms revealing the scuffed silver manacles she wore clamped tight on each wrist. A dozen feet behind them, Gin's growl grew louder.

"What is he going on about?" Josef grunted, rolling his shoulders to test the new bandage arrangement.

"The usual," she murmured.

Josef scowled. "I can make him stop if it's bothering you."

Nico shook her head. "Eli needs them for his plan, and things like that stopped bothering me long ago." She reached into her coat and pulled out a clean shirt, which she held out to the swordsman.

Josef took it and pulled it over his head, ignoring the pain in his chest. "I'll talk to Eli about it, then. You shouldn't have to put up with that idiocy just so he can get another five thousand on his bounty."

"I'd put up with more for less," Nico said. She caught his eye and gave him one of her rare smiles. "The higher we make his bounty, the better the bounty hunters get. Soon you'll have the kind of fights you've been searching for."

"Fights seem to find us no matter what Eli's bounty is," Josef grumbled, but he was grinning when he looked at her. "Still, that Coriano and his awakened blade will be a challenge worth remembering. If the higher bounty attracts more of that sort of opponent, all of this stomping around in the woods will be worth it." He paused. "Which isn't to say I'll agree to another of your idiot kidnapping ideas, Monpress."

He turned around and folded his arms over his chest. A moment later, Eli stepped out of the underbrush with an enormous sigh.

"Too much suspicion will lead to an early grave," he said, strolling over to stand beside Nico.

"I would argue it's the other way around," Josef said. "So, did you need something, or did you just come out here to bother us?"

Eli made a great show of looking hurt. "For your information, I came out to see if you were all right. Nico was still putting your chest back together when I drifted off last night, so when you weren't in the hut when I woke up, I decided to investigate. Now I'm glad I did. What's this about an awakened blade?"

Josef plunged the Heart of War into the soft ground and leaned on it. "The swordsman I fought had an awakened blade."

"Must be a good one considering it put a hole in your tough hide," Eli said. "Good thing yours is better. We'll make short work of him if we see him again."

"I'm not going to use the Heart," Josef said solemnly.

"Josef, not this again," Eli groaned. "You're the swordsman; you decide how you fight. I respect that, but every time you get this way, half your blood ends up on the ground. If things go down the way they're looking like they will, we're going to have to make a quick exit, and that's hard enough without Nico having to drag your sword-riddled carcass across the countryside. The Heart of War chose you for a reason, and it wasn't to get carted around the world on a strap. Can't you just smash the swordsman and take the easy win for once in your life?"

"An easy win is meaningless," Josef growled. "If I'm going to get stronger, I have to defeat Coriano on my own, the right way."

"Nonsense!" Eli smiled. "We think you're plenty strong already, don't we, Nico?"

Nico stared at him. "Do you think your bounty is plenty high?"

Eli's grin faded. "Point taken." He shook his head. "Fine, do whatever you want. Just don't do something stupid like die on us, all right?"

Josef snorted. "Who do you think I am?"

"For the sake of our friendship, I'm not going to answer that." Eli met Josef's glare with a wry grin. "Now, I'm going back to the hut to mind our guests. Can you two handle getting the costumes?"

"Shouldn't be a problem," Josef said, pulling his iron sword out of the ground and resting it on his shoulder. "The real question is, will the Spiritualist follow orders?"

"Oh, yes," Eli said, nodding. "She's in this neck deep now. When Renaud showed his true colors, he put her duty to Spirit Court doctrines on the line. She'd break just about any law to keep her oaths to the spirits. So while she may try and moralize us to death, I think we can count on her not to flub the plan."

"Just make sure you actually *have* a plan this time," Josef called as he walked back toward the hut for the rest of his weapons.

Eli folded his arms over his chest, glaring at the swordsman's bandaged back. "Do you believe that?" he grumbled. "And after all the scrapes I've gotten him out of."

Nico shrugged. "With all the scrapes you get him into, I think it works out about even."

"Don't you start, too," Eli sighed. "In the year you've been with us, have I ever let us down? Don't you trust me yet?"

"Josef trusts you," Nico said, starting toward the hut as well. "That's enough for me."

Eli sighed again, louder this time, but Nico didn't look back. Shaking his head, he jogged after her, stopping a moment to say good morning to Gin, who was still growling, before joining the others in the hut.

"You know this is a terrible plan," Gin growled.

"Yes," Miranda said, pulling the long tunic dress over her head. "You've told me so every ten minutes since sunrise."

They were in the tiny space behind the forester's hut, wedged between the trees and the crumbling stone. Gin was slouched by the hut's corner, his body blocking the opening to the clearing so Miranda could have some privacy while she changed into the costume Josef had shoved into her hands a few minutes ago, when he and Nico had finally returned from wherever they'd been. She'd never been so happy to see them. A whole morning alone with the king and Eli had almost been more than she could stand.

"Disguise yourselves and sneak into the castle?" Gin snorted, making the low-hanging branches dance. "How are you going to get through the doors with no spirits? Wait for the thief to charm them all? And he didn't say a thing about what you'd do when you actually got in. I'm telling you, it's never going to work."

"I wouldn't be so sure about that," Miranda said, finding the opening for her head at last. "Eli's terrible plans have an interesting habit of working out."

Gin rolled his eyes. "Because his kidnapping plan went *so* well."

"Up until us, yes it did," Miranda said, giving him a sharp look. "I don't like this any more than you do, mutt, but we're in deep now, so we might as well do our best."

Gin kept grumbling, but Miranda ignored him. She smoothed the bulky dress over her shift with a final wiggle, and then, reaching awkwardly behind her, tied it with the strings sewn into the back. Next, she reached up and pulled her hair as tight as she could, knotting it in place at the base of her neck with a bit of twine. She grabbed the thick veil from a waiting branch and draped it over her forehead, letting the rest hang down her back so that her red hair was completely covered. Last of all, she fixed the small cap at the crown of her head with a long stickpin that held the whole affair in place. She gave her head an experimental shake to make sure the veil wouldn't slide off. When it stayed put to her satisfaction, she turned around.

"There," she said, putting her hands on her hips. "How do I look?"

Gin eyed her up and down. "Like a librarian."

"Such flattery!" Miranda folded her hands over her chest dramatically. "Be still, my trembling heart!"

"What? That's the point, right?" Gin said, getting up.

Miranda grinned at his confusion and tucked her discarded clothes under her arm before pushing her way through the giggling trees. Gin padded after her, muttering under his breath.

The tiny clearing outside the hut that served as Eli's hideout had become quite crowded since Nico and Josef had returned. Most of the space, however, was taken up by the new additions. Laid out on a ratty blanket, two men and a woman, dressed only in their underclothes, were sleeping peacefully in the tree-dappled sunlight—castle servants, the sources of the costumes. King Henrith was crouched beside them, his hands moving in worried circles on his knees. He had traded out his filthy silk clothes for what looked like a set of Josef's spares, though it was hard to tell without the knives. The bad fit and the king's dour expression as he hovered over the unconscious servants made him look like a refugee from a tragedy play.

"I don't see why you had to knock them out like this," he muttered.

"It was the simplest way to get the sizes correct," Josef said in a bored voice. He was lounging beside the hut, with his back propped against the ever-present camouflage thatch of branches provided by Eli's arboreal admirers. His enormous sword was stabbed into the ground beside him and a pile of throwing knives was spread out in the grass at his feet. His normal array of cross-belted sheaths was gone, and in their place he wore the chain and blue surcoat of a House Allaze royal guard, which, judging from the gaps at the shoulders, had recently belonged to the narrower of the sleeping men. "They'll wake up soon enough, no worse for wear."

"And you'll be here, sire," Eli chimed in, fastening the cuffs of his valet's coat. "A free evening off work and a touching reunion with their monarch. I'd say we're doing them a favor."

"What I don't understand," Miranda said, kneeling beside the distressed king, "is why we're stealing costumes to sneak into the castle when Josef and Nico already snuck into the castle to grab these three."

"We did nothing of the sort," Eli said. "Every servant doesn't live in the palace, you know. Josef spotted this lot walking into town from the outlying village. He merely gave them an involuntary night off. Oh, don't look like that." He waved his hands at Miranda's horrified expression. "If Josef says they'll be fine, they'll be fine. He's a professional. He does this all the time."

Josef nodded sagely at the pile of knives he was polishing. Somehow, Miranda failed to find the gesture comforting.

"Of course," Eli put his hands in his pockets, "the real question here is why we had to resort to this in the first place. I thought you said you had a contact in the palace?"

Miranda shook her head vehemently, making her veil fly. "There's no way I'm letting you drag Marion into this, not after she already stuck her neck out for me once. Just look what you did to one of her coworkers." She pointed at the unconscious girl, whose librarian uniform dress Miranda was now wearing. "Besides," she muttered, "I spent a good deal of time correcting her ideas about wizards. I don't want her meeting you lot and getting the wrong impression all over again."

"You cut me to the bone, lady," Eli said, clutching his chest. "Are you implying that I blacken the reputation of wizardry?"

Miranda cocked an eyebrow at his theatrics. "The Rector Spiritualis wouldn't have sent me out here if you were doing it a benefit, Mr. Monpress."

"Ah yes, the great Etmon Banage." Eli smiled. "How nice of him to draw the line between good wizard and bad wizard so clearly. Truly a civic-minded man."

"Master Banage is twice the wizard you are, thief," Miranda hissed, leaping to her feet. "How dare you even mention—"

A black blur shot in front of her face, and Miranda flinched as the long, pitted blade of Josef's sword came into focus an inch from her nose. The swordsman was lounging against the hut with his arm extended, holding the enormous blade between Miranda and Eli with one hand.

"Children," he said, "not now."

Miranda blinked nervously. The sword hung in the air in front of her. This close, she could see the deep gouges from a lifetime of battles that ran like canyons along the blade, though the sword's surface was like no metal she had ever seen. It was blacker than pot iron, and dull as stone. Its cutting edge was uneven, splashed here and there by a redder darkness, like old blood that could never be scoured off. The blade looked impossibly heavy, but Josef's arm was firm as an iron beam, and the sword did not once waver in his grip.

His point made, Josef plunged his blade back into the moss

beside him and calmly resumed cleaning his knives as though nothing had happened.

Miranda turned to Gin as much to get away from Eli's triumphant grin as to fix the small bag containing her rings to the rope around his neck.

"I could eat him for you," Gin growled in her ear, his eyes on the swordsman. "It wouldn't be any trouble."

"No," Miranda said, adjusting the small bag, her fingers lingering over the familiar shapes outlined through the soft doeskin. "Without you around, we'll need someone who can look threatening. Besides, he'd probably give you indigestion."

"Without me?" Gin snorted. "I'm going with you."

"No, you're not. We've been over this." Miranda pulled his head down, bringing his orange eyes level with her own. "If there's one thing we do know about Eli, it's that he's a master thief. If he says he can get us in, then I believe him, but even Eli can't work miracles, and that's what it would take to sneak your fluffy face past the walls. No, your job is to stay and guard the king. The Powers know he can't guard himself."

Gin glanced over at the king, who was prodding the passed-out guard with his finger, and gave a mighty sigh. "All right," the dog growled and shuffled over to sit next to Henrith, who looked none too pleased by this turn of events, "but I'll be listening."

"I'll call if I need you," she said.

Gin snorted, but left it at that.

"All right," Eli said. "If the girl and her puppy are finished saying their good-byes, let's get a move on."

Josef nodded and stood up, his ill-fitting armor clanking loudly. Since his outfit didn't have room for his usual arsenal, he had been forced to make do with a knife in each boot, one behind his neck, and one at his waist. Still, he could almost pass for a normal soldier.

Almost, that is, until he ruined the whole look by fastening his black sword across his back with a leather strap.

"You can't wear that," Miranda said, pointing at the blade. "What's the point of wearing disguises if you're just going to give it away by carrying that monstrosity around? I mean, if I left my rings, surely you can go an hour without your sword?"

Josef looked her straight in the eye and pulled the strap tighter. "If the Heart stays, I stay."

"I hate to admit it, but she does have a point," Eli said, frowning. He went into the cabin and came out a few moments later, carrying a few sticks and a leather sack. "Just a second," he muttered, laying his materials carefully on the dirt. He kneeled beside them and began to talk in a low, soft voice. Miranda tried to listen, but it was impossible to get close enough to hear what he was saying without making it obvious that that was what she was trying to do. At last, he scooped up the shortest stick and, with a few more words, bent the wood into a circle as easily as one would coil a length of rope.

Miranda watched in amazement as Eli laid the loop of wood and the two remaining straight sticks on top of the leather bag.

"When you're ready," he said.

No sooner did the words leave his mouth than the bag sat up. With a lively wiggle, the leather sack undid its seam and began wrapping itself around the wood, forming a tube around the two longer sticks. When the leather had wrapped itself as far as it could go, it pulled itself tight, and the thread from the seam stitched itself lengthwise up the edge of the long, leather tube. When it was finished, Eli held up a long, but otherwise perfectly normal-looking, spear quiver, the exact size and shape to hide the Heart of War.

Eli thanked the quiver several times before handing it to Josef, who slid his sword into the leather with his own nod of thanks.

"How did you..." Miranda pointed a limp finger at the quiver that had been three sticks and a bag less than a minute ago.

"Easy enough," Eli said. "I've had the bag for a while. He always had higher ambitions than luggage, so he was happy to help. The sticks were greenwood, and they love any chance to move around a bit before they dry brittle." He walked over to Josef and examined his handiwork. "It's too bad we don't have any spears to really complete the effect."

He kept talking, but Miranda's mind was too dumbfounded to make sense of it. She was still processing the enormous list of impossible things she'd just watched him do like it was nothing, like he did this every day. Talking to trees was one thing, but to make something new, just by talking, it was unbelievable. Not even the great shaper wizards could craft spirits without opening their own souls at least a little. This was like the wood and leather had decided to do him a favor, just because he asked. If she'd tried to do something like that without getting one of her servants to act as a middleman, the wood would have ignored her completely. Yet it did what Eli asked joyfully, as if he were the one who needed impressing, and not the other way around. She watched Eli as he talked, his long hands moving in elegant circles, and, not for the first time, Miranda caught herself wondering just what he really was.

"Are you feeling all right?"

Miranda jumped. Eli was looking at her quizzically. "You were staring and not listening."

"It's nothing," Miranda muttered, fighting down her blush at being caught. "Let's just get going."

Eli shrugged and turned to follow Josef as he led the way toward the castle. Nico joined them at the edge of the clearing, fading out of the woods like a ghost. Miranda jumped when she saw the girl, half because of her sudden appearance, and half because she hadn't noticed Nico was missing in the first place. Then she realized that Nico didn't have a disguise.

"Wait, doesn't she need—"

"No," Nico said, without stopping or looking back.

Gin padded back over to her, his eyes on the girl. "Watch yourself," he growled, "and don't forget what she is. Demons can't be trusted."

"Duly noted," Miranda said, and she gave his fur a final ruffle before jogging into the forest after Eli and the others.

Though they were only half a mile from the city, it took over an hour to reach the wall. This was mostly because Josef led them in a crazy zigzag through the brush. They crossed back over their path more than once, and he insisted on keeping to the tall undergrowth and away from the game trails, so that with every other step Miranda had to beat back a branch or untangle her skirt from a nettle bush. To make things worse, Eli stopped every five minutes or so to murmur quietly to this tree or that rock. She made it a point to listen covertly, but so far as she could tell, his little talks were of the most mundane kind, an exchange of pleasantries, maybe a comment about the weather, like a country wife chatting with her neighbors. As he talked, he would do them little favors, flicking an ant away or scraping some moss off the peak of a rock so it could feel the sunlight. That was strange enough, but the truly amazing thing was the way the sleepy spirits perked up as soon as he spoke to them. Miranda could almost feel them leaning forward, eager to tell him anything he wanted to know. Whatever brightness Gin had been talking about, it seemed to have a universal effect.

Miranda expected Josef to complain about the seemingly meaningless stops, but he accepted Eli's little chats with bored inertness, as if he had long since argued every point of the process five times over and couldn't be bothered to care anymore.

At last, they had reached the edge of the forest, where the king's deer park met the city's northern border. The trees ended a good twenty feet from the wall, leaving a broad swath of open ground carpeted with overgrown grass and saplings. Josef made them crouch in the scrubby bushes at the edge of the clearing as he scouted ahead. While they were waiting for the swordsman to come back, Miranda took the opportunity to satisfy her curiosity and she crept over to where Eli was crouched in the grass.

"Okay," she whispered, "I give up. Is the weather talk some kind of code?"

"What?" Eli's eyebrows shot up. "No, no, I'm just building good will."

Miranda gave him a confused look. "Good will?"

"It's a harsh world," Eli said. "You never know when you'll need a little good will from the local countryside."

Miranda was skeptical. A mossy rock didn't seem like much of an ally. "So you weren't doing reconnaissance or anything?"

"Sorry, no," Eli said, shaking his head.

Miranda frowned. "But—"

"Quiet."

Miranda and Eli both jumped at the sudden command. Josef was kneeling in the tall grass not a foot away from them, glaring icily. Miranda hadn't even heard his approach.

"We move now," he said.

"Wha—" Before Miranda could even form her question, Josef took off for the city wall at a dead run, Nico and Eli right on his heels. Miranda took a deep breath and charged after them, covering the space of open ground between the trees and the city wall faster than she had ever moved in her life. She slammed into the wall and dropped to a crouch just in time. No sooner had she reached the stones than a small troop of guards appeared out of the woods only a few feet from where they'd been hiding just moments before.

Miranda clapped her hands over her mouth as the soldiers fanned out. They patrolled the edge of the forest in a wide sweep, poking their short spears into the underbrush. Finding nothing, the leader waved his hand, and the unit faded back into the woods. Only when the sound of their boots had died to a whisper did Miranda release the breath she'd been holding.

"That was lucky," she said.

"Luck's got nothing to do with it," Josef said in a low voice, peering at her through the grass. "Those patrols have been sweeping the area all day. If it wasn't for the fact that the forest doesn't want them to find us, all the luck in the world wouldn't have gotten us this far."

Miranda started, and Eli winked at her from his hiding place farther down the wall.

Josef gave Miranda a look of grudging approval. "Nice sprint, by the way."

"Thanks," she muttered. "What now?"

"Now we have to find that panel," Josef said, turning to the wall. "It should be close."

"It's here." Nico's quiet voice made Miranda jump. Nico was crouched on Josef's right, one small white finger sticking out of her voluminous sleeve to point at the iron square, barely larger than a laundry chute, set into the wall beside her.

"What is it?" Miranda asked, leaning in for a better look.

"A bolt hole," Eli said, crawling over to crouch beside Nico, "in case the royalty need to make a fast exit. Very common in cities like this." He gave the iron door an experimental push, but it didn't so much as rattle. He tried again, harder this time, but he might as well have been pushing the wall itself. "Hmm." He frowned. "This one seems to be locked."

Miranda gave him a puzzled look. "Isn't this how you got in last time?"

"Of course not," Eli said, looking insulted. "First rule of thievery, never use the same entrance twice."

Miranda rolled her eyes. "How many 'first rules' of thievery do you have?"

"When one mistake can mean your head on a pike, every rule's a first rule," Eli said cheerfully.

The thief ran his long fingers along the door's edge, which was set flush against the stone. Miranda watched with growing uncertainty. There wasn't even a keyhole, so far as she could see. When he had tapped every inch of the metal, Eli leaned back, brow knit in thought.

"Can't you just talk it open?" Miranda asked, moving a little closer. "Like you did with the prison door?"

"I could," Eli said, "but—" He reached into his coat pocket and drew out a small leather case, monogrammed in gold with an ornate capital *M*—"sometimes a simpler solution suffices."

He flipped the case open, revealing a startling selection of lock picks. Carefully selecting the longest and thinnest, he leaned down until his nose brushed the door. He held out his hand, and, without further prompting, Josef handed him a knife. Eli expertly wedged the slender blade into the hair-thin crack between the iron and the stone. Then, using the blade as a lever, he carefully lifted the door out of its niche. It opened just a fraction before sticking again with a soft clang.

"Lever and padlock," Eli muttered, switching out the thin lock pick for a slightly longer one with a crooked head. "Josef, if you would."

Josef took the knife from him and held it where Eli pointed, putting just enough pressure on the lever to keep the opening as large as possible without snapping the blade. Eli took a pair of delicate, extremely-long-nosed pliers out of his case and, using both hands, neatly slipped the pliers and the lock pick through the knife-thin crack.

He gripped with the pliers and began to deftly maneuver the lock pick, wiggling it right, then left, then right again, like he was trying to hook something. At last there was a loud click. Eli released the pliers and a muted crash came through the iron as the padlock hit the ground on the other side. He tucked his tools back into their leather case and opened the door with a flourish. The whole operation had taken less than a minute.

When he caught Miranda gawking, Eli's grin became unbearably smug.

"What were you expecting?" he said, still grinning. "I'm the greatest thief in the—*ow*!" He yelped as Josef punched him in the arm.

"Enough bragging," the swordsman grunted. "Inside, quick. The patrols move in a circle, you know."

Still rubbing his injured arm, Eli slid feet first into the dark bolt hole. Nico went next, casually wedging herself, bulky coat and all, through the narrow opening.

"You next," Josef said, looking at Miranda.

She swallowed. Suddenly, the bolt hole looked impossibly narrow and abysmally deep. However, she had an image to maintain as a Spiritualist, and that image did not include being afraid of holes, no matter how narrow or deep they might be. She sat down stiffly and began easing herself in, feet first. Just when she'd managed to convince herself it wasn't going to be that bad, she heard the crunch of men moving through the forest. She looked frantically over her shoulder in time to see the first patrolman reach the edge of the forest. She was about to whisper a warning when Josef shoved her, hard. Miranda yelped and lost her balance, sliding the rest of the way down the bolt hole. She landed in a pile on a cold, hard-packed dirt floor. A second later, Josef landed on top of her. The iron door clanged shut above them, and the room plunged into darkness.

CHAPTER 18

The next few seconds were a confused, painful scramble as Miranda did her best to get out from under Josef. The man was amazingly heavy and, she grunted as she cracked her ribs against his elbow, full of sharp edges. It didn't help that the ground was horribly uneven. Just when she'd finally managed to untangle herself from the swordsman, a soft, yellow glow winked to life. Miranda's relief was almost physically painful as the darkness resolved itself into familiar shapes. They were in a root cellar. Other than the four of them being in it, it was a very normal root cellar, with potatoes, apples, and turnips rolling across the floor where Miranda and Josef's landing had knocked them loose from their bins.

Eli held up a tiny blackout lamp, one shutter cracked just a fraction, the source of the unsteady light. "Nice landing," he said with a grin.

"I would have been fine if someone hadn't pushed me," Miranda hissed, hurling a potato at Josef.

"If I hadn't pushed you, we would have been spotted," Josef said, catching the potato in midair, "and that would have been that."

"Well, now that we're all here and uncaught," Eli said, swinging his lamp toward the squat wooden door half hidden behind a large bin of potatoes, "let's get on with it."

Miranda stood up, slipping a little on the rolling tubers. "Where are we?"

"Under the city, inside the walls," Eli said, popping the crude lock on the wooden door with a wiggle of his lock pick. "I told you, we're in the bolt hole. Most castles would have their own tunnel to safety in case of invasion, but Allaze is so close to the river, a deep tunnel would flood, so it looks like they had to make do with linking a bunch of cellars together."

"Lucky thing for us, in any case," Josef said, walking through the door Eli held open and into the next cellar.

Nico followed close behind him, stepping between the rolling potatoes as if she had no problem seeing in the dark. Miranda tried to mimic her path, but ended up slipping on her second step. She fell with a stifled yipe, catching the demonseed's shoulder at the last minute. The strange, thick material of the girl's coat shifted like a living thing under her fingers, and Miranda jerked her hand away. Despite the Spiritualist's full weight landing on Nico's shoulder, the smaller girl had not so much as stumbled. She turned to meet Miranda's horrified look.

"Go ahead, Spiritualist," she said, her pale face impassive. "The lamp's more for you than for us."

Had that sentence come from Eli, Miranda would have brushed it off as bluster, but the strange glitter in Nico's eyes left no doubt in her mind that the girl spoke the truth. With a muttered thanks, Miranda slipped by, pressing herself against the grimy wall to make sure she didn't brush the strange, moving coat again, and hurried into the adjacent cellar where Eli was already popping the next door.

After that, Miranda kept as close to Eli as her pride could bear, desperate to stay in the tiny circle of light. The next door led to another cellar, which led to another. Sometimes they would walk through a short tunnel, crossing under a road, Miranda guessed, and then it was on to another door and another person's hoard of vegetables. Mostly, the cellars were pitch black, but a few times they would open a door to see light streaming through the floorboards above their heads. When this happened, Eli would close the shutter on his lamp and they would scurry to the next cellar like mice in a larder.

One room, however, was nearly disastrous. After a long series of dusty, empty cellars, Eli had picked up the pace. Then, after finding a door that wasn't locked at all, he opened one right next to Cook picking out vegetables for supper. They all froze in the doorway, and Miranda was sure their game was up. However, nothing happened. Minutes passed, and the cook just kept sorting through vegetables, singing in an off-key, nasal voice, not a foot away from them. Finally, she finished picking her potatoes and, still singing, tromped up the ladder, her swollen ankles wobbling unsteadily as she swung her armful of tubers in time to her song, and Miranda realized the cook was sodden drunk.

"Thank the Powers for cooking wine," Eli said when the cook closed the door behind her. "Let's go."

After almost half an hour of navigating the endless maze of doors, the cellars took a noticeable turn for the affluent. The floors shifted from hard-packed dirt to laid stone, and there were wine casks and brandy stores as well as the standard potatoes and beets.

"Getting close now," Eli whispered, lowering the shutter on his small lamp until it gave off only a splinter of light.

As they passed from cellar to cellar, Miranda began to wonder how they would know the castle door when they saw it. Every cellar they entered now seemed to have two or more locked doors leading off it. It wouldn't surprise her if the nobles had their own network of secret tunnels down here, running from house to house to facilitate liaisons and any other secret activities the rich indulged in. As each cellar led to another just like it, she began to get the panicky feeling that they were lost in the underground maze of passages, going around and around in circles forever. Then, Eli opened a triple-locked door, and Miranda realized she needn't have worried.

At the end of the next cellar was a heavy iron door. It was the same size as the other cellar doors, but the stone wall it was set in looked both older and sturdier than the walls around it. At the door's center, set so deep Miranda could have stuck her finger up to the first knuckle into the grooves, was the seal of House Allaze.

Josef snorted. "I thought this was supposed to be a secret entrance."

"Secret from outsiders, yes," Eli said. "But you don't want some maid or delivery boy coming down here and opening it by mistake."

"No chance of that." Miranda shook her head. "How do we get it open?"

"Leave that to me," Eli announced. He reached into the small leather bag he wore under his valet coat and pulled out two small glass bottles filled with clear liquid. "Two weak acids," he said, holding the bottles up, "used in metal working to etch patterns. Normally, it would take either of these a month to go through that much metal. However, these particular bottles of acid happen to hate each other."

"Hate each other?" Miranda frowned. "How did that happen?"

Eli swirled the bottles innocently. "I might have played the gossipmonger a bit too well. You see, acid spirits, though volatile and dangerous, aren't very bright. They are, however, very quick-tempered." As he spoke, the liquid began to slosh. Just a little at first, so that Miranda thought it was because of Eli's swirling, but by the time he finished speaking, the acids were practically boiling in their bottles.

"Now," Eli said, shaking the bottles violently, "we just have to get them good and mad, and—" He hurled both bottles at the door, landing them smack on top of each other. The glass shattered, and the acids fell on each other with a roar, sinking through the iron door like boiling water through fresh snow.

"A good fight does wonders for them!" Eli shouted over the din of the spirits' war.

"That's horrible!" Miranda shouted back. "Using a spirit's feelings like that, it's abusive!"

"Not at all." Eli looked hurt. "I'm treating them like living things, which is a lot more than I can say for the blacksmith I bought them from. Look, it's even waking up the door."

The acids' fight was indeed getting the door's attention. It squealed and ground on its hinges, trying to get away from the brawl that was eating through its core. The din was deafening, and Miranda clapped her hands over her ears. Eli cringed at the worst of it, but otherwise seemed content to watch the show. Josef just stood there, watching the door with bored interest. Nico crouched closer to the hissing metal than Miranda would have dared, staring in fascination as the hole in the door grew wider.

Finally, the acids fought themselves out, leaving a warped, melted hole in the iron just large enough to fit a small fist through. The door whimpered, and Eli rubbed it gently, whispering apologies and promising to have it recast as soon as possible. Whether he meant it or not, the words seemed to put the door at ease, and as it drifted back to sleep, Eli reached his hand through the melted hole and popped the lock on the other side.

"Swordsmen first," Eli said, swinging the door open.

Josef put his hand on his sword hilt and eased his way into the black tunnel.

"All clear," he whispered, and the rest of them hurried through the doorway, mindful of the spots where the last remnants of the acids were still steaming.

The hall on the other side was smaller than the cellar it joined.

In fact, it was barely larger than the door itself. They walked single file, with Josef leading the way, absently twirling two knives in his hands. Miranda went next, followed by Eli, with Nico trailing behind as usual. For her part, the Spiritualist kept to the absolute center of the hall, as far as she could get from the cobwebby walls. Here and there, small roots had pushed through the ceiling, and she realized they must be under the palace grounds. Unseen things scuttled in the dark behind them, making Miranda's skin crawl. Apparently, Josef didn't like the scuttles either because he stopped suddenly, causing Miranda to nearly run into him.

"What now?" she whispered, regaining her balance.

Josef threw up his hand to silence her. She glowered at the command, but said nothing. Behind them, something skittered again, and Josef turned on his heel. Miranda didn't see the knife leave his hand, but she heard it hit. A squeal erupted behind them, and the skittering stopped. Eli whirled around, holding his lamp high. The light fell across their dusty footprints and, right at the edge of the glow, was a squirming, dying rat with Josef's knife sticking out of its side.

"Getting paranoid?" Eli muttered, lowering the lamp. "It's not like you to kill the wildlife."

"It's not paranoia." Josef walked over to reclaim his knife. "Have you ever seen a rat act like that?"

"What are you talking about?" Miranda said.

"Rats are scavengers and foragers," Josef said. "This one's been following us since the first cellar. What kind of rat leaves a cellar full of food to follow people into an empty hallway?"

Miranda hurried over to the dying animal and hovered her hand over its head. Sure enough, she could feel the faint echo of Renaud's spirit slipping away as the rat's movement stilled. She snatched her hand back.

"Josef's right," she said.

"If he has control of the rats, that could be a major problem," Josef said, looking at Eli. "Even you can't sneak past rats."

"He can't control all of them," Miranda said, rubbing her hand on her skirt. "Controlling lots of small spirits is harder than controlling one large one."

"He wouldn't need to control all of them," Eli said thoughtfully. "Rats talk among themselves, and two wizards aren't exactly inconspicuous. Two or three informants would be enough."

Josef pushed past them and began walking in quick, impatient strides down the dark hall toward the castle. "We'll just have to assume Renaud knows we're down here," he said. "And that means we need to be somewhere else."

Miranda hurried after him. The dark, dirty tunnel was the last place she wanted to face another of Renaud's mad spirits. The swordsman set a grueling pace, not running but walking so fast they might as well have been. The tunnel around them was growing lighter or rather, less dark. She still couldn't see anything beyond the lamplight, but the tone of the darkness was shifting to something friendlier, more human. Even so, the tunnel seemed to go on forever, and Miranda's legs were beginning to ache. The gardens hadn't seemed this long when she was aboveground. As the tunnel went on and on, she started to wonder if this wasn't some new trap they had stumbled into.

At last, she saw real light up ahead. Josef slowed his pace a fraction and then came to a complete stop. Eli held up the lamp, revealing a wrought-iron gate kept closed with a simple chain and padlock. The chain had rusted long ago, and Josef was able to reach through the iron bars and yank it off without difficulty. The gate swung open with a creak, and they piled into the final room of their journey.

"Great," Miranda said, "more potatoes."

"Ah," Eli countered, "but these are royal potatoes! We're here."

Miranda looked around skeptically. The stone cellar, with its bins of root vegetables and its cold, earthy smell, was uncomfortably like every other wealthy cellar they'd tromped through. On the opposite wall, dim light shone through the cracks of a squat wooden door. Eli blew out his lamp and set it on the lip of the potato bin. He put his finger to his lips and then, slowly and silently, opened the door.

The hallway beyond was lit with indirect firelight from the room at its end. Distorted voices echoed up and down its length, and Miranda could make out the shadows of servants as they sat around the hearth. Eli craned his neck out as far as he could, then pulled back, grinning.

"All right," he said, brushing the last bits of cobweb off his valet's jacket, "time for phase two. Ready, Nico?"

The girl nodded and pulled her coat tighter.

"Wait," Miranda whispered. "What's phase two?"

Eli shook his head and put his finger to his lips before stepping out into the hall. Miranda made a rude gesture at his back and crept after him.

CHAPTER 19

Something's not right," Josef muttered.

"You've got a point," Eli said, thunking his slab of bread against his wooden plate. "This bread's two days old at least."

Miranda hunched over her stewed beef and said nothing. The three of them were crowded around a small table in the kitchen surrounded by a crowd of servants who were all eating their dinners with determined efficiency. So far, phase two had consisted of sneaking into the kitchens and blending in with the other servants for the dinner rush. No one had noticed them, but they weren't getting any closer to Renaud, and, even worse, Nico was nowhere to be seen.

"We're wasting our time," Miranda grumbled, shoving her plate away. "There was no need to get food as well."

"Nosunse," Eli said around his enormous mouthful of beef. He swallowed with gusto. "A servant who rejects food? Now *that* would stand out. Besides, why let it go to waste?" He took another bite.

"They have only two guards at the door," Josef went on, ignoring them both, "and no one checking the servants. The cooks didn't even look sideways at us."

"Maybe they don't know we're here," Eli said. "The spying rat we caught could have been the only one. Or maybe they know we're in the castle, but they weren't expecting us to come to the kitchens. Or maybe my plan is actually working. The whole point of breaking in at dinner was to catch the shift change so no one would notice three newcomers."

"Or maybe they're just incompetent," Miranda said, remembering how the castle had reacted when she'd arrived for the first time. "Renaud may be in charge, but Mellinor is still Mellinor. Common sense seems to be as forbidden as wizardry in this country."

"You have a point," Josef said, leaning back in his chair and pretending to drink while he scanned the room. "But this was too easy even for incompetence. Mellinor may be slack, and I don't know about Renaud, but Coriano isn't someone who would leave an opening like this, not unless he was planning something."

"Coriano?" Eli wiped his mouth with a greasy napkin. "Didn't he run off?"

"He's a swordsman; he only retreated. Besides"—Josef dropped his hand to where the carefully wrapped Heart of War was leaned against his leg—"the Heart can feel his sword. They're calling to each other."

"Josef," Eli said patiently, "for the last time, you're not a wizard. You can't hear a damn thing that sword is saying."

"I don't have to hear him to know what he wants," Josef growled. "You're just mad you can't talk to him." Josef flashed Miranda a conspiratorial grin. "It's the only spirit we've found that won't talk to Eli."

"Who'd want to talk to a spirit that chose you, anyway," Eli muttered, reaching for his spoon to finish the last of his impromptu dinner. "He must have horrid taste."

"Enough," Miranda said, shoving Eli's bowl out of reach before he could take another mouthful. "We're wasting our time. What are we waiting for, anyway?"

A chorus of screams erupted from the kitchen, and Eli's face broke into an enormous grin. "That."

A crowd of cooks poured screaming out of the kitchen, followed by a thick plume of white smoke. The servants at the front tables started to panic, screaming "fire." The soldiers ran forward, shouting for order as the servants rushed the doors to the kitchen gardens. While the overwhelmed guards yelled and tried to keep people from trampling each other, Eli and Josef calmly got up and jogged toward the now unguarded door to the upper castle. Miranda watched the panic in shock for a moment and then stood up and stomped after the thief.

The main hall of the servant level was even more crowded than the dining room. Alarm bells were ringing up and down its length, and the smell of wood smoke and burning tar hung heavy in the hazy air. Servants seethed from the dozens of interconnecting hallways like ants out of an overturned hill, shouting and shoving as they rushed the exits. Eli let them surge past him, nimbly working his way upstream along the wall. Only when a platoon of guards carrying buckets appeared at the far end of the hall did he change course and duck down one of the small connecting corridors.

"I can't believe it!" Miranda whispered fiercely as they half walked, half ran down the narrow hall. "You started a fire just so you could get past some guards? Do you *ever* consider the consequences of your actions!?"

"We didn't start a fire," Nico's voice said calmly.

Miranda jumped and whirled around. At first, she saw nothing but the empty hallway filled with hazy smoke, dark except for the sputtering wall sconces set at wide intervals. Then, Nico appeared from the shadows a foot behind them, as if she had emerged from the wall itself, looking very pleased with herself.

Miranda refused to be intimidated. "What did you do?"

"Nothing bad," Nico said. "I just let the furnace know what I was, and now it's trying to burn down the castle."

"You deliberately terrified a fire spirit?" Miranda gasped. "That's horrible!"

Nico crossed her arms over her chest, her brown eyes perfectly calm. "I didn't terrify it. I introduced myself. It was the furnace's decision to try and kill me by burning everything. Don't worry, though; it's a slow, fat spirit. The servants will have no trouble holding it back, if they can get over their own panic."

"Don't you dare blame the furnace," Miranda said. "Spirits are panicky by nature, fire spirits especially. It's our job to protect them from things like this, not scare them witless."

"*Your* job, you mean." Nico turned away. "Don't assume that everyone thinks like you."

Miranda's face reddened, but before she could retort, Nico vanished into the shadows as suddenly as she had appeared.

"How does she do that?" Miranda said, crossing her arms over her chest.

"She's always been like that," Eli said, giving the Spiritualist a little push down the hall. "Didn't I tell you she didn't need a costume?"

Miranda shook her head and let him jostle her down the corridor. They had gone only a few steps when Nico popped back into view, making Miranda jump again.

"I forgot to tell you," she said to Eli. "Renaud is in the treasury. I overheard the valets complaining about it when I was getting in position. He's been in there since last night, apparently."

Miranda's eyes went wide. "The treasury? You're sure?"

Nico shrugged. "That's what I heard. Apparently, he's been spending all his time staring at a support pillar."

"Well, there's no accounting for taste," Eli said. "Maybe he's never seen one before. I don't think he got out much."

"You're sure it's a pillar?" Miranda's voice was pleading. "Are you sure you didn't mishear?"

"I don't mishear," Nico said flatly.

Miranda clenched her hands together. "Oh, dear."

Josef, who had been quiet all this time, stepped forward to block her way. He planted himself in front of the Spiritualist, looking down at her with a stony expression. "Why is a pillar bad?"

"I'll have to explain later," Miranda said, pushing past him. "We need to get to the—"

"No," Josef said, grabbing her arm. "You'll explain now."

He looked up and down the corridor. Behind them, in the main hall, servants were still running madly for the exits. Josef shook his head at the panic and marched Miranda in the other direction. He tried the first of several small, inconspicuous doors. When it opened, he shoved Miranda inside. Nico and Eli followed suit, cramming themselves into the small closet.

"What are you doing?" Miranda hissed, fighting Josef's hold.

"You haven't been open with us," Josef said, tightening his grip. "You were the one who asked for our help, Spiritualist. You don't get to string us along, telling us whatever you think we need to know. I'm not going a step farther until you tell us why Renaud being in the treasury is enough to make you go white."

Miranda briefly considered lying, but Josef's face was murderous in the dim light filtering through the warped cracks in the closet door. She swallowed against her dry throat and decided it was time to come clean.

"It's not like I was hiding it," she said, slumping against the back wall. "I just didn't think it would be an issue."

"Obviously it is," Josef said, releasing his grip. "Talk."

"Fine," Miranda said. "I wasn't just wandering through Mellinor when I found out you three had stolen the king. I was sent here by the Rector Spiritualis."

"Figures," Eli said. "That old windbag probably couldn't stand having a country in the Council that didn't buy into his Spiritualist mumbo jumbo."

"Ignore him," Josef said, cutting off Miranda's retort before she could open her mouth. "Why did the Rector send you?"

Miranda shot Eli an icy glare. "We received a tip from Coriano that Eli was in this kingdom."

Josef arched an eyebrow. "Coriano works for you?"

"Worked," Miranda corrected him. "We couldn't let *someone*"—she glared at Eli—"continue to ruin our good reputation, so the Spirit Court paid Coriano to tip us off since he was following your trail anyway. Everything was fine until I got here. Then Renaud bought Coriano out from under us."

"That's the problem with mercenaries," Eli said. "They always live up to their name."

"Stop interrupting," Josef said flatly. "What about the pillar?"

Miranda shook her head. "When Master Banage sent me here, we didn't know the king was the target. He thought Eli was after an obscure wizard artifact that has been in Mellinor's possession since its founding, Gregorn's Pillar."

"Obscure?" Eli looked insulted. "Why would I want to steal something no one's heard of?"

"Gregorn," Josef said and frowned. "I've heard that name before."

"I'm not surprised," Miranda said. "Gregorn was Mellinor's founder, and, despite their current rhetoric, he was actually quite a famous, and quite a nasty, enslaver."

"What does Banage care about the pillar then?" Josef asked. "He's not an enslaver. Why would he want something that belonged to one?"

"To keep it away from other wizards who want to follow Gregorn's path," Miranda said.

"What's it do, then?" Josef asked. "Does it amplify powers somehow, or call spirits to you?"

Miranda began to fidget.

"I'm not actually sure," she admitted at last. "Master Banage never told me exactly. All I know is that it's bad news for everyone if a wizard gets his hands on it." Master Banage's exact words had been 'soul-imperiling danger for both the human and spirit worlds,' but after Eli's earlier comments, she didn't think they would appreciate the gravity of that statement.

Eli scowled at her. "I thought the Spirit Court was around to keep stuff like that under control."

"We do," Miranda snapped. "Why else do you think Master Banage sent me to keep the pillar from being stolen? I'm a fully initiated Spiritualist! I'm not exactly an errand girl."

"So why let it sit in Mellinor all this time if it's so dangerous?" Josef scratched his chin. "Seems awfully irresponsible."

"We're a neutral power!" Miranda threw up her hands. "We can't just waltz in and demand a country's national treasure! Besides, in case you forgot, Mellinor hates wizards. Gregorn's Pillar is perfectly harmless to normal people; so leaving it in a country where wizards are deported on sight seemed like an acceptable risk."

"Let me get this right"—Josef bent down to look her straight in the eye—"you think that Renaud, an enslaver, is trying to get this pillar, which is named after another enslaver, and is, in your words, 'bad news' if a wizard gets his hands on it." He arched an eyebrow at Miranda. "Don't you think you should have told us about this earlier?"

"I'm sorry!" Miranda sputtered. "I really didn't think it was going to be an issue! Renaud grew up right above it, so I figured if he knew about the pillar at all, he would have gotten it years ago, before he was banished."

"He wouldn't have had access to it when he was a prince," Eli said. "The treasury vault can be opened only by the king's direct order."

Everyone turned and looked at him, and Eli took a step back.

"What? I did do *some* research on Mellinor. That was my first plan, actually—get Henrith to open the vault for me—but then I figured kidnapping would be much more high profile."

Miranda slapped her hand against her forehead. "Well," she said, "that clears things up nicely."

"Does it really matter?" Eli said. "I mean, our objectives haven't changed. Get Renaud, get the money, get away. The plan is still rolling smoothly. We'll just have to be more careful. Besides"—he rubbed his hands together—"sneaking into a treasury sounds much more profitable than sneaking into a throne room."

Miranda grunted, but she could think of nothing sufficient to counter all that was wrong with that sentence. Eli grinned and opened the closet door, spilling them out into the dark hazy hall.

"Look," Miranda said, balancing herself against the sooty wall, "even if you're right, and the plan is still valid, we don't know where the treasury is. Since we made it this far with only a spying rat for trouble, it's a safe bet Renaud doesn't have the Pillar yet, but if anyone recognizes us, we'll be up to our neck in guards and, shortly after that, enslaved spirits. We don't have time to wander around lost."

"So we'll ask someone." Eli smirked and pointed over her shoulder. "In fact, I think I've spotted someone who can help us."

Miranda whirled around, and her eyes widened in shock. Standing at the junction where their small corridor met the madness of the main hall, still as a statue with her hands pressed against her mouth despite the other servants pushing past her, was Marion. As soon as Miranda made eye contact, the girl rushed forward, and the Spiritualist barely had time to catch her breath before the librarian's hug crushed it out of her.

"Oh, Lady Miranda," she gasped. "I knew you'd be back! I knew it! The king's not really dead, is he?"

Miranda clutched the girl's shoulders awkwardly. "No, Henrith's alive. He's with Gin, and safe."

Marion looked up at her, eyes glowing with delight. "Really? Oh, thank goodness." She looked around at Eli and Josef. "Who are these? Reinforcements from the Spirit Court?"

"More or less." Miranda grinned, and Eli rolled his eyes. "Listen"—she pushed Marion back so she could look the girl in the eyes—"Marion, this is serious. We need to get to the treasury."

Marion nodded vigorously and grabbed Miranda's hand, pulling her to the end of the corridor. "This way," she said, turning down a tiny hallway Miranda hadn't noticed before. "With the main halls like that, it's faster to take the servants' passages."

Miranda nodded and resigned herself to being dragged. Eli took up position right behind her, with Josef bringing up the rear. As usual, Nico was nowhere to be seen. Marion led them through a maze of narrow halls and then down a flight of stairs. This led to more hallways and then more stairs, until Miranda could hardly believe all of this labyrinthine tunneling fit inside the same castle she'd bullied her way into only days before.

As they followed the twisting hall down yet another stair, something occurred to her, and Miranda looked over her shoulder at Eli. "How did you know it was Marion?" she whispered. "I never told you what she looked like."

"Simple," Eli whispered back. "Who else in this place would possibly be happy to see you?"

Miranda couldn't help but chuckle at the truth of that, and she turned her attention back to the stone hall as Marion led them past the turn-off for the prisons and down yet another narrow stair, heading deeper and deeper into the castle's foundations.

CHAPTER 20

Marion led them deeper than Miranda had imagined the castle could reach, down below the prison, below the foundations, and into the very heart of the stone that lay far below the fertile soil of Mellinor. Though the city was low lying, there was no sign of water here, no seepage over the years as one would expect to find this deep below the surface. Only the ancient, wooden support beams and the occasional fluttering light of the lamps broke the monotony of the smooth, dry stone as the narrow hallways and connecting stairs descended deeper and deeper into the earth.

Finally, at the base of the longest stairway yet, they reached a small wooden door.

"This is as far as I can take you," Marion said, turning to face them. "The treasury hall is just beyond here, but I've never been inside myself. Actually," she said and blushed sheepishly, "servants aren't even allowed past the prison, but I spent a lot of time memorizing drawings of the castle back when I was the Master Architect's assistant, before I got promoted to librarian."

"Well, thank the Powers for that," Eli said, smiling charmingly. "You've been a most effective guide, Lady Marion."

Marion's blush spread as Eli took her hand and guided her back toward the stairs. "I must insist that you return now. You've risked far too much helping us."

"It was the least I could do," Marion mumbled. She looked shyly at Miranda and dropped into a sudden, haphazard curtsy. "Thank you, lady. Good luck!"

She whirled around and scrambled back up the stairs as fast as she could go. Miranda watched her with a faint smile. Only when the girl's footsteps had safely faded away did she turn back to the grim task before them.

Josef had pressed himself against the wooden door and was peering through the gaps in the boards with one eye. Nico was crouched below him, peeking under the crack where the door met the floor, while Eli hovered impatiently behind them both. "How does it look?" he asked.

"Interesting," Josef said. He stepped aside so Miranda and Eli could have a look.

Miranda pressed her eye against the crack, and her breath

caught in her throat. On the other side of the door was the treasury hall Marion had mentioned. It was much larger than Miranda had expected, roughly a hundred feet from end to end and wide enough for ten men to stand shoulder to shoulder. She knew that last bit for certain, because that's how they were standing. The corridor was absolutely packed with soldiers. They were standing at attention in tight rows running from wall to wall down the entire length of the carved hall. Each soldier carried a tall, wooden shield in one hand and an iron-tipped spear in the other. Bright torches hung from every bracket on the blackened walls, filling the entire corridor with light. At the end of the hall, almost hidden by the bristling spears and peaked helmets, the top edge of the iron treasury door was visible, a black spot in the dancing light.

"That explains why there were no guards outside," Josef whispered. "They must have packed the entire army in there. Even if we were invisible, we couldn't sneak through without shoving half a platoon out of the way."

Miranda bit her lip. "Nico"—she looked down at the girl—"couldn't you just do your, um, disappearing thing to get past them?"

"It doesn't work like that," Nico said. "It's too far to go in one jump. I'd have to land in the middle of them. Anyway, what would I do when I got there? You all would still be here."

"Well," Josef said, "I guess there's nothing for it." He walked back up the stairs a little ways and took hold of one of the wooden support beams. Bracing his foot against the stone wall, he dug his fingers into the wood and began to pull. The wood squealed under his grip, and the old stone crumbled. Josef pulled harder and, with a cracking sound, yanked the beam free of its anchors. Miranda gaped like a landed fish as the swordsman swung the six-foot beam over his shoulder like it was made of straw. The noise had drawn some attention. Shouted orders and the sound of shields slamming down filtered through the thin door. Josef, however, walked calmly down the stairs past Eli and the gaping Miranda and paused just in front of the door, beside Nico.

"Ready, girl?" he said.

To Miranda's amazement, Nico's pale face lit up in an enormous smile. "Always, swordsman."

"Wait," Miranda whispered. "What are you—"

Josef lifted his foot and, in a motion too fast for Miranda's eyes to follow, kicked down the door. Time slowed to a crawl as all the soldiers turned toward the sound, and for one endless, silent moment, no one moved. Then, Josef's wooden beam caught the closest soldier square in the chest, and the hallway erupted.

The soldiers surged forward, shouting and brandishing their spears. The alarm horns rang out deafeningly close, and the stone floor trembled under the pounding boots as the wave of armed men crashed into the small doorway. Josef swung his beam in huge arcs, sweeping soldiers off their feet and slamming them by the half dozen into the mosaic walls. He waded into the thick of them, the Heart of War securely strapped across his back, its leather disguise falling off in ragged chunks as it deflected strokes that would otherwise have landed in the swordsman's spine.

Miranda tried to run forward, but Eli's hands wrapped around her shoulders and flung her with surprising strength against the doorframe.

"Let me go!" she shouted. "That idiot's going to get us all killed!"

"Too late for that!" Eli shouted back. "He's already going. If you interfere, he'll have to watch out for you, and then he really will die." He eased his grip a fraction. "Trust him," he said. "Josef's the best there is."

Miranda wanted desperately to believe the thief, but at that moment a resounding twang cut through the battle as the archers in the back released a flight of arrows into the fray. She watched in horror as the arrows sailed over the crowd, almost scraping the smoke-stained ceiling before arcing downward straight at Josef's unguarded head. Right before the barbed tips landed, they vanished. Suddenly, Nico was there, standing on his shoulders, her enormous coat swirling around her like water, the arrows clutched in her bony hand. She tossed them aside just in time to knock the next volley out of the air, effortlessly shifting her balance to match Josef's swings, for the swordsman kept going as if she wasn't there. Josef was laughing, moving in long, rolling arcs down the chaotic corridor, the beam flying in front of him and the Heart guarding his back. Whenever he left an opening, soldiers of all sizes and builds would lunge for it, only to be caught by a well-aimed kick and then swept into the wall with the others as the beam came down.

Miranda watched in amazement, not bothering to fight Eli's grip any longer. "He's a monster," she whispered.

"Yes," Eli whispered back. "That's why the Heart of War chose him."

When Josef's path of destruction had almost reached the treasury door, Nico launched herself off his shoulders and began laying waste to the last few lines of archers, most of whom had dropped their bows and were frantically fighting with short swords. Nico moved between them like a shadow, jabbing each man twice between the ribs before he fell to the ground clutching his stomach, unable to do more than gurgle in pain. By the time she reached the end of the archer line, the remaining soldiers were fleeing in panic, stumbling down the hall as fast as they could and paying no attention to Eli or Miranda as the two stepped out of the shelter of the small stair.

The hallway was a mess. Soldiers lay slumped in moaning piles against the cracked stone walls, their bloody splashes obscuring the rolling mosaics. Still, while badly battered, almost all were alive and groaning pathetically as Miranda and Eli hurried past them. Josef sighed loudly, leaning the battered, bloody, but still intact wooden beam against the wall beside the treasury door. He was sweaty, dirty, and breathing hard, but he could have been plowing a field or digging a ditch for all Miranda could tell. There wasn't a wound on him. Nico was the same way, leaning against the wall with a satisfied grin.

"That," Josef panted, "was the best five minutes of this whole"—pant—"awful"—pant—"job."

"Glad someone's having fun," Eli said, rolling one of the unconscious soldiers away from the door. "Now, let's see if the reward was worth the mess."

He took a step back and looked up at the enormous iron door with a low whistle. "Impressive." He grinned wide. "Now I see why Renaud didn't just enslave his way in as a boy. Sandstorms are chaotic and stupid, easy to control if your will is stronger. But metal, especially thick, old metal like this?" He rapped his knuckles on the door's surface, making a strange, metallic echo down the ruined hall that only made him grin wider. "You'd use up all your energy just waking it up, never mind controlling it."

Miranda stepped forward, running her fingers over the smooth, cold iron. "Can you open it?"

If possible, Eli's grin grew wider still. "Who do you think I am?" he said, putting both hands palm down above the door's handle. Miranda snorted, but said nothing, stepping back to watch him work. A moment after Eli's hands settled on the iron, his expression changed from cocky to quizzical. He gave the door a push with his palms, and it swung inward with a faint scrape.

Miranda blinked in amazement. "I guess you're not all talk."

"High praise indeed," Eli said, stepping back. "I wish I could claim it, but that wasn't me. The door's unlocked."

Josef walked over to him and stared hard at the metal door, which was slowly drifting open under its own weight. "You realize," he said quietly, "this is probably a trap."

"We've been walking into a trap since we got here, most likely." Eli looked sideways at Josef. "You said so yourself."

Josef shrugged and picked up his beam again. "Too late to worry about it now."

"Let's get this over with," Eli said, and shoved the door as hard as he could.

The metal slab swung open easily, and an old, cold wind ruffled their hair. The light from the hall torches extended only a foot from the threshold. Beyond that, the treasury stretched out into flat blackness, without depth or end. Miranda took a tentative step forward, reaching out, but she felt no spirits, mad or otherwise. The groans of the soldiers outside faded as soon as she crossed the threshold, and the scrape of her boot was frighteningly loud in the sudden stillness.

All at once, Josef shuddered as if he'd been thrown into an icy pond. He stepped forward, staring determinedly into the featureless dark. "I know you're there," he said. "Come out."

His voice echoed in the darkness, the words repeating over each other and then fading again. For a long moment, nothing changed. Then, a few yards in front of them, a match flared to life, illuminating a pair of eyes, one blue, one clouded silver.

"Hello, Josef," he said. "What took you?"

CHAPTER 21

Not whom you were expecting?" Coriano smiled and touched his match to the wick of a glass lamp that dangled from his hand. The light flared up, illuminating the empty walls that ran in a smooth arch until they disappeared into the darkness overhead, beyond the lamp's reach. Underfoot, the flame sent shadows scurrying across the stone floor decorated with the stained outlines of removed shelves and trunks. The makers of those stains were gone, however, leaving only dust, cobwebs, and occasional woodchips behind. By the time the lamp's flame steadied, it was painfully obvious that the heavily guarded treasury was completely empty.

Miranda stepped forward. "Where is Renaud?"

"Forget him," Eli said. "Where's the treasure?"

"Where is the treasure, indeed," Coriano said. "Did you know that, among bounty hunters, you're famous for your unpredictability, Eli? They never understand when I tell them how, in one aspect, you're steady as the sun. Miranda would know best." He flashed her a cold smile. "I gave her the same advice as I gave all the others: If you want to catch Eli Monpress, simply put yourself between him and what he wants. Because his only constant is that, once he decides something is his, he's never able to let it go, not even to save his own skin."

"Then," Miranda said, "all those soldiers outside?"

"A necessary deception." Coriano tilted his head. "Anything less than a full guard and you might have guessed something was wrong. I even let that librarian wander around in the hope that she would take you to the small stair, just to make it seem really authentic."

Miranda's face went scarlet, but before she could open her mouth, Eli grabbed her shoulder.

"Well done, then," Eli said, pushing Miranda back and taking her spot beside Josef. "You've found me. However, you still haven't caught me."

"But it's not you I'm after," Coriano said. "It's the man who follows where you lead." A sudden flash of white cut the dark as Coriano drew his sword and aimed the point directly at Josef's chest. "Master of the Heart of War, we have unfinished business."

Josef brandished the dented, bloody support beam like a club in front of him, a broad smile breaking across his face. "Let's finish it, then."

"Are you mad?" Miranda grabbed Josef's arm. "Weren't you listening? Renaud could be claiming the pillar right now. We don't have time for pride fights!"

"If you're looking for the new king," Coriano said, "he's in the throne room. Back through the treasury hall and straight up the main stair four flights. The first door on the right will take you to the promenade hall, and you just follow the flags to the throne room itself. He's got the entire contents of the treasury up there on my advice, so I could set my trap and he could work on his pillar in peace."

Miranda's hands began to shake. "You're letting him work on the Pillar? Do you have any idea what that could mean?"

"No," Coriano said, "and neither do you. Does it matter?"

"Of course, it matters!" Miranda's voice echoed through the empty cavern. "You were there in the clearing. You should know better than most that the man has nothing but contempt for the spirits! If he gets that Pillar, there won't be a spirit in the world that can stand against him, and every spirit he conquers will go as mad as that sandstorm. Doesn't that mean anything to you?"

Coriano raised his white blade and brought the red-wrapped hilt to his lips. "The only spirit I care about is Dunea," he whispered, "my River of White Snow, and all she cares about is beating him." He pointed the tip of his sword at the hilt of the Heart of War poking over Josef's back. "Everything else is meaningless."

Miranda growled, but Josef stepped in front of her, his enormous back and the great sword strapped across it blocking everything else from view. The swordsman looked over his shoulder, and Miranda's blood went thin at the look in his eyes. Even when he had waded out into the sea of soldiers with nothing but a stick of building material, he hadn't looked as large or as deadly as he did now.

"Nico," he said. "Protect Eli and the girl." He turned back to face Coriano. "This is my fight."

A cold hand grabbed Miranda's and she looked down to find Nico dragging her out of the treasury.

"We'll meet you upstairs," Eli said, jogging after the women. "Don't lose."

Josef didn't answer, but Miranda saw him grin as he turned to face Coriano, the beam brandished before him. Coriano raised his white sword in greeting as the enormous treasury door drifted shut, obscuring them from view.

"We can't just leave him!" Miranda shouted, fighting Nico's grip. "Shouldn't we help? We could beat Coriano and go upstairs together!"

"You don't get it, do you?" Eli grabbed her shoulders and spun her around. "Do you think Josef's my servant? That I can just order him around?" He was breathing hard now, and his face was more serious than she had ever seen it. "'Do not postulate where you do not understand,'" he sneered, his voice warped into a biting mimicry of her own. "Maybe it's time you listened to your own advice, Spiritualist. Josef Liechten travels with me by his own choice. When he says 'This is my fight,' that's what it means. His fight, not ours to interfere with because it doesn't match what we want to do."

"But he's your friend!" Miranda shouted. "You can't just leave him to die! Coriano would have had him last time if Renaud hadn't released the storm. What makes you think he'll survive?"

"He won't lose." The absolute surety in Nico's voice struck Miranda like a hammer. The girl looked up at the Spiritualist, her enormous black coat twitching around her calm, pale face. "Josef's the strongest swordsman in the world," she said. "He won't lose to someone like Coriano and his arrogant white sword."

Miranda stared blankly, trying to think of an answer to that, but Nico was already gone, picking her way through the groaning soldiers and toward the stairs. Eli shot Miranda a look that dared her to say something more and started after the girl. Miranda took one last, long look at the treasury door. Then, with a heavy sigh, she turned and followed the other two through the ruined hall, past the splinters of the tiny servants' door where Josef had made their entrance, and up the broad main stair that led back to the upper levels of the palace.

After getting lost twice, they found the door that opened into the throne room's approach. The long hall had changed dramatically since Miranda and Marion had pushed their way through the crowd that had gathered to see Renaud ages ago. Black mourning banners hung from the vaulted ceiling in place of the Mellinorian flags, and the sconces on the walls burned low behind black shades. The edge of the newly risen moon was visible through the high windows, but the watery glass and high, swift clouds distorted into ghostly shadows what light the moon shed, leaving the lofty hall as gloomy as a cemetery forest. Eli, Miranda, and Nico crept along the wall, scurrying from fat stone pillar to fat stone pillar, but it soon became obvious that such precaution was unnecessary. The promenade hall was empty.

"Where is everyone?" Miranda said, stepping out into the dim light.

"Probably still fighting the fire," Eli said, cocking an eyebrow at Nico. "I really hope you didn't underestimate the situation. Henrith won't thank us for getting his throne back if the castle burns down."

"It won't." Nico glided silently through the gloom. "That furnace wasn't smart enough to manage anything as spectacular as burning down an entire castle."

"Comforting words indeed," Miranda said, shaking her head. "Come on. The throne room is this way."

They half walked, half ran the length of the long promenade. The golden doors to the throne room loomed large, glowing silver in the dim moonlight, and, as they discovered when they reached them, locked tight.

"Not even locked," Eli said, running his hands over as much of the ornate gold work as he could reach. "The doors themselves have been sealed somehow." He got down on his knees and tried to peer underneath, but the doors were set flush with the marble floor, without so much as a hair crack to look through.

"Nico," Eli said, stepping back. "If you would be so kind."

Nico nodded and shook her hands free of her bulky sleeves. Bracing her boots against the slippery marble, she slammed her palms against the metal and started to push. The doors groaned under the pressure and began to bow inward. Cracks sprouted in the carved gold, growing in cobwebby spirals as Nico pushed harder. With a soft, peeling crack, large sections of the gold began to flake off, revealing the dark metal beneath. The door squealed, and the marble under Nico's feet began to crack under the pressure, but the iron core of the doors beneath the soft gold did not budge. Nico gritted her teeth and pushed harder still, growling under her breath. The stone supports around the doors began to creak. Grit fell from the ceiling. Small showers of dust at first and then fist-sized bits of stone started coming down like hail.

"That's enough!" Eli shouted, ducking the falling rocks. "You're going to bring the ceiling down on our heads!"

Nico stepped back, panting. The doors, though mangled and dented with two Nico-hand-shaped craters, remained defiantly shut. Miranda bent down and picked up one of the larger flakes of gold leaf from the debris scattered across the floor. "The great, golden doors of Mellinor," she said and handed the piece to Eli. "Just a gilded fake."

"Gold is an impractical material for making doors, anyway." Eli crumpled the gold foil and deftly slipped it into his pocket. "Well," he said, "I wanted to be quick about this, but I guess there's no choice."

Nico stepped aside, and Eli took her place in the marble crater that had been smooth floor a minute before. He laid his hands on the dented metal and began whispering in the gentle tone Miranda had labeled his spirit sweet-talking voice. He was barely two words in when he jerked back, clutching his hand as if he'd been burned.

"We have a problem," he announced. "I can't talk to the doors."

"What's wrong?" Miranda picked her way through the rubble toward him.

Eli gazed grimly up at the twisted metal, shaking his hands vigorously. "They're terrified. So terrified, in fact, I'm surprised they're still standing."

Miranda looked at Nico, but Eli shook his head. "Not her. Demon fear is different, vindictive. This is enslaver work. Renaud's scared them shut."

Miranda raised her eyebrows skeptically and brushed her hands against the doors. As soon as her fingers made contact, white-hot pain shot up her arm. It went through skin, muscle, and bone and straight to the core of her spirit, and it was all she could do not to burst into tears. Her hands jerked away of their own accord, taking shelter in the cool, smooth cloth of her skirt. The burning remained, however, and with it an echo of terror so great that it made her legs watery. In the moment she touched the doors, one iron-clad command had overshadowed everything. It rang through the metal, greater than the fear and heavier than the pain, an unbreakable order: Don't move.

"That bastard." Miranda looked up at Eli, her face pale with fury. "We have to stop him. I don't care if he's after Gregorn's Pillar or not. Anyone who would do this to a spirit can't be allowed to live."

"For once, we agree." Eli reached up and began to unbutton his valet jacket, and then the white shirt underneath. "I hadn't meant to use this just yet," he said, "but I can't let Josef find us standing around, can I?"

He turned, and Miranda cringed before she could stop herself. His jacket and shirt hung open, revealing his bare chest. A series of angry red burns ran in a swirling pattern from his collarbone to just above his navel. Before she could ask what caused such an injury, the burns began to hiss. Smoke rose up from the marks in a white plume, curling into a cloud that smelled faintly of charred flesh. The temperature in the room began to rise. It was a pleasant, dry heat at first, but it increased exponentially with every breath Eli took. The ball of smoke above the thief's head blackened as the heat grew. Sparks flashed at its center, faintly at first, then more violently, until the cloud was popping like a greenwood bonfire. Despite the fire show happening less than a foot above him, Eli's face was calm and his eyes were closed, as if he were asleep. The cloud was as hot as a smelter now, and Miranda took a step back as the hissing and snapping reached a crescendo. With a final crack, a tremendous blast of hot air and smoke shot out of the cloud, and every lamp in the hall snuffed out at once.

For a moment, the world went black, and then bright red light, more intense than any fire, blossomed in the air above Eli. The light swirled and grew, blending smoke and fire to form feet, then legs. A broad-barrelled chest three times as tall as Miranda flashed in the darkness, growing muscular arms, boulder-sized fists, and shoulders like fiery mountains. Finally, with a new burst of heat, the remaining light condensed into an enormous flame-wreathed head whose pointed crown brushed dangerously near the peak of the hall's vaulted ceiling. Fully formed, the creature stretched languidly, sending a shower of sparks down around him. Red light rippled along the new-made muscles, tracing the intricate connections between limb and trunk as the creature's surface hardened from smoke and fire into red-hot stone. When it was done stretching, it tilted its enormous head down. Glorious, fiery swirls moved like weather fronts across its face as the great hinge of a mouth opened wide, dripping fire.

"Eli," it said. "It is good to see you."

Eli pulled his coat closed, covering his now unmarred chest. "You, too, old friend."

Miranda could not believe what she was seeing. The enormous spirit glowed like the heart of a smith's fire, but the solidity and weight reminded her of Master Banage's great stone spirits. The heat coming off it was more powerful than Kirik's at full burn, and the giant hadn't even done anything yet.

"A lava spirit," she said, not bothering to hide the amazement in her voice. "I've never met a wizard who could take one as a servant, not even Master Banage."

"You still haven't met one," Eli said. "Karon isn't a servant. He's my companion."

"But," Miranda gaped, "how do you control him?"

"I don't," Eli said, grinning. "I ask."

The enormous, burning spirit looked from Eli to Miranda, then back again. "You're keeping strange company these days," he rumbled.

"Only temporarily," Eli assured him. "Now, I was hoping you could do me a favor. I need these doors open."

Karon glared at the doors. "That's a powerful command they're under. I may have to kill them."

"At this point, that might be a mercy," Eli muttered. He looked at Miranda, whose distress was obvious, and he sighed. "Be gentle, if you can. The Spiritualists have always been a bunch of bleeding hearts."

Karon nodded and turned to the doors. Miranda could feel them shaking through the marble, still too scared to open even when faced with death. As the lava spirit stepped forward, Nico and Eli retreated behind one of the support pillars, and, a moment later, Miranda followed. The hall shook as the lava spirit positioned himself in front of the trembling doors. Karon pounded his fists together a few times, getting them white hot. Then, with a hiss, he slammed his glowing hands into the quivering metal. The doors screamed when he made contact, filling the air with the bloody stench of iron. Melting gold flowed in glowing rivers down the door's surface as the remaining scrollwork and flourishes dissolved under Karon's fire like marzipan dipped in steam. Karon ignored the wealth flowing around him and wedged his glowing fist deeper into the iron's screaming heart. At last, the terrified metal could hold no longer, and the doors began to slip away. Iron dripped like wax from Karon's fingers, falling in large, hissing black drops to splash against the stone floor. Back in the hall, Miranda huddled behind Eli, cringing away from the splatters of liquid metal and the smelter blast of Karon's heat. Her left hand clutched the empty finger where Allinu's ring normally rested. Never in all her life had she wished so hard for her cool mist spirit.

At last, the heat faded, and Miranda felt the thunderous stomp of Karon stepping back. She peeked around the corner. All that was left of the golden doors of Mellinor was a gaping hole, its melted edges bleeding liquid metal onto the blackened, cracked floor.

Karon looked over at Eli, who was admiring the wreckage from a distance.

"Good work," the thief said, nodding.

The lava spirit's face rippled in what Miranda guessed was a smile. Eli strolled forward, stepping without hesitation over the still-smoking metal. "Very good work indeed," he said, grinning up at Karon. "Now, if you don't mind, I'd like it if you could hang around a bit longer. I have a feeling I'll need your help again sooner than I'd like."

Karon nodded and squatted by the ruined doors, watching with intent as Eli stepped over the smoking threshold.

Beyond the circle of Karon's ambient glow, the throne room was as dark as the treasury had been. Miranda stepped forward, squinting against Karon's glare, and, as her eyes adjusted, the room began to take shape. The first thing she noticed was that the royal banners that had lined the far wall were gone. So were the elegant lamps, chairs, and end tables that had once ringed the open room. In their place, the entire contents of the treasury—golden statues, jewelry, weaponry, overturned chests of embroidered silk, everything—had been stacked along the walls in sloppy piles. But most upsetting of all was what lay directly ahead of them. At the far end of the room, at the foot of the dais steps, the gilded throne of Mellinor lay on its side, broken and splintered, as if it had been kicked off its perch. In its place, standing like a trophy at the top of the tall dais, was a squat, gray pillar.

CHAPTER 22

The two swordsmen stared at each other long after the sounds of the footsteps of the fleeing wizards had faded. Coriano held his white sword delicately in front of him, the blade shimmering with its own pearly brilliance. Brighter than the lantern at the bounty hunter's feet, the sword glowed like the moon in the dark, empty treasury. Josef kept his eyes even with it, letting them adjust to the light.

Coriano took an experimental step forward, but Josef's only response was to tighten his grip on the heavy beam and hold his ground. Coriano stepped back again, resting his sword wearily on his shoulder. "You can drop your oversized matchstick," he said. "I'm not going to roll over when you come swinging like those fools in the hallway. Draw your sword."

"You set all this up just to fight me," Josef said. "Well, here's your chance. Come when you're ready."

Coriano chuckled. "You think this is about you? Don't flatter yourself, Mr. Liechten. You are just the trappings. You know what I'm after." His good eye flicked up and focused just above Josef's left shoulder, where the Heart of War's hilt waited. "Draw."

"The Heart is my sword," Josef said. "It chose me, so I'll decide when to draw. If you're so keen to cross blades with it, make this worth my while."

Coriano's eyes narrowed, and there was no hint of humor in his expression when he raised his sword again. "Have it your way."

Coriano lunged, and Josef raised his beam just in time to keep the white blade from burying itself in his neck up to the hilt. The sword cut through the solid hardwood like it was taffeta, and Josef was forced to duck as the swing carried over his head. But Coriano was waiting. As soon as Josef's head went down, the swordsman's knee hit him square in the ribs. The blow opened Josef's chest wound and sent him sprawling. He hit the stone floor hard and brought what was left of the beam up just in time to save his stomach from the next blow. The sword sliced clean through the wood again, but this time, Josef was prepared. At the split second when the white edge was buried deep in the beam, he twisted the beam. The blade caught, and Coriano's eyes widened as, with one enormous heave, Josef sent beam, blade, and swordsman hurtling through the air.

Coriano ripped his sword free and landed neatly. The beam clattered to the ground behind him, sending a shower of dust and splinters into the air. Josef struggled to his feet, clutching his chest, which was bleeding freely again. He drew his short sword and dropped into a defensive position.

"You can't be serious," Coriano said, sounding almost annoyed. "You can't really expect to beat my Dunea with that metal hunk. She was made by Heinricht Slorn himself, the greatest master of Shaper wizardry the world has ever known. She was forged to be a killing blade in the hands of a master swordsman. This is her purpose, her nature, and you would face her with a sword so deep asleep, it doesn't even know which side its edge is on? Be reasonable, man. You won't be able to land a touch, much less a blow."

Josef grinned. "Only inferior swordsmen blame their swords, Coriano."

Coriano's eyes darkened. "We'll see."

He lunged again. Josef sidestepped, sliding his blade along the flat of the white sword, going for Coriano's knuckles. The older swordsman spun, and the white blade flew up to bite into Josef's left shoulder. Josef gritted his teeth and dropped to one knee, spoiling the blow and saving his tendon, but the shallow cut was enough. Pain shot down his arm, and he felt himself going off balance. The cut had sliced through the leather strap that kept the Heart of War in place, and the enormous sword's weight threatened to topple him. He twisted, slipping out of the harness before it could pull him to the ground. The Heart of War rang like a bell as it hit the stone floor, and the entire room vibrated with the deep, clear sound.

Josef didn't have time to see where it had fallen. Coriano's sword was coming again, a high blow aimed at his right shoulder. Josef dodged and swiped at the one-eyed swordsman's side, hoping to catch him off balance, but Coriano's white blade was there before Josef saw it move, and the top third of Josef's short sword clattered to the ground.

Coriano returned his sword to the ready position. "We've been here before, Josef," he said calmly. "We both know how it ends. Pick up your true blade and fight."

Josef's downswing caught Coriano off guard. The jagged edge of the broken blade bit deep into the bounty hunter's leg, and only the older man's speed saved his artery from being cut clean through. Coriano danced away, sword flashing. Josef grinned and swung his stub of a sword, flinging an arc of Coriano's blood onto the dusty ground.

"One touch," he said.

Coriano didn't answer. He lunged with a snarl, and they began a complicated dance around the treasury. Coriano's blows fell lightning fast, and it was all Josef could do to dodge them. There were no wasted strokes in Coriano's style, every white flash was a killing blow, and only Josef's instincts, sharpened over years behind the sword, saved his skin from a new collection of holes. He blocked when he could, but the white blade whittled his sword to shavings. By the time they came around again to where the Heart had fallen, he was down to a chunk of hilt.

Josef was panting now, and even Coriano was looking strained. He was leaning to the right, favoring his uninjured leg, but even though the pain must have been blinding, the one-eyed swordsman never gave an opening. His sword flashed like a silver fish, and Josef gasped as the tip flew across his chest, leaving a burning trail. He stumbled, and the broken hilt flew out of his hand and clattered off into the dark. A hard kick followed the cut, and Josef found himself on his back again, gasping painfully, with Coriano standing over him. The swordsman's face was twisted in disgust. He laid his white sword against Josef's neck, where the artery pulsed, and the blade's light flickered.

"She's angry," Coriano whispered. "Angry enough that even your deaf ears should be able to hear her. All this time, chasing you through country after country, and when we finally catch you, this is all you can give us." He flicked his wrist, and the white sword's tip plunged into Josef's previously injured shoulder. "You're slow, and your guard is sloppy. You rely on gimmicks and refuse to fight with your full strength. Is this the master of the Heart of War?" He plunged his sword into Josef's other shoulder. "The greatest awakened sword in the world, with all of humanity to choose from, why did it choose you?"

The white sword slid down his blood-soaked chest, and Josef bit his tongue to keep from screaming.

"You are a waste of time," Coriano sneered, and, with a smooth thrust, he plunged his sword into Josef's stomach. When Josef struggled, Coriano looked him square in the eyes and twisted the blade, wedging it deeper. "You're not even worth dragging back for your bounty," he whispered, his voice sharp and deadly as the metal in Josef's flesh. "Lie here and rot, Josef Liechten."

He yanked his white sword out, and Josef couldn't stop the groan as his own blood ran hot and free down his sides and onto the cold ground. With a final disgusted look, Coriano turned away, casually wiping his blade on his sleeve.

He walked over to the Heart of War, still lying abandoned where Josef had dropped it. Its surface was ink black in Dunea's pearly light as Coriano kneeled, running his fingers over the sword's dull, dented edge.

"Not a whisper," he murmured. "Not even a presence. Can this truly be the Heart of War?" He glanced over at Josef's prone body. "They say it was forged at the dawn of creation. The Heart of War is a legend that Dunea and I have dedicated our lives to finding, the greatest awakened blade, the ultimate test."

He reached out and grabbed the Heart's crudely wrapped hilt, but when he pulled, the sword did not budge. He scowled and pulled harder. The sword stayed completely still, as though it were part of the floor.

"The weight of a mountain," Coriano murmured, rocking back on his heels. "It is the real thing, the true Heart of War. Only the hand it chooses can lift it." He traced the hilt one last time, and the awe on his face faded. "How tragic that we should meet it now, when it chose so poorly."

He stood up, sliding the River of White Snow back into her sheath. "The Heart will lie here, then, until it chooses a new master." He looked sadly at Josef. "You, on the other hand, will be carted off and buried alone as a thief. A fitting end for the man who failed his sword and denied us our great ambition."

He shook his head and turned away, limping toward the treasury door. Josef lost track of the uneven footsteps' sound almost as soon as they began. The dim cavern was growing darker, and the cold stone pulled at him until he was as heavy and motionless as the floor itself. However, even as the sound around him faded, the mantra in his head grew stronger, one word echoing through his fading consciousness.

Move.

It had been there since he took the first blow, soft at first, easily lost in the heat of combat. Now, when things were still and his life was leaking out of him, it was deafening.

Move.

Move.

MOVE.

Josef closed his eyes. He had to be very close to death indeed to hear this voice. Finally, he answered. "I can't."

Get up, it shouted, loud enough to make him wince. He turned his head slightly. The Heart of War was barely a foot away. All he had to do was reach out, but his arm would not move.

Take me, the deep voice said. *Fight with me.*

"I can't," Josef said again. "How will I become stronger if I rely on you to win my battles?"

The strange voice sighed. *If you don't draw me, Josef Liechten, you will die here, and this pathetic weakness will be the height of your achievement.*

Slowly, his breath coming in short, shallow gasps, Josef moved his arm. Slowly, he dragged his hand across the stone floor, now damp and sticky with his blood. He reached out, one finger at a time, inch by painful inch, and gripped the long, crude handle of the dull, black sword.

Now—the Heart of War gave a satisfied sigh—*we can begin.*

Coriano had just reached the iron treasury door when he heard the scrape of metal on stone. He looked over his shoulder, and his good eye widened. At the center of the room stood Josef Liechten. His head was down, and his wounds were still bleeding sluggishly, but he was standing straight, in a fencer's ready position, and in his hand was the Heart of War.

Coriano turned and drew his sword. Dunea was quivering with anticipation, her light bright and eager, but the Heart of War looked no different than it usually did, and Coriano felt a stab of disappointment.

"Is your blade still asleep?" he asked, circling. "All awakened swords gain their own light as they grow. I expected the Heart to shine like the sun, but you can't even manage that."

Josef didn't respond. He stood perfectly still, breathing deeply. This close to death, he could feel Coriano's sword—a sharp, cold, feminine, bloodthirsty presence. By contrast, the sword in his hand was heavy and blunt, but with that weight came the absolute knowledge that, when he swung, it would cut.

Coriano raised his sword. "If you disappoint me this round, swordsman," he said, sneering, "I'll take your head."

He sprang forward, aiming high to strike Josef's injured right shoulder. However, right before his blow landed, Josef moved. His actions were slow and deliberate, so different from his frantic dodges before. The Heart of War moved with him, following the curve of his blood-streaked arm. Together, they struck, forcing Coriano to change up in midstride, bracing Dunea with both hands to block the blow.

It was like being hit with a mountain.

Coriano flew backward, slamming into the wall. His ribs cracked like kindling, and only his instinctive reaction to tuck in his head saved his skull from shattering against the stone. However, before he could even process his body's reaction, Dunea's voice shot through the blinding pain, and he almost retched. The River of White Snow was screaming, her light undulating in wild patterns across her blade, save for one section. Where the Heart had struck, the white steel had caved in. Coriano could not believe what he was seeing. Nothing he'd fought before had ever been able to scratch his awakened sword. He opened his spirit without hesitating, forcing his calm over her panic, forcing her to straighten out. She extended slowly, reasserting her shape. As she drank in his calm, he felt her spirit sharpen to a cutting edge. He looked up and found Josef waiting, still standing in the middle of the room, the Heart of War held loosely in one hand.

Coriano pushed away from the wall, forcing himself to ignore the pain. This was it at last, their shared ambition, a true duel between awakened blades. His palms were sweaty against Dunea's red-wrapped hilt as he took his ready position. This was what they had been training for. This moment was why they had chased Josef across half the known world. He held Dunea before him, and her light was nearly blinding. He'd never felt her so alive, so ready to strike. He brought his spirit as close to hers as he could and matched her killing instinct with his own, a musician tuning a chord to its true tone. When there was no more dissonance between them, he leveled her blade at Josef's chest and lunged.

He moved faster in that moment than he had ever moved before. With his spirit fully opened and roaring through him, his body felt as quick and weightless as sunlight. Only Dunea had weight, a heavy, killing quickness that could slice through bone, stone, and steel. Together, they were on Josef before he could have seen their movement, sword and swordsman moving as one to strike the larger man's heart.

Josef moved as if underwater, slowly and deliberately raising his blade. It was as though he lived in a different world, where time was a physical thing, a sticky morass between seconds that he swam through like a carp, faster than sound, faster than light, and inexorable as gravity. Even at his own blinding speed, Coriano could only watch as Josef turned, set his footing, and lifted the Heart of War to receive Dunea's blow. He saw it happen, and yet Coriano could not change his strike. He could not move fast enough.

There was a flash of blinding light when Dunea struck the Heart, and Coriano felt himself falling. He hit the ground hard, skidding across the stone until he came to a stop several feet behind Josef. He lay still, unable to breathe from the impact, and tried in vain to see where he was. The room was suddenly very dark. For a breathless second, he lay there in confusion, and then he felt the warm slickness coating his stomach, and he understood.

His hand was stretched out in front of him, still clutching Dunea's hilt. Just above the guard, the white blade ended in a ragged edge of torn metal. The rest of the sword was in a dull, tangled heap a few feet in front of him, and though he reached out to her with the shredded remains of his spirit, the sword did not answer. The River of White Snow was broken, and her light had gone out.

Coriano's anguished cry echoed through the dark, empty room, and Josef forced himself to turn. The Heart of War's spirit was still coursing through him, and he had felt it tear through the white sword and into Coriano's chest as if his own arm had been the cutting blade. Coriano was lying in a quickly spreading pool of blood. His shoulders were shaking, and his hand still clutched his sword's guard, the only part of the blade that was still snowy white. As if he knew he was being watched, Coriano forced himself to roll over. When his face came into view, his skin was as strained and white as his sword had been, marred only by the dark purple stain of his scar and a thin trickle of bright blood on his lip.

Josef could feel the Heart's power receding, but before he buckled, he forced himself to take a step forward. He plunged the dark blade into the stone floor and rested his weight against it. "You got your wish," he said, panting. "Was it worth it?"

Coriano's fingers tightened on the ruined hilt, leaving dark finger prints on the crimson silk. "No," he breathed at last. "Nothing is worth losing her." He brought the broken sword toward him, clutching it to his chest. "But it was the only end that could make us happy." He smiled. "Our souls will remember your name, Josef Liechten, and when we are reborn, we will hunt for you. Do not disappoint us..."

The last words were a hiss as Coriano's final breath left his body and he lay still, Dunea's hilt cradled against his chest. Josef watched as long as he could as the Heart's power faded. As it ebbed, the pain of his wounds came crashing back, and his heavy, tired body faltered under the impact. He slumped against the dull edge of his blade, fighting to breathe.

High above him, through the tons of stone, the castle began to quake.

CHAPTER 23

I see you've ruined my doors."

Renaud's voice slid through the darkness. Miranda jumped and squinted futilely against the lava spirit's light, but still she saw nothing. Only when Renaud turned his head could she see him clearly, standing on the dais by the pillar.

"They were ruined long before I got to them," Eli said, stepping forward. Karon bent down and glared menacingly through the warped remains of the doors, casting his fiery light over everything. Miranda and Nico walked under him to stand beside Eli.

"Step away from Gregorn's Pillar, Renaud," Miranda said.

"Well, well," Renaud said. "I told the lie myself, but I never thought it would turn into the truth. The Spiritualist and the wizard thief, working together."

"Your crimes dwarf his, at the moment." Miranda's eyes narrowed. "Give up, Renaud. There's no sandstorm to save you this time."

"I have no need for such childish ploys." Renaud turned back to face the pillar. "Not anymore."

"Stop!" Miranda shouted. "Listen to reason! Gregorn was the most feared enslaver who ever lived. He was not the kind of man to leave a boon for his ancestors. Whatever he left in that pillar will only hurt the balance between man and spirit that all life depends on, even yours, Renaud. If you use it, I guarantee the power you gain won't be worth it in the end. Step away, now!"

Renaud chuckled at her vehemence. "It's far too late for that, Miranda."

He shifted, turning toward Karon's light, and Miranda's eyes went wide. The enslaver's arms were buried in the pillar. Not just buried, eaten, up to his elbow. Where they met its surface, the pillar had corroded, leaving a black, gaping hole that glistened in the firelight like a rotten wound. As she watched, the pillar made a soft, wet sound, and another inch of Renaud's arms disappeared inside. Miranda covered her mouth, fighting not to be sick.

"Beautiful, isn't it?" Renaud sighed, gazing lovingly at the pillar's rotten surface. "Gregorn's greatest accomplishment lies just beneath this shell. Even now, the lineage of Gregorn in my flesh and blood is eating away at his barriers. When it is finished, Gregorn's legacy will be mine at last."

"You're mad," Miranda said, regaining her composure. "Anything Gregorn conquered as a wizard died with him long ago. What treasure could he have left you?"

"The only kind that matters," Renaud said calmly. "A spirit."

"Nonsense," Miranda scoffed. "No bond between human and spirit, not even an enslavement, can last past the wizard's death."

"Ah, but you see," Renaud said as the pillar ate another inch of him, "Gregorn's not dead."

It took Miranda a few moments to find her voice after that pronouncement. Fortunately, Eli spoke for both of them.

"What do you mean 'not dead'? It's been four hundred years. You're kidding yourself if you think anything human can hold on that long."

"The human will is the greatest force in this world," Renaud said. "It can conquer any spirit, any natural force, even time, if only the wizard can master himself. Gregorn's will conquered a spirit powerful enough to raise Mellinor from the inland sea. A spirit so strong, so dangerous, that nations trembled at Gregorn's feet for three months before the strain of controlling the spirit finally destroyed his body."

"As it should," Miranda spat. "I hope that spirit crushed—"

"His body," Renaud said, cutting her off, "not his will. Our bodies, our shells are fragile. They age and die, but while we have will, we have life. Gregorn understood this in a way your Spirit Court, with all its self-censorship in the name of arbitrary *balance*, never could. When his flesh began to fail him, my ancestor used the last of his power to enslave the only human soul a wizard can control, his own."

"Impossible," Miranda said grimly. "You can't enslave yourself any more than you could lift yourself off the ground by grabbing your own shoulders."

"That is the blindness of your discipline," Renaud sneered. "You Spiritualists are so quick to dismiss things, aren't you? So quick to say this is impossible, or that is impossible, and so, when the impossible happens in front of you, you're as blind and deaf as any human." He looked up at the pillar triumphantly. "Gregorn mastered himself and turned his own dying body into a pillar of salt, binding his spirit to this world. He left only one decree to his followers: form a kingdom around him and never let another wizard within its borders so that their spirits could not interfere with the delicate balance of his control."

Renaud leaned into the gaping, black blot that had now consumed over half of the pillar's surface, caressing it like a lover. "That's the real reason behind Mellinor's wizard ban," he whispered. "The reason why I was forced to grow up as a stranger in my own home, the reason I was banished, and the reason I returned. Everything in Mellinor grew from that one purpose: to protect Gregorn's control. Everything in this kingdom still serves her first king. Everything here exists so that this spirit who raised kingdoms and frightened nations, the spirit Gregorn gave up rebirth to gain, could never, ever escape him.

"That, Spiritualist," Renaud said, grinning cruelly, "is the true power of the human spirit, which you, with your rings and your self-limitations, will never reach."

Miranda trembled with rage, but before she could speak, Eli stepped forward.

"If you're so impressed by all this," he said casually, "why are you even here? If everything in Mellinor is in service to Gregorn, what are you doing to that pillar except undermining a greater wizard's work?"

"Taking what is mine," Renaud hissed. "I am Gregorn's heir, the first wizard in the Allaze family since Gregorn himself." He thrust his hands deeper into the pillar, which shuddered and ate.

"It is time for a new wizard king in Mellinor. Time for me to receive at last what my ancestor has held in trust for me for all these years. Together, we shall finish what Gregorn started. We will crush the trembling world into submission until every spirit waits on my demands and every wizard depends on my whim."

"Don't fool yourself!" Miranda cried, her voice shaking with barely restrained anger. "Gregorn isn't holding anything for you. A man who was willing to give up rebirth and sleep in a salt pillar for eternity just to keep a stranglehold on a spirit isn't the type to quietly pass on his legacy to a new generation. Even if that pillar eats you whole, Gregorn will never give that spirit to you!"

"Any other time you would be right, Spiritualist," Renaud said. "But what you don't realize is that, at this point, he doesn't have a choice." The enslaver looked at the place where his arms met the pillar, and his haughty smile became a mad grin. "After four hundred years, his soul has degraded so far past human, he's no better than the salt he's trapped in."

As he spoke, the black surface of the pillar began to bubble and hiss. Renaud laughed and plunged his hands in deeper. Then, with a sickening thrust, he threw open his spirit, and Miranda gasped as the black, sickening weight of his triumph-drunk will rolled over her.

The pillar groaned as Renaud's spirit crashed against it, stabbing into the black wound where his arms were buried and pressing down, forcing the hole wider. The black taint on the pillar's surface bubbled and hissed as Renaud forced himself in, using his spirit as a wedge. The harder he pressed, the faster the dark stain spread, eating what was left of the pillar's knobby gray surface as rot from an infected wound devours a limb. With a final, triumphant stab of his spirit, Renaud's arms disappeared into the sucking maw. His head followed, then his chest and his legs until, finally, he vanished completely. The pressure of his opened soul still pounded through the room, but the man himself was gone, eaten by the pillar, which was now entirely covered in the slick, black rot.

The second the last inch of his heel disappeared into the pillar, a wailing scream cut through the air. Miranda slapped her hands over her ears, but it was no use. The spirit scream cut straight to the well of her soul. It was worse than the sound the sandstorm had made, for that had been many small voices and the effect had been broken up. This scream was one enormous, anguished cry that set her teeth on edge and brought tears to her eyes, but worst of all, worse than anything, was the ghost of a human voice behind it.

Black sludge began to pour off the pillar's surface, oozing from the hole Renaud left behind him and pouring onto the marble floor. It eroded the stone where it touched, hissing loudly as it washed down the dais steps, and the smell almost made Miranda vomit. The liquid stank of rotten meat, like open sewage on a hot day. The stench filled the room to bursting, until Miranda could feel it eating her skin.

"What is it?" she choked out, looking frantically at Eli.

"Gregorn," Eli said, his voice muffled by the handkerchief he'd covered his nose and mouth with. "Or what's left of him. Renaud's forcing him out."

The ooze from the pillar showed no sign of stopping. It flowed down the dais to pool on the floor. The stone floor hissed and cracked as the acid spread across it with frightening speed, and yet the pillar showed no signs of slowing. Above it all, Renaud's spirit hung like an iron weight, and the fearsome spirit wail went on and on—almost human, yet never stopping for breath. When the black pool reached the center of the throne room, Renaud's spirit jerked and the pool froze, quivering like a caught leaf.

"Gregorn," the enslavement boomed through Renaud's voice, sending enormous ripples through the black liquid. "Kill them."

The wailing scream spiked, and the black sludge began to boil. No, Miranda took several steps back; not just boil, grow. The pool was rising, bubbling up into an enormous mound of black slime between them and the pillar on the dais. It grew and grew, and as it grew, its screaming deepened, until there was nothing human in it at all.

Eli looked up at the quivering, putrid, acidic sludge that was all that remained of the world's greatest enslaver, and his face paled. "Well," he whispered, glancing sideways at Miranda. "You're the Spiritualist, how do we stop it?"

"I have no idea," she confessed. "I've never even heard of something like this."

High above them, the peak of the mountain of ooze had reached the highest point of the vaulted ceiling. When it touched the stone, it wailed again, sending a rain of acidic globs down on top of them.

"Wonderful," Eli said, dodging the spray. "Just bleeding wonderful." He sighed deeply, though Miranda couldn't imagine how he managed it, considering the stench, and he looked over his shoulder at the lava spirit, still waiting in the hall. "It's never easy, is it?"

"Easy is boring," Karon rumbled, stepping through the ruined doorway.

"I hoped that was what you'd say." Eli smiled. "Well," he said and turned back to the blob, "let's have some fun, then."

Miranda felt the lava spirit's answering laugh deep in her stomach. The castle shook to its foundation as Karon charged forward, his glowing stone feet cracking the floor with every step, and his flaming fist aimed straight at the center of the quivering pile of black liquid. The blob that had been Gregorn surged forward to meet Karon midway, and Eli, Miranda, and Nico dove for cover as the two spirits collided in an explosion of black steam.

CHAPTER 24

Miranda hunched over, gasping for breath. For once, Nico and Eli were right down on the floor with her, coughing and choking as the black steam burned their lungs. Eyes watering, Miranda looked up in time to see the thick, acidic clouds swirling off Karon's molten fist as the lava spirit prepared to swing again.

"Wait!" Miranda choked out, but the lava spirit didn't hear her. His fist slammed into the slick mound that had been Gregorn, but the blob barely flinched. Instead, it sucked in the blow, sending tarry tendrils up Karon's glowing arm, trapping the spirits together. Black steam churned around them as the spirits screamed together. Karon struggled against Gregorn's grip, but the more he fought, the tighter the black tar adhered. Finally, with a great, rumbling cry, the lava giant opened his enormous mouth and breathed a column of white-hot fire over both of them. The blob shrieked and pulled away, showering acid that immediately evaporated in the shimmering heat. A fresh wave of black steam surged across the room, covering everything in a stinging, inky cloud.

"You have to stop him!" Miranda wheezed in the direction she'd last seen Eli. "If he keeps evaporating the liquid like that, we're going to suffocate before he can make a dent!"

Somewhere in the black clouds, Eli coughed a few words, and the roaring of Karon's fires stopped. Almost instantly, the clouds began to clear. Wiping her eyes furiously, Miranda squinted up to see Karon frozen in midswing. Eli coughed again, and the lava spirit nodded. Karon brandished his smoking fist one last time at the black blob and vanished in a great puff of ash, which blew back to Eli.

"What are you doing?" Miranda shouted, struggling to her feet as Eli closed his shirt over the reemerging burn. "I didn't mean get rid of him entirely!"

"Can't have it both ways!" Eli shouted back. "Watch out!"

Denied its target, the acid blob screamed louder than ever, sending a rain of black sludge showering down. Miranda, Eli, and Nico ducked as the fist-sized globs struck the wall behind them, and sank deep in the dissolving rock.

"He'll melt the palace into slag at this rate!" Eli shouted over the spirit's wail.

"We have to do something!" Miranda cried.

"You tell me!" Eli cowered as more acid spattered around them. "I'm out of good ideas!"

"I'd take a bad one, at this point!"

Still screaming madly, the mound of sludge shivered from base to tip. Suddenly, with a sickening, liquid snap, a torrent of black water began to pour out of its base. It was as if a dam inside the sludge had burst, sending a river of foamy, black liquid roaring across the floor straight toward them. It happened so quickly, Miranda couldn't do anything except watch in horror as the wave rushed at her. Only when the black tide washed over the piles of discarded treasure, dissolving the carved mahogany and precious metals in the time it took to catch her breath, did Miranda's instincts gain the upper hand on her fear. She spun around and dashed for the far wall, her feet skidding across the marble. As soon as she was close enough, she launched herself at the wall, and her grasping fingers caught the edge of a decorative niche. She hauled herself up, tossing over the stone bust of some Mellinorian king or other to make room, and pressed her body as far back into the crevice as she would fit. Eli followed her lead, climbing into the alcove next to hers.

"Nico," he shouted, "there's a shelf a bit higher up you could jump to."

But Nico didn't answer. Miranda peered over the lip of his hiding place. Several feet below, the girl was standing at the base of the wall, stoically watching the black tide as it rushed toward her.

"Nico," Eli said more urgently, leaning out of his crevice and thrusting out his arm. "Take my hand!"

"Josef told me to protect you," Nico said, not even looking at him.

"Don't be an—" He gasped and ducked as a black wave crashed against the wall, sending burning spray up the walls around them. Miranda turned away in horror as the black surge covered Nico's lower body, and waited for the scream.

But there was no scream, not even a pained gasp. Miranda turned back. Nico was standing in inky liquid up to her knees. Smoke rose in white plumes where the acid touched her, yet her posture was as calm as ever. She might have been wading in a warm river for all the attention she paid the black water eating at her legs.

At the center of the room, the black blob quivered, and the tide of black sludge receded with a sucking hiss. Miranda watched in spellbound horror as the girl's legs came back into view, bracing for the worst. However, while Nico's trousers, boots, and the hem of her coat were completely dissolved where the acid had submerged them, her pale skin was untouched, as were the heavy silver manacles she wore on her ankles.

Gregorn screamed in angry confusion as Nico took a step forward, her bare, uninjured feet moving through the sludge of the dissolved treasure in quick, light steps. As she walked, a soft, dry sound cut through the spirit's wailing. It sounded like dust blowing through grass, and it took Miranda a few seconds to realize that Nico was laughing. The girl hopped clear of the treasure detritus and stood before the screaming sludge spirit, tilting her head back so she could see all of him at once. When she spoke, her voice was full of that horrible, dry dust laughter.

"You think you can beat us with that?"

The black sludge froze in midshriek and hung there, quivering. Nico watched for a moment, and then she raised one bony hand to her throat, and the temperature in the room plummetted.

In one smooth motion, Nico tossed her coat to the ground. Without its bulk to hide her, she was skeletally thin. Her threadbare shirt was sleeveless, and her bony arms hung like cracked branches from a crooked trunk. Her silver manacles glowed with their own light, casting weird shadows across the acid-etched floor as she reached up to take off her hat.

"Nico…" Eli's voice held a warning, but if the girl heard him, she ignored it. "That stupid girl," he whispered.

Miranda didn't have to ask what he meant. Without the coat to hide her, the girl's aura was inescapable. Predatory menace rolled off her in waves, stirring Miranda's deepest instincts to run, to get out. But she could not move. Deep, irrational, primordial fear had turned the air to glue, snaring her soul like a rabbit under a wolf's paw. She could do nothing except cower in her alcove and watch, gasping in the acidic air and waiting for the threat to kill her or pass by. For the first time, she understood why all spirits fear a demonseed, and why Gin had been so adamant about killing the girl, no matter how small or controlled she seemed.

"Can't you stop her?" Miranda whispered through gritted teeth.

"Only Josef can stop her when she gets like this." Eli was pressed so far back in his alcove Miranda couldn't see him anymore. "You might want to get down," he whispered.

Nico stretched her arms out, flexing her shoulders. One by one, the thick manacles at her wrists, ankles, and neck popped open with a hard, metallic snap. Each time, the silver clung to her for a moment, screaming angrily, but even fully awakened metal can't fight gravity. The manacles hit the floor with a crash, cursing Nico all the way down. As soon as she was free of their touch, the small girl's posture changed completely.

The Nico who stood at the center of the circle of cast-off clothes and silver restraints was an entirely different creature than the Nico who had entered the throne room with them. Her thinness was no longer awkward, but deadly and cutting, like garrote wire. Her movements were languid as she dropped lazily into a stance, her newly freed hands flourished in front of her.

With a thin smile Nico stared up at the enormous sludge. Then the dim moonlight seemed to bend around her, and she vanished.

The sludge roared as shadows, blacker than any simple darkness, streaked across its surface, appearing and vanishing in an instant, like black heat lightning. It was nauseating to watch, but Miranda could no more look away than she could sprout wings and escape. Everywhere the shadow touched, a large section of acidic sludge vanished. It wasn't that it got knocked away, or that the creature was pulling it back. Where the darkness landed, that piece of the blob was simply gone. Within a few seconds, the acid spirit looked like a mouse-nibbled biscuit, and the fear in the room was suffocating. The stones were screaming, the unlit lamps were screaming, the gold-plated decorations, the remaining contents of the treasury, the glass windows, the air itself, *everything* in the throne room was screaming nonsense in a state of full panic. The voices stabbed Miranda's ears, filling them to bursting, but all she could do was press herself tighter against the screeching wall and watch wide-eyed as Nico winked into view, landing neatly at the center of the throne room.

Gregorn's sludge was about half the size it had been. It lay at the far end of the room, whimpering pathetically, but still protecting the dais as it had been commanded to do. Nico, on the other hand, looked healthier than Miranda had ever seen her. Her pale skin was flushed and glowing. Her body was no longer skeletal, but strong and supple. Her legs were longer and her torso more filled out. She also looked taller, a suspicion confirmed by the new gap between the hem of her shirt and the waist of her trousers. It was as if she'd aged ten happy, healthy years, and yet the freezing, predatory menace rolling off her was stronger than ever. She glided across the corroded stone, and the acidic sludge shrank back, but it would not give up its position in front of the dais, not even when Nico stopped a foot away from its trembling base.

"Nico!" Eli's voice was thin and strained, but the fact that he could speak at all was a miracle. "Don't do it, Nico!"

The girl ignored him. With a triumphant cry, Nico plunged her bare hand deep into the acid's center. If Miranda had named the spirit's scream a wail before, the cry it gave now reduced its earlier sounds to whimpers. Gregorn's spirit thrashed on the end of Nico's arm like a speared fish, slinging acid in huge arcs. But, despite its struggles, the spirit was shrinking. It was now not more than double the height of the dais. Then it was no taller than Gin, and still it was shrinking, its cries growing smaller and smaller. When the sludge was no larger than Nico herself, a new shape began to emerge. The black tar narrowed and separated, revealing long appendages. Ribs appeared at its center, and its peaked top became a rounded head. Two legs, barely more than tar over bone, appeared at the base, and shoulders like knives led to twig-like arms. Finally, the last of the sludge disappeared altogether, and Nico stood over the kneeling, black form of an old, skeletal man.

Wisps of hair still sprouted from his head, plastered down by black tar, and his face, his face was still human. Sunken eyes grayed over with cataracts looked pleadingly up at his conqueror. His cracked, black lips moved pathetically, but no sound came out. Black tears pooled in the hollows of the ancient enslaver king's cheeks as he looked up at her, his ruined hands rising slowly to grasp Nico's wrist where her hand was buried deep in his hollow chest.

With a final, cruel smile, Nico yanked her hand free, and what was left of Gregorn toppled to the ground. He made no sound as he fell, the last of his human features crumbling to dust even before they struck the pitted stone. Nico shook the dust off her fingers, and Miranda knew as surely as if she'd been standing over him herself that Gregorn's spirit was dead.

"Nico." Eli's soft voice made Miranda jump. She hadn't seen him leap down from his alcove, but the thief was standing a dozen feet behind the demonseed. Cautiously, he held out his hand, the largest of Nico's manacles, her neck piece, dangling from his fingers. "You did well," he said. "You did as Josef asked. Now it's time to come back to us."

The girl turned slowly, regarding him through slitted eyes that flashed in the darkness with their own flickering light. The room was deafeningly silent. Everything seemed to be holding its breath as Nico considered him.

"Come back?"

Her voice was different. The dry dust scrape that had been just a whisper before now completely overwhelmed her natural sound. It was so alien, so strange, that if Miranda had not seen Nico's lips moving, she would not have been able to name the speaker as human. Nico took a step forward, moving with unnatural grace toward the thief until she was only a few inches from Eli's outstretched hand. Then, with casual cruelty, she reeled back and punched him.

Eli didn't try to dodge. He took the blow full in the chest, and it sent him flying backward. He landed with a bone-snapping crunch on the scarred marble, the silver manacle clattering off into the dark. The second he hit the floor, Nico was on top of him again with another of her gut-wrenching, light-bending jumps. She grabbed the thief around the neck, lifting him off the floor.

"Come back?" she hissed, glaring at him with eyes that opened wider than human eyes should. "To what? I see how you treat the girl. A weapon, a *servant.* Our kind do not serve, thief!"

"I'm talking to Nico, not you," Eli said coldly. "You're just an interloper, a deadbeat tenant. We treat Nico as a partner, which is far more than I can say for you, bug."

She roared at that, drawing her fist to hit him again, but before she could strike, there was a silver flash in the thin space between them. Nico screamed and flailed backward, dropping Eli on the ground. Breathing hard, the girl reached down and wrenched something out of her chest. She tossed it to the ground where it landed with a clatter, and Miranda recognized one of Josef's knives. Eli grunted and rolled over, another knife ready in his hands.

But Nico's white skin was knitting itself back together as Miranda watched, and she crept toward Eli like a hunting spider. "You treacherous thief," she hissed. "How dare you take his blades!"

"Ah-ha," Eli said, coughing as he sat up slowly. "So there is some Nico left in there." He tucked the second knife back into his sleeve. "Listen to me, Nico. This isn't the real you. You're human, Nico. Still human, even now. Josef didn't nearly die five times over rescuing you just to have it end like this, in this nowhere kingdom." He held out his hand, his face kind and pleading. "Come back to us."

Nico paused and stared at his hand, and for a moment, the inhuman light in her eyes flickered out. Then it was back brighter than before. She lifted her clenched fist, ready to bring it down on the thief's unguarded head, but before she could swing, a tremendous crash stopped everything. Glass exploded above them, and Nico looked up just in time to see the swirling mass of gray fur and knife-sharp claws crash through the high window right before it landed on top of her.

Miranda pressed her hands to her mouth. The relief mixed with fear was almost more than she could bear. "Gin!"

Gin had Nico in his mouth. He shook her fiercely before flinging her as hard as he could against the stone wall. Her impact cracked the marble, and she slumped to the floor, her limbs bent under her at unnatural angles. Gin bounded to one side, putting himself between the crumpled girl and Miranda.

"I came as soon as I felt her," he growled, never taking his eyes off Nico's motionless body. "I told you, didn't I? Demons can't be trusted."

Miranda jumped down from her alcove and ran to him, flinging herself face down into his swirling fur.

"The king?"

"Still hiding and safe enough," he said quietly. "Not that any of us are 'safe' at this point." He voice thickened to a snarl as Nico stirred. "Get the thief."

Miranda nodded and looked around for Eli. The thief was still on his back where he had fallen, coughing painfully.

She ran to help him. "Can you stand?"

Eli nodded and took her offered hand, groaning as she pulled him to his feet.

Gin gave a warning growl. Nico was stirring, her cracked limbs righting themselves as they watched.

"What do we do now?" Miranda said.

"We do what we should have done when this mess started," Gin said. "We kill her."

"The dog might be right," Eli whispered, his voice thin and pained. "At this point, without Josef, I don't know anything else to do. Every moment she spends like this, our Nico goes further away. But whatever we do, let's do it quickly, otherwise"—he tapped his foot on the acid damaged stone—"the castle will do it for us."

Miranda froze. Now that he'd pointed it out, she didn't know how she'd missed it. Now that Gin had injured the demon and broken the spell of fear, every spirit in earshot was awake and calling for blood. Every piece of the throne room, from the broken glass to the stones under their feet, rumbled with desperate anger. Showers of dust cascaded from the ceiling as the marble strained against its mortar. Even the support pillars were edging closer, preparing to break free and let gravity do the rest, even if it cost them their lives, if that's what it took to kill the demon.

With a sickening series of cracks, Nico sat up. She stretched out her arms, and the joints snapped back into place. As she moved, the terrified dust flung itself off her, creating a low cloud that obscured her movements. Even so, Miranda could feel when Nico turned, feel the girl's regard sliding over her skin. Then Nico opened her eyes, and Miranda's blood turned to lead. The girl's eyes, which were too large to be human anymore, glowed with a steady, otherworldly light. They shone bright as candles through the terrified dust, brilliant but illuminating nothing. The rest of her face was lost in shadow, but Miranda could see clawlike hands scraping as the girl edged to the rim of her crater, and that was enough.

Nico moved along the wall, gathering herself for another leap, but Gin didn't give her the chance. He charged with a howl, barreling toward the demonseed. She snarled in answer and sprang to meet him, winking through the darkness faster than Miranda could follow. But Gin's sight was better than Miranda's, and the ghosthound's teeth caught Nico's arm just before she landed a killing strike on his skull. She whipped her other arm around and caught his jaw before he could bite down, stopping his momentum like an iron wall. Gin struggled against her grip, and Nico cackled, her terrible eyes narrowing to glowing slits. She slammed her feet into the screaming stone and lifted the ghosthound off the floor. Gin yelped in surprise as Nico swung him over her head and slammed him into the cracked wall where she had landed before. The hound rolled as he flew, landing on his feet. His paws barely touched the stone before he pushed off again with a roar, barreling straight for Nico. The demonseed had no time to dodge before the flat of Gin's head hit her square in the chest and the two of them went flying in a tangle of shifting fur and snapping fangs. But when they landed, Nico was on top. With a triumphant cry, she plunged her claws into Gin's back, and the ghosthound howled. He fought her as hard as he could, rolling and snapping, trying to knock her off, but her hand was deep in his muscle, and he couldn't dislodge her. Dark red blood flowed down his sides, matting his fur and hiding his patterns. His movements grew sluggish, but he would not stop fighting, even when his legs collapsed. Miranda's throat was raw before she realized she was screaming, though she couldn't make sense of her own words, or if they were words at all.

Without thought or warning, her spirit flung itself open, and Miranda's power roared to life. Spirit voices shot through her, clearer than ever before, flooding every sense until she could almost taste where one soul ended and the next began. Without thinking, she swept her spirit across them. The response was immediate. Every spirit was desperate for action, desperate to fight the intruder. A direction was all it took. She thrust her hand toward the demonseed, and the spirits leaped forward, screaming vengeance. A volley of broken glass, stone, and metal came from every corner of the throne room to strike Nico wherever there was room to strike. The impact ripped her hand free of Gin's back, and she toppled over. The marble floor was ready for her. The moment she hit, the stones sank beneath her, going as soft as clay at Miranda's command. As soon as Nico was mired, the stone surged over her arms, legs, chest, and neck before hardening again, pinning the demonseed to the ground. Miranda ran forward, flinging out her hand. The throwing knife that Nico had flung away clattered across the tiles and leaped into her grip. Miranda clamped her fingers on the hilt as she jumped, aiming the point to land deep in Nico's exposed throat.

But the blow never connected. The demonseed ripped her legs free of the stone at the last moment and caught Miranda in the chest. The Spiritualist grunted in pain as the new impact hit the old bruises, and she tumbled backward, cracking her head on the stone floor. Nico sprang to her feet, flakes of dead stone falling off her like dried mud.

"Stupid girl," she hissed, her eyes glowing like lanterns in her shadowy face. Her hand shot out, grabbing Miranda around the throat. Miranda struggled violently as Nico lifted her off the ground, but her head was ringing and the demonseed's grip was like iced iron against her skin. Nico pulled her close, close enough that Miranda could smell the strange, metallic stench of the girl's transformed skin. The demonseed's mouth curled into a sharp-toothed grin as she dangled Miranda from her outstretched arm, the Spiritualist's legs still kicking weakly as her air ran out.

"That's enough."

The deep voice cut clean through the spirits' clamor, leaving only silence in its wake. Nico froze, her lantern eyes flicking past Miranda to the tall figure standing in the ruined doorway, outlined by the falling dust.

Josef stood lopsidedly, Heart of War under his shoulder, like a crutch. Very slowly, he hobbled past Eli, who was still on the floor, clutching his ribs, past Gin, who lay motionless on the ground, and stopped right behind Miranda.

"Put her down."

Nico obeyed, and the Spiritualist landed in a heap on the shattered floor, coughing and clutching her throat. Neither the demonseed nor the swordsman paid her any attention. They stood face to face, Nico cowed and heaving, Josef still and calm. With great effort, he shifted his weight to his own feet and lifted the Heart of War over Nico's trembling body.

"Time to come home," he said, and he brought the sword down.

Miranda could barely breathe. She knew the Heart of War was an awakened sword, but that did not describe what happened next. As the blade connected with Nico's shoulder, the Heart of War's spirit opened like a wizard's. Miranda had never even heard of a spirit that could open its soul, yet the Heart's presence was doubling and doubling again, growing exponentially until it filled the hall with its oppressive, immobile weight. It was as if a mountain had fallen on the castle with the sword at its center and Nico beneath it. She crashed to the floor, and Josef followed her down, sinking to his knees.

With a shuddering sob, Nico started to shrink, the terrifying light in her eyes fading away. Her claws dulled into fingers, and her frame shriveled to skin and bones again. As she shrank, the aura of fear receded, and Miranda felt the spirits calming as the Heart of War's weight pushed them into a deep sleep. Only when the room was still did the Heart's spirit begin to pull back. When the mountain was just a sword again, Josef lifted the black blade and slammed it into the stone beside Nico's head. She was lying on the floor with her eyes closed, small and feeble again, as if nothing had happened. Josef slumped down the dull blade of his sword, resting on his elbow beside her.

"Stupid girl," he muttered, brushing the wild black hair out of her sleeping face with a gentle finger. He smiled and, his eyes rolling back in his head, fell forward to lie beside her, the Heart of War standing over both of them like a guard.

Miranda didn't realize Eli was moving until he crawled past her, Nico's silver restraints tucked under his arm. He pulled himself to her and began clamping the manacles back into place, a grim look on his face. "Gin's still alive," he whispered roughly, locking the silver ring onto Nico's neck. "Get him up and get them out of here." He nodded toward Josef and Nico. "We're not safe yet."

At this point it was meaningless to argue. Miranda climbed slowly to her feet and stumbled toward Gin's collapsed body, almost crying with relief when she saw his bloody chest rise and fall.

"Gin," she whispered, fisting her hands into his coarse fur. "We have to move."

The ghosthound's orange eyes cracked open, and he shifted just a little. "Gin." She shook him, blinking back tears. "Come on, mutt. We have to get you out of—"

"Leaving so soon?"

She had never hated Renaud's voice as much as she did at that moment. She turned slowly, putting her back against Gin's shoulder. On the other side of the throne room, still safe on its dais, the pillar waited. But, she squinted in the dim light, it was different now. All the black, rotten sections had vanished and, instead of its original dingy gray, the pillar's surface was now white and fragile as crusted snow.

A wave of spirit pressure burst out from the dais, and the room began to shake. Long cracks raced across the snowy surface of the pillar, and as they spread, the castle began to shake from its foundations. Showers of white dust poured down as cracks blossomed across the marble arches that held up the roof. Fissures sprouted on the walls, running like dust-bleeding capillaries from floor to ceiling as the stone spirits, already traumatized by multiple enslavements and a demonseed, finally started to lose their grip. Whole sections of wall began to come loose as Miranda watched, shattering the glass windows as the ceiling's weight began to shift.

Then, as suddenly as it had started, the shaking stopped. The room became deathly still, as though the world were holding its breath, waiting.

In the silence, the pillar split open.

CHAPTER 25

Gregorn's Pillar split cleanly. The crystallized salt fell away in two neat halves, dissolving into fine crystals that spattered like wet snow against the marble. Where the salt crumbled, watery light swelled in its place, blue and calm like the noon sun seen from the bottom of a clear lake. At the light's heart, casting long, dancing shadows across the ruined stone floor, was Renaud.

He stood at the center of the dais, the last of the salt falling around him, and across his shoulders, draped like the pelt of some mythic beast, was a glowing waterfall. It roared in a torrent over his shoulders and down his back, and then, just before it spilled onto the floor, it hit the wall of Renaud's open spirit and turned in midair. The water's own momentum forced it back up his chest and over his shoulder, where the cycle began again, an endless circle of water churning in furious anger. But no matter how it writhed and tossed, its flow was contained by the barriers of the enslavement. Renaud's control was well entrenched, and the water could not break free even enough to wet his clothes, which were completely dry despite the flood rushing across them.

Renaud held out his hand and the water followed his movements, charging down his arm to form a long, thin spike at the tips of his fingers, which he leveled at Miranda's head.

"That's two kings of Mellinor your little group has murdered," he said. "Not to mention the destruction of our throne room. I don't think anyone could object to your execution, at this point."

"The only murderer here is you, Renaud," Miranda hissed, clutching Gin's fur. "Release that spirit!"

Renaud chuckled, and the water flowing across his shoulders roared even faster. "I don't think you want me to do that. I see now why Gregorn was willing to die to keep this spirit. He's barely awake, but just look what he can do."

Renaud swung his arm, and the spike of water flew out in an arc, striking the wall like a cannon shot. The stones exploded outward, sailing into the night. Wind rushed in, and Miranda ducked as a shower of rubble flew toward her. When Renaud pulled back his hand, the entire northwest corner of the throne room was gone, leaving a gaping hole where the wall had been.

The stones in the roof squealed, but with one of their corner supports gone, it was a losing battle against gravity. One by one, they hurtled to the ground, cracking the floor where they hit. Renaud cackled, and the water's light flashed wildly around him, shifting from blue to white to almost black in sickening confusion.

"Renaud!" Miranda shouted, putting her arms up in a desperate attempt to shield herself and Gin from the falling rocks. "Enough of this! You're going to destroy everything if you keep this up!"

"And what do I care?" Renaud's voice trembled with the force of the spirit he held back. "Mellinor is mine to do with what I like!" He held out his hand again, and the water rushed over it in a fountain of white spray. "This is the heart of Mellinor," he shouted, raising the water high over his head. "Everything else is just an empty shell!"

As he clenched his fist, Miranda could hear the water's own deep voice, warped by the enslavement, screaming in frustration as it fought Renaud's hold. And as it screamed, the palace began to shake worse than ever.

"We have to get out of here!" Miranda turned frantically to Eli, trying to cover Gin's head as ever-larger pieces of ornamental stonework crashed down around them. "That idiot won't stop until he brings the whole place down!"

Eli looked up from where he was fixing the last of Nico's restraints, but whatever he'd been about to say was interrupted as a large chunk of stone arch landed not half a foot away from Josef's head, covering them all in a shower of grit.

"All right," Eli growled. "That's it."

The naked fury in his voice shocked Miranda out of her protective crouch, and she looked up just in time to see another, fist-sized stone hurtling toward Nico's unprotected shoulder. Eli caught it without looking and hurled it as hard as he could at Renaud's grinning face.

"Do you think this is fun?" he shouted. "Do you think this is a game? Is beating us so important that you'll bring down your own roof to do it?"

Renaud shattered Eli's stone with a flick of his hand. "Don't flatter yourself, Monpress. This was never about you. You and your collection of oddities were just in the wrong place at the wrong time when fate decided to hand me my birthright." He grinned maniacally. "Consider this my thanks, a throne room for your tomb, my way of repaying the unknowing kindness you did me."

The water hissed as he spoke, changing its flow as Renaud's triumph rippled through his wide-open spirit, subtly altering the shape of the enslavement. Suddenly, Miranda had an idea.

"You might want to watch your captive before you speak of kindness," she said, turning to face Renaud head on. "I don't know what that spirit used to be, but Gregorn died trying to control it." She smiled her most infuriating smile. "No matter what you say about birthrights, Renaud, you're no Gregorn. I give you fifteen minutes before the water breaks your soul and eats you alive."

"What would you know about control, girl?" Renaud thrust out his hand, and a wall of water surged down from the dais, rising over Miranda in a great wave. "You Spiritualists know nothing about control! You go on and on about balance, about our duty to the spirits, but we wizards are the ones with the power! The spirits obey *my* will, even one who bested Gregorn!" He was shouting now, his face scarlet. This close, Miranda could feel the chains of his enslavement vibrating with his rage, and the suspended wave he held over her head began to tremble. "Soon," Renaud crowed, "even you will learn that this is the proper balance! With the wizard on top, and the spirit below!"

"If that's the case," Miranda said and smiled at him through the wall of water. "If you're so in control"—just a little more—"why is your shirt wet?"

Renaud's arm shot up to his shoulder. Sure enough, his black shirt was soaked through. He snatched his hand away, but not before a tremor of uncertainty fluttered through the enslavement that held the water captive. A tremor was all it needed. The wave roared in triumph and crashed against the enslavement's barrier. Renaud staggered and slammed his control down again. Then, with a snarl, he crashed the suspended wave down on Miranda's head.

The force of the water knocked Miranda off her feet. She spun in the freezing, dark water as the current batted her back and forth, crushing the air out of her lungs. Her chest burned as she tried desperately to hold on to what breath she could, but no matter how she struggled, the water would not let her go. It hadn't been enough, she realized as cold crept in. He'd regained his control too quickly. But even as she sank, she could still feel the echo of Renaud's uncertainty, and far below her in the icy depths, she felt a tremble of hope. As the water darkened around her, the last bubble of Miranda's breath drifted from her lips in the shape of a request. Deep at its heart, as far as possible from the iron walls of the enslavement, the water listened.

Eli was on the move as soon as the wave crashed down. Enslaver, king, Gregorn's heir, whatever he decided to call himself, Renaud was still human, and he could concentrate on only so many things at once. Eli didn't know what had possessed Miranda to taunt a man bent on destruction, but she had his full attention, and the thief was determined not to let the opportunity pass him by.

Using the water to keep himself out of Renaud's line of sight, Eli crept to the fallen ghosthound.

"Mutt," he whispered, poking Gin's side. "Wake up, mutt. Your mistress needs you."

The ghosthound was unresponsive. Only the shallow rise and fall of his chest showed that he was alive at all. Eli put a little more weight into his voice. "Gin, wake up. Miranda's going to die."

The ghosthound's breathing hitched as the spirit voice trembled through him, and one of his ears swiveled in Eli's direction.

"You are very forceful, aren't you, wizard?" Gin's voice was barely a whisper. "I'm an inch from death myself. If you have the energy to use your tricks, why don't you save her?" The ghosthound opened one enormous orange eye and focused its menacing gaze on Eli. "We both know you can."

The thief grimaced. "I'd like to, but the price of playing the hero isn't one I can afford right now. It's you or nothing, mutt."

"Not... quite..." Gin closed his eye, but one of his ears flicked toward the water, and Eli looked up.

Miranda's body hung limp at the heart of the wave. On his dais, Renaud was grinning triumphantly, but as the enslaver lowered the water to get a better look at her, the Spiritualist's head jerked up. She met Renaud's grin full on, and her spirit opened like a flower.

Despite having no bound spirits to resonate the power, Eli took a step back as her spirit washed over him. It filled the room, warm and strong as a desert wind. There was no fear in it, no doubt, only the practiced, controlled power of a master Spiritualist nearing the peak of her craft, and that power struck Renaud like a wave of lead.

The enslaver fell to the ground, unable to move. With so much power coursing through the room, Eli could almost see the outline of Miranda's fully opened spirit bearing down, not on Renaud himself, but on the channels of the enslavement, cutting away the banks that held the water spirit captive. Using the current's own ebb and flow, Miranda sawed the cutting edge of her soul against the prince's overstrained will. With every surge of Miranda's power, the feedback through Renaud's connection with the spirit slammed him into the floor, grinding him into the stone. Cracks began to appear in his enslavement, and the well-contained wave began to sprout leaks. Shouting in triumph, Miranda and the water pushed together one last time. Then, with an explosive crack, Renaud's control shattered, and water burst in every direction.

The wave holding Miranda splashed to the ground, and she landed on her back, soaked and gasping beside Gin. The ghosthound shifted his head so that his nose pressed against her heaving side.

"I told you before, thief," he said, looking at Eli as he nudged Miranda into a sitting position. "My mistress is no weakling."

Miranda looked at Gin in confusion, still coughing, but there was no time to ask what he was talking about. Renaud was still on the ground. Miranda's spirit had closed when she fell, but the effects on the enslaver didn't seem to be fading.

"What did you do to him?" Eli said, reaching down to help her up.

"Exactly what he did to me," she said, taking his hand and letting him pull her to her feet. "He's learning the ultimate difference between Spiritualists and enslavers. You see, *my* spirits serve me willingly, so when I'm knocked on my back from spirit feedback, *my* servants don't try and take advantage of the situation." Her face broke into a triumphant grin. "Renaud's may not be so considerate."

With a thundering roar, the water surged toward the dais. Renaud raised his head, his spirit swinging wildly as he tried to reassert his control, but nothing he mustered could stop the wall of furious water rolling toward him, growing larger and faster with each moment. By the time it reached the dais, the wave's crest brushed the collapsing roof. In a final act of desperation, Renaud threw the brunt of his power at it, stopping the wave for a moment at its peak. But the enslaver's exhausted, overextended will could not hold back the water's rage, and his soul crumpled. The wave crashed down with a scream, shattering the stone dais. Miranda got one last look at Renaud's body as the water tossed him up, his pale face contorted in terror as he plummeted head first back into the swirling water and disappeared beneath the waves.

The moment he hit, the whirling spirit light in the water vanished, plunging the room into total darkness. Miranda gripped Gin's fur, letting the ghosthound's heavy breathing be an anchor for her thudding heart. Slowly, her eyes adjusted, and the world began to reinstate itself. The wind whistled softly through the shattered windows and the gaping hole in the wall, peeking in to see what the fuss was about before quickly blowing away. From the darkness where Renaud had fallen came the gentle sound of flowing water, but Miranda could see nothing. The dim moonlight seemed to avoid that section of the throne room. The quiet stretched on and on, and, at last, Miranda took a tentative step forward. She jumped back immediately as something freezing and wet touched her foot. Shivering, she pressed herself against Gin's warmth and squinted into the darkness.

In the indirect glow of the moonlight, she could just make out a thin layer of water spreading out from the ruined dais. It ran past the fallen stones, over the ruined floor, and under Josef and Nico's bodies. Gin shivered when it touched him, and Miranda tore a strip out of her ruined skirt to try and stem the flow.

"We have to move," she muttered. "This water's like snowmelt. They'll die if they sit in it much longer."

"I think temperature is the least of our worries," Eli muttered, staring into the darkness where the dais had been.

Before she could ask what he meant, a flash pulsed in the darkness and warm, blue light blossomed through the room. Blinking the spots out of her eyes, Miranda turned toward the dais as well, bringing her hands up to shield her eyes. In front of them, floating above the pile of rubble that had been the royal seat of Mellinor, was a tall column of pure, clear water. It hung in the air as if weightless, spinning slowly. The light at its heart was blinding bright, like the glint on a far-off wave. Water poured from its sides like a fountain, rushing in little streams down the rocks to join the spreading pool that was quickly carpeting the entire room in clear, cold water. The turning column slowed, then stopped, and though it had no face, no distinguishing features, Miranda felt its gaze land on her.

"Wizard," the deep, deep voice shook the castle to its foundations, making little waves in the freezing shallows the throne room had become. "Thank you for freeing me from Gregorn's legacy. You have saved me from a life of madness and servitude, and I owe you a great debt. To show my appreciation, I will hold back my waters until you and your companions have escaped."

Miranda stared at the water, dumbfounded. "Hold back your waters?" She looked down at the shallow river lapping at her feet. "Spirit," she whispered. "Who are you?"

The castle trembled again as the water chuckled, sending little waves splashing against her calves. "I forget," he rumbled. "My imprisonment has been a long time by my reckoning, but how much longer is it for you humans, with your lives like mayflies? Very well, as another part of my thanks, I will give you my name." The pillar of water twisted and brightened until its light banished the shadows from the room. "I am Mellinor, spirit of the inland sea."

CHAPTER 26

The inland sea…" Miranda's voice wavered.

"All of this land was once my basin," the spirit rumbled. "From the foothills of the mountains to what is now desert, it was all mine. Until that man came." The water's light turned a deep, angry blue. "Though he trapped me deep in the cold stone and stinging salt, I remembered sunlight and moonlight, the wind on my waves, and the madness did not take me." His voice trembled, and the water began to flow more quickly. "Now, thanks to you, I shall feel the sun and wind again. I shall retake what was stolen, and, after so long alone, my waters shall lap against my shores once more."

"An inland sea," Miranda said again. She looked up at the brilliant spirit, shaking to her toes with something that had nothing to do with the freezing water covering her feet. Now she understood how this spirit could have overpowered even the great Gregorn, and why the famous enslaver had used his own life to keep it trapped. The pillar of water floating over the ruined dais was no common spirit that could be trapped in a ring or compressed into a ball. This was the glowing heart of a Great Spirit, one of the masters of the spirit world. Miranda swallowed against the lump in her throat. A Great Spirit who wanted its land back.

"Wait!" Miranda stumbled forward. "Great Spirit Mellinor, wait. Mellinor, that is, the kingdom Mellinor, which now lies in your basin, is home to thousands of people. Millions of spirits have made homes there since you were trapped four hundred years ago. If you reclaim your land, then all of those people and spirits will drown."

"And what concern is that to me?" Mellinor rumbled. "If it was not for that enslaver, those spirits would never have taken root here. They should be grateful for the time they had."

"I know Gregorn did you wrong," Miranda cried. "If I could undo your imprisonment, I would, believe me! But those people, those spirits are innocent! Please, you can't just drown them!"

"Do not tell me what I can and cannot do, wizard!" The spirit's deep voice was choppy with rage, and the column of water swelled into a breaking wave. "I take no more orders from your kind," the water roared, and Miranda braced for impact.

"Now, just a moment." Eli stepped in front of Miranda, hands in his pockets. His voice was bland and casual, but something in his tone was enough to stop the wave in midcrash. "Is that any way to talk to the Spiritualist who risked her own life to free you?"

The water retreated a bit. "And who are you to defend her?"

"Just a common thief who doesn't like the idea of drowning." Eli smiled. "But this girl here"—he slapped Miranda on the shoulder—"she teamed up with her enemies, disobeyed her orders, and stuck out her own neck, all to keep Gregorn's descendant from enslaving you. Now," he said, arching an eyebrow, "don't you think you should at least hear her out?"

The wave fell a bit, almost as if it was embarrassed. "Very well," it gurgled. "She may speak."

Eli nodded and nudged Miranda forward. For her part, Miranda was too shocked to do much besides gape.

"You can't talk to a Great Spirit like that," she hissed when Eli nudged her again.

"I just did," Eli whispered. "Now you'd better do your part, or we're all in the drink." He pushed her hard, and she stumbled out right in front of the wall of water.

She straightened up, squinting into the blinding light. The spirit loomed over her, and she wished more than anything she had not left her rings behind. Even if her spirits' powers were nothing to the sea before her, maybe they would at least have some idea how to talk to it.

"Great Spirit," she started shakily. "I know we have no right to prevent you from reclaiming your land, but if you could just wait a day or two, I'm sure we could move people and some of the spirits out of the way. Then you could reclaim your basin, and we could limit the loss of life."

She finished hopefully, smiling up at the glowing water. It did not respond. Miranda's smile faltered, and she began to fidget. "Of course, it might take some convincing to get people to—"

"Are you finished?" the great wave rumbled.

Miranda jumped. "More or less."

"Then I have heard you out. Your offer is unacceptable. I will not delay my freedom for the convenience of those who have profited from my imprisonment."

"Now hold on," Eli said, stepping up to stand beside Miranda. "If you're a Great Spirit, isn't it your responsibility to watch over the lesser spirits?"

The wave turned, angling the peak of its foaming crest directly at Eli's head. "What do you know of that, human?"

"I'm right, aren't I?" Eli said, staring up at the swirling water with his arms crossed over his chest. "I know your imprisonment was awful, but, enslaved or free, you're still a Great Spirit. Those animals and trees and all the rest living on what used to be your land, they're yours to guard just as much as the fish that lived in you when this was all sea. Even if things have changed, you can't just turn your back on them."

Without warning, the shallow water at Eli's feet geysered up, lifting the thief clear off the ground until he was level with the wave's crest.

"What would a human know of the pain of enslavement?" the spirit roared. "Who are you to lecture me when it was your kind who created this situation? You humans disgust me. You came from nowhere—blind, short lived, half deaf—and yet you were given dominion over the spirit world? Understand this, boy"—the geyser of water surged higher still, pushing Eli almost to the ceiling—"I take no more orders from your kind."

With a flick of his current, the great spirit sent Eli hurtling across the ruined hall. For a gut-wrenching moment, Eli flew silently through the dark. Then he struck the crumbling wall with a deathly thud and tumbled with a splash to the ground. Miranda held her breath, waiting for him to move, to breathe. But he did not stir. The ripples around him stilled, and Miranda felt her stomach turn to ice. Without thinking, or knowing what she could do if she reached him, she hurled herself forward, slipping and skidding across the wet floor. Before she had gone more than a few steps, a wall of water erupted, blocking her path.

She whirled on the spirit, eyes flashing. "You had no right!" she shouted. "Thief or not, he helped us, helped *you*." Her spirit roared open, stronger and brighter than it had ever been and sharp as a spear as she leveled it at the water's glowing heart.

"Come then, little girl," the wave rumbled, rising up. "If this is how your kind repays kindness, it's better I kill you like this than leave you to dirty my waters later."

"Miranda!" Gin howled, struggling to stand. "He's a Great Spirit, Miranda! Don't be an idiot!"

But Miranda's rage had taken her further than his voice could reach. With a roar, she hurled the sharpened edge of her spirit at the sea's glowing heart as the water at her feet erupted, covering everything in a great, white wave.

Eli lay on his back where he had landed, trying not to think. He tried not to think about the pain or the freezing water that soaked his lower body. He tried not to think about the waves of spirit power rolling over each other just a few feet away. He especially tried not to think about the frantic, desperate edge on the fiery spirit he had come to recognize as Miranda's, and what that kind of desperation meant for their odds of survival.

Worried about her? a familiar, silky voice whispered in his ear.

Eli started, sending a new wave of pain through his body. The sultry voice chuckled. *Such a pretty little wizardess, and so concerned for your safety*, she tsked in his ear. *These little dalliances of yours make me less inclined to help you.*

"It's not a dalliance," he muttered. "And I didn't ask for your help."

A thin, white line appeared in the air above him. It hung for a moment, shedding its ghostly white light in a surgical stripe across his chest. Then, with a sound like silk sliding through sand, a white hand reached through the cut in the air to cup his chin. Long, feminine fingers, whiter than moonlit snow, stroked his bleeding cheek, leaving a burning touch behind that was almost painful, yet never enough.

I rather like you this way, she murmured, tracing the bridge of his nose. *Broken and helpless. It reminds me of when I first found you.* That *time, you accepted me with open arms.*

"Time is a fickle master," Eli said, closing his eyes against the light. "He changes many things."

You're full of sayings today. The disembodied hand brushed past his lips and slid down his neck to his chest, tapping the gaping wound the stones had torn open when he hit the wall, just below Karon's burn. Eli sucked in a breath when she touched the ragged skin, and he felt her chuckle against his skin. *Your time is about to end, if you stay like this. Such a pity, I hate watching you squander my gifts.* Her white fingers moved in circles along his rib cage, tracing the bloodstains on his torn shirt. *Of course*, her voice slid seductively along his ear, *I could help you, if you asked nicely.*

Eli turned away. "Do what you want, Benehime."

She laughed gleefully as he said her name, and a second disembodied hand snaked through the white opening to join the first. Her palms slid over his open wound and, still laughing, she pressed down. Overwhelming pain lanced though Eli's body, darkening his vision and slamming his teeth together. It was as if every wound, bruise, cramp, and discomfort from the past twelve hours was happening again, only all at once, and amplified. He gasped and tried to jerk away, but Benehime's hands pinned him to the icy floor as surely as if he were nailed there. The pain went on and on, until he was sure it would never end and he would be stuck like this forever. Then, like the sun coming out from behind a cloud, it stopped. The pressure lifted from his chest and breath thundered back into his body.

As he lay on his back in the shallow water, gasping like a landed fish, Benehime's white hands moved to cup his cheeks. *Next time, I'll make you beg*, she murmured, trailing her burning touch across his skin one last time before drawing her hands back through the white cut in the air. *I will see you soon, my favorite star.*

The white line faded with her voice, leaving Eli staring at the empty air. It took a few moments more for her overwhelming presence to fade completely, and as his soul righted itself, he realized he could barely feel Miranda's spirit at all anymore.

Miranda was on her hands and knees in the water beside Gin's flank, panting. Her librarian's outfit was dirtied beyond recognition, and her pinned hair had tumbled in a wet tangle down her neck, clinging to her skin like red seaweed caught in the tide hole of her shoulders. She was soaked and shivering, her eyes dull and weary, but she was not beaten. They were huddled in a small circle, with Josef and Nico's heads propped on Gin's paws to keep them from drowning in the shallow water that rode in hand-high waves across what was left of the marble floor. The fact that Gin did this without complaining was proof enough of how serious the situation was. Two feet above them, held back only by the invisible bell jar of Miranda's open spirit, the wall of black water rippled in threatening patterns.

Mellinor surrounded them on all sides, his powerful current beating steadily against the thin bubble of Miranda's spirit. Each time the water crashed down, she felt her mind drowning under the endless, tireless power. Each time, it pushed her right to the edge of buckling, but each time she rallied and met the crash strength for strength, keeping their tiny bubble intact for another few seconds before the next wave hit and the struggle started all over again.

In the tiny space between the surges, the grim corner of her mind that could still think on things besides mere survival wondered why she bothered to resist.

She had done well, at first. After Eli went down, she'd been able to go blow for blow with the water for a little while. The great spirit was powerful, but his imprisonment had left him slow and weak. However, the longer he spent in the open air and moonlight, the more his power returned, and as he had gained strength, Miranda had exhausted hers. Slowly, inch by inch, the great spirit had pushed her back until he washed her under entirely. Now, trapped in a bubble with her air running out, it was all she could do to survive another wave. Of course, the grim corner muttered, just surviving wasn't winning. She wasn't even sure what the standards of victory were in a fight like this. Even if she had been stronger, more resilient, even if she hadn't let herself be trapped, her enemy was a great spirit of an inland sea. She could no more defeat him than she could defeat a mountain.

So why was she holding out, her doubt whispered. What hope was she trying to preserve? There was no help coming, no knight to ride to her rescue. Even if she could somehow get a message to the Spirit Court, Master Banage was the only wizard strong enough to have a chance against Mellinor, and he would never raise his soul against a great spirit, not even to save her. Hopelessness welled up in her chest, and Miranda choked back a sob, almost losing her rhythm as another wave crashed down. As she struggled to keep their last few feet of air intact, she couldn't banish the thought that, even if she did somehow get out of this alive, Master Banage would never forgive her for fighting a great spirit. Especially seeing as she was doing it to protect two bounty-carrying criminals and a demonseed. Perhaps it would be kinder to everyone if she dropped her shield and let the water carry them away.

"Just concentrate." Gin's gruff voice was frighteningly close to her ear, but the sound of his growl lovelier at that moment than any music in the world. "Great spirits may be old and flashy, but they're still spirits. The strength of their souls is limited by their physical form.

Your strength, a wizard's strength, is limited only by your will. That's the secret I learned back on the steppes, when I first decided to follow you." He pressed his wet muzzle hard against the small of her back. "I will watch your back, mistress, so never let your will falter."

Miranda turned and clung to him, burying her face in the coarse fur of his long nose. "I will not let you down."

The waves pounded harder than ever against the shell, but Miranda met each one blow for blow, and no water got through. With every failure, Mellinor roared and foamed, his waters churning as he struck again and was again defeated.

But just as Miranda steadied herself into this new pattern, a surge of oddly familiar spirit power shot through the black water like an arrow, freezing everything with one word.

Stop.

The waves stopped. The water stopped. Even Miranda paused, pressing her hands to her mouth to keep from crying out. Even though the word had not actually been spoken, she would know that spirit voice anywhere. It was Eli.

CHAPTER 27

Like someone had opened a drain, Mellinor's waters poured away. Miranda's bubble shattered, and she toppled over, gasping at the fresh air. Mellinor's water was still ankle deep on the floor, but the spirit's attention wasn't on her any longer. The wave had reformed itself above the shattered dais, and all its attention was focused on the gangly figure standing at the far end of the room in a circle of shattered marble.

"What a pain," Eli said, running his hands through his wet hair. "We go to all this trouble, and the spirit at the heart of everything turns out to be an ungrateful jerk." He stepped out of the crater he'd made when Mellinor threw him and smiled up at the enormous wave. "It's time to go."

"I go nowhere, boy," the sea spirit hissed, pulling his water closer.

"We'll see." Eli's smile widened, and he opened his spirit.

The room changed. Every spirit, from the stones underfoot to the air overhead to the clothes on Miranda's body, was suddenly wide awake and focused on Eli like he was the only thing in the world. His open spirit was quick and airy as it raced through the throne room, but there was something different about it, something Miranda had never felt in a spirit before, wizard or otherwise. It felt like light. There was no other way of describing it.

Eli walked casually, seemingly oblivious that he was the object of so much attention. As he walked, the spirits made way. The dirt from the flood rolled aside when he came near, so did the fallen stones and the broken glass, making a clear path. Miranda watched in amazement as the room rearranged itself to make Eli's walk easier. Even the marble trembled as he stepped on it, not with fear, but with anxiousness, as if it wanted more than anything to make a good impression as he walked the last few steps to the crumbled dais.

Mellinor had shrunk to a wavering ball. He floated over the pile of stones flashing between nervous gray and deep blue.

Eli stopped when his boots were almost touching the shattered rock that had been the first step of the dais stairs. He put his hands in his pockets and looked up at the quivering water. "Now"—the word hummed with power—"I need you to get up."

It was not an enslavement, as Miranda had been bracing for. It was a request. Mellinor shivered, sending tall waves across his surface. "How is it possible?" the water whispered. "How was I allowed to toss you like that when you bore her mark? Had I but known, had you shown me…"

"None of that matters now," Eli said. "Just get up. You're ruining what's left of Henrith's throne room."

The remaining loose water leaped back into Mellinor's sphere, and the floating ball of water churned as the sea spirit tried to make himself smaller. The best he could manage was still twice Eli's height. He was about to try again when Eli's voice stopped him.

"That's good enough," the thief said. "Now, please understand that we are, in fact, very sorry all of this happened to you. You have every right to be angry at Gregorn and his descendants, but you need to understand our position. This kingdom"—he pointed toward the ruined windows where dawn was just beginning to tint the sky—"it's not yours any more. You need to move on."

The sphere of water spun slowly on its axis, its light muted to a deep, cold blue. "Where would I go? My home was here, my seabed and my fish. Without the land, I am nothing. A homeless spirit is no better than a ghost."

"You'll go where all water eventually goes," Eli said gently. "To the ocean."

"The ocean?" The light at the spirit's heart fluttered madly. "Not there. I'll die before I go there. You'll have to kill me first."

"Why are you so afraid?" Eli said. "All of your water has been through the ocean thousands of times."

"But he hasn't."

Eli sighed and turned to watch Miranda hobble toward them, clutching her sides. Her face was pale and exhausted, and fresh yellow bruises stood out stark on her pale, waterlogged skin. Her eyes, however, were determined as she dropped to the ground beside the thief, breathing heavily.

"Water spirits flow in and out of each other," she gasped. "Rain falls and makes creeks that flow to rivers and, eventually, as you say, to the sea, but," she said and looked up at the slowly turning water, "a sea is more than the water that passes through it. Even the smallest creeks have their own souls separate from the water that fills them. You can't just blithely send that soul to fend for itself in the ocean."

"She speaks the truth," Mellinor rumbled. "The ocean is a hungry mass too large to have a cohesive soul of its own. As soon as I joined the waves, that mob of water spirits would tear me apart. They would split me into smaller and smaller pieces with each tide, and with every split I'd grow weaker and stupider, until I could no longer remember my own name."

Eli shook his head. "You'd still be alive."

"To what end?" Mellinor's light flashed wildly as the water heaved. "I'd be worse than a ghost. At least if I dry up here, I can die as myself, with my soul intact and entirely my own."

"Is that really what you would prefer?" Eli said.

The sphere bobbed in the approximation of a resolute nod. "If you won't let me have my land, yes."

Eli thought a moment, then nodded gravely. "Very well, we'll do as you ask."

Miranda looked up at Eli, horrified. "You can't just kill him."

"That's how he wants it!" Eli shouted, spinning to face her. "Were you listening at all? Why do you care, anyway? As I recall, he was trying pretty hard to kill *you* when I interfered."

"He's in this position because of us!" Miranda yelled back. "If it wasn't for Gregorn, none of this would have happened. We have a duty to make things right!"

"Make things right?" Eli flung out his arms to take in the whole of the ruined throne room. "Miranda, look around! Do you really think the masters of Mellinor are going to be happy if we tell them that everyone in the country has to move? Do you think they'll even listen? Even if they did, how long would it take to get everyone safely out? A week? A month? What's Mellinor here going to do while he waits, hang in the air? He'll evaporate before the masters finish their committee meeting. You know as well as I do that a displaced spirit has two choices: find a home or die. I don't want the second option any more than you do, but there's no place for him here, and he won't take my compromise and go to the sea, so guess where that leaves us." Eli crossed his arms and glared down at Miranda. "He's made his choice, so, for once, can you put aside your Spiritualist dogma and just let the spirit be?"

Miranda pushed herself up, her fists shaking with fury. "I won't let you kill him."

Eli met her glare head on, and they stood that way for several moments, like children having a staring contest. Finally, when it was clear she wasn't going to back down, Eli flung up his hands.

"All right," he said. "If you're so concerned, *you* deal with him."

Miranda blinked; she hadn't expected him to turn this back on her. "I don't know what to do."

Eli made a series of frantic "you see?" gestures, which Miranda ignored. Instead, she looked down at her hands. They seemed so bare and fragile with only the one small ring on her pinky. She blinked hard, then blinked again, and her head shot up. "I could take him as a servant."

Eli stopped flailing and stared at her blankly.

"He could live with me," she said, pointing at the small ring. "Then he would have a home but no one would need to be displaced."

Eli's eyes flicked skeptically from her to her pinky finger and back again. "It's an interesting idea, but you can't keep him in that, you know."

She looked down at the ring in surprise. "What? Oh, no, not this one. I mean, it's empty, but there's no way even a fraction of his spirit would fit. Besides, I'm saving it. Look," she said and took a deep breath, "forget the ring. I'm not even talking about the ring." She pointed at her chest. "I could do what you did, with the lava spirit."

"Karon was an entirely different set of circumstances," Eli said, glancing up at the hovering water. "He was also much smaller."

"I'm not saying it would be the best living situation," Miranda huffed, "but I'm pretty sure it beats the rest of our alternatives."

Eli stoked his chin, considering. "I can't lie to you," he said, "it's an incredibly stupid, reckless idea that you'll probably regret. Still, I can't think of a technical reason it wouldn't work. Of course, in the end, it's not really up to us."

They turned to look at the spirit, who bubbled as he considered the idea. "Servitude to a wizard," he sloshed thoughtfully. "You'll forgive me if I'm skeptical about putting myself in a human's hands again."

"Well," Eli said, slapping Miranda hard on the back, "I can't vouch for her character, but I'd bet money she beats dying here."

"True enough, wizard," the spirit rumbled. "I don't see as I have much choice in the matter."

"It must be by choice," Miranda said, ignoring her aching sides and straightening up to her full height. "I can only take servants who follow me willingly. However, it would be nothing like Gregorn's bond, I can promise you. As my servant, you would be subject to my command, but, in return for your service, I can offer you the Spiritualist's vow that I will never force you to act against your will or keep you if you wish to leave. I will never cast you aside for any reason, and, so long as I have breath, I will do my best to keep you from harm. I offer you power for service, strength for obedience, and my own body to act as your shore, but that is all I can give." Clenching her hands at her sides, she looked up at the churning water. "Is it enough, Mellinor?"

The water spun slowly on its axis, his light shifting softly as he thought. "It is enough, Spiritualist," the water said at last. "Your pledge is accepted."

The great sphere of water splashed to the ground. Mellinor rolled forward, forming a wave as he had before, but this time the water that engulfed Miranda was warm and gentle. It flowed up her body and snaked around her shoulders, pausing just a moment in front of her eyes, as though the spirit was weighing what he saw there one last time. Whatever the test, she must have passed, for the water rippled approvingly and, in one smooth motion, slid into her mouth.

Miranda tensed, eyes wide, as the spirit poured down her throat. From the moment she decided to offer her body as a vessel, she'd tried to ready herself for the feeling, but this was so wildly different from anything she'd ever experienced, all her mental preparations seemed laughable now that she was up against the reality. It wasn't like her other spirits. Those had felt like gaining a new limb or a close confidant. This was like gaining a new soul.

Mellinor's power surged through her body as the sea poured into her, filling every hidden nook, every fold of her spirit, even the ones she hadn't been aware of until that moment. It filled the well of her soul to overflowing, and still the water came. As the spirit's strength went on and on, she realized at last how small and pathetic her earlier attempts to fight him had been and how much he had been holding back as he tried to batter her into submission. A wave of regret surged through the water, and she instinctively forgave him everything. All that they had done wrong was pooled together now, one great ocean of fears and regrets that threatened to swallow her. Yet Mellinor's reassurances buoyed her up, and she realized that he was just as much a part of this as she was. They were horse and rider now, servant and master, spirit and human. Unequal, yet the same.

When she opened her eyes at last, she found herself on her back with no memory of how she'd gotten there. Her body ached at every joint, and yet, it all seemed so far away. Time moved in fits and starts. It should have been dawn by now, she was sure, but the throne room was darker than before. She felt a pressure under her shoulders, and she lolled her head back to see Eli crouched over her, his face closed and thoughtful. He had his arms hooked under hers and was dragging her across the floor. Miranda started to wonder where he was taking her, but then her drifting attention was caught by the wonderful sound that filled the air.

"What is that noise?" she whispered, or thought she whispered. It was hard to be sure. She wasn't quite clear yet where she ended and Mellinor began, but Eli seemed to understand.

"Rain," he said, laying her down beside Gin. "Not even your belly could hold all that water, so I sent what was left to putter itself out."

She nodded languidly. It all seemed very sensible. "Where are you going now?"

"If I told you, it would be no fun at all." Eli smiled. He reached into his jacket and pulled out something white and square, which he tucked into Miranda's skirt pocket. "Sleep well, little Spiritualist," he said, standing up with a wink. "I'm sure we'll meet again."

Miranda nodded peaceably and closed her eyes. Within seconds, everything but the lovely sound of the rain had fallen far away, and she slipped easily into a deep, dreamless sleep.

CHAPTER 28

Miranda woke slowly, her mind rising like a bubble from her deep sleep. Below her, Mellinor was still sleeping, his currents deep and calm at the bottom of her awareness. She let him be and drifted upward, the dandelion fluff of her thoughts coming and going on their own time. Everything felt wonderful, like she was floating in a warm, lavender-scented cloud while someone played music in the distance. She winced, off-key music. Unbearably off key. Her thoughts began to thicken into consciousness, falling into place while worries filled the cracks between them. Suddenly, she wasn't quite as comfortable. She hovered for a moment on the edge of sleep, fretting, and finally decided that if she was awake enough to fret about waking she might as well go all the way. At least then she could stop the awful music.

She opened her eyes to find herself buried at the center of a large feather bed. An elderly maid dozed in a chair by the bed's foot, her soft snores stirring the dust motes that hung suspended in the honeyed sunlight pouring down from the high windows. The awful music came from behind a large folding screen, which split the already small room in half. Miranda shifted experimentally, and she jumped as something heavy rolled across her chest. With some effort, she freed one of her hands from the tightly tucked sheets and groped clumsily across the comforter. After a few uncertain moments, her fingers closed around a soft leather pouch filled with the heavy, familiar shapes of her rings. An incredible feeling of relief rushed through her, and she sighed contentedly. At the sound, the sleeping maid leaped from her chair.

"Lady," she clucked, shuffling across the thick carpet to pull the sheets tighter. "Please do not move."

"Is she awake?" an excited voice called from behind the screen. There was a shuffle, and then King Henrith came bounding into view, a handsome but sloppily tuned tenor vikken dangling from his left hand. His cheeks and neck were wrapped in white bandages and there was an angry gouge across the bridge of his nose, but otherwise he looked quite well compared to the last time she'd seen him. The maid backed away reverently as he approached, and Miranda sank a little deeper into the bed.

"I was hoping you'd wake up during one of my visits," the king said, grinning. "Of course, I haven't been able to visit very often. Things have been busy, but I did think you'd enjoy some music." He held up the poor vikken by its strings. "How did you like my—"

"It was lovely," Miranda cut in. "How long have I been like this?"

"Well," the king said and scratched the top of his chin, which was the only section of his beard that wasn't covered in bandages. "Three days, I think. Really, it feels longer."

"Three days?" She clutched her ring bag. "Eli is gone, I take it?"

"Yes," Henrith said, sounding annoyed, "and all the loose gold with him, what wasn't melted to slag, anyway. Honestly, I don't think we could have expected better. I was more distracted by the state of the room and, of course, you and my brother. We thought you were dead as well, but your beast told us that you were merely suffering from exhaustion, so I asked one of the girls—"

"Gin told you?" Miranda sat up in a rush, but the pain that shot through her skull at the movement sent her right back down again.

"Well, he didn't tell us exactly." The king sat down on the nightstand. "One of the other wizard chaps spoke with him."

"Other wizards..." Miranda closed her eyes. This conversation was veering rapidly in directions she didn't think her battered mind could handle right now. "I'm sorry," she muttered. "Could you start over? From the beginning, please."

"There's not much to it," the king said. "They arrived right after I did. That night, when the shaking started and your dog ran off, I just couldn't stay put. I kept hearing these awful sounds. It was like the forest itself was trying to get away from something."

Miranda remembered the terrifying aura of Nico's uninhibited powers and shuddered. The king didn't seem to notice.

"I decided it was time to stop hiding, so I made my way back to the castle only to find everyone out in the yard because of a fire in the kitchens or some such. The kitchen staff had it well in hand, but with all the noises from the throne room and the stories the wounded soldiers were telling, no one wanted to go back in." The king chuckled. "Nobody believed I was who I said at first. It took me a good hour to convince them I really was their king, and then it was another two hours after the water stopped pouring out of the castle before I could get together a group bold enough to go inside and see what all the fuss was about.

"I'm still not quite clear on what happened," Henrith said, frowning. "But the wizards showed up about half an hour after we found you and just sort of took charge." He gave her an amused look. "It's funny, after four hundred years without them, Mellinor's suddenly up to its neck with wizards."

"These wizards," Miranda said, reaching into her leather bag, pulling out the thick, gold loop of her Spirit Court signet, "do they wear rings like me? Are they Spiritualists? How many are there?"

"That's the strangest thing," Henrith said, adjusting his bandages. "They wore no rings, and they didn't say anything about the Spirit Court. The serious fellow who leads them said he was with the League of Something or Other."

Miranda froze. "The League of Storms?"

"Yes! That's the one!" Henrith grinned. "There were more than fifty at the beginning—seemed to pop right out of thin air, gave us quite a fright, I can tell you—but most vanished again after an hour or so. Now there are maybe eight or nine. Still, they're doing a great job fixing the damage Renaud did to my throne room, and at no expense to us, so I'm inclined to let them be. Though I would like to ask you for your version of what happened that night. The doctors demanded we take it slowly so as not to risk your... Where are you going?"

Miranda had swung her feet over the edge of the bed and was shoving her rings back onto her fingers. "Thank you for your hospitality, my lord," she said in a rush. "The Spirit Court will not forget such kindness, and I will of course be happy to relate what happened in the throne room, but I can't afford to waste any more time in bed."

"Are you sure you should be getting up?" Henrith said, eyeing her suspiciously. "The doctors still aren't sure what's been wrong with you."

For a moment, Miranda considered trying to explain the dangers of opening one's spirit for prolonged lengths of time, especially to such an extreme degree as she had, and then accepting a new spirit on top of that. However, seeing the concerned look on Henrith's face, she opted for something less explanatory and more understandable.

"It's just exhaustion," she said, sliding to the edge of the fluffy mattress while ignoring the increasingly urgent calls from her muscles that standing would be a very bad idea. "I was a bit overzealous with my abilities. Luckily, I recover quickly."

Henrith arched an eyebrow at her but didn't say anything as

she took a deep breath and, gripping the heavy bed frame like a lifeline, hauled herself to her feet. It hurt every bit as much as she'd expected, but she firmly ignored the pain and set about looking for something more substantial than a woolen nightgown. Fortunately, some thoughtful servant must have anticipated this, and a delighted smile spread over Miranda's face when she saw her riding suit, freshly laundered and mended, laid out on the dresser under the window. Using the heavy furniture to support her sleep-weakened legs, she hobbled along the wall to the dresser. When she picked up her jacket, something white tumbled out of the pocket and landed on the thick carpet by her feet.

"Ah," the king said. "We found that with you, in the pocket of the librarian's uniform you, um, borrowed. It looked important, so I told them to keep it here for you."

Miranda bent down and picked up the rectangular object. It was an envelope. She turned it over. Stamped at the center of a large glob of green sealing wax was a fanciful, calligraphic *M* that she recognized all too well. However, what caught her breath was the name written across the fold in neat, precise capitals.

"Etmon Banage," she read, frowning in confusion. What in the world could that thief have to say to her master? She slid her thumbnail under the wax, but, right before it cracked, she thought better of it. No matter the source, opening the Rector Spiritualis's private mail was not a wise career move. Squishing her curiosity, she tucked the unopened letter back into her coat pocket and reached instead for her freshly pressed shirt. She draped it over her arm and turned around, looking at the king expectantly.

He looked back at her, smiling pleasantly, and showed no signs of leaving.

"Thank you for your concern, Majesty," she said pointedly. "I really do appreciate it, but I've had my time to lie about. I must do my duty."

"Fine, have it your way." The king sighed sullenly, tucking the vikken under his arm. "Just don't blame us when you get sick again. I'll wait for you in the garden."

She dropped a half curtsy as he walked back behind the screen. She heard the footman greet him, and then the scrape of the door as he left. When it closed, she gave herself a little shake and, with the maid's stony assistance, began the painful work of getting dressed.

Fifteen minutes later, Miranda was dressed and on her way to the throne room. She probably should have gone to meet Henrith in the garden first, but the League of Storms took priority over just about everything, even courtesy. She felt ten times herself again back in pants with her rings and Eril's pendant in their rightful places. Her spirits were in an uproar, both at being left behind and at the new interloper they could feel through Miranda's skin. She sent a warning thread of energy down her arms, and the ruckus quieted instantly. Miranda felt guilty forcing them down after everything that had happened, but dealing with the League of Storms was not an activity that bore distraction.

She paused at the end of the corridor and smoothed over her hair with her fingers one more time. When she was satisfied that she looked as collected and competent as she could make herself without a mirror, she turned the corner into the promenade hall and stopped dead in her tracks.

The throne room looked nothing at all as it had when she'd last seen it. The marble floor was smooth again, with no sign that it had ever been scoured by the acidic soul of a dead enslaver. The colored-glass windows were unbroken, filtering the sunlight into colorful streams that played across the gracious golden fixtures and delicate ornamental stonework, all of which was back in its proper place. The roof had been restored to its original graceful arch, and the walls were smooth and straight again, as though they'd never been broken. Only the great golden doors were immune to this miraculous repair. They hung sadly from their hinges in a cascade of melted gold and iron slag, just as Eli's lava spirit had left them.

Men in austere black coats were standing in pairs over the few remaining spots where the damage was still apparent. Most of them seemed to be lost in deep contemplation, studying the last bits of wreckage as if the shattered stones were works of art. As she watched, one of them waved his hand, and a cracked stretch of wall righted itself before her eyes.

"Should you be up, Lady Spiritualist?"

Miranda jumped at the voice, and she turned to see a handsome middle-aged man in a long black coat standing a few feet behind her with a polite smile on his face.

"My apologies," the man said and held out his gloved hand. "I did not mean to frighten you. I am Alric, deputy commander for the League of Storms."

Miranda took his offered hand firmly, keeping her eyes locked on his face. This was not the time to show weakness. "Miranda Lyonette."

"Ah," he said, smiling, "Master Banage's young protégé."

"How unfair," Miranda said, taking back her hand. "You know who I am, but I've never heard of you, Sir Alric."

"The League lives to serve, lady. We have no need to make a show of our achievements." He smiled as he spoke, but the thin-lipped expression did not reach his blue eyes. "Now"—he took her arm and began walking her toward the throne room—"to business. I was hoping you would wake up before we finished our work. I have several questions I'd like to ask you about the night all this unpleasantness occurred."

Miranda nodded. "You want to know about the Great Spirit."

"Of course not," Alric said. "That's your realm, lady, not ours.

Our interest lies in the one called Nico." He stopped, and his grip on her arm tightened. "You know what she is, of course." He smiled at her. "Tell me, then, why did you let her escape?"

Miranda stepped back, putting some space between them. "It was my duty to see to the welfare of the spirits first," she said, keeping her voice steady and neutral. "Considering the extraordinary circumstances that night, I judged her to be the lesser threat."

"The 'lesser threat'?" Alric chuckled. "I sincerely doubt that."

As he spoke, his pleasant smile took on a sinister tint and, despite the warm sunlight, a shiver ran down Miranda's spine. Suddenly, she was uncomfortably aware of just how powerful a wizard the man standing in front of her was.

"That night," Alric said, "the demonseed inside the girl awakened, correct?"

"She did change," Miranda said, choosing her words carefully. "But things were happening very quickly, and I have no experience with demons. Some of your members must have been close by, since you arrived in Mellinor in such a timely fashion. Surely you can ask one of them."

"The League can move quickly when it needs to," Alric said. "And seeing how every spirit within a hundred miles of this place was in a screaming panic on the night in question, we felt it necessary to move very quickly indeed. Thus, imagine our surprise when we arrived and found not only no demonseed but no spirits that would tell us where it had gone. I was hoping you could shed some light on the subject."

"I've told you what I know," Miranda said coldly. "She changed, and my ghosthound was injured trying to subdue her. However, one of Eli's companions was able to bring her under control, and she changed back."

"Awakened demons don't just 'change back.'" Alric leaned closer. "Isn't there something else you'd like to tell me?"

"No." Miranda glared stubbornly.

Alric's blue eyes grew colder still, but before he could speak, a man's voice called his name from the throne room.

Miranda jumped at the low, rumbling sound. Alric gave her a final warning look before turning on his heel and marching back into the throne room where the man who'd called him was waiting. The man was standing at the center of the sun-drenched hall and was wearing the same long black coat as all the rest, but Miranda was positive he hadn't been there when she'd arrived—there was no way she could have missed a man like that. He was enormously tall, close to seven feet, and every inch of him—the ready tenseness of his broad shoulders, the lightness of his boots on the stone, the clenched hand on the hilt of his long blue-wrapped sword—spoke of a man who lived for one purpose: to fight. To fight and win.

He turned as Alric approached, and his silver eyes flicked to Miranda for only a moment, but a moment was enough. She felt blinded by the intensity of his attention, the sheer weight of his focused gaze, enough to make her lungs falter. She hung on his look, pinned like a fly, until his eyes flicked down to Alric, and the air came thundering back.

Without a word, she turned on her heel and fled. Her spirits were wide awake, yet oddly silent, their attention buzzing against her shaking fingers. She shoved her hands in her pockets and walked faster. So that was the Lord of Storms. For the first time, she understood why Banage had been so adamant about leaving demon matters in League hands. The silver-eyed man did not look like someone who took well to having his affairs meddled in. She almost felt bad for Eli and Josef. If the Lord of Storms himself was here looking for Nico, it was only a matter of time before they found her. Alric had said that awakened demons don't go back to sleep and, whatever Josef's sword had done, Miranda believed him. She shuddered, remembering the flickering glow of Nico's lantern eyes. Despite Eli's pleas, she didn't see how something like that could ever go back to being human. Hopefully, the thief and the swordsman would have enough sense to give her up quietly when the Lord of Storms came, or there wouldn't be enough of them left for her to catch, much less bring back to Banage.

That thought nearly made her sick, and she put the whole affair out of her mind. Whatever horrors were yet to happen, it wasn't her problem anymore. That thought cheered her up immensely, and she threw open the door to the stables with remarkable gusto for someone who'd spent the smaller half of a week in bed.

Gin was where she knew he would be, sprawled at the center of the stable yard, eating a pig. The stains on the cobbles around him spoke of many such meals, and she stopped at the edge of the walkway, putting her hands on her hips with a mock glare. "Are you eating them out of house and home?"

"Nice to see you, too," Gin mumbled between chews. He licked his chops and rolled to his feet. Miranda winced when she saw the long, still-healing gash that ran across his shoulders, interrupting the flow of his undulating patterns.

"It's not as bad as it looks," he growled when he saw her expression. "I'm not made of paper, you know."

Miranda walked over and reached up to scratch behind his ear. "I'm glad to see you doing so well."

"So am I," Gin said, but he leaned into her scratching. "So, where now?"

"Home," Miranda said. "I have to let Master Banage know what happened, especially now that the League's involved. I think our Eli hunt is going to get a bit more hairy from here on."

"If Banage lets us keep going," the hound said. "League nonsense aside, Eli still got away with the increased bounty and more than eight thousand in loose gold. Banage isn't going to be happy about that part, and he's not the forgiving type."

"Let's cross that bridge when we reach it," Miranda said, giving him a final pat. "Finish your pig, we're leaving as soon as I find where they put the rest of my things."

They left that afternoon, after Miranda said good-bye to Marion and paid her respects to the king. Henrith was in a bit of a panic when she found him, for the league members had left just a few minutes before, vanishing as mysteriously as they had appeared.

"It really is too much," he said, slumping down in his chair. "First we have no wizards, then we have too many, and now none again."

"It doesn't always have to be that way," Miranda said, sipping the tea he had insisted she try before leaving. They were sitting in the rose garden behind the main castle, just below the throne room's windows. It, like the rest of the palace, had been repaired, but here and there the plants were bent at odd angles where the falling stones and overflowing water had crushed them. Deep inside her, Mellinor shifted uncomfortably at that thought. Miranda sent a warm reassurance before setting her cup down and meeting Henrith's dejected gaze. "The Spirit Court would be delighted to send a representative. We might not be as flashy as the League, but no country was ever worse off for having a Spiritualist."

"I think I may take you up on that offer," the king said thoughtfully. "After all, of all the wizards who've tromped through my kingdom over the past week or so, you're the only one who did right by us, and we won't forget that."

"Your Majesty flatters me," Miranda said and smiled. "Perhaps I can do you another good turn. I'm going home to Zarin to give my report to the Rector Spiritualis. Master Banage is a powerful man, and he might be able to convince the Council of Thrones to throw out Mellinor's part of Eli's bounty. I think coercion of a monarch counts as extenuating circumstances enough to justify a slight bending of the rules."

The king set down his teacup. "I appreciate the offer, but it won't be necessary. After all this ruckus, I think thirty-five thousand is the least we can do to reward the person crazy enough to catch Eli Monpress." He smiled broadly. "I hope, lady, that it will be you."

"I'm not sure if that's a compliment," Miranda said, laughing. "But I shall do my best, all the same."

In the end, he gave her three bags of the tea to take with her. She bundled them into her pack, along with the generous store of sandwiches, fruits, nuts, and bread from the palace kitchens, and secured the lot across Gin's lower back. Then she climbed into her spot right behind the ghosthound's ears and let him put on all the show he liked as they bounded over the gates and out of the town. Once on the road, she was careful not to comment when he set a slower pace, and if she made them take more breaks than they usually did, Gin didn't mention it. So, in this casual way, they crossed the borders of Mellinor and followed the trade roads north and a little east toward Zarin, the wizard city at the heart of the world.

Far to the west, on the other side of Mellinor, Eli was having a harder time of things.

"I give up," he said, turning his back on the deep, fast river he had spent the better part of an hour trying to convince to pull back its waters long enough for them to cross.

"Why don't you just give it an order?" Josef said from his perch on the enormous bag of gold. "Worked well enough on the big lake spirit back there, why not a river?"

"It was a sea spirit," Eli growled. "And that was totally different." He turned his scowl toward Nico, who was sitting on the ground beside Josef drawing patterns in the sand with a split twig.

"This is all your fault, you know," he said, pointing at her. "If you hadn't been so careless and ripped your coat to shreds, the river would have no idea what you are, and we would have been safely across thirty minutes ago. Now it thinks we're part of some vast, demonic conspiracy and is looking for a way to drown us."

As if to prove his point, the river chose that moment to splash several rocks onto the shore, which landed in the sand inches from Nico's bare knees. Eli shook his head and glanced forlornly upriver. "Nothing for it, we'll have to find a bridge and cross like normal people. Fortunately, I think there's one in our direction."

"Our direction?" Josef scratched his chest where the bandages poked above his shirt. "Where are we going, anyway?"

"Isn't it obvious?" Eli said. "We can't get anything done with Nico in that condition. We're going to get her a new coat."

"A new coat?" Josef cocked an eyebrow at the wizard. "Is that all?"

"Yes," Eli said, starting up the sandy bank. "So make sure you don't lose any of that gold. If we're lucky, we'll have just enough to pay for it."

"We've got enough gold to purchase a fully stocked villa and the noble title to go with it!" Josef said, kicking the bag with his boot heel. "What kind of coat are we buying?"

But Eli was already a good distance ahead, digging through the maps in his shoulder bag and muttering to himself. Josef rolled his eyes and stood up. With a grunt, he heaved the bag of gold onto his back and balanced it on the flat of his sword while he tied it in place. Then, with the Heart of War secured over one shoulder, and the bag of gold tied across the other, he tromped down the bank after the thief. Tossing down her twig, Nico stood and followed, fitting her small, bare feet into the swordsman's large tracks. Every few minutes, the river would send a new volley of rocks at her, which she dodged easily, never taking her eyes off Josef's back. She stayed less than a step behind him the whole way, one thin hand clutching the tattered remains of her coat and the other stretched out in front, her long fingers resting on the cutting edge of the Heart of War's blade.

ACKNOWLEDGMENTS

To my parents for raising me; Lindsay for finding me and giving the most wonderful advice; Matt for being my champion; and Devi and everyone at Orbit for taking a chance, thank you.

Last but not least, thank you Steven. You are, and always shall be, the original Eli.

VOLUME 2

The Spirit Rebellion

To my parents, for more reasons
than I can fit on one page

PROLOGUE

High in the forested hills where no one went, there stood a stone tower. It was a practical tower, neither lovely nor soaring, but solid and squat at only two stories. Its enormous blocks were hewn from the local stone, which was of an unappealing, muddy color that seemed to attract grime. Seeing that, it was perhaps fortunate that the tower was overrun with black-green vines. They wound themselves around the tower like thread on a spindle, knotting the wooden shutters closed and crumbling the mortar that held the bricks together, giving the place an air of disrepair and gloomy neglect, especially when it was dark and raining, as it was now.

Inside the tower, a man was shouting. His voice was deep and authoritative, but the voice that answered him didn't seem to care. It yelled back, childish and high, yet something in it was unignorable, and the vines that choked the tower rustled closer to listen.

Completely without warning, the door to the tower, a heavy wooden slab stained almost black from years in the forest, flew open. Yellow firelight spilled into the clearing, and, with it, a boy ran out into the wet night. He was thin and pale, all legs and arms, but he ran like the wind, his dark hair flying behind him. He had already made it halfway across the clearing before a man burst out of the tower after him. He was also dark haired, and his eyes were bright with rage, as were the rings that clung to his fingers.

"Eliton!" he shouted, throwing out his hand. The ring on his middle finger, a murky emerald wrapped in a filigree of golden leaves and branches, flashed deep, deep green. Across the dirt clearing that surrounded the tower, a great mass of roots ripped itself from the ground below the boy's feet.

The boy staggered and fell, kicking as the roots grabbed him.

"No!" he shouted. "Leave me alone!"

The words rippled with power as the boy's spirit blasted open. It was nothing like the calm, controlled openings the Spiritualists prized. This was a raw ripping, an instinctive, guttural reaction to fear, and the power of it landed like a hammer, crushing the clearing, the tower, the trees, the vines, everything. The rain froze in the air, the wind stopped moving, and everything except the boy stood perfectly still. Slowly, the roots that had leaped up fell away, sliding limply back to the churned ground, and the boy squirmed to his feet. He cast a fearful, hateful glance over his shoulder, but the man stood as still as everything else, his rings dark and his face bewildered like a joker's victim.

"Eliton," he said again, his voice breaking.

"No!" the boy shouted, backing away. "I hate you and your endless rules! You're never happy, are you? Just leave me alone!"

The words thrummed with power, and the boy turned and ran. The man started after him, but the vines shot off the tower and wrapped around his body, pinning him in place. The man cried out in rage, ripping at the leaves, but the vines piled on thicker and thicker, and he could not get free. He could only watch as the boy ran through the raindrops, still hanging weightless in the air, waiting for the child to say it was all right to fall.

"Eliton!" the man shouted again, almost pleading. "Do you

think you can handle power like this alone? Without discipline?" He lunged against the vines, reaching toward the boy's retreating back. "If you don't come back this instant you'll be throwing away everything that we've worked for!"

The boy didn't even look back, and the man's face went scarlet.

"Go on, keep running!" he bellowed. "See how far you get without me! You'll never amount to anything without training! You'll be worthless alone! WORTHLESS! DO YOU HEAR?"

"Shut up!" The boy's voice was distant now, his figure scarcely visible between the trees, but his power still thrummed in the air. Trapped by the vines, the man could only struggle uselessly as the boy vanished at last into the gloom. Only then did the power begin to fade. The vines lost their grip and the man tore himself free. He took a few steps in the direction the boy had gone, but thought better of it.

"He'll be back," he muttered, brushing the leaves off his robes. "A night in the wet will teach him." He glared at the vines. "He'll be back. He can't do anything without me."

The vines slid away with a noncommittal rustle, mindful of their roll in his barely contained anger. The man cast a final, baleful look at the forest and then, gathering himself up, turned and marched back into the tower. He slammed the door behind him, cutting off the yellow light and leaving the clearing darker than ever as the suspended rain finally fell to the ground.

The boy ran, stumbling over fallen logs and through muddy streams swollen with the endless rain. He didn't know where he was going, and he was exhausted from whatever he had done in the clearing. His breath came in thundering gasps, drowning out the forest sounds, and yet, now as always, no matter how much noise he made, he could hear the spirits all around him—the anger of the stream at being full of mud, the anger of the mud at being cut from its parent dirt spirit and shoved into the stream, the contented murmurs of the trees as the water ran down them, the mindless singing of the crickets. The sounds of the spirit world filled his ears as no other sounds could, and he clung to them, letting the voices drag him forward even as his legs threatened to give up.

The rain grew heavier as the night wore on, and his progress slowed. He was walking now through the black, wet woods. He had no idea where he was and he didn't care. It wasn't like he was going back to the tower. Nothing could make him go back there, back to the endless lessons and rules of the black-and-white world his father lived in.

Tears ran freely down his face, and he scrubbed them away with dirty fists. He couldn't go home. Not anymore. He'd made his choice; there was no going back. His father wouldn't take him back after that show of disobedience, anyway. Worthless, that was what his father had written him off as. What hope was left after that?

His feet stumbled, and the boy fell, landing hard on his shoulder. He struggled a second, and then lay still on the soaked ground, breathing in the wet smell of the rotting leaves. What was the point of going on? He couldn't go back, and he had nowhere to go. He'd lived out here with his father forever. He had no friends, no relatives to run to. His mother wouldn't take him. She hadn't wanted him when he'd been doing well; she certainly wouldn't want him now. Even if she did, he didn't know where she lived.

Grunting, he rolled over, looking up through the drooping branches at the dark sky overhead, and tried to take stock of his situation. He'd never be a wizard now, at least, not like his father, with his rings and rules and duties, which was the only kind of wizard the world wanted so far as the boy could see. Maybe he could live in the mountains? But he didn't know how to hunt or make fires or what plants of the forest he could eat, which was a shame, for he was getting very hungry. More than anything, though, he was tired. So tired. Tired and small and worthless.

He spat a bit of dirt out of his mouth. Maybe his father was right. Maybe worthless was a good word for him. He certainly couldn't think of anything he was good for at the moment. He couldn't even hear the spirits anymore. The rain had passed and they were settling down, drifting back to sleep. His own eyes were drooping, too, but he shouldn't sleep like this, wet and dirty and exposed. Yet when he thought about getting up, the idea seemed impossible. Finally, he decided he would just lie here, and when he woke up, *if* he woke up, he would take things from there.

The moment he made his decision, sleep took him. He lay at the bottom of the gully, nestled between a fallen log and a living tree, still as a dead thing. Animals passed, sniffing him curiously, but he didn't stir. High overhead, the wind blew through the trees, scattering leaves on top of him. It blew past and then came around again, dipping low into the gully where the boy slept.

The wind blew gently, ruffling his hair, blowing along the muddy, ripped lines of his clothes and across his closed eyes. Then, as though it had found what it was looking for, the wind climbed again and hurried away across the treetops. Minutes passed in still silence, and then, in the empty air above the boy, a white line appeared. It grew like a slash in the air, spilling sharp, white light out into the dark.

From the moment the light appeared, nothing in the forest moved. Everything, the insects, the animals, the mushrooms, the leaves on the ground, the trees, the water running down them, everything stood frozen, watching as a white, graceful, feminine hand reached through the cut in the air to brush a streak of mud off the boy's cheek. He flinched in his sleep, and the long fingers clenched, delighted.

By this time, the wind had returned, larger than before. It spun down the trees, sending the scattered leaves dancing, but it did not touch the boy.

"Is he not as I told you?" it whispered, staring at the sleeping child as spirits see.

Yes. The voice from the white space beyond the world was filled with joy, and another white hand snaked out to join the first, stroking the boy's dirty hair. *He is just as you said.*

The wind puffed up, very pleased with itself, but the woman behind the cut seemed to have forgotten it was there. Her hands reached out farther, followed by snowy arms, shoulders, and a waterfall of pure white hair that glowed with a light of its own. White legs followed, and for the first time in hundreds of years, she stepped completely through the strange hole, from her white world into the real one.

All around her, the forest shook in awe. Every spirit, from the ancient trees to the mayflies, knew her and bowed down in reverence. The fallen logs, the moss, even the mud under her feet paid her honor and worship, prostrating themselves beneath the white light that shone from her skin as though the moon stood on the ground.

The lady didn't acknowledge them. Such reverence was her due. All of her attention was focused on the boy, still dead asleep, his grubby hands clutching his mud-stained jacket around him.

Gentle as the falling mist, the white woman knelt beside him and eased her hands beneath his body, lifting him from the ground as though he weighed nothing and gently laying him on her lap.

He is beautiful, she said. *So very beautiful. Even through the veil of flesh, he shines like the sun.*

She stood up in one lovely, graceful motion, cradling the boy in her arms. *You shall be my star*, she whispered, pressing her white lips against the sleeping boy's forehead. *My best beloved, my favorite, forever and ever until the end of the world and beyond.*

The boy stirred as she touched him, turning toward her in his sleep, and the White Lady laughed, delighted. Clutching him to her breast, she turned and stepped back through the slit in the world, taking her light with her. The white line held a moment after she was gone, and then it too shimmered and faded, leaving the wet forest darker and emptier than ever.

CHAPTER 1

Zarin, city of magic, rose tall and white in the afternoon sun. It loomed over the low plains of the central Council Kingdoms, riding the edge of the high, rocky ridge that separated the foothills from the great sweeping piedmont so that the city spires could be seen from a hundred miles in all directions. But highest of all, towering over even the famous seven battlements of Whitefall Citadel, home of the Merchant Princes of Zarin and the revolutionary body they had founded, the Council of Thrones, stood the soaring white spire of the Spirit Court.

It rose from the great ridge that served as Zarin's spine, shooting straight and white and impossibly tall into the pale sky without joint or mortar to support it. Tall, clear windows pricked the white surface in a smooth, ascending spiral, and each window bore a fluttering banner of red silk stamped in gold with a perfect, bold circle, the symbol of the Spirit Court. No one, not even the Spiritualists, knew how the tower had been made. The common story was that the Shapers, that mysterious and independent guild of crafting wizards responsible for awakened swords and the gems all Spiritualists used to house their spirits, had raised it from the stone in a single day as payment for some unknown debt. Supposedly, the tower itself was a united spirit, though only the Rector Spiritualis, who held the great mantle of the tower, knew for certain.

The tower's base had four doors, but the largest of these was the eastern door, the door that opened to the rest of the city. Red and glossy, the door stood fifteen feet tall, its base as wide as the great, laurel-lined street leading up to it. Broad marble steps spread like ripples from the door's foot, and it was on these that Spiritualist Krigel, assistant to the Rector Spiritualis and bearer of a very difficult task, chose to make his stand.

"No, here." He snapped his fingers, his severe face locked in a frown even more dour than the one he usually wore. "Stand here."

The mass of Spiritualists obeyed, shuffling in a great sea of stiff, formal, red silk as they moved where he pointed. They were all young, Krigel thought with a grimace. Too young. Sworn Spiritualists they might be, but not a single one was more than five months from their apprenticeship. Only one had more than a single bound spirit under her command, and all of them looked too nervous to give a cohesive order to the spirits they did control. Truly, he'd been given an impossible task. He only hoped the girl didn't decide to fight.

"All right," he said quietly when the crowd was in position. "How many of you keep fire spirits? Bonfires, torches, candles, brushfires, anything that burns."

A half-dozen hands went up.

"Don't bring them out," Krigel snapped, raising his voice so that everyone could hear. "I want nothing that can be drowned. That means no sand, no electricity, not that any of you could catch a lightning bolt yet, but especially no fire. Now, those of you with rock spirits, dirt, anything from the ground, raise your hands."

Another half-dozen hands went up, and Krigel nodded. "You are all to be ready at a moment's notice. If her dog tries anything, *anything*, I want you to stop him."

"But sir," a lanky boy in front said. "What about the road?"

"Never mind the road," Krigel said, shaking his head. "Rip it to pieces if you have to. I want that dog neutralized, or we'll never catch her should she decide to run. Yes," he said and nodded at a hand that went up in the back. "Tall girl."

The girl, who was in fact not terribly tall, went as red as her robe, but she asked her question in a firm voice. "Master Krigel, are the charges against her true?"

"That is none of your business," Krigel said, giving the poor girl a glare that sent her down another foot. "The Court decides truth. Our job is to see that she stands before it, nothing else. Yes, you, freckled boy."

The boy in the front put down his hand sheepishly. "Yes, Master Krigel, but then, why are we here? Do you expect her to fight?"

"Expectations are not my concern," Krigel said. "I was ordered to take no chances bringing her to face the charges, and so none I shall take. I'm only hoping you lot will be enough to stop her should she decide to run. Frankly, my money's on the dog. But," he said and smiled at their pale faces, "one goes to battle with the army one's got, so try and look competent and keep your hands down as much as possible. One look at your bare fingers and the jig is up."

Off in the city a bell began to ring, and Krigel looked over his shoulder. "That's the signal. They're en route. Places, please."

Everyone shuffled into order and Krigel, dour as ever, took the front position on the lowest stair. There they waited, a wall of red robes and clenched fists while, far away, down the long, tree-lined approach, a tall figure riding something long, sleek, and mist colored passed through the narrow gate that separated the Spirit

Court's district from the rest of Zarin and began to pad down the road toward them.

As the figure drew closer, it became clear that it was a woman, tall, proud, redheaded, and riding a great canine creature that looked like a cross between a dog and freezing fog. However, that was not what made them nervous. The moment the woman reached the first of the carefully manicured trees that lined the tower approach, every spirit in the group, including Krigel's own heavy rings, began to buzz.

"Control your spirits," Krigel said, silencing his own with a firm breath.

"But master," one of the Spiritualists behind him squeaked, clutching the shaking ruby on her index finger. "This can't be right. My torch spirit is terrified. It says that woman is carrying a sea."

Krigel gave the girl a cutting glare over his shoulder. "Why do you think I brought two dozen of you with me?" He turned back again. "Steady yourselves; here she comes."

Behind him, the red-robed figures squeezed together, all of them focused on the woman coming toward them, now more terrifying and confusing than the monster she rode.

"What now?" Miranda groaned, looking tiredly at the wall of red taking up the bottom step of the Spirit Court's tower. "Four days of riding and when we finally do get to Zarin, they're having some kind of ceremony on the steps. Don't tell me we got here on parade day."

"Doesn't smell like parade day," Gin said, sniffing the air. "Not a cooked goose for miles."

"Well," Miranda said, laughing, "I don't care if it's parade day or if Master Banage finally instituted that formal robes requirement he's been threatening for years. *I'm* just happy to be home." She stretched on Gin's back, popping the day's ride out of her joints. "I'm going to go to Banage and make my report." *And give him Eli's letter*, she added to herself. Her hand went to the square of paper in her front pocket. She still hadn't opened it, but today she could hand it over and be done. "After that," she continued, grinning wide, "I'm going to have a nice long bath followed by a nice long sleep in my own bed."

"I'd settle for a pig," Gin said, licking his chops.

"Fine," Miranda said. "But only after seeing the stable master and getting someone to look at your back." She poked the bandaged spot between the dog's shoulders where Nico's hand had entered only a week ago, and Gin whimpered.

"Fine, fine," he growled. "Just don't do that again."

Point made, Miranda sat back and let the dog make his own speed toward the towering white spire that had been her home since she was thirteen. Her irritation at the mass of red-robed Spiritualists blocking her easy path into the tower faded a little when she recognized Spiritualist Krigel, Banage's assistant and friend, standing at their head. Maybe he was rehearsing something with the younger Spiritualists? He was in charge of pomp for the Court, after all. But any warm feelings she had began to fade when she got a look at his face. Krigel was never a jolly man, but the look he gave her now made her stomach clench. The feeling was not helped by the fact that the Spiritualists behind him would not meet her eyes, despite her being the only rider on the road.

Still, she was careful not to let her unease show, smiling warmly as she steered Gin to a stop at the base of the tower steps.

"Spiritualist Krigel," she said, bowing. "What's all this?"

Krigel did not return her smile. "Spiritualist Lyonette," he said, stepping forward. "Would you mind dismounting?"

His voice was cold and distant, but Miranda did as he asked, sliding off Gin's back with a creak of protesting muscles. The moment she was on the ground, the young, robed Spiritualists fanned out to form a circle around her, as though on cue. She took a small step back, and Gin growled low in his throat.

"Krigel," Miranda said again, laughing a little, "what's going on?"

The old man looked her square in the eyes. "Spiritualist Miranda Lyonette, you are under arrest by order of the Tower Keepers and proclamation of the Rector Spiritualis. You are here to surrender all weapons, rights, and privileges, placing yourself under the jurisdiction of the Spirit Court until such time as you shall answer to the charges levied against you. You will step forward with your hands out, please."

Miranda blinked at him, completely uncomprehending. "Arrest? For what?"

"That is confidential and will be answered by the Court," Krigel responded.

"Powers, Krigel," Miranda said, her voice almost breaking. "What is going on? Where is Banage? Surely this is a mistake."

"There is no mistake." Krigel looked sterner than ever. "It was Master Banage who ordered your arrest. Now, are you coming, or do we have to drag you?"

The ring of Spiritualists took a small, menacing step forward, and Gin began to growl louder than ever. Miranda stopped him with a glare.

"I will of course obey the Rector Spiritualis," she said loudly, putting her hands out, palms up, in submission. "There's no need for threats, though I would like an explanation."

"All in good time," Krigel said, his voice relieved. "Come with me."

"I'll need someone to tend to my ghosthound," Miranda said, not moving. "He is injured and tired. He needs food and care."

"I'll see that he is taken to the stables," Krigel said. "But do come now, please. You may bring your things."

Seeing that that was the best she was going to get, Miranda turned and started to untie her satchel from Gin's side.

"I don't like this at all," the ghosthound growled.

"You think I do?" Miranda growled back. "This has to be a misunderstanding, or else some plan of Master Banage's. Whatever it is, I'll find out soon enough. Just go along and I'll contact you as soon as I know something."

She gave him a final pat before walking over to Krigel. A group of five Spiritualists immediately fell in around her, surrounding her in a circle of red robes and flashing rings as Krigel marched them up the stairs and through the great red door.

Krigel led the way through the great entry hall, up a grand set of stairs, and then through a side door to a far less grand set of stairs. They climbed in silence, spiraling up and up and up. As was the tower's strange nature, they made it to the top much faster than they should have, coming out on a long landing at the tower's peak.

Krigel stopped them at the top of the stairs. "Wait here," he said, and vanished through the heavy wooden door at the landing's end, leaving Miranda alone with her escort.

The young Spiritualists stood perfectly still around her, fists clenched against their rings. Miranda could feel their fear, though what she had done to inspire it she couldn't begin to imagine. Fortunately, Krigel appeared again almost instantly, snapping his fingers for Miranda to step forward.

"He'll see you now," Krigel said. "Alone."

Miranda's escort gave a collective relieved sigh as she stepped forward, and for once Miranda was in complete agreement. Now, at least, maybe she could get some answers. When she reached the door, however, Krigel caught her hand.

"I know this has not been the homecoming you wished for," he said quietly, "but mind your temper, Miranda. He's been through a lot for you already today. Try not to make things more difficult than they already are, for once."

Miranda stopped short. "What do you mean?"

"Just keep that hot head of yours down," Krigel said, squeezing her shoulder hard enough to make her wince.

Slightly more hesitant than she'd been a moment ago, Miranda turned and walked into the office of the Rector Spiritualis.

The office took up the entirety of the peak of the Spirit Court's tower and, save for the landing and a section that was set aside for the Rector Spiritualis's private living space, it was all one large, circular room with everything built to impress. Soaring stone ribs lined with steady-burning lanterns lit a polished stone floor that could hold ten Spiritualists and their Spirit retinues with room to spare. Arched, narrow windows pierced the white walls at frequent intervals, looking down on Zarin through clear, almost invisible glass. The walls themselves were lined with tapestries, paintings, and shelves stuffed to overflowing with the collected treasures and curiosities of four hundred years of Spiritualists, all in perfect order and without a speck of dust.

Directly across from the door where Miranda stood, placed at the apex of the circular room, was an enormous, imposing desk, its surface hidden beneath neat stacks of parchment scrolls. Behind the desk, sitting in the Rector Spiritualis's grand, high-backed throne of a chair, was Etmon Banage himself.

Even sitting, it was clear he was a tall man. He had neatly trimmed black hair that was just starting to go gray at the temples, and narrow, jutting shoulders his bulky robes did little to hide. His sharp face was handsome in an uncompromising way that allowed for neither smiles nor weakness, and his scowl, which he wore now, had turned blustering kings into meek-voiced boys. His hands, which he kept folded on the desk in front of him, were laden with heavy rings that almost sang with the sleeping power of the spirits within. Even in that enormous room, the power of Banage's spirits filled the air. But over it all, hanging so heavy it weighed even on Miranda's own rings, was the press of Banage's will, iron and immovable and completely in command. Normally, Miranda found the inscrutable, uncompromising power comforting, a firm foundation that could never be shaken. Tonight, however, she was beginning to understand how a small spirit feels when a Great Spirit singles it out.

Banage cleared his throat, and Miranda realized she had stopped. She gathered her wits and quickly made her way across the polished floor, stopping midway to give the traditional bow with her ringed fingers touching her forehead. When she straightened, Banage flicked his eyes to the straight-backed chair that had been set out in front of his desk. Miranda nodded and walked forward, her slippered feet quiet as snow on the cold stone as she crossed the wide, empty floor and took a seat.

"So," Banage said, "it is true. You have taken a Great Spirit."

Miranda flinched. This wasn't the greeting she'd expected. "Yes, Master Banage," she said. "I wrote as much in the report I sent ahead. You received it, didn't you?"

"Yes, I did," Banage said. "But reading such a story and hearing the truth of it from your own spirits is quite a different matter."

Miranda's head shot up, and the bitterness in her voice shocked even her. "Is that why you had me arrested?"

"Partially." Banage sighed and looked down. "You need to appreciate the position we're in, Miranda." He reached across his desk and picked up a scroll covered in wax seals. "Do you know what this is?"

Miranda shook her head.

"It's a petition," Banage said, "signed by fifty-four of the eighty-nine active Tower Keepers. They are demanding you stand before the Court to explain your actions in Mellinor."

"What of my actions needs explaining?" Miranda said, more loudly than she'd meant to.

Banage gave her a withering look. "You were sent to Mellinor with a specific mission: to apprehend Monpress and bring him to Zarin. Instead, here you are, empty-handed, riding a wave of rumor that, not only did you work together with the thief you were sent to catch, but you took the treasure of Mellinor for yourself. Rumors you confirmed in your own report. Did you really think you could just ride back into Zarin with a Great Spirit sleeping under your skin and not be questioned?"

"Well, yes," Miranda said. "Master Banage, I *saved* Mellinor, all of it, its people, its king, everything. If you read my report, you know that already. I didn't catch Monpress, true, but while he's a scoundrel and a black mark on the name of wizards everywhere, he's not evil. Greedy and irresponsible, maybe, and certainly someone who needs to be brought to justice, but he's nothing on an Enslaver. I don't think anyone could argue that defeating Renaud and saving the Great Spirit of Mellinor were less important than stopping Eli Monpress from stealing some *money*."

Banage lowered his head and began to rub his temples. "Spoken like a true Spiritualist," he said. "But you're missing the point, Miranda. This isn't about not catching Monpress. He didn't get that bounty by being easy to corner. This is about how you acted in Mellinor. Or, rather, how the world saw your actions."

He stared at her, waiting for something, but Miranda had no idea what. Seeing that this was going nowhere, Banage sighed and stood, walking over to the tall window behind his desk to gaze down at the sprawling city below. "Days before your report arrived," he said, "perhaps before you'd even confronted Renaud, rumors were flying about the Spiritualist who'd teamed up with Eli Monpress. The stories were everywhere, spreading down every trade route and growing worse with every telling. That you sold out the king, or murdered him yourself. That Monpress was actually in league with the Spirit Court from the beginning, that we were the ones profiting from his crimes."

"But that's ridiculous," Miranda scoffed. "Surely—"

"I agree," Banage said and nodded. "But it doesn't stop people from thinking what they want to think." He turned around. "You know as well as I do that the Tower Keepers are a bunch of old biddies whose primary concern is staying on top of their local politics. They care about whatever king or lord rules the land their tower is on, not catching Eli or any affairs in Zarin."

"Exactly," Miranda said. "So how do my actions in Mellinor have anything to do with some Tower Keeper a thousand miles away?"

"Monpress is news everywhere," Banage said dourly. "His exploits are entertainment far and wide, which is why we wanted him brought to heel in the first place. Now your name is wrapped up in it, too, and the Tower Keepers are angry. Way they see it, you've shamed the Spirit Court, and, through it, themselves. These are not people who take shame lightly, Miranda."

"But that's absurd!" Miranda cried.

"Of course it is," Banage said. "But for all they're isolated out in the countryside, the Tower Keepers are the only voting members of the Spirit Court. If they vote to have you stand trial and explain yourself, there's nothing I can do but make sure you're there."

"So that's it then?" Miranda said, clenching her hands. "I'm to stand trial for what, saving a kingdom?"

Banage sighed. "The formal charge is that you did willfully and in full denial of your duties work together with a known thief to destabilize Mellinor in order to seize its Great Spirit for yourself."

Miranda's face went scarlet. "I received Mellinor through an act of desperation to save his life!"

"I'm certain you did," Banage said. "The charge is impossible.

You might be a powerful wizard, but even you couldn't hold a Great Spirit against its will."

The calm in Banage's voice made her want to strangle him. "If you know it's impossible, why are we going through with the trial?"

"Because we have no *choice*," Banage answered. "This is a perfectly legal trial brought about through the proper channels. Anything I did to try and stop it would be seen as favoritism toward you, something I'm no doubt already being accused of by having you brought to my office rather than thrown in a cell."

Miranda looked away. She was so angry she could barely think. Across the room, Banage took a deep breath. "Miranda," he said, "I know how offensive this is to you, but you need to stay calm. If you lose this trial and they find you guilty of betraying your oaths, you could be stripped of your rank, your position as a Spiritualist, even your rings. Too much is at stake here to throw it away on anger and pride."

Miranda clenched her jaw. "May I at least see the formal petition?"

Banage held the scroll out. Miranda stood and took it, letting the weight of the seals at the bottom unroll the paper for her. The charge was as Banage had said, written in tall letters across the top. She grimaced and flicked her eyes to the middle of the page where the signatures began, scanning the names in the hope she would see someone she could appeal to. If she was actually going to stand trial, she would need allies in the stands. However, when she reached the bottom of the list, where the originator of the petition signed his name, her vision blurred with rage at the extravagant signature sprawled across the entire bottom left corner.

"Grenith Hern?"

"He is the head of the Tower Keepers," Banage said. "It isn't unreasonable that he should represent them in—"

"*Grenith Hern*?" She was almost shouting now. "The man who has made a career out of hating you? Who blames you for stealing the office of Rector out from under him? He's the one responsible for this 'fair and legal' accusation?"

"Enough, Miranda." Banage's voice was cold and sharp.

Miranda blew past the warning. "You *know* he's doing this only to discredit you!"

"*Of course I know,*" Banage hissed, standing up to meet her eyes. "But I am not above the law, and neither are you. We must obey the edicts of the Court, which means that when a Spiritualist receives a summons to stand before the Court, no matter who signed it or why, she goes. End of discussion."

Miranda threw the petition on his desk. "I will not go and stand there while that man spreads *lies* about me! He will say anything to get what he wants. You know half the names on that paper wouldn't be there if Hern hadn't been whispering in their ears!"

"Miranda!"

She flinched at the incredible anger in his voice, but she did not back down. They stared at each other for a long moment, and then Banage sank back into his chair and put his head in his hands, looking for once not like the unconquerable leader of the Spirit Court, but like an old, tired man.

"Whatever we think of Hern's motives," he said softly, "the signatures are what they are. There is no legal way I can stop this trial, but I can shield you from the worst of it."

He lowered his hands and looked at her. "You are my apprentice, Miranda, and dear as a daughter to me. I cannot bear to see you or your spirits suffer for my sake. Whatever you may think of him, Hern is not an unreasonable man. When he brought this petition to me yesterday, I reacted much as you just did. Then I remembered myself, and we were able to come to a compromise."

"What kind of compromise?" she said skeptically.

"You will stand before the Court and face the accusations, but you will neither confirm nor deny guilt."

Miranda's face went bright red. "What sort of a compromise is that?"

Banage's glare shut her up. "In return for giving Hern his show, he has agreed to let me give you a tower somewhere far away from Zarin."

Miranda stared at him in disbelief. "A tower?"

"Yes," Banage said. "The rank of Tower Keeper would grant you immunity from the trial's harsher punishments. The worst Hern would be able to do is slap you on the wrist and send you back to your tower. This way, whatever happened, your rings would be safe and your career would be saved."

Miranda stared at her master, unable to speak. She tried to remind herself that Banage's plans always worked out for the best, but the thought of sitting silently while Hern lied to her face, lied in the great chamber of the Spirit Court itself, before all the Tower Keepers, made her feel ill. To just be silent and let her silence give his lies credence, the very idea was a mockery of everything the Spirit Court stood for, everything *she* stood for.

"I can't do it."

"You must do it," Banage said. "Miranda, there's no getting out of this. If you go into that trial as a simple Spiritualist, Hern could take everything from you."

"It's not certain that Hern will win," Miranda said, crossing her arms over her chest stubbornly. "Tower Keepers are still Spiritualists. If I can tell the truth out in the open, tell what actually happened and show them Mellinor, let the spirit speak for himself, there's no way they can find me guilty, *because I'm not.*"

"This is not open for debate," Banage said crossly. "Do you think I like where this is going? This whole situation is my fault. If you had another master, this would never have grown into the fiasco it is, but we are outmaneuvered."

"I can't just sit there and let him win!" Miranda shouted.

"This isn't a game, Miranda!" Banage was shouting, too, now. "If you try and face Hern head-on, you will be throwing away everything we worked together to create. You're too good a Spiritualist for me to let you risk your career like this! You know and I know that you are guiltless, that your only crime was doing the right thing in difficult circumstances. *Let that be enough.* Don't fool yourself into thinking that your fighting Hern on this will be for anything other than your own pride!"

Miranda quaked at the anger in his voice, and for a moment the old obedience nearly throttled her with a desperate need to do what Master Banage said. But Mellinor was churning inside her, his current dark and furious, his anger magnifying hers, and she could not let it go.

Banage must have felt it, too, the angry surge of the great water spirit, for she felt the enormous weight of his spirit settle on top of her as the man himself bowed his head and began to rub his eyes with a tired, jeweled hand.

"It's late," he said quietly. "A late night after many long days is no time to make weighty decisions. We'll pick this up tomorrow. Maybe after a night's rest you'll be able to see that I am trying to save you."

Miranda's anger broke at the quiet defeat in his voice. "I do see," she said, "and I am grateful. But—"

Banage interrupted her with a wave of his hand. "Sleep on it," he said. "I've given orders for you to be under house arrest tonight, so you'll be comfortable at least. We'll meet again tomorrow for breakfast in the garden, like old times. But for now, just go."

Miranda nodded and stood stiffly, mindful of every tiny noise she made in the now-silent room. As she turned to leave, she stopped suddenly. Her hand went to her pocket and fished out a white square.

"I'd almost forgotten," she said, turning back to Banage. "This is for you."

She laid the envelope on his desk. Then, with a quick bow, she turned and marched across the great stretch of empty marble to the door. Pulling it open, she plunged out of the room and down the stairs as fast as her feet could carry her.

Banage watched the door as it drifted shut, the iron hinges trained after centuries of service to never slam. When the echo of her footsteps faded, Banage let go of the breath he'd been holding and let his head slump into his hands. It never got easier, never. He sat for a while in the silence, and then, when he felt steady enough to read whatever she had written him, he let his hand fall to the letter she had placed on his desk.

When he looked at the letter, however, his eyebrows shot up in surprise. The handwriting on the front was not Miranda's, and in any case, she never addressed him as "Etmon Banage." Curious, he turned the letter over, and all other thoughts left his mind. There, pressed deep into the soft, forest-green wax was an all-too-familiar cursive *M*.

Banage dropped the envelope on his desk like it was a venomous snake. He sat there for a few moments staring at it. Then, in a fast, decisive motion, he grabbed the letter and broke the seal, tearing the paper when it would not open fast enough. A folded letter fell from the sundered envelope, landing lightly on his desk. With careful, suspicious fingers, Banage unfolded the thick parchment.

It was a wanted poster, one of those mass-copied by the army of ink-and-block spirits below the Council fortress. An achingly familiar boyish face grinned up at him from the creased paper, the charming features older, sharper, but still clearly recognizable despite more than a decade's growth. His mocking expression was captured perfectly by the delicate shading that was the Bounty Office's trademark, making the picture so lifelike Banage almost expected it to start laughing. Above the picture, a name was stenciled in block capitals: ELI MONPRESS. Below the portrait, written in almost unreadably tiny print so they could fit on one page, was a list of Eli's crimes. And below that, printed in tall, bold blocks, was WANTED, DEAD OR ALIVE, 55,000 GOLD STANDARDS.

That's what was printed, anyway, but this particular poster had been altered. First, the 55,000 had been crossed out and the number 60,000 written above it in red ink. Second, the same hand had crossed out the word WANTED with a thick, straight line and written instead the word WORTH.

"Eli Monpress," Banage read quietly. "Worth, dead or alive, sixty thousand gold standards."

A feeling of disgust overwhelmed him, and he dropped the poster, looking away as his fingers moved unconsciously over the ring on his middle finger, a setting of gold filigree of leaves and branches holding a large, murky emerald as dark and brooding as an old forest. He stayed like that for a long, silent time, staring into the dark of his office. Then, with deliberate slowness, he picked up the poster and ripped it to pieces. He fed each piece to the lamp on his desk, the heavy red-stoned ring on his thumb glowing like a torch as he did so, keeping the fire from spreading anywhere Banage did not wish it to spread.

When the poster and its sundered envelope had been reduced to ash, Banage stood and walked stiffly across his office to the small, recessed door that led to his private apartments. When he reached it, he said something low, and all the lamps flickered, plunging the office into darkness. When the darkness was complete, he shut the door, locking out the smell of burnt paper that tried to follow him.

CHAPTER 2

Eli Monpress, the greatest thief in the world, was strolling through the woods. His overstuffed bag bounced against his back as he walked, and he was whistling a tune he didn't quite remember as he watched the late afternoon sunlight filter through the golden leaves, bringing with it a smell of cold air and dry wood. So pleasant was the scene, in fact, that it took him a good twenty paces to realize he was walking alone.

He stopped on his heel and spun to see Josef, his swordsman, sitting twenty paces back in the middle of the path with Nico, Josef's constant shadow, sitting beside him. Beside her, Josef's famous sword, the Heart of War, stood plunged into the hard-packed dirt, and beside it lay the enormous sack of gold they'd liberated from Mellinor's sadly destroyed treasury. Despite the fine weather, none of them looked happy.

Eli heaved a dramatic sigh. "What?"

Josef stared right back at him. "I'm not taking another step until you tell me exactly where we're going."

Eli rolled his eyes. *This again.* "I told you before. I told you this *morning*, we're going to see a friend of mine about getting Nico a new coat."

"I didn't ask what we were going to do when we got there." Josef folded his arms over his chest. "I asked you, *where are we going*? We've been walking vaguely north for days now, and since yesterday we've been walking in circles around the same four miles of woods. This is the second time today we've passed that beech tree, and I'm tired of lugging your ill-gotten gains." The sack of gold jingled as his large fist landed on it. "Admit it," the swordsman said, giving Eli a superior sneer. "You're lost."

"I am not." Eli threw out his arms, taking in the scant undergrowth, rocky slopes, and slender, white-barked trees of the small valley they were in the middle of climbing out of. "We're in the great north woods, which the Shapers call the Turningwood, and the Council of Thrones doesn't have a name for because we left the Council maps a while ago. Specifically, we are in the Thousand Streams region of the Turningwood, a name you might appreciate, considering all the valleys we've had to climb through. Even more specifically, we are in the northeast corner of the Thousand Streams, where the streams are slightly less numerous. A little farther north and we'd be in the foothills of the Sleeping Mountains themselves, and a little farther east and we'd hit the frozen swamps on the coastal plain. So, as you see, I know exactly where we are, and it is exactly where we are supposed to be."

Despite such a grand display of navigation, Josef did not look impressed. "If we're where we're supposed to be, why are we still walking?"

Eli turned and started up the hill again. "Because the house of the man we are looking for isn't always in the same place."

"You mean the man isn't always in the same place," Josef said, making no sound of following him.

"No." Eli panted as he reached the crest of the valley. "I mean the house. If you don't like it, complain to him."

"*If* we ever find him," Josef said.

Eli shook his head and started down the other side of the hill, wishing that the swordsman would apply his stubbornness to something useful, like being a perfect gold carrier, or finding them something tastier than squirrel to eat. By the time he'd reached the bottom of the next valley, Josef had still not crested the ridge of the one before. Eli grimaced and kept walking, though more slowly and with one ear out for the sound of jingling gold, which would tell him if this was just a Josef bluff or if he was actually going to have to go back and push the man up the hill. Fortunately, the decision was rendered moot when he took another step forward and found nothing but air.

He yelped as the world spun upside down and sideways. Then, with a sharp pain in his ankles, it stopped, and he found himself hanging high in the branches of a tree. Blinking in surprise, Eli looked down, or up, depending, and saw he was strung up by his ankles in the branches of a large oak. That much he'd been prepared for, but how he was hanging took him by surprise. Instead of ropes, a knot of roots with dirt still clinging to them bound his feet, ankles, and lower legs. They moved as he watched, creaking with a sound very much like snickering. He was still staring at the roots and trying to figure out what had just happened when he heard Josef come over the hill. Eli craned his neck and started to yell a warning, but it was too late. The second Josef was off the rocky ravine, a snaking cluster of roots erupted from the ground and grabbed his feet. The swordsman flew into the air with a lurch and came to rest neatly beside Eli.

"Well," Eli said. "Fancy meeting you here."

Josef didn't answer; he just scowled and bent over, wiggling his foot. There was a flash, and a long knife dropped out of his boot before the roots could tighten. The swordsman caught it deftly an inch from Eli's face and bent over, reaching for the closest root.

"I wouldn't do that," Eli said, glancing up, or down. "It's a bit of a drop."

Josef followed his gaze. The ground swung dizzyingly a good thirty feet below them, but the drop was made even longer by the enormous hole the roots had left when they'd sprung. Josef shook his head in disgust and stuck the knife into his belt. "I thought you were friends with trees."

"For the last time, it doesn't work like that," Eli said. "That's like saying, 'I thought you were friends with humans.' Anyway, don't be a grouch. We've found it! This is the Awakened Wood that guards the house."

Josef sighed. "Wonderful. Fantastic welcome. Is your friend always this friendly, or are we a special exception?"

Before Eli could answer, a woman's voice interrupted.

"Eli Monpress." The words were heavy with laughter. "I wouldn't have thought we'd catch you."

Both men craned their necks. Directly below them a tall young woman in hunter's leathers stepped out from behind the tree they were dangling from, a smug smile on her tan face. She was very young, not more than sixteen, and lanky, as though she hadn't quite grown into her limbs yet. She crossed her long arms over her chest and stared at them as though daring Eli to try and talk his way out of this one. Eli opened his mouth to oblige her, but he never got the chance. From the shadows behind the girl, a pair of white, thin hands in silver manacles shot out and closed around her throat. The girl's eyes bulged and she dropped to her knees as Nico flickered into sight behind her.

"Release them," Nico said in a dry, terrifying voice. "Now."

"No, Nico!" Eli shouted. "She's not going to—"

The rest of it was lost in the girl's roar as she ducked and tumbled forward, using Nico's own iron grip to take the smaller girl with her, slamming them both into the ground with Nico on the bottom. As soon as she was on top, the girl elbowed Nico hard in the ribs. Nico gasped, and her grip faltered. The girl shot up, rolling gracefully to her feet. When she turned around, she had a long, beautiful knife in her hands, the blade glowing with its own silver light.

Nico was back on her feet in an instant, and for a breathless moment the two watched each other. Then the girl in the hunting leathers shook her head and slid her knife back into the long sheath on her thigh.

"I begin to understand why you needed that coat," the girl said, not taking her eyes off of Nico. "Let them down, gently please."

The tree made a sound like a disgruntled sigh and lowered its roots, releasing Eli and Josef just a little higher than would have been a safe drop. The men landed hard in the dirt, and while Josef was on his feet almost immediately, Eli took a bit longer to get his breath back.

"Hello, Pele," he coughed, trying to discreetly determine if his back was broken. "Always a pleasure."

Pele arched an eyebrow. "Can't say I feel the same." She glared at Nico, who was still watching her from a crouch. "Must you always bring such trouble?"

"Trouble is my element," Eli said, sitting up. "And is that any way to greet a customer?"

"Your custom is usually more trouble than it's worth," she said with a frown. "Get up. I'll take you to Slorn."

"Wait," Josef said. "You mean Slorn as in Heinricht Slorn? The swordsmith?"

"He makes a lot of things besides swords," Pele said crossly. "But yes, that Slorn, and he's going to be testy if you make him wait. Now follow me, quickly. We've wasted enough time rolling in the dirt."

"And whose fault was that?" Eli muttered, but the girl was already disappearing into the woods, slipping between the trees like a passing sunbeam.

"You never told me you knew Heinricht Slorn," Josef said, walking over to where he'd dropped the Heart of War. He almost sounded hurt.

"I couldn't," Eli said, picking the leaves out of his hair. "Not talking about him is part of knowing Slorn. He'd never sell me anything if he thought I'd been spreading his location about, or the fact that he really exists. Most people think he's a myth made up by the Shaper Wizards to sell more swords. When that tree sprung, I was half afraid he was going to have the Awakened Wood toss us out altogether because I'd brought you two. But, seeing he sent his daughter out to greet us, I think it's safe to assume we've captured his interest enough to at least get our pitch in."

"Daughter, huh?" Josef said, picking up the Heart and sliding it into its sheath on his back. "She's pretty good to throw Nico around. Must be some kind of family."

"That's one way of putting it," Eli said, wincing as he stretched his bruised back. "We should get moving, though. Pele was right about Slorn's hatred of waiting. The man is brilliant, but..." He paused, brushing the dirt off his coat as he searched for the right word. "Eccentric."

Josef snorted. "Funny way of putting it, coming from you."

Eli just gave him a look and set off through the trees.

Though she'd entered the woods only moments before them, there was no sign of Pele's passing. Eli, Josef, and Nico stumbled in the direction she'd gone, following the dry streambed that was the best they could do for a path. Now that Pele had come out to greet them, the trees were whispering openly, and what they had to say made Eli's ears burn.

"Honestly," he muttered, kicking a sapling as they passed. "She's *right here.*" He looked over his shoulder. "Don't listen to them, Nico! They're just a bunch of prejudiced, gossipy old hardwoods with nothing better to do."

The trees rustled madly at this, but Nico just kept walking with her head down, giving no sign that she heard his voice or theirs. Eli looked away. The girl was looking bad. She'd been unusually quiet since they'd left Mellinor, even for Nico, and while she'd been eating as normal, she seemed to be getting thinner. Eli didn't know if that was just the effect of seeing her without her bulky coat all the time, or if he just thought she was larger than she was, but he'd heard Josef talking to her about it as well, at night when the swordsman thought he was asleep. Also, no one, wizard or otherwise, could miss the way her manacles danced on her wrist, jittering across her skin even when she was sleeping. That was new since she'd lost the coat, and Eli didn't like it one bit. Overhead, the trees were whispering again, and Eli gritted his teeth, picking up the pace as they pushed through the thickening woods.

Fortunately, they didn't have much farther to go. The woods opened up just a few steps later, and they found themselves at the edge of a sandy-bottomed valley. At the center, sitting crooked on what had been the sandy bank of a now-dead stream, was a house. It was two stories and heavy-timbered, with a shingle roof and a tall chimney made of river stones. It was a handsome house and well constructed, but quite normal looking until you got to the foundation. There, things took a turn for the bizarre. Where a normal house would have sat on the ground, or stood on stone supports, this one crouched on four wooden legs. They were made of the same dark wood as the cabin, beautifully carved with scales and lifelike wrinkles right down to the clawed feet. At first glance, this could have been passed off as eccentric architecture, but then the legs moved, like an animal shifting its weight, and the house shifted with them.

"No matter how many times I see it," Eli said, "I never get used to it." He set off across the sand, dragging Josef, who was still gawking, along behind him.

Thanks to the legs, the house's doorstep was a good five feet off the ground. The gap was covered by a set of rickety stairs that would have been suspect in a normal building, let alone a moving one.

"I hate this part," Eli said, grabbing the rope banister as the house shifted again. "I'm already feeling seasick."

"Just go," Josef said, giving him a push. Eli grunted and stumbled forward, pulling himself up enough to knock on the door.

It was opened immediately by a scowling Pele.

"Took you long enough," she said, stepping back. "Come in and don't hang on the stairs. They're set to go any day now."

"Ever the charming and comforting hostess," Eli said as he lurched into the house. Josef and Nico followed more gracefully, and Pele shut the door behind them.

They were standing in a tiny entryway lined with pairs of oiled boots and racks of heavy coats. Eli pressed himself against the wall, partially to make room for Pele to get by and partially to steady himself against the sway of the house as it rocked on its spindly wooden legs. If the motion bothered Pele, she didn't let on; she simply turned and motioned for them to follow her down a long, narrow hallway riddled with doors to other rooms. They passed a sitting room stuffed with books, a small kitchen with a warm hearth and a heavy table piled with chopped vegetables, and even a stone-tiled bathroom complete with an iron tub and a barrel full of steaming water. As they walked, Eli could hear the house adjusting to accommodate their presence, the scrape of chairs scooting themselves under tables when they passed the kitchen, or open books slamming shut on the library desk. Josef must have heard it, too, for the swordsman's hands went to rest on the blades at his hip. Eli let him be nervous. Explaining the complex ecosystem of Slorn's house was more work than he had the patience for at the moment.

The long hallway ended at a closed door. Pele stopped and knocked softly. Almost instantly a deep voice inside rumbled, and Pele pulled the handle.

Almost too late, Eli remembered this was Josef and Nico's first time visiting Slorn. A warning of some sort was probably wise.

"Remember," he whispered over his shoulder as they stepped through the door. "Don't stare."

Josef gave him a confused look, but then they were walking through the door and his eyes went wide as Eli's meaning became clear.

They were standing at the end of a long, well-lit room with a cheery fire in the hearth and a dozen lamps swinging from the tall rafters. Long as the room was, it was mostly taken up by a heavy table large enough to seat eight full-grown men, but which was currently covered with everything from pieces of driftwood to incredibly intricate parts of unknown machinery. At the table's head, an enormous man sat hunched over, working an iron ingot between his enormous hands like a potter works clay. At first glance, he could have been one of the giant, northern woodsmen, but with one slight, important difference. At his shoulders, where his neck should have been, rose the furry head of a black bear.

It was a sharp change, human skin suddenly giving way to black fur, as though the man's own head had been chopped off and a bear's put in its place. But other than the horrible wrongness, it was a natural transition. The man part of him looked like any other man, and the bear part looked like any other bear. His nose was black and wrinkled and it quivered under his slow breathing. Yellow teeth glinted in a jaw that could crush a man's head, but his dark, wide-set eyes were calm and thoughtful as they watched the iron yield to his hands. Although Eli knew what to expect, a shudder ran from his feet to his head. No matter how many times it happened, seeing Slorn was always a bracing experience.

"You're staring," said a gruff voice, more growl than speech. The bear looked up, his dark eyes passing over Eli's shoulder to the man behind him. "I heard Monpress tell you not to do that."

Eli heard the creak of leather as Josef's hands tightened on the knives at his hip, and the bear-headed man made a low rumbling sound that was eerily close to a chuckle. "Don't insult my house with those dull blades, swordsman. Unless you mean to draw the monster on your back, or the monster at your side"—his dark eyes flicked to Nico, who was pinned to Josef's arm—"I suggest you calm down."

Josef relaxed slightly, and the bear grinned, a disturbing sight. "Come," Slorn said. He tossed the iron down and motioned to the bench. "Sit and tell me how I might get rid of you."

"Now, Heinricht," Eli said, plopping down at the table across from him, "is that any way to treat your customers?"

"I'm a craftsman," Slorn said, resting his furry chin on his knuckles. "Not a shopkeeper. Get to the point."

Eli leaned forward. "You see that timid little thing beside my swordsman?" he whispered conspiratorially. "I need you to make her a new coat."

Slorn's dark eyes flicked over to the girl who was huddling in the doorway, as far from the bear-headed man as she could get, her eyes wide and disturbingly bright. They stared at each other for a long minute, then Slorn gave Eli a tired glare.

"When you asked for a cloth that could hide a demonseed's presence," he said, "and manacles to hold it down, I made them. I did it in thanks for the great service you had done me, and I asked no questions. But the debts between us are paid, Monpress. I took the risk of letting you find me today out of respect for our history together, but understand that doing what you ask now will put me in a very tenuous position. What compensation have you brought to make it worth my while?"

Eli's smile brightened, and he motioned to Josef. The swordsman hefted the sack of Mellinor's gold, which he had lugged halfway across the known world for this purpose, walked over to the table, and set it down with a very satisfactory thump. Eli reached out and undid the leather strap, letting the gold spill out in a glittering cascade.

"A king's ransom," he said smugly. "Well, part of one. There's enough in there to buy you a castle, though it'd be up to you to put legs on it. I think that should more than cover one little coat."

Slorn looked at the pile and then at Eli. "I asked you what compensation you'd brought. All I see here is a lot of money."

Eli's smug expression faltered just a hair. "Surely even the great Heinricht Slorn needs to buy things on occasion."

"If I wanted *money*"—Slorn spat the word with disgust—"I could get more than this from far better company." He leaned back, folding his arms over his massive chest. "What else did you bring?"

"False hopes, apparently." Eli sighed. "Look, bearface, we're in a bit of a bind." His hand shot out and grabbed Nico's wrist, pulling her out from behind Josef and pinning her arm to the table before she could react. He pressed it down, letting the sound of the manacle rattling against the wood make his point for him.

"I don't have to tell you what that means," he said softly, meeting Slorn's dark, animal stare. "You made them. If you don't want gold, tell me your price and I'll steal it for you, but if you're not going to help us, just say so and we'll get out of your fur."

Nico tugged her hand out of Eli's grasp, but he didn't look at her. He kept his eyes on the bear-headed man, who was scratching his muzzle thoughtfully.

"Perhaps we can come to an arrangement," Slorn growled at last. "I've been doing some work on my own, and I think I can make your girl a coat better than the one before. Something made to withstand your"—he paused, looking them over—"harsh lifestyle. In return, however, I want you to do a job for me."

Eli arched his eyebrows. "And what kind of job would this be?"

"Something right up your alley, I'd think," Slorn said. "I'm afraid that's all I can tell you before we have an agreement."

Warning bells sounded in Eli's head, and he gave the crafter a suspicious look. "It's not usually my policy to make deals without knowing what I'm getting into."

Slorn shrugged. "If you don't like it, you're free to go and find a coat elsewhere. Better decide quickly, though. Your demonseed is starting to make the furniture nervous."

As if on cue, the bench they were sitting on started to rumble and tried to tip backward. Josef slammed his feet and leaned forward, pinning it with his weight. Eli shook his head and turned back to the bear-headed man.

"You make a good point," he said. "All right, we'll take your job, *but*"—he pointed his finger directly at Slorn's snout—"you're making the coat first. Nico's an important part of my team. I need her in peak condition if we're going to do a job, especially one you won't tell me about beforehand."

On the other side of Josef, Eli heard Nico straighten up, and a warm feeling of satisfaction went through him. Perhaps the girl wasn't as unfeeling as she made out.

Slorn, however, did not look convinced. "How do I know you won't just run off?"

Eli clasped his chest. "You wound me! I would never risk losing your good opinion, or all the nice toys you keep making me."

"Fair enough," Slorn said, standing up. "You have your deal. Pele, take the girl upstairs and measure her. I'll start on the cloth tonight."

Pele nodded and pushed off the wall she'd been leaning on. She looked at Nico and jerked her head in the direction of the tiny staircase that led to the house's attic. "This way."

If possible, Nico's face went paler. She looked at Josef, almost like she was asking permission, but the swordsman just stared right back at her. Biting her thin lip, Nico left Josef's side and crept up the stairs after Pele, keeping her arms crossed over her chest and staying as far from the walls as she could. When she reached the tiny landing, she gave Josef and Eli one last terrified look before Pele ushered her into a brightly lit room and shut the door behind them.

"They won't be long," Slorn said, moving across the room with surprising lightness for such a tall, broad man. "We need to move quickly. The manacles were never meant to do their job alone."

"I thought the coat was just a cover," Josef said, standing up. "A front to hide what she is so the spirits won't panic."

"That's part of it," Slorn answered. "But demons feed on all parts of a spirit, including fear. In the absence of its cover, the seed has been gorging, and not just on the fear around the girl, but on her own as well. As it eats, it grows, and as it grows, the girl's fight to keep her mind becomes harder and harder." The bear-headed man knelt down by a chest that opened instantly for him, the lid popping up of its own accord. "I cannot undo the damage that has already been done, but I can slow down the process by hiding what she is, cutting off the demon's food source and allowing Nico to regain some measure of control."

He stopped searching through the trunk and turned to look at them, his bear eyes dark and sad. "You understand, of course, that this is only a delay. No matter how many layers of protection we swaddle the girl in, so long as she lives, her seed will continue to grow. Whether it comes tomorrow or a year from now, the end will be the same. The demonseed will eat her, body and soul, and there will be nothing you can do."

He was looking at Eli as he spoke, but it was Josef who answered, and the vehemence in his voice made them both flinch.

"Nico is a survivor," the swordsman said. "When I found her, she was a breath away from death. I waited for her to die, but she didn't. She kept breathing. Every breath should have been her last, but she always found another. She'll beat this, too, bear man, so make the damn coat."

Slorn stared at him in abashed silence, but Josef ignored him and stood up. "I saw a bath on the way in." He slid the Heart of War from his back and dropped it on the table with a resounding gong from the iron and a painful shudder from the wood. "If Nico asks, that's where I'll be. If anyone else needs me, they can wait."

With that, he turned and stomped off down the hall. Slorn watched him go, looking as astonished as a bear could. Eli just watched from his seat at the table, grinning like a maniac.

"He certainly doesn't mince words," Slorn said, turning back to the chest.

"No," Eli said and grinned wider. "That's why I like him."

Slorn shook his head and turned back to the chest.

Eli watched him for a moment, but he could see the work settling on the bear-headed man's shoulders like a vulture, and he decided it was time to move somewhere more comfortable before Slorn forgot him completely.

"I'm going to freshen up as well," he announced. "I presume the guest bedroom is still in the same place?"

"More or less," Slorn said. "Top of the stairs, third door on the right."

"Third door, much obliged." With a gracious nod, Eli gathered his bag and set off up the stairs, leaving Slorn alone in the great room. On the broad worktable, the enormous pile of gold glittered in the fire light, forgotten by everyone.

CHAPTER 3

Gin was asleep in the flower bed that surrounded the low building where Miranda kept her chambers when she was in Zarin. His legs kicked in his sleep, sending the well-turned dirt flying, and his shifting patterns swirled in strange, spiraling shapes across his body, all except for the patch between the shoulder blades. There, the wound from his fight with the demon girl Nico stood out like a red brand beneath the dried layers of green polluce the stable master had smeared over it. It looked better than before, but it would never be part of his patterns again. Even in his sleep, he seemed to favor the wound, cringing away from it whenever he rolled over.

Suddenly, his dream running stopped. He lay perfectly still, except for his ears, which swiveled in quick circles, each moving independently from the other. The night was as quiet as a city night could be, but Gin jerked up, his orange eyes wide open, watching the corner of the building. A few moments later, Miranda flew around it. She saw him at once, and ran toward him, moving strangely, keeping her breathing almost too regular and her face down so that the last evening light couldn't touch it. This was probably to keep Gin from seeing that she was crying, but his mistress had never fully appreciated just how much his orange eyes could pick up, especially in low light.

Still, he played along, rolling over and sitting up properly as she came near, his tail wrapped around his paws. Miranda didn't slow when she reached him, didn't say a word. She slammed into him and slumped down, and though she never made a sound, the salty smell of tears filled the air until he had trouble breathing. After several silent minutes, Gin decided to take the initiative. After all, if they needed to escape, it would be best to do it now, before the lamps were lit.

He lowered his head until he was level with hers. "Are you going to tell me what's wrong?"

Miranda made a sound somewhere between a curse and a sob. Gin growled and nudged her with his paw. "Don't be difficult. Spit it out."

"It makes me so angry!" Her answer was a whip crack, and Gin flinched. Miranda muttered an apology, scrubbing at her eyes in a motion he was probably not supposed to notice. "It's just…How could they do this to me? How could they betray me like this? All my life, from the moment I understood that the voices I heard were spirits, all I've wanted was to be a Spiritualist. To do good and defend the spirits and be a hero and all the stuff they tell you when you start your apprenticeship. And now here I am, on trial for making the decisions the Spirit Court trained me to make. It's not *right*!"

That last word was almost a wail, and she buried her head in her hands. Gin shifted anxiously. He hadn't seen her this upset in a long time.

"Try to remember that I've been in a stable having cold, foul-smelling gunk smeared on my back all evening," he said. "Could you be a little more specific?"

Miranda leaned back against him with a huff and, in a quick, clipped voice, told him everything. The arrest, her meeting with Banage, the accusations, and Hern's compromise.

"A compromise, can you believe it?" she said, digging her fingers into the dirt. "Extortion is more like it."

"Being a Tower Keeper doesn't sound so bad," Gin offered.

"It *wouldn't* be," Miranda said, "if I were getting the promotion for any reason other than Hern playing on Master Banage's sense of duty toward me! Oh, I hate to think what other concessions Master Banage had to make to get that out of Hern. The man is a slime."

"But if Banage already made the concessions, why not take the offer?" Gin said, sweeping his tail back and forth. "The problem is the Tower Keepers thinking your actions reflect badly on them, right? So let them have their trial. If you're right and Hern's only doing this to make Banage look bad, why give him more fodder by fighting? He can't find fault if you keep strictly to the role of the dutiful Spiritualist."

Miranda gave him a sideways look. "That's a very political answer for a dog who always says he doesn't understand politics."

"I don't understand politics," Gin growled. "But I understand pride, and that's what this is really about. Sometimes the price of doing the right thing is higher than we realize when we do it. Knowing the consequences, would you have acted differently in Mellinor?"

Miranda froze and thought for a second. "No," she said firmly.

"There you have it," Gin said with a shrug. "So pay the price. Take the out Banage bought you, appease the Tower Keeper's pride, and move on."

"I will not," Miranda said. "Maybe it is about pride, mine as much as anyone's, but I cannot, *will* not, bow to Hern's bullying. Those things he accuses me of *did not* happen, and I will not stand by while he smears my name and my spirits with his lies."

"So, what, you're just going to throw Banage's help away?" Gin growled. "What about the part where losing this trial could lose you your spirits? Your pride is your own, and I respect your right to beat yourself bloody over it, but we're not something to be thrown away so cheaply."

"That won't happen," Miranda said fiercely, gripping her hands until her rings cut into her fingers. "Trust me, we've got right on our side. We won't lose, especially not to Hern."

Gin looked at her, his orange eyes narrowed to slits. "And would you bet all of us on that?"

Miranda didn't answer. They sat in silence for a while, staring out at the darkening streets. Gin sat very still, watching in the way that spirits watch. He could see each of Miranda's spirits, the flow of their souls pulsing softly with the beating of her heart. Each spirit shone softly with its own unique color, and below them, buried deep within Miranda's own bright soul, Mellinor's spirit turned in his sleep. The Great Spirit was enormous and alien even to Gin, ancient beyond comprehension, yet it was also a part of Miranda now, and dear to him because of it, even beyond the natural reverence he owed a Great Spirit. Each glowing spirit, even Mellinor, had a tendril reaching out from its core. These were the bonds, the strong, deep network of binding promises, at the center of which was Miranda. All of them, even the tiny moss spirit, had abandoned their homes to follow her. From the moment they'd sworn their oaths, she'd become their center, their Great Spirit, their mistress, worthy of service. The thought of being taken from her made him afraid in ways he hadn't felt since he was puppy. Yet the Spirit Court could do that, if it chose. Miranda's oath had forged the bonds, but every one of those promises had been made under the authority of the Court. So long as Miranda believed in that authority, the Court owned her rings and the spirits inside, even him. As with all human magic, it all came down to will. So long as Miranda wasn't willing to go against the organization she'd pledged her life to, they were all bound to the Spirit Court's whims. Still, the choice was Miranda's, and despite what he'd said, Gin knew her well enough to know her decision. So he waited patiently, watching as the city lamps flickered on, the tiny fire spirits winking to life as the lamplighters walked the districts, filling the dark streets with soft, dancing light.

When Miranda answered at last, her voice was small but steady. "Gin," she said, "I have always lived my life according to principle. I believe more than anything that there is right and there is wrong, and that the gap between them is wider than any words can bridge. No amount of good intentions or clever plans can turn one into the other. What we did in Mellinor, for Mellinor, was the right thing. I will not sit by and let anyone say it wasn't."

"Does that mean you're going to fight?"

"Yes," Miranda said and smiled, tilting her head to look up at him. "To the great inconvenience of everyone involved."

"The life of principle is never convenient," Gin said with a toothy grin. "At least not that I've seen."

Miranda laughed, and Gin got up with a long stretch. "Now that that's decided," he growled, "you should get inside. You're crabby when you haven't slept."

Miranda stood up stiffly, brushing the dirt off her trousers and looking forlornly at the deep rut Gin had made in the flower bed. "The garden committee is going to kill us."

"Eh," Gin said, shrugging. "You're already on trial for treason. What more could they do?"

Miranda rolled her eyes at that, but she was smiling. As Gin nosed her toward the door of her building, she caught his muzzle in her hands and gave him a serious look.

"Thank you," she said, "for being a pushy ass."

"What else am I here for?"

Miranda shook her head and walked into her building, trudging up the stairs to the tiny suite of rooms the Spirit Court allotted all traveling Spiritualists. Gin watched her until she was out of sight, then moved out to the alley to watch the light come on in her window. The lamp flickered, and then, a minute later, the room went dark again. Satisfied that things would be fine until tomorrow, Gin ambled back to his flower bed and flopped down, resting his head in a soft, sweet-smelling clump of something silver-green with furry leaves, and, after scarcely two breaths, promptly fell back to sleep.

Far away from the low, plain buildings where the common Spiritualists kept their rooms, at the other end of the Spirit Court's district where the architecture took a turn for the large and ornate, Grenith Hern was sitting on his balcony enjoying a bottle of wine. Bright light from his sitting room shone through the open double doors, highlighting the graying gold of his long, straight hair and casting his shadow in perfect contrast on the empty street below, a fine, trim figure in fine, trim clothing. This was not by chance. Hern often sat this way in the evenings, for he enjoyed the picture he presented, and the view of the city was very fine.

From here he could look down the ridge to see the lamps flicker on, one pair at a time. As he watched them, he couldn't help thinking, as he always did when he spent his evenings at home, how, if he were Rector Spiritualis, he would have put every lamp spirit in the city under the control of a single fire, so that they could all be lit at once. The current method of lighting with a pair of lamp lighters walking around telling the lamps when to flare was old-fashioned and inefficient, not to mention a horrible waste of an opportunity to make the Whitefall family owe the Spiritualists a favor for something that would cost the Court very little. Still, there was nothing to be done as he was merely Head of the Tower Keepers, and he certainly wasn't about to give Banage the idea.

Hern sighed at the waste and refilled his glass, his lace cuff holding itself neatly out of the way of the dark wine. He was just about to take a sip when he heard the sound he'd been sitting on the balcony waiting to catch: the whisper of dust as it moved up the smooth white marble of his townhouse walls. He turned his chair to face the far corner of his balcony as a stream of dark-colored dust began to collect in the tray he'd left out for it. He waited patiently as the dust gathered, forming a thin layer at first, then growing to a large pile. As it collected, a smell began to collect in the air, char and smoke, and it quickly became clear that the powder on the tray was not, in fact, dust, but fine, gray ash.

When the last of the ash had collected, Hern leaned forward, a smile on his slightly lined but still handsome face. "You're early. I hope it's good news."

The ash sighed, sending a smell of burnt hardwood into the air. "For your information, it's been a very difficult day. I will never get used to moving about in such a spread-out fashion, being stepped on and losing bits of myself in the street. It's not to be borne."

Hern made a tsking noise. "Come now, Allio. You're far more useful as a pile of ash than you ever were as a tree."

"I'm glad you think so," the ash snapped, sliding away from Hern in a sulk. "Considering it was your fault I got burned."

Hern shrugged. "You knew the risks when you took the oath. Come, enough complaining. What news do you bring?"

The ash made a grumpy sound, but it gathered itself into a neat pile and began its report. "I put myself in Banage's office, just as you told me. Sure enough, he had the girl brought straight to him. They had quite the argument." The ash rippled wistfully. "Now *those* are Spiritualists. Such conviction, and the spirit the girl had in her, I haven't seen the like since I was rooted in my own forest."

Hern kicked the tray, and the ash quickly got back on topic. "Banage did just what you said he would. He made the offer and left out all the particulars."

"And?" Hern prompted.

"And she didn't take him up on it," the ash finished. "He cut her off and sent her away before she could deny him outright, but I get the impression she's not the kind to take the easy road."

Hern leaned back in his chair, feeling very pleased with himself. "She'll fight for certain, then. I'd bet money on it."

"You'll have to if you want to win," the ash said. "It's one thing to scare old Tower Keepers into signing a paper, but something else again to get them to vote against her in front of the whole Court. You're going to need to put your gold where your mouth is before this is over, I think."

"Ash doesn't think," Hern snapped. "Leave the details to me. Anyway, money won't be an issue. The duke will be coming into town tomorrow, and this is as much an issue for him as it is for me. In the meanwhile, I want you to go to every Tower Keeper who came into town for this event and invite them over. I feel the need to throw a party."

"*Every* Tower Keeper?" the ash said. "Master, I've been out all day. I can't spend all night crawling through town bringing your invitations to *every* Tower Keeper. It's impossible, I—"

"Allio," Hern said, drumming his fingers on his chair, his rings glittering in the light. "I have twenty-one other spirits making demands on my energies. It's very tiring, and I've been thinking I should cut the dross. Now, more than ever, is the time to prove yourself useful. After all, I think I have already been kinder than most, keeping you as my spirit even after the unfortunate burning incident. What a shame if I were forced to give you up now, just because you weren't willing to put in a little extra effort, don't you think?"

The ash swirled on the platter, making little hissing noises. After a few turns, it stopped and lay flat in a defeated heap. "Of course, Master," it said softly. "I wouldn't dream of disappointing you."

"I know you wouldn't," Hern said with a cool smile. "Off with you, then."

The ash bowed and slithered off the platter, disappearing over the balcony's edge with a soft rasp. Hern, however, was already up, walking into his parlor and yelling for his housekeeper to wake up and prepare the kitchen, for he was going to have guests. Once the old woman was roused, Hern locked himself in his office and pulled out the notes he'd prepared for just such an occasion. Making Banage compromise to save his favorite had been sweet, but this promised to be far sweeter, and his face broke into an enormous grin as he leaned over and began to write out his speech.

By the time the first of the Tower Keepers arrived, he was well into his conclusion and feeling more confident than ever that here, at last, was his chance to take something precious from Banage once and for all. When he dropped his pen and went out to greet his guests, he was all confident smiles and charm, and for once, not a bit of it was faked.

CHAPTER 4

The sun was barely over the valley edge when Eli emerged, yawning and disheveled, from the house on legs. As he climbed down the rickety steps, he noticed with surprise that the house was about fifteen feet farther down the dry riverbed from where it had stood the night before. Eli paused a moment, wondering whether he should be concerned that he'd slept right through the move, but he let it go with a shrug. Such things were to be expected when you visited Slorn.

On the flat stretch of sand where the house had stood yesterday, Slorn was already hard at work. He was standing still, stroking his muzzle with long, patient fingers. All around him, laid out in a rough circle with the bear-headed man at its center, was an enormous collection of sewing materials. There were bolts of cloth, enormous spools of thread, skeins of yarn, scissors, buttons, needles, everything you could think of to make a coat. For the most part, Slorn just stood there, still as a statue, but every few minutes he would walk over to one of the objects, a length of silk, say, or a pin poked in a wad of dyed wool, and stare at it hard, like it was the only thing worth looking at in the entire world. He didn't seem to notice Eli, not even when the thief walked up to the edge of his circle and cleared his throat. Eli, quickly tired of not being noticed, left the craftsman to his flotsam and went to look for his swordsman.

He didn't have to go far. Josef was on the opposite side of the house, where the dry river had cut below the tree-lined bank. Nico was with him, as always, perched on a flat white stone with her chin in her hands, watching. She was wearing an outfit that must have been Pele's at one point, a girl's cut sleeve shirt and matching large-pocketed pants that actually fit, for once. It was a nice change from her usual threadbare attire, but her hard look warned off any compliments Eli might have made before she turned her eyes back to Josef.

For his part, the swordsman paid his audience no attention whatsoever. Despite the cold morning air, Josef was shirtless. He'd taken off the bandages as well, and the wounds from his fight with Coriano stood up in red, puckered lines against his pale, scarred skin. The Heart of War was in his hands, its black, dull blade like a hole in the morning light. He held it out in front of him, the muscles in his arms straining against the weight, as though he'd been holding it like that for a long, long time. Then, without warning, Josef pulled the blade back and swung. The enormous sword moved lightning fast, almost too fast for Eli's eyes to keep up with it, flying toward the thin trunk of a sapling. Just before it hit, the blade stopped with a whistle of terrified air, its notched, dull edge quivering less than a hair's width from the sapling's smooth white bark. The tree creaked and shuddered, dropping a snow of tiny, white-green leaves to join the growing pile at its base.

"It's a good thing Slorn's on the other side," Eli said, taking a seat next to Nico. "I don't think he'd like you scaring his trees naked."

Josef pulled back the Heart to its first position. "Daily training is the breath of swordsmanship."

"Profound," Eli said. "But can't you breathe on something less excitable?"

Josef lowered his sword and looked at him. "Do you mind?"

Eli shrugged and leaned back on the warm stone, watching in silence as Josef prepared to take another swing. As the swordsman moved, Eli couldn't help but notice how Joseph's injuries seemed to be dragging on him. Though Josef never flinched or showed any sign of pain, there was a hitch in his movements at the point in the swing when his arm stretched too far, a certain pause in his steady breaths that made Eli supremely uncomfortable.

"Josef," he said hesitantly, "we're going to be here for another day at least; why don't you take a break? Enjoy the scenery or something?"

"I am enjoying it," Josef said as he swung his sword again at the poor, terrified sapling.

"Why are you training so hard, anyway?" Eli said. "Don't most swordsmen let their old wounds heal before they start prepping to get their next ones? You beat Coriano. Can't you let it go for just a little bit?"

Josef stopped midswing and plunged the Heart into the sandy creek bed.

"Eli," he said, leaning hard on the hilt of his sword, "do you know how I beat Coriano?"

Slightly taken aback, Eli guessed, "Thoroughly?"

"I used the Heart," Josef said, nodding to the blade. "So, though he is dead and I am alive, I lost. It was the Heart who beat him, not me."

"But the Heart can't move without you," Eli pointed out.

"Don't mistake the Heart's power for mine," Josef said bitterly. He straightened up, pulling the blade out of the sand and returning it to first position. "All my life, I've had one goal: to push myself as far as I can go. To be the strongest I can be. If I let the Heart win all my battles for me, then what's the point of even holding a sword?"

The question didn't require an answer, and Eli didn't offer one. Point made, Josef turned his attention back to his sword, preparing for the next swing. Seeing that any further conversation was pointless, Eli shoved his hands in his pockets and walked back toward the house in search of breakfast.

An hour later he was bathed, dressed, and helping himself to a plate of fruit, bread, and whatever else he could find in Slorn's pantry when Josef and Nico finally came in. The girl took a seat on one of the stools along the wall, but Josef walked straight through the kitchen to the large water barrel, grabbing a bucket from the shelf as he passed. He dipped the bucket in the barrel, filling it to the brim with the cold water and, after a bracing breath, proceeded to dump the whole thing over his head. Eli jumped back with a yelp, dancing away from the flying water as Josef gave himself a shake.

"You're a wonderful houseguest, you know that?" Eli said, wiping the water off the table. Josef just shrugged and helped himself to an apple from Eli's plate. He leaned against the heavy wooden table as he ate, staring through the window. Outside, Slorn was still standing in his circle of sewing materials, his bear head warped to monstrous size by the wobbly glass.

"He gives me the creeps," Josef said quietly, taking a bite out of what had been Eli's apple.

"How so?" Eli said. "Is it because of the—" he made a gesture, outlining a muzzle in the air in front of his face.

"More than that." Josef looked around at the small, tidy kitchen. "This whole place has been giving me the creeps since we came in. Rugs that slide out of the way before you step on them, cabinets shutting themselves when they've been left open. It's not natural. And then there's the constant feeling that we're being watched." Josef grimaced. "It's like the whole house is alive."

Well, Eli thought, munching a block of yellow cheese, it had been bound to come up sooner or later. He was only glad he didn't have to give this explanation in front of Slorn. The bear-headed man was a stickler for particulars, and Josef explanations required lots of glossing over.

"Not alive," Eli said, "*awake.* Like an awakened sword, only this time it's cabinets and plates." He held up his empty breakfast plate. "Awakening an entire house is pretty extreme, but that's Slorn for you."

Josef gave him a flat look that was dangerously close to not caring, and Eli tried again. "I know 'wizard stuff' isn't exactly your forte, but try and follow me here. You know about awakened blades, right? Well, this is an awakened house. Unlike a sword, though, a house isn't just one spirit, but hundreds, maybe thousands, all working together. That's how it moves. The legs work with the supports, which work with the nails, which work with the hearth. None of these could move the house on its own, but together they're far more powerful. The secret is getting them to work as a team. It's called 'spirit unity,' and it's a very secret and well-guarded Shaper wizard technique. Even I don't know exactly how Slorn does it, especially with so many small, sleepy, mundane spirits. I've tried asking, but he bites my head off every time I bring it up, something about respecting Shaper secrets."

"So Slorn's a Shaper," Josef said, looking out the window. "I've heard stories, but I've never met one."

"And you're not likely to," Eli said with a shrug. "They keep to themselves. Of course, technically, you still haven't met one. Slorn's an ex-Shaper."

Josef's eyebrows shot up. "What, did he get kicked out?"

"Kicked out or left on his own." Eli said. "I don't know which for sure. But I do know it had something to do with how he got that head."

They both looked out the window where the bear-headed man was still working, this time kneeling in the sand and drawing something with a long stick, muttering to himself.

"How *did* he end up like that?" Josef said softly. "Did the Shapers curse him or something?"

"Powers, no," Eli said, laughing. "There's no such thing as a curse. Slorn's head is his own doing, though, again, I don't know the particulars. I've known Slorn for a long time, but he's tight-lipped about the past. He's had that head the whole time I've known him, though. All I know is that it used to be the head of the great bear spirit that watched over these woods. The bear and Slorn made some kind of deal, and Slorn ended up with a bear's head but a man's body and mind. I don't know why he did it, but I know one thing for sure." Eli pointed two fingers at his eyes. "Those black eyes of his aren't just for show. They're bear eyes, real ones, and they can see as spirits see."

Josef gave him a curious look, clearly not comprehending how impressive this was, so Eli explained further. "You know how wizards are humans who can hear the voices of spirits, right? Well, even the best wizards can't see the spirit world. We can feel it sometimes, especially if the spirits are very strong, but we can't see it. It's like we as a species lack that sense, like our eyes are only half functional, seeing only half of the world. That's why spirits are always complaining about human blindness, because to them, we are blind. Most spirits don't even see as we do. Like this table." He knocked on the heavy wood he was leaning against. "It has no eyes, no sense of vision as we think of it; yet to it, we're the blind ones. But Slorn's different." Eli turned to gaze out the window. "He can see as they see, and that gives him a tremendous advantage as a craftsman. The things he makes are literally on an entirely different level from other goods, even other Shaper stuff, because Slorn is the only human crafter who can actually *see* what he's doing."

Josef pursed his lips. "Why in the world did the Shapers kick him out, then? If he's that good, I'd think they'd be after him like mad."

"They would be," said an annoyed voice behind them. "If they could find us."

Eli, Josef, and Nico whirled around to see Pele leaning against the doorway, looking cross. Eli relaxed when he saw her, but Josef looked put out, and Nico looked deadly furious. Neither of them was used to people being able to sneak up on them. For her part, Pele just crossed her arms and gave the three of them a sour look.

"Next time you decide to gossip about your host," she said, "don't do it inside his awakened house. When I tell you the walls have ears, it's not a figure of speech."

"Don't be prickly, Pele," Eli said. "If your walls were listening, they know I didn't say anything to my companions I haven't said directly to Slorn's face. Have a little faith in me, darling."

Pele looked skeptical. "Slorn wants to see you outside. All of you."

Eli, Josef, and Nico exchanged a look, then stood up and filed out. Pele brought up the rear, but Eli hung back, letting the swordsman and the demonseed outpace them.

"So," he said quietly, glancing at Pele, "it's 'Slorn' all the time, now?"

"Shaper tradition requires distance between a master and his pupil," Pele said. "Technically, as my father, he shouldn't be teaching me at all, but it's not like there's anyone else." She looked up as they exited the house, staring north at the distant snowcapped mountains. "I don't even remember the Shaper mountain."

"Well," Eli said, putting an arm around her shoulder, "you're not missing much. It's dreadfully boring."

Pele shot him a glare, and Eli removed his arm before she did it for him, hurrying down to the riverbed to stand beside Josef at the edge of Slorn's circle.

Slorn himself was standing at the center beside the carefully stacked pile of materials that had passed his rigorous examination. His bear face was impossible to read, but his movements were anxious as he motioned his guests closer.

"I've finished material preparations for the coat," he said gruffly. "But before I begin the cloth, I'll need to take one final measurement."

"What?" Josef said. "Did the girl miss an inch last night?"

"This measurement can't be taken with tape," Slorn said. "This coat doesn't just hide Nico's body; it hides the nature of her soul, and what lives inside it. For that, I need to take Nico up into the mountains." His dark eyes flicked to Josef. "Alone."

"Why?" Josef said, hand drifting to the Heart's hilt. "What do you need that you can't do here?"

"Those are the terms," Slorn said. "If you don't like them, you can leave."

Josef looked supremely uncomfortable, and Eli was about to say something to deflect the tension when Nico stepped forward, her cracked-leather boots soundless on the packed sand. "I'll go."

Eli blinked in surprise. "Are you sure?"

Nico just gave him a scathing "of course" look over her shoulder before going to stand at Slorn's side. The bear-headed man nodded and turned to Pele. "Bring these"—he pointed to the pile of materials at his feet—"to my workroom. Eli, you and your swordsman can put the rest back into storage."

Eli gaped at him. "What part of our deal says we're your grunt labor?"

But Slorn had already turned and started walking toward the woods, Nico following close behind him. Pele just grinned and started gathering the chosen materials. A moment later, Josef started picking things up as well. When it was clear he wasn't going to be able to get out of this one, Eli sighed and started lugging bolts of cloth into his arms, muttering under his breath about Shaper wizards and the dreadful decline in service. Josef, however, was ignoring him. The swordsman picked up the balls of yarn and yards of cloth with only half an eye to what he was grabbing. His real attention was on the trees, where Nico and Slorn had vanished into the forest's shadow, and nothing Eli said could draw him away from them.

Nico and Slorn moved silently through the forest. They followed no path, but they did not need one. The trees parted for them, the young hardwoods creaking softly as they lifted their branches. Slorn nodded his thanks as he passed. The trees rustled in return but then grew still as Nico walked by.

They walked without speaking until they reached the foot of a steep, leaf-strewn slope. There, Slorn began to climb, his heavy boots moving surely over the slick leaves. Nico followed more cautiously, digging her hands into the wet leaf litter to keep from slipping. They climbed for a long time, and as they got higher, the trees began to change. Slender oaks and birches gave way to heavier, darker trees Nico couldn't name. They clung to the slope in great knots of root and stone, looming enormous and dark, their black leaves blotting out the sunlight until the ground was a dim patchwork of shadows.

As they climbed in the dark, the need to flit ahead through the shadows was overwhelming. Why, something inside Nico whispered, should she crawl like an animal? She could have been at the top ten times over by now. But Nico forced the feeling down. Such thinking was dangerous. Shadows were the demon's highway, and moving through them, even for a short jump like this, always made her feel like a shadow herself. Without her coat, it was easy to lose focus, to forget to come out of the dark. Easier for the thing inside her to go places it shouldn't, the places in her mind where she hoarded her humanity. A cold, clammy feeling began to wrap around her, and Nico shook her head, focusing her attention to a dagger point on Slorn's back as they trudged on. To stay with Josef, to stay human, she needed to keep her mind clear, sharp. It was only a little longer. She would see what Slorn wanted her to see, and then go back. Easy, simple. She repeated those words again, and deep in the dark behind her eyes, something began to snicker.

Finally Slorn stopped. They were high now, the air cold and heavy with the smell of snow. The strange trees were shorter here, thinner, and Nico caught glimpses of blue sky through the branches. Yet the sun seemed to shy away from them, leaving the thin woods at the top of the slope darker than ever. Everything was quiet. Despite their height, no wind rustled the trees, and no animals moved in their branches. The slope was still, a heavy, unnatural stillness that pressed down on Nico like deep water, and she had the strong feeling she should not be here.

"What you are feeling is the valley's warning," Slorn said softly, turning to face her, his gruff voice grating against the silence. "We woke it years ago and tasked it with keeping things away."

Nico looked around, confused. She didn't see a valley, just the slope and the strange trees. Slorn saw her confusion, and he motioned for her to look at him, his voice becoming deathly serious.

"What I am about to show you," he said, "you must tell no one, not even your companions. If you cannot promise me this, I cannot make your coat. Will you promise?"

Nico looked up at him hesitantly. No one, not even Josef, had ever asked her to promise something. She thought about it a moment, weighing the weight of a secret against the necessity of her coat and her own growing curiosity, and then she nodded.

Slorn turned and walked up the slope, motioning for her to follow. Nico did, slowly, fighting against the growing certainty that she should turn around and run while she still could. She was so focused on putting one foot in front of the other that she almost didn't see Slorn's shape flicker ahead of her, as though he'd walked through a curtain of water. A step later, Nico felt it rush over her as well, intensely cold and strange, as if the air itself was moving to let her pass. It was only for a moment, and then the world around her changed. She was standing beside Slorn, still on the slope, still surrounded by the strange trees, only now she was balanced on the edge of a knife-sharp ledge looking down at a valley that had not been there a moment before. It was a small, narrow thing, barely fifteen feet across and maybe thirty feet long, more like a fissure in the slope than a valley. There were no trees growing nearby, yet the light was somehow dimmer than ever. When she looked down into the cleft, shadows flowed like a river, making it impossible to tell how far down the crack in the stone went.

Nico frowned. She wasn't used to shadows hiding things from

her. But as she leaned forward to get a better look, a familiar, terrifying feeling crashed into her. It took her over, passing through her senseless body like a spear and landing hook first in her mind. No, deeper. This feeling, the sense of grasping claws, of an endless, gaping, ravenous hunger, of being trapped, of being crushed, was deeper than mind or thought. For an eternity, it was all Nico could do to hold on to the tiny flickering light of herself until, inch by inch, the darkness subsided. Rough, warm hands were shaking her shoulders. She didn't remember falling, but Slorn was helping her to her feet. Already the feeling was fading like a dream, but deep inside her, something curled closer, drinking it in.

"I'm sorry." Slorn sounded genuinely upset. "I didn't know it would affect you like that."

"What is it?" Nico whispered, shrinking away from the ledge. Yet even as she asked, she knew. She knew the demon hunger as well as she knew her own breath. Slorn's answer was to step aside, and very slowly, Nico looked again. The gully was the same; so were the shadows, but the overwhelming wave did not come back. Relieved, Nico stared into the darkness until it gave way, and the dark bottom of the valley came into focus. It was a dry, dead place. The bottom was sandy, as if water had flowed there once, long ago. Now there was nothing but rocks and the scattered leaves of the dark trees lying dry and brittle on the sand. And at the farthest, deepest end, sitting cross-legged on a large, flat stone, was a woman in a long, black coat.

She sat very still, her head bowed so that her hair, wispy and dark, fell to hide her face. Her hands, skeletally thin and pale, were folded in her lap, while at her wrists, gleaming dully in the dark, a pair of silver manacles trembled. She wore a silver collar at her neck as well, and rings on her ankles. All of them were shaking, buzzing like bees against her skin so that, even this far away, Nico could hear the faint, hollow clatter of rattling metal.

The woman gave no sign that she saw Nico and Slorn on the ridge above her. She sat as still as a doll, the shaking bindings at her wrists the only movement in the gully. Yet the more Nico stared, the more the woman's very stillness seemed to move and crawl. The cold feeling began to gnaw at Nico again, and she was forced to look away.

"Is she alive?" Nico said, looking back at Slorn.

"Oh yes," Slorn said, looking down at the woman with a sad look in his dark, animal eyes. "Very much alive."

"She's a demonseed." It scarcely needed to be spoken, but Nico said it anyway, as if having it out clear and simple like that could somehow make the woman in the dark less terrifying.

"That she is," Slorn said softly. "Her name is Nivel. She is my wife."

"Your wife?" Nico's voice was trembling now. She knew very little about things like wives, but it seemed wrong that the woman should be alone here in the dark under the open sky, miles away from home.

Slorn must have followed the same line of thought, for his answer was fast and defensive. "It was her choice," he said. "She chose to live here in the valley so that when she awakened she could not hurt her husband, her child, or anyone else. The valley helps her by keeping innocent spirits away. No rain falls inside those walls, no trees sprout, no wind blows."

"Nothing to feed the demon," Nico finished softly. "But how does she live? Humans must eat."

Slorn clenched his fists. "In the five years since I lowered her down there, Nivel has taken neither food nor water. She doesn't sleep and she doesn't move. But her will, her human will, is still there, still fighting. So, in the only way that truly counts, she's still my Nivel. Still human, even now."

Nico didn't see how someone who never ate or slept could be

called human, but she held her tongue. Slorn looked down at the woman in black again and his voice grew very sad.

"Over the last decade I have pledged everything: my life, my work, my place as a Shaper"—he raised his hand to his furry face—"even my humanity to finding a way to bring Nivel back from the brink. Yet for all my work, all I've managed is to slow the inevitable. The coats I make, the manacles, these are all just stopgaps, ways to starve the demon, to restrain it and keep it distracted." Slorn bared his teeth. "Ten years and I am no closer to finding a cure than I was at the beginning." He looked at Nico. "Do you understand why I am telling you this?"

Nico shook her head.

"Because, unlike your swordsman, I refuse to give false hope. That's why I brought you here." Slorn took Nico's shoulders and turned her to face the dark gully again. "Look sharply. What you see down there is your future, the unavoidable end. I've heard about what happened in the throne room of Mellinor. I know you've gone over the edge and come back. It's a trick not many can pull off, but no one returns unscathed." His hands tightened on her shoulders. "No one is strong enough to play with the demon and come back every time. No one can hold off the demon forever. Even if you resist with everything you have, a demonseed is something outside of human or spirit understanding. It is a predator, and we, all of us, humans and spirits, are its prey. Just as the sheep cannot fight the wolf, we cannot fight the demon. Eli brought you here for a coat, but I cannot make one for you until you understand completely that it is only a crutch, not a cure. No coat or shackle, no human implement, no magic, no spirit can stop the thing that is inside you."

Nico looked him straight in the eye, shrugging her shoulder out of his grip."That may be," she said, "but your wife is still alive, and so am I. So long as we're alive, we can fight." It was the first thing Josef had taught her.

"Still alive, as you say." Slorn sighed. "But as for the fight..." He looked down into the valley, and the look of grief on his face was the most human expression Nico had seen him make. "The only way for you to understand is to ask her yourself."

Nico's eyes widened and she turned back to the dark valley. The woman, Nivel, sat still as ever, but then, almost imperceptibly, Nico saw her fingers twitch. Her hand rose from her lap, lifting straight up like a marionette's hand on a string, and the thin, limp fingers curled in a beckoning motion. Beside Nico, Slorn stood perfectly still, watching the woman as her hand fell back to her knees.

Nico swallowed. "Is it safe for me to go down there?"

"Of course not," Slorn said. "Nothing is safe in your condition, but you have less to fear than anything else. So far as I know, demonseeds don't eat each other."

That didn't make her feel any better about dropping into the dark, but Slorn was settling down on the ground, obviously not going anywhere. Realizing that this was what he'd brought her up here to do from the beginning, Nico decided to see it through. She took a deep breath and then, very carefully, stepped off the cliff edge.

It was a shorter fall than she'd expected, another trick of the unnatural shadows that filled the valley. She landed badly in the sand, but righted herself automatically. Now that she was down in it, the valley was darker than ever. She could see nothing, not even the stone walls of the cliffs that boxed her in. The only sound was the metallic rattle of the woman's buzzing manacles. Nico could feel her own restraints trembling against her skin in answer, matching the rhythm. As the sounds merged, her vision began to sharpen. Not lighten, for there was no more light than before. Even so, she could see clearly now despite the dark. And there, in front of her, was Nivel.

The woman was closer than she'd realized, her bare feet almost touching Nico's legs. Nico jumped back, and the woman in the chair made a thin, hollow sound, like sand blowing over metal. It took Nico a moment to realize Nivel was chuckling.

"You have good instincts."

The woman's voice was a rasp, a mere shaping of breath, as though she'd long since screamed her throat away. Her eyes, bright as lanterns in the unnatural darkness, glittered behind her long, matted hair. Behind them, shapes and shadows flickered in unnatural forms. Even so, meeting the woman eye to eye, Nico felt a strange feeling of kinship and, with it, a strong urge to run away as fast as she could.

"Heinricht gave you the speech, did he?" Nivel said. "He gives it to every demonseed before sending them to me. Still, you are the first I've seen in a very long time. I thought maybe he'd finally given up." She sighed, a cutting, rasping sound. "My poor, faithful bear."

"Other demonseeds?" Nico said, startled. "He's sent others here?" It seemed impossible. Surely the League of Storms would shut any operation like that down in an instant.

"A few," Nivel said, waving her hand. "We'd hoped to learn something, but the demonseeds we could get were too small and weak to be any use. The League never lets them get too big, you see. But you"—her eyes locked with Nico's—"you're different."

Fast as a shadow, Nivel's hand shot out, grabbing Nico's wrist and dragging her closer. Nico fought by instinct, but the woman's grip was filled with a demonic strength even greater than hers, and Nico found herself on her knees beside Nivel, her face inches from the woman's own. This close, she could smell death and rocks and something else, a sharp, acidic bite that tugged at memories she didn't want to recall.

Nivel's eyes glowed brighter as she looked Nico over before releasing the girl with a suddenness that made Nico stumble.

"You're no usual seed, are you?" Nivel said as Nico picked herself up. "Old, far older than you look, and with a seed that appears to have blossomed many times, yet never freed itself." She tapped her fingers against her knees and a purely human look of inquisitive interest passed over her face. "Tell me, how did you get that way?"

"I don't know," Nico said. "I don't remember anything before Josef found me."

Nivel looked supremely disappointed, and the light behind her eyes flickered. "So it told me before I'd even asked the question. I hate it when the bastard is right."

Nico looked at her, confused. There was no one else in the valley save themselves. Not even a spirit. Nivel caught her surprised look and smiled a pleased smile.

"Well, child," she said, "if you don't know what I'm talking about there might be hope yet."

Nico's heart beat faster. "Slorn said there was no hope. That was why he brought me up here."

"Heinricht's doesn't believe in false assurances," Nivel said, smiling. The expression softened her face until she looked almost human again. "He's always been a realist. But there's a difference between being a realist and being a defeatist. Just because no one has ever beaten their demon doesn't mean you're going to give in, does it?"

Nico shook her head.

"I thought so." Nivel chuckled, the same dry sound as before. "In that case, strange little demon girl, let me give you some hard-learned advice." She caught Nico's eyes with her glowing gaze. "There will come a time when my words mean something to you. I may not have Slorn's eyes, but even I can see you've been using your seed too much of late. It's quickening, growing like a babe in the womb. Someday, possibly very soon, it will wake. When that happens, if you remember nothing else, remember what I tell you here."

Nivel leaned forward, lowering her voice to a bare, scraping whisper, and Nico leaned in to listen.

"Demons," Nivel said, "are predators. Creatures of power and control. But as a human, you are unique among all spirits. Your soul is your own, and you must never give your control over, no matter what. When the voice speaks, do not listen to it, do not take its advice, and do not talk back to it, no matter what it says. Do you understand?"

Nico shook her head.

"You will," Nivel said. "I'm glad I could tell someone. Though we won't meet again, I would feel guilty if I never warned you."

Nico's eyes widened. "Never again? But I've never met someone else like me. I've never had—"

Nivel shook her head. "There are no mentors in this life of ours, child. Even now, the demon inside me is trying to find a way to use you to free itself. In a few minutes, I won't have the strength to keep it back. I have fought this battle of inches for ten years, but it will be over soon. The demon is now as strong as I am. We are perfectly balanced. Yet it can get stronger, and I can't. All it would take is a bite of a spirit. A wind, a few drops of rain"—Nivel's glowing eyes ran over Nico's body—"a little girl, and the demon could shed me like snakeskin and fly free. That's why I told Slorn to put me in this valley, where all the spirits have withdrawn, leaving nothing to eat. Here, I can keep it in check. But," Nivel's rasping voice cracked, "it's been five years since I sat down on this stone, and I'm tired. So tired."

"But you're still alive!" Nico said. "So long as you have that, you can fight."

Nivel laughed, a sad, empty sound. "No one's will is strong enough to hold out alone forever. Just staying alive isn't enough. You need something to live for. A purpose. Mine is Slorn. I left him and Pele alone, and yet he still kills himself trying to find a way to bring me back. I thought that if he was willing to fight for me, to attempt the impossible, then I owed it to stand strong for him. That belief has kept me going far beyond my time. Even so, everything ends."

As she spoke, the manacles on Nivel's wrists began to rattle more incessantly, and Nico winced as the cold, dark feeling began to creep over her again. Nivel took a breath and closed her eyes tight. "You should go now," she said quietly.

Nico clenched her jaw. "I won't say farewell," she said, standing up. Her hand shot out, and she grabbed Nivel's fingers. "We'll meet again, so don't give up."

With that, Nico released her grip and turned around, marching toward the stone wall. When she reached the sheer cliff she began to climb, her impossibly strong fingers finding grips on the most minute cracks and wrinkles in the stone.

Nivel watched her go, cradling the hand Nico had seized, savoring the surprised feeling of the unexpected contact.

I hope you're happy, a deep, smooth voice said in her head. *You just let the death of your world go on her merry way. We should have eaten her when we had the chance.* It sighed deeply. *You'll regret this. Mark my words.*

Nivel just smiled and ignored the voice, as she always had, watching as Nico pulled herself over the edge of the cliff and vanished into the sunlit world above.

High overhead, Nico spilled herself out onto the dry leaves, panting and letting her eyes adjust to the light. Slorn was waiting where she'd left him, sitting solemnly on the dirt.

"So," he said slowly, "you have met the truth of demonseeds face to face. Do you still want me to make your coat?"

Nico stood up, brushing the leaves off her clothes. "Yes," she said. "Nothing has changed."

Slorn grinned, showing a great wall of sharp yellow teeth. "You have passed the final measure, then. Come," he said and stood up. "Pele and the rest should have things ready by now."

Nico nodded and followed him back down the slope and through the strange, black trees, stopping every few steps to look back over her shoulder, even after the valley had long since vanished from view.

CHAPTER 5

Miranda delivered her decision to Master Banage over breakfast. They argued, but it was the same ground they'd covered the night before, and nothing new was resolved. In the end Banage relented, for what could he do? It was her career and her neck Miranda was risking, and he could not force her to take the easy road. Their parting was short and bitter as Miranda excused herself to prepare for the trial.

Back in her room, she took more care with her preparations than usual. Using Karon's heat to warm the water in the basin, she washed her face and teeth, taking special care with her eyes, which were red ringed and raw from crying and lack of sleep. Next, she dug out the tin of powder her sister had given her ages ago and brushed the white base over her ruddy cheeks, hiding her dark circles as best she could. When she was as pale and serious as she could make herself, Miranda opened the trunk at the end of her bed and began to dress. She'd picked out her clothes the night before, choosing her favorite pair of worn trousers and a soft, light shirt to go under the heavy silk robes that were mandatory for formal Court functions. She had set out her official set this time, blood-red silk with white and gold designs in long, geometric patterns. It was hideous. The fabric was stiff and musty from being in her trunk for so long, but it marked her status as a vested and sworn Spiritualist of the Court even more than her rings did, and that was exactly the impression she was trying to make.

When every one of the robe's impossible buttons was finally fastened, Miranda sat down on her bed and took off each of her rings in turn. With great care, she rubbed each one with a soft cloth, waking and soothing the spirit inside before sliding them back onto her fingers. When the rings were done, she fished Eril's silver-wrapped pearl from his place next to her skin and, after a cleaning coupled with a firm reminder of the dire repercussions of acting out, laid him on top of her robes. Finally, she brushed out her hair as straight as it would go and bound the red mass back in a severe braid so that her face was not obscured from any angle.

Ready as she could make herself, Miranda locked her room and walked down the stairs to the street where Gin was sitting beside the door, waiting for her.

"You know," Miranda said, scratching his head, "since you're not technically a bound spirit, you don't have to come with me today."

Gin gave an undignified snort and trotted off down the narrow walk between the buildings, leaving her to follow.

A group of Krigel's red-robed guards met them at the side entrance to the tower. Miranda let them lead her and Gin up the low stairs and through the broad side hallways to the back door of the long, opulent room that served as the Court's waiting chamber.

Like all rooms in the tower, the waiting chamber was built on a grand scale, which was good, considering she was there with a fifteen-foot-long ghosthound. Even with Gin, however, Miranda felt as though the room would swallow her up if she let it. It was austere, designed to impress the age and power of the Spirit Court on its occupants, usually minor nobles and representatives from the Council who needed help with flooding river spirits or petulant winds that tore up their crops. Since it was only her this morning, the lamps were dark, and the dim, gray light from the high windows made the room's otherwise luxurious ambiance feel gloomy and cold.

Her guards, who hadn't spoken a word since she'd met them, took their places at the many doors that led into the room, and Miranda, after looking around lost for a bit, took a seat on one of the cushioned benches across from the largest door, which led into the Court itself. She knew from experience that that was where they would come for her. She had waited here once before, the day she took her oaths. Sitting there, she felt the same nervous weight in her stomach. Back then it had felt exciting; now it just made her feel ill.

Through the heavy wood she could hear the shuffling as the gathered Tower Keepers took their places. Muted conversations washed in and out, and over them all rang a smug, laughing voice she'd heard only a few times in her life but recognized instantly. How could anyone forget Hern's superior sneer?

Gin twitched beside her, lowering his head to whisper in her ear. "It's not too late. You can still take the out."

"No," Miranda said. "I need only a majority vote to have all charges against me thrown out. Every person in that room is a Spiritualist, which means every single one of them, even Hern, has taken an oath to protect the Spirit World." She folded her hands tightly in her lap. "What I did in Mellinor was not wrong or abusive, and I have the spirit inside me to prove it. For every ring in that Court, I have a measure of hope that their masters will see the truth and make the right choice."

Gin shook his head as the muted conversations vanished and the room beyond the heavy doors fell into silence as the Court convened. "I hope you're right."

"So do I," Miranda whispered, clutching her rings tighter than ever.

They sat in nervous silence until, at last, the great door opened and the bright light of the Court shone in. Even though she knew it was coming, the shock of the brilliant Court chamber after the dim waiting room threw Miranda off balance for a moment. Then she was in control again, and she marched through the doors and up the steep steps with her head high and Gin right behind her.

The Spirit Court's hearing chamber was a circular room that took up the entirety of the tower's second floor. High overhead, hanging from the tall, arched ceiling, white fires burned in silver sconces without fuel or heat, their sharp light blending with the sunlight that filtered through the tall, milky glass windows. Enormous rings of wooden benches ran along the outer edge of the room, spiraling down from the walls in a series of interlocking tiers, but only the bottom rings were filled. Tower Keepers sat primly in their formal robes, their ringed hands draped over the high wall that separated them from the open floor and the raised stand at its center, where Miranda would make her case.

Directly across from the doors where she had entered, an enormous bench loomed over everything else. It towered above the polished marble floor, carved from wood so old it had lost all its color and was now solid black beneath the layers of polish. Sitting behind the great bench on a chair as regal as any throne was Master Banage. He was dressed in a coat of pure white with a high collar that framed his face like a snowdrift, making him look ancient and distant, an infallible king of judges. Around his neck he wore the Mantle of the Tower, the regalia of the Rector Spiritualis. It was styled as a chain. Each link was a knot of heavy gold holding a great stone, and each stone held one of the spirits bound, not to any one Spiritualist, but to the Court itself, passed down from rector to rector, the living symbol of the Spirit Court's pledge of protection, justice, and equality to the Spirit World.

It was an awe-inspiring sight that was as much a part of the Spirit Court as the tower itself, and with every step she took toward the stand, Miranda felt the weight fall heavier on her shoulders. The age, the power, the majesty of the Spirit Court threatened to crush her, and no matter how many times she told herself that this was exactly the intended effect, the impact was not lessened. By the time she reached the stand, climbing the three little steps so that she stood at the apex of the Court's scrutiny, even Gin's presence couldn't stop her hands from shaking.

"Spiritualist Miranda Lyonette." Banage's voice boomed down from the high bench, warped into a fearsome specter of itself by the room's strange acoustics. "The Spirit Court has gathered to hear the charges brought against you by your peer, Spiritualist Grenith Hern, Master of the Towers, concerning the incidents that occurred in the kingdom of Mellinor."

Banage looked down at the man who was sitting front and foremost in the first ring of seats. There, dressed in a well-tailored robe of expensive crimson silk embroidered with gold flourishes, was Grenith Hern himself. He was young for a Tower Keeper, scarcely into his forties, and clearly he had been very handsome at one point. His hair, though graying, was still a flaxen blond, and he wore it long and braided down his back like a dandy. However, any appearance of youthful inexperience was banished by the immense collection of rings that glistened on his hands, which he draped casually over the bench that separated him from the open floor. He had necklaces as well, jeweled chains nearly as ornate as Master Banage's, and bracelets glittering beneath the cuffs of his robe.

Banage looked down. "Speak your complaint, Spiritualist Hern."

Hern stood up with a gracious nod and turned to face Miranda, meeting her glare with a warm, confident smile.

"My complaint is one of a most serious nature." His smooth voice rang out through the great room. "I charge that Miranda Lyonette, in violation of her duty and her oaths, did conspire with the noted criminal Eli Monpress to gain access to the spirit known as Mellinor, a Great Spirit overpowered and imprisoned by the dreaded Enslaver Gregorn, and thought destroyed more than four hundred years ago. Despite her orders to apprehend Monpress, Spiritualist Lyonette instead worked with him to win over Mellinor, already weakened and confused from the long Enslavement and imprisonment, with threats and guile. Furthermore, in payment for this assistance, Spiritualist Lyonette bought Monpress time to escape by destroying the throne room of Mellinor, putting countless lives in danger."

Banage gave him a cold look. "This is your charge?"

Hern nodded. "It is."

"And what punishment do you seek?"

Hern turned to look down at Miranda, and his smile became a cruel smirk. "Banishment," he said, low and cold. "Banishment from the Spirit Court by stripping of rings, rank, and privileges, including entry to Zarin or any other safe haven maintained by the Court."

A great murmur went up among the crowd. Miranda let the sound wash over her, keeping her eyes straight ahead. She had expected this, she told herself, but still, hearing the actual words turned her spine to water. When the noise quieted down, Banage leaned forward from his high seat to look down at Miranda and spoke as gently as the acoustics of the room allowed. "How do you answer these charges, Spiritualist Lyonette?"

Miranda met his eyes one last time, and took the plunge.

"I call them nonsense." Her voice rang out through the chamber. "It is true that I was sent to Mellinor to capture Eli Monpress, but when I arrived in Mellinor, I found a far greater crime against the spirits than anything Monpress was capable of. As you should all know, for I went into this at great length in my report, the prince, Renaud, who lost his throne thanks to Mellinor's ancient prejudices against wizards, had turned to Enslavement to get it back. He awakened and Enslaved a Great Spirit left by his ancestor, the Enslaver Gregorn, in the artifact we know as Gregorn's Pillar, the same artifact I had been sent to Mellinor to ensure Monpress did not steal. Despite my efforts, Renaud successfully shattered the pillar and took control of the weakened Great Spirit of the now-dry inland sea Mellinor. However, with Monpress's help, I was able to free Mellinor from Renaud's control and destroy the Enslaver."

By the time she finished, the crowd was whispering madly. Hern raised his hand, and the noise stopped.

"A fascinating story," he said. "All of which matches what the Kingdom of Mellinor itself reported to the Council, of course. Yet, the question still remains: How did all of this end up with Monpress escaping and you with the Great Spirit?"

Miranda glared at him. "After Renaud's death, Mellinor rightfully demanded that the land Gregorn had stolen from him, what was now the Kingdom of Mellinor, be returned. However, there were, are, people living on that land, and millions of spirits who would perish if it returned to a sea. I could not let that happen. Yet a spirit without its land is a ghost with nowhere to go, and Mellinor had survived too much to die moments after winning his freedom. So we came to a compromise: Mellinor would leave the kingdom to its new inhabitants, and I would give him a new home using the only vessel large enough for a spirit of his power, my own body."

"Your body?" Hern gave her a distasteful look, which he made sure everyone saw. "Highly unorthodox, and very dangerous for both spirit and Spiritualist. Your idea, I take it?"

"Yes," Miranda said. "But then, wouldn't any Spiritualist risk their life to save a Great Spirit?"

"Their own life, yes," Hern said. "But have you thought of what happens if you die like that, Miss Lyonette? With a small ocean inside you?" He held up his hand, gesturing with his jeweled rings. "A *stone* is stable, durable, but humans are fragile creatures. That dog of yours could turn feral and eat you, and in the course flood all of Zarin."

Gin growled savagely, but Miranda put her hand on his muzzle and yanked his fur until he stopped. When she felt sure he wouldn't start again, she released her grip and answered Hern as calmly as she could. "I did my best with the options I had. I had to make a choice that night, and I chose to preserve as many lives as possible, spirit and human. What Spiritualist would do otherwise?"

"What Spiritualist, indeed?" Hern said, his voice growing coy and condescending. "You try to play to our sense of pity, to hide your true intention behind pure motives. But we are not so easily fooled as that poor, befuddled water spirit."

Miranda blinked, astonished by this new attack, but Hern did not let up.

"Do you think we've looked the other way throughout your astonishing career?" he said, looking around the Court. "How could we? You came to the Court from a wealthy Zarin family, finished your training in two years instead of the standard three, and from the moment you took your apprentice's oath, no one would suit you as a mentor save Etmon Banage himself, the new favorite to become Rector Spiritualis."

Miranda clenched her fists. "I don't see how any of this has any bearing on—"

"Don't you?" Hern snapped. "Look again. Your entire life within the Court has been one of achievement and ambition. It's no secret that Banage is grooming you to be his successor. The special missions he sends you on are all highly irregular, and we won't even begin to talk about the misappropriation of Court funds in hiring a bounty hunter, one Coriano, to track down Monpress."

An enormous swell of noise went up at this, and Banage banged his desk for order.

"Hern," he said, "if you have a problem with my policies, you will bring them up with me personally. In this trial, you will limit your statements to the matter at hand."

"Of course." Hern's tone changed again. He was all sincerity now. "I merely mentioned this ugly situation to give our good Keepers a rounded look at the character of the woman whose fate we are deciding." He turned back to Miranda. "After all, when her history of ambition and disrespect for Spirit Court regulations are considered, should we really be surprised that, when the opportunity arose in Mellinor to bind a Great Spirit, something no Spiritualist has done since the oaths were codified, Miranda Lyonette seized upon it?"

Gin snarled, and this time, Miranda didn't stop him. "This is ridiculous!" she cried. "How can you stand there and pull these lies out of thin air? However badly you think of me, what part of my story, of *anything* that has happened, could make anyone believe what you're saying? If I were this ambitious monster you make me out to be, then surely I never would have just let Eli escape!"

"Ah," Hern said, "but that was the deal, wasn't it? Looking the other way in exchange for his help. Of course, you'd fail in your mission, but who could fault you for failing to catch the famously uncatchable Eli Monpress? Such a small blemish is easily overpowered by the prestige of being the master of a Great Spirit.

Frame it that way and suddenly your plan is quite understandable. Just another shortsighted and selfish grab for power hidden under good intentions."

Miranda looked around in disbelief as the Tower Keepers nodded. "Where is your proof?" she shouted. "My report, Mellinor's own report, the truth itself, do these mean nothing to you?"

"Proof?" Hern lashed back. "The proof is in your report!" He held up a stack of papers for all to see. "If taking Mellinor was not your final intention, why then did you pair up with Monpress instead of contacting the Spirit Court for backup according to the standard procedure for dealing with powerful Enslavers?"

Miranda flinched. "There was no time."

"No time?" Hern said, astonished. "If Mellinor had time to send a bounty request to the Council, surely you had time to contact a nearby tower? The only reason I can see for your silence was that you wanted to keep your doings a secret from the Court. You paired up with a thief who wouldn't question your actions, and in return you quietly looked the other way while he ran off with half the contents of Mellinor's treasury."

"There are no towers in Mellinor!" Miranda shouted. "Or anywhere nearby. That's why I was sent there in the first place rather than leaving things to the local Tower Keeper. As for looking the other way, I was unconscious when Eli escaped because I had just taken in a Great Spirit! And if you don't believe that Mellinor came to me of his own free will, then I invite you to ask him yourself!"

A great swell of talk rose up from the stands, and Miranda stood in the middle of it, stiff as stone. This was her biggest hammer, and she'd meant to save it until later, but Hern certainly wasn't playing for a long trial. If she was to have any hope of winning, she couldn't afford to dance around. Still, Hern looked cool and collected, giving her a little go-ahead motion with one narrow, jewel-covered hand, and that made her more nervous than any of his earlier bluster.

Banage silenced the court with a wave of his hand. "Spiritualist Lyonette is correct," he announced. "Since the complaint is that she gained the spirit Mellinor under false pretenses, the resolution seems simple enough. We will question the spirit to see if it has been mistreated." He looked down. "Miranda, if you would."

Miranda nodded and closed her eyes, reaching down into the deep well of her spirit where Mellinor slept. He woke as soon as she brushed him, and a strange sensation rushed through her body, as though she were pouring out of her skin. It wasn't uncomfortable, but neither was it pleasant, and it went on for what felt like a very long time.

When the sensation finally faded, the sound of water filled her ears. She opened her eyes and saw Mellinor hovering beside her. The Great Spirit of the inland sea had changed since she'd offered her soul as his shore. He still appeared as a great orb of water, crystal clear and glowing with his own shifting blue light, but he was smaller now, barely as tall as she was. She'd known he had to shed some of his size to live inside her, but actually seeing the once enormous globe cut down to something more manageable was a shock. Still, Mellinor did not seem troubled at all by his new stature. He hovered, turning to watch the wizards in the stands as they gawked openly. The more they gawked, the brighter the light in the water became, and Miranda got the distinct feeling that, diminished as he was, Mellinor was still the largest spirit most of them had ever encountered firsthand, and the ball of water knew it.

Banage leaned forward on the bench. "You are Mellinor," he said, almost hesitantly, "Great Spirit of the inland sea?"

"I was." Mellinor's voice was like a crashing wave. "But my sea is long gone to grass and trees, so now I am Mellinor, beholden to Miranda."

Hern leaped at this. "Beholden? You mean oath bound?"

Mellinor gave him what passed for a dirty look among water spirits. "Formalities are pointless. I accepted her offer of sanctuary and sustenance in exchange for service on the understanding that I am free to leave whenever I wish, which I currently do not."

"So," Hern said, ignoring Mellinor's distaste, "you were given the choice of servitude or... what?"

He left the question hanging, and Mellinor's water swirled. "I see where this is going, human," the water spirit rumbled. "I am not bound to answer to you."

"But your mistress is," Hern said. "Answer the question, service or what?"

Miranda felt Mellinor give her a questioning prod. She nodded and, with a watery sigh, the Great Spirit answered. "Return to the sea. When I was free from the Enslaver, I attempted to reclaim my land. Miranda Lyonette and Eli Monpress stopped me, for it would mean the death of millions of spirits, as well as thousands of your kind. Monpress meant to return me to the sea, and defeated, I would have gone. It was Miranda who stopped him. Had she not offered the Spiritualist's pledge to me, I would be lost right now, my soul pounded to nothingness beneath the waves. Servitude to a good master is a small price to pay for escaping that end."

Miranda beamed at the glowing water, but Hern's smug smile only grew wider.

"So," he said, "just to make sure I have this right. You were given the choice between death at Monpress's hands or service to Spiritualist Lyonette?"

"I don't like how you say it," Mellinor rumbled. "But if you insist on reducing a complex situation to its most base components, then yes, that is technically correct."

Hern turned to look out over the rows of Spiritualists, spreading his arms to encompass them all. "Though it scarcely needs to be spoken," he said in a ringing voice, "I would like to remind everyone present of the first rule of servant spirits, as it is written in the founding codex of our order: 'Servitude of a spirit is by the spirit's choice alone.' *Choice*, my friends, a spirit's informed, free choice is the cornerstone of all the magics of the Spirit Court. What happened that night in Mellinor was not choice. We already have a name for when the only options are death or service." His face clenched in a disgusted sneer. "*Slavery*. That night Spiritualist Lyonette and the thief Monpress put Mellinor in a situation where there was only one outcome. Though he took the oath, Mellinor did not enter her service by his free will, but rather because there was no other choice." He paused gravely for a moment, letting that sink in. "Though it doesn't fit the technical definition," he continued at last, "I think we can all agree there's little else to call it but Enslavement."

"Are you stupid?" Miranda shouted, all her calm crumbling around her. "You heard it straight from Mellinor! He's here because he wants to be! *I saved his life!*"

Everyone was shouting now. Spiritualists shot up from their seats, arguing over each other in increasingly loud voices while Banage shouted for order. Gin was growling furiously, with his ears flat and his claws out, digging into the stone. Only Hern was quiet, watching the chaos as a victorious commander watches the routing of his enemy. Miranda was so angry she could barely see straight, but Mellinor's anger dwarfed her own. It throbbed through their connection like a tide as his surface shifted from calm blue to an angry, choppy, steel gray.

After several minutes Banage finally regained order. When the room was quiet, he nodded at the water spirit. "Do you have anything else to add?"

"Only this." Mellinor's voice was like a breaking glacier. He turned to Hern, and his water grew very dark. "I have been

Enslaved, Spiritualist. I know the madness, the agony, and the humiliation better than any spirit who still has their mind intact. If you presume to call my contract with Miranda Enslavement again, then I will exercise that free choice you claim to value so highly to drown you where you stand. And none of those weak flickers you wear so gaudily on your fingers would be able to stop me."

Hern blanched, and Banage let him squirm for a moment before turning to Miranda. "Spiritualist Lyonette, please control your spirit."

Miranda had a choice answer for that, but a look at Banage stopped her tongue. As much as she would love to let Mellinor do what the spirit was aching to do, any hope of beating the charges against her would vanish if she didn't stay to the right side of Court law, which meant no drowning. With great effort, she tugged at Mellinor's connection, and the spirit reluctantly pulled back, but his cold light never lost its focus on Hern until the last wisp of water vanished.

"You have all heard the charges," Banage said. "The accused will now exit the chamber while the Court deliberates."

Dismissed, Miranda climbed off the stand and marched across the open floor, doing her best to ignore the whispers that followed her. Behind her, she could hear Hern chatting with the Spiritualists around him, his voice ringing confident and cheerful over the hum of the crowd. Her heart sank in her chest as she walked through the double doors the apprentices held open for her, returning to the dark waiting chamber.

"That pompous idiot," Gin growled, pacing in cramped, little circles through the long waiting room while the apprentices secured the door behind them. "You should have let Mellinor drown him."

Miranda didn't answer. She plopped down on the bench

against the far wall and put her head in her hands. On her fingers, her rings were awake and asking questions, buzzing through their connection. With great difficulty, she sent them firm, reassuring waves of confidence. Everything would be fine. Slowly, her rings quieted, the smaller spirits first, and finally the larger ones. Even Mellinor settled down under the pressure. Tired from his earlier anger, he burrowed deep into the corners of Miranda's mind where she rarely went, his mood dark and brooding and well suited to her own.

When they were all still, Miranda lifted the pressure and sat back, staring up at the high windows. She rarely lied to her spirits, but she wasn't above withholding a truth, especially one that had not come to pass yet, and things *could* still turn out in the end.

She closed her eyes. Even thinking it felt foolish. Everything would be all right? She didn't see how they could have gone worse. She'd needed to make a glorious defense. Instead, she'd lost her calm and let Hern lead her in circles away from her carefully prepared arguments. Miranda gritted her teeth. She'd let him play her for a fool from the very beginning, from that first night in Banage's office when she'd read his name on the petition.

Miranda leaned back, letting her head thunk against the cold stone wall. She'd been such an idiot. All this time, she'd truly believed that if she could only tell her story, show them Mellinor, prove that Hern's case was completely unfounded, then the Tower Keepers would be on her side. Yet she could see them now in her mind's eye, the robed figures, their faced turned toward each other, whispering, their ringed hands drumming impatiently on the stands. They hadn't come to Court today to be convinced, to test innocence. There'd been no questions, no demanding of proof, no calls for witnesses, nothing. The Tower Keepers who came today had come to see an unpleasant bit of necessary business through, just as Banage had warned her. She clunked her head against the stone wall again, a little harder this time. Stupid, that's what she'd been. Stupid and naive, thinking things would be the way she wanted just because that's how she believed they should be.

She could hear Gin's claws on the stone as he paced. He'd been right that night in the garden. Coming here today, naked like this, with only her spirits and her word behind her, it had been a prideful thing to do. She had gone in with her head held too high to see the shaky ground beneath her feet, and now…

Miranda raised her hands quickly, pressing her fingers hard against her eyes to block the wetness that threatened to roll down her cheeks. She could not be weak, not now. But Hern's voice, smooth and triumphant as he announced the punishment, was circling through her mind.

Banishment from the Spirit Court by stripping of rings, rank, and privileges.

Her hands began to tremble. She had known from the beginning that this was the risk she was taking, but, at the same time, she had not truly understood what was at stake. Banishment she could handle. Rank could go as well, and everything else. But her rings? She turned her hands over, pressing the stones of her rings against her cheeks. She could feel her spirits moving inside them, turning as they slept. Each one was tied to her by a promise, a sacred pledge she'd thought would last until her death. Could she lose that?

The crack of the doors interrupted her thoughts, and Miranda had just enough time to scrub her eyes before two red-robed Spiritualists entered the waiting room. They didn't look at her, only opened the doors and stood at either side, waiting for her with downcast faces. Miranda got up from the bench with a terrible feeling of dread. Had the Tower Keepers reached their decision so soon? Surely not. It had been barely ten minutes. Could they even take the vote that quickly? Yet the young Spiritualists stood waiting to escort her, and Miranda had no choice but to take her place between them. Without a word, they led her up the stairs into the bright light of the Court, and with every step she took, Miranda felt her hope grow fainter.

This time, her walk through the Court was very different. She was the same, marching in with her head high and her face a calm mask over her fear. She was still a Spiritualist after all, at least for the next few minutes. The circular room, however, had changed in the short time she'd been waiting. Before, the first two rings of seats had been nearly full. A slim showing, but still, people had been there. Now, the great Court was almost empty. Only a few Spiritualists sat sprinkled across the benches, mostly faces she knew, Banage's supporters. Everyone else seemed to have left after the vote. Probably too cowardly to stay and watch the aftermath, she thought darkly.

Hern was there, of course, lounging in his chair like a patron at a boring play, though he did look up to give Miranda a smile, which she did her best to ignore, focusing instead on Master Banage. For once, however, the sight of her mentor brought her no comfort. Even beside the snowy whiteness of his collar, his face looked pale and worn. For the first time his hair looked more gray than black, and his blue eyes were sad and tired when they met hers. If she'd had any hope about the verdict, it died then, but she walked to the stand the same as ever, straight and proud, with Gin stalking behind her like a silent, silver mist.

"Spiritualist Lyonette," Banage said when she had climbed the steps and taken her place on the stand. "You have heard the accusations brought against you and given your answer. Your case has been debated by the leading members of the Spirit Court, and we have come to our decision by majority vote. Are you prepared to hear our verdict?"

Miranda gripped the brass railing that surrounded the stand. "I am."

Banage looked down at the desk in front of him. "Spiritualist Lyonette, this assembly finds you guilty of conspiring with the criminal Eli Monpress for the purpose of obtaining the Great Spirit Mellinor under false pretense and in violation of your oaths. As punishment, you are hereby banished from our assembly. Your titles and privileges within the Court, including all pacts, promises, or agreements made in its name, are now considered void. You will surrender your bound spirits and leave this city at once."

Master Banage's voice was soft and calm, yet every word struck Miranda like a hammer, rattling her mind until all she could do was stare at him dumbly. She heard footsteps behind her and turned to see two young Spiritualists she didn't recognize walking toward her, one with a large pile of sand stalking behind her like a tiger, the other walking beside what looked like a centipede made of stone.

They were moving slowly, and Miranda had plenty of time to look down at her hands. Her rings glittered on her fingers, each one shining with its own tiny light, innocent, completely unaware of what was about to happen. Mellinor, however, knew things were wrong. He moved under her mind, a shadow under the water that was her conscious, restless and thrashing. Miranda closed her eyes, feeling the pull of her spirits, the bond of the vows she had made them, the vows that had just been pronounced void. It felt the same as ever, an iron cable tying her soul to her spirits.

Standing there on the stand with the Spiritualists advancing toward her, Miranda faced her choice. Truly faced it, for the first time. Honor the Spirit Court or honor her spirits. When she saw her situation like that, laid bare of all its pomp, she realized she'd already chosen. All that was left was to act.

The thought terrified her, but not nearly as much as it would have an hour ago. After all, a voice that sounded suspiciously like Eli's whispered in her head, *What more could they do to you?*

The approaching Spiritualists were an arm's length from Gin's tail when Miranda turned to face them.

"Eril," she said softly, "distraction."

A great cackling laugh rose up from the pendant on her chest, and Eril burst forth in a blast of wind that nearly knocked her flat. He howled as he circled, overturning empty chairs, scattering papers everywhere, and the room erupted into chaos. Hern shot out of his chair, but his voice was lost in the gale. The other Spiritualists were standing as well, thrusting out hands covered in bright glowing rings, but Miranda had no time to watch them. The Spiritualist with the sand tiger shouted something, and her spirit sprang forward, meaning to trap Miranda in an avalanche of sand. As it leaped, Miranda threw out her hand. A blast of water flew from her fingers, meeting the sand creature head-on. The wall of water engulfed it, and sand flew out in all directions with a rasping scream. The girl who commanded it cried out as well, and another ring on her hand flashed, but Miranda was too quick.

"Skarest," she ordered, and lightning crackled down her arm, jumping in a white arc from her finger to the girl's chest. The Spiritualist flew backward with a great cracking sound, landing in a sprawl on her back across the room.

"Skarest!" Miranda shouted, horrified.

"She'll be fine," the lightning crackled smugly. "Watch your back."

Miranda whirled around just in time to see the other Spiritualist send his stone centipede skittering forward, but even as she opened her mouth to call Durn, her own stone spirit, Gin leaped over the spirit and landed on its Spiritualist. The stone monster froze as the ghosthound picked the boy up by his collar with one claw and tossed him into the benches. The rock centipede scurried over to its fallen master, but other spirits were joining the fray now. Hern had jumped down from the seats onto the chamber floor, his hands wreathed in a strange blue fire that matched the flashing stone at his neck.

Seeing they were about to be horribly outnumbered, Miranda hurried over to Gin. "Time to go!"

"Where?" Gin growled, kneeling down so she could jump on his back. "We're in the heart of the Spirit Court. I'm all for leaving these idiots in the dust, but you picked a really bad place to rebel."

The Spiritualists in the benches had their spirits out now. Everywhere Miranda looked she was ringed in by spirits of every type and size beginning to move down out of the gallery to the floor.

"There." Miranda pointed at the high windows.

"It's too narrow," Gin snapped. "We won't get through."

"Well, try anyway," Miranda said, getting a death grip on his fur.

Gin growled and dropped into a crouch. She could feel his muscles tensing, gathering strength, and then, in a single, explosive motion, he jumped. Miranda had never seen him jump like this. It felt as if they were flying. They soared over the benches, over Hern, who could only watch openmouthed, lifting his flame-ringed hands too late. Gin and Miranda flew past Banage, and Miranda turned to catch one last glimpse of her mentor. What she saw, however, was not what she'd expected. Despite the fiasco going on in his Court, Banage had not moved. He simply sat there at his seat, watching her. Then, without warning, he smiled, and his spirit welled up around her.

She'd felt him open his spirit wide before, but this was different. The stones on his chain of office glowed like sunlight, and Miranda's bones hummed with power. Not just Banage's power, but the power of the Rector Spiritualis, the wizard tied to the interconnected spirit of the Spirit Court's tower and the great sleeping spirits that lay beneath Zarin itself.

Banage flicked his fingers and the room shook with an enormous groan. It lasted only a second, but it was enough. Ahead of them, the too-narrow window they were flying toward suddenly slid away, the milky white glass that was never meant to open dropping down to let them through. It didn't stop there, though. Next, the stone that ringed the window began to peel outward, the white marble bending and curling like an opening flower, creating a hole just large enough for Gin. Miranda barely had time to gawk before they were through, soaring out of the tower and into the clear morning air.

For one glorious moment they flew high and free with all of Zarin spread out before them. Then, in a slow, inevitable arch, they began to fall. Miranda felt Gin's legs kick, then begin to scramble in the empty space, and she realized something was wrong. They were too high, even for Gin, and falling at the wrong angle.

For a single, breathless moment, they tumbled in free fall, the sky and ground swapping places in sickening circles as they hurdled the three stories down toward the cobbled courtyard. Miranda gripped Gin's fur and opened her mouth to scream, but no sound came. Instead, Mellinor poured out of her. Later, thinking back, she could never recall if she had asked him or if the water spirit had acted on his own, but she had never been so happy to see the impossibly blue water.

Mellinor plummeted ahead of them in a great wave, falling to the pavement below and forming a vast pool of water. She watched, her terror overcome by amazement, as the water shaped itself into a great, floating well a dozen feet deep, or tall, depending on how you saw it, and Miranda realized she had better hold her breath.

Gin hit the pool with a great splash, and it was all Miranda could do to hold on as the force of the water threatened to scrape her off the ghosthound. But Mellinor caught her, his water absorbing the impact. She regained her seating just as Gin's feet touched the ground. The water held them a moment longer, until Gin had his balance, and then, with a heady rush, Mellinor poured back into Miranda. She went stiff, gasping for breath as the water spirit returned to her, and she would have fallen off if her fingers had not already been tangled in Gin's fur so tightly. Then Mellinor was back where he always was and they were standing in the courtyard, dry and safe, with the sound of spirits clamoring above them.

Gin didn't give Miranda time to assess the situation. As soon as the water was gone, he burst forward, nearly running over a handful of gawking people. Miranda could only hold on and keep her head down as the ghosthound jumped the wall that separated the Spirit Court from the rest of the city. No one tried to stop them as they ran through the busy streets and made a beeline for the southern wall.

"We'll hit the south fields," Gin said, his voice barely audible over the rush of the wind and cries of the people forced to jump out of their way. "Make a show. Then when Zarin's out of sight, we'll circle back east and lose ourselves in the farmland. Lots of hiding places there. We can rest and decide where we're actually going."

Miranda nodded against his fur, happy to let him decide. She looked down at her fingers knotted in Gin's fur, at the rings that pressed into her skin. Then she looked back over her shoulder at the great tower of the Spirit Court standing straight and white over the city. She regretted it immediately as a surge of emotion choked her throat, and she ducked her head, burying her face in Gin's neck. She did not look at anything again until they were far, far away.

Etmon Banage eased his spirit a fraction, and the stones that Miranda and Gin had just gone sailing through folded in again, the window sliding back into place as though it had never moved.

Below him, the solemn chamber was in complete uproar. Hern stood by the empty stand, his hands still wreathed in his blue fire spirit, shouting orders. The other Spiritualists weren't listening. They were busy withdrawing their retinues and helping the poor pair who had tried to confront Miranda get back on their feet.

When Hern realized he was getting nowhere, he marched to the foot of the great bench and glared upward.

"Banage!" he shouted. "Have you gone soft in the head? Why did you let a convicted criminal escape?"

"That window is a priceless part of our tower," Banage answered matter-of-factly. "The ghosthound was going through it, one way or another. Would you rather I let it be broken?"

"Don't play that line with me," Hern growled, pointing a finger wreathed with blue flame. "You knew. You knew she would try to escape!"

Banage arched his eyebrows at the younger man. "You were the one who pushed her into the corner, Hern," he said. "Miranda is a strong, proud Spiritualist. Is it surprising she pushed back?"

Hern gritted his teeth and lowered his hands, the flames sputtering out. "It makes no difference; she's a traitor and a criminal now. We'll hunt her down sooner or later."

"Perhaps," Banage said, unfastening his stiff collar. "But your involvement in this matter is at an end, Hern. I suggest you put it out of your mind."

Hern glared at him. "What do you mean? I'm not finished until that girl's rings are dust."

"The pursuit and apprehension of traitors is the sole purview of the Rector Spiritualis." Banage removed his heavy chain next and handed it to Krigel, who had stepped forward to help him. "Rest assured, I will give this matter the attention it deserves."

Hern glared murder at him. "I will not let you bury this," he said, his voice taut. "Do not think this is done, Etmon!"

"I would never allow myself such luxuries," Banage answered, but Hern was already off, marching through the chaotic hall, his robes flying behind him like fantastic wings. A handful of the remaining Tower Keepers fell in behind him, leaving the room nearly empty.

"Well," Krigel said when they were gone, "that was a fine fiasco."

"Yes," Banage said, sinking back down into his chair. "I seem to have a talent for making troublesome enemies."

Krigel sniffed. "Any man who wasn't Hern's enemy would be no friend of mine."

Banage nodded absently, staring up at the window.

Krigel followed his eyes. "If you don't mind my saying, sir, that was very unlike you. What possessed you to do it?"

"What," he said, "let her escape? It certainly wasn't the proper thing to do." He paused, and a thin smile spread across his lips. "Let's just say it felt more right than letting Hern win."

"I see," Krigel said. "And are you saying that as the Rector Spiritualis or as her master?"

"Both," Banage said. "She made her choice and she chose her spirits. I can't say I would respect a Spiritualist who chose otherwise, not as mentor or as Rector. Now"—he stood up—"back to work. Tell me, which traveling Spiritualist reported in last?"

"That would be Ziggot," Krigel said. "He stopped in last week and left promptly a day later to investigate reports of spirit abuse by pirates on the Green Sea."

"Good," Banage said, nodding. "Notify anyone who asks that Ziggot is now in charge of catching Miranda Lyonette and bringing her to face trial."

"But he's on a boat by now," Krigel said. "Even relaying through the towers, it will take weeks to inform him of his new assignment."

"Too bad," Banage said. "I suddenly have the strong feeling that no one but Zagget is right for this job."

"It's Zigget, sir," Krigel said.

"Whatever." Banage shrugged, looking around at the scattered papers and overturned benches. "Put him on it and make sure Hern knows, and get someone in here to clean this up."

"Yes, Rector." Krigel bowed.

Banage patted him on the shoulder and walked down the stairs and out of the chamber, running his hand along the wall as he went. Beneath his fingers, the stone tower whispered that the white dog and its master were already outside the city, running south and east across the plains. Smiling, Banage pulled back his hand and started up the stairs, feeling much better than he'd expected to feel.

CHAPTER 6

As soon as Slorn announced he would start the coat, he vanished into his workroom and did not come out for food or sleep. The first day of waiting passed quickly enough, but by the second Eli was getting dangerously bored.

"You know," Josef said, "it's a sign of maturity to be able to entertain yourself."

They were sitting around the table in the main room. Josef had all his knives, swords, and throwing spikes laid out by size, and he was carefully sharpening them with a contented look on his face. Nico was sitting beside him, reading some book of Slorn's she'd picked up the day before, one of Morticime Kant's fourteen-volume *A Wizarde Historie*. This activity had surprised Eli for two reasons: one, that Slorn kept that kind of trash in his house, and two, that Nico could read. She'd never given any signs that she was literate before, but there was so little he knew about her, it wasn't safe to assume anything. Anyway, that had been yesterday's realization. Today, he was slumped over the hard chair by the fire, bored out of his mind.

"An active mind requires stimulation," he grumbled, tilting his head to look at Josef. "We can't all be happy sharpening knives all day long."

Josef just kept dragging his long knife over the whetstone with practiced ease and said nothing. Realizing he wouldn't get an argument, Eli swung himself up with an exaggerated sigh and looked again at the sealed door to Slorn's workroom. The only interesting thing going on in the whole house and Slorn was too stingy to let him watch. Still, there was always a way.

"What are you doing?" Josef asked as Eli began to stalk across the room.

"Broadening my mind," Eli answered, carefully laying his fingers on the door. It was good, hard wood, and already awake. Eli smiled and began tapping his fingers against it.

Before he could say anything, the door said, "Don't even think about it."

"Come now," Eli said softly. "Surely dear Heinricht wouldn't mind if I checked in on him. It's not often I get to watch a master at work. Just a peek, what do you say?"

"Absolutely not." The door held itself firmer than ever. "And if you're considering schmoozing anything else, I'll tell you right now you can save your breath. Every stick of furniture in this house is under strict orders to make sure *you* keep out of the way."

Behind him, Nico made a sound almost like a snort. Eli gave her a cutting look over his shoulder before turning back to the door, which had pulled back so far it was digging into its frame.

"I wouldn't dream of getting in the way," he cooed. "No one wants him to finish quickly more than I do. I just want to learn. How can you deny me that? Come on, I don't even have to see. Just let me listen in." He leaned forward, putting his ear against the gap in the boards. "Slorn loves knowledge above all else. How could he object to just a little listen?"

The door gave a shriek and Eli jumped backward, slapping a hand over his ear to stop the ringing. The door's shriek faded to a loud, off-key humming, and Eli sighed, rubbing his ear with his palm.

"All right," he said. "I get it. You can stop now."

The door hummed louder.

"I guess this is one of those times I should be glad I can't hear spirits," Josef said, looking down at the sword he was sharpening with a smile that was slightly larger than the blade warranted.

"In this house, that's all the time," Eli grumbled. "Does Slorn awaken only the rude ones?"

"I hardly think following orders makes a spirit rude," came a growly voice. The door ceased its humming, and everyone turned to look as Slorn himself stepped into the room looking very tired and very annoyed.

"Slorn," Eli said. "How nice to see you again. I was beginning to worry work had eaten you for good."

"I find it hard to work with so much noise going on." Slorn folded his arms over his chest. "Aren't thieves supposed to be quiet?"

"Only when quietness is called for," Eli said.

"I'm so sorry, Heinricht," the door said. "I was only trying to protect your privacy, and—"

The bear-headed man silenced it with a wave. "You did well. I was coming out anyway."

Eli brightened. "Is it done?"

"Mostly," Slorn said, turning back toward his workroom. "Come in and see, but don't touch anything."

Eli sprang across the room and fell in behind him, giving the grumbling door a dazzling smile as he passed. Josef put down his sword and followed at a more reasonable pace, with Nico bringing up the rear.

Eli had been trying to get into Slorn's workroom since his first visit, and he was not disappointed. The room was in strict order and absolutely full of curiosities. Shelves filled every available bit of wall, and every available bit of shelving was covered with bins of scrap cloth, animal hides, and enormous spools of thread, some of which were glittering, others almost invisible. There were bins of metal as well, all obscurely labeled in Slorn's spidery writing as "resentful" or "pleasant," and one locked chest on the top shelf bore a red sign that read "bloodthirsty—for blade cores only."

There was a large forge in the corner, which was surprising, considering there was no chimney on this side of the house, but it was cold and its anvil had been pushed to the side. Instead, a large loom took up what little floor space there was. It sat empty now, but its shuttles were twitching with exhaustion, coming down off of two days of solid work.

Eli hopped around like a magpie, examining the tool racks, the shelves of materials, the half-finished projects, anything he could get to. Josef, obviously not seeing what the excitement was about, strolled along behind him looking decidedly bored until he spotted something that made him stop midstep. He grabbed Eli's sleeve, pulling the thief away from the chest of glass knobs he'd been gawking over, and nodded toward the wall. Eli followed his gaze, letting out a low, impressed whistle.

There, hanging from a large iron peg, was a sword unlike any they'd seen. To start, it was enormous, larger even than the Heart of War. The blade, guard, and handle were all the same dark metal, a steel blacker than iron with a red tinge that made Eli shudder. Strangest of all was the edge. The heavy, black metal tapered on one side, sharpening, not to a sword edge, but to a row of jagged, bladed teeth. They ran in an uneven line, like teeth in a sea monster's jaw, and every one of them gleamed killing sharp. The sword's surface had a strange, matte finish that made the blade look darker than it was, but when Josef reached out to touch it, Slorn was suddenly there, grabbing his hand halfway.

"I said don't touch," the bear man growled.

"Slorn," Eli said, sliding between the two men with a smile. "I thought you didn't make swords anymore."

Slorn let go of Josef's hand with a low rumble. "I don't, usually. That's a custom order for another client." He glared at the sword. "The rabid piece of junk took me almost two months to finish and it's not friendly, so I'd appreciate it if you left it alone."

Despite the warning, Josef leaned in, more interested than ever. "It must weigh what, two hundred? Two fifty?"

"A ton," Eli said. "Who's it for, a mountain?"

"I have clients who are mountains," Slorn said, "but no. And I was told weight didn't matter, so I didn't bother to weigh it. Can we move on, please? I don't have all day."

He stepped aside, motioning them to the far back corner of the workroom. Eli went cheerfully, Josef less so, but what they saw next put the sword out of their minds. In the corner stood a dressmaker's dummy half eaten by something that looked like liquid night. Eli blinked and looked again, letting his eyes adjust to the soft light of the workshop, and slowly, the blackness arranged itself into the shape of a woman's coat.

It was a long coat with a wide collar, flared sleeves, and

buttoned straps to hold it closed. Silver flashed at the neck, and when he looked harder, Eli realized the flashes were needles. A small army of needles swam through the black fabric, moving in perfect unison, dragging the shiny black thread behind them. Still, despite that all this was happening less than three feet in front of him, Eli had a hard time seeing what the needles were doing. The light from the tall floor lamp seemed to slide around the coat, almost like the yellow glow was deliberately avoiding it. Eli marveled at the effect, wondering what kind of fabulous cloth Slorn had used, but when he looked at the scraps that lay scattered about on the floor, he realized the fabric was actually no blacker than any dark wool.

He mentioned this to Slorn, and the bear-headed man smiled wide.

"That's the new layer of protection I put in." His voice had an uncharacteristic note of bragging in it, the pride of a workman who has just made something unique. "It's not that the coat is so black, but that the lamp can't see it. Watch this."

He grabbed the coat's sleeve and began to move it toward the lamp. The closer he got to the light, the darker and less substantial the coat became.

"How did you do that?" Eli asked, snatching the sleeve out of Slorn's hand to get a better look at it.

"The law of type," Slorn answered proudly. "Most spirits who emit light are fire spirits in one form or another. They all have the same type. It's like a spirit species." He added that last bit for Josef, who looked completely lost.

"But the law of type merely states that spirits of the same type share strengths and weaknesses," Eli said, giving the coat's fabric an experimental tug, amazed at the strength of it. "What does that have to do with not seeing?"

Slorn chuckled. "Let's just say that spirits who share a type also share the same blindnesses. For example, fire spirits as a whole are very direct. They don't bother with things they can't burn. To take advantage of this, I simply wove the spirits in the coat together in a way that, for the spirits, makes it look like resting water, which is of no interest to flames."

"Wait," Josef said. "So you're saying fire doesn't see water?"

"No," Slorn shook his head. "I'm saying that, since deep, standing water is generally not a threat to fire spirits, they are almost universally uninterested in it, and so feel no need to illuminate it." He gave Josef an amused look. "Why do you think lakes look so black at night?"

"Clever," Eli said, letting the sleeve fall back to its position. "Very, very clever. So we've got a coat that is almost invisible in firelight. That will be very useful in our line of work."

"Doesn't work in sunlight, though," Slorn said, frowning. "The sun's a different matter entirely, so don't get overconfident."

"No worries," Eli said. "I'm confident in my confidence. What else did you put in?"

Slorn shook his head and turned back to the coat. "It's a vast improvement over the previous coat. It's stronger and more flexible, though still thick enough to keep even the most persistent spirits from seeing what's inside, not that they would know to try. To the spirit world, this coat and anything it hides are just a blank, no more interesting than a sleeping nest of small water spirits or a pile of finely ground sand. Plus, the needles are putting a hood in as we speak, so there won't be the problem of losing the hat anymore, though she will look a little out of place in warmer climates."

"She'll look a little out of place anywhere besides a cultist convention." Eli grinned. "Fortunately, we're not concerned with appearances." He looked over at Nico. "What do you think?"

Nico's eyes were wide. "I want to try it."

"Go ahead," Slorn said, stepping aside.

The needles finished the last stitches on the hood as Nico stepped forward. She reached out, almost hesitantly, and took hold of the coat by the collar, gently sliding it off the dummy's shoulder and onto her own. It fell around her like a cloak, seemingly far too big, and yet her hands peeked out perfectly from the long sleeves while the hem ended just below her knees. She gave it an experimental shake, and the coat swirled around her like a current.

"Well?" Josef said.

Nico held out her arms. "It's heavy," she said, surprised.

"Not nearly as heavy as it should be," Slorn said, "considering what's in it. That coat contains almost a hundred feet of cloth, all folded and crunched around itself to give the spirit an actual size and power much greater than its form would suggest. There's wool and silk and steel in the weave, all picked for their complementary personalities and strong sense of duty. Out of that mesh of spirits, I have imprinted a new soul with properties greater than its component parts." Slorn ran his fingers over the smooth, black fabric. "This cloth will stop arrows, knives, and even a sword thrust from anything except an awakened blade. On your shoulders, it's better than any normal armor ever could be, because all the pieces of this coat, the thread, the cloth, the buttons, are part of one awakened spirit given a single purpose: to protect the spirit world from panic and destruction by concealing the demon and protecting the demon's prison"—he nodded at Nico—"you. If you are the strongbox that holds the demon, they are the vault around you, or that's how the spirit sees itself." Slorn smiled. "I made it rather zealous, so you'll have to be careful. The coat will follow you as its captain and obey any orders you give so long as they do not contradict the purpose I used as the foundation of its creation—preventing the demonseed from escaping into the world."

"Wait," Eli said. "Follow her orders? How? Nico's not a wizard."

Slorn looked at him, astonished. "Of course she's a wizard. Only wizards can become demonseeds. Normal human souls are far too flimsy to contain a demonseed to maturity."

A stab of betrayal hit Eli in the gut as he turned to Nico. "You were a wizard all this time? Why didn't you tell me?"

For the first time since he'd know her, Nico looked hurt. "You didn't ask," she said softly. "And it didn't seem important. Besides, it's not like I can talk to spirits casually, being what I am."

Eli opened his mouth to ask more questions, but the murderous look he was getting from Josef was enough to make him close it again. Fortunately, Slorn took that moment to change the subject altogether.

"Now that you've seen the work," he said, "it's time to talk about the price."

"I was wondering when we'd get to that." Eli sighed. "Well, never let it be said that I am a man who doesn't pay his bills. What can we do for you?"

Slorn sat down on the edge of his wooden table. "Have you heard of the Fenzetti blades?"

"Of course," Eli said. "I'm a thief. I've heard of everything you can put a price on, and the price on a Fenzetti is higher than most. There are, what, five total in the world? All held by collectors who won't sell them for love or money."

"There are ten, actually," Josef said, "including the half-finished piece Fenzetti was working on when he died." He raised his eyebrows at Eli's incredulous expression. "What? I'm a swordsman. Fenzetti blades are famous swords. It's not hard to see the connection. What I want to know," he said, shifting his gaze to Slorn, "is why does the world's greatest awakened swordsmith want one? Fenzettis are novelty items, prized for their supposed indestructibility, but they're hardly great works of sword making.

Any swordsman, wizard or not, would gladly trade a Fenzetti for one of Heinricht Slorn's blades."

Slorn's mouth twitched. "It's not supposed indestructibility. The swords made by Fenzetti are impossible to break by any known means. Fenzetti was a Shaper wizard, you see. This was hundreds of years ago, far before my time, but he was legendary as one of our most creative craftsmen and guild masters, presiding over an uncommonly experimental and productive period of Shaper history. Now, traditionally, Shapers keep a large stockpile of rare materials for their work, including materials no one else really knows about—things the spirits bring them, oddities, stuff no one else understands. The objects we call Fenzetti blades are made of such a substance. The Shapers named it bone metal, for its off-white color, and for a while it was a subject of great interest among the Shaper crafters. It's not often you get your hands on an indestructible substance. Unfortunately, this indestructibility also made the bone metal completely unworkable. You can't melt it or scratch it, can't crush it or hammer it, and no one has ever successfully woken a bone metal spirit. After a few years of frenzied study, most Shapers wrote bone metal off as an interesting but useless substance. What good is a material that can't be turned into anything?"

"Fascinating history lesson," Eli said. "But when does Fenzetti come in?"

"I was getting to that," Slorn said crossly. "Of all the Shapers, Fenzetti was the only one who ever figured out how to work bone metal. Over a twenty-year span, he made a series of unbreakable swords from the material. Still, even the great Fenzetti could do only crude work with bone metal, and I've heard that even the few pieces he considered his masterworks aren't much to look at. But then"—Slorn grinned—"I'm not exactly looking to hang one on my wall. I want the metal."

"Well, in that case," Eli said, "why not just buy bone metal? Why go through the trouble of stealing a Fenzetti?"

"Because bone metal is so rare in nature it might as well not exist," Slorn said, annoyed. "What bone metal there is, the Shapers keep in their storehouses under their mountain. As I think should be abundantly clear by this point, they're not just going to sell the stuff to me, and I don't think you want to try robbing the Shaper mountain again."

"No," Eli said, laughing. "Once was enough for me, thanks. I guess Fenzetti blades it is. Do you want any one in particular?"

"A large one would be preferable," Slorn said thoughtfully. "But I don't have a particular blade in mind. Whatever you can get quickly will be fine."

"Quickly may be relative," Eli said. "But a deal is a deal, and you certainly did come through on your end."

"Are we settled then?" Slorn said.

"Yes." Eli grinned and stuck out his hand. "One coat for one bone metal blade, even trade."

Slorn shook his hand firmly and then shuffled them out of his workroom, Nico still happily swirling her coat. As they filed out into the main room, they found Pele there waiting for them. Her face was pale and anxious, and her hair was windswept and wild, as if she'd been standing in a gale, though the trees outside were perfectly still.

"Slorn," she said quietly. "The weather's changing."

Eli gave her an odd look. Weather talk wasn't usually something Pele mentioned with that kind of gravity. Slorn, however, stopped midstep and pricked up his round ears, listening.

"You're right," he said, at once as serious as she was. "The pressure is changing." He looked to Eli. "You've got the coat, so you'd best be leaving now. The weather changes quickly here. We need to move the house."

"If you say so." Eli felt uncomfortably like he had just missed something very important. "Wasn't like we had much left to do, anyway."

It took them about five minutes to get everything assembled. The kitchen packed them a bag of sandwiches and fruit that Eli took with such effusive thanks, the counters were nearly quivering with happiness. Josef, meanwhile, packed up his knives suspiciously, keeping his eyes on Slorn and Pele as they went around closing cabinets and shuttering windows. Eli didn't blame him. It was hard to feel the urgency for a storm when the sky was blue and bright.

But as they trundled down the stairs and out onto the dry stream bed, Eli began to feel it too. The pressure was falling, making his ears ache, and though the air was still and calm, he could smell rain. High overhead, the clouds were moving quickly.

Slorn and Pele saw them to the edge of the woods, but the moment Eli, Nico, and Josef stepped into the shade of the trees, their hosts turned and went back inside the house without looking back, as though they were deliberately trying not to see which way their guests left.

When the door shut behind them, the house shuddered. There was an enormous creak of bending wood, and the house's foundations began to move. The four spindly legs straightened and stretched their chicken-feet talons, leaning forward, then backward, so that the house rocked like a ship at sea, and Eli felt sure he was going to be sick just watching. Then, when all the legs were stretched, the house shuddered and took a step forward. The wooden limbs rippled like muscle, and the house was off, walking in long strides down the dry streambed and disappearing into the woods with surprising speed, leaving only a thin line of chimney smoke behind it and no footprints at all.

Josef gave a low whistle as he watched the line of smoke vanish behind the trees. "No wonder the bastard was so hard to find." He looked over at Eli. "So, you're his friend; are the storms here that dangerous or was the bear man spinning a story to get rid of us?"

"I don't think that's the case," Eli said quietly, looking south. There, barely visible over the treetops, the black smudge of a storm front was building on the horizon. That much wasn't so unusual; the weather in the mountains was finicky, but something was off. The clouds around the storm front were drifting south, yet the dark thunderheads were plowing straight north against the wind, and moving fast.

"Come on," Eli said. "I don't think we want to be around when that hits."

Josef nodded and they began to move east, following the streambed, walking as fast as they could go in the loose sand. Behind them, the storm rolled on, veering slightly west in the direction Slorn's house had gone.

The walking house stopped on a rocky cliff at the edge of the Awakened Wood. It turned twice in a circle and then crouched on the cliff's edge. As soon as the house stopped swaying, Slorn opened the door and stomped down the rickety steps, his bear face unreadable. Pele was right behind him, and they took their positions in the high, scrubby field that led up to the cliff.

The storm rolled over the forest, lit from within almost constantly by arcs of blue-white lightning. The treetops tossed sideways where it passed, yet no rain fell. Slorn and Pele hunched against the wind as it came, howling and heavy with the ear-splitting pressure of the storm. The clouds flew overhead, blotting out the afternoon sun, and the cliff went as dark as rainy midnight. Slorn could feel Pele shivering next to him, and he put a hand on her shoulder, steadying her as they waited in the dark.

Lightning flashed all around them, jumping between the

clouds in spidering arcs. Then, with a crack that split all hearing, a single tree-sized bolt struck the ground in front of Slorn, blinding what little night vision he had gained. But no light could blind the world Slorn saw through his spirit sight, and as the clap of thunder followed on the lightning's heels, he saw it appear. A primordial storm, such as had not been seen in the world since creation, stood before them, an epic war of air and water spirits and the lightning spirits they birthed, embroiled in an endless conflict hundreds of miles across. Yet all of this was bound into the shape of a tall man in a black coat carrying a long sword, crushed together by the white mark Slorn dared not look at. The flash of the lightning faded, and Slorn let his normal eyes, the bear's soft-focusing, near-sighted vision, take over. It was best not to look at the Lord of Storms as he truly was for too long.

For a long, awkward moment, no one spoke. Finally, Slorn took the initiative, lowering himself in a small bow. "Welcome, as always, my lord. What can we do for you?"

"Spare me the gracious-host routine," the Lord of Storms said. His voice was impatient, and he was looking around, his flashing eyes seeing through everything. "I'm just here to get our new recruit his sword."

The Lord of Storms stepped aside to reveal another man standing behind him. Slorn's eyes widened in surprise. He hadn't even seen the man until now, though that was due to the Lord of Storm's control over his thunderheads. There certainly was no other way Slorn could have missed the monster of the man who stepped forward. He was taller even than the Lord of Storms, and nearly twice as wide. His head was clean shaven and crisscrossed with pale, puckered scars. His black coat, which was too small, he wore open and fluttering in the wind, the sleeves ripped off to make room for his bulky, overmuscled arms. His face had the strange, smashed look of a brawler's, the bones broken too often to ever sit right again. Yet what made Slorn look away in disgust wasn't his crooked fingers or his sharp-toothed, murderous sneer, but the sash he wore across his bare chest.

It was a strip of crimson fabric tied over one shoulder of his ripped coat. The cloth had several long, telling splatters streaked across it that left little to Slorn's imagination, but even more disturbing was what was sewn into the sash. All across the red cloth, sewn in with surprising care, was a collection of what Slorn could only guess were trophies. There were broken sword hilts, some of them with their spirits still whimpering in pain, bits of jewelry still splattered with lines of dark, dried blood, and other things Slorn didn't look at too closely.

"This must be the one you told me about," Slorn said carefully. "Your new, nonwizard recruit." It had to be. There was no way a wizard could wear what the man was wearing and not go mad.

"Yes," the Lord of Storms said. "Spirit deafness is a bit of a hindrance, but you don't have to hear to kill demons. Sted here has proven he can get the job done, so I've decided to make him a full member of the League." He smiled at Slorn, a terrifying sight. "The sword's the last bit he needs. I presume it's ready?"

"Yes," Slorn said. "Pele, take Mr. Sted here to his new sword."

To her credit, Pele didn't hesitate. She stepped forward and motioned for the enormous man to follow her. As they disappeared into the house, Slorn took the opportunity to broach the subject hanging over their heads.

"So," he said, looking at the Lord of Storms. "It's not often you escort a new recruit to pick up a sword yourself. Is Sted that good?"

"Hardly," the Lord of Storms said. "Sted's a brawler. He was born a brawler and he'll die the same. I only hope we can squeeze a few dead demons out of him before it happens." He turned to face Slorn, and his expression grew murderous, a sure sign that the time for small talk was past. "You need to consider the company you keep more carefully, Slorn."

Slorn crossed his arms. "So long as I fulfill my contract to provide the League of Storms with awakened blades, I am free to pursue whatever other side projects I desire. This is our agreement."

The Lord of Storms sneered. "I allow your little dalliances with that thing you keep up in the mountains only because the Weaver managed to convince my lady you would be the one to find a cure for the demon infestation. That generosity does not extend to Monpress's pet monster. I may be forbidden from interfering in the thief's actions, but that doesn't mean I have to stand by and watch while you sell him tools to hide the demon from us."

So the Lord of Storms had been warned off Eli by the Shepherdess. Slorn had suspected something of the sort. It wasn't like the League to let something like Nico run free. He tucked that bit of information away for future use.

"All I gave Eli was a coat to replace the girl's ruined one," he said. "Surely you don't want the demon terrifying the countryside and causing panics."

"Spare me," the Lord of Storms snarled. "Know this, Shaper: This is not the way of things for much longer. Do you think that boy's my lady's first favorite? Or her last? The time is coming, very soon, when the Shepherdess will grow tired of Monpress's antics. I suggest you think long and hard about where your loyalties fall when that day comes."

"When that day comes," Slorn said slowly, "I know exactly what I will do."

"Good," the Lord of Storms said. "The League of Storms has existed since the world began, and in all that time you're one of the best swordsmiths we've ever had. It would be a great shame to lose you." He paused, and gave Slorn a long, hard look. "Great, but not unbearable. Do I make myself clear?"

Slorn smiled. "Immensely."

Inside the house, Pele lit the lamps with a wave of her hand as she led the way to her father's study. The man behind her, Sted, was talking in a loud, brash voice, as he'd been since she'd closed the front door behind him.

"So," he said, keeping too close behind her. "You're the bear man's what, servant? Lover?"

"Apprentice," she answered curtly, leading him into the den.

"Ah." She could see him grinning. "Thought you looked a little rough for a concubine, but we are pretty far out. Where are we, anyway? The boss wouldn't tell me."

"We're in the Turning Wood," Pele said, coming to a stop at Slorn's workroom door. "That's all I can tell you. Slorn's location is a League secret."

She opened the door to the workroom and led him inside. "I must ask you not to touch anything," she said. "No spirit in this workshop may be touched by outside hands without Slorn's permission."

"Why would I want to touch this junk?" Sted growled, glaring at the scraps of cloth left over from Nico's coat. "Where's my sword?"

Pele stood aside and motioned to the black blade on the wall. Sted stopped in his tracks. He stared at the sword, eyes wide. "Is it magic?"

"It is awakened," Pele answered, turning to look at the jagged-toothed blade as well. "Since you are spirit deaf, Slorn made the blade from a stock of ore with a very straightforward personality. This sword has only one desire: to destroy all that stand before it.

Not a sophisticated weapon, but we were assured a straightforward blade would be best for a man of your"—she paused—"talents."

If Sted caught the insult, he showed no sign. He reached out greedily for the blade, but Pele moved faster, gripping the handle right before him.

"As I said, no touching." She met his angry glare. "The sword doesn't know you, and it would be happy to take your hand off. Before I can hand it to you safely, you'll need its name."

Sted snorted. "What do I look like, some duelist fop? I don't bother with names for my swords."

"No, you don't name it," Pele said crossly. "This is an awakened sword. It has its own name." Gasping a little at the weight, Pele carefully took the sword down from its peg, wincing as she always did at the pure blood thirst that permeated the metal. "This is Dunolg," she said, turning the blade so that the hilt was toward Sted, "the Iron Avalanche."

Sted grinned, taking the sword with a steady hand. "A proud name." He gave it a test swing, which was quite unnerving in the tiny room. "It fits," he said, nodding. "Yes, this sword will do nicely. I can feel it. We'll cut anything that dares stand before us."

Pele stepped back as Sted swung the sword again, his scarred face lighting up with ghoulish delight as the wicked, toothed blade cut through the air. It whistled as it swung, a low trill of pure, violent hunger that made Pele sick to her stomach. When she had helped Slorn forge the blade, she hadn't been able to imagine the kind of man who could form a bond with such a monster. Now, as Sted tied the jagged blade to his hip with a length of stained leather, she was sorry she'd found out.

Slorn and the Lord of Storms were waiting in silence when Sted and Pele exited the house. Sted started to say something about his new sword, which he wore proudly on his hip, but one look at his master's face was enough to silence him. Without a word, he took up his place beside the Lord of Storms. When he was in position, the Lord waved his hand, and then, without a good-bye or a thank-you, they were gone. There was no lightning this time; they simply vanished into the dark. The moment they were gone, the unnatural clouds began to roll away, retreating as quickly as they had come, and sunlight burst back onto the high ridge.

Only when the storm front was far in the distance did Slorn let out the breath he'd been holding.

"Father," Pele said softly, "was it right to give that man *that* sword?"

"Right has nothing to do with it." Slorn ran his rough hands over the fur between his ears. "It was work, Pele, nothing more." With that, he turned and walked back into the house. "Let's move."

Pele sighed. When her father got like this, there was no point in asking for more explanation. She simply hurried after him, climbing the rickety steps as the house began to shudder. As soon as she was inside, the house took off down the ridge, heading north, toward the mountains.

CHAPTER 7

The Spirit Court's tower was not the only great building in Zarin. Across the city, past the dip in the ridge made by the swift Whitefall River, the white-painted stone and timber buildings that made up most of the city took a turn for the elegant. The roads steepened as they climbed up the ridge, cutting back and forth until they reached the highest arch of the city's rocky backbone. There, perched like a coral on a jut of bare rock, stood the Whitefall Citadel, fortress of the Whitefall family, the Merchant Princes of Zarin, and official home of the unprecedented organization they had founded, the Council of Thrones. Though not as tall or as mystical as the Spiritualist's white tower, it was nonetheless magnificently impressive. The castle stood apart from the city, separated from the steep road by a long bridge that stretched across a natural gap in the ridge. Perched as it was on an outcropping, the citadel seemed to float all on its own, a great, airy fortress of flashing white walls and soaring arches. But most impressive of all were the famous towers of Zarin. There were seven in all crowning the inner keep, so tall they seemed to scrape the sky itself with their hammered gold spires.

Despite its grandness, these days the citadel was mostly for show. It remained the symbol of the Council, and its seven towers stood in proud relief on every gold standard the Council mint pressed, but the enormous bureaucracy that kept the Council turning over had long ago outgrown the soaring towers of its home fortress, spilling into the mansions and trade halls of the surrounding slopes. These days, the only people who actually stayed in the fortress were the Whitefall family of Zarin and any actual nobles who deigned to come to Council functions themselves.

On the fifth floor of the citadel's inner keep, where everything was as luxurious as money and station could make it, one such man, Edward di Fellbro, Duke of Gaol, was having tea in his rooms. For most nobility, especially those with lands as rich as Gaol, this act would have involved at least three servants, yet Edward was alone, calmly finishing a modest plate of fruit and bread at the corner of his enormous dining table, which was covered, not in cornucopias of exotic fruits and sweetmeats, but with maps.

They were spread out neatly end to end, maps from every region in the Council Kingdom in different styles and time periods, some old and worn, some whose ink had hardly dried, yet every single one of them was dotted with the same meticulous red markings. Sometimes they were *X*s, sometimes circles or squares, and very occasionally a triangle. No matter the shape, however, the same tight, neat notation was listed beside each one, usually a number and a short description, and always marked with a date.

Duke Edward stared at the maps intently, his thin face drawn into a thoughtful frown as he took a sip from his teacup only to notice it was empty. Scowling, he held out his cup, and an elegant teapot on four silver legs waddled over to refill it. The pot trembled as it moved, its worked golden lid rattling softly as it poured. The duke glared at the pot and it stopped rattling instantly, moving back to its spot in the tea service with murmured apologies and careful bows so as not to drip.

Edward saw none of it. His stare was already back on the maps, flicking from point to point in no discernible order. From his posture, he might have stayed like that indefinitely, but a knock on the carved door interrupted his contemplation.

"Enter," he said, not bothering to hide the annoyance in his voice.

The door opened, and one of the Council pages, dressed head to toe in the ridiculous white and silver finery Whitefall made all his servants wear, stepped timidly into the room.

"Spiritualist Hern to see you, my Lord," the boy announced with a low bow.

Edward put down his fork and pushed his plate away. "Send him in."

The boy stepped back, and the duke's unexpected guest sailed into the room. Sailed was the right word. Edward had never met anyone as preoccupied with his appearance as Hern. The

Spiritualist was in full regalia today, a tight green coat embroidered with blue and silver in the imitation of peacock feathers, with tall, turned, and pointed cuffs hanging down over the glittering, knuckle-sized jewels of his rings.

"I swear, Edward," he said, collapsing onto a cushioned lounge by the window as the boy closed the door, "your quarters get smaller every time you come to Zarin. And they've got you up on the fifth floor this time, with all those stairs." He pulled out a handkerchief and patted his flushed face. "It's intolerable. I never understood why you don't just take a house in the city like everyone else."

"I see no point for such a useless expense," the duke said dryly. "Besides, the part of my Council dues that covers these rooms is too dear already. A rich lord does not stay rich by indulging in redundant expense."

"So you like to say," Hern said, helping himself to a cup from the tea service, which he held out for the nervous teapot to fill. "What's that you're working on there?" He nodded toward the spread of maps. "Plotting to expand your lands? Going to take over the Council Kingdoms?"

"Hardly," the duke said. "They wouldn't be worth the bother."

"So what are these for, then?" The Spiritualist actually sounded fascinated, a sure sign that he was only trying to get Edward talking and comfortable. It was the same song and dance they went through every time Hern visited, and Edward had long since learned it was faster to just go along than try and force the Spiritualist to get to his point sooner. Besides, he hadn't explained his system in a long while, and explaining something to others was a useful exercise for uncovering faults in execution.

"These," he said, leaning forward and stretching out his hand to tap one of the red markings on the map in front of him, "are the movements of Eli Monpress."

Hern blinked. "The thief?"

"Do you know any other Monpresses?" Edward gave him a scathing look. "You asked, so pay attention. Each red mark denotes where he's been active since he first appeared five years ago." He moved his fingers over the maps without touching them, tracing a path between the markings. "The *X*s are confirmed robberies, the circles are unconfirmed incidents that I believe were his work, and the squares are crimes attributed to Monpress, but which I don't believe he had a hand in."

"And how do you make that judgment?" Hern said, blowing on his tea.

"I look for a pattern." Edward was pleased with the question. A chance to talk through his logic was always welcome. "All men have patterns. It's human nature, even for someone as famously unpredictable as Monpress. Look here." He moved his finger over the *X* closest to him, far south of Zarin, covering the dot that denoted the desert city of Amit.

"Monpress's first crime we know of was here, the theft of the Count of Amit's cash prize for the annual Race of the Dunes. He also stole the winning horse, which he then used as a getaway. He's next seen a few months later"—his finger ran up the maps, heading far north to the very top of the Council Kingdoms—"here." He tapped a red *X* in an empty spot of the map, somewhere in the wilderness between the Kingdom of Jenet and the Kingdom of Favol. "He ambushed the wedding procession of the Princess of Jenet and stole her entire dowry, including nearly eighty pounds of gold brick, fifty horses, a hundred head of cattle, and all of the bride's wedding jewelry."

"I've heard of that one," Hern said with a laugh. "The story I heard said he did it all by himself, but surely—"

"I think that was the case," the duke said. "Before the swordsman and the girl came into the picture a little over a year ago,

Monpress always acted alone. For the Princess of Jenet, witnesses say he talked the road itself into changing its path, leading the whole procession into a sinking mire that he could reportedly walk over like it was dry land."

"Come, that's impossible." Hern waved his jewel-covered hand. "I've got two top-notch earth spirits, and even I couldn't convince an entire road to move."

Edward raised his eyebrows, tucking that fact away for future use. "Well," he said, "however he managed it, the road story fits Monpress's pattern."

"Which is?" Hern said, slurping his tea.

The duke gave him a flat look. Even if he was only feigning interest, surely Hern wasn't that dense. "Look at the history," Edward said slowly. "Monpress's crimes are always robberies, and not just robberies, but thefts on a grand scale, usually against nobility. They are never violent, save in self defense, and usually leave little question as to who the perpetrator was."

"You mean the calling card." Hern nodded.

"Indeed." Edward reached up to the very top of his maps and unclipped the small stack of white cards he'd pinned there. They were all roughly the same size, and though a few were on cheaper paper, they all had the same basic look: a white card stamped at the center with the same fanciful, cursive *M*.

"They started out handwritten," the duke said, shuffling through the cards carefully so as not to get them out of order. "Then after his third crime, when his bounty was raised to five hundred gold standards, they were all printed. The early ones are still cheap, but for the past two years, he's used a variety of high-quality stocks, though never the same one twice." The duke smiled, tapping the cards on the table to line them up again. "Monpress is vain, you see. He's a glutton for attention. That's the way you can spot a fake Monpress crime."

He spread his hands over the maps, coming to rest on one of the red squares just north of Zarin. "Here," he said. "Two years ago someone broke into a money changer's house, killing one of his apprentices in the process. The thief left a Monpress calling card, and that was all the local authorities needed. However, anyone who's spent time studying Monpress knows that, whoever committed that crime, it wasn't Eli. First off, a money changer's office is far too small a target. Second, the murder of the apprentice, very unlike him, but the real sign here is the lack of flair. It's such a simple, unsophisticated crime. Uninventive. For me, that alone is enough to absolve Monpress of guilt in this matter."

"Impressive," Hern said, making a good show of actually looking impressed. "Are you going to take all this over to the bounty office, then? Earn a little goodwill from the Council? The northern kingdoms are still rather miffed at you for raising the toll to use your river last year."

"I calculate my toll based on the damages their drunken, irresponsible barge captains inflict on my docks," the duke said. "If they have a problem with that, then they are free to reimburse me directly or hire better captains. As for Eli," the duke said, returning the stack of cards to its place at the top of the map, "I would never dream of giving my findings to a group as disorganized and sensational as the Council's Bounty Office. If they think they can just throw money at a problem as complex and nuanced as Monpress and make it go away, then they deserve the runaround he's giving them."

Hern gave him a sly look over his teacup. "Thinking of collecting the bounty yourself, then? I didn't think fifty-five thousand was a large enough number to interest a man of your wealth."

"Do not make assumptions about my interests," the duke said, sitting back. "Only a shortsighted fool thinks he is wealthy enough not to take opportunities presented."

"How interesting to hear you say that," Hern said, sitting up and putting his teacup aside. "As it happens, a new opportunity has just opened up for me."

The duke smiled and mentally calculated Hern's timing. Five minutes from arrival to broaching of actual point, faster than usual. Hern must have something big on the line. "How much?" he asked, tapping his fingers together.

Hern looked taken aback. "Edward," he said, "what makes you think—"

The Duke of Gaol gave him a cutting look. "How much, Hern?"

"Ten thousand gold standards," Hern said, crossing his legs and draping his arms over the back of the couch. When the duke gave him an incredulous look, he just shrugged. "You asked, I answered. I've a rare opportunity here, Edward. Remember what I wrote you a few days ago about forcing Banage to exile his own apprentice to a tower? Well, the girl lived up to her reputation better than I'd thought possible and rejected the deal entirely. Fortunately, I got wind of this before the trial, and just this afternoon I had her convicted of treason."

"Sounds like a done deal," the duke said. "Why do you need my money?"

"Well," Hern said and took another long sip of his tea. "A treason conviction is a serious matter, Edward, especially for a girl as promising and protected as Banage's little pet. It all happened very quickly and I had to make a few promises the night before to see it through."

"I see," the duke said. "And these 'promises' add up to ten thousand gold standards? What happened to the thousand I gave you last month?"

"Gone," Hern said with a shrug. "How do you think I got the signatures for her accusation? Whether they're Tower Keepers or apprentices, all Spiritualists have an obsession with duty, and that makes getting them to do anything very expensive. Frankly, Edward, you got that trial on the cheap. Any other time and it would easily have cost twice that much to put Banage's favorite on the spot. But this Mellinor business was such a mess. People were already nice and scared and looking for someone to blame, and who better than the girl at the heart of it?"

"And what does this have to do with me?" the duke said. "So far, all I've heard is the usual Spiritualist politics, and I have quite enough politics of my own to deal with. Why should I give you ten thousand standards to fund more?"

Hern's eyes narrowed. "Don't get cheap on me, Fellbro. This is as much for your benefit as mine. Fifteen years now I've been Gaol's Tower Keeper, and for fifteen years I've been keeping idealists like Banage out of your land. We don't need to go into what would happen if an investigation of Gaol was requested, but you'd be amazed how fast the Spirit Court's policy of noninterference with sovereign states can vanish if they judge the cause worthy enough. Such an investigation could be especially troubling if they teamed up with your enemies in the Council, who would love to see a return to lax tariffs and rules of your father's time. I have worked tirelessly for years now to keep your secrets, and all I've ever asked in return is a little monetary assistance in my efforts to reform the Court. Ten thousand is pocket change for a man like you. We both know it, so don't try and pretend I'm being unreasonable, or else I may have to start suddenly remembering things about Gaol you'd rather I didn't."

Edward gave the Spiritualist a disgusted look. Still, the man did have a point, and it had been a while since he'd dipped into the Spirit Court management part of Gaol's budget. "You're sure that ten thousand will buy the result you're after?"

"Certain." Hern leaned forward. "Miranda Lyonette was one of Banage's key pillars within the Court. It's no secret he's been grooming her to be his successor. Crushing her is the closest we can come to striking a direct blow at Etmon himself. Even though she managed to flee Zarin before her sentence could be carried out, the deed is done."

"She escaped?" The duke arched his dark eyebrows. "That was careless of you, Hern."

"Doesn't matter," Hern said, shaking his head. "She can't run forever, and in any case, her reputation is ruined. She'll never work as a Spiritualist again, and Banage is left alone and bereft, robbed of the apprentice he loved like a daughter. The old man is weakening, a bit at a time. Soon, with enough money and pressure, the damage will be irreversible. We'll rip Banage's control of the Court wide open, and then all I have to do is be in the right place at the right time with the right incentives and the Spirit Court will be mine, and, through reasonable extension, yours."

He finished with a smile the duke found discomfortingly overconfident. Using money to sway circumstance in your favor was one thing, but when you started outright buying people to act against their conscience, a situation could quickly slide out of control. Still, he'd requested Hern as his Tower Keeper exactly because the man knew how to play the Spirit Court. If he couldn't trust him now he'd have lost a lot more than ten thousand gold.

"One more question," the duke said carefully. "This Miranda Lyonette, she's the one the Court sent to Mellinor after Monpress, correct?"

"Yes," Hern said. "Her failure there was what got her into this mess."

The duke nodded. "And do you think the Spirit Court will be sending anyone else after Eli while this is going on?"

"No," Hern said. "I think the Court has had quite enough of Monpress for a while."

Duke Edward nodded absently, staring down at his maps.

"How fortuitous." He looked back at Hern. "I'll send a notice for the ten thousand to your house after I've warned my exchequer. He'll assist you as usual in collecting the money from my accounts in Zarin. And if you need more, Hern, don't bother coming over. Just send a letter with a documented list as to why. All of this beating around the issue is inefficient."

Hern's eye's widened at that, but his smile never flickered. "Lovely chatting with you too, my lord," he said, standing up with a graceful swirl of his coat.

"Send in the page on your way out," the duke said, reaching across the table to grab a sheaf of blank stationery and an ink pot from his desk.

Hern shot him a dirty look, but the duke was already absorbed in whatever he was writing, his pen scratching in neat, efficient strokes across the paper. With a sneer at being treated like a valet, Hern left the duke's room in a huff, grabbing the first page he saw and literally shoving the boy toward the duke's door before it had even finished closing.

The boy stumbled into the duke's parlor, blinking in confusion for a few moments before recovering enough to drop the customary bow.

"You," the duke said without looking up from his note, which he was folding into thirds. "Take this to the printing office on Little Shambles Street. Give it to Master Scribe Phelps, and *only* Master Scribe Phelps. Tell him that fortuitous circumstances have necessitated an acceleration of my order, and he is to have the numbers outlined on that note ready for distribution at the points written beside them by tomorrow morning. Repeat that."

"Printing office, Little Shambles Street, Master Scribe Phelps," the boy repeated with the practiced memory of a trained page who got this sort of request quite often. "I am to tell him that fortuitous circumstances have necessitated an acceleration of your order, and he is to have these numbers ready for distribution at the points written beside them by tomorrow morning."

The duke handed him the folded note without a word of thanks, and the boy shuffled out, wishing that, just once, the duke would bother to tip for such feats of memory. He never did, but that was part of why Merchant Prince Whitefall charged the old cheapskate double for his rooms.

When the page was gone the duke stood alone at his table going over his plans step by step in his head. He did this often, for it gave him great pleasure to be thorough. Phelps would balk at having to print thousands of detailed posters and have them packed for distribution in one night, but a successful man seized opportunity when it arrived. The Court's interest in Monpress had been the last uncontrollable element. If they were putting off their investigation thanks to this business in Mellinor, now was the time to strike. Accelerating the pace made him nervous, but he fought the feeling down. Surely this apprehension was merely a product of being in Zarin, where things were messy and chaotic. In a week, all his business here would be done and he'd be on his way back to Gaol, where everything was orderly, controlled, and perfect.

Just thinking about it brought a smile to his face, and he reached down for his teacup, newly refilled by the creeping teapot, which had already returned to its place on the tea service. Yes, he thought, walking over to the tall windows, sipping his tea as he watched Hern climb into an ostentatious carriage in the little courtyard below while, behind him, the page hurried toward the gates with the letter in his hands. Yes, things were going perfectly smoothly. If the printers did as they were paid to do, then tomorrow the net woven of everything he'd learned over years of following Monpress would finally be cast. All he had to do was sit back and wait for the thief to take the bait, and then even an element as chaotic as Eli Monpress would be drawn at last into predictable order.

The happiness of that thought carried him through the rest of his day, and if he drove particularly hard bargains in his meetings that afternoon, no one thought anything special of it. He was the Duke of Gaol, after all.

CHAPTER 8

Down the mountains from Slorn's woods, where the ground began to level out into low hills and branching creeks, the city of Goin lay huddled between two muddy banks. Little more than an overgrown border outpost, Goin was claimed by two countries, neither of which bothered with it much, leaving the soggy dirt streets to the trappers and loggers who called it home. It was a rowdy, edge-of-nowhere outpost where the law, what there was of it, turned a blind eye to anything that wasn't directed squarely at them, which was just how Eli liked it.

"Aren't you glad I talked you out of making camp and coming down in the morning?" Eli said, strolling down the final half mile of rutted trail out of the mountains.

"I still don't see why you wanted to come here at all," Josef said. "I passed through here about two years ago chasing Met Skark, the assassin duelist. It was a mangy collection of lowlifes then too, and Met wasn't nearly as good as his wanted posters made him out to be. Still," he said, smiling warmly, "Goin did have some lively bar fights once the locals got drunk enough not to see the Heart, so it wasn't a total waste."

Eli looked at him sideways, eyeing the enormous wrapped hilt that poked up over Josef's broad shoulders. "I don't see how anyone could get that drunk."

"The strained liquor they brew in the mountains is strong stuff." Josef chuckled. "They don't call it Northern Poison for nothing."

Goin was surrounded by a high wall of split and sharpened logs set into the thick mud. The northern gate was closed when they reached it, but the guard door stood wide open.

"Sort of defeats the point of a gate in the first place," Eli said, standing aside as Josef and Nico ducked through.

Josef shook his head. "Can't say I blame them for not bothering."

Eli sighed. The man had a point. Inside the wooden wall, the town was a maze of wood and stone buildings, dirt streets, flickering torches, filthy straw, burly, drunk men, and foul smells. Hardly a high-value target, even for the least discerning bandits.

"Civilization at last," he mumbled, covering his face with his handkerchief. "This way."

He led them deeper into the town, stepping over drunks and dodging fistfights, turning down blind alleys seemingly at random until he stopped in front of a small, run-down building. There was no sign, nothing to separate the building from the dozen other run-down buildings around it. Josef glared at it suspicously, but Eli smoothed his coat over his chest, checked his hair, then stepped forward to knock lightly on the rickety wooden door.

On the second knock, the door cracked open and a hand in a grubby leather glove shot out, palm up. With a flick of his fingers Eli produced a gold standard, which he dropped into the waiting hand. It must have been enough, for the door flew open and a burly man in a logger's woolen shirt and leather pants welcomed them in.

"Sit down," he said, motioning to a fur-covered bench. "I'll get the broker."

Eli smiled and sat. Josef, however, did not. He leaned on the wall by the door, arms crossed over his chest. Nico stayed right beside him, her eyes strangely luminous beneath the deep hood of her new coat.

The large man vanished through the little door at the rear of the building, leaving his guests alone in the tiny room, which was uncomfortably warm thanks to the red-hot stove in the corner and smelled like dust. A few moments later, the man came out again, this time trailed by a tall, thin woman in men's trousers and a thick woolen coat, her graying hair pulled tight behind her head. She walked to a stool by the stove and sat down, looking Eli square in the eye as the large man took up position behind her.

"The fee is five standards a question," she said.

"That's a bit steep," Eli said. "One is traditional."

"Maybe in the city," the woman sneered. "This far out, customers are few and far between. I have to eat. Besides, you don't pay the doorman in gold if you're bargain shopping. Five standards or get out."

"Five standards then." Eli smiled, flashing the gold in his hand. "But I expect to get what I pay for."

"You won't be disappointed," the woman said as the man took Eli's money. "I'm a fully initiated broker. You'll get the best we have. Now, what's your question?"

Eli leaned forward. "I need the location and owners of all the remaining Fenzetti blades."

The woman frowned. "Fenzetti? You mean the swords?"

Eli nodded.

"A tough question." The woman tapped her fingers against her knees. "Good for you I had you pay up front. Come back in one hour."

"No worries." Eli smiled. "We'll wait here."

Neither the woman nor her guard looked happy about that, but Eli was a paying customer now, so they said nothing. The woman stood up and disappeared into the back room. The man took up position by the door she'd gone through, watching Josef like a hawk.

"Well," Eli said, fishing through his pockets, "no need to be unfriendly, Mr. Guard. How about joining us for a game?" He pulled out a deck of Daggerback cards. "Friendly wagers only, of course."

The guard glowered and said nothing, but Eli was already dealing him a hand with a king placed invitingly faceup. The guard's expression changed quickly at that, and he moved a little closer, picking up his cards. After winning the first five rounds, the guard had warmed up to them immensely. So much so, in fact, that he scarcely noticed his luck going steadily downhill after his initial streak. Eli kept things going, asking him innocent questions and distracting him from the cards in his hand, which only seemed to get worse as the rounds went on. To Josef, who was used to Eli's fronts, it was clear that the thief's attention was only half on the game. His real focus was the door the woman had disappeared behind and the strange sounds that filtered through the thick wood. The noise was hard to place. It sounded like a sea wind, or a storm gale, yet the torches outside the tiny, grimy window were steady, burning yellow and bright without so much as a flicker.

Almost exactly one hour later, by Josef's reckoning, the door opened and the woman came back into the room. By that point, the guard had been losing for nearly forty minutes, and four of

Eli's five gold standards were back in the thief's own pockets. The woman shot her guard a murderous look, and he jumped up from the bench, leaving his hand unplayed (a good thing, too: his pair of knights would never have beaten Eli's three queens) as he dashed to his place behind her. Eli only grinned and gathered his cards, tucking them back into his pocket before he turned to hear his now greatly discounted answer.

With a sour expression, the woman flipped open a small, leather-bound notebook. "I was able to get the locations of eight Fenzetti blades," she said. "You don't look like the sort who's trying to buy one, so I'll skip over the part about how none of these are for sale. Of the eight I could locate, five are held by the Immortal Empress."

Eli made a choking sound. "The Immortal Empress? Couldn't you start with something in an easier location? Say, bottom of the sea?"

"You paid only for location and owner," the woman said. "Them being impossible to get is your problem."

"All right," Eli said, sighing. "Well, that's five out of the way. How about the other three?"

The woman ran her finger down the page. "One is owned by the King of Sketti."

"Sketti, Sketti," Eli mumbled, trying to remember. "That's on the southern coast, right?"

"It's an island, actually," the woman said, nodding. "Large island in the south sea. Four months from Zarin by caravan, five by boat."

Eli grimaced and motioned for her to continue.

The woman flipped to the next page in her book. "There's rumored to be a Fenzetti dueling dagger in the great horde of Del Sem. It hasn't been seen in eighty years, though, not since Rikard the Mad lived up to his name and started giving out his family's treasure to anyone who promised to banish the demon he was convinced lived in his chest."

Eli frowned. "So that one could be anywhere, really."

The woman nodded and closed her book. "I'd say Sketti is your best option. Would you like to buy another question?"

"Not so fast," Eli said. "You said there were eight known blades. You've only told us seven so far. Where's the last one?"

"Oh," the woman said. "That one might as well be at the bottom of the sea for all the chance you have of getting your hands on it. It's currently held by the Duke of Gaol."

"Gaol?" Eli whistled. "He's supposed to be richer than most countries put together. Rules over a beautiful and boring little duchy like it's his private playground, or so I've heard. Where does the impossible part come in?"

She gave him a look of disbelief. "Where have you been?"

She got up and walked over to a small wardrobe set against the corner. It looked like a simple coat closet, but when she opened it Eli saw it was full of papers, organized into wooden nooks with small, scribbled labels. She dug around for a moment and then returned carrying a rolled-up poster.

"I can't believe you haven't seen these. They've been plastering them up in every city, town, and waypost across the Council Kingdoms for the past week. The printing cost alone must have been a fortune."

Eli took the poster from her and carefully unrolled it. It was very large, twice the size of the bounty posters and covered in splashy block printing surrounding an engraved illustration of the most formidable fortress Eli had ever seen.

"Edward di Fellbro," he read aloud. "Duke of Gaol, Liegesworn of the Kingdom of Argo, so on and so forth." He scanned down the enormous list of titles that always seemed to follow anyone important, looking for the actual announcement. "Ah," he said. "Here we are. It's an announcement for the duke's new stronghold. Look here"—he motioned Josef and Nico over—"'...this new, impenetrable fortress, a wonder of modern architecture and security built on impenetrable bedrock, was created to protect his lordship's priceless family heirlooms, the famous treasures of Gaol.'"

Eli's eyes flicked back and forth, his grin growing wider by the word. "Powers," he cackled. "There's three paragraphs alone on the thickness of the walls!"

"Mm," the broker said, nodding. "It goes on like that the whole way through. People thought it was funny at first, him making such a big deal over it in places that didn't even know there was a Duke of Gaol. Who advertises a fortress, anyhow? But the tune changed after rumors got round 'bout what he did to the first couple of thieves he caught. Cruel doesn't begin to describe it. So, unless you're Eli Monpress, I'd count this target out. No sword, Fenzetti or whatever, is worth that kind of suicide mission. Stick to Sketti."

Eli nodded thoughtfully, rolling the poster back into a tube. "Can I keep this?"

"Sure." The woman shrugged. "As I said, they're everywhere. I'll just get another."

"Much obliged," Eli said graciously, standing up. "Thank you for a very thorough answer, Miss Broker. I'll make sure to recommend your services."

The woman gave him a sharp look. "It's customary to tip," she said. "Especially considering how you managed to cheat my idiot here out of most of my fee."

Eli gave her an innocent smile, but she arched an eyebrow. "I told you," she said. "A girl has to eat, and if you won't play fair by me, then I might be forced to write a letter to these sword owners."

"You make a good case," Eli said, and his hand flashed, sending four gold standards flying across the room in rapid succession. The woman caught them easily, and she nodded her head in thanks as the thief and his companions ducked through the low door and into the night.

"Well," Josef said, walking in step with Eli through the narrow dirt streets, "that was surprisingly informative. If I'd known brokers were so useful I would have tried harder to find one."

"They're everywhere if you know what to look for," Eli said, spinning the rolled-up poster between his fingers. "Though they're really at their best when you're looking for something physical. They don't handle manhunts well. I didn't expect such a thorough answer from a broker in an end-of-nowhere town like Goin, but I guess I should have known better. Brokers, wherever they are, always know what's going on. Someday, when I get bored enough, I'll find out how they do it."

"Well," Josef said, "at least we know where we're going. I've never been to the southern coast, but there are several good swordsmen along the islands I've been meaning to test out. This seems like a good opportunity."

"Josef, Josef, Josef," Eli said. "What are you talking about? We're not going to Sketti. There's no way I'm wasting the half a year it'll take to go all the way down to the south coast, and then come all the way back on what is essentially a pro bono project." He flashed a smile at Nico. "No offense, dear, but your coat isn't worth *that* much. Besides," he said, unrolling the poster again with a gleeful grin, "why would we pass up an opportunity like this?"

"I see several in bold print," Josef said, looking over his shoulder.

"*Look* at this!" Eli cackled. "'Impenetrable fortress'? 'Impossible to infiltrate'? '*Thief-proof*'? It's practically an invitation!" Eli slapped the paper with the back of his hand. "This, my friends, is a challenge! And I never turn away from a challenge."

"Or a trap," Josef grumbled. "Come on, Eli, think. The only

reason to put up a notice detailing your fantastic security is if you're desperately trying to ward off thieves, or fishing for them. Considering he's putting up posters in nowhere mud-hole towns miles from his borders, I'm going with the latter. *Especially* when the bait seems tailored to a certain famous thief with a kingdom-swaying bounty who's well known for his love of impossible targets. Powers, he might as well just hang up some 'Welcome Eli' banners and be done with it."

"You might be right," Eli said, rolling the poster back into a tube. "But that just makes it even more irresistible. Besides, the duke's lands are in Argo. That's barely a week away from here if we acquire some transportation. Even if we just go over to take a look and decide it's impossible, we've still hardly lost any time. Besides, if this trap for me is as transparent as you seem to think, then there are bound to be dozens of bounty hunters hanging around, and you did say you wanted a good fight."

"I wouldn't call most of the trash that comes after us a 'good fight,'" Josef grumbled, but even his gruff tone couldn't hide the spark of interest. "Of course," he added, a few moments later, "we never know when we might run into another Coriano."

"That's the spirit." Eli grinned, clapping him on the back. "Come on, let's go find some food and then see if we can't find a ride out of here. I don't know about you two, but I'm *really* sick of walking."

Neither Josef nor Nico disagreed with that statement, and so the three of them went off in search of a tavern whose kitchen was still open and whose floor wasn't currently a wrestling ring.

As it turned out, finding a meal was the hardest part of the night. The taverns of Goin lived up to their reputation as rowdy dumps where beer counts as food and a broken nose is considered part of a good night out. This worked for Josef, who had a bit of fun tossing the locals around under the guise of "securing a table," but Eli was having trouble finding anything on the dinner boards of the few places that offered food that wasn't a concoction of meat, grease, and dirt. After several hungry, bloody hours, the night rolled around into predawn, and Eli was finally able to buy a sack of day-old bread from a baker who had just opened his shop.

Obtaining transportation was significantly easier. Most of the stable hands were drunk, and the stable locks were old and rusted. With about five minutes' work Eli had them a very respectable-looking covered merchant's cart and a team of sturdy but unexceptional brown horses to draw it.

Josef and Nico both frowned when they saw the horses. Horses were always a risk. They were very sensitive to threats, especially demons, and were prone to panic if Nico came too near. Slorn's new coat was working wonders, however, and the horses barely noticed when Nico climbed up over the driver's bench and into the back.

"I could get used to this," Eli said, jumping up after her. "Remind me to thank Slorn again."

"Don't get too happy," Josef said, climbing in last and taking the driver's seat. "We're not out yet."

He took off the Heart and laid it gently in the cart. Next, he undid all of his scabbards, handing his blades one by one to Nico. Finally, he pulled up his collar and buttoned his cuffs, hiding the scars on his arms and jaw, and slouched over the horses with a petulant expression on his face. Eli nodded in approval. If it wasn't for the strange, watchful look in his eyes, even he would have been hard-pressed to label Josef as anything other than a big farmer with a bad temper.

Their ride out of town was uneventful. If the guards had any suspicions about how a merchant cart that had been driven into town by an old woman the night before was now being driven out by a surly man in his twenties, one look at Josef's shoulders was enough to convince them it wasn't really important. They rode in silence for about twenty minutes before Eli tapped Josef on the shoulder and the swordsman pulled the cart over to the side of the empty road.

"Cover for me," Eli said, hopping down. "I'm going to see if I can't speed things up."

Josef nodded and leaned back, undoing his cuffs and flipping his collar back to its usual flat position. Nico started handing him his belts of knives as Eli undid the harnesses on the cart horses and let them wander over toward the clumps of grass that grew between the wagon ruts.

"There," Eli said, tossing the harness on the ground. "Either they'll find their way home or some deserving soul gets new horses. Never let it be said that I never gave back to the people."

"You're a regular public servant," Josef grumbled, belting on his swords. "What now?"

"Now," Eli said, "we get moving."

He crouched down beside the right front wheel and gave it a friendly pat. "Good morning," he said cheerily.

For a few moments, nothing happened. Then, slowly, the wheel began to creak as it finally woke up. "What's good about it?"

"Well," Eli said, looking around, "to start, it's a lovely dry day on a nice even road with a downward slope. Doesn't get much better, I'd think."

The wheel wobbled. "That's because you're not down here being dragged along by those cloppy-cloppy beasts, going so slowly you got moss in your joints, having mud kicked at you morning, noon, and night. No day's a good day when you're in the rut, I tell ya."

"Ah," Eli said, keeping his voice low so the other wheel wouldn't wake up too soon and spoil the plan. "Today's a bit different, friend. You see, the horses are gone, and I've got a bit of a challenge for you, if you're interested."

"Challenge?" The wheel perked up. "What do you mean?"

"Well," Eli said, "you see that wheel over there?" He pointed at the left front corner of the cart. "He told me, just now, that you're over your prime, off circle, and that he can outroll you any day of the year."

The wheel creaked with fury. "Oh, he did, did he? Put on only last year and already looking to replace me, eh? Well, I'm sound as any wheel you'll find, and if he wants to try me, tell him he can go ahead. I'll match any horse he cares to try!"

"Oh, we're not talking horses, friend." Eli shook his head. "This is an open challenge. The two of you in a flat-out race, no horse, just you, him, and the open road, winner take all."

"No horses?" The wheel balked. "How'm I supposed to roll, then?"

"Oh, that's easy," Eli said. "You just roll forward."

"What, you mean like downhill?"

"Or uphill," Eli said. "Anywhere! Just roll."

"Don't know 'bout that," the wheel said. "Last time I tried that I fell over. I hate falling over."

"No worries there," Eli said. "The cart will keep you up, and I'll be in the seat acting as the referee and laying out the course. What do you say, want to try a race? Prove who's the better wheel?"

"Won't be much of a competition," the wheel cackled. "Just give the signal and I'll show you how a cart's supposed to move."

"Excellent," Eli said, standing up. He left the wheel muttering threats at its axlemate and leaned toward Josef, dropping his voice to a whisper. "I'm just waking the front two for now. When they catch on, we'll switch the wheels and start again with the pair in the back."

"I have no idea what that means, but all right," Josef said, pulling himself back into the cart. "Just don't get the cart too excited. It's a long trip."

"Won't be when I'm done," Eli said, walking around the cart to the left wheel to start the process again.

A few minutes of excited whispering later, the whole cart began to shake. Eli leaped into the driver's seat and grabbed hold of the bench. "Hang on," he said, grinning at Nico and Josef. "Here we go."

He'd barely finished speaking before the cart launched forward, rattling down the overgrown road at a breakneck pace.

Josef clung to the cart for dear life as the trees flew by and the sky danced overhead. Eli was laughing and shouting directions and encouragement to the wheels, who were spinning as though their lives depended on it as they screamed insults at each other.

"Don't you think this is a little conspicuous?" Josef shouted over the wheels.

"Not at all!" Eli shouted back. "This is nothing compared to how some Spiritualists travel. If we're lucky, people will think we're Shaper wizards. No one's stupid enough to mess with Shapers, and they ride stuff like this all the time, though their horseless carts are a lot nicer, not to mention smarter. I could never pull this stunt on Shaper goods. Ah," he said, breathing deeply, "I love common, sleepy spirits. They're so open to suggestion."

Josef looked at him blankly, but Eli just grinned wider.

"What? No point in going slow through that if we don't have to, right? Don't worry so much."

Josef had an answer for that, but experience told him to save his breath. The thief would do what he wanted, and this *was* faster. So he made himself as comfortable as he could in the pitching cart and dug out one of his throwing knives. At least the cart gave him a good chance to practice catching his knives in an unstable environment, and Josef wasn't the kind to let opportunity pass.

From her place in the back of the cart, Nico watched Josef as he flipped the razor-sharp knife, catching it first with his right hand, then his left. Behind her, the green forest whirled by in a blur as they bounced at full speed down the road toward Gaol.

CHAPTER 9

They had to switch the wheels only once before they reached the border of Argo. The roads had been quiet and empty, barely more than cart tracks as they skimmed the northern edge of the Council Kingdoms. They had seen no one and, more important, no one had seen them.

"Well, it makes sense," Josef noted as their cart rolled to an exhausted stop by the signpost marking the official border. "That glorified goat track was the worst excuse for a road I've ever seen."

"Why should they keep it up?" Eli said, climbing stiffly off the cart. "It's not like anyone with money goes through there. Who'd take a narrow road through the middle of nowhere now that the Council's opened the rivers? Still"—he patted the exhausted wheels—"across the top of the Council Kingdoms in three days. I'd like to see a riverboat do that."

"No one would ever accuse us of traveling normally." Josef shrugged, helping Nico down. "Can the cart keep going?"

"No," Eli said. "They've earned their rest. Help me out," he said, leaning down. "After all that, the least I can do is leave them free."

They undid the wheels and left them propped in the rocks beside the cart. Then, with a thankful farewell, Eli, Nico, and Josef set out down the overgrown path into Argo.

"All right," Josef said, setting a brisk pace. "What now?"

"Now, we make for Gaol." Eli reached into his pack and pulled out his map. "Argo is divided into four autonomous duchies, each about the size of a small kingdom itself. Argo's really more like a collection of kingdoms than somewhere like Mellinor, where one king calls all the shots. That's probably why it was one of the first major players to join the Council of Thrones. It was already used to the idea of governance by committee. Anyway, Gaol is the southernmost duchy, taking up the whole of the Fellbro River Valley just before it joins the Wellbro and they both change their names to the Whitefall River as the water enters Zarin's territory. That's part of why Gaol is so rich. The Fellbro River connects the northwest quarter of the Council Kingdoms with everything else. There's enough trade coming down that waterway to keep even the greediest merchant happy, and not so much as a kernel of wheat passes through without Gaol levying some kind of tariff. Now, we're currently in Eol, the northernmost and relatively poorest duchy of Argo. All the attention's on the river traffic, so I expect that if we can stay on foot and on the border here we can just walk into Gaol with no questions asked."

Josef shot him a look. "That simple, eh?"

"With us? Never," Eli said, laughing. "If we can get into Gaol's capital, which, I might add, is also called Goal, thanks to the stupid and confusing naming conventions of the northwest kingdoms. Anyway, if we can get in unmolested, we'll have Slorn's sword and be out of here in a week, tops."

"A week?" Josef said. "You said kidnapping the King of Mellinor would take a week."

"Give or take a major inconvenience," Eli said, shrugging.

"Kidnapping was a new area for us. There were bound to be slip-ups. This is good old-fashioned theft, and no Spiritualists in sight to mess it up. I think we'll be all right."

Nico and Josef exchanged a look behind Eli's back as they followed the thief south, down the overgrown road and into the rolling hills of Argo.

It took them two days to reach Gaol's border, mostly because on the second day it began to rain. It was a drenching, cold rain blown down from the mountains, and it made the going miserable. Eli, drowned and sulking with his blue jacket wrapped tight around him, mentioned something about stopping every mile or so, but nothing came of it. The mountain forests had stopped at the Argo border, logged to make room for sheep and cattle grazing, but it was poor land up here and the ranchers' homes were spread thin. They passed a few farmhouses, their inviting plumes of smoke smelling of cooking and warmth, but the travelers didn't stop. Eli had learned his lesson about nosy farmers on multiple occasions, and even a miserable, wet walk wasn't enough to make him try one of those doors.

"Not much farther," he said, tilting his head so the water would have a harder time going down his neck.

"So you keep saying," Josef said. The swordsman paid no more attention to the rain than a bull does, and the water rolled off him with scarcely a notice. Nico kept in step with him, kicking her thin feet so the mud wouldn't build up on her boots. Eli grumbled something about traveling with monsters and kept his own pace, moving his feet carefully so as not to lose a boot in the quagmire the road had become. It was a complicated process, which was why he didn't notice that Josef and Nico had stopped until he ran face-first into Josef's back.

"Powers!" he muttered, stumbling back. "What *now*?"

Josef just nodded at the road ahead of them. Eli squinted into the rain, confused; then he saw it too. About ten feet ahead of them, the rain stopped. The road went on, the hills went on, but the rain didn't. Eli walked forward, sloshing through the mud until he was on the edge of where the weather suddenly cut off. There, in the middle of the road, was a line. On one side, it was a miserable, cold, wet rain; on the other, the weather was sunny and the road was dry.

Squinting through the rain, Eli leaned forward until his nose was almost touching the invisible barrier separating rain from sun. "Well," he said softly, "that's odd."

"That's one way to put it," Josef said.

Eli tilted his head back and squinted at the sky. The disconnect seemed to go all the way up. Even the gray clouds stopped at the line, swirling and turning over on each other at the border as if they'd hit an invisible wall.

"Very odd," Eli muttered.

Josef glared at the division. He didn't like unexplainable things. "Any ideas on what could cause something like this?"

"Well," Eli said, tapping his fingers against his wet chin. "It could be some kind of agreement between the local spirits. I doubt it, though. Spirits have their own politics, but something this precise smacks of human interference."

Josef frowned. "A wizard who likes sunshine, then?"

"That'd be my guess," Eli said, poking at the line between wet and dry with his boot. "Not a Spiritualist, though. They'd consider something like this, I don't know, rude. Not their style at all."

Josef nodded, and they stood there staring at the anomaly for a moment longer. Then Eli shook himself.

"Well," he said, "no point in standing in the drink when we don't have to. That's our road, so we might as well stop worrying and enjoy the sunshine."

He strode forward, crossing the border between rain and sun

with only a tiny hesitation. He felt nothing as he crossed, just the welcome warmth of sunlight on his wet shoulders. Now that he was on the dry side, the air was cool and bright and the dry road was solid and even, a welcome change from the rutted mud slick they'd been shuffling through all day.

Once they were all in the dry they shook out their soaked clothes and sat in the thick grass on the roadside while they drained the water out of their boots. Now that they could see the sun, it was clear that the afternoon was quickly passing, so after a short rest, they pressed on, following the road down out of the hills into a green valley.

The land on this side of the rain was very different from the scrubby hills they'd been plowing through since abandoning the cart. The brown grass and rocky outcroppings had been replaced by orderly orchards and green pastures. The road was well maintained, with neat stone walls dividing it from the farmland and not a single rut in the hard-packed dirt. In the distance, picturesque farmhouses made of gray stone and whitewashed wood nestled between the hills like plump, roosting chickens. Sleek horses grazed in green fields while roosters with deep-blue tails strutted on white fences, crowing occasionally as the sun sank lower.

"It's like we walked into a painting," Josef said. "*Cottages at Sundown* or something."

Eli brushed self-consciously at his dirty clothes. He hated being dirty in general, but being dirty here felt like an insult to the bucolic perfection. "Funny, I figured the richest province in the Council Kingdoms would be a little less pastoral."

Josef shrugged. "Even rich people have to eat."

"I just hope this place has something worth picking up besides the Fenzetti," Eli said. "All I'm seeing is a lot of grass and livestock, and I'm *not* doing horses again. I swear, the more valuable their bloodline, the harder they bite."

"I don't think you have to worry about that," Josef said. "There's the town."

Eli looked up and saw that Josef was right. At the bottom of the hill they'd just crested stood a large, lovely town. Gray stone buildings with steep red roofs stood in orderly squares divided by broad, paved roads. The city was hemmed in on all sides by a high stone wall, though it looked more like an ornamental barrier to separate the city from the country than an actual, defensible position. On the far side of the city from their position, a river hemmed in by bridges and dock houses glittered in the evening light, and above it, sitting on a jut of rock like a crow on its perch, was the duke's citadel.

Even if the poster hadn't had a picture, Eli would have recognized the building. Perfectly square, with tiny windows and a black exterior, it was radically different from the charming buildings that surrounded it. Guards walked the perimeter, tiny glittering figures with polished hauberks guiding thick-shouldered dogs on leather leads. Though it was still early evening, torches burned on the citadel walls, their light reflected by mirrored panels set right into the stone, bouncing the light back and forth so that every shadow was illuminated. These felt like unnecessary precautions, however. Even without the guards and the lights, the thick walls of the citadel positively reeked with inaccessibility. Eli felt his pulse quicken. It was a challenge, a true challenge, and he could hardly wait to begin.

Josef caught his gleeful look and folded his arms over his chest. "We're doing this carefully, remember?"

"Oh, I remember." Eli grinned. "It would be a shame and a waste to do it any way but right." He clapped his hands and turned to his companions. "First order of business, setting up base camp. I'm thinking docks."

"Sounds good," Josef said. "Lots of people go through there.

It's hard to remember them all. Even the best guards won't notice three new faces."

"Close to the city, too," Eli said, eyeing the river. "And plenty of escape routes."

"That's settled, then," Josef said, veering off the road. "Let's go."

Eli and Nico followed the swordsman as he left the road and cut straight down the steep embankment toward the river. They hit the water south of town and followed it up, slipping past the wall through one of the dozens of dock gates and up onto the river walk. The river itself was a good fifty feet across and deeply trenched for the large, low-running barges that floated down it. Piers jutted out into the murky green water, connecting the boats to the long, low storehouses that pushed right up to the river's edge. River crewmen were gathered in knots by the iron fire troughs, smoking pipes and roasting fish on skewers over the hot coals. These clusters were few and far between, however, and other than the river men, the docks were empty.

"Better and better," Eli said quietly.

They chose one of the storehouses on the end, a small affair with an older lock, which took Eli five seconds flat to pick, and plenty of dusty cargo that wasn't going anywhere.

"Perfection," Eli said, craning his head back to look up at the last light of evening as it streamed through the tiny, glassless windows high up on the two-story walls. "And with daylight to burn."

"I'll take care of the groundwork," Josef said, setting the Heart down in a corner. "Nico, secure the building. Eli, do whatever it is you do."

"Right," Eli said, plopping down on a crate and kicking off his wet boots. "I'll get right on that."

Josef made a "forget it" gesture as he walked out the door. Nico had vanished the moment Josef assigned her duty, and so Eli was left alone. He took his time wiggling out of his wet coat and fanning out his shirt so the white cloth wouldn't dry crinkled. Finally, when he was beginning to feel human again, he stood up and strolled to the center of the dusty warehouse.

"All right," he said to the empty room. "Let's get started."

It was fully dark when Josef slipped back into the storehouse, carrying a bag of food and a long list of new troubles. But when he opened the door, he realized he wasn't the only one who'd had bad news. Eli was sitting in the far corner of the room, surrounded by boxes and looking more frustrated than Josef had ever seen him look.

He put down his bag and walked over, crouching next to the thief. "What's wrong?"

"It's the boxes!" Eli exclaimed, far too loudly. "They won't talk to me!"

Josef flinched at the desperate edge in his voice. Anything that put Eli this out of whack was going to be a problem.

Eli glared at the boxes. "They won't talk to me at all. Not at all! It's like they're not even spirits!"

"Eli," Josef said slowly, "they are just crates. We'll find something else—"

"It doesn't matter if they're crates or cupcakes!" Eli cried. "They're spirits, and they're not talking. Spirits *always* talk to me, unless they're under an Enslavement not to, but I don't feel anything like that here. Just crates who *won't talk.*"

"Maybe they're shy?" Josef said and sighed. "Anyway, we've got bigger problems than not-talking crates. Something's off in town."

"Off?" Eli said. "Off how?"

"Hard to explain, really." Josef ran his hand through his short hair. "To start, it's spooky quiet. Everything's so neat. Plus, the streets emptied out as soon as the sun went down. No taverns, no drunks, nothing but guards, clean streets, and quiet."

Eli shrugged. "Gaol's a peaceful, quiet town full of decent, boring people. I realize you might not have much experience with those, but it's hardly something to get alarmed about."

"There's quiet and then there's quiet," Josef snapped. "I told you, this was spooky quiet. And"—he reached in his pocket—"these are all over town." He took out a piece of paper and unfolded it, revealing a familiar grinning face above a large, bold number. Fifty-five thousand standards.

"They didn't even get the bounty right," Eli said, grabbing the poster. "I'm worth *sixty* thousand."

"Who cares about the number?" Josef growled, snatching the paper back. "I knew this was a trap from the moment you got all wide-eyed over that poster for the citadel back at the broker's, but the bounty posters confirm it. We should sneak out tonight before it slams shut on our heads."

"Sneak out?" Eli cried. "Josef, we just slogged through two days of rain to *get* here. We're not going to just turn tail and leave."

"Weren't you listening?" Josef said, grabbing Eli's arm. "It's one thing to get caught in an ambush, but it's just plain stupid to stay in one after you've spotted it. Part of fighting is knowing when to retreat."

"As you are so fond of pointing out," Eli said, snatching his arm back, "I'm not a fighter. And we're not leaving."

"You should leave," whispered a quiet voice. "You seem like a nice wizard. We don't want you to die."

Eli spun away from Josef. "Well, hello there," he said. "Looks like you *can* talk!"

The crates around them jumped. "Shh!" the voice hissed. "Not so loud! If we're caught talking to you it's the end for us."

"What?" Josef whispered, looking around.

"It's the crates," Eli whispered back, grinning like a madman. "They're agreeing with you." He patted the swordsman on the back and then leaned in to whisper to the wooden crate. "What do you mean 'the end'? Who would catch you?"

The crate fell silent again, leaving the question hanging. Then, in a voice that was scarcely more than a whisper of dust on wood, it said, "The watcher."

Eli frowned, confused. "Watcher?"

"The duke's watcher sees everything," the crate said, trembling. "We're not allowed to talk to wizards, but you're the nicest, brightest wizard we've ever seen, so please, leave. We don't want you to get caught."

Eli was about to ask another question when a sharp crack from the highest crate on the stack interrupted him.

"Watcher!" the crates cried in unison. "It's coming! Say nothing! Ignore the wizard!"

"Get out of here!" Eli's crate whispered frantically.

"What's coming?" Eli whispered frantically, running his hands over the dusty wood. "What do you mean 'watcher'?"

But the crates had shut themselves down again, and in the silence, Eli heard a low sound.

"What is going on?" Josef said again, more urgently this time.

"Shh!" Eli hushed him, hunkering down among the crates.

Josef gave him a cutting look, and then he heard it too.

It sounded like a strong wind rushing between the buildings, only it didn't rush. The roaring sound lingered, moving up the river slowly, patiently, and in a manner that was wholly disconnected with the entire idea of wind. It hit the wooden walls of the warehouse like a wave, rattling anything that wasn't nailed down, whistling as it tore through the high windows. Then it was gone, moving methodically down the line of dock houses, leaving only the terrified silence of traumatized crates in its wake.

Eli glanced at Josef and the two of them crept back to the center of the storehouse. Nico was there waiting for them, though Eli hadn't seen her come in. She was simply there, and she didn't look happy about it.

"Something just came by," she whispered once they were close.

"So we heard," Eli said. "Did you catch what it was?"

Nico shook her head. "I want to say it was a wind, but I've never felt a wind like that."

Eli bit his lip thoughtfully, but Josef looked like his mind had just been made up.

"So," he said, "we've walked into a trap full of terrified spirits and winds that aren't winds. Is that enough to convince you this job is going to be more trouble than it's worth?"

"One day." Eli faced Josef, holding up one finger. "Give me one day to scout the situation. Tomorrow night, we'll make the hit or leave. Either way, it'll be done." He looked up at the high windows. "There's something going on here. First, the line in the rain; now this. Surely you're as curious as I am about what's going on here?"

"Of course I'm curious," Josef said. "But I don't let my curiosity get me stuck in situations I can't get out of. That's the difference between you and me."

"Come now," Eli said. "I've never been in a situation I couldn't get out of."

Josef gave him a look. "There's a first time for everything."

Eli chuckled. "Well, if we're going to be compressing three days of prep into one, let's get things rolling. But first, I'm going to secure our position."

"How do you mean to do that?" Josef said. "You just said the spirits wouldn't talk to you."

"For this, they don't have to," Eli said, walking back over to the crates.

"Excuse me," he said, his voice soft and sweet. "I appreciate the warning earlier, and I have one more favor to ask you."

The crates rattled uncomfortably, and Eli put up his hands.

"It's nothing big. In fact, you were probably going to do it anyway. All I want is for you to go to sleep. Just ignore me, forget I'm here, and I swear I won't do anything wizardly to wake you up."

The crates rattled at this, confused, and a splintering voice from the back cried, "How can we sleep? You're a wizard. Now that we're awake, it's not like we can just not notice you."

Eli sat down cross-legged in front of them. "Just try," he said softly.

The crates creaked uncertainly, but Eli didn't move. He simply sat on the floor, his eyes closed, his face calm, as the warehouse grew darker and darker. Presently, the nervous noises from the crates grew quieter, and then stopped altogether. The warehouse fell as silent as any old, forgotten place.

Quiet as a cat, Eli stood up and walked away from the crates and over to the little corner by the door where Nico and Josef were huddled around a tiny lamp, quietly eating the food Josef had brought.

"We good?" Josef said, tossing Eli a round loaf of bread.

"We're good," Eli answered, flopping down beside them.

"So," Josef said. "I know I'll regret asking, but what did you do?"

"I put them back to sleep," Eli said tiredly. "Small, normal spirits are almost always asleep unless a wizard wakes them up. Of course, the problem here is that, once a wizard wakes up a spirit, it's hard for them to go back to sleep if the wizard's still there. It's like trying to go to sleep when someone's in the room waving a lantern around. I simply quieted my presence. Think of it as throwing a blanket over the lantern. The lantern's still there, but it's not such a bother. It's an old trick I learned back in my thieving apprentice days, actually. It's not always good to be noticeable when you're trying to be a thief. So long as I don't do anything wizardly or otherwise make a scene, I should seem almost normal to any watching spirits."

"Great," Josef said, "a plan that depends on you not making a scene."

"I just wish I knew what was going on," Eli said, ignoring him. "The only thing that can get spirits that riled up is a wizard stepping on them, but there's no Enslavement I can feel. I don't think I'd miss it if there was one. It's not a subtle thing."

"So it's a mystery," Josef said, leaning back against the wall with the Heart propped against his shoulder. "Let the Spiritualists deal with it. Spiritual mysteries are what they're there for, when they're not bothering us."

"How can you be so blasé?" Eli said around a large mouthful of bread. "Don't you want to know what's going on?"

"Sure," Josef said. "But wanting to know is a terrible reason to do anything. It only causes trouble, and not the good kind either, the stupid, time-wasting kind. Just let it go. We're on a deadline, remember?"

"How could I forget?" Eli grumbled, lying back.

They sat in silence for a while before Nico leaned forward and blew out the lamp. Lying there, in the dark, Eli meant to think more about the crates and the wind and all the other strange things. He needed to think about them because, despite Josef's cracks about curiosity, the first rule of thievery was never go into a job if you didn't understand the territory. This was a dangerous game, with more uncontrollable factors than he was comfortable with. But, despite his best intentions, the weeks of hard travel pulled at his body, and he was asleep as soon as the light went out.

High overhead, the windows rattled in the dark as the strange wind passed by again.

The night air above Gaol was still. Far off on the horizon, lightning flashed from distant storms. Even so, no rain-heavy wind swept the fields of Gaol and the clouds did not cross the duchy border. They knew better.

Down in the streets, however, a wind moved slowly. It sent the tall oil lamps flickering, disturbing the steady pools of light they shed on the paved streets. It dipped into alleys, under barrels, and through attics. It roared as it went, a cruel, howling sound, and never strayed from its path, moving with almost painful slowness until it had made a full circuit of the town. Only then did the wind pick up speed. It turned and rose, flitting over the rooftops and toward the center of town where the duke's citadel crouched on its jutting rise, every bit as sullen and formidable as the posters made it out to be.

The strange wind circled the base of the fortress once and then turned and climbed the glum wall to the top, the only part of the gloomy structure that varied from the blocky architecture. Here, crowning the top of the citadel, was a series of interlocking towers. They were short and hard to see from the ground, but being on top of the citadel they provided a breathtaking view of the city and the countryside around it. At the center of the fortress, nestled between the towers, was a small courtyard garden filled with small, neat plants, all carefully arranged into beds by color and size. It was here the wind stopped, spiraling down and slowing to an almost stagnant crawl before the man who sat on a reed chair at the center of the garden going over a stack of black-bound ledgers by the light of a steady lamp.

The wind hovered a moment, hesitantly, but the man didn't look up from his ledger until he had finished the row. Only then, when each figure had been noted in his short, meticulous handwriting, did Duke Edward look up at the empty space where he knew the wind was waiting. "Report."

"My lord," the wind whispered, "two things. First, Hern has arrived."

"Has he?" The duke set his ledger aside. "That's unexpected."

"He went straight to his tower as soon as he was through the gate." The wind made a chuckling sound. "He doesn't seem very happy about being back."

"Interesting," the duke said. "What's the second?"

The wind's whistle grew nervous. "I caught a blip of something over by the docks this evening."

The duke scowled. "A blip? Explain."

"Well," the wind said, "it's hard to describe to a blind man—"

The duke's glare hardened, and a small surge of power rang through the garden. All at once, the wind found the words.

"It was like a flash," it said. "And then it was gone. I passed over twice but never saw it again. Could have been a hedge wizard, some spirit-sensitive riverboater who never developed his skills past listening for floods."

"But you don't think so," the duke said.

The wind jerked at this, surprised, and Duke Edward smiled. He'd always been good at picking up what wasn't said. It was a useful skill for people and spirits alike.

"I don't know what it was," the wind said, finally. "But nothing ordinary shines that brightly."

"I see," the duke said. "I trust discipline is being maintained."

"Of course," the wind huffed. "Your spirits speak to no one."

"Good," Edward said. "Keep an eye on this blip. Tell everyone that I want tight patrols tonight. The bait has been spread far and wide. Our little mouse may be in the trap already."

"Yes, my lord." The wind spun in the closest equivalent a wind can give to a bow. "Anything else?"

The duke thought for a moment. "Yes, on your next round, send Hern over. I'm curious what he's doing back in Gaol so soon after my investment in his success in Zarin."

"Of course, my lord," the wind chuckled. It had never liked

Hern much, and it delighted in the chance to make the Spiritualist come when called like he was one of his own fawning ring spirits.

"Thank you, Othril," the duke said. "You may go."

The wind circled one more time before blowing away. When he was gone, the duke opened his ledgers again and returned to marking numbers.

Nearly an hour later, one of the duke's house servants came into the garden to announce Hern's arrival. Duke Edward had long since finished his accounting and was now using the time to work with his vines. He ordered them one way, then another, sending them twisting up the stone walls of his garden and along the narrow breezeway door that looked out over the dark western hills. He heard Hern enter but didn't turn his attention from his vines until they had worked themselves into the desired double spiral.

When he finally turned to greet his guest, he found the Spiritualist standing in the doorway and looking quite put out.

"So," Hern said slowly, "you wanted something?"

"Straight to the point, this time," Edward said, sitting back down in his chair. "You must be in a foul mood."

"Being ordered from my bed by a *wind* after a long journey has that effect."

"I'll make this quick then," Edward said, his voice clipped and clinical. "I gave you money to dominate the Spirit Court in Zarin. Why, then, are you back in Gaol?"

Hern gave him a cutting look. "Politics isn't like your garden, Edward. I can't force things into the shape I want." The Spiritualist began to pace. "Banage has been working his connections in Zarin tirelessly. You'd think escaping a trial for treason was a heroic effort! The ink on her banishment edict is barely dry, but all I hear is *poor Miranda*, the noble, oppressed Spiritualist who threw away honor and safety to uphold her promise to her spirits.

The whole Court is eating it up, even the Keepers who voted against her, and it's making things very difficult." Hern stopped there a moment, reaffirming his composure. Edward, for his part, simply watched and took note.

"As it stands," Hern continued in a tight, calm voice, "Zarin is no longer the optimal place for me to pursue my objectives, so I've returned to regroup. I've got some sympathetic and influential Tower Keepers coming in tomorrow to discuss our next move. It is vital we counter Banage's spin on the facts before he sways the whole Court back under his cult of personality."

"Mmm." The duke nodded, turning back to his vines. "See that you do. I would hate to think that my investment in you was a bad one, Hern."

The Spiritualist stiffened, but said nothing. Edward smiled. It pleased him to know that Hern understood the difference between them here. Hern might have influence in Zarin, but this was Gaol. Here, there was no power, no authority that the duke did not control.

"It is late," Hern said at last. "Please excuse me."

Edward waved, listening as Hern turned and left. When the man was gone, Edward picked up his ledgers and his lamp and walked toward the door. When he reached it, he stopped and turned to his garden. He looked at it for a moment, the well-balanced colors, the sweet fragrance of the flowers, all in perfect order. Satisfied, he said, "Good night."

As soon as the words left his lips, every flower in the garden snapped itself shut. With that, Duke Edward of Gaol took his lantern and went down the empty halls to his bed.

CHAPTER 10

Far, far west of Gaol, far west of everything on the barren coast of Tamil, the westernmost Council Kingdom, Gin ran through the sparse grass with a bony rabbit hanging from his teeth, his swirling coat making him almost invisible in the clouds of cold, salty sea spray. The land here met the water in great cliffs, as though the continent had turned its back on the endless, steely water, and the ocean, in retaliation, bit at the rock with knife-blade waves, eating it away over the endless years into a large and varied assortment of crags and caves, yawning from the cliffs like gaping mouths below the dull gray sky.

Gin followed the cliff line until he reached a place where the coast seemed to fold in on itself. Here, moving his paws very carefully on the wet, smooth stone, he climbed down into a hollow between two pillars of rock. It was narrow, and he had to scramble a few times to keep from getting stuck. Then, about ten feet down, the rock suddenly opened up, dropping him into a large cave.

It was dim, but not dark. Gray light filtered down through the cracks overhead and through the wide mouth of the cave that looked out over the ocean. Little ripples of shells and sea grass on the sand marked the high-tide line, filling the cavern with the smell of salt and rotting seaweed. Gin landed neatly on the hard sand and turned away from the roaring sea, trotting up toward the back of the cave where a small, sad fire sputtered on a pile of damp driftwood. Beside it, hunched over in a little ragged ball, was his mistress.

He dropped the rabbit in the sand beside the fire and sat down.

"Food," he said. "For when you're done moping."

Miranda glared at him between her folded arms. "I'm not moping."

"Could have fooled me," Gin snorted.

She reached for the rabbit, but just before her fingers touched the torn fur, Gin scooted it away with his paw.

"Are you ready to talk about where we're going next?"

Miranda sighed. "We're not going anywhere."

Gin's orange eyes narrowed. "So we're just going to live out our lives in a sea cave?"

"Until I can think of somewhere better," Miranda snapped. "We're fugitives, remember?"

"So what?" Gin said. "If anyone is actually looking for us, it's probably Banage trying to set this mess straight."

"This isn't Banage's problem," Miranda said, meeting Gin's eyes for the first time. "I was the one who decided to do things the hard way, and I failed." She buried her head in her arms again. "If I can't be a good Spiritualist, then at least I'll be a good outcast and vanish quietly, not make a scene to embarrass the Court further."

Gin shook his head. "Do you even hear how ridiculous you're being? Do you think it'll make everything better if you keep playing dutiful Spiritualist to the end?"

"Supporting the Spirit Court *is* my duty!" Miranda cried. "I'm not playing, mutt."

"No," Gin said. "You're hiding and licking your wounds. What good are you to the Spirit Court if you're only using it as a reason to run away?"

"*Run away*?" Miranda's head snapped up. "I don't get to just stop being a Spiritualist, Gin! I have oaths! I have *obligations*!"

"Exactly," Gin said. "But to us first. I thought you'd already made this decision back in Zarin, but now I'm not so sure. What matters more, Miranda, the Spirit Court or the spirits? Will you deny your oaths to us to save Banage's honor? Would he even want you to?"

Miranda looked away, and Gin stood up with a huff. "Just remember, you're doing no one any good hiding in this hole," he growled, trotting toward the cave entrance. "Eat your rabbit. Next time you get hungry, you can go out and catch your own dinner."

Miranda stayed put until he left. When his shadow vanished into the sea spray, she grabbed the rabbit and began to dress it.

Stupid dog, she thought.

She skewered the rabbit on a stick and arranged it over the coals. Gin might be a particularly perceptive dog, but he was still a dog, and he didn't understand. If she made a scene, things would only get worse for Master Banage, and that would be intolerable. Banage had been the one trying to help her, as always, and she'd thrown it back in his face. As Miranda saw it, she had only one option left, one final duty: disappear, fade into the world, and never give Hern another inch of leverage against her master.

Miranda sat back against the cave wall, digging her fingers into the hard-packed sand as the rabbit began to sizzle. Outside, the gray ocean crashed and foamed, throwing cold spray deep into the cave. She grimaced. Gin was right about one thing: They couldn't stay here forever. She had no spare clothes, no blankets, and she was filthy with sea grime and sand. Even her rings had cataracts of salt on them. Still, she didn't know where else to run, or what to do when she got there. When she tried to imagine life separated from the Spirit Court, her mind went blank.

She supposed that was understandable. She'd been in the Spirit Court since she was thirteen, and from the moment she'd taken her vows the Court had been her life. That, she'd always suspected, was the main reason Banage had accepted her as his apprentice over all the others. She was only one who would work the hours he worked. But she'd done it gladly, because when she was doing the Spirit Court's work, she felt as if she was doing something that mattered, something worthwhile. It gave her purpose, meaning, confidence. Now, without the Court, she felt like a block of driftwood bobbing on the waves, going nowhere.

She leaned back, staring up at the firelight as it danced across the smooth curve of the sea-washed stone. The wind blew through the cave, whistling over the rock like it was laughing at her. Then, out of nowhere, a voice whispered, "Miranda?"

Miranda leaped to her feet with her hands out, ready, but the cave was empty. Only the fire moved, the little flames clinging for life in the high wind. She pressed her back against the wall. A trick of the wind? Spirits sometimes mumbled as they went, especially winds, who seldom slept. Yet the voice had been clear, and it had certainly said her name.

She was turning this over frantically in her head, trying to keep a watch on everything at once, when her eyes caught something strange. At the mouth of the cave, silhouetted by the strip of sunlight, a figure landed.

Miranda blinked rapidly, but it didn't change what she saw. With the light at their back, she couldn't tell if it was a man or a woman, but it was certainly human, even though she'd just seen it do something a human shouldn't be able to do. Whatever it was had not walked up or climbed down—it had *landed* in front of her cave. Landed neatly, as though it had hopped down off a step, but that made no sense at all. The cliff was nearly a hundred feet tall.

Even as she was trying to sort this out, the figure ducked under the cave's low entrance and walked forward with quick, sprightly steps. Miranda pressed her back to the wall and sent a tremor of power down to her rings only to find that they were already awake and ready, glimmering suspiciously. As the figure stepped into the circle of the firelight, Miranda saw that it was a man. She placed him at late middle age, maybe older, with gray hair and skin that was starting to droop. He had an intelligent, wrinkled face and large spectacles, which gave him the air of a kindly scholar. This effect was aided by the long, shapeless robe he wore wrapped several times around his bony shoulders so that he looked like someone who'd lost a fight with a bed sheet. Other than the robe and the spectacles, he wore no other clothes she could see. Even his feet were bare, and he took care to walk only on the sand, stepping around the washed-up patches of sharp, broken shells.

Miranda didn't move an inch as he approached. Nothing about him was threatening, yet here was a stranger who'd appeared from nowhere, and she was a wanted fugitive. But even as the thought crossed her mind, she felt almost silly for thinking it. Anyone could have seen that the man wasn't from the Spirit Court. If the lack of rings wasn't proof enough, the fact that he just walked up to a Spiritualist, who had all her spirits buzzing, without a trace of caution completely tossed out all suspicion of Spirit Court involvement. That left the question, what was he?

As he approached, the wind continued to roar, drowning out all other sounds. It blew the sand in waves and whipped the man's robes around him, though, miraculously, they never tangled in his arms or impeded his legs. When he reached Miranda's fire, the man sat down gracefully, like a guest at a banquet, and gestured with his hand.

The moment he moved his fingers, the wind died out, and in the sudden silence, he extended his hand to Miranda.

"Please," he said, smiling. "Sit."

Miranda didn't budge. It took a strong-willed wizard to work with a wind, and she wasn't about to give him an opening just because he was polite. "Who are you?"

"Someone who wants to help you, Spiritualist Lyonette," the man said pleasantly.

"If you know that much," Miranda said, relaxing a fraction, "then you should know it's just Miranda now. My title was stripped last week."

"So I have been told," the man said. "But such things matter very little to the powers I represent." He motioned again. "Please, do sit."

Curiosity was eating at her now, and she inched her way down the wall until she was sitting, facing him across the fire.

"I'm sorry," the man said, taking off his spectacles and cleaning them on his robe. "I have been rude. My name is Lelbon. I serve as an ambassador for Illir."

He paused, waiting for some kind of reaction, but the name meant nothing to Miranda. However, the moment Lelbon spoke, she felt a sharp, stabbing pressure against her collarbone. At first, she thought the man had done something, but then she realized it was Eril's pendant driving itself into her chest.

Careful to keep her face casual, she sent a small questioning tendril of power down to her wind spirit. The answer she received was an overwhelming, desperate need to come out.

"Eril," she said softly, pulling on the thread that connected them, giving permission. The pendant's pressure stopped and the wind spirit flew out. For once, however, Eril did not rush around. Instead, he swirled obediently beside Miranda, creating little circles in the sand.

"Sorry, mistress," the wind whispered. "Illir is one of the Wind Lords. To not pay my respects to his ambassador would be unthinkably rude."

Miranda tensed. "Wind Lords?"

"Yes," Lelbon said. "The West Wind, specifically."

"And this Illir," Miranda said carefully, "is the Great Spirit of the west?" It seemed like a tremendous area to be under the control of one Great Spirit, but with spirits it was always better to suggest more power rather than less, so as not to risk offending. From the way her usually intractable wind spirit was acting, Miranda guessed that Illir was not someone you wanted angry with you.

"Great Spirit isn't the most accurate description," Lelbon said with the slow consideration of someone who thrived on particulars. "Great Spirits have a domain: The river controls its valley, an ancient tree guards its forest, and so forth. Winds are different. They can cross dozens of different domains over the course of their day, and since they do not touch the ground, local Great Spirits have little control over them. So, rather than be part of the patchwork of grounded domains, the winds have their own domain in the sky, which is ruled by four lords, one for each cardinal direction. Whenever a wind blows in a direction, it enters the sway of that lord. Illir is the Lord of the West. Therefore, when a wind blows west, it is under the rule of Illir." He smiled at the space where Eril was circling. "Any given wind will blow in all directions during its lifetime, and thus owes allegiance to all four winds. Angering any of them could mean shutting off that direction forever."

"A terrible fate." Eril shuddered. "It is our nature to blow where we choose. Losing a direction for a wind is like losing a limb for a human."

Miranda nodded slowly, a little overwhelmed. She'd never heard of any of this, not from her lessons in the Spirit Court or her travels, and certainly not from her wind spirit.

"Don't look so fretful." Lelbon smiled at her wide-eyed look. "There's no reason for humans, wizard or otherwise, to know the obligations of the winds. Most spirits don't even understand how it works. They don't need to. The winds handle their own affairs."

"So what are you?" It felt rather personal to ask, but she had to know. "Are you human or..."

Lelbon laughed. "Oh, I'm human. I'm a scholar who studies spirits, wind spirits in particular, which is how I stumbled into my current position. The West Wind is an old, powerful spirit, but also rather eccentric and very interested in the goings-on of humans. In return for letting me study him and his court, I serve him as messenger and ambassador whenever he needs a face people can see. Most people find talking to a wind directly to be quite disconcerting."

"That's one way to put it," Miranda said, glancing sideways at the empty spot where Eril was spinning. "But why did Illir send you to talk to me? What does the West Wind want with a former Spiritualist?"

The man pursed his lips thoughtfully. "Your reputation among spirits who care about this sort of thing is quite exemplary, Miranda Lyonette. Particularly your daring rescue of the captured Great Spirit Mellinor."

Miranda jerked. "You know about that?"

Lelbon chuckled. "There is very little the winds do not hear, and it was hardly a small event. Next to that, the technicalities of Spirit Court politics and who is or is not officially a Spiritualist aren't important. All I need to know is would you be willing to do a job for us?"

Miranda sat back. "Thank you for the compliment, but I'm afraid you've come to the wrong person. You would be much better off taking your plea to the Rector Spiritualis in Zarin."

"Ah," the man said. "My master has already determined that the Spirit Court is not in a position to offer the assistance we require, which is precisely why I was sent to find you. Won't you at least hear our offer?"

Miranda frowned, then nodded. After all, what harm could there be in just hearing him out?

Lelbon smiled and leaned closer. "As I explained, the Wind

Lords, while very powerful spirits, aren't technically Great Spirits, in that they don't have dominion over a specific area. Even so, they, like all large, elder spirits, have a duty to protect and look after spirits less powerful than themselves. So it has always been. Now, this arrangement seems simple enough on the surface, but in reality it's a delicate balance of responsibilities. The winds are required to act on whatever problems they see in the domains they cross over. Yet, as they have no real dominion over any spirits except wind spirits, this often means nothing more than reporting the problem to the local Great Spirit, who deals with the trouble in its own way, if at all."

"Doesn't sound very reliable," Miranda said.

"That depends on the Great Spirit," Lelbon said. "If they are open to outside assistance, things go smoothly, the problem gets dealt with, and everyone moves on. However, if the Great Spirit does not welcome interference in their affairs..." He trailed off, looking for the right word. "Well, let's say that things can get complicated, which brings us to my offer."

"Let me guess," Miranda said. "Your lord has found trouble somewhere where the local Great Spirit doesn't want him."

"More or less," Lelbon said, smiling. "I can't go into the particulars of the goings-on. My master is already trespassing on dangerous ground simply by seeking you out. All we're asking you to do is go to the place and make your own assessment as a neutral party. That's the job. We would pay your expenses, of course, and my master would be very grateful."

For a long moment, Miranda was very tempted. It sounded like an interesting problem, and it must certainly be urgent if the West Wind would rather pull her in than wait for the Spirit Court to assign someone. But...

"Strictly for curiosity," Miranda said slowly. "Where would I be going?"

"Are you familiar with the land surrounding the Fellbro River?" Lelbon said. "The duchy called Gaol?"

Miranda froze. "Gaol?"

"Yes," Lelbon said. "Medium-sized holding, about four days' ride from Zarin."

"I know where it is," Miranda muttered. This changed everything. Gaol was where Hern kept his tower. "Look," she said. "You seem to know a great deal about me, so you know I can't go to Gaol. That's Hern's land. If I was seen there at all, everyone would think I was there for revenge. Anywhere else I could maybe help you, but not Gaol."

"It is precisely because of your history with Hern that we chose you," Lelbon said seriously.

Miranda's eyes widened. "You think Hern is involved?"

"Let me put it this way," Lelbon said, leaning closer. "If he were doing his job as a Spiritualist, would we need to ask your help? We need *you*, Miranda, exactly as you are. No one else will do."

They stared at each other for a long moment and then Miranda looked away. "I'm sorry, I can't. I've muddied the Spirit Court's reputation too much as it is already. If I go and make a scene in Gaol, I'll be no better than the thief Monpress. Tell your master thank you for the offer, but I can't do it."

They sat in silence, and then, slowly, Lelbon stood up.

"Well," he said, "if that's your final decision, I won't insult you with arguments. However"—he reached into the folds of his white robe and drew out a little square of bright, colored paper—"should you change your mind, just give us a signal."

He pushed the folded paper into Miranda's hands before she could refuse and turned away, padding across the sand toward the cave's mouth. Belatedly, Miranda stood up and hurried after to show him out. It was only good manners, though she felt a bit ridiculous playing hostess in a cave. Even so, Lelbon smiled graciously as she ducked with him under the cave's low-hanging lip and out onto the stony beach.

"I am sorry," Miranda started to say, but the man shook his head.

"All I ask is that you think about it. After all"—his soft voice took on a cutting edge—"you are the Spiritualist. You must decide how best to uphold your duty."

Miranda winced at that, but said nothing. Lelbon smiled politely and, after a little bow, walked away down the beach. She watched him go, feeling slightly awkward. After his dramatic and mysterious arrival, she'd thought for sure his exit would be something more dramatic than ambling down the stony beach. But the old man kept walking, his bare feet deftly dodging the patches of stone and broken shells, growing smaller and smaller behind the clouds of sea spray. She was about to turn back into her cave when she caught a motion out of the corner of her eye.

Far down the shore, she saw Lelbon raise his hand, as if he were hailing someone. As his hand went up, a great wind rose, whipping Miranda's hair across her face as it barreled down the beach. It reached Lelbon seconds after passing her, and the old man's shapeless robe belled out around him like a kite. As she watched, his bare feet left the sand. He soared up with the wind, the white of his robe like a seabird against the dull gray sky, and vanished over the cliffs. Miranda ran into the water, hoping to see more of his amazing flight, but the sky was empty, and the old man was already gone.

She was still staring when the sound of something heavy landing in the sand behind her made her spin around. Gin crouched behind her, panting as if he'd run the whole cliff line. "What's going on? What was that enormous wind?"

"Wasn't it amazing?" Eril said before Miranda could even open her mouth. "It was one of the great winds who serve the west. I've never met a wind so large!"

"What was a great wind doing here?" Gin growled, glaring at the sky.

"Trying to give us a job," Eril said, whirling so that his words blasted into Miranda's face. "I can't believe you turned him down! Illir is the greatest of the Wind Lords, and you passed up the chance to do him a personal favor?"

"Wait, what?" Gin looked at the wind. "What kind of job?"

"One we're not taking," Miranda said firmly, sending a poke of power at Eril. "If it had been anywhere else, maybe, but there isn't a spirit in the world who could make me go to Gaol."

As she was saying this, Eril was talking under her in a frantic rush, filling Gin in on the particulars of Lelbon's request. Gin listened, the fur on his back standing up in a ridge by the time the wind finished.

"Is it true?" he said, orange eyes flashing as he looked at Miranda. "You turned down a plea of help from a spirit who sought you out?"

"Don't look at me like that!" Miranda shouted. "I didn't make us fugitives to turn around and walk straight into Hern's backyard! Would you have me make everything we went through in Zarin worthless?"

"Better than making your entire career as a Spiritualist worthless!" Gin shouted back. "We are your spirits, Miranda. We serve you because we believe in you. The Miranda I follow would never turn down a spirit's plea for help."

"Weren't you listening to anything I've said?" Miranda cried. "Master Banage—"

"Banage would never forgive a Spiritualist who turned her back on her oath to the spirits in order to serve the Court." Gin was snarling now. "And you know it."

"That's not fair!" Miranda said. "This isn't that simple!"

"Isn't it?" Gin growled, turning away. "You told me not too

long ago that there was right and there was wrong, and no amount of words could bridge the gap between the two. Maybe it's time you considered your own words, and what those prized oaths of yours really mean."

With that, the dog took off down the beach. Miranda could only stare after him, fuming. She felt Eril slide back into his pendant, curling back into place with a long, disappointed sigh, leaving her alone on the long, thin stretch of rocky beach. Suddenly too tired to go back into the cave, Miranda sat down in the sand, digging her bare feet under the smooth rocks and staring out at the pounding waves.

To serve the spirits, to protect them from harm, to uphold their well-being above all else, that was the oath all Spiritualists took the day they received their first ring. Miranda looked down at the heavy gold ring on the middle finger of her left hand, tracing the smooth, perfect circle stamped deep into the soft metal. It was supposed to represent the circle of connection between all things, from the smallest spirits to the greatest kings, and the Spirit Court's duty to promote balance within that connection.

The ocean spray blew her hair wild around her face as she turned to look where Gin had gone. Balance and duty, right and wrong. Even as she thought about it, she could almost feel Banage's disdainful look. After all, Banage's deep voice echoed in her head. What greater shame could there be for the Spirit Court than a Spiritualist who turned her back on a spirit in need?

She reached into her pocket and took out the flat, folded square of colored paper Lelbon had given her. She turned it carefully, unfolding the delicate paper again and again until she held nearly four feet of colorful tissue streaked with reds, greens, and golds in her hands. There was nothing written on it, no note, no instructions, but when she reached the center of the square, the paper ended in a sharp point tied to a long string. Feeling a bit silly,

Miranda stood up, careful to hold the fluttering paper out of the water. She walked to the edge of the beach and released the paper into the wind. It whipped up, colored streamer flapping as it soared into the sky, anchored by the string Miranda wrapped around her fingers. For a long moment the colored kite danced in the sea wind, dipping and bobbing. Then, without warning, a wind snatched the kite out of her hand. The bright, colored paper flew up into the sky, turning little cartwheels as the wind blew it off, dancing and dipping westward, over the sea.

Miranda watched the kite until it vanished behind the clouds, and then she turned to find Gin. She didn't have to go far. He came trotting up almost at once, looking immensely pleased with himself.

"I knew you'd come around," he said, tail wagging. "Are we leaving now or do you still need to get something?"

Miranda looked back at the cave. Her little fire had already flickered out, and everything else she had was on her back.

"Don't think so," she said. "Ready when you are."

"I've been ready for the last five days," Gin grumbled, lying down so she could climb up. When she was steady, he jumped, taking the first rocky ledge in one leap. The beach swung crazily below them, and Miranda felt all her blood running to her feet. By the third jump, Gin's claws were scraping on bare stone, and Miranda closed her eyes to keep from being sick. Then they were on flat ground at the top of the cliff face, and Gin was asking her which way to go.

"East and south," Miranda said.

"How far?" Gin asked, loping over the scrubby grass.

"I don't know." Miranda bit her lip. "If we go east, we'll hit the road to the river, but if we cut cross-country, two days' hard running?"

"Right," Gin said, nodding. "We'll be there tomorrow morning."

"Tomorrow morning?" Miranda scoffed. "You can't fly, mutt."

"No?" Gin grinned. "Watch me."

He picked up speed, racing over the low hills faster and faster until it was all Miranda could do to hold on.

"Gin!" she cried over the wind. "You can't keep this up all the way to Gaol!"

"You worry about what we do when we get there," he shouted back. "Leave the running to me."

After that, Miranda gave up and held on. Clinging to the ghosthound's shifting fur, she tried to think of what she'd do when they reached Gaol, but her mind was blank. After all, she didn't even know what they were looking for, and though Lelbon had said the West Wind would help, she didn't know what kind of help a great wind spirit considered appropriate, or if she'd recognize it when it came. Still, being on the road again, running toward a purpose, these made her happier than she'd been since arriving in Zarin, and she contented herself with holding on as the rocky fields and scrubby grass streaked by. Overhead, the cloudy sky grew dimmer as evening approached.

CHAPTER 11

Eli woke up to bright sunlight in his face and Josef's boot poking his ribs.

"Get up," Josef said. "The situation's changed."

Eli sat up, rubbing the grit out of his eyes. When he looked again, Josef was gone. He blinked a few times, trying to figure out if he'd dreamed the whole uncomfortable event, and then he spotted the ladder nailed to the wooden wall of the warehouse beside the door.

It was a hairy climb. The ladder was nailed to the wall with no allowance for footing, and he wasn't actually awake enough for this sort of thing. Still, a few moments later he wiggled through the trapdoor to the sloped roof to find Nico and Josef lying belly down on the wooden shingles, staring across the water. The warehouses, being, as they were, by the river, were at the lowest point of Gaol. From the roof, however, you could see into the city proper, which seemed to be in some commotion.

"The sun's barely up," Eli said, yawning. "What is it, a bakers' riot?"

"Not sure," Josef said, eyeing the crowds that filled the broad streets leading up to the citadel. "Those are hardly bakers, unless bakers in Gaol make bread with swords. I was going to guess peasant riot, but the crowd's far too calm, and nothing's happening at the citadel. So now I'm thinking conscript army, and seeing as we're knee-deep in a thief trap made for Eli Monpress, I'd say that crowd has your name on it."

"Well," Eli said, "they're going the wrong way."

He was right. The well-armed crowd in the street was heading away from the docks, marching uphill toward the keep.

"I wonder," Eli said, standing on his toes to get a better view. "We should head down and find out what's going on."

Josef glared at him. "What did I just say last night about curiosity?"

"Josef," Eli tsked, "this isn't just curiosity; it's groundwork. You gave me a day and a night to pull this job, and I can hardly steal a Fenzetti blade from here. Come on." He smiled, heading for the trapdoor. "Let's get dolled up."

He vanished down the ladder. Nico and Josef exchanged a long-suffering look before getting up and following.

Though years of thievery and natural inclination had given Eli a quick hand and inventive eye for improvised disguises, he always kept the staples on hand. There were some things you simply could not count on improvising. The moment he reached the floor of the warehouse, he ran to his pack and began pulling things out. He had a surprisingly large pile before he found what he was looking for: a small, carefully wrapped package tied with string. Eli undid the knots deftly and the package spilled open, revealing a cascade of golden, flowing hair, the crown jewel of his costume collection.

He shook the wig out a few times, but it needed very little. Wigs of this quality never did, if you stored them right. Eli didn't know how much it had cost, but he guessed quite a bit since its previous owner, the Princess of Pernoff, had seen fit to store it in the safe with her jewels. Eli had relieved her of both that night, and though the jewels were long gone, the wig remained one of his favorite possessions.

Using his fingers, Eli brushed his short hair back until it was flat against his head, and then, leaning over, slid the wig on with practiced ease. When he came up again, he looked remarkably different. The pale golden locks hung in subtle waves around his face, setting off his pale skin in a way his own dark hair never had, making him look delicate and noble in a fragile way, something he took full advantage of.

"Powers," Josef said, jumping off the ladder. "Not that thing again."

"I'll stop wearing it when it stops working," Eli said, pinning the wig into its final position with a half-dozen tiny hairpins. "See if there's anything workable in the crates. I saw one addressed to Freeman's Clothier in Zarin that might have something good."

Josef walked over to the pile of wooden boxes and began reading the faded shipping manifests. He had to move several to get to the crate Eli had mentioned, but when he cracked it open, they were not disappointed.

"Perfect," Eli said, grinning.

Inside was a neatly folded stack of brocade jackets, obviously intended for some tremendously overpriced shop in Zarin. Eli pawed through them, finally picking out a garish red-and-gold peacock pattern that matched the wig perfectly and, as an added bonus, caused Josef to sigh in disgust. Unfortunately, the only coat in the box that would fit over Josef's broad shoulders was a hideous green monstrosity that he refused to wear. Finally, Josef settled for a thick, black shirt from his own pack.

"I guess that will do," Eli said and sighed. "Just be sure to scowl a lot; that way no one will get close enough to notice the mended stab holes and bloodstains."

"I do wash it," Josef said. "Anyway, it fits me better than the guy I took it off."

Eli gave him a startled look. "I don't think I want to hear any more about your brand of shopping."

Josef shrugged. "It's not like he was using it."

Eli left it at that.

In the end, Josef decided to bring only the twin short swords he wore at his hips and the knives he could hide in his clothing. He and Eli agreed that walking into town covered in blades as he usually was would be asking for trouble, especially when they were trying to be discreet. Of course, this also meant Josef would have to leave the Heart, something Eli had a much harder time convincing him of.

"I don't see why this is a big deal," Eli said. "You hate having to use the Heart anyway."

"That's not the issue here," Josef said, crossing his arms stubbornly. "It's plain stupid to walk into an unknown situation, with armed men gathering in a city we know is a trap, and not bring our best weapon."

"Come on," Eli pleaded. "It's common knowledge you're with me these days. Carrying that thing is like walking around with a giant signpost: 'Here's Josef Liechten! Please stab!' If you're going to bring it, there's no point in disguises at all."

Josef scowled. "I don't think—"

"Just leave it here," Eli interrupted. "It's not like it could get stolen anyway, seeing as you're the only one who can pick it up. Besides"—Eli's voice smoothed to warm honey—"you're Josef Liechten, the greatest swordsman in the world. Surely *you* can take a few armed men without the Heart."

Josef gave him a dangerous glare. "Don't treat me like one of your idiot spirits." He pulled the enormous black blade off his back and dropped it. It fell like a hammer, sticking point-first in the wood floor. "I'll leave the Heart because you make a good case, but don't ever try and con me again, Monpress."

"Point taken," Eli said softly, but Josef was already stalking toward the door.

"You deserved that," Nico said, standing up from the crate she'd been sitting on.

"Thanks," Eli said sarcastically, but his heart wasn't in it. He looked over at Nico. "Sure you don't want a disguise? Just for a change?"

"No." Nico gave him a little half smile. "Nothing in those crates can do this."

She stepped forward into a long shadow cast by one of the dividers that separated the windows and vanished. Eli blinked. He'd seen Nico do her shadow thing dozens of times, but never that cleanly. It was like she'd simply disappeared.

"Slorn did a good job with this coat," she said behind him.

Eli jumped and whirled around. She was several feet away, sitting on a crate a few rows up, shaking her oversized sleeves with a kind of visceral happiness, like a cat playing with a stunned mouse.

"So I see," Eli said. "Shall we go?"

But the crate was already empty, and Nico winked into existence again beside Josef, who was standing impatiently at the door.

"Right," Eli muttered, hurrying to catch up.

The city of Gaol was a beautiful, well-laid-out place. Every road was perfectly straight, every house perfectly kept. Small gardens glowed like jewels behind the low stone walls, and every sign was painted in matching colors without a single scuff or faded letter. Even the paving cobbles were set at perfect right angles with their cracks swept meticulously clean.

Over all of this order flowed a constant stream of ordinary people, men and women, with identical swords belted at their sides. They were moving in close knots, talking together in quiet, nervous whispers. None of them looked happy to be there, but they moved at a good pace, making their way toward the citadel at the city center to join the growing crowd.

"Amazing!" Eli stood on tiptoe to get a better look. "It's like they turned the town upside down, shook out the people, and gave them swords. What is this, community military service?"

"Stop gawking," Josef said, tugging the thief down by his gaudy coat. "You're supposed to be a traveling merchant, remember?"

"I think it's perfectly in character for me to gawk," Eli said, batting Josef's hand away. "Haven't you ever met a merchant?"

They were walking toward the center of town down one of the main roads. Eli, as the merchant, stayed out in front, while Josef, the hired sword, kept a few paces behind. Nico, as usual, was nowhere in sight, but Josef's practiced eye spotted her flitting in and out of the gloom between the buildings, a tiny, girl-shaped patch of darker shadow. They were following the crowd toward the duke's fortress, its hulking, boxy shape black against the clear morning sky. Ahead, the road opened out into a square that was even more packed than the street they were on. Eli paused, frowning at the armed crowd, and then, quick as a bird going for cover, ducked into the nearest door, forcing Josef to turn sharp if he wanted to follow.

The doorway led to a bakery. It was a tiny shop, just a few benches and a counter separating the actual ovens from the customers. Still, like everything in Gaol, it was immaculately neat. Boards covered in precise lettering detailed the startling variety of baked goods and sweetmeats the shop offered. Hearing the door, the baker pulled himself away from the small window that overlooked the crowded square and came to the counter, a sour look on his flat face.

At once, Eli launched himself into character, his grin growing snide and arrogant as he flipped a handful of silver bits from the local currency casually between his fingers.

The baker's expression became infinitely more gracious at the glitter of silver. "What can I get for you, sir?"

"Hmm," merchant Eli droned, not bothering to look away from the window. "Give me a half dozen of those little fruit things, and a loaf of whatever's cheap for my boy here. Something hearty—these swordsmen eat you out of house and home."

Josef didn't have to fake his scowl, and the baker's red face paled. "Of course, sir, at once."

He went over to the shelves and began pulling things down with the hesitant clumsiness of someone who didn't usually do this himself.

"Where are your apprentices?" Eli said, casually leaning on the spotless counter. "I can't imagine you run this shop alone."

"Oh, no," the baker said and laughed. "But you know how boys are. They ran off to the square as soon as they heard the news. The duke's called in the conscriptions, the whole lot, word is." He huffed as he set out the tarts. "I'm just thankful I got dispensation on account of my shop, or I'd be grabbing my sword too."

"Conscriptions?" Eli said. "Why? Is Gaol under attack?"

"Oh, no." The baker shook his head. "Who'd attack Gaol? No, sir, word everywhere is that Eli Monpress robbed the duke's fortress last night."

The silver coins stopped flashing in Eli's hand.

"Really," he said, almost too casually. "How do you know it was Monpress? Did they catch him?"

"No," the baker said, fishing a loaf of brown bread out of the bin. "There's been no official word yet, but if they'd caught the thief, I doubt Duke Edward would bother with conscripts." He gave Eli a wink. "*That's* how we know it was Monpress. Who else would warrant mobilizing the whole country to catch him?"

"Who else, indeed," Eli said. "But it's been hours since the robbery if Monpress robbed the citadel last night. Wouldn't the thief have escaped by now?"

"I don't see how he could have," the baker said, packing Eli's order into a small wicker basket. "The duke closed the gates before dawn this morning. They say Monpress can move through shadows and kill guards just by looking, but that's rubbish. Whatever his bounty, he's human, and nothing human could have gotten through the duke's security."

"Why do you say that?" Josef asked, glaring at the baker from his place on the wall. "The thief got in, didn't he?"

The baker jumped and looked at Eli, obviously waiting for him to discipline his guard, but Eli was staring out the window, studying the citadel and the growing crowd with intense interest. Realizing he wouldn't get any backup from that quarter, the baker sullenly packed the last of Eli's pastries into the basket. When he was done, he had to wait a moment while Eli tore himself away from the window, but the pile of silver Eli tossed on the counter quickly smoothed over any hurt feelings.

"Thank you, sir," the baker said, bowing graciously as Eli swept out of the bakery with Josef on his heels.

The moment they stepped onto the street, Eli veered hard right, and they ducked down a narrow but shockingly clean alley. Nico was waiting for them, and she helped herself to one of the pastries from Eli's basket as soon as he was close.

"What's going on?" she asked, biting into the corner of the flaky tart.

"Someone got here before us," Josef said, leaning against the wall with his arms crossed. "I'd like to know who."

"I have an idea," Eli said carefully, picking a tart out of the pile. "But I'd have to get a look at the scene of the crime to be sure."

"What?" Josef said. "You mean *inside* the citadel? The one surrounded by armed guards?"

"Well, I certainly can't tell anything from out here," Eli said.

Josef frowned. "You do realize this could all be part of the trap."

"What?" Eli said, his mouth full of sweet pastry. "Fake a robbery so I'd come and investigate? That's a bit of a long shot. Think of it like this: We're here for a Fenzetti blade. Now, if another thief did break in, he either took the blade with him or had to leave it. Either way, we have to go into that citadel, either to pick up the thief's trail or get the blade for ourselves. The way I see it, we've just had the opportunity of a lifetime dropped in our laps. They're getting their orders now, but in a few moments, that whole crowd of citizen soldiers is going to start tearing this town apart looking for Eli Monpress. By going into the citadel, we'll be going to the only place they're *not* going to be looking. No thief good enough to get into the Duke of Gaol's citadel would ever return to the scene of the crime. When you look at it that way, the citadel's the safest place in the city for us to be right now."

Josef gave him a long look, casually sliding a dagger in and out of his sleeve as he thought about it. "That's some twisted Eli logic," he said at last, "but I'll bite. Anyway, sneaking into a citadel sounds a lot more interesting than hiding in a warehouse until dark."

"Ah," Eli said, licking the last of the tart off his fingers. "But that's the brilliant bit of the plan. We won't be sneaking. They're going to let us in all nice and legal."

Josef arched an eyebrow. "How are you going to manage that?"

Eli only smiled and shoved the wicker basket at him. "Just eat your breakfast. I've got to do some shopping. Be back in five minutes."

Josef barely had time to grab the basket before Eli was gone, ducking back out into the street with a flash of fake golden hair and vanishing expertly into the crowd. Josef stood there, holding the basket and watching where Eli had been for a moment, and then he sighed and sank back against the wall.

"Never boring with him, is it?" he said, fishing the loaf out of the basket and biting deep into the warm, dark bread.

Nico shook her head and helped herself to another tart.

Ten minutes later, Eli popped back into the alley carrying a small velvet bag in his fist and grinning like a cat who'd just eaten a coop of canaries. Josef stopped twirling the empty breadbasket between his fingers and straightened up. "What did you buy?"

"Take a look," Eli said and opened the drawstring, upturning the velvet bag over his open hand. There was a faint tinkling sound, and a glittering cascade fell out of the bag into Eli's waiting palm. They were rings. Jeweled rings in a rainbow of colors, all set in gold bands of various thickness. Some of the stones were round and smooth, others were cut to sharp points that refracted the morning light in glowing colors, and not a single one was smaller than the first knuckle of Eli's thumb. They were, in short, the tackiest, gaudiest jewelry Josef had ever seen.

"Powers, Eli," Josef said, picking up a ring set with a ruby that was almost larger than the embellished band it was attached to. "I hope you stole these. I can't imagine paying good money for something this ugly."

"Oh, I paid for them," Eli said, shoving the rings onto his fingers. "But not much, don't worry. They're glass. Fakes. I saw them in the window of one of the stores as we were walking up. They're what gave me the idea for how we're going to get into the citadel, actually. Look." He held up his newly adorned hands and wiggled his fingers. "Remind you of anyone?"

He'd crammed the rings onto every finger, thumbs included. His right pinky actually had two rings, both smaller gold and pearl bands that looked like something a father would buy for his spoiled daughter. But he was right, the effect was familiar, and Josef began to understand.

It didn't seem possible, but Eli's grin grew even wider. "Come on," he said, turning on his heel. "This is going to be the most fun I've had all year."

Josef stepped out after him. Nico, still licking her sticky fingers, kept right on the swordsman's heels.

CHAPTER 12

Gin made good on his boast. He ran like the wind itself, his long legs eating up the miles as they ran cross-country, on road and off. His orange eyes were completely unhindered by the darkness, and he stopped only when Miranda made him, which she did as much to catch her breath and unclamp her aching hands from his fur for a bit as to make the dog himself rest. Still, they made the journey from the western coast to the edge of Argo, the kingdom of which Gaol was the most prominent duchy, with time to spare, crossing the border shortly after dawn.

As they ran, Miranda had plenty of time to worry. She had no money or supplies, just what she'd had with her under her Spirit Court robes the day of the trial, which was precious little. Alone and in exile on the beach, she hadn't given it much attention. Now, however, all she could think was that this was a sorry start to a job. What she needed was some money, a cleaning up, and maybe a writ or other official document that could give her a new identity. As she was, no papers, no money, no authority, her hair thick with salt and her clothes stained with sea spray, she didn't even know if they'd let her through the city gate.

At their second stop, however, something happened that made Miranda realize she wasn't giving the West Wind enough credit. After two hours of hard running, Miranda coaxed Gin to a stop by a creek. While he drank, she stretched her legs, which ached from holding on to the ghosthound so tightly for so long. But as she was bending over to touch her toes, she felt something flutter against her fingers. She jumped in alarm and looked down to see it was a note, the paper money some kingdoms issued for internal use instead of coins or council standards. The note fluttered, and she snatched it between her fingers before it could blow away again. It was from the kingdom of Barat, which she vaguely remembered being somewhere south and west. Miranda studied the note intently before slipping it into her pocket. The number printed on the corner was modest, and she didn't even know if she could find somewhere that would accept it outside of Barat, but it was more than she'd had a moment ago, so Miranda counted it a lucky find and let the matter drop.

The next time they rested, it happened again. This time a small rain of silver coins from Fenulli, a city-state hundreds of miles away, landed inches in front of Gin's nose. After that, every time they stopped, more money appeared, always from countries to the west, and always in small amounts, yet their pile was growing. By the time they reached the Gaol border, Miranda's pockets were bursting, and she was feeling much more confident about the whole affair. She was still going over the particulars in her head, how she would change the money, what she would say if anyone commented ("My father collected currencies," or "We're a traveling act," which would explain the dog nicely), when she realized Gin was acting oddly. They were still at the Gaol border, off the road but in sight of the signs, standing in a little valley just below a well-kept vineyard, but Gin showed no signs of moving on. Instead, he was pacing back and forth, in and out of the duchy.

"What is it?" she asked, too tired to be as concerned as she should be.

"Look at the ground," Gin growled, his nose against the grass. "See anything odd?"

Miranda looked at the ground. It looked like field grass to her, with a few stones scattered about. Fortunately, Gin answered his own question before she had to admit her ignorance.

"The grass is wet here," Gin said, pawing at the ground on the non-Gaol side of the border, "but dry here." He jumped the little gully that marked the beginning of the duchy and nosed at the bright green, but bone-dry, Gaol grass. "It's like that all through here," he snorted, raising his head. "Like it didn't rain on Gaol at all. What kind of weather acts like that?"

Miranda frowned and squinted upward, but the sky was the same rainwashed clear blue as far as she could see on both sides of the border. She looked back at the ground, and her frown deepened. What kind of weather indeed?

"We are here to investigate strange happenings," she said. "This would certainly count, but it can't just be that the rain is acting odd. I don't think the West Wind would need us for something like that. Let's go farther in. Maybe we'll find more oddities."

Gin nodded and they trotted up the hill into Gaol itself. They kept the road in sight but stayed to the ridges and trees, Gin slinking lower and lower as the farms grew denser. Still, everything they saw looked perfectly normal. Idyllic even, so much so that Miranda began to wonder why they'd been sent here at all.

"I never knew Gaol was so pretty," she said delightedly as they crossed a stone bridge over a clear, babbling brook. "Why in the world does Hern spend so much time scheming in Zarin when he's got this to come home to?"

"Well, I don't like it one bit," Gin said. "It's too open and too neat. Even the grass growing in the fields is lined up in a grid. It's unnatural."

"Better get used to it," Miranda said, signaling him to stop at a picturesque stand of shaggy fir trees. "Because you're going to be waiting here while I go change this money and gather information. I saw a sign for an inn and trade house a little ways back. It'll be a start, if nothing else."

Gin snorted. "I'm not going to wait here while you wander off."

"We're trying to keep a low profile, remember?" Miranda said, jumping down. "Ghosthounds aren't exactly inconspicuous."

Gin rolled his eyes at that, but he sat down, which meant he was going to go along. Miranda smiled and checked her pockets one last time. The mix of coins and paper ruffled pleasantly under her fingers. Satisfied, she ran her hands through her windblown, salt-stiff hair and bound it back in a stiff braid. When she was as presentable as she could hope for, she left the trees and made her way down the hill to the large, charming lodge at the bottom, whose bright painted sign advertised lodging, baths, and all manner of trade and services for travelers.

Miranda swerved west and came up to the inn on the road as though she'd been walking on it the whole time. The main building was set back from the road itself, behind a large yard for caravans to turn around in. However, the turnaround was empty this morning. So were the stables, Miranda noted as she climbed up the wooden steps and opened the door to the inn. The building was just as charming inside as it was outside, with large wooden beams across the ceiling, warm lamps hanging on the walls, and a large stone hearth surrounded by benches. Feeling decidedly out of place in her dirty clothes, Miranda put on her most competent face and walked over to the dry-goods counter, where an old man was sorting through a large accounts book below a neatly lettered sign advertising money changing.

"We don't trade any council standards," he said as she approached. "Local currency only."

"I wasn't going to—" Miranda started, then dropped it, fishing her money out of her pockets instead. "Local is fine. Can you change these?"

The man stared at the strange collection of currencies as though Miranda had just emptied a fishing net on his desk and gave her a look sour enough to curdle cheese. "This ain't the Zarin exchange, lady."

"Just change what you can," Miranda said. "Please."

The man sneered at the pile, and then, with a long-suffering sigh, began to sort the notes and change into stacks.

"So," Miranda said, leaning forward just a little. "Quiet day?"

"Quiet?" The man snorted. "Try dead. The duke's called conscription and suspended all travel, or didn't you notice the empty road?"

"I just arrived," Miranda explained. "What do you mean 'called conscription'? Is there a war brewing?"

The man laughed loud and hard. "Council'd hardly allow that, would they? No, the duke can call conscription for whatever he likes. This here is a duchy in the old way. Old Edward owns everything, every field, every house, every business, even this one. We're all of us working for him, one way or the other, and conscription duty ain't any harder than farm work. Anyways, no one would say no to him even if he wasn't landlord and employer. You don't say no to the Duke of Gaol. Not if you want to keep the things what make life worth living."

Miranda grimaced. This duke sounded like a monster. That was one good thing about being here on her own rather than on the Spirit Court's business: She wouldn't have to introduce herself to the duke before getting to work. "Well," she said and smiled. "Why has he called conscription this time? Is there an emergency?"

He gave her a look as if she was stupid. "Didn't you hear? Eli Monpress robbed the duke last night. Stole him clean. Word is the treasury is empty."

It took every ounce of Miranda's discipline to keep her face calm, but inside, she was shrieking with joy. Eli Monpress here? Now? She couldn't even imagine a stroke of luck this fantastic. If she could somehow get her hands on Eli, why, even Hern couldn't keep her out of Zarin.

She looked up to see the innkeeper staring at her, and Miranda realized she must be grinning.

"That's too bad," she said, forcing her face into courteous disinterest. "I hear Monpress has a nice bounty. Did the duke catch him?"

"No word on that yet," the innkeeper said, shrugging. "The citadel's been shut up tight. But look at it this way: Would the duke shut down trade and close the borders if he had the thief in a cell?"

He might, actually, if he'd done any research on Eli, Miranda thought, but she kept it to herself.

"Doesn't matter none anyway," the man continued. "The duke will catch him all the same. This is Gaol, after all." He smiled, pushing a small stack of silver coins across the counter.

"Sixty-four exact," he said. "Take it or leave it, but you won't find better for the paper around here."

Miranda had no idea if that was good or not, but she took the money without complaint. The coins were thin pressed, and each was stamped with a man's face in silhouette, which the block lettering on the edges identified as belonging to Edward, Eighteenth Duke of Gaol.

It must have been a nice bit of money, for the innkeeper's tone softened considerably. "Anything else, miss?"

Miranda thought a moment. "Yes," she said. "I'll need a new set of clothes. And some soap."

The man raised his eyebrows, but he turned around and got a paper-wrapped bar from the shelf behind him.

"Soap," he said, slapping the bar on the counter. "One silver. As for clothes..." He walked over to the corner and opened the first of a series of large chests set against the wall. "My daughter's work," he said, pulling out a stretch of brown homespun. "Five silvers each. Just pick out what you like."

Miranda walked over with a grimace. The chest was full of dresses. Farmer girl dresses. With little motifs of daisies on the trim and sleeves. A quick look through the other chests showed more of the same. The man's daughter was apparently prolific, and very fond of daisies. Seeing this was all she was going to get, Miranda settled on a long, rust-colored dress with a wide skirt that looked like it would do for riding, and, most important of all, long sleeves that went down over her fingers to hide her rings. The color didn't clash with her hair too badly, and the stitching, though large, was sturdy. Satisfied, she paid the man for the soap and the dress, and he even wrapped it up for her for free, cementing her suspicion that she was being vastly overcharged.

Miranda shoved the package under her arm. Before she turned to leave, however, she asked one final question.

"Sir," she said, "did it rain last night?"

"Of course not," the man sniffed. "It's Wednesday."

Miranda gave him a funny look. "What does that have to do with rain?"

"This is Gaol," the man said. "It only rains on Sundays."

Miranda just stood there a moment, stunned, while in her head, several little pieces clicked into place.

"Thank you," she said. "Thank you very much."

The man just made a harumphing noise before going back to his ledger.

Miranda walked up the road until she was out of sight of the inn's windows, then sprinted up the hill to where Gin was hiding. She'd worried he would be asleep, but the dog was awake and waiting.

"What's going on?" he asked as soon as she ducked under the shaggy treeline.

"Strange and wonderful things," she answered, peeling off her shirt. "Mellinor, could I get some water?"

The water spirit complied, and she was sopping wet in an instant. Peeling the soap out of its waxed-paper wrapping, Miranda began to scrub her face and hair. She relayed her conversation with the innkeeper as she washed, occasionally breaking to ask Mellinor for more water, which he gave immediately, for he was listening as well.

"Eli Monpress! Do you believe the luck?" Miranda said again, leaning over to wring out her hair.

"Lucky indeed," Gin said. "But go back to that bit about the rain. As I've heard it, only a Great Spirit can order the rain, and only then if it's got the cooperation of the local winds. How is a human doing it?"

"Maybe he's Enslaving the Great Spirit of this area," Miranda said, wincing as she picked at a knot of tangles rooted at the back of her neck.

"Preposterous," Mellinor rumbled, giving her a bit more water. "If this place was Enslaved, we would have known miles ago. The whole world would have known. Trust me, a land whose Great Spirit is Enslaved does not look like this."

The water slung outward, taking in the lovely hills, rolling farmland, and flowering orchards. Miranda was going to point out that Mellinor had looked pretty nice to her when she'd arrived, but then she remembered that spirits probably saw something completely different and she kept her mouth shut, washing the last of the soap out of her hair in silence.

"Well, whatever's happening, it's not good," she said, squeezing her hair dry. "Time to ask the spirits what's going on."

She pulled the dress over her head, the thick fabric catching on her wet skin. When the dress was in place, she knelt on the needle-strewn ground and pulled the green stone ring off her little finger.

"Alliana," she said softly, placing the ring on the ground, "say hello to the grove for us."

The moment the ring touched the ground, a circle of bright green moss began to spread over the brown needles. It spread to the base of the nearest tree, the moss's tiny rootlings prodding the bark. But as the moss crept up the fir tree, its quiet, tiny sounds became frustrated.

Finally, almost five minutes later, the moss retreated, and Alliana herself spoke up. "It's no good, mistress," the moss said, sounding quite put out. "I can't get the tree to talk. I couldn't even talk to the sapling sprouting below it. I don't understand; green wood is normally very chatty."

Miranda frowned. "You're saying they wouldn't wake up?"

"No, they're awake," the moss grumbled. "They just won't talk. I don't know what kind of land this is, but its spirits are *frightfully* rude."

Miranda bit her lip. This was an unexpected problem. "Try another tree."

They tried five altogether, but every time it was the same. The trees would not talk. None of the spirits in the little grove would. Finally, Alliana asked to go back to sleep, as this was all too frustrating for her, and Miranda drew her back into the moss agate.

"All right, I give up. What's going on?" Miranda said, sliding the ring back onto her finger. "Could it be Eli? What did he call it, building goodwill with the countryside?"

"No amount of goodwill does that," Mellinor said, flicking a spray of water at the reticent trees. "And I doubt even the thief has this kind of reach. Normally, I'd say Enslavement. I never knew anything else that could shut up young trees once a wizard woke them up, but they don't seem frightened, just worried." The water made a thoughtful splashing sound. "No, something is wrong in Gaol, and I doubt it's only here. The West Wind was right to be worried."

"So what are we going to do about it?" Gin said, tail twitching.

"Start at the top," Miranda answered. "If anyone can tell us what's going on, it's the Great Spirit of Gaol. Since the Fellbro River is by far the largest spirit in this area, I'm going to guess it's either in charge or knows who is, so we'll start with it, and for that, we're going to the capital."

"The capital?" Gin gave her a look. "The river runs all down the duchy's eastern side. Why do we need to go to the capital?"

"Because it's only three miles away, *and* because Eli's in the capital." Miranda smiled, shaking her sleeves until they fell down over her rings, hiding them completely. "Nothing wrong with a little bonus."

"I thought you said Eli had already robbed the duke," Gin said. "Wouldn't he be long gone by now?"

"Come on," Miranda said. "This is Eli we're talking about. When has he ever just run away? I don't think he even could, not with an entire treasury. Even Nico's not that strong. No, I bet he's hiding in the capital, waiting on his chance to waltz out while everyone goes crazy around him. Who knows, maybe he's still in the duke's citadel." She grinned. "After all, 'the last place a man looks is under his feet.'"

Gin gave a long sigh. "It's a dark day indeed if you're quoting the thief." He lay down. "Come on, let's get going. I did a little scouting while you were gone. If we keep low, we can hide behind copses and hedge walls almost all the way."

Miranda glared at him. "You were supposed to wait here."

Gin just wagged his tail, and Miranda shook her head before climbing on.

"Just *try* and remember to be sneaky," she whispered as they crept out of the fir trees.

"Who do you think I am?" Gin snorted. He slunk up the hill, keeping behind the vineyards until he reached a stretch of trees and bushes that did indeed shelter them for the next few miles, just as he'd said it would.

When they reached the outskirts of Gaol's walled capital, Miranda left Gin hidden in an empty barn. He was much easier to convince this time around. Even Gin admitted there was no way he could sneak into a city, and besides, the night's running was catching up with him. Miranda left him sleeping under the straw in the hayloft, and then, strolling casually out of the barn, she started for the city.

With the embargo on travel, she'd expected it would take some finagling to get into Gaol's capital—a bribe for the guards, maybe, or some wall climbing. But as she got closer, she realized it wasn't going to be a problem. The road was full of people, farmers mostly, from their clothes, and almost all of them wearing swords. These must be the conscripts, she realized. The duke was apparently building himself quite an army. Because of this influx, the guards at the large gate were letting people in without much question. No one, however, was coming out. Miranda held her breath and kept her head down as she passed through the gates, but the guards didn't even speak to her. For once, she was very grateful to be ignored.

Gaol's capital was as lovely as the countryside around it, with a high, thick wall, a grid of neatly paved streets lined with iron street lamps, and tall, close timber and stone buildings with tiled, sloping roofs.

"It's every bit as orderly as the land outside," Mellinor whispered in her ear as she turned onto one of the side streets. "The Great Spirit must be a horrible taskmaster."

"I don't think the Great Spirit's the problem," Miranda muttered. This was a wizard's doing, she was certain. But how, and why? Those were the questions she was here to answer. As for who, though, she had a pretty good idea already. She looked northeast, where the pointed roof of an instantly recognizable tower poked over the rooftops. This was Hern's territory, after all, and as she thought about it, several strange things in Hern's past began to make sense, like how he'd refused year after year to take an apprentice of his own. She'd always chalked that up to self-importance combined with laziness, but if he were hiding something in Gaol, suddenly his not taking an apprentice would be cast in a new light. Same with his stubborn refusal to let other Spiritualists do any studies in Gaol, and his insistence that no Spiritualists cut through the duchy on their way to other places. He'd claimed his duke disliked Spiritualists disrupting his duchy by riding through on strange creatures, and since Hern was powerful and influential, and going around Gaol was a simple matter, no one had thought to question that explanation.

Well, Miranda thought, glaring at the tower, that was about to change. With a final sneer, she turned and started walking downhill toward the river.

As she went deeper into town, the crowd got thicker. Everyone, men and women, was carrying swords. Some moved in orderly groups through the streets, conscripts who'd already received their orders. Others, people who'd come through the gate with her, were still pushing toward the citadel, which seemed to be the heart of the whole operation. By the time she'd reached the edge of the town center square, the crowd was shoulder to shoulder. Miranda pushed her way through as best she could, but it was clear she wasn't going to get to the river this way. She scowled at the wall of backs in front of her and started looking around for a side street she could take down to the water. That's when she spotted him.

There, pushing his way through the crowd not five feet from her, was Hern. He was overdressed as always in a bright blue coat with silver embroidery, and looking hurried. The rings on his fingers glittered dangerously as he elbowed his way past a belligerent, and very large, pair of farmers. Once he was past, he gave the crowd a sneering look and turned down a side street lined with large, beautiful houses. As soon as he was around the corner, Miranda followed him.

"Miranda," Mellinor said in a warning voice. "What are you doing?"

"Think about it," she whispered, sneaking through the crowd. "Hern's secretiveness, strange things going on with the spirits in Gaol, the West Wind asking me, Hern's enemy, specifically to investigate? It doesn't take a genius to put it together."

"That may be," Mellinor said, "but don't forget your own words.

You didn't want to take this job specifically because of Hern. I don't like Hern any more than you do, but the world hasn't changed in the last day. You said it yourself: if anyone sees you here, they're going to think it's revenge. Take your own advice, ignore the pompous idiot and keep going for the river."

"The river will still be there in an hour," she said under her breath. "I can't miss an opportunity like this. Think, if I can prove that Hern's behind whatever is going on here, I can destroy his credibility, maybe even get a retrial. It would be even better than catching Monpress. Even if it's just that he knows what's going on and hasn't reported it to the Court, that would be enough to throw mud all over his career." She stood on tiptoe, catching a glimpse of Hern's blond head through the crowd, before ducking down again. "No," she said. "He has to be up to something. The Spirit Court referendum is coming up any day now, and he wouldn't dare leave Zarin and miss the run-up for that unless he had a very good reason. I'm going to find out what that is."

Mellinor didn't like that one bit, but he didn't say anything else. Miranda trailed Hern for two blocks. It was nervous work. All the houses faced the road, and there was no cover for her to hide behind once they left the crowds. But Hern never so much as looked behind him. He just marched in that pompous, hurried way of his until he reached the steps of a large, expensive-looking inn. Here, he went up the stairs, nodding to the boy who opened the door for him, and vanished inside. A moment later, Miranda followed. The boy didn't open the door as readily for her, but a coin changed his mind and Miranda found herself in the opulent entry hall of a wealthy inn in a wealthy town. Hern was at the far end of the room, talking with two men Miranda recognized as Tower Keepers. Just as she spotted them, a well-dressed servant walked over to escort the men up the stairs.

"Miss?"

Miranda jumped, startling the waiter who was hovering at her elbow. "Can I help you, miss?"

"Yes," Miranda said, pointing at the stairwell Hern had just disappeared up. "What's up those stairs?"

"The private dining rooms, ma'am," the man answered skeptically, eyeing her rough clothes.

"Good," Miranda said. "I'd like one. How much?"

"It's fifteen silvers for a private meal," the man said. "We've got grouse and pheasant in a plum glaze, with—"

"Sounds lovely," Miranda said, shoving the money at him. "Show me up."

The man's haughty expression vanished when the money hit his hand, and he cheerfully led her up the stairs. There were several dining rooms, but only one of the doors was closed. She picked the door beside it, and the waiter showed her into a small room with a dining table and a little stand in the corner with water, stationery, and a jug of flowers. Best of all, it had a simple plank wall separating it from the closed dining room next door. She could just barely hear the buzz of voices coming through the wood, and then Hern's haughty laugh.

"This is perfect," Miranda said, nodding. "You may go."

The waiter gave her a confused look, but bowed and left, shutting the door behind him. The minute he was gone, Miranda got down on the floor beside the wall and pressed her ear against the planks. The men's voices drifted through, muted but understandable.

"It's a mess is what it is," one of the Tower Keepers was saying. "We voted against the girl like you said and nothing's changed except Banage is more self-righteous than ever. Also, the tide in the Court's on his side now. My position as head of the committee on Forest Spirit management is threatened."

"You knew the risks." Hern's voice was bored. "But you took my money all the same. You think your committee head position's in danger now, just wait until the Court hears about how you took a bribe to bring down Banage's favorite."

Miranda's eyes widened. She shot off the floor and grabbed the stationery from the table, as well as the ink pot and pen. Here was Hern admitting to everything she'd suspected. She had to get it down on paper so she didn't forget a word.

Both of the Tower Keepers were angry now, accusing Hern of threatening them, trying to call his bluff, but Hern's voice was as calm as ever.

"Gentlemen," he said, "we can go up together, or we can go down together. Your choice."

The men grumbled, and Miranda got the feeling Hern was giving them that same haughty, implacable look he'd given her the day of the trial. It must have worked, for a few moments later he started asking them about the situation in Zarin.

Miranda was writing furiously when the door to her room clicked. She sprang off the floor and into her chair just as the waiter entered with a covered dish.

"First course," he said cheerily. "Mushroom soup with cream and a bread tray. Your main course will be up in just—"

He stopped as Miranda frantically put a finger to her lips. The voices from the other room had stopped as well, listening. Then she heard their door open. They were also getting their first course. Miranda let out a sigh of relief, and then she flashed the waiter a dazzling smile.

"Sorry," she said. "It's been a very long trip. All I want to do is sit quietly for a while." She stood and pressed a stack of coins into his hand. "Don't bother with the other courses," she whispered. "I just want to be left alone."

"Yes, lady," the waiter whispered back taking the coins gladly. "Whatever you like."

She smiled and waved as he left, and then, as soon as the door was closed, she grabbed the soup and a hunk of bread and sat right back down on the floor, readying her pen and paper for whatever else Hern might admit.

Out in the hall, the waiter counted over his new wealth. The crazy lady had given him ten coins to *stop* serving her. Well, he wasn't going to complain, and he wasn't going to let the rest of the dinner she'd bought go to waste. He was hungry, too, and the slow-roasting pheasants had been tempting him all day. Grinning, he put the money in his apron pocket and hurried down the stairs to the hotel's register. It was dangerous to carry this much money around. The other waiters would filch it the first chance they got, which was why everyone gave their tips to the register. Sure, he took a five percent cut, but it was a small price to pay for knowing your money wouldn't vanish altogether.

The register took his coins no questions asked, and, after noting the amount, threw them into the strongbox with all the other cash. He closed the lid, plunging the coins into darkness. The moment the light went out, the coins began to talk. They buzzed like rattler snakes, spreading gossip, telling what they'd heard, but the waiter's coins' story quickly rose to the top. A wizard with rings, powerful ones, spying on Master Hern. The duke must be told!

This was the message given to the strongbox, who in turn told the beam of the wall it was set into, who told the eaves it supported, who told the lamp on its post outside. The lamp, then, did what it had been ordered to do and switched itself on. A moment later, a strange, slow wind blew through the street, circling when it reached the glowing lamp. It heard the story and, judging it important, carried the coins' words over the rooftops, over the growing crowd in the square, and up to the very top of the citadel, where its master waited.

* * *

Back in the hotel, Miranda was almost giddy. Over the course of their lunch, and what sounded like a few glasses of wine, Hern had laid out a dozen plans to bring Banage down, any one of which would be a grievous violation of his oaths. She'd gotten them all down, marking the ones that seemed to be already in progress. It was a dizzying list. Hern had apparently been bribing Tower Keepers for years, which explained why Master Banage had been having so much trouble with them. She was not really surprised to hear that Hern had been buying votes, but to actually learn the full extent of his reach from his own lips was amazing, and it was all she could do to get it down. By the time their waiter brought the brandy, she had ten pages of close-scribbled notes full of dates, names, and specifics, and she was almost bursting with the urge to wrap everything up and take it to Banage herself, exile or no.

But as the men in the other room settled down with the brandy glasses, an unexpected knock interrupted them. Miranda jumped, thinking it was her waiter again. But the knock was at the other door, and she heard the scrape of chairs as Hern got up to see what was going on. There was a creak as he opened the door, followed by words too quiet for Miranda to make out, and then the crinkle of paper.

"What is it, Hern?" one of the Tower Keepers asked.

Hern didn't answer. She heard the scrape of his boots as he walked across the room. Not back to his seat, but to the wall that Miranda was crouched against. He was so close she could hear his breath. She held her own, not daring to make a sound.

A moment later, Hern spoke one word. "Dellinar."

Miranda's eyes widened. It was a spirit's name. In the split second after, time slowed to a crawl. She turned and grabbed her papers, shoving them into the pocket of her dress as she called for

Durn, her stone spirit. He could stop anything of Hern's, Miranda was sure, buying her time to get to the window. They were only one flight up; she could make it. But even as her lips formed Durn's name, the wall between the rooms exploded in a shower of splintered wood and snaking green vines. The plants sprang like tigers, snapping around her ankles, her waist, and her wrists, slamming her to the floor so hard she saw spots. More vines wrapped around her arms and her head, sliding across her open mouth to gag her. She struggled wildly, but then the vines twined around her throat, nearly cutting off her breath. She looked up and saw Hern kneeling beside her, a wide grin on his face.

"What you feel is my vine spirit about to crush your windpipe," he said calmly. "If your spirits try anything, he will take off your head."

Miranda spat an obscenity at him, but all she managed was strangled sound as the vine twisted tighter.

Hern leaned over so that he was in front of her, and he waved a piece of paper. "Lovely bit of warning," he smiled, glancing down at her scattered notes, which had fallen from her pocket when she fell. "Good timing too. I must remember to thank dear Edward."

There was shouting out in the hall, and Miranda caught a glimpse out of the corner of her eye of soldiers entering the room. "Spiritualist Hern," a stern voice announced. "Duke's orders, both you and the spy are to report to the citadel at once."

Hern glowered. "I have this well under control, officer."

The soldier didn't even blink. "Duke's orders," he said again.

Hern rolled his eyes. "Very well," he said. "But first"—he made a florid gesture with his jeweled hand. Miranda gasped and began to kick as the vines wrenched tight. She reached frantically for her spirits, but it was too late. The plants cut into her skin, binding her limbs and cutting off her air. Her body grew impossibly heavy, and she lay still, her lungs burning for air.

"Pick her up." Hern's voice was very far away. "And mind the vines."

Hands slid under her and she felt herself lifted. Guards' faces blurred across her vision, and then she saw nothing.

CHAPTER 13

The crowd in front of the citadel was thinning, the conscripts getting their orders from a group of guards in full uniform at the gate and moving off in organized packs toward different sections of town. The peasant soldiers organized with remarkable efficiency, and Eli got the feeling that the duke called in conscripts fairly often. Eli waited until the coast was clear, lounging casually on a bench by a fountain in one of the little parks just off the main square while Josef waited tensely behind him with Nico. Eventually, the last of the conscript groups moved off and most of the uniformed soldiers trudged back into the citadel, leaving only a small knot of guardsman and a lone officer at the door.

Seeing his opportunity at last, Eli stood up and walked toward the square, Josef and Nico trailing along behind. Just before he stepped out into the open, Eli paused and closed his eyes. When he opened them again, his demeanor had changed. His posture was perfectly straight, his shoulders square, his face intent and uncompromising. When he stepped out into the square he didn't walk across the cobbles; he marched straight over the open ground to the broad steps at the front of the Duke of Gaol's impenetrable fortress.

The knot of six guards and their decorated officer stood at attention at the top of the stairs before a heavy iron door. They pulled closer as Eli approached, gripping their spears suspiciously. Eli ignored the warning and walked until he was just shy of the first step. There, he stopped and planted both feet with iron stubbornness.

"If you're here for the conscription," the officer said skeptically, "you're too late to avoid the fine. If you give your name to Jerold here, I'll be sure the duke knows you showed up, but—"

"Don't be stupid," Eli sneered, tossing his golden hair. "I'm no conscript. I am the Spiritualist Miranda Lyonette, head of the Spirit Court's investigation into the rogue wizard Eli Monpress. I heard that he struck this fortress last night, and I demand access to the scene of the crime."

The guard just stood there, blinking in confusion. Whatever he'd expected the man marching across his square to say, this certainly was not it. "You," he said slowly, "are Miranda Lyonette?"

"Yes," Eli said, looking extremely put upon.

The guard looked at the guard next to him. "Isn't Miranda a girl's name?"

"How dare you, sir!" Eli cried. "I'll have you know it is an old family name. Honestly, am I to be constantly hounded by the ignorance of others? A girl's name, *really*."

The absolute scorn in his voice did the trick, and the guard's face went scarlet. "Forgive me, sir. I meant no offense. It's just, well, do you have proof of your identity?"

"Proof?" Eli rolled his eyes dramatically. "You insult my name and then ask for proof? Honestly, do I look like I have time for this idiotic song and dance?"

"Anything will do," the guard said. "Some sort of identification from the Court, or—"

"You know anyone beside Spiritualists who wear rings like these?" Eli held up both his hands, letting his gaudy glass rings catch the sun. "What do you want, a writ signed by Banage himself?"

"That would be good, actually," the guard said as politely as possible. "I really can't let you in without papers of some—"

Eli went positively livid. "You dare, sir! I just made the two-day trip from Zarin to Gaol in under four hours. Do you think I had the time to wait for those Court bureaucrats to give me papers? When you're chasing Monpress, time is of the utmost importance! Already, the trail is getting colder, and for every second you waste I lose hours in the hunt for the thief. If you won't let me in, then I will make sure your duke knows exactly who is responsible for letting his thief get away!" Eli looked about. "Where is your duke anyway? Bring him here at once!"

The guard blanched. "You see, the duke is terribly busy, and without proper identification, I'm afraid I can't—"

"Afraid?" Eli's eyes narrowed. "You'd best be afraid, doorman! Somewhere in that brick of a citadel is a spirit who saw how Monpress did what he did. Even now, that spirit is falling asleep. If it falls asleep entirely it will likely forget what it saw, and if that happens—" Eli paused for a deep, shuddering breath. "You don't even want to know what I'll do, but one thing is certain." His eyes narrowed, pinning the guard captain with a killing glare. "*Should* that happen, I will make sure everyone, from Zarin's highest seats of power to the Duke of Gaol himself, knows that *you* were the reason why."

The guard bowed, his face pale and sweating. "Apologies, Spiritualist Lyonette; I never doubted you were who you claimed to be. But I'm afraid I still can't give you access to the treasury without permission from the duke. If you could wait just a—"

"I will not!" Eli said with a flippant wave of his ringed fingers. "Powers, man, you've already been robbed blind! What are you afraid I'm going to do in there, steal your dust? Just show me and my assistants to the scene of the crime and I can get to work finding your thief, which I'm sure will make your duke much happier than you interrupting him with stupid requests."

The guard was sweating profusely now, and Eli took his chance for the final push. "Listen very carefully," he said slowly, twitching his spirit just a fraction so that the gaudy rings on his fingers glittered with malice. "If I lose the trail because of your delays, you will wish you'd never heard of Spiritualists. Do you understand?"

"Of course, Master Spiritualist," the guard said, waving his men toward the doors. "Right this way."

The pack of guards opened one of the great iron doors, and Eli, Nico, and Josef followed the guard captain into the citadel.

In the sky overhead, the wind that had been circling since Eli first stepped out into the square changed direction, blowing up the stone wall to the top of the citadel and through the window of one of the stubby towers at its crown. The tower was all one room, large and circular, with a long table at its center. A cluster of men stood around it, all dressed in the same drab uniform. Most of them looked like dressed-up farmers taken from their fields and thrust into uniforms, which was what they were. They were the conscript leaders, and they all wore the same quiet, obedient expression as they watched the head of the table where Duke Edward was pointing out markers on the city map carved into the table's smooth, wooden top.

The duke was in the middle of laying out details about how he wanted the perimeter handled, but he stopped midsentence as the wind blew by.

"Is this about Hern again?" Edward said.

"Not this time," the wind answered, blowing in circles above the farmer-generals. "Someone claiming to be a Spiritualist just bullied your idiot door guard into letting him and his assistants into the citadel."

The duke scowled. "A Spiritualist? One of Hern's cronies?"

"No," the wind spun. "I don't think it's really a Spiritualist, either. Didn't even look like a wizard to me. It was a yellow-haired man, said his name was Miranda Lyonette."

The duke's eyes widened. "Miranda?" He pursed his lips. "Considering Hern just sent word that he is escorting *Miss* Lyonette to the citadel as we speak, I find that hard to believe." He scratched his beard. "Whoever it is, I'll investigate myself. We can't afford another contingency at this point. The situation is bollixed enough as it is. Speaking of which, any news from the spy?"

"Not yet," the wind whispered. "I'll go check again."

"Thank you, Othril," the duke said. "I trust you'll notify me if anything else odd happens."

"Of course, my lord," the wind huffed.

Edward waved his hand and the wind flew off back to his patrol, shooting out over the citadel's edge. When he was gone, Duke Edward turned back to his officers, all of whom had waited patiently through what seemed to them to be a one-sided and nonsensical conversation.

"Gentlemen," the duke said. "It seems we have a rat in our cupboard. Those of you already assigned positions, please take your soldiers to their places. The rest of you, come with me." He swept past the table and toward the door. "We have an intruder to catch."

The officers saluted and went their separate ways, calling for their seconds to rally the conscripts as they trundled down the rickety stairs into the citadel proper.

The inside of the fortress of Gaol was not what Eli had expected. As soon as the guard led them through the iron doors, he'd looked eagerly for narrow halls, high ceilings, archer decks, thief catches, all the wonderful things highlighted on the poster. But the hall they entered was low and perfectly ordinary. Little hallways branched off of it leading to barracks, small offices, meeting rooms, and equipment caches. The walls were of uninspiring thickness, the architecture unremarkable, and there was only one portcullis, not five, as the poster had boasted. In short, it was a normal citadel built on a conservative plan, and perhaps a bit on the cheap.

Eli was supremely disappointed.

"*This* is the great citadel of Gaol?" he said, gazing around in disgust. "Where are the six-foot walls? The multitiered locks? Where are the booby traps? The poster promised traps in every room!"

The guardsman's hairy face turned a bit red. "Well," he mumbled, "that's just advertising. Those posters of the duke's were just a precaution. Tell the thieves how impossible it is and they just give up, right? Far cheaper than actually building some supercitadel. Anyway, I'd say it worked. We've had no trouble from thieves since word got around about how secure the fortress was."

"No trouble until last night," Josef pointed out.

"Well, that's Monpress," the guard huffed. "He hardly counts. Don't worry, though; the duke'll catch him, Sir Spiritualist, make no mistake."

"Oh, certainly," Eli said with disgust, eyeing the hallway, which had now widened out into a large common room. "How did the duke know it was Monpress, anyway?"

"Well," the guard said, "who else could it be?"

"Who else, indeed?" Eli said, smiling, while Josef rolled his eyes.

The officer led them out of the common room through a flimsy doorway and into a hallway even smaller and drabber than the ones before it. Eli glowered at the man's back. So far, the "thief-proof citadel of Gaol" was a monstrous waste of time. If not for the

Fenzetti, and if he wasn't so curious about someone impersonating him, Eli would have called the whole thing off the moment they passed the unlocked weapon cabinets. Only when they were almost to the center of the citadel did Eli finally spot something promising. Their guide had led them around a corner and into a small hallway set back from the main thoroughfare. Unlike the others, this hall was long and narrow, with a ceiling tall enough for archer stands to be placed over troops. Best of all was what waited at the end. There, at the far side of the hall, standing beside a large stone hearth and chimney, was an immense metal door. Its surface was perfectly smooth, without even a knob or handle. It was set flush against the stone without groove or crack, no way to get leverage at all. It stood black and impenetrable in the firelight as they approached, and Eli immediately began to perk up. This was more like it.

When they reached the fire pit the guard captain stopped and began to feel around in his pockets, muttering apologies.

"Sorry, sorry," he said. "It's something different every time." He drew out a small sachet wrapped in white paper. He laid it in his palm, weighing it experimentally before lobbing the packet, paper and all, straight into the banked fire. The paper curled and blackened, its edges cracking as sweet-smelling smoke—Eli picked out cinnamon and thyme—rose in a white plume. Then, without warning, the fire burst upward in a full roar, blasting the tiny hall with a wave of heat.

"You again?" a flickering voice bellowed as the fire churned, but the guard just mopped a bit of soot off his balding head, completely unaware that the fire was speaking to him.

The flames slumped down sullenly. "I know," it mumbled. "Open the door, close the door. I never get to sleep. It's been years. I don't know. No rest, no sleep, nothing but work..." The voice wavered like smoke in the wind and then faded as the fire dropped back to its usual size, leaving only the smell of burnt cinnamon. Somewhere below them, machinery began to grind and the great door in front of them rolled aside.

"There you are," the guard said. "That's the magic gate. Don't understand how it works, but I suppose it beats pushing that slab open with your shoulder, eh?"

"Indeed," Eli said, doing his best to convey the absolute disgust he was sure a Spiritualist would have felt at seeing a fire spirit used in that way. It wasn't hard. He felt kind of sour himself. He didn't know what kind of operation Gaol was running, but wizards who overworked their spirits deserved to be robbed blind. He only wished he'd been the one to do it. His thoughts drifted back to the terrified crates, but he forced himself to stop. Whatever was going on here, he didn't have time to deal with it. Anyway, it didn't matter. Once word got out that Eli Monpress had robbed Gaol, the Spiritualists would start showing up in droves. They would deal with whatever abuses were going on in Gaol. That would be his gift to the spirits, and it would have to be enough. Right now, he needed to find out who was taking advantage of his reputation before the situation got out of control. He had a suspicion, but for once he really hoped he was wrong; otherwise things were going to get very, very annoying. Just thinking about it made him feel tired, and he quickly turned his attention back to the task at hand.

The room beyond the treasury door was massive. It was perfectly square, with bright, mirrored lanterns burning high overhead that Eli suspected were also spirit powered, since he could see no way a servant would get up that high to light them. The harsh, brilliant light fell over what must have once been an impressive and large collection, but was now just a neat grid of empty shelves with only telltale holes in the dust to show there had ever been anything there.

"The entire holding of the di Fellbro family," the guard said, almost teary. "Gone."

"Not all gone," Eli said, pointing across the room to where a large golden lion still took up half a shelf.

"Aye," she guard said. "The thief left a few pieces. Some we think were too large for him to carry. Others, well, we honestly don't know why he left them."

Eli nodded and leaned closer. "Confidentially, friend," he said conspiratorially, "how close are your men to catching Monpress?"

The guard's face went red. "Hot on his heels, sir. I can't tell you the details, of course. Security must be upheld."

"Of course," Eli said, smiling graciously. "Thank you, Captain, we'll take it from here."

The captain twisted uncertainly. "Actually, sir, I'm afraid I'll have to stay. I couldn't leave anyone, even a Spiritualist, alone in here."

"Suit yourself," Eli said with a shrug. "We won't be long."

The guard nodded and took a seat on the ledge of the hearth, but Eli had already stopped paying attention to him. He walked across the room to the lion and kneeled down to peer into its open mouth. Josef stood behind him, eyes roving over the empty shelves, while Nico wandered off toward the far end of the room, staring up at the high ceiling.

"So," the swordsman said quietly, "think they're actually close to catching the thief?"

"Not a chance," Eli said, running his fingers over the lion's mane. "He wouldn't have let us in if they had a lead. For all they know, this stuff just vanished in the night. The guard's probably sticking around because he's hoping we'll give him something he can use. Look here."

His fingers paused their roving just behind the lion's left paw, and Eli bent down almost to the ground, peering intently at the gold with a knowing smile. "Thought so, this is a fake. Actual Golden Lions of Ser have a tiny blessing to the volcano of Ser stamped into their left paws. This one has nothing."

"It's not real gold?" Josef said, drumming his knuckles on the lion's head.

"Oh, no, it's real gold." Eli stood, brushing off his knees. "But whoever robbed this place wasn't your common cat burglar. Look at the shelves, not a one out of place. Even the dust is undisturbed. This room seems completely secure, far more so than anything we walked through to get here. I've been on the lookout since we stepped through the door and even I can't figure out how the thief got in, or got out again with what had to be a wagonload of priceless artifacts. However, I can tell that whoever did this was patient, educated enough to spot a fake, discerning enough not to want one, and very, very good. That narrows the list down quite a bit."

"So you know who it was?"

Eli rolled his eyes. "Let's just say there's only one man I know who can pull a job like this, but if we're going to find him, I'm going to need to see a list of the duke's business contacts."

Josef looked at him, thoroughly confused. "Business contacts?"

"It's our only chance. He certainly didn't leave a clue here." Eli craned his head around, scanning the shelves. "Well," he said cheerfully, "at least the Fenzetti blade is missing."

"How is that a good thing?" Josef said.

"If the thief took it, we know it wasn't fake."

"Or wasn't here to begin with," the swordsman grumbled.

"No, no." Eli shook his head. "If the broker said it's here, then it's here. Their information is always reliable; that's why you pay through the nose for it."

While he was speaking, Nico appeared beside Josef. The swordsman instantly stopped listening to Eli and turned his attention to her.

"Men with swords are filling the hallway," she said quietly. "And someone is talking with our guard."

Eli spun around. Sure enough, there was their guide at the door in deep, frantic conversation with someone Eli couldn't see. As he watched, whoever it was ran off, and the guard took up position at the center of the door.

"The game is up," Josef said, looking at Nico. "I'll take the front. See if you can't find another exit."

Nico nodded and they broke, leaving Eli staring at empty space.

"What are you planning?" he whispered loudly, trotting after Josef as the swordsman ran for the door.

Josef didn't answer. He reached the door and stared down the guardsman, who had turned to face them, a short sword held in his shaky hands.

"I am sorry, Sir Spiritualist," he said, peering over Josef's shoulder at Eli. "Orders from the top. The other guards are coming right now. I have nothing but respect for your organization, but please, surrender quietly."

Eli stared at the guard as if he'd grown a second head before he remembered his cover story and snapped back into character.

"Surrender?" he shouted, beyond indignant. "I am here on the business of the Spirit Court! I am apprentice to the Rector Spiritualis himself, head of the Eli investigation! When it comes to Monpress, I *AM* the highest authority! And I demand that you tell those men to stand down and let us pass!"

Eli had himself in a fury now, and it was working. The guard was sweating bullets, but he still didn't move. Behind him, the clink of metal boots on stone was deafening as the guards marched down the hall, filling their only escape with a wall of armed men, and not the conscripts from outside either, but professional soldiers.

Eli was about to start a new round of threats when Josef threw out his arm, cutting him off.

Josef looked down at the guard. "You seem like a nice fellow," he said. "Sorry about this."

Quick as a cat, Josef stepped forward, sliding inside the man's guard and pinching his inner arm just below the joint of his armor. The guard cried out in pain, and his sword fell from his now-limp hand. The second it dropped, Josef spun him around and gave him a push. The man went flying into the hallway, straight into the first pack of guards. They scrambled to catch him, but the guard's weight sent them lurching backward. By the time they recovered, Josef filled the door completely. He drew his swords and stepped into a defensive position, spinning the blades in whistling arcs, an enormous grin on his face.

The soldiers in the hall surged forward, swords drawn, and as they crashed into Josef, the swordsman did what he did best. He planted his feet and, with a great roar, swept his swords, one high, one low, into the crowd. The soldiers, trained to fight in formation, all held their weapons at the same height. Josef's swords sang over and below them, past their defenses. The man on the far left had it worst. Josef's swords slammed into his armor at the shoulder and the thigh, flinging him sideways into the soldier on his right. Josef carried the momentum, throwing himself into the sweep. His weight, the force of his blows, and the unexpected angle were too much for the men, and they smashed into the far wall, grunting in pain and surprise. Swords clattered to the stone as they tried to catch themselves, but it was no use. The moment they were off balance, Josef spun and slammed them again, with his leg this time, beating them against the wall and into the doorman, who'd just finished getting up.

What had been a coordinated charge was now a mess of men on the floor. Josef grinned and fell back to the door, not even winded. The second line of soldiers got their swords ready and were starting to push past their fallen comrades when a whistle sounded. It was a high trill, and the moment it went off, the guards began to pull back.

Josef fell into his defensive crouch, but the hallway was emptying rapidly until only one man stood at the far end. He was tall and thin, with neatly trimmed black hair streaked with gray, and a bored, slightly annoyed expression. His eyebrows arched when he saw Josef.

"So," he said, "you're our Spiritualist?"

"Depends," Josef growled. "Who's asking?"

The man fixed him with a cold stare. "I am Edward di Fellbro, Duke of Gaol."

"The man himself," Eli whispered, peeking around the corner. "Why is he here? Aren't dukes supposed to lead from the back?"

Josef ignored him, tightening his grip on his swords. "Look," the swordsman said. "I'm not going to bother feeding you a story. We're just here looking for the thief, same as you. No need to get nasty. Just back off now before more of your soldiers get hurt."

"Back off?" The duke chuckled. "You're in no position to be giving orders, boy. But I have no mind to waste time and money forcing you out. Surrender now and I'll let you keep your life."

"And if I don't?" Josef said.

Edward just smiled, a cold, thin smile, and moved his mouth, saying something Josef couldn't quite make out.

From his place against the wall, Eli gave a little squeak. "Josef!" he cried. "Get back!"

Josef jumped backward a second before the hearth beside the treasury door erupted in a wall of white-hot flame. Almost before he could recover, two flat stones came sailing through the fire. Josef's sword knocked the first one aside before he'd even realized what it was, but the next one clipped him on the shoulder, and he grunted in pain.

Eli jumped forward, grabbing the stone from where it had

fallen and turning it over in his hands. It was a paving stone from the hall outside, and as he touched it, he could hear the rock babbling in terror.

"Josef, watch out," Eli said. "He's a wizard."

"I guessed that," Josef grumbled, rubbing his shoulder. In the doorway the flames were dying down, revealing the duke again. He hadn't moved from his place at the end of the hall, only now he had a pile of paving stones in front of him. They were stacked neatly, leaving a large, bare patch on the floor around him. He smiled at Josef and casually tossed a paving stone in his hand.

"The offer of surrender is still open," he said.

Josef opened his mouth to tell him exactly what he could do with his offer, but at that second, the duke saw Eli crouched on the floor, his blond wig askew. The duke's pale, lined face went white as snow, and he opened his mouth in a shout that drowned out Josef's comeback.

"Eli Monpress!"

Eli jumped and looked just in time to see every single one of the paving tiles shoot forward. They flew from the duke in a flock of loosed fury, flying through the air faster than stone was ever supposed to move. They flung themselves at Eli, and they would have done some terrible damage had Josef not grabbed the thief by his gaudy collar and tugged him down at the last second.

The paving stones whistled inches over their heads, but Eli barely had time to get some air back into his thundering lungs before he heard the duke's voice roaring through the keep. "Spirits of Gaol! Your duke commands you! Crush the intruder!"

"Hold on now," Eli said, looking up from his crouch. "You can't just order a building like—"

The walls began to shake. In the hall, stones ripped themselves from the supports while dropped weapons picked themselves up off the ground. Everything, nailed down or not, began to lift and turn toward the doorway where Eli and Josef were crouching.

"Nico," Josef said. "We need that exit."

Behind them, the room was quiet. Out in the hall, things were beginning to speed forward.

"Nico!" Josef shouted.

At once, she appeared beside them, whether through her shadow stepping or just her terrifying speed, Eli couldn't tell. She flung back her hood, her scraggly black hair standing straight up, her eyes bright as candles, and a familiar wave of fear washed over the room. She pushed Josef aside and turned to face not the hallway or the things flying down it, but the enormous treasury door. Her hand shot out, the silver manacle jerking and shaking on her wrist, and her fingers dug into the iron like it was river mud.

Deep in the stone under their feet, something screamed. Nico ignored it, digging her fingers deeper, her glowing eyes narrowing to slits as she spoke a command.

"Move."

The enormous door moved faster than Eli had ever seen iron move. Bits of stone went flying as it surged forward, slamming itself shut with an impact that shook the keep.

For a moment, everything was silent, then there was dull clatter as the flying object collided with the now-shut door. The duke was shouting on the other side, but the sound was very far away. Then, all at once, the room began to scream.

Eli and Nico both slammed their hands over their ears as the terrible sound swept over them.

"What did you do?" Eli shouted.

"I closed the door," Nico said, her voice thin and strained as she pulled her hood back over her head.

"I can see *that*," Eli said. "My problem is with *how* you did it."

"What?" Nico glared at him, her eyes bright as lanterns. "It worked, didn't it?"

"Oh, sure," Eli said, rolling his eyes. "Solved the crazy wizard problem, but you can't just do that to spirits!"

"You've told me to scare spirits before," Nico said grudgingly.

"That's different," Eli snapped. "Giving spirits a little scare is one thing. It doesn't hurt anyone and it moves things along, but that's not what you did. You sank your fingers into that metal and gave it an order, and that, Nico, is not good. That door can't say no to you when you've got your teeth in its throat. Giving spirits orders they can't say no to is no better than Enslavement, and we don't do that. Besides, now we're trapped in a screaming, panicked vault that, as you mentioned earlier, has *no other exit*."

Nico turned away, scowling. Eli grabbed her shoulder to turn her back around, but Josef stepped between them.

"Save it," he said, sheathing his swords. "Let's find a way out. Quickly. We're losing structural integrity."

He was right. Large streams of grit were falling from the ceiling as the stone arches that held up the vaulted ceiling fought to get free and crush the demon. Chunks of rock clattered down the stone walls, landing in a series of crashes that were only getting louder.

"We're not finished," Eli said, pointing at Nico. Then, without another word, they split to search for some way, any way, out.

"All right," Eli shouted, scanning the shaking walls. "The thief got in, and he didn't take the main door. I can promise you that. Look for something unusual."

"Could you be more specific?" Josef yelled, staring blankly at the quivering wall.

"I don't know." Eli ran his fingers over the shivering, weeping rock. "Discolored stone, a corner out of place, anything that could mark a secret door or passage, maybe a bricked-over window. I'll take a mouse hole at this point."

"Can't you just do something wizardly?" Josef said, dodging a chunk of stone that fell right where his head would have been.

"I don't exactly think these spirits are in the mood to chat!" Eli shouted back.

Josef gave him a rude gesture just as Nico cried out, "Here!"

Argument forgotten, Eli and Josef ran over to find the girl standing in front of what looked like a perfectly normal patch of wall behind a toppled shelf.

"What?" Eli said, looking around frantically. "I don't see anything."

"Neither do I," Nico said. "But listen, it's not screaming."

She was right. While the other stones were in full-on panic, the patch of wall in front of them, a little eight-brick square, was perfectly silent. Now that Eli looked, it wasn't shaking either. It was a rock amid the chaos, and now that he saw it, he wondered how he could have missed it earlier.

He stepped in close to the stone and ran his fingers across it, very gently. It felt hard, like stone, but different—soapy and almost hollow when he tapped it. A slim grin crossed Eli's face. He raised his foot and, taking aim, gave the wall a good, hard kick. A clean, sharp crack appeared down the middle of the block of wall, and the stone crumbled to dust, revealing a dark tunnel just the right size for a man to crawl through.

"What was that?" Josef said.

Eli waved him away, focusing instead on what was waiting inside the tunnel. A few feet in, leaned carefully against the tunnel's wall, was another square of wall identical to the one he'd just broken, and stuck to it was a small, white card. Eli reached in and snatched the card between his fingers. There was no printing on it, no identification, just a sentence written in neat, masculine cursive.

Thought you would need this.

Eli cursed under his breath and shoved the card in his pocket. "All right," he said. "Let's move."

"What was that?" Josef said again. "Is this a trap? Is it safe?"

Eli gave him an incredulous look. "Anything's safer than this! Get in the tunnel! And watch that square. One whack at the wrong place will cause it to crumble."

Without further hesitation, Josef crawled in, pressing himself against the wall to squeeze by the square of fake wall. Nico followed right behind him, buried deep in her coat. When they were through, Eli paused for a moment and dug around in his pockets, pulling out a large, white card printed with an elaborate, cursive *M*.

"First rule of thievery," he muttered to himself. "Never waste an opportunity."

With that, he tossed the card toward the center of the room. It swooped through the air and landed at the foot of the fake Lion of Ser. Eli nodded and ducked into the tunnel. Crawling on his hands and knees, he turned and, very, very delicately, lifted the square of fake wall. Behind them, the dusty remains of the old fake stones were already indistinguishable among the grit and rubble showering down from the ceiling. Satisfied that they wouldn't be followed, at least not immediately, Eli gently plugged the entrance. The square of fake wall fit perfectly, as he'd known it would, and the tunnel plunged into darkness. Their path secured, Eli turned and made his way down the tunnel after Josef and Nico.

The tunnel ended unceremoniously twenty feet later in the ceiling of a wine cellar. Josef and Nico were already waiting when Eli jumped down, and Josef reached up to press the loose boards on the ceiling back into place behind him, leaving no sign that they'd ever moved.

Eli stood doubled over for a moment, catching his breath. When he'd coughed up enough dust to start a mortar company, he straightened and took off his gaudy red coat, which was now a dull, pinkish gray.

"Come on," he said, shoving the balled-up coat behind an ancient wine barrel. "Let's go."

"We're getting out, then?" Josef said, slapping the dust out of his shirt.

"Nope," Eli said. "We're going to get our Fenzetti."

Josef gawked at him. "Are you mad? The duke knows you're here. The jig is up. Only thing for us to do now is get out with our skins. Anyway, you don't even know where the other thief is. How are you going to find him when there's a whole duchy out there looking for you?"

"I know how to find him," Eli said, taking off his wig and carefully placing the dusty blond mess into his pocket for cleaning later. "He certainly hasn't left Gaol."

"Why wouldn't he?" Josef said. "You said he was smart. Leaving seems like the smart thing to do."

"Ah," Eli said, smiling. "But you're forgetting the first rule of thievery."

"Which one?" Josef sighed. "You have a hundred at least."

"This one is very important," Eli said, stepping up to the cellar door and putting his ear against the coarse wood. "The last place a man looks is under his own feet." He paused for a moment, holding his breath, and then opened the door with a flourish. "After you."

Josef stomped out, followed by Nico. But as she passed, Eli caught the edge of her sleeve. She looked over her shoulder, her eyes still suspiciously bright.

Eli tightened his grip. "I'm sorry if I was rough earlier, but I meant what I said. I know you did it to save us, but you really can't go around doing that to spirits. There's a lot I don't know about how you work, Nico, and I'm sorry I haven't helped you like I should, but there's a big difference between giving a spirit a little scare and giving it an order."

Nico looked away. "I had to. Josef—"

"Josef can't say this because he's not a wizard," Eli said. "What you did back there was as bad as any Enslavement, if not worse. At least in Enslavement there's a battle of wills the spirit could maybe win, but no spirit can win against you. Demon fear is simply too strong. I'm being serious, Nico. Don't do it again, all right?"

Nico clenched her fists. On her wrists, her manacles began to shake softly, but Eli held on to her coat until, at last, she nodded.

"Promise?"

Nico nodded again, and he released her sleeve. Josef was waiting for them on the other side of the door, arms crossed over his chest. "What was that about?"

"Nothing," Eli said and smiled. "Let's get moving."

Josef gave him a skeptical glare, but he nodded and let Eli lead the way out of the cellars. Nico trailed behind, her face hidden by the long hood of her coat.

The wine cellar was at the bottom of a warren of cellars that ran under the keep. Fortunately, the warren let out into the kitchen yard, which was where they made their escape, blending in with the mass of kitchen workers and other menials who were all gathered at the edge of the keep, presumably to watch the excitement. Whistles were blowing everywhere now, and hordes of conscript patrols were racing through the streets and toward the citadel. In all the confusion, no one noticed three more scruffy, dirty people, and they were able to duck down a less-fashionable side street without trouble. Once they were a block from the castle, Eli changed direction, guiding them through the winding streets seemingly at random until he came to a stop in front of a modest building that, if the sign outside was correct, housed a trading company.

"Wait here," Eli said. "I'll be right back."

He flashed them a knowing smile and vanished around the back of the building. Josef, fed up with arguing, slumped back against the wall while Nico took her time brushing the dust off her coat. A few minutes later, Eli emerged from the front door carrying an enormous ledger and grinning like a maniac.

"Powers," Josef said. "How much did you have to bribe a clerk for that bit of work?"

"Nothing," Eli said. "Things are too hot for bribery right now, so I nicked it. I *am* the greatest thief in the world, you know."

Josef rolled his eyes.

"Not like there was anything to it," Eli said, flipping through the book as he walked. "I could have stolen the whole office for all the clerks cared. They were all pressed against the windows like it was going to be revolution in the streets. Gaol must be a boring place if this is all it takes to make the town go crazy."

Eli flipped the pages back and forth and then stopped, tapping his finger on an entry toward the end of the book. "Here we go," he said. "Fennelle Richton, masonry expert and antiques appraiser under contract with the Duke of Gaol for ornamental stonework, currently residing at the Greenwood Hotel. That's by the docks, I think."

Josef looked at the entry, which was one of hundreds that ran down the page. "How do you know this is our man?"

"Fennelle and Richton are the main characters in *The Tragedy of the Scarlet Knight.* It's his favorite opera."

"His?" Josef said. "His who?"

"You'll see soon enough." Eli turned on his heel and set off for the docks, Nico and Josef close behind them. In the distance, voices grew louder as the northern corner of the duke's famous fortress collapsed in on itself in a great shower of rubble.

CHAPTER 14

The citadel shook and rumbled as bits of it collapsed. Edward, Duke of Gaol, ignored the stones clattering to the floor around him, staring instead at the smooth surface of the closed iron door to his treasury. He'd heard of Monpress's demon, of course, but dismissed it as another rumor, one up there with tales of Monpress's ability to turn invisible. That said, to see it in action himself, in his fortress, was a well-deserved lesson in making assumptions.

Even now, minutes after the initial wave, the demon panic was still flooding through the air. The shouts of people outside echoed down the shaking halls, tiny and distant under the rumbling of the terrified stone. The duke ignored them. He simply waited, patiently, with his hands crossed behind his back. The moment the demon panic began to ebb, he opened his spirit.

At once, every stone was still. The duke's will filled the castle, crushing all resistance, stomping down on fear. He laid his hands firmly on the wall beside him, feeling every stone in the castle as they lay subservient before him. Only then, when he was certain he had every pebble in the citadel's full attention, did he give his command.

"Clean yourself up."

The fortress obeyed. Stones jumped off the floor and refitted themselves into place. Cracks mended themselves, and he felt the citadel groan and shake as the collapsed northern corner shuddered and then rebuilt itself. When the duke lifted his hand from the stone, there was no sign there had been a panic at all. Even the scuff marks on the stone from Josef's fight with the soldiers were gone.

The duke shook his hands with a sigh and turned to face his gawking officers, who'd come running in the moment the citadel stopped moving.

"It's a miracle," one of the young guards whispered.

"No," the duke said. "It's business as usual." He glared at the soldier. "I'm not just some wizard, boy. I'm the Duke of Gaol. Everything here is mine to command, the stones, the water, the winds, and you. Don't ever forget that. Now"—he pointed at one of his officers—"you, take your men and get the courtyard under control. I want the conscripts back in position by the river and everyone else in their houses. Full lockdown. I don't want to see so much as a stray cat on the streets, understand?"

"Sir!" The officer saluted and motioned his men down the tunnel.

Edward looked over the remaining soldiers. "The rest of you, stand by. I have one final problem to attend to, and then"—he smiled—"we're going thief hunting."

The soldiers saluted and stood at attention. Satisfied, Edward turned back toward his treasury. Out of everything in the castle, only the treasury door remained out of place. It alone was still bashed and dirty, and still stubbornly closed. The duke walked forward slowly, deliberately, letting his open spirit go ahead of him as a warning, but the door did not move.

"Why?" the duke asked softly. "Why so willfully disobedient?"

"I can't help it, my lord," the door shuddered. "She ordered me closed. I must obey."

The duke leaned in, his voice very low and very cold. "Whatever Monpress's girl can threaten is nothing compared to what I'm about to do to you if you *do not open.*"

The door gave a terrified squeak and began to thrash in its track, but no matter how it fought, it could not roll back.

"Please, my lord," it panted. "Mercy! She struck something deep, I'm afraid. A strange mix of demon fear and wizardry. I've never felt anything like it! Please, just give me a few minutes to overcome the fear and I swear I'll obey. I beg you, my lord!"

The duke waved his hand. "Time is a luxury I do not have." He glared at the stones on either side of the door. "If you cannot open, then I'll find something that will."

He snapped his fingers at the wall beside the door, and all at once, the mortar began to crumble. Stones popped themselves out of their sockets and landed in a neat pile on the floor. Robbed of its support, the door began to wobble. Duke Edward stepped back and motioned for the blocks to keep coming. The door held out for an impressively long time, but soon, as more and more of its supporting structure was removed, not even its will was enough to stand against gravity. It fell with a long, tragic cry, crashing to the floor in an enormous cloud of dust.

The duke turned to his soldiers. "Get some rope and take this hunk of metal outside. Set it up at the center of the square where the rain can hit it. We'll see what a few years of rust can do for its temperament."

The soldiers, spirit deaf and not quite understanding what was going on, ran to obey him. At his feet, the door began to sob, a terrible, squealing metal sound, and something made a little crackling noise at the duke's elbow. Edward looked over and saw his fire, the fire that connected all the hearths in the citadel, flickering hesitantly.

"My lord," it crackled. "Don't you think that's a little harsh? He was wounded by a demon, and—"

"Would you like to join him out in the yard?" the duke snapped.

"No, sir," the fire answered immediately.

"Then don't say another word." The duke straightened up, watching as the soldiers came back with the rope and began looping it around the heavy door.

"If it can't serve as a door," the duke said, "then it can at least serve as an example. Disobedience will not be tolerated."

"Yes, sir," the fire whispered again, but the duke was already off, walking over the poor sobbing door and into his empty treasury.

The cracks and broken stone had been repaired here as everywhere, but the shelves were still in disarray. He put them back with an impatient wave of his hand, noting that the false Lion of Ser and a few of the other cheap pieces were still in place. There was, however, no sign of the thief's escape. Duke Edward walked in a slow circle, scanning the wall, running things over in his mind, but he got no further than he had this morning when he'd first investigated the crime scene. He'd been sure before, but he was now positive that the first robbery had not been Eli's work. So why had Eli come?

Pride was the obvious answer. Monpress was a prideful man. He might have come looking for clues as to who would impersonate him. Yet that seemed too simple an explanation. If his studies had taught him anything, it was that Monpress never did anything simply. Also, it was too fast. The robbery had only happened this morning, which meant Monpress must have already been in town. That made him smile. His bait had worked. At least that part of the plan had stayed on track. His smile faded, someone had sprung the trap early, and he meant to find out who. Still, today's events had convinced him that the situation was salvageable. Monpress was in town. He'd probably been planning his own heist when he heard about the impostor and came to investigate. That certainly matched what he knew of Monpress, but still, something was off.

Edward walked in a slow circle around the room. Eli's exit

bothered him. The thief was known for his flash, and the demon trick with the door had certainly been flashy, but after that, nothing. He'd vanished just as smoothly as the thief last night. He briefly entertained the idea that the two thieves might be in league, but he dismissed it almost as quickly. Monpress wasn't the kind to share glory.

He was still walking and thinking when he spotted something white on the floor. He stooped to pick it up, turning it over in his hand. It was a card, marked the same as all his others, with the fine, cursive *M*. Smiling, Edward slid the card into his coat pocket. Cocky to the last, that was Eli. He couldn't bear to leave any credit unclaimed. But as he straightened up, his eyes caught something else out of place. There, straight ahead, the wall was uneven.

Edward stared at it. He'd ordered all the bricks to square themselves when he'd righted the citadel. Was this more disobedience or just simple incompetence? He stepped in for a closer look, brushing the crooked stones with his fingers. As he touched the smooth cut surface, his eyes widened, and several mysteries clicked into place.

Othril blew in through the front door of the citadel, pausing to stare at the sobbing bulk of the treasury door as the guards struggled in teams of twenty to drag it down the steps. After a moment of gawking, the wind hurried on. It was best not to question things like that, and he had news for the duke that could not wait.

He found the duke in the treasury, which wasn't surprising, staring at the wall, which was. Othril circled uncertainly overhead. Interrupting the duke while he was working was never something that ended well, but neither was withholding a time-sensitive report. He was still warring between those two bad choices when the duke made the decision for him.

"Othril," he said, pointing at the square of wall in front of him. "Look there and tell me what you see."

Othril swooped down to the duke's level and stared at the stone. "Nothing," he said. "I see nothing at all. Why?"

"Nothing," the duke said. "I thought so."

He reached forward and grabbed the stone. The blocks crumbled in his grasp like flaky pastry, revealing a tunnel.

A tremor of panic shot through Othril. It had been his job to inspect the castle. His job to find anything untoward. The duke was not forgiving of failure. Fortunately, Duke Edward looked more annoyed than angry.

"It's a mash-up," he said, picking up a large chunk of the fake wall and crumbling it in his hands. "Tiny specks of stone and sand too small for consciousness, and thus below the notice of awakened spirits, bound together in brittle glue and then stamped to look like a wall." He paused, shaking his head. "It's actually brilliant in a simplistic way. How else would you hide a tunnel from a wizard who knows every spirit in his castle than to make something those spirits can't see? Not Eli's work, of course. Far too subtle. Still," he sighed, "one can't help being a little impressed by such a simple and effective escape."

"Yes, well," Othril said, "about that. I came to let you know that the spirits have reported in and we're ready to move into position." The wind paused. "Do you still want to go ahead with the plan, my lord? If you're certain he's not Monpress, perhaps we should wait."

"No," the duke said, standing up. "We're absolutely going ahead. Monpress is in town, and he's also looking for the impostor. This may well be our chance to catch two thieves for the price of one."

"Monpress is here?" Othril said, astonished. "But I haven't—"

The duke gave him a cold look, and Othril backed away. "Of course, my lord. As you say."

The duke nodded. "What about our other business? Is the Spiritualist secured?"

"Yes," the wind said, used to the duke's sudden subject changes. "And the measures to make sure she stays that way are in place, as you ordered. Hern was gloating the whole time, though his cronies looked less pleased. He swears she's the real Miranda Lyonette, the one who worked with Monpress in Mellinor. She won't wake for another hour or two, but she apparently knows Eli better than most. Are you going to go talk to her?"

"Of course not," the duke said. "In an hour or two, everything should be over. Besides, no amount of information is worth dealing with extremists like Banage and his sympathizers. I have far too many contingencies as it is. No, so far as I'm concerned, she's Hern's problem now. I'm just keeping hold of her for the moment, since Hern can't keep a prisoner to save his life. It's his love of gloating. He gives them too many opportunities for escape."

"What about her dog?" the wind asked. "I've been hearing reports from the countryside about a dog."

"As I said," the duke said, walking out of the treasury, "Hern's problem. Moving on, is the city ready for lockdown?"

"Of course," the wind said. "Has been for hours. All we're waiting on now is for the conscripts to finish clearing the last of the nonenlisted townsfolk back into their homes."

"Good." The duke smiled as he walked down the front steps of his citadel. "It may not be unfolding quite as I designed, but the trap is still in place. Eli will come, mark my words. Just be ready to tighten the noose when you hear the signal."

"Yes, lord duke," the wind said, spiraling up into the cloudless sky as the duke made his way across the square shouting for his officers.

On a black cliff above the gray northern sea stood a great citadel. It was cut from the same black stone as the cliff, or perhaps it was part of the cliff. After so many years it was difficult to tell. It stood tall and sharp, looming over the choppy waves and the desolate strip of shore far below like some great weapon dropped in an ancient battle of giants. Yet it stood alone. There was no town nestled in the rocky field at its base, no houses on the barren hills beyond. Nothing but stone and sand and wind-dwarfed trees and the citadel, its windows dark beneath the grudging noon light that filtered through the ashy clouds overhead.

Midway up one of the leaning towers, sitting at a broad desk that faced one of the larger windows overlooking the sea, Alric, Deputy Commander of the League of Storms, was dealing with the morning's crises. A demonseed had awakened in the desert that spanned the southern tip of the Immortal Empress's domain. So far, it had eaten three dunes, a cactus forest, a small nomad camp, and the agent who'd been sent to deal with it. Alric listened carefully to the wind spirit who'd come with the report, his thin-lined face set in a thoughtful frown as the wind blustered about the size of the demon and how it had already eaten a great desert storm and didn't Alric know they were all doomed?

When the wind finally blew itself out, Alric turned to the large, open book that took up most of his desk, and he flipped to the last page. Taking his sharp pen, he neatly crossed out the name of the now-deceased agent. It was a shame. The boy had shown promise. He flipped forward a few pages and decided to put one of his senior agents on the desert problem. Ante Chejo was an excellent swordsman and a level thinker, and he was from that part of the empire. He would do nicely. Decision made, Alric made a note next to Chejo's name in the great book and called in a runner. The silent, somber-suited man was at his side instantly. Alric gave him the orders and the runner left to find Chejo.

Thanking the wind for the message, Alric sent it to wait in the courtyard with stern assurances that Chejo would take care of things from here on. The wind didn't seem convinced, but it left, blowing out the window in a blustery huff and leaving Alric to deal with the other fires that were already flaring up.

There were rumors of a possible demonseed on the southern jungles of the Council Kingdoms and a new report of something off the north coast of the White Wastes, which was probably just a leviathan but had to be investigated all the same. There were reports piling up from agents in the major cities on demon cult activity, fund movements, and possible candidates for the League as well as the usual panic reports from spooked spirits that had to be investigated, compiled observations from each of the great winds, and equipment requests from the League armsmaster. It was the same rubbish over and over, but they had to be sorted, all the same.

He was about halfway through the morning's work when something fell onto his desk with a clatter. He looked up. It was a bound and capped tube stamped with the seal of their post in Zarin. Alric frowned. It was not unusual for a message to simply appear on his desk. That was part of the system the League of Storms had always used to spread information quickly, set up long, long before he was born. What was unusual was that Zarin would be sending a report now when he'd just received their morning report thirty minutes ago. He popped the seal with his finger and began to read.

Fear pulse reported at midmorning, Gaol. Spirit destruction, mass panic, suspect five weeks or higher. Request backup.

Alric read the message twice in rapid succession before letting it curl back into a scroll. He hunched forward, his frown deepening. This was a problem. A fear pulse was League jargon for the wave of demon panic that was generally the first warning when a new demonseed finally devoured its human host and became active on its own. Yet Merick, his man in Zarin, had placed the demon at five weeks of unrestrained growth, which was simply not possible. No demon could escape League notice for five weeks, especially not somewhere as populated and civilized as Gaol. But Merick was an experienced League member and not one for embellishment. If he said five weeks, then that's what they were dealing with.

Alric pushed the message away and leaned back in his chair to consider his options. There were only two demons remotely that active outside of the Dead Mountain itself, Slorn's wife and Monpress's pet. Alric drummed his fingers on the table. Nivel was well contained, but Eli's creature was another matter. If she was the source of the fear Merick reported, then this was going to be a complicated situation. The White Lady had forbidden the League to hunt that specific demon. The Lord of Storms had made that much clear, though he didn't say why and obviously wasn't happy about it. Still, the League couldn't just ignore a mass panic in a highly populated area. Their mission was to promote order, and order depended on rapid, predictable response. They could cause another panic even worse than the first if they didn't show up. Alric tapped his fingers thoughtfully, turning the problem over in his head. Slowly, a plan began to piece itself together.

Smiling slightly, Alric took the message and carefully slid it under a stack of other finished papers. Powerful as she was, the White Lady could not read minds. He had no proof that the disturbance in the report was Monpress's demon. There was no physical description, no witness reports. All he had was a dire message and a request for aid, and following up on such things *was* his job. If he never let on to his suspicions, how was she to know that the accidental elimination of the Monpress demon was less than accidental? He just had to make sure he put the right agent on the job. Someone strong enough to take on a demon of that size and a good enough swordsman to deal with her guardian, not to mention prideful enough to take on the Heart of War. But at the same time, he needed a man ignorant enough not to realize whom he was fighting, and whose loss wouldn't be a crippling blow to the League when the Lady took her vengeance.

Fortunately, he had just the man in mind.

Smiling slightly more than was appropriate, Alric summoned a runner. The dour man appeared instantly, stepping into Alric's office through a narrow slit in the air. It opened soundlessly, a cut in the fabric of reality from one place to another, in this case, from the common room to Alric's office. Instant travel was yet another of the niceties of League membership, a necessity when you had to travel around the world on short notice, and one that League members designated as runners were particularly skilled at.

Alric smiled at the runner as the cut in the air closed behind him. "Bring me Berek Sted."

The runner raised an eyebrow. "Sted, sir?"

"Yes," Alric said. "And if he drags his feet, just tell him he'll finally get to test that bloodthirsty sword of his."

If possible, the runner's face grew even more sour. "Yes, Sir Alric."

The runner vanished, slipping through a new slit in space so quickly even Alric didn't see it open. Five minutes later, the enormous man with his sash of hideous trophies and a great, jagged blade worn naked at his side walked into the room.

"Ah," Alric said, turning to face his guest. "Just the man I wanted to see."

Sted didn't answer. He sat down on the heavy bench in the corner, glowering at Alric while the wood creaked under his weight.

"I have a job for you," Alric said. "A demon has appeared in Gaol. Most likely a girl. I want you to investigate."

"A girl?" Sted's voice dripped with disgust. "I don't fight girls."

Alric gave him a flat look. "I realize you're new to the League, but try to remember that what you're fighting is the thing inside the girl. Demons take the body that serves their purpose."

"I don't fight girls," Sted said again. "Send someone else."

"This is not open for debate." Alric's voice was as cold as a dagger in a snowbank. "If you want to keep your League privileges"—his eyes flicked to the sword at Sted's side—"I suggest you learn some discipline."

Sted narrowed his eyes, but said nothing. Alric let him stew a minute before continuing.

"Killing the girl may not be simple," he said. "She travels with a protector, a swordsman who wields a famous awakened blade."

Sted grinned and slapped the sword at his side. "Couldn't be better than mine."

Alric's thin mouth twitched. "This sword has had many names, but it is best known by the name it took for itself, the Heart of War."

Sted's eyes widened. "The Heart of War, the *real* Heart of War? Why didn't you say that earlier?"

"This isn't a pleasure trip, Sted," Alric snapped. "Your mission is to eliminate the demon girl and secure the seed inside her quickly and quietly. Avoid confrontation with her companions if at all possible. Even spirit deaf, your membership in the League gives you a sense for demons. If she's active, you should be able to find her easily enough."

"Aye, aye," Sted said, standing up. "Quick and quiet. Got it. I'm ready now, so go ahead and open me a door to Gaol."

Alric turned back to his ledger. "You're a fully initiated League man," he said. "Open it yourself."

Sted grumbled a long string of curses. Then a moment later, Alric heard the unmistakable soft sound of the cut in reality, and the grumbling vanished. When he glanced over his shoulder, the room was empty. Alric turned back to his ledger with a smile. Either way this gamble played out was good for him. If Sted lived up to his brutal reputation, Alric would have the Monpress demon out of his hair for good. If the girl or her swordsman defeated him, well, that wasn't really a loss either. He wouldn't have to put up with Sted's insubordination anymore, and, while the loss of the sword would be lamentable, Slorn could always make more.

That thought cheered Alric up immensely, and he set to work sorting through the rest of the day's business with a smile.

CHAPTER 15

The man Eli was looking for was not at the hotel he'd been listed under in the ledger. However, the desk clerk, after a little cajoling and a few carefully palmed coins, pointed Eli toward the docks where Mr. Richton was due to set sail for Zarin that afternoon.

"Are you sure this is our thief?" Josef asked as they walked down the curiously empty street toward the river.

"Positive." Eli grinned from under the brim of his large hat. It was his compromise, since his wig was dirty now, but he might as well have gone bareheaded. They hadn't seen a soul since leaving the clerk's office, a fact that was making Josef very nervous indeed.

They made their way along the back alleys to the dock the clerk had mentioned. There was only one ship moored on the long wooden jut, a large, respectable-looking trade vessel running low in the water, heavy with cargo.

Josef looked at it skeptically. "Kind of a slow getaway vehicle."

"Not if no one's looking for you," Eli said, jogging out onto the dock.

On the deck, barefoot sailors were tying off ropes and doing the final work of getting the barge ready to go. One of them, a large river man in a black shirt and red scarf, who seemed to be the leader, looked their way just long enough to glare.

"Shove off," he grunted.

"Now, now," Eli said, smiling warmly as he walked up the plank from the dock to the ship's deck. "Don't be so hasty. We're here to see Mr. Richton. It's very urgent."

"Oh yeah?" The man straightened up slowly. "Name?"

"Gentero," Eli said without missing a beat.

The sailor gave him a funny look, but he nodded and walked across the deck to the small cabin at the prow. He knocked once before sticking his head in. A few seconds later he waved them over.

"Mr. Richton says go in," he announced, going back to his work.

Eli thanked him, but the sailor didn't notice; he was busy tying off the rope he'd been working on when they arrived and grumbling about bloody merchants and their inability to keep a bloody timetable.

Eli, Josef, and Nico walked across the deck to the cabin. Without bothering to knock, Eli pushed the wooden door open, and the three of them ducked inside. The cabin was small, but very well decorated. A colorful, gold-tasseled rug covered the plank floor and bright, mirrored lanterns anchored in the corners above flip-out seats filled the room with warm light. Bright paintings of exotic city skylines were nailed to the walls, making up for the lack of windows. A large desk was built into the wall directly across from where they stood, and sitting at it, dressed in a well-cut navy coat, was a handsome, older gentleman. Silver streaked his close-clipped fox-red hair and neatly trimmed beard, but his face was only lightly lined. He wore silver-rimmed spectacles low on his hooked nose and behind them, his quick, brown eyes missed nothing as he turned to face them.

"Gentero," he said thoughtfully in a soft, urbane voice. "The trickster. Wrong opera, but quite appropriate."

Eli shoved his hands in his pockets. "I never liked *Tragedy of the Scarlet Knight*, anyway."

"No," the man said, closing the fold-down writing table where he'd been working. "You never had any taste for subtlety." His eyes flicked from Josef to Nico. "Aren't you going to introduce me?"

Eli sighed. "Nico, Josef, meet Giuseppe Monpress. He is, for lack of a better insult, my father."

The man stood up and held out his hand. "Pleasure."

Josef just looked at him. "I thought we were here to find the thief who robbed the duke ahead of us?"

"We are," Eli said. "That's him."

"Bit of a family business," Monpress said, sitting down again.

"*You're* the one who stole the duke's treasury?" Josef said.

"What bits of it were worth the taking," Monpress said. "Quite honestly, when you factor in the setup costs and expense of fencing such well-known artifacts, I'm not sure I made any money at all on this venture."

"Then why did you do it?" Eli said.

The tone in his voice made Josef hesitate. He'd never heard Eli sound quite that sharp. Eli, however, wasn't paying attention to him or Nico. His focus was entirely on the smiling man sitting at the desk. "You never pull a job without running the numbers three times through. You used to say that anything less than fifty percent profit wasn't worth the breath to talk about. So why did you rob Gaol?"

Monpress gave him a dry look. "You mean, why did I take your target?"

"However you want to put it," Eli said, crossing his arms over his chest.

"Because it was made for you," the older Monpress said. "Come, you must have realized that this whole fiasco—the citadel, the bragging, the posters plastered on every wall for two hundred miles in any direction—was all bait in a trap for you. Of course you did, and yet here you are, ready to waltz in like an *idiot,* just like always."

"Traps aren't a bother if you go in with your eyes open," Eli said through clenched teeth. "It was a challenge. And I still don't understand why you felt the need to impersonate me."

"I did nothing of the sort," Monpress said. "I only robbed them. They decided it was you. And no wonder, with the way you carry on. I mean, a *challenge*? Did you listen to nothing I taught you? Thievery is about finesse, about getting in, getting out, and being long gone before anyone thinks to check the safe. It's *not* about having your face on every wall or being so well known that any noble with a budget shortfall can lure you into his lands."

Eli shot him a murderous glare, and the older Monpress took a deep breath. "I don't know why we're even having this discussion," he said, his voice calm again. "Like it or not, I still feel an obligation to watch out for you. I headed for Gaol as soon as I saw them putting up the posters in Zarin. The whole thing was so obvious that I knew it was only a matter of time before you came running. I *had* hoped to be done with the whole affair well before you crossed the border. After all, challenge or no, even you wouldn't bother breaking in when there's nothing left to steal. I thought if I couldn't stop you from taking the bait, I could at least disarm the trap." His eyes narrowed. "Obviously, I forgot how quickly you can move when your unfortunate flair for the dramatic makes you take leave of what little sense you have."

The two men glared knives at each other, and for a moment Eli looked as if he was about to turn on his heel and march out. Then he shook his head and shoved his hands in his pockets. "You know what?" he said. "I don't care. I don't even know why I was surprised to find you here. You always were a meddling old man who never knew when to leave well enough alone. But it doesn't matter. That 'thief-proof' citadel was a joke I wouldn't want to be known for breaking into anyway. However, we are here for something other than just the joy of breaking in. I need an item from the duke's collection, a Fenzetti blade."

Monpress looked appalled. "That thing? Why? Fenzettis are impossible to fence."

Eli smiled secretively. "Let's just say I have a buyer who's already paid in full."

"A buyer?" Monpress said, theatrically impressed. "That's a first for you. I was beginning to side with the popular opinion that you eat everything you steal."

"That's one of the nicest things they've said about me." Eli grinned. "Are you going to give us the Fenzetti or not?"

Monpress stood up with a long sigh and walked to the far corner of the cabin. He lifted the plush carpet to reveal a hidden hatch, which he yanked open.

"After you," he said, nodding to the narrow ladder descending into the hold below.

After a skeptical look, Eli went first, then Josef and Nico. Monpress came down last with a lantern, which he hung from the hook on the low ceiling. The hold took up most of the ship's lower level. It was just tall enough to stand in and it was packed absolutely full of goods. There were bolts of fine cloth, casks of wine, enormous spindles of thread, wooden bowls, porcelain, all stacked in open-top boxes stamped with Gaol's label.

Josef looked around in disbelief. "Wait," he said. "If being a merchant is just your cover, where did all this stuff come from? Is it stolen too?"

"Powers, no," Monpress said, laughing. "It's all purchased from the duke's own shops. Every stitch of cloth or drop of wine on this vessel has been paid for in full, and then paid for again in tariffs, and insured."

Josef shook his head. "Sounds expensive and troublesome."

"For certain," the old thief answered. "But it's all part of a properly executed job. I stole the best of Gaol's family treasures, all of which are easily recognizable, and all of which the duke is probably searching for quite adamantly at this very moment. However, the Duke of Gaol is, before all else, a businessman. Even in crisis, the last things he'd want to search are his own insured goods."

Monpress reached over to the pile of cloth beside them and lifted the top bolt. There, nestled between the folds of burgundy damask, was a beautiful set of gold plates.

"White Tower Dynasty," Monpress said. "Probably older than Gaol itself. Lovely design, too. I think those are my favorite pieces."

"Hiding stolen goods in purchased ones," Eli said, trying not to look impressed. "Classic. I have to say the insurance is a nice touch. Even if you did get stopped, the duke's guards wouldn't do more than a cursory inspection for fear of breaking something."

"First rule of thievery," the elder Monpress said, laying the cloth down again. "Always hide where it costs money to find you."

Josef burst into laughter, and Eli shot him a sharp look. "It wasn't that funny."

"No, no," Josef gasped between laughs. "It's just that I see where you get it now."

"Really?" Monpress smiled, gripping Eli's shoulder. "I'm so happy to hear he remembers *some* of what I taught him. If he can only learn to control his flamboyant nature, he might actually make a good thief someday."

"I don't know what you're talking about," Eli said, ducking out of the older man's grasp. "I'm already the greatest thief in the world, or haven't you heard?"

Monpress gave Eli a serious look, killing the mirth in the room. "If you were actually any good, I wouldn't have heard," he said quietly. "If you were actually the best thief in the world, no one would know you were a thief at all, even after you'd robbed them blind."

"What?" Eli said. "You mean like you? How many months did you play merchant to set this up? You had a tunnel into the treasury, so I'm guessing at least three. In the last three months I've stolen the Golden Horn of Celle, the original painting of the *Defeat of Queen Elise*, *AND* the King of Mellinor."

"Three months?" Monpress smiled. "That would have been a feat indeed, considering the posters went up only two weeks ago. And for your information, the tunnel was already there, one of the duke's many cost-cutting measures to save stone. All I had to do was cut the initial entry into the treasury and make the fake panels, which took about two days. I spent the next three moving everything before the duke found out."

"Well, it doesn't matter," Eli said. "The point is that the jobs I pull are—"

"I know, I know, very impressive." Monpress sighed. "Your exploits are reported far and wide. But what do you have to show for it? You're hunted by everything that cares for gold, and yet look at you. Threadbare coat, worn boots, you look like a common cutpurse. It's embarrassing to watch you drag the name Monpress through the dirt and not even making a good living at it. If you wanted fame, you should have chosen another profession, or have you forgotten the most important rule of thievery?" His eyes narrowed. "A famous thief is quickly a dead one."

"Sorry if I don't put too much faith in that one," Eli said, crossing his arms. "I've been famous for years, and I'm still alive. My head is worth more than you've stolen in a lifetime, old man."

"Oh, I wouldn't count on that," Monpress said quietly. "I get by. But unlike some, I don't feel the need to turn every theft into a carnival."

"Uh-huh," Eli said. "A few hundred thousand more and my bounty will beat Den the Warlord. I'll be the most wanted man in all of the Council Kingdoms, and they *still* won't be able to catch me."

"Well," Monpress said icily, "that will be a red-letter day indeed."

The two men stared at each other, and the hold grew very uncomfortable. Just as things were getting really heavy, Nico spoke.

"The boat is moving."

Both Monpresses blinked in surprise.

"I guess our good captain decided it was time to go," the elder Monpress said. "River types can be so impatient."

"Well," Eli said, "not that it hasn't been a pleasure catching up, but I'm not interested in crawling to Zarin on a riverboat with you, old man. We'll just take that Fenzetti off your hands and be on our way."

Monpress arched an eyebrow, but led them to the back of the hold, stopping in front of a pile of rolled-up woven rugs in a rainbow of colors stacked against the wall. The old thief stood on tiptoe and reached for the one on the very top. He caught the edge with his fingers, then paused and looked over his shoulder.

"Sir swordsman," he said, "if you would be so kind. I'm afraid my arms aren't what they used to be."

Josef shrugged, and Monpress stepped back as the swordsman grabbed the rug. He swung it down with a grunt, and it landed hard on the wooden floor of the ship.

"Heavier than it looks," Josef said, panting slightly.

"Must weigh a ton to have you out of breath," Eli said, kneeling down. "Let's see it."

He gave the rug a push, and it began to unroll, dumping its hidden treasure onto the floor with a dull clatter. For a moment, they all just stared. The thing on the floor was whitish gray, metal, but not at all shiny, and a little longer than Josef's arm. Its matte surface had a strange, smooth texture, almost like it was made of soap. It was sword-shaped only in theory, and Eli had to look at it from several different angles to figure out which end was the point and which was the hilt.

Curious, Josef picked it up and gave the white blade a swing. It wobbled through the air, off balance and ungainly, and Josef stuck it into the deck floor, glaring when the dull point couldn't even pierce the wood.

"Fenzetti blade," he grumbled. "More like Fenzetti bat. It doesn't even have a sharpened edge."

"To be expected," the elder Monpress said. "There's not a force in the world that could put an edge on bone metal. That's part of why they're so hard to sell. Fenzettis are immensely rare, valuable historical pieces that demand a high price. But, in the end, who wants to pay through the nose for an ugly, dull sword?" He shrugged. "Hopeless situation."

"Good for you that we're taking it off your hands, then," Eli said, grabbing a folded square of crimson-dyed linen from the stack beside him and tossing it to Josef. "Wrap that thing up and let's get out of here."

Josef nodded and started to bind the cloth around the blade. But just as he was tying it off, the boat began to pitch. They all flailed for purchase as the hold lurched below their feet, listing high on the starboard side like a skiff at sea instead of a flat-bottomed riverboat loaded with cargo.

"What's going on?" Eli said, getting his feet back under him.

"I think it's the wind," Monpress said, holding onto a support beam as the boat started to level out again.

"Wind can't do that," Josef snapped, but Nico held up her hand.

"Listen," she whispered.

They listened. Sure enough, above the sailor's cursing and the creaking of the boat was another sound, a deep, howling roar.

Josef slammed his feet on the ground as the ship finally righted itself. "What kind of wind—"

He never got to finish because, at that moment, both Nico and Eli slammed their hands over their ears. Monpress and Josef exchanged a confused look.

"Powers," Eli gasped.

"What?!" Josef shouted.

"It's the spirits," Nico said, her voice strained. "They're all yelling. It's deafening."

Josef's eyes narrowed. "Demon panic?"

"No," Nico looked up, very confused. "They're shouting an alarm."

Josef's eyebrows shot up. "An alarm?"

"Yeah," Eli said. "And it gets worse. We've stopped moving."

He was right. Though the boat was still rocking from its sudden jump, they weren't moving forward like before. They weren't moving at all.

"Fantastic," Monpress said. "You know, the only time I ever have trouble like this on a job is when you're with me, Eli."

Eli rolled his eyes and walked over to the closest crate. He plunged his hand between the bolts of wool and came out with a jeweled cup. It was vibrating in his hand and, for those who could hear it, screaming like a banshee.

"Easy," Eli said gently.

The cup ignored him, squealing and spinning in his hand.

"Shut up," Eli said, loading a bit more force into his voice.

It was enough. The cup froze in his hand, looking slightly dazed, or as dazed as a cup could look.

"Thank you," Eli said. "What are you doing?"

"Raising the alarm," the cup said. "You're a thief."

"Am I?" Eli said. "And how would you know? You've been stuffed between textiles all morning."

"The wind was the signal," the cup said haughtily. "No one steals from the Duke of Gaol! He's already got you surrounded, and when he catches you, we'll finally be rewarded for years of loyal watching! Finally, after so long things will be—"

Eli shoved the cup back in the wool, muffling it.

"What?" Josef said, gripping the Fenzetti blade with both hands as if it was a bow staff.

"It's a trap," Eli said. "Looks like most of this treasure was awakened and set to report their thief's location. Apparently we're surrounded." He glared at the old Monpress. "Why do you never hire a wizard? If you'd just had someone to poke at all this before you hid it, you would have known."

The old thief folded his arms over his chest. "Not everything runs by wizard rules," he said. "And in case you haven't noticed, now is scarcely the time for blame." He glanced upward. Sure enough, boots were thumping on the deck above their heads. "Either my sailors have suddenly decided to wear shoes, or we should beat a hasty retreat."

"Right," Eli said. "Is there another way out?"

"Of course," Monpress said, beckoning them to follow him. "You're with me, remember?"

On the dock, Duke Edward watched the stopped ship with a satisfied smile. Below his feet, the river was perfectly still, holding the boat like a fly in amber as his soldiers swarmed over it.

"Excellent work, Fellbro."

"Thank you, my lord," the river said, its deep voice strained from the pressure of holding the water back. "Are the soldiers almost finished? I don't think I can keep this up for much longer."

"You'll keep it up until I tell you otherwise," the duke answered, motioning for another group of soldiers to move into position on the far bank.

"But"—the river began to tremble—"with all due respect, my lord, you're asking an imposs—"

"Fellbro," the duke said, staring down at the water, which had gone perfectly still, "do you remember when you first swore obedience? What happened that year?"

The water didn't answer, so the duke continued. "Do you remember how I dammed your flow and poisoned your water?" Edward leaned closer. "I do. I remember the great floating islands of dead fish, the stench, the flies. How anything that drank your water died within the day. Do you think that was pleasant for either of us?"

"No, my lord," the river said.

The duke leaned closer still, his voice a cutting whisper. "And do you think I would hesitate to do it again?"

The river's water sank away from him. "No, my lord."

"Then I suggest you stop complaining and find a way to obey me," the duke said, straightening up. "Do not forget your station, Fellbro."

"Yes, my lord," the river murmured, its water dark and murky.

Satisfied, the duke turned to see his soldiers beat down the hold door while another group moved to secure the cabin. He was watching with pleasure when a strong wind blew down beside him.

"Everything's in place," Othril said, panting. "I must have flown across the duchy twice over, but everything is ready on your order. Though"—the wind turned to the boat, ruffling the duke's graying hair in the process—"we might not need it. The soldiers are almost into the hold, and there's no other way out. Maybe you overestimated his abilities."

"I overestimate nothing," the duke said, nodding toward the stern of the boat.

Right where the back of the boat met the water, something was shaking. Then, with a soft crack, the hull popped open and a plank splashed into the water a few feet from the long pier where the soldiers had boarded. The moment the plank hit the water, a small figure dressed in shapeless black jumped out, landing neatly on the dock. The figure was followed by a large man carrying a long, wrapped package, and then an older gentleman who jumped quite gracefully for his age. Last of all, a gangly, dark-haired man leaped from the boat. His jump was awkward, and he almost missed the dock altogether, but the larger man grabbed him at the last moment, pulling him onto the dock, and they started running just as a hail of arrows launched after them from the bow of the ship.

"Othril," the duke said quietly. "Close the trap."

The wind spun into the sky, shrieking like a kettle. The sound rang out to every corner of Gaol, and the city obeyed.

"Eli!" Josef shouted. "Now would be a good time for something impressive."

They were racing through backstreets. The soldiers weren't far behind, and though the narrow turns kept the arrows down, who knew how long that would last. But after that horrible, shrieking howl, the soldiers had become the least of their problems.

From the moment the sound rang out, the town itself had turned against them. The paving stones rumbled, trying to trip them, shutters unlatched themselves and swung freely, aiming right for their faces. Shingles flew from rooftops like arrows, forcing them to duck quickly or risk a caved-in head. Josef kept them moving, turning down smaller and smaller alleys, trying to get some cover. But whenever they changed direction, the street lamps, which suddenly seemed to be on every corner, began to flicker brightly, signaling their location to the soldiers chasing them.

"This is ridiculous," Josef shouted, parrying a flying butcher knife as they ran past an open kitchen window. He had both his swords out now, with the Fenzetti blade tied across his back. Nico was right behind him, batting roofing tiles, cutlery, and snaking clotheslines out of the air with the whiplike sleeves of her black coat. The awakened fabric moved with her like a living thing, growing and shifting its size to fit her needs. Eli would have been mightily impressed if he'd had the chance to watch, but he was crouched between Josef and Nico, shielding his head with his hands and stomping on the rattling paving stones whenever he could. Monpress jogged quietly behind them, seemingly immune to the onslaught.

"Eli," Josef grunted as he chopped a flying rake in half, "what are we dealing with here? Is it another wizard, like the one in the citadel? An army of them?"

"Nothing so simple," Eli said. "No one's giving orders. The spirits are just going crazy." He grimaced. "They're going on about taking me alive for the duke and all the things he's going to do to me. It's fairly disturbing, actually."

"Well, you're a wizard too," Josef shouted. "Do something!"

"I can't!" Eli snapped back. "The spirits here won't talk to me, remember? Anyway, they're so worked up I'd have to Enslave them just to get their attention. They keep shouting, 'For the glory of Gaol' and 'For the duke.' "

"So the duke's the wizard in charge?" Josef said, kicking over a beam before it fell on them.

"Either that or he's got the best propaganda program ever," Eli said. "Anyway, that still doesn't explain how he got the whole city to spontaneously awaken. It's actually kind of amazing. I've never seen anything like it."

"Save the praise," Josef said, cursing when the alley they'd been running down suddenly let out into a large square. Without missing a beat, Josef changed direction midstride, kicking a door that tried to open in his face so hard it fell off its hinges. "We need to get out of here *now*."

"Might I suggest we head north, then?" the elder Monpress said.

Josef whirled to look at him. The older man smiled patiently, jogging along to keep pace. "I have an emergency exit prepared," he explained. "It should still be open."

"Why didn't you say something earlier?" Eli said, exasperated.

"You always get upset when I try to help," the older thief pointed out. "You can't also get upset when I don't."

Eli opened his mouth to say something stinging, but Josef shut him up with an elbow in the ribs. "Save it," the swordsman growled, and then nodded to Monpress. "Lead on."

The thief smiled and took the lead, turning them down a breezeway between two houses. With Monpress leading, their journey was far less hectic. The man knew the city like the back of his hand, and every time their way seemed blocked, he found another path. In this way they reached the northern wall with comparatively little fuss. Getting past it, however, was another matter entirely.

"Oh, dear," Monpress said.

The city wall, which had been a thick wall of average height when they first entered the city, was now almost fifty feet tall. Even worse, the once simple, straight stones were stretched at almost impossible angles so that the wall was now much wider at the top than it was at the bottom, creating a curving slope that would have had them almost upside down if they tried to climb it. It was also covered in knife-sharp spikes that twitched as they watched, ready to spear any climbers.

"So," Eli said. "Where's your exit?"

"There." The older Monpress pointed at a squarish stone about thirty feet off the ground above them. "Of course, it was much lower before."

"Of course," Josef said, lowering his swords.

"Well," Eli said, looking at Josef, "if it's that tall, it can't be that thick. Can't you just break it down?"

"Sure," Josef said, "if I had the Heart, which I don't because someone said don't bring it."

Eli ignored the comment and looked at Nico. "Want to give it a punch?"

Nico shrugged and walked up to the wall. She stared at the stones for a few moments, and then, pulling her fist back as far as it would go, she punched the wall with all her might. A great cracking sound echoed through the town, and Nico spun back, gripping her fingers. The wall, however, stood firm. The spot where she'd hit was slightly dented, but otherwise whole.

"No use," Nico said, shaking her hand furiously. "The spirits are standing strong. Whatever convinced them to stand up straight also convinced them to hold tight."

Josef sneered at the stones. "I bet the Heart could still break it."

"I'm sure," Eli said, putting his hands on his hips. "But as you said, we don't exactly have it handy." He glared up at the wall. "Nice and trapped, aren't we? And the final blow should be showing up any moment." He nodded toward the lamp at the end of their alley, which was blinking like mad.

"*Surely* you've got some clever plan," Josef said, sheathing his swords.

"I'm working on it," the thief muttered.

"You may want to work faster," Nico said, feeling the ground. "If you believe the paving stones, we'll have soldiers here in less than a minute."

Eli frowned, glaring at the blinking lamp, then down at the paving stones, and then back to the lamp. Finally, he shook his head.

"All right," he said. "We'll try this." He turned to the elder Monpress. "You've always got at least three safe houses. Do you think you have one that isn't compromised yet?"

"One, maybe," Monpress answered. "It won't stand up to a serious search, though."

"That's all right," Eli said. "It doesn't need to. Here's what we'll do. All of this noise is to catch me, right? So we'll split up. You three will go for the safe house."

Josef scowled. "And what will you do?"

Eli looked at him plainly. "I'm going to turn myself in."

Stunned silence was his answer. Josef was the first to recover.

"Are you crazy?" he shouted. "I don't know about wizard stuff, but I'm pretty sure there won't be any doors to charm this time, Eli. If the duke was good enough to trap us like this, he's certainly good enough to keep you in chains."

"Don't worry," Eli said. "Even without the spirits, I'm Eli Monpress. There isn't a prison in the world that can hold me." He winked at the elder Monpress as he said this, but the old thief just rolled his eyes.

"Anyway," he continued, "I'll break out and meet you at the safe house. Whatever the duke did to wake up the town, he can't keep it up forever or he would have done it the second he saw me, back at the treasury. I don't actually know how he managed this, but simple spirits need a huge amount of energy to stay awake, which I doubt the duke can provide indefinitely. The town will have to go back to sleep sooner or later, and that's when we'll run. Sound good?"

"No," Josef grumbled, "but I'll take it." He glared at Eli as he walked away. "Don't get yourself killed, idiot."

"Thanks for the encouragement," Eli called back, but the others were already jogging down the alley away from him.

Smiling, Eli began to jog the other way.

He ran along the wall, waving at each light as it lit up when he passed. The little alley he was on widened into a street as he reached his chosen destination, the city's northern gate. Sure enough, as he'd guessed, there was a small knot of conscript guards, half a dozen at least, standing at attention before the closed doors. They were rough-looking boys mostly, farmers' sons, Eli guessed, and all gripping their swords like fire pokers as they stared wide-eyed at the twisting, awakened city.

Moving silently along the wall, Eli snuck up behind the smallest boy and, after adjusting his clothes and smoothing back his hair, Eli tapped the young conscript on the shoulder. The boy jumped two feet with a deafening yelp, dropping his sword. The other guards held together more admirably, whirling to face Eli with their swords drawn. Eli, surrounded on all sides, leaned back against the gate and raised his hands with a charming smile.

"Congratulations," he said. "You've caught Eli Monpress."

He had time for one last grin before all six guards jumped him.

CHAPTER 16

The rest of the army arrived just as the guards threw Eli on the ground. The career soldiers were on him at once, pushing the conscripts aside and slapping enough iron on Eli's wrists to make a miner jealous. The boys protested and won the right to be the ones to march Eli to the citadel, which they did with great cockiness. Eli went right along with it, grinning and waving as best he could with his shackled hands. He actually liked getting caught a great deal. People were always so excited.

By the time they reached the steps of the citadel, every soldier in Gaol, conscript and professional, was marching with them, shouting and cheering. But the merry mood vanished when a tall man in somber clothes came down the steps to meet them. Eli gritted his teeth. It was the wizard from before, and he looked unpleasantly smug as he took Eli's chain.

"I want the conscript troops on patrol," he said, wrapping the chain around his hand. "Keep the city on lockdown until I give the signal to stop. Guardsmen, I want you inside the citadel. Double posts at all times."

"Yes, my lord." The response was a dull roar from a thousand throats as the soldiers saluted and began to break into units. The man watched them for a moment and then, keeping Eli's chain taut, turned and walked the thief into the citadel.

"Let me guess," Eli said, struggling to keep up. "You're the duke, right?"

"Correct, Mr. Monpress," the duke said. "I am Edward di Fellbro, Duke of Gaol, and your master now, so you will hold your words unless spoken to."

"I'm afraid there's a bit of a mix-up," Eli said. "The only master I answer to is myself."

The duke's answer to that was a long, thin smile as he led Eli up the stairs to the very top of the fortress. As they walked, the fortress responded. Doors opened on their own to let them pass, chairs scooted out of their way, and curtains pulled back to make room.

"That's an impressive trick," Eli said, marveling as a pair of washbuckets rolled themselves behind a corner, out of the duke's sight. "How do you manage it?"

"I am a firm believer in obedience," the duke answered. "You'll learn it as well, soon enough."

When they reached the smaller nest of towers and courtyards at the top of the citadel, the duke marched Eli around a garden and through a heavy door and into a well-appointed study. The large stone room had many windows looking out across the city and the countryside beyond. As soon as they were inside, however, every window but the last closed its shutters, and the heavy door locked itself behind them.

When the room was secure, the duke let go of Eli's chain.

"You may take off your manacles now, Mr. Monpress," the duke said, settling himself comfortably in a high-backed chair. "There is no need for this to be uncomfortable unless you force me to make it so."

Eli stared at the gray-haired man, not quite sure what to make of him. But the duke just sat there, waiting, so Eli turned around and fished a straight pin out of his sleeve with his teeth. He picked the manacle lock in five seconds flat and turned back around, tossing the irons on the carpet at the duke's feet.

"Any other tricks while I'm performing?" Eli said. "Should I dance?"

"You should sit," the duke said, gesturing to the stool in the corner.

Seeing no point in refusing, Eli sat.

"So," Eli said, "you've caught me. Congratulations! Shouldn't you be sending someone to the Council to collect your reward?" He looked around at the opulent study, the colorful tapestries and carved-wood tables. "I have to admit, I always hoped it would be a poor country that caught me, or some honest bounty hunter. Someone who could use the money. Gaol scarcely seems in need of sixty thousand standards."

"It's not an amount to scoff at," the duke said. "But you should know, Mr. Monpress, I didn't catch you for the bounty."

Eli stopped. "You didn't?"

"No," the duke said. "I must admit, Mr. Monpress, you've been an immensely interesting hobby. You first came to my attention three years ago, when you stole the crown jewels of Kerket. Since then I've been following you closely, and you've never disappointed, every theft grander than the last. It's really quite remarkable."

"I'm always delighted to meet a fan," Eli said with a pleased smile. "But you didn't have to go through all this effort if you just wanted to meet me. I do respond to letters, you know."

"I know," the duke said absently. "I have several of yours. Intercepted in travel and bought for a price higher than I was wise to pay."

Eli gave him a shocked look. "You *bought* my mail?"

"Yes," the duke said. "To learn more about you. To learn how to catch you. As you see, it paid off. Here you are."

"Here I am," Eli said. "And are you satisfied?"

"I must admit," the duke said, looking Eli over, "I didn't expect you to be quite so like the caricature you present to the world. You seem every bit as cocky and irresponsible as your deriders make you out to be. I had hoped to find the real Monpress a man of greater depth than the boy in the posters."

"Well, you did just trap and arrest me," Eli said. "I could hardly be expected to show my true colors under such conditions."

"Quite so," the duke said and nodded. "But we shall see what you are made of soon enough."

Eli swallowed. Something in the way the duke spoke hinted that he wasn't using the phrase in a figurative sense.

"So," Eli said, shifting in his chair. "If you didn't catch me for the sixty thousand, and you didn't catch me for the conversation, why am I here?"

The duke gave him a thin smile. "*Fifty-five* thousand, which is what the Council lists as your bounty, is hardly enough money to justify the great expense and enormous trouble of catching you. Especially once we factor in what the Council will take back in taxes, tariffs, and fees. I'd be surprised if there was enough left over to pay Gaol's Council dues."

"Then why bother?" Eli said. "Conscripting that army of millers, farmers, and shopkeepers outside must have been an enormous headache, and let's not forget the spirits." He glared at the duke. "I don't know how you got control over so many spirits at once, or what you threatened them with so that they won't talk to me, but I can guarantee that if the Spiritualists ever find out about your little dictatorship here, they will come down on Gaol like a swarm of locusts. Seems a great risk on your part for a reward you claim not to want."

"Don't flatter yourself too much," the duke said. "The spirits of Gaol have been mine since long before you appeared."

"So what then?" Eli leaned forward. "Did you just catch me to prove something? Personal challenge? If so, bravo and well done; can I go now?"

The duke chuckled and leaned back in his chair. "Catching the uncatchable thief does bring a certain feeling of accomplishment—pleasant enough, but meaningless in the end. I'm a duke, Mr. Monpress, and as a duke I must think as a country, not as a man."

He stood up from his seat, pacing back and forth like a professor expounding his theory. "As I said earlier, I've followed your exploits for some time now, and over the years, I've noticed something of a discrepancy. Let's take your robbery of Kerket. The crown jewels consisted of eight pieces, including the scepter of Kerket, which contains the Sea Star, the largest sapphire in the world. Technically priceless, though I imagine you would get only around ten thousand standards for it on the open market, and that's *if* you could find a buyer willing to take the risk. Still, ten thousand standards, and that's just one jewel in one piece of the set. Any normal thief would have retired to a life of luxury after that, but you, you show up in Billerouge not a month later to steal seven paintings from the royal collection. Again, technically priceless, but I estimate fifteen thousand for each at least, likely more.

"How strange, then," the duke said, fanning his fingers as he spoke, "that none of these famous items have ever re-emerged. In fact, *nothing* you steal ever shows up again. Every time you're spotted, you're wearing the same threadbare clothing. You seem to have no lands, or, if you do, you certainly spend no time on them, considering you're spotted in a different country nearly every month. So far as I can tell, you travel mostly by foot, primarily through wilderness, and of all the hundreds of reports I've collected from the Council about your exploits, not a single one has mentioned you ever spending more than twenty standards at a go." He stopped and looked at Eli. "Do you see where this is headed?"

Eli shrugged, and the duke gave him a slow smile.

"You've been on the Council bounty list for what?" He shrugged. "A little more than three years? I estimate that in that time you've stolen approximately three hundred and fifty thousand Council standards' worth of goods, not counting what was stolen from my own treasury." His grin widened. "To put that in perspective, three hundred and fifty thousand standards is more than the entire yearly tariff income of the Council of Thrones. *That* is the number that caught my attention, Mr. Monpress, not the fifty-five thousand those idiots in Zarin say you're worth."

Eli tilted his head to the side. "It sounds so impressive when you put it like that. I never actually added it up myself."

The duke shot him a scathing look. "I find that very hard to believe."

Eli just smiled, and the duke moved on. "Now, Mr. Monpress, I have answered your question. I must insist you answer one for me."

"I'm a firm believer in fairness," Eli said, crossing his legs. "What do you want to know?"

The duke crossed over to the single open window and looked out at the rooftops and neat green fields of his country. "There is something I wanted to ask if I caught you," he said, his voice for once not commanding, but curious. "These thefts of yours are always elaborate, some quite dangerous. I've heard stories of you walking right past piles of gold brick to steal a wooden statue, simply because it was more famous. At first, I thought you must be a collector, but then you go and steal the payroll for the entire Marcheron Shipping Company."

"Oh, yes," Eli said, laughing. "I thought I'd really lose my neck that time. Those pirates are quick with a knife, and I didn't have my swordsman then."

"Yes, yes." The duke turned to look Eli in the face. "But what I want to know is why? Why do you steal these things? It's obviously not for the money. You've had more money than any one man could spend in his life for years now."

"Don't estimate what a man can spend," Eli said and chuckled.

"If you spent half of what you steal, you'd be your own economy," the duke scoffed. "You can stop the conceited-boy act. There's no audience for you here. Just tell me the truth. Why do you steal what you steal? Why do you live this"—he stopped, grasping for the right word—"this *vagabond* lifestyle? You're obviously intelligent, driven, not to mention a powerful wizard. So why? What is your motive? Why do you do it?"

"Well," Eli said slowly. "First, it's fun. A man needs something to do with his life. As for motive, mine is grander than most. That fifty-five thousand you didn't want to scoff at earlier? I can't even be bothered with such a number. Such a tiny sum isn't even a tenth of my ambition." Grinning at the duke, Eli leaned forward, his voice lowered to a conspiratorial whisper. "One day, this head on my shoulders will be worth one million in gold."

The duke's look narrowed to a glare. "I'd said you were driven, but now you prove to be delusional as well. One million in gold? You'd be worth more than any four kingdoms put together. The Council would never allow such a bounty. A sum like that could destroy the balance of power on the continent. It's an impossible goal."

"Perhaps," Eli said and nodded, "but an impressive one, nonetheless."

"But you have yet to answer *why*," the duke said. "Why set such a number for yourself?"

Eli paused, tapping his fingers thoughtfully against his knee. "A bounty is a unique thing," he said. "Some overly nice people would say that a man's life is priceless, but as you so eloquently pointed out, things are worth what people will pay. In that way, a bounty is like a price tag, isn't it? And who doesn't like large numbers? Especially when applied to one's self."

The duke tilted his head, his brow furrowing from effort to decide if Eli was being facetious. In the end, he must have decided it didn't matter, for he walked across the room and stopped in front of Eli with a patient smile. "Well, whatever you claim your reasons to be, your goal is tragically to die unfulfilled when I turn you in for the bounty."

"Come on," Eli said, scooting to the front of his chair. "Surely with all the money flying around, actually turning me in for the bounty would be superfluous."

"But I must turn you in," the duke said. "If I start selling your stolen treasures without turning you in, everyone will think we're in league together. Once you're caught, however, I can claim your treasures as my own. Finder's rights. Also, that fifty-five thousand, minus taxes, will just about cover the expense of catching you."

"Are you sure you should be telling me this before I tell you where I keep my treasures?" Eli said. "I mean, when you put it that way, I feel absolutely no inclination to help you. Shouldn't you at least pretend to offer me my freedom? Keep the carrot dangling?"

The duke gave him a withering look. "I do not lie, Mr. Monpress. Such fawning embellishment wastes my time and yours."

"Then I hope you have something spectacular planned," Eli said. "Because I can't think of a single reason why I should go along with you."

"Oh, you will," the duke said. He fixed Eli with a slow, cutting smile, and waved his hand. The second his fingers moved, the chair Eli was sitting in threw itself backward. Eli hit the wall with a thud that knocked his breath out, but he didn't bounce off it. The moment he touched the stone, the blocks changed shape. The stone moved like living clay, wrapping around his legs, arms, waist, and neck, pinning him spread-eagle to the bare wall of the study. He was still trying to blink the spots out of his eyes as the duke walked over and pressed a gloved hand against his shoulder.

"I have a great deal of experience with bringing objectors around to my point of view," he said softly. "You see, Mr. Monpress, everyone has something they find intolerable. All you have to do is discover what that is, and then, whether it's a Great Spirit or a man, it becomes your willing servant."

"Sorry to disappoint," Eli said, gasping against the stone's chokehold, "but I'm afraid life as a thief has made me remarkably tolerant."

"That's all right," the duke said. "Life as a duke has made me remarkably patient." He gestured at the stone. "We'll start with the simplest, physical pain."

Eli sucked in a breath as the braces holding him in place began to move slowly and inexorably away from one another, stretching him in all directions.

"The stretching is a slow buildup," the duke said calmly, a connoisseur explaining the intricacies of his art. "The pain will become greater and greater as the joints are stretched past their limits, disjointing the shoulders, knees, elbows, possibly the hips, though most never get that far. I don't normally go to these lengths. Most people find even the idea of pain intolerable, but I try to keep in practice."

Eli grunted in reply, panting as his arms stretched farther. The stone crushed into his skin as it pulled, stretching him like taffy. He could feel his sinews pulling, his bones creaking at unnatural angles until he had to clench his teeth to keep from whimpering. The duke saw this, and gave Eli a pleasant smile.

"We can stop at any time," he said. "Just tell me what I want to know and this will all be over. Otherwise, the pain will continue to grow until you pass out. When that happens, we'll rest an hour and then start again. Just remember that this situation is completely within your control. One concession, that's all it takes."

"You know," Eli said, gasping as something in his shoulder began to make a horrifying creaking sound, "for someone who claims to have studied me as long as you have, you don't know me very well. If you'd paid any attention, you'd have stuck with the carrot. Being bullied just makes me more stubborn, and life with Josef has made me very blasé about pain."

"We'll see," the duke said, resuming his seat by the window. "I can wait."

A moment later, the something in his shoulder snapped, and even Eli's clamped teeth couldn't stop the scream that came next.

"Sorry about the cramped conditions," the elder Monpress said, passing Josef a bottle of wine and a set of mismatched cups. "This place was never meant to hold more than one person."

"We've been in worse," the swordsman said.

They were crowded into an attic with a sloped ceiling that Josef had to almost double over to fit under. He and Nico were sitting shoulder to shoulder on the wrapped Fenzetti while Monpress sat opposite, cross-legged on top of the trapdoor.

They'd made it to Monpress's hideout with relatively little trouble. Once the soldiers captured Eli, the streets had emptied to nothing. Now they were waiting for dark, and while, technically, everything was going according to plan, Josef couldn't shake the feeling that the situation was rapidly spinning out of control. For one, they hadn't received a signal from Eli. Whenever he'd let himself get caught before, he'd always sent a signal of some kind. This time they'd gotten nothing. It could be because Eli couldn't cajole the spirits in Gaol like usual, but Josef had a bad feeling about it.

Monpress, however, was keeping busy. He'd already changed clothes from his somber merchant outfit to what looked to Josef like a set of ragged black pajamas. The cloth looped and tied in a dozen places, held close to the old man's surprisingly lithe body by an intricate network of straps. Once he was dressed, Monpress began slipping tools into hidden pockets with a silent efficiency that impressed even Josef. In addition to two small knives, he had a host of crooked hooks, pliers, straight pins, and other metal objects Josef recognized from Eli's thief tools but couldn't put a name to. He was wrapping his feet in padded cloth when Josef finally gave up and asked him what he was doing.

"Isn't it obvious?" Monpress said. "I just took a large chunk from my schedule to keep Eli out of trouble. Yet here I am, Eli in jail, and myself trapped in an attic with no treasure at all for compensation. So, I'm going to do the only thing I can do to mitigate my losses. I'm going to spring him."

"Wait," Josef said. "Don't bother. I'm going for the Heart as soon as it's dark. I'll just get him then."

Monpress looked at him skeptically. "You're going to beat an entire army with one sword?"

"No," Josef said. "The sword is for the wall. I don't need the Heart to fight common soldiers."

"Is that so?" Monpress chuckled. "I hope you don't mind if I try my way as well? Just for variety's sake?"

"Do what you want," Josef said. "Whatever happens, we're getting out of here tonight."

"I couldn't agree more," Monpress said, pouring himself a glass of wine from the bottle in Josef's hands. "Drink up; it's a good bottle. Be a shame to waste it."

Josef eyed the bottle skeptically. "No, thanks. I'm sure it's good, but I don't drink when I have to fight."

"Wise man," Monpress said, sipping at his own glass. "I only hope Eli can pick up a little of your forethought."

"Not a chance," Josef said. "He's categorically against considering the consequences of his actions." He looked at the old thief. "You seem like a cautious man. How did you end up with a son like Eli?"

"Oh, he's been like that ever since I've know him."

Josef scowled. "That's an odd thing for a father to say."

Monpress shrugged. "Well, you need to understand that I'm not actually his father. He showed up on my doorstep ten years ago very much as he is now. Smaller, of course, but every bit as ridiculous. I don't know how he found me. I make it a point of not being findable—hazard of the business—but there he was, standing in the snow outside my mountain lodge, asking could I teach him to be a thief."

Monpress took a long drink from his cup. "I turned him away, of course, but he wouldn't go. I don't even know how he got up there. I'd bought the lodge for its seclusion, so we were miles up in the mountains, but the boy had no horse or warm clothing. It was like he'd just appeared out of thin air. I turned him away several times, but he was so insistent about learning to be a thief, I realized I might have to kill him to get rid of him. Whatever my faults, I'm not a killer. Besides, there was a storm lurking overhead, and I'm not so heartless as to send a boy out into the weather. So I acquiesced and let him come in, just for the night. He's been my ward and apprentice ever since, and a sorry one at that." Monpress smiled, swilling the wine in his glass. "Still, infuriating as he is, one can't help getting attached to the boy, which is how I'm in the mess I find myself in today."

He raised his cup in salute and then downed the rest in one gulp. Josef scowled. He knew so little of Eli's life before they met, but it wasn't surprising to hear he'd been a thief's apprentice, and even less surprising to hear he'd sweet-talked his way into it. But who had he been before he'd taken the name Monpress? Just as Josef opened his mouth to ask, a strange, soft sound on the roof drove all talk of the past from his mind.

They all froze, listening. Josef motioned the others to stay quiet before leaning over to peer out the tiny, grimy window. Outside, he saw nothing but the same roofs and eaves he always saw. No strange movements, nothing out of place, just the last glow of the setting sun on the red tile. He was about to pass the sound off as something innocent, a cat maybe, or the house settling below them, when it sounded again, a low creaking, like something large was walking on the tile above them.

Very, very slowly, Josef opened the window and climbed outside. It was a tight fit, but he made it soundlessly, getting both feet on the roof before slowly peeking over the edge at the roof of their hideout.

The moment his eyes cleared the eave, it launched at him.

Josef flew backward, skidding down the tile. His short swords were in his hands before he knew what was happening, and it was a good thing, because the blades were his only protection from the ball of shifting white fur, claws, and teeth on top of him as they both slid down the roof.

"Oh, *Powers*," he growled through gritted teeth. "Not you again."

The ghosthound snarled, and Josef took the initiative, kicking the dog hard on the flat spot between his front legs. Gin yelped and jumped away, landing lightly on the roof's peak just as Nico winked in from nowhere and grabbed his neck. Gin howled and kicked, tossing her into the air, but she turned in flight, landing neatly beside Josef, who was sheathing his swords.

"Easy, puppy," Josef said. "I'd love to make a coat out of you, but this isn't exactly the best place."

As if to prove him right, the lamppost on the street below them began to flicker frantically and, a moment later, whistles sounded in the distance.

"If you're looking for Eli," Josef said, "he's not with us."

"I know," Gin growled, keeping low against the tiles. "I'm not here for him."

Josef glanced at Nico, who repeated what the dog had said. Gin, meanwhile, was watching the evening sky through slitted eyes.

"We need to move," he said. "That wind is coming. Follow me."

With that, he hopped off the roof.

Nico repeated this to Josef, who repeated it to Monpress, who was just climbing out the window to see what was going on.

"We might as well follow," the old thief said. "This hideout was blown the second you got out the window. We'll be up to our necks in guards in a moment."

"Or worse," Josef muttered, looking down at the tiles under his feet, which were beginning to rattle. "Come on."

He reached through the window to grab the Fenzetti blade, and they walked to the edge of the roof where Gin had jumped off. It was a two-story drop, but fortunately most of it was covered by a sturdy trellis. Nico climbed down first, then Monpress, who was remarkably agile for his age, and Josef brought up the rear. Gin was waiting at the bottom, and he led them around a corner to a large stone storehouse. It was an ancient thing, with great cracks between the stone overgrown with plants. Still, it was big enough for all of them, just barely, and they got inside just before the strange, howling wind passed overhead.

"All right, dog," Josef said, crossing his arms. "You lost us our hideout and nearly blew our cover altogether, so what do you want? Where's your master?"

Gin glared at him, then looked at Nico. "Don't tell me you're the only one who can understand me?"

Nico shrugged, and Gin rolled his eyes. "Fine," he growled. "Tell your sword boy that his second question answers the first. I'm here looking for Miranda. She went into town this morning and never came out. Then all the spirits started going crazy, so I decided to come get her. I know she's in the citadel, and I smelled the thief in there as well. It doesn't take a genius to put two and two together. But even I can't get into a castle crawling with guards and winds who do nothing but watch, so I sniffed you out, swordsman." Gin wrinkled his nose. "Not that I could miss you. Do you even know what a bath is?"

Nico repeated this, leaving out the bath comment, and Josef gave the dog a skeptical look.

"We didn't even know the Spiritualist was in town," he said. "She certainly didn't go in with Eli. She's probably helping the duke. Catching Eli is her job, after all."

"It's complicated," Gin growled. "But she's not with the duke. Miranda wouldn't help anyone who treated the spirits this way. Common little spirits were never meant to be awake this long. It's going to kill the town if it keeps up. Miranda wouldn't put up with something like that to catch a hundred Elis. However, she is in the citadel, along with your thief, and I don't imagine either of them wants to be there. So if you're planning a rescue, then I want in."

Josef listened as Nico repeated the dog's words, rolling his eyes when she got to the end. "If you just wanted to come along there was no reason to jump us."

Gin grinned, showing a spread of long, sharp teeth. "I figured my negotiating position would be stronger if I had your head in my mouth, but this works too."

Nico gave him a horrified look, and didn't pass the message on.

Monpress, however, was sitting back against the stones, stroking his neatly trimmed beard with a thoughtful calmness not usually witnessed in the presence of ghosthounds. "Dog," he said, "you can understand what we're saying, correct?"

"Of course," Gin snorted. "Human speech is the simplest form of communication."

The thief chuckled as Nico translated. "Well, then, if you're willing to follow directions, I think we can come to an arrangement."

"That depends on the directions," Gin growled. "Who are you anyway?"

Nico answered that one. "He's Eli's father. He's a thief too."

Gin gave her a sideways look. "He doesn't smell anything like Eli."

Nico passed that on to Monpress, who laughed. "I'll take that as a compliment. I am Giuseppe Monpress, and I have many occupations. For the last few days, I served as a masonry and antiques expert. This morning, I was a thief. Right now, I'm simply a mentor trying to save his lost charge from his own cockiness. Does that answer your question?"

"In a roundabout sort of way," Gin growled, but he nodded just the same.

"Excellent," Monpress said. "As I was saying, I'm no wizard, but I can guess that the Duke of Gaol is the one controlling the town. If there's one thing living in Gaol taught me, it's that the duke controls everything within his borders, no matter how trivial. The man doesn't know the meaning of the word delegate. I wouldn't be surprised if he had a personal contract with every paving stone in Gaol. This level of attention to detail has gotten him where he is, but it's also a tremendous handicap, which we are going to use to our advantage. Look here."

He leaned over and began to sketch an outline of the citadel on the shed's dirt floor with one of Josef's knives, which Josef hadn't even felt him take. "We'll create a series of catastrophes, each requiring the duke's attention. Mass destruction seems to play well to each of your strengths, so I don't think this will be a problem. While the duke is putting out fires, I will locate and free Eli and the Spiritualist. Can you tell me where they are in the citadel?"

Gin nodded. "Once I'm inside."

"You'll be with me, then," Monpress said after Nico translated. "Once we've set the first distraction, you'll point me toward our targets. After that, you keep the attention off me while I do the extraction and then provide us with a quick getaway. You can run faster than a horse, can't you?"

Gin's toothy grin needed no translation, and Monpress turned to Nico and Josef. "We'll be depending on you two after we finish the jailbreak. Your job will be to cause enough flash that any report of prisoners going missing is lost in the noise, but not bring so much heat down that you become prisoners yourselves, or die in the process."

"Shouldn't be a problem," Josef said. "Let me get the Heart and I'll put a hole the size of a wagon in that outer wall. Maybe a couple. That should solve both the getaway problem and the distraction."

"I leave that to your discretion," Monpress said, making a mark at the corner of the citadel closest to the river. "We'll exit here, at the stables, so make your first hole on the northern wall. We'll rendezvous at the northern border of Gaol. I've got one final hide-out there. Nothing fancy, but it should last long enough for a simple switch. From what I've seen, the duke's reach ends at the Gaol border, so all we have to do is cross the line and we're free. Aside, of course, from the usual pursuing guards and whatnot, but I'm sure you have experience avoiding those."

"Tons," Josef said, grinning.

Nico frowned at the diagram. "It's kind of a blunt plan."

"Circumstances have given me blunt instruments. You do your best with what you're given."

Nico's mouth quirked at that, and she seemed satisfied. Josef, meanwhile, snatched his knife back and stood up, settling the blade back into his sleeve. "I'll need an hour to get the Heart and get into position."

"That's fine," Monpress said, standing up as well and dusting the dirt off his black, padded suit. "We'll need full dark anyway, so that gives us just the right amount of time. I won't be able to give a signal when we start. Can I trust you to be in position on time?"

"One hour," Josef said, walking to the rickety shed door. "We'll be there."

He paused for a moment, listening. Satisfied the coast was clear, he opened the door and slipped out into the alley, Nico right on his heels like a little shadow. Monpress watched them go, a skeptical look on his face.

"The girl I'm not worried about," he said and sighed. "But I have to admit, the thought of our success depending on that swordsman's ability to sneak to the river and back without causing a scene is not very reassuring."

Gin chuckled and settled down with his chin on his paws, his ears swiveling for any hint of sound. A moment later, Monpress sat down as well, and together they waited in silence for full dark to fall.

CHAPTER 17

Eli felt like a wad of kneaded dough. His breath came in ragged hiccups, his muscles ached, and his vision was almost black. The duke had called the first rest seconds before he passed out, but Eli wasn't sure he'd made it in time. Passing out still seemed like a valid option. Currently, however, he was awake, more or less, and being carried down a long hall suspended between the bulky arms of two enormous men. The duke ghosted ahead of him, a tall, dark shape among dark shapes.

They'd gone down a dozen flights of stairs, and the part of Eli's mind that wasn't whimpering in the corner realized they must be deep underground. The air was old, dusty, and cold enough to make his teeth chatter by the time they finally stopped in front of a deep-set iron door.

"My strongest prison," the duke said, standing aside as one of the guards unlocked the fist-sized padlock. "Also, my only prison. As most situations can be solved via the strategic use of force, I normally find them a waste of time. This one, however, I had made especially for you, Mr. Monpress, just in case you lived up to your reputation."

As he talked, the guard got the door open and carried Eli through and into a low, wide room. The only light came from the duke's own torch, but it was enough to make Eli wish he couldn't see. The dark stone walls were covered in strange metal objects, most of them sharp. There was a rack of hand and foot manacles in various sizes, as well as racks of other things he vaguely recognized from some of the more horrible dungeons he'd broken out of, but he had never worked up the courage to study the implements closely. There was also a large, locked grate in the middle of the floor, almost like a drain, and Eli shuddered to think what that was for.

But the guards walked past all that, dragging Eli to another iron door at the back of the room. This door the duke unlocked himself, standing in front so Eli could not see what he was doing and whispering something Eli couldn't make out. The door opened soundlessly to reveal a cell the size of a large closet stacked with bales of dark-colored hay.

Eli wanted to quip something about how nice it was of the duke to consider his comfort, but all he managed was a gurgling sound as the guards tossed him in. He landed on the hay with a grunt, the door clanging shut behind him.

"One hour." Eli could hear the duke's smile through the iron. "Then we'll begin again. Think on your answer."

Their footsteps faded away and the prison's outer door slammed shut, leaving Eli lying in the straw in utter black silence.

When he heard the outer door close, Eli sat up stiffly. His fingers went to his belt pocket and pulled out a small ring of heavy keys that had, moments ago, been in the guard's pocket. He felt them in the dark, and a small grin spread over his face. They'd have to beat him worse than that to slow his pickpocketing.

With a low groan, Eli pulled himself over to the door and set about looking for the keyhole. The duke had said one hour, but Eli wasn't about to wait that long. In one hour he intended to be with

Josef and Nico as they plowed a hole out of the city. However, those happy thoughts were quickly put out of his head as his finger ran along the door's pitted metal surface from floor to ceiling, and found nothing. No lock, no hinges, just metal that jutted almost seamlessly into stone.

Eli bit his lip. He had to be missing something. What he needed was a light. So he closed his eyes and reached down, prodding the lava spirit that slept in the burn on his chest.

"Karon," he whispered. Then again, a little louder. "*Karon.*"

His chest warmed as the lava spirit stirred sleepily.

"Could I bother you for a light?"

The spirit mumbled sleepily, and a warm, orange light began to shine from under Eli's shirt. Now that he could see, he noticed the door did have an opening, a small slit right at eye level, probably for guards to check on prisoners without opening the door. Otherwise, the light only confirmed what his fingers had found earlier. No lock, no handle, no hinges, nothing.

"Come on," Eli muttered, running his hands along the door's edge, tapping it with his fingers. As he tapped, he felt the door move away. It was a tiny, stubborn motion, but Eli jumped when he felt it, and everything fell into place. Of course, he realized, rolling his eyes. The hunk of iron was awakened, and probably terrified loyal like everything else in this pit of a country.

With a frustrated groan, Eli sat back and contemplated his next move. Something dramatic would be a nice change. Maybe he could get Karon to blow the door down in a shower of fire. He was turning this idea over when his nose caught the hint of something odd, a grassy, chemical smell, almost like lamp smoke. At once, the warm light from his chest went out.

"*Powers*, Eli." Karon's deep voice made his ears ring. "What are you doing, calling me like this? I could have killed us both."

Eli scowled. "What are you talking about?"

"You're covered in oil," Karon said. "I nearly set you alight."

Eli reached down in alarm, patting his shirt with quick hands. Sure enough, his clothes were slick with something that smelled faintly of grain. He grimaced. Lamp oil, cheap smoky stuff too, but when... He reached down to the hay bales and gave an enormous sigh. He remembered thinking they looked dark when the guards threw him in. Now that he had his hands in them, and was thinking of something other than getting out, it was clear they were drenched in oil. No fire spirits.

"Fantastic," he muttered, flopping back into the straw. No point in avoiding it since he was already covered. "What a fine mess."

Fine mess was a pretty way of putting it. Royally screwed was more accurate, or completely bollixed. Eli folded his arms across his chest. They still hurt horribly; so did his legs. Eli clenched his teeth. He hated pain. He also hated being trapped, but he had no one to blame but himself this time. He thought back to the duke's words in the library, before the pain had become too much. He'd let himself get predictable. How many times had he gotten himself caught? A dozen in five years? Two dozen? He shook his head. Far too many, that was for sure.

"You're getting lazy," he muttered at the dark. "Lazy and predictable."

Saying it actually made him feel worse, but he always tried to be honest with himself. First rule of thievery: If you can't be honest with yourself, you'll never fool anyone else. He rolled over, ignoring the horrible cramping in his back. Telling the duke what he wanted was out of the question. Even if he'd asked for something simple, Eli was categorically against bullies. He turned over again, trying to find a way he could lie without feeling like he was crushing something that had already been crushed too many times that day. It wasn't like he could take another round of the duke's questioning. He had to escape. Had to, and quickly, and he would get right on that as soon as breathing didn't feel like swallowing knives.

A while later he was still lying there, warring between making himself move and ignoring the necessity, when he caught a glimpse of light. It flashed red through his closed eyes, but when he snapped them open, the brightness was gone. Instead, the room, which had been pitch black, was now filled with cool, gray light. The itchy straw was gone from under him as well, and he was lying on something soft and yielding. Without warning, a gentle, cool hand touched his face, and Eli sucked in his breath at the burning touch the fingers left behind.

Just when he'd thought things couldn't get worse.

What? a lovely, musical voice chuckled behind him, *No hello?*

"Hello," he said through gritted teeth. "What are you doing here?"

Do I need an excuse? White hands, paler than fresh snow in moonlight, drifted down his chest to settle over his heart. *It pains me deeply to see you in trouble, dearest. Does love need a motive to come to the aid of the one she cherishes?*

Her voice was piercingly sad. Eli didn't fall for it for a moment.

The Lady sighed when he didn't answer, and her fingers ran over Eli's bruised body, leaving a burning feeling wherever they touched. *Look at what that man has done to my beautiful boy.* There was anger in her voice now, cold and sharp. *All you have to do is say the word and I will avenge you. Open yourself, show these common spirits whom you belong to, and this city will worship you as it should.*

"I don't belong to anyone," Eli said. "And I don't want your help."

The roving hands froze, and suddenly he found himself being whirled around. A terrible strength slammed him to his knees on the floor so that he was facing her as she stood before him, terrifying in all her glory. Perfectly straight white hair tumbled around a white face, spilling over her lovely shoulders, across her lovely body to the floor, where it flowed across the stones like moonlit rivers. Her eyes were pure white, the irises only defined by a shimmer of iridescent silver and the flutter of white lashes. She was naked, but her nakedness was not a shameful thing. Beside her inhuman whiteness, it was Eli who felt exposed.

Wherever her light touched, spirits woke, no matter how small or insignificant, and as they woke, they began to reverence her. The stones, the straw, the iron of the door, the tiny spirits of the air, everything, every bit of the world worshiped at her feet. Yet the White Lady ignored their praises. Her entire focus was on Eli alone. Slowly, gracefully, she reached forward and tangled her hands in his hair, pulling him close until his face was inches from her bare stomach.

You belong to me, she whispered, her voice shivering and terrible. *From the moment I saw you, you were mine. It was I who saved you, I who gave you everything you have. Because I love you, I have let you run free, but do not think for a moment that you are anything but mine.* She pulled his head up, almost breaking his neck as she brought his face to hers. *Do not forget what you are.*

"How could I?" Eli said, his voice wheezing with pain. "You keep showing up to remind me. But there's one thing you're wrong about," he said. "I don't belong to anyone but myself." The White Lady's hands trembled, and for a moment, Eli thought she was going to rip his head clean off. Then she began to chuckle. *So rebellious*, she cooed, ruffling his hair. *So arrogant. You haven't changed at all, have you? Refusing my help when I came all this way to save you. How selfish, but I always loved that about you, dearest boy.* She kissed his forehead. *Very well, beat yourself bloody if you must. But remember*—her hands gripped his head like a vice—*whatever you say, you do belong to me. I have been extremely tolerant, but push too hard, darling star, and I will take you back whether you like it or not. Then, things will be as they were before, when you were my darling little boy who loved me more than anything.*

"That was a long time ago," Eli said, leaning away from her touch. "Things change, Benehime."

Her hands caught him again and yanked him to his feet, putting his face inches from her own. She bent down with painful slowness, laying a cold kiss on his mouth. *I'll see you soon*, she murmured against him. *My favorite star.*

"Not if I can help it," Eli grumbled, but the room was dark again. The Lady was gone. Suddenly his legs felt as weak as jelly, and he flopped into the straw. For several moments, all he could do was sit there and adjust. Benehime's presence was intoxicating, and recovering once she left was a little like waking up after drinking an entire bottle of grain liquor. He was experienced with it, though, and recovered his mind with quick efficiency, especially when he realized he might still be able to take advantage of the awed spirits. But by the time he thought to try it, the door and the stones around it were already solidly ignoring him.

Of course, Eli sighed, flopping back over, she took the memory of her visit with her for everyone but him. She was too wise to be leaving him freebies like that. Her help never came for free. Well, she could wait forever, because there was no way he was ever going to come begging to her. Whatever she said, he was through being her pet.

Gritting his teeth against the pain of moving, Eli slid off the straw and knelt beside the door. No prison was perfect, he reminded himself. Even without his tools or wizardry, the duke was kidding himself if he thought he could keep Eli Monpress locked up. Feeling slightly better at this thought, he began patiently running his fingers along the door cracks, looking for the small oversight that would spell his freedom.

Miranda woke in the dark with her head throbbing. She was lying on her stomach with her arms under her, as if she'd fallen. She didn't remember falling, but her arms were asleep, so she must have been like that for a while. The memory of her capture was scattered and hazy, but she recalled Hern's face and the choking pain from the vines before everything had gone black. Even now, her head burned like someone was holding a brand to it. She tried pressing her fingers against her forehead, and a wave of blinding pain flashed through her. Miranda spat curses that would have made her mother faint and snatched her hand away. That bastard Hern would get what was coming to him, she thought bitterly, as soon as she got out of—

Miranda froze. Her fingers, the fingers she'd just pressed to her head, were empty. She held up her hands, waving them right in front of her face. It did no good; she couldn't see them, but then, she didn't need to. The feeling of bare skin against her cheek was enough.

"No," she whispered, curling over, her empty hands skittering across the unseen floor, desperately looking for what she knew was not there. "No no no no no."

Her rings were gone. All of them. So was Eril's pendant. And not just gone, but so far away she couldn't even feel the familiar tug of their connection on her spirit. Frantically, she flung her soul open, reaching out, calling for her spirits. Calling and waiting, but there was no reply.

Fear deeper than even the demon panic flooded through her, and her mind began to race. How long had she been out? How long had her spirits been without their connection? Where was Gin? Where was she, and how could she get out? She had to get out. She had to escape right now, before her rings died out.

"They won't die out," tsked a voice deep inside her. "Your spirits are stronger than that. Have a little faith, Miranda."

The low, watery voice in her ear made Miranda jump, and she cracked her head hard on the wall behind her.

"Sorry," Mellinor said.

"It's all right," Miranda whispered. "I've never been happier to hit my head in my life. Thank goodness you're still here."

"I live inside you," Mellinor said, matter-of-factly. "How would they take me?"

"Good point," Miranda said, sinking into a sitting position on the cold floor. "Did you see who took my rings?"

"No," Mellinor said and sighed, creating a strange feeling of water moving over her mind. "But I did get a lesson in the limitations of using a human body as a vessel. It turns out, if you're unconscious, I can't see anything. I heard them fighting, though."

"They fought for me?" Miranda was unexpectedly touched.

"Of course," Mellinor said. "As well as they could, anyway. Their abilities are very limited without you up to channel power to them. I couldn't even get out to help. I can't leave your body without injuring it if you're not awake to let me go. Yet another inconvenient lesson for today."

"This is kind of a new thing for all of us," Miranda said. "Let's get out of here."

"My thoughts exactly," Mellinor rumbled. "What first?"

Miranda blinked in the pitch dark. "How about some light?"

Mellinor made a bubbling sound, and Miranda felt cool water running through her. At once, soft light, like moonlight seen from deep underwater, began to fill the tiny cell, and she got her first good look at her prison.

"Good grief."

She was kneeling in a circular pit that might have been an old well. The walls were smooth, so either the prison had been cut into a solid block of stone, or they were deep underground, cut into the bedrock. The walls finally ended fifteen feet up at a metal grate sitting atop her cell like a well cap and held shut by a thick padlock. Above the grate, she could see nothing but darkness.

The cell itself was more spacious than she'd originally thought, however. She had enough room to sit down, if not to stretch out. Other than herself there was a wooden bucket, presumably to be used as a toilet, and a great deal of gray dust. It covered everything: the floor, the walls, and even, she realized with disgust, her clothes where she had been lying.

Miranda stood up, slapping at her skirt, but the dust clung to the fabric almost like it was sticky. It was on her hands too now, gray and fine as dried silt. She rubbed at it fiercely, but the powder stuck to her, forming dark little rivers in the creases of her skin. She held her hands to her nose. The dust had an odd scent that was strangely familiar. Very lightly, and sure she was being very foolish, Miranda licked her finger. The stuff had a horrid, alkaline taste, and that was all she got before the tip of her tongue went numb.

"Thought so," Miranda said, coughing. "It's graysalt. The servants used to put it down as a rat poison when I was a child."

"And you licked it anyway?" Mellinor said, horrified.

"Well, it's not lethal to humans," Miranda said, scraping her numb tongue with her teeth. "As a dust it's harmless, but get it wet and it becomes a paralytic. So the rats would run through and then get it wet when they tried to groom the dust off, and bam, dead rat."

"Good thing you're not a rat then," Mellinor grumbled.

"No," Miranda said, "but I'm trapped like one just the same. Look"—she pointed at the piles of gray dust on the floor—"there must be pounds of it down here. Sure, it's nontoxic now, when it's dry, but if we were to get it wet there's more than enough here to paralyze me from head to toe, maybe for good."

She peered up at the locked grate, high overhead. Even if she could reach it, she didn't think she could break the lock without Durn or one of her other spirits. Mellinor could, maybe, if he got enough pressure, but in her experience, lots of pressure meant lots of water, which was precisely what they couldn't have.

"Well," Miranda grumbled, "nice and trapped. I must admit I never expected something this ingenious, or cheap, out of Hern. Twenty pounds of graysalt probably cost less than one of those bottles of wine he had with dinner."

Mellinor shifted inside her. "Actually, I don't think we're in Hern's tower."

Miranda frowned, and the spirit explained. "Generally speaking, spirits who spend a lot of time around Spiritualists are pretty active, but it's quiet as the dead down here."

"That's no different from anything else in Gaol," Miranda said. "Hern's got a stranglehold on this place."

"You keep saying that," Mellinor murmured. "But something's been bothering me. You said before that Hern was always in Zarin, right?"

"Right," Miranda answered.

"Well," the water rippled in her head, "whatever's controlling the spirits in Gaol, it's acting like a Great Spirit. That kind of control doesn't work if the controlling power's not constantly in contact with the land, like a Great Spirit is. A land without a Great Spirit becomes sleepy and stupid, more so than usual. Just look at my old basin. But this land is disciplined, and easily woken. That's not something you see when the commanding power is always somewhere else."

Miranda bit her lip. Mellinor made a good point, and he would be the expert on this sort of thing. "But," she said, "if it wasn't Hern, then who? Who's running Gaol?"

"The duke, of course," said a cheery voice above her.

Miranda looked up in alarm, biting back a curse as she whacked her head again. She knew that voice, she realized, rubbing her poor, abused skull, but she certainly hadn't expected to hear it here.

"Monpress?"

"Who else?" Eli's laughing voice was muted, like he was behind something large and heavy.

"What are you doing in here?"

"I was caught." She could almost hear his shrug. "It happens from time to time. The trouble, as always, is keeping me caught. I was just exhausting my options when I heard your voice. Now, I think I can safely assume, unless your little oration about the powdered poison was a cruel and elaborate ploy, that you are also an unwilling guest of our illustrious host, Duke Edward?"

"Duke Edward?" Miranda stood up. "The Duke of Gaol?"

"No, the Duke of Farley," Eli said, sighing. "Yes, the Duke of Gaol. As I said, he's the one running everything. Whose castle do you think we're in?"

"Nonsense," Miranda said. "The duke isn't even a wizard."

"Who told you that?" Eli scoffed. "Just because a man doesn't wear rings or have WIZARD written across his forehead doesn't mean he isn't one."

Miranda shut her mouth. Now that she thought about it, everything she knew about the Duke of Gaol came from Hern's annual reports. This situation was getting stranger by the minute.

"So," she said slowly, "the Duke of Gaol is a wizard, and he's the one controlling the spirits, not Hern?"

"I don't know who Hern is," Eli said, "but that's correct. Now that you know, however, I can't imagine it makes you any happier to be locked up, so how about we work together and get out of here? It'll be just like Mellinor, only with less enslavement and near-drowning."

"*Me*," Miranda cried, "help *you*? Do you have any idea how much trouble helping you has caused me?"

"Not in the slightest," Eli said. "But think on this: I wouldn't be sitting here talking if I had a way out, would I? I'm proper trapped, same as you. Now, the duke will be back in less than half an hour to take me away, and after that, I don't think I'll be coming back. Are you really going to let a wizard who runs his spirits through a system of fear and intimidation be the one to catch me?"

Miranda scowled. The thief had a point. She'd put Monpress to the side while she focused on getting dirt on Hern, and it had landed her in here. If circumstance had delivered the thief, and possibly her freedom, right into her hands, who was she to argue? Plus, she now knew who was behind the strange happenings in Gaol. If the duke had indeed set himself up as the tyrant Great Spirit of Gaol that would certainly fit the West Wind's concern. If she played things carefully, she could very well walk out of Gaol with everything she'd come here to get, and that was worth taking a risk. After all, she thought and glared at the grimy filth on her skin, what did she have to lose?

"All right," she called back up. "What do you want me to do?"

"Catch!" Eli shouted, and she heard the jingle of something metal flying through the air before a set of keys landed with a jangle on the grate to her cell. They tottered there a moment, and then fell. She caught them in her outstretched hand.

"I don't believe it," she said. "How did you get keys? And how did you know what cell I was in?"

"You *are* the only source of light in the room. It's kind of hard to miss," Eli said. "As for the first part, who do you think you're dealing with? I'm Eli Monpress, the—"

"Greatest thief in the world. Yes, I know," Miranda sighed, looking up at the lock high, high overhead. "How am I supposed to use these?"

"I can't do everything for you," Eli said. "Figure it out, and do it fast. The duke could come in at any moment."

"Right," Miranda grumbled. "No pressure." She looked around at the walls for anything she could use as a grip to climb, but they were smooth, almost glossy, and she couldn't find so much as a hairline fracture. Jumping was out of the question. Even standing on tiptoe on the wooden bucket, stretching with all her might, she couldn't reach the halfway mark. She put her fists on her hips, scanning the cell. There had to be a way.

Her roving eyes stopped on the bucket under her feet. It was wide and low like a wash bucket, which was probably what it had been before being repurposed. It was made of cheap, light wood, but the joints were tight and waxed to hold water. Suddenly, she began to smile.

"Mellinor," she said, "could you flood this cell?"

"Theoretically," the water answered. "It's dry, but I could probably get enough water out of the air to do it, but I thought we weren't going to risk the powder."

"We're not." Miranda grinned and clunked her heel against the bucket.

She felt the water's attention flit down to the floor, and then Mellinor heaved a sigh like a tide. "Miranda, be reasonable. I don't think that thing is buoyant enough to float, let alone support you. Even if it did, I'd be turning the cell into a pool of toxic sludge. One slip and you'd be paralyzed forever."

"That's just a risk we'll have to take," Miranda said. She patted her chest where the water's glow was the brightest and gave her spirit a confident smile. "If any water can float this bucket safely to the top, it's you."

"Flattery might work on the dog, but it gets you nowhere with me," the water grumbled. "I'll try, but only if you understand that once we start, we can't stop. I can't just send the water away again if it has nowhere to drain."

Miranda flipped the keys over in her hand. "All you have to do is get me to the grate. I'll take it from there."

"All right," Mellinor said. "Brace yourself."

Miranda stepped into the bucket. "Ready," she said.

"The undersides of your wrists are clean, so I'll use those." Mellinor's voice was moving through her, collecting at her hands. "Roll up your sleeve and hold out your arm."

Miranda did as he asked, holding her hands out in front of her. What happened next was painless, but almost too intense to watch. The water spirit poured from the clean skin of her lower arms, flowing out of her pores like milk squeezed through cheesecloth. It hit the ground with a great splash, sending a splatter of the poison dust onto her skirt. Miranda closed her eyes and thanked whatever luck there was that she'd chosen the dress with thick, long skirts. Under her feet, the bucket groaned as water flowed around it, yet it did not start to float. Mellinor was completely out of her now, and she pulled her arms back, carefully holding them away from the parts of her dress that were still dry and dusty. The water kept rising as Mellinor pulled moisture from the air, the tiny specks of water too small to have consciousness, and into his body. When the water was less than a finger's width from the lip of the bucket, the wooden slats beneath her feet finally began to wobble. The bucket left the ground with a pitch that made Miranda scramble. After that, she braced herself against the stone with both arms, using the straight walls as a guide as Mellinor gently floated her bucket up.

Even with Mellinor's glow, the foaming water was filthy and foul smelling. Balancing became more and more difficult the higher they went, as the bucket began to bob on the swirling current. Miranda flailed her arms, keeping upright by pushing herself off the walls, first one way, then another, as the waves took her. Just when she'd finally gotten the rhythm of it, the game changed. She felt wetness in her boots. When she looked down between sways, she noticed about an inch of water on the low end of her makeshift boat.

Miranda gasped and jerked away, causing the bucket to pitch, and she almost fell in completely. She caught herself at the last moment, bracing against the wall as the water kept rising. Now that the water had found a way in, more and more of it was pushing up through the bucket's cracks. Miranda bit her lip. Another moment and it would be up to her ankles. It was time to take a risk.

The grate was right above her, though still a foot out of reach. Before she could psych herself out, Miranda jumped. She jumped straight up, toppling the sinking bucket with her momentum. For a moment, her reaching hands caught nothing. Then her fingers slammed into the iron bars of the grate and she held tight.

"Mellinor!" she cried, grabbing the bars with her other hand as well and pulling her legs up. "Stop the water!"

The water stopped instantly, and for a moment Miranda hung there, gasping for breath as she clung to the bars. Only a moment, though, and then she was on the move again, pulling herself along the grate until she was right beside the iron padlock. It took several tries to find the right key, and then a great deal of pushing once she found it, for the lock was trying its best not to give in. But, in the end, purpose overwhelmed even spirit determination, and the lock snapped open. Unfortunately, in her hurry to get out, Miranda had neglected to determine which direction the grate opened. As it happened, it opened inward, something she found out very quickly when the grate swung down, taking her with it.

She yelped as the grate swung wildly, slamming her against the wall and knocking her breath out. But the hinges hadn't been oiled in a while, and the grate, after its initial bout of movement, creaked to a halt, leaving her startled, upside down, and dangling mere inches above the foul water.

"Miranda," Eli whispered frantically. "Are you all right?"

"More or less," Miranda groaned, pulling herself around the

grate. She climbed up the lattice of iron bars and then, with a final heave, onto the stone floor of the prison itself. The moment she hit flat rock, she flopped over, gasping, and didn't move for at least a minute.

"Well," Eli said, his voice floating through the dark, "at least it's never dull, being with me."

"Shut up," Miranda gasped, pushing herself upright. Mellinor's light was dimmer, thanks to the gallons of filthy water he had commandeered, but it was still enough to see by. As she'd expected, she was in a prison, though a strange one. It was all one long room with a wide variety of equipment, from a selection of manacles to things she didn't recognize and didn't want to, bolted to the walls. There were not, however, any cells she could see.

"Where are you?"

"Turn left," Eli said. "Your left. I'm the door at the far back."

Miranda turned as he said and found herself facing what she'd thought was an iron wall. Looking closer, however, she picked out a small rectangle cut at eye level and, peering out through the gap, a pair of familiar blue eyes glittered in the dim light.

"Hello," Eli said. "Mind letting me out?"

Miranda stumbled over to the door. It didn't seem to have a lock or hinges or a handle or anything normally associated with doors.

"I see why you had to give me the keys," she said, running her finger along the smooth door crack. "I suppose the door isn't in a talking mood?"

"No more than anything else in this country," Eli said with a sigh.

"We'll need to knock it down, then," Miranda said. "Wait here."

"Like I could wait anywhere else."

Miranda ignored him, walking back over to the pit where Mellinor was still swirling. She knelt by the edge and peered into the water, which was already looking clearer.

"Losing the sediment?"

"As much as I can," the water rumbled. "This stuff feels awful. It's all slick and heavy, and whatever personality it had before is long gone thanks to the processing. I see why they use it to kill rats."

Miranda grimaced. "Glad I didn't fall in it. Think you've got enough water to knock down a door?"

"That depends on the door," Mellinor said, swelling up in a wave and looking where she gestured. It studied the door for a moment and then vanished back into the pit.

"Tell the thief to get ready," he called, his watery voice echoing up from the bottom of the cell.

"I've been ready," Eli called back. His voice was farther away now, and Miranda guessed he was pressing himself against the back of his cell. "Just do it."

Mellinor gushed and thundered, but right before he erupted in a geyser, Eli cried "Wait!"

The water stopped and Miranda groaned in frustration. "What?"

"It occurs to me," Eli said, "that the duke was probably prepared for me, a trapped and notorious wizard thief, to do something desperate, like Enslave the door holding me in. Before you knock it down, you might check for traps."

"Traps?" Miranda said. "What kind of traps could he have against Enslavement?"

"Humor me?" Eli said sweetly.

Miranda shook her head and walked back over to the door. She didn't see anything, just the iron wall of a door set into the stone. Still, she ran her fingers along all the seams anyway, just to be sure. She was about to tell the thief he was being paranoid when she felt something unusual at the very top of the door. A thin bump, almost like a wire, ran up from the top of the door to the stone ceiling. Standing on tiptoe, she followed it with her fingers until she hit a loose brick in a wall that didn't have any bricks. Frowning, she reached up gently with both hands and gave the brick a tug. It came away easily, revealing a large metal tin attached to the wire she'd followed. She lifted the tin down gently. It was heavy in her hands and sloshing with a liquid she could already guess wasn't water. Sure enough, it was full to the brim with a black, inky substance Miranda recognized from when Mellinor's water first touched the powder in her cell. It was the poison, and from the look of it, very concentrated. If Eli had Enslaved the door or opened it or busted it down in any way, this stuff would have drenched him, paralyzing him completely. A good thief catch, she had to admit, much better than burning oil or anything that could kill or disfigure. The best bounty depended on him being alive and recognizable.

Very, very carefully, Miranda emptied the tin in the far corner of the prison, standing back as the black liquid pooled in a low spot on the stone. When it was all gone, she went back to Mellinor and told Monpress to get in position.

"Whenever you're ready," he called back.

Miranda gave the signal and the water burst up in a geyser, shooting out of the pit before turning in midair, like water in a pipe, and barreling straight for Eli's cell door. It hit the iron like a hammer and the metal squealed, but didn't give way. The water wasn't finished, though. Mellinor gathered himself in the door's cracks, pushing his water between the stone and the metal. With no hinges, the door depended on its resolve to stay upright, but no resolve was strong enough to hold with water in every crevice. It clung for a few moments more, and then, with a defeated squeal, the door fell forward, crashing to the ground.

Almost before it hit, Eli jumped out. He was dirty and pale, his short black hair standing up at all angles, but he was beaming as he grabbed Miranda's hand and gave it a vigorous shake.

"I knew I could count on you," he said, clasping her hand tightly in his. "I always told Josef, if there's one Spiritualist with her head on right, it's Mira—"

He was interrupted by the clink of a lock closing. Eli looked down. The hand that was shaking Miranda's now had a manacle around its wrist, the other end of which Miranda was fastening around her own. It was one of the manacles from the rack on the wall, and she locked it in place with a key from the key ring he'd given her before tossing the entire ring into the pit of her former cell.

"Eli Monpress," she said, grinning like her ghosthound, "you are now under the authority of the Spirit Court."

Eli looked down at his wrist, wiggling his hand against the tight, sharp, metal band. "That was a dirty trick."

Miranda didn't stop smiling. She held out her hand, and Mellinor blasted himself against the prison's outer door, popping the hinges. The door fell over with a squeal of metal on stone, and Mellinor returned to Miranda, leaving the excess water he had gathered to drain away back into Miranda's cell.

Eli watched as the keys vanished under a layer of filthy, poisoned water. "A *very* dirty trick," he grumbled as she dragged him out into the hall.

"I don't want to hear it," she said, walking quickly and quietly, using Mellinor's light to guide her. "You're the master of dirty tricks."

"I thought you were above all that," he said, letting her drag him. "And you *know* it's not going to work."

"Maybe not for long," she said, "but if I can keep you under control for even an hour, it will be worth it." She came to a stop at another door, a wooden one this time, blocking the entire hall. It was locked, of course, with a padlock that looked very similar to the one on her cell.

"Well," Eli said. "I doubt your little spout spirit there has enough water to bash this one in. If only we still had the keys."

Miranda silenced him with a jab to the ribs and pressed her ear against the door. She could hear shouting on the other side, shouting and guard whistles. They didn't seem to be coming her way, though. She bent down lower to examine the lock when the door rattled softly. Miranda jumped, slapping her hand over Eli's mouth as she pressed them back into the wall. The door rattled again, and there was an almost inaudible click as the lock popped open.

Miranda dampened Mellinor's light to nearly nothing and then reached up to grabbed an unlit torch from the wall bracket above her. She brandished the torch like a bat as the door opened. The moment a head came into view, she braced herself and brought her makeshift weapon down with all the force she could muster.

A second before it would have conked his head, her target dodged. He spun, a shadow in the dark hall, grabbing her arm as he went. She barely had time to gasp before she was on the floor with her arm wrenched behind her and the stranger's knee in her back.

"Well," a cultured voice whispered just above her head. "Eli, what are you doing, letting the lady go first?"

The pressure vanished from Miranda's back, and she felt the chain jerk as Eli rolled over on the floor beside her.

"*Letting her go first?*" the thief sputtered. "Whose idea do you think this was?"

The man, whoever he was, ignored Eli completely, and a black-gloved hand swooped down to help Miranda to her feet.

"Apologies, my dear," he said kindly. "The boy never could learn manners."

Miranda took the hand gingerly, very confused, and lifted her head to see a tall, thin man in late middle age with a handsome, cultured smile wearing wrapped clothes in varying shades of black.

"Giuseppe Monpress," he said, before she could ask. "You must be Miranda. Gin has told us all about you."

"Gin?" she said, her voice rising in a rush of hope. "Is he here? What do you mean you're Monpress?"

"It's not a terribly uncommon name," the man said. "And your hound is currently making a fine distraction running circles around the duke's men. Now"—he took her arm, the one that wasn't chained to Eli, whom the man seemed to have forgotten—"we should hurry. The duke's a clever man. He'll tear away from the ruse soon enough. We've got a little time before Josef and Nico's cavalry shows up, however. Meeting you here has put me ahead of schedule."

"Well, good for you," Eli said, elbowing his way between them. "I, however, am in a hurry to miss my date with the duke, so if you don't mind..."

He made a series of gestures toward the door. The older Monpress shrugged and, gesturing for Miranda to go ahead, let Eli lead the way up the narrow stairs to the maze of tunnels that ran below the citadel, speaking up only to correct the thief when he was taking them in entirely the wrong direction.

CHAPTER 18

Josef and Nico snuck through the empty streets. Above them, lights flickered behind the wobbly glass windows in the upper stories of the lovely houses, but Josef and Nico saw no one. Though it was still early, all the restaurants were dark and closed, same with the taverns, and even the inns. Whatever command of the duke's had cleared the streets earlier was obviously still in effect, and now that Eli was caught, even the patrols were off the streets, leaving Nico and Josef to run in the shadows behind the watchful lamps and toward the dark river and the docks beyond.

"At least the paving stones aren't trying to trip us anymore," Josef grumbled, stomping harder on the cobbled street than was strictly necessary. "I guess Eli was right when he said the spirits couldn't keep it up forever."

"Or they just aren't looking for us," Nico said. "Spirits are famously bad at finding nonwizards. Humans all look the same to most spirits."

"Lucky us," Josef said, hopping up the stairs toward the tall bridge that was the only way across the river. They kept to the back line of storehouses, ducking behind crates and barrels until they reached the dusty, neglected warehouse they'd slept in the night before. Josef flipped the rusty lock with impatient fingers. He could almost feel the Heart inside, waiting for him. The door opened with a groan, and they slipped inside.

With the docks empty, there were no fires burning in the braziers outside. Without the ambient light, the warehouse was ink black, forcing Josef to stop at the threshold and let his eyes adjust. Nico went on ahead of him, striding confidently into the dark. That was typical. The dark never seemed to slow her down, which was why he jerked to attention when her soft footsteps stopped.

His hand dropped to the sword at his hip. He could just barely see Nico in front of him, a spot of darker shadow gone completely rigid. Keeping one hand on his sword and the other on the dagger in his sleeve, Josef crept forward until he was pressed against Nico's back.

"Someone's here." Her voice was scarcely more than a breath.

Josef stared over her shoulders, but he saw nothing but shadowy outlines and dusty beams. She pointed at the darkness ahead of them, and Josef squinted. He could make out details now, the edges of crates, the forgotten tools lining the walls, and, directly ahead of them, the dark, solid shape of the Heart of War leaning against the corner, right where he'd left it. He was about to ask Nico to be more specific when something shifted in the dark, and then he saw it as well. Sitting on the stack of crates beside the Heart was an enormous, dark shape. At first Josef thought his eyes were playing tricks on him, that the shadows were stretched out, for no man could be that large. Then the shape jumped down, landing on the wooden floorboards with a crash that rattled the building to its foundation.

Josef stumbled, gripping the hilts of his sheathed swords, white-knuckled as the dark figure stretched out his hand, pointing one long finger, not at Josef, but at Nico, who was trembling in front of him. The man, for Josef could now see it was a man, smiled, his teeth glinting in the dark, and spoke a command.

Don't move.

Even Josef, spirit deaf, could tell the words were more than words. The moment they left the man's lips, Nico went down. She fell hard, straight down without catching herself, landing on the floor with a bone-splitting crack. Josef was at her side in an instant, but wherever he touched her, her coat was as hard as iron. Even the air felt like stone around her skin. Her body was rigid, the frantic darting of her eyes and the slight noise of her panicked breaths the only sign she was still alive.

Josef was still trying to get her up when he heard the clank of enormous footsteps coming toward him. Leaving Nico with a curse, he drew his swords with a singing scrape of metal and turned to face the enormous man closing the distance between them.

But the man wasn't looking at him. He didn't even seem to notice the blades in Josef's hands. He was staring at the girl lying on the floor.

"You were hard to find, little demon." His deep voice was still terrible, but it was at least mostly human this time. "I don't know how you hid yourself, but no matter. No one hides from the League forever."

Josef stepped over Nico and took up position between her and the approaching man. "What did you do to her?" he shouted. It looked like wizard stuff to him, but Eli had always told him wizards couldn't control other people.

"League benefit," the man said, walking slowly. "I gave the spirits around her something to do. The League is the arm of the White Lady, so their nature binds them to my command when it comes to demon hunting. They'll stay like that, squishing her down, until I tell them otherwise."

Josef had no clue what the man was talking about, but he had other worries. Now that he was out of the deep shadows, the man wasn't as large as Josef had initially thought, but he was no less a monster. He stood seven feet tall at least, and was wide enough to make his height seem normal. His head was shaved clean, and scars that stood out white against his deeply tanned skin ran from the top of his skull to the tops of his bushy eyebrows. A long cut had scarred his face into a permanent sneer, and his nose was crooked from multiple breaks. He looked like a man who'd spent his life brawling, and he carried his enormous frame with a fighter's grace. Across his bare chest, he wore a wide, red sash festooned with a host of strange objects—jeweled rings, sword hilts, necklaces, talismans, and even, Josef cringed, a preserved hand curled in a fist.

Above the ghastly collection, a long black coat with a high collar sat awkwardly on the man's monstrous shoulders. The sleeves were ripped off, revealing muscular arms covered in mismatched tattoos. The coat looked too small for him, but anything would look small on this man. Anything, that is, except the sword he wore at his side. That suited him perfectly. Its pommel was the size of an orange, and the hilt was wrapped in thick leather until it was almost as large as the guard above it. He wore it naked, with no sheath, the dark blade out and lying bare against his coat so that the wicked, toothed edge tore at the fabric until the dark cloth was nearly in tatters. It was eerily familiar, but the blade looked so at home on the man's hip that it took Josef a few moments to recognize it as the sword he'd seen in Slorn's workshop.

"Ah," Sted said, laying a hand on the sword's hilt. "You like my new baby, yes? You must be the demon's guardian." He looked Josef up and down. "Aren't you a bit puny to be the master of the Heart of War?"

Josef ignored him. "Who are you? What are you here for?"

"What kind of question is that?" Sted cackled. "Don't you see the jacket?" He flipped his torn collar. "I'm Berek Sted, best killer in the League of Storms, and I'm here to kill the demon."

Josef raised his swords. "You'll find that harder than you think."

"Really?" Sted laughed. "I like you, swordsman. Tell you what, I'll make you a deal. See, I kind of owe you. When I got to Gaol, I couldn't find the girl. I've never been good at finding demons and all that League mumbo jumbo. But I could feel the Heart." His scarred face grew almost wistful. "Any swordsman worth the name can feel a sword like that. It's a force of nature. So I followed it and waited and, sure enough, here you are. I hate owing people, so how about I make you a deal to call it even?"

Josef scowled. "What kind of deal?"

"A fighting chance," Sted said. "It goes like this: You give me a good fight, something to make me remember why I put up with the League. If you beat me, I'll let the girl go and tell old Alric I couldn't find the demon."

Josef stared at the man. "Wait," he said. "You're a member of the League of Storms, and you're offering to let the demon go if I fight you and win?"

Sted shrugged. "The League is work, you know? You look like you know how to give a good fight, and I always say pleasure before work. Anyway," he chuckled, "it's not like I'll *lose.*"

Josef glanced down at Nico. She was still on the floor, prone and flat against the boards. He did a quick calculation in his head. They had a little under half an hour before they were supposed to meet the elder Monpress and Eli at the wall. Not much time, but it wasn't like he could ask the man to wait. He'd just have to be quick. In any case, he thought as his hand tightened on his sword, wasn't this the kind of challenge he'd been looking for?

"All right," Josef said. He bent over, laying the wrapped Fenzetti on the floor beside Nico. "You've got your deal."

Sted's scarred face broke into an enormous grin. "Wonderful! If you put up a good enough show, I might even add something of yours to my trophies." He cackled and pounded his chest, making the grim collection on his sash clatter.

"I'll pass," Josef said, dropping into a defensive crouch.

"Suit yourself," Sted said. "Start whenever you're ready."

Josef balanced on the balls of his feet, swords out. The Heart was on the other side of the room still, but that was fine. He was going to win this without the Heart's help. Across the room, Sted watched him, arms slack at his sides. Josef chose his spot carefully, a stretch of unguarded muscle to the left of Sted's ribs, just above his stomach. When he could almost feel his sword cutting the man's flesh, he sprang.

He threw himself forward, moving with a speed that would have impressed Coriano had the other swordsman been alive to see it, and dashed hard to the right, making a feint toward Sted's leg. Then, at the last second, he swung his swords around to bite into his true mark, plunging the flashing steel straight into Sted's flesh. But as the blow came down, Josef knew something was wrong. Sted wasn't blocking. It wasn't that he'd seen through the feint; he hadn't even moved. The man just stood there, smiling as Josef rushed him, not even flinching when both of Josef's swords landed in his undefended side.

Josef felt a shock move up his arm as the strike hit, but it was all wrong. The impact was far too strong. It was like hitting stone, not flesh. Josef slid with the blow, letting his momentum carry him past Sted. The moment he was behind the larger man, Josef flipped his swords, turning and thrusting them into Sted's back. Again, the blades struck true, and again that horrible reverberation went up his arm, only this time it was accompanied by a sharp crack. Josef's eyes widened, and he jumped, landing in a crouch on a crate several feet away.

He held his swords in front of him, grimacing at the two inches missing from the top of his left-hand weapon. The tip had snapped clean off, leaving a square nub where the point should have been. But Sted, who had just taken four killing blows, stood the same as ever. He looked over his shoulder at Josef, and then reached behind him, picking the broken tip of Josef's sword out of his coat. Beneath the holes the swords had torn when they entered, his skin was smooth and whole.

When he turned, Josef saw Sted's side was also uninjured, the skin not even reddened from the strike. Sted's grin grew wider as he watched the realization sink in.

"You know," he said slowly, tossing the broken sword tip casually in his hand, "when you get an invitation to join the League of Storms, they give you a gift, sort of a consolation prize for leaving your life behind. Some guys choose a longer life, some choose an endless supply of beautiful women, some just want to get drunk with no consequences. *I* didn't want any of that. Instead, I asked for skin that couldn't be cut." He grabbed the sword tip midtoss and jabbed the broken end straight into the soft flesh below his wrist. Josef flinched, but the jagged metal slid harmlessly over Sted's skin without leaving so much as a scratch. Point made, Sted tossed the sword tip over his shoulder, where it clattered across the unseen crates and vanished into the dark.

"I probably should have told you that before you agreed to the fight," Sted said, sinking into a combat stance for the first time. "You can still run if you want."

Josef's answer to that was to lob his broken sword right at Sted's head. Sted dodged easily, but Josef was already moving, running along the crates. He flipped a knife into his empty hand and, before Sted could turn to face him, launched himself at the larger man.

Again, Sted didn't try to dodge. Josef came in high, aiming for Sted's shoulder. But then, at the very last second, he switched up and thrust his knife hand up, stabbing not for the shoulder, but straight at Sted's left eye.

Sted caught Josef's arm before the blow could land, and he heaved the swordsman off. Josef landed with a crash in a pile of crates, filling the air with dust. Sted watched where he had landed cautiously, but when the dust cleared, there was Josef. He was sitting cross-legged on the splintered crates with both his blades still in his hands, and looking enormously pleased with himself.

"So," he said, grinning. "Judging from that little display, uncuttable skin doesn't account for the eyes. I wonder what other parts your 'gift' missed?"

Sted grinned back. "Why don't you come see?"

Josef leaped forward. This time, he went for Sted's grinning mouth, holding his sword like a spear. Just as he was about to land, Sted drew his own sword, the great iron monster at his side, and met Josef's blow with one of his own. The two swords crashed in a shower of sparks, and Josef's blade shattered. Sted carried the blow, striking Josef straight across his now-unguarded chest.

Josef grunted as the jagged blade bit through his shirt and into his skin. He felt his ribs crack as the impact of Sted's strike blew through him, and then he was flying backward in free fall. He hit the wall with another blow that knocked what little breath he had left from his lungs and toppled to the ground. For a moment, he felt nothing, saw nothing, heard nothing but the blood pounding in his ears. Then, finally, his lungs thundered back to life, and pain exploded through him. He lay gasping for a moment, barely aware of Sted's hulking shape as the man came to stand over him, holding his enormous, jagged sword in one steady hand.

"The skin wasn't the only gift I got." Sted's voice was far away as Josef tried to roll over, tried and failed. He looked up, his blurry vision barely making out the shape of Sted's sword as he held it over Josef's prone body.

"Meet Dunolg," the enormous man grinned, "the Iron Avalanche."

Josef groaned and dropped his broken sword. Normal blades were no use against an awakened sword. He'd already learned that the hard way. Nothing for it now, he thought bitterly. He'd have to use the Heart. But the great sword was all the way across the room, and Sted was already raising his blade for the final blow.

Then, just as Josef was trying to think of a way to dodge, his fingers brushed familiar fabric, and he had an idea. Sted dropped his sword down on Josef's bleeding chest, but just before the blow landed, Josef grabbed the wrapped bundle of the Fenzetti blade and held it over him. Sted's sword crashed down, the jagged edge meeting the wrapped fabric with a deep, golden sound, like a great bell. For a moment, the swordsmen stared at each other as the sound rang through them, and the cloth fell away to reveal the bone-white blade holding back the jagged black one.

Josef used the moment of confusion to roll out of the way,

sliding the Fenzetti's dull blade along Sted's with a shower of red sparks. He came up on his feet with the sword in front of him. His breath was back, his chest aching but bearable, and, most important, he was holding a sword Sted couldn't break. The Fenzetti sat awkward and heavy in his hands, but he held it steady, watching as Sted turned to face him.

"What kind of sword is that?" Sted spat. "It doesn't even have a cutting edge."

"A cutting edge is hardly necessary for you," Josef answered. "Since I can't cut you, we'll see how you stand up to bludgeoning."

Sted glared at him. "I didn't give you this deal so that we could play-fight with dull sticks." He stood aside, pointing at the enormous black blade in the corner, still leaning where Josef had left it. "Pick up the Heart," Sted growled. "Stop this dancing and give me a real fight."

Josef just grinned and brandished the Fenzetti blade, leaning in to balance the skewed weight. "The Heart is my sword," he said. "I use it when I choose. You challenged me; you fight by my rules."

Sted stabbed his sword into the wooden floor. "That's how you want it?" He took off his coat, throwing it on the ground. It landed with a great crash, and Josef realized with a grimace that it was weighted, enormously so if the dent it made on the floor was any indication.

"That's how you want it," Sted shouted again, flexing his now-bare shoulders and rocking his head from side to side, cracking his neck in a hail of popping bones. "All right, little swordsman." He grabbed his sword again. "Here I come."

Josef barely had time to raise his sword before Sted was on top of him, the jagged blade flashing and flying across the Fenzetti's bone-white surface. He pushed Josef back, and back again, raining a flying onslaught of jagged teeth across the dull blade of the Fenzetti. It took every ounce of Josef's skill just to keep away, and even when Sted's openings were enormous, which was common, the man was throwing everything into his attack, and Josef couldn't break away from his defense long enough to take advantage of them. Sted was laughing now, pushing Josef back faster and faster with each blow, taunting him endlessly.

The Fenzetti, however, was living up to Slorn's promise. No matter how hard Sted attacked, no matter what angle his blade hit the uneven, bone-colored edge, the Fenzetti never faltered. It formed an impenetrable wall in front of Josef, so long as he was fast enough to block. That, Josef thought, gritting his teeth, was the hard part. The sword's unevenness and bad balance pulled at his muscles, but he didn't dare slow down. Still, he was quickly using up his strength, and at this rate it was only a matter of time before he made a mistake. When that happened, it would be over.

"Yes," Sted said, laughing, as his sword flew. "I know what you're thinking. I've seen it in every man's eyes, right before the end." He thrust straight and then cut left, forcing Josef to overreach in the scramble to guard his shoulder. "It's just one missed block, and down you go." Sted switched up his attack again. "After that, there's nothing left to do but butcher the girl. I'll cut the seed right out of her heart." Sted followed his words with a thrust that sent Josef spinning backward from the force.

Josef stumbled, looking for footing, and his feet touched something yielding. He threw his weight at the last minute and glanced down in surprise to see that he was standing over Nico. He hadn't realized they'd come back around the room. She was still exactly as she had fallen. Only her eyes moved. They looked at him, bright and wide and filled with an emotion he couldn't name but that he felt all the way to his core. The desperate need to fight, to live.

Sted was charging again, and Josef jumped to the side, leading him away from Nico, but the look in her eyes followed him, and, slowly, shame began to grow in his mind. All this time, from the moment he first found her dying in the mountains, she'd struggled to keep living, to never lose the battle against the dark creature that lived inside her. And here he was, playing, throwing that struggle away because of his pride. Because he didn't want the Heart to win for him again.

He looked down at the crooked sword in his hands, at the white metal that turned awkwardly in his grip. He couldn't win like this. He wasn't good enough to win like this, not yet, but that didn't mean he was free to lose. After all—he turned, letting Sted drive him toward the far corner of the warehouse—this wasn't just his battle anymore.

On Sted's next blow, Josef let go of the Fenzetti. It flew out of his hands, and Sted, not expecting the sudden lack of resistance, fell off balance. It was only a moment, but it was enough. Josef sprang backward, reaching for what he couldn't see but knew was there. For a moment he felt nothing, and then his fingers closed around the wrapped hilt of the Heart of War. Grinning, he brought the black blade around. The cloth unraveled like a veil, fluttering away into the dark to reveal the black, pitted blade. Its matte surface was impossibly old, crisscrossed with the scars of ancient battles no one but the blade itself remembered anymore. It sat confident and comfortable in Josef's hand, the blade perfectly balanced against his weight, ready.

Sted grinned like a mad dog and, swinging his sword in an arc, took up a fencing position, the first Josef had seen him use.

"Now," Sted growled. "Now we will fight. Now we will have the kind of battle worth dying for."

As he spoke, his sword began to glow brighter. Its light swelled red-silver, the color of blood in cold water, filling the room. The Heart, however, stayed as dark as ever, but the feel of it, the endless strength, flowed in a torrent down Josef's arms as he raised the blade for a swing.

What happened next happened in an instant. Josef charged forward, gripping the Heart's long hilt with both hands. He was moving with the Heart's impossible speed now, the kind of speed where the air is like jelly, and everything, every step, every heart-beat, slows to a painful crawl. Even so, even as he barreled down on top of him, Josef saw Sted lift his sword, setting it across his chest to block the Heart's blow. It was the first defensive position he'd taken in the entire fight, and he took it just in time as the Heart, and the mountain of force behind it, crashed into him.

Time snapped back as they collided, and there was an enormous crash. Sparks flew from the clashing blades while wood and debris went everywhere as Sted's braced feet ripped the floor-boards to pieces, fighting to stop Josef's momentum. Finally, half-way across the room from where Josef had struck, they stopped in a great cloud of dust. Josef stood panting. He could barely see anything, but the Heart was still in his hand, and he could see Sted's crouched outline below him. It was over. No sword, awakened or not, had ever taken a full-on blow from the Heart and survived. And yet, even as the thought floated through his head, the dust began to settle, and his eyes widened. There, beneath the Heart's blade, was Sted's jagged sword, bent where the Heart had struck, but not broken. Its light shone brighter and hungrier than ever, and behind it was Sted, baring his teeth in triumph.

"Is that all?" he roared.

And then he pushed back, throwing his tremendous strength into his sword until Josef was the one crouching under him.

Josef rolled before the man's weight could crush him completely, his mind spinning wildly. How had his attack not worked? The Heart was unbeatable. It never lost. Sted should be dead, but he was on the attack wilder than ever, and Josef had to scramble to knock his blows away. Once again, Josef was falling back, but the Heart was not the unbalanced stick the Fenzetti had been. It danced in his grip, blocking Sted's blows and then snaking up to strike the gaping openings in Sted's defense. But even the Heart's blows slid off Sted's impenetrable skin. Josef struck again and again, harder and harder, but it did no good. Sted's skin remained unmarred. Sted's attacks, however, were beginning to get through. The long fight with the Fenzetti, his earlier wound, the enormous initial blow with the Heart, it was all taking its toll. Josef could feel himself getting slower, and cuts began to appear on his body as his parries grew closer and closer.

With every new cut, Sted's smile fell farther, and his blows grew more vicious. "Come on," he said, dragging his jagged sword across Josef's shoulder, leaving a deep trail of jagged cuts. "Come *on.* You're just swinging your sword. Fight me! Show me the Heart of War!"

He crashed an overhanded blow down on Josef's head as he said this, forcing Josef to duck and roll. Josef was openly panting now. Blood ran down his sides, hot and slick under his shirt, but there was no time to stanch it. Every ounce of strength went into keeping Sted's sword away.

"How disappointing," Sted sneered, catching the Heart's edge and dragging Josef up until they were eye to eye. "You're not even a swordsman, are you? You're just a man with a *sword.*"

He screamed the last word, matching it with a thrust at Josef's unprotected stomach. This time, it was too fast. Josef couldn't dodge. The jagged sword bit into him, and pain exploded. His vision went dark, his mind blanked out, and only his clenched muscles kept the Heart in his hand. Breath came in ragged gasps as he struggled to keep his eyes on Sted, yet he couldn't do anything, couldn't even raise his sword to block as Sted slowly, languidly, tossed him aside.

Josef landed on his stomach, the air crushed out his lungs, the Heart of War landing with a deep, resounding gong beside him.

For a moment, Josef just lay there, not breathing, not moving, not knowing if he was dead or alive. Then air thundered back into his lungs, and reflex took over. He pressed his hand to his bleeding side, trying to stop his lifeblood from washing out onto the floor. He steadied his breaths and looked for his sword. It was right beside him, inches from his fingers. He forced himself to reach out. The Heart could get him through almost anything. All he had to do was touch it.

But when his fingers were a hair's breadth away from the Heart's hilt, an enormous boot came down on his wrist, crushing his hand and pinning it to the ground.

Sted looked down at him, his scarred face disappointed. "Just a man with a sword," he spat. "And to think the Heart of War chose someone like you." He knelt down and grabbed Josef by the hair, lifting his head up to whisper in his ear. "This next blow is for your sword. An act of mercy. I'm going to set it free from such an unworthy master. Who knows"—he grinned against Josef's skin—"maybe it will choose me."

"The Heart wouldn't have anything to do with you," Josef growled, spitting the words.

Sted dropped him back onto the floor. "How would you know?" he said, turning Josef over with his foot so that he was lying on his back. "You aren't even strong enough to protect a little girl."

And with that, he brought his jagged sword down on Josef's stomach. Josef cried out in pain, a hitching, sobbing sound. Sted just held him down with his boot, pushing the sword in deeper. When Josef stopped struggling, Sted pulled his blade out and slung it in an arc, flinging Josef's blood across the room.

He picked up his cast-off coat and wiped his blade clean. Then he turned and started toward Nico, the clomp of his boots the only noise in the warehouse. He walked with his sword out, the curved blade awake and glowing hungry red. Yet, for all that he was her death walking to meet her, the girl wasn't looking at him. Her eyes were focused on the swordsman's body.

Subtly, almost imperceptibly, her hand twitched. Her head moved very slightly off the ground before being slammed down again. Her leg kicked a fraction, like a child's in the womb. Sted saw this, and walked a little faster.

"I'm impressed you can move under the weight of the command," he said. "I'm told that takes a tremendous amount of will. You must have been a very strong wizard before the demon took you."

Nico didn't even look at him as he spoke, but her hand edged forward, her short nails digging into the wooden floor.

"You'll only hurt yourself if you keep trying," Sted warned. He was a dozen feet from her now. "I'm no wizard, but the order you're under has nothing to do with spirit talking. It's a tool given to League members by the Lord of Storms himself, a sharing of his gift from the Shepherdess, or some such. I'm told it commands the spirit world's inborn hatred of demons to create a crushing weight. Supposedly, with practice, a skilled League member can control its strength, make it less painful on the victim." He stopped just short of her outstretched hand, grinning wide. "I never saw much point in that."

He nudged her with his boot, turning her over, and held his sword above her exposed throat, just above her silver collar, which, for once, lay perfectly still against her skin. "Time to go to work," he said, sighing. "May whatever is left of your human soul find peace with your precious swordsman in the next life."

He swung his sword up in a whistling arc, and then brought it down. A great cloud of dust and debris went up as the jagged blade crashed through the girl and into the floor, obliterating everything. The deed done, Sted straightened up, swinging his sword back to inspect the damage. But as the dust began to clear, his confident smile faded. He could see the black outline of the girl's body, clearly crushed by his sword, and yet there was no smell of fresh blood. He waved his arms frantically to clear the last of the dust, and his teeth clenched in a snarl. There, in the crater his sword had made, flat and empty as a shed skin, was the girl's coat.

He whirled around just in time to see the girl, surprisingly thin and bony in her torn shirt and threadbare trousers, clutch the swordman's body before vanishing again into the shadows.

Sted snatched the shed coat with the point of his sword and tossed it away. "What are you?" he bellowed. "A damned cicada? Come out and fight!"

Silence was his answer.

On the other side of the warehouse, behind a stack of crates she'd scouted out yesterday as a potentially useful hiding place, Nico gently set Josef's body on the floor. At some point after Sted's final blow, his hands had managed to grip the Heart, which was the only way she'd been able to move it. The black sword followed no hand but Josef's.

Quiet as a shadow, Nico pulled a length of dyed silk out of the crate beside her and wrapped Josef's wounds as best she could. She worked quickly, tugging the bandage with shaking hands. Even though he was spirit deaf, Sted was a League hunter. Without her coat, it was only a matter of minutes before he found her.

She looped the crooked bandage over Josef's chest one last time and tied it tight. The blood was already seeping through, but it would have to do. She was out of time.

Nico ran her hand over Josef's face, feeling his dim, ragged breath on her fingers. "Keep breathing," she whispered. "This time, I'll save you."

With that, she vanished, skipping through the shadows to the far end of the warehouse. She reappeared behind the pile of splintered wood Josef had crashed into earlier. Sted's back was to her. He was standing near where she'd hidden Josef, studying the crates. Soundlessly, Nico reached up to the line of dusty tools hanging from the rack above her and took down a heavy iron hammer. It woke instantly at her touch, and she could feel it getting ready to scream.

"Don't." The command was a whisper, but it was more than enough. The hammer froze in place, terrified, and Nico lifted it to her mouth, her lips moving against the cold, trembling metal. "Strike him quietly and true," she whispered, "or I'll eat you whole."

She felt guilty as she spoke, and the image of Eli's serious face as he held her sleeve flashed through her mind. Nico crushed the feeling. The thief had had it easy. He didn't understand that survival meant doing what had to be done. Anyway, beating Sted and saving Josef meant far more to her than a stupid hammer. Decision made, she drew back her arm and, taking careful aim, threw the hammer as hard as she could. It flew unnaturally straight, balancing itself as it spun, and landed right at the base of Sted's skull.

The swordsman stumbled and roared, whirling around to face his attacker. This time, Nico didn't blink away. She stood her ground, staring Sted straight in the face as he raised his arm to throw the immobilization on her again.

"You said you wanted a fight," she growled, dropping into a crouch.

Sted's arm fell. "I don't like to fight girls," he said with a sneer. "But for that"—he kicked the fallen hammer—"I'll make an exception. I only hope you're more of a challenge than your guard, demon."

Nico's answer was to flit behind him and slam her fist into his back, right below his liver. Josef had already learned Sted was uncuttable, but every human had the same organs. Still, punching Sted was like punching a rock, and about as effective. The League man didn't even grunt. Instead, he spun with his blade, forcing Nico to skip away through the shadows or get sliced in half. She emerged panting on the other side of the room, shaking her hand to get the feeling back. Sted turned slowly to face her, looking cockier than ever.

Nico clenched her fists, pressing her buzzing manacles against her skin. Without her coat she could feel the spirits all around her, easy prey, easy power. She could feel the demon inside her waking, scenting food. The spirits were beginning to wake as well, to notice what she was, and she could feel the panic growing. She couldn't fight like this much longer, and from the look on his face, Sted knew it.

"Jump while you can," he said, walking toward her with terrible, slow steps. "Every power you use gives me more allies. Soon, you won't even have a place to stand."

As if to prove him right, the boards beneath her feet began to groan, working up the courage to snap and trap her. Nico leaped before they got the chance, blinking through the dark to the air above Sted's head. Sted just laughed and raised his sword to block.

At that moment, deep inside Nico, in the places she never went, something woke, and the wailing demon panic exploded all around her.

CHAPTER 19

The outside of the duke's citadel was utter chaos when Eli, Miranda, and the elder Monpress finally emerged from the tunnels below. Soldiers were running everywhere, carrying rope and spears, far too busy to notice three people in the shadows as they rushed to get to the square. Squinting into the dark, Miranda could see why. Even from this angle, she could see the cobblestones moving like waves, chasing something she couldn't see. There were clouds overhead as well, winds ripping across the sky, forming a tiny tornado right in front of the citadel. From the top battlements, she could hear the duke shouting orders, his voice carried far and wide by the spinning wind. He was shouting for them to catch something.

"Ah," Monpress said, locking the door again behind them. "Splendid."

"Splendid?" Miranda said, looking in horror as a sheet of roofing tiles flew off a nearby house at whatever was circling in the front courtyard. "This is utter madness."

"Chaos is the thief's best friend," Eli said with a shrug. "Where's our ride?"

"Busy, from the looks of it," Monpress said, pointing at the courtyard.

"Ride?" Miranda said. "Do you mean—"

She cut off midsentence as Gin appeared around the corner, followed by a hail of clay roofing tiles. He was running full tilt. They barely had time to jump out of the way before he barreled past. He gave Miranda a wink as he flashed by, and she saw at once what he was planning.

"Get in a line against the wall," she said, jerking Eli's chain and pushing Monpress with her other hand. "Be ready to jump on when I say so."

"Jump on?" Eli said. "You mean throw ourselves at the dog when he comes around again?"

"Pretty much," Miranda said, hiking up her skirt and tucking it under her belt so it wouldn't get tangled. "Get ready, here he comes."

They all whirled to look at Gin. He was still running full tilt away from them with the stones right on his tail. But just as he was about to hit the tall bank that separated the castle grounds from the river, he dropped to a crouch and skidded to a stop. The stones, not made for high-velocity anything, sailed straight over him, landing with a splash in the river beyond. The moment they were over his head, Gin was back on his feet racing toward Miranda. She held out her hands, motioning for Eli and Monpress to do the same. The ghosthound ran low, and as he passed they grabbed on to the thick fur of his back. Gin's momentum took them off their feet, and suddenly they were flying along with him down a side alley while the wind howled overhead.

"Letting yourself play decoy," Miranda said, digging her fingers in a little harder than was necessary as she climbed into position on his back. "That was a foolish thing to do, dog."

"Well, hello to you too," Gin panted. "Ask the old man if we're still going for the wall."

Miranda glared at him, but turned and relayed the question to the elder Monpress, who was helping Eli get into place.

"So far as I know," he said. "I haven't heard anything from Josef or Nico."

"You probably won't," Eli said, grabbing Gin's fur with both hands as the dog raced through the night. "Even if he sent a message, we'd never get anything through all this mess. I can barely hear myself think with the town like this."

He was right, Miranda thought with a grimace. The whole town seemed to be shouting all at once. And not just spirits, but guards and alarm whistles too. Gin had his ears back as he ran, taking a crazy path through the back alleys as he ran north and a little west, toward the wall.

"Wait," Miranda shouted. "We're escaping? What about my rings? I can't leave without my rings!"

"We can't go back for them now," Eli shouted over the din. "Not unless you want to fight the entire town."

"The duke took your rings?" Gin panted, alarmed.

"No, I think Hern did," Miranda answered. "We have to go back."

"Well, look at it this way," Eli said. "Now that you're out, those rings are the only power this Hern fellow has over you. He's certainly not going to risk them on something trivial."

"Oh, that's comforting," Miranda said, bending low on Gin's back. But the thief had a point. They couldn't turn around, not without getting killed. She didn't like it, but for now she'd get out, maybe try and make contact with the West Wind, get some backup. Maybe she could get word to Banage. Even if it came from an exile, the Spirit Court couldn't ignore something like this, and then the duke would *really* have something to worry about. Of course, she thought as she ducked under a shop sign that was swinging wildly at her head, they'd have to get out first.

Gin hopped over a low shed, and suddenly they were at the wall, still stretched to an impossible height and bristling with spikes. They ran along it, looking for some sign of Josef and Nico, a bashed-in bit of wall, some knocked-out guards, anything, but there was nothing. Gin slowed, panting, and sniffed the air.

"No good," he growled. "Neither the swordsman nor the girl has been anywhere near this place for hours."

"They've got to be somewhere," Eli said, looking around frantically. "It's not like Josef to be late for anything."

"Well, something must have happened," Gin snapped back, "because he's not here, and we shouldn't be much longer. This city's on the verge of tearing itself apart trying to do that man's bidding. I'd hate to see what it'd do to us."

"Wait," Miranda said suddenly, her eyes bright. "Hold on, you just gave me an idea." She stood up on the dog's back, looking out over the dark city. The streets glowed, some with lampposts, some with torch light from the pursuing guards, but in the distance, the river glittered dark and slow, strangely peaceful in the light of the half moon.

"Gin," she said, "we're going back to our first plan."

"What?" he said, then he paused. "Oh, I get you."

Miranda nodded. "Take us to the river."

"The river?" Eli cried as Gin launched himself back the way they had come. "Are you mad? The river's at the center of the mess we're trying to get out of!"

"You want to solve a problem," Miranda said, "you start at the top. Now be quiet." She jerked the chain holding them together. "Prisoners shouldn't talk this much."

The elder Monpress laughed at that and tipped his head to Miranda, who smiled back. Eli, seeing he was getting nowhere with these people, folded his arms over his chest and focused on not falling off as Gin wove a crazy path down to the river.

The Duke of Gaol stood on his battlements, shouting orders to his spirits as the lampposts signaled the ghosthound's position. They had reached the wall already, but were turning back, probably realizing they were trapped.

Good, he thought. Let them scramble. He had other problems at the moment, starting with the one standing directly beside him.

"For the last time, Hern," Edward said, "go back to your tower."

Beside him, Hern went pale with anger, gripping the battlements with clenched fingers. "I will not," he said. "You promised me, Edward! You promised to keep that girl locked up, and then you go and throw her together with Monpress? What were you thinking?"

"If anyone should be angry, it's me." He glared at the Spiritualist. "Helping you almost cost me my thief. If I hadn't taken precautions by keeping the city secure on multiple levels, both of our quarries would have flown by now. So save your bluster for your Court and kindly get out of my way. In case you haven't noticed, I have other problems besides Monpress slipping his leash."

As if on cue, a wind rose up from the south, and he turned to meet it.

"Othril," he said when he felt the wind on his face. "Report."

"The south docks are in a full demon panic," the wind said quickly. "Big one, too, though not as flashy as the treasury. I put up a quarantine as you ordered. Not even a cockroach is going to cross the boundary without your say-so. That should contain the panic somewhat, but you know we can't keep a lid on these things for long."

"We won't need to," Edward said. "This is a ploy by Monpress, a distraction for his escape. Now that he's out, it should be calming down."

Hern shook his head. "What kind of reckless idiot uses a demon panic to cover his escape?"

"When you hunt Monpress, you must be prepared for everything," Edward said. "Othril, follow Monpress and the Spiritualist girl. Now that they've realized the wall is trapped, they might try the river."

"That would be good for us," the wind said. "Fellbro's water will catch them like flies in honey."

"With Monpress you can only corral, never anticipate," Edward said. "Watch him and report to me at once if they change direction."

"And check for the girl as well," Hern added. "She must be contained."

Othril stopped midgust, and Hern felt the strange, itchy sensation of a powerful wind spirit staring at him. Edward, however, waved the wind away, and it blew into the night.

"Hern," Edward said when the wind was gone. "Never presume to give orders to my spirits again."

"Well," Hern said, shifting his hands so that his rings glittered menacingly, "you hadn't mentioned it, and I wanted to be sure you did not forget what you owed me, Edward."

The duke spun around and grabbed Hern's hands before the Spiritualist could move, squeezing his fingers until the gemstones dug painfully into Hern's flesh.

"You forget yourself," the duke whispered, his voice low and dangerous. "Never forget where you are. You might have sway in Zarin, but *I rule Gaol.* So long as you are on my lands, you obey *me.*"

Hern was gasping in pain, his rings flashing under the duke's hands, but the duke's spirit was like a vise across them, and they could not leave. He held the Spiritualist like that until Hern nodded, falling to his knees. Only then did Edward release his grip.

"Do not make me remind you again," he said quietly, turning back to the battlements.

Hern retreated, grumbling empty threats under his breath as he slunk back to the far wall with as much dignity as he could muster. Edward ignored him. Hern's lot was firmly entrenched in Gaol. He could alert the Spirit Court to Gaol's activities, but it would mean the end of his own career as well, and Hern was far too selfish for that. That settled, Edward dismissed the Spiritualist from his mind, focusing instead on the blinking lamps that marked the ghosthound's position as it ran a winding path through the back alleys of his city and toward the black line of the river.

Gin burst out of the cover of the narrow alley and onto the dock and turned sharply, leaving the pursuing hail of roofing tiles and weather vanes and other trash to soar out past him, straight into the river. Panting, Gin slowed down a fraction, bringing them right up beside the water, which flowed dark and murky in the flashing lamplight.

"We're here," the dog growled. "Now what?"

"Now we do what I should have done this morning," Miranda said, getting into a crouch on his back. "Put control of the city back where it belongs, with the Great Spirit." She glanced skeptically at the river as they ran along with it. It didn't look like an enraged spirit, but maybe the duke had some kind of binding on it. Well, she thought, reaching back to tie her hair tight, she'd know in a second.

"I'll meet you on the other side," she said, scratching Gin's head. "Don't get caught."

"Never do," Gin snorted.

"Wait," Eli said, tugging on the chain that connected them. "Before you do anything rash, aren't you forgetting something?"

"Not that I can recall," Miranda said, turning toward the river. She gave Eli one last smile. "Hold your breath."

And then she jumped, taking Eli with her. For a moment they soared through the air, Miranda tucking gracefully, Eli flailing to keep his head upright, and then they landed with an enormous splash in the dark water. The moment they hit, Mellinor was there, surrounding them in a clear, bubbling flow, forming a protective pocket of air around them as they sank down into the muddy river. It was deeper than Miranda had expected, going down a dozen feet between the docks. All light from above vanished after the first foot, leaving only Mellinor's own watery glow to light their way as they sank deeper, coming to rest on the black silt at the bottom.

Miranda stood inside the bubble Mellinor had made. Eli followed more slowly, shaking the water out of his hair.

"Why is it every time we get together, I get drenched?"

Miranda ignored him. They had limited time before their air

ran out, and considering the duke certainly knew where they were, she didn't think things would end well if they had to surface. It was now or never, so she put Monpress out of her mind and, standing very still, opened her spirit.

It was like stepping into another world. She could feel the enormity of the river's spirit flowing around her, dark and slow and inexorable. Yet even as she marveled at the size of it, she could feel that something was wrong. The flow of the water felt pinched, hobbled, almost like it was being squeezed through something, yet there was nothing there. Stranger still, and more alarming, was the water's silence. Though she could feel the power of the river, she heard nothing, no threats, no demands for her to state her identity or purpose, nothing but the quiet sound of the water as it crept by.

"Mellinor," Miranda whispered. "What's wrong with it?"

"I'm not sure," the glowing water answered. "There's no Enslavement, but what kind of river doesn't respond to a wizard with a blazing open spirit standing at its heart?"

"Maybe it's shy?" Eli offered.

"Or maybe it's under a binding we can't feel." Miranda stepped forward until she was at the very edge of Mellinor's bubble. She hated doing this. Not only did it feel like a vaguely abusive display, it was unspeakably rude. Still, they were on a strict timetable, and the river certainly wasn't going to cooperate on its own.

"River Fellbro!" she cried, pouring the weight of her spirit into the words until they buzzed with power. The water around them hitched as her voice struck it, and for a moment, the river was still. Then, as though nothing had happened, the water began flowing again, darker and murkier than ever. Miranda, panting from the power she'd put into her call, looked around in confusion. She'd thought for sure even a Great Spirit wouldn't ignore something like that.

She was gathering herself for another try when Eli's hand brushed her shoulder. She looked at him, startled and scowling, but he just pointed at a spot in the water behind where she was standing. There, in the clouds of swirling silt, was a face. It was large, about as wide as Miranda was tall. Its features were murky, shifting in and out as the water flowed, and it did not look pleased.

The dark, silted eyes roved over them as a muddy, brown mouth opened. "Go away."

Its voice was like a wet slap against their ears, but Miranda reached out with her spirit, catching the river as it tried to fade. "We will not," she said firmly. "Great Spirit Fellbro, I come before you as a representative for all the spirits of Gaol currently under the thumb of Edward di Fellbro, Duke of Gaol. It is the Great Spirit's duty to protect those in its charge, yet your spirits live in fear and slavish obedience because their Great Spirit will not stand up for them. I feel no Enslavement on you, no madness. Why, then, do you ignore your duty?"

The silted face glowered and turned away. "How easy it is for you to talk," it grumbled, "coming here at the end of things. We're the ones who have to live with the duke day in and day out." The river looked at her, and Miranda shuddered as the weight of years pressed against her through his gaze. "There are worse things than being Enslaved."

"I don't think you know what that means," Mellinor growled, his water flashing brilliant blue. But Miranda raised her hand.

"What kind of threat could the duke use," she said softly, "to make you abandon your duty?"

"All kinds," the river said. "He is a powerful man with all of humanity's destructive nature at his aid. He's threatened to dam me up, pollute my water, reroute my flow to another river, the worst kind of things you can think of. With all that, Enslavement seems kind of superfluous, don't you think?"

"So you abandoned your spirits?" Mellinor roared. "All to save yourself?"

"Not forever!" the river roared back. "Judge all you want, but you never lived with the duke. We have to, and we suffer every day for it. Our only consolation is that, awful as he is, the duke is only human. He'll die sooner or later, and then we'll be free. But for now, we do as he says, all of us, even me, because no humiliation, no suffering he puts us through is worse than what he would do to us if we disobeyed."

Miranda opened her mouth to answer, and so did Eli, but it was Mellinor who spoke first, his water almost boiling with rage.

"You rivers," he sneered. "Always flowing downhill, always taking the easy way out. You let him walk all over you just because he won't live forever?"

"Don't talk so mighty, lost sea," the river rumbled, sending ripples through their bubble. "What right do you have to judge us? It's not like you're so pure. I know you, Mellinor. We've all heard of your failure, the sea defeated by a wizard. Rage all you want, but I had no mind to follow your path into madness. A few years of shame is nothing compared to hundreds trapped under a dead wizard's thumb. I just did what you should have done, and I have kept my lands."

"Then your lands are poorer for it," Mellinor rumbled, his water spinning faster and faster, "saddled with such a coward!"

"Live a year in Gaol and you'd understand!" Fellbro shouted. "I only did what I needed to survive!"

"Mellinor!" Miranda said sharply. "Enough! This isn't—"

A great tide of power cut her off. Mellinor's spirit welled up inside her, choking her breath, pushing his way free. He poured out of her, pushing the black water of the river back in a great, shining wave. Through it all, Miranda could only stand there, the conduit of his power, until, all at once, he was gone. The emptiness hit her like an avalanche, and she toppled over. Eli caught her just before she hit the mud, pushing her back onto her knees. But even like that, Miranda could barely keep her balance. She clung to his wet shirt, staring up at the great white wave above them as it invaded the river.

"What is he doing?" she said, her voice trembling. "Why didn't he listen? We're supposed to be *helping* the river."

Eli gave her face a little slap, startling her back into the present. "He's being a Great Spirit," he said, nodding up at the glowing water. "I warned you about this, back in Mellinor, but you were the one who wanted to be his vessel, as I recall. You can't complain now when he acts according to his nature."

"He's going to ruin everything," Miranda groaned, staring helplessly as Mellinor's white water invaded the dark river. "We need the river on our side. This isn't the time for fighting!"

"I think Mellinor knows a lot more about being a Great Spirit than either of us," Eli said softly. "Trust him."

Miranda gave him a sideways look. "Must you be so smug about everything?" she grumbled. "I should have left you up top."

"I told you to," Eli said. He pointed up with a grin. "Now things are getting going; watch."

Miranda looked up. Mellinor's blue water was invading the dark river in every direction. She could feel Fellbro's fear as it fought the sea for control of its water, but Mellinor's rage was ironclad, and he did not fall back.

"Mellinor!" The river's roar had a pleading edge to it. "Don't do this!"

"You have betrayed your station, Fellbro." The blue water foamed and flashed.

"You have no right!" the river shrieked, its murky waters racing away. "This is my land! Mine! I will run it as I see fit!"

But Mellinor's water pressed on without mercy or hesitation, and when he spoke, his voice echoed from all directions. "You relinquished your right to rule the moment you gave your powers away to save your own water. You have acted in a way unbecoming of a Great Spirit, and you know the price for that, same as the rest of us. Therefore, as Great Spirit of the Inland Sea, I, Mellinor, claim your rights as restitution on behalf of your spirits." The river trembled and fought, but Mellinor's wave ate everything as his final decree rang out. "Your water is now mine."

With that, the river's face shattered, and the entire river flashed the color of sea foam. The wave of power took Miranda and Eli off their feet, tumbling them along the river bottom as the bubble collapsed. But before they could come to harm, the water caught them gently. It carried them in a swell up from the depths, and they broke the river's surface with a gasp, sucking clean, fresh air into their lungs.

All around them, the river had changed. What had been a dark, stagnant flow now glittered a deep, deep blue. The water glistened with its own blue light, and she could feel the familiar weight of Mellinor's spirit all through it, comforting and a little apologetic.

"I am sorry," the water whispered. "I know you wanted a peaceable solution, but we spirits have our own laws that must be upheld."

"No," Miranda said, shaking her head. "Being a Spiritualist means understanding and respecting my spirits' natures. But"—she slapped the water, sending a splash up in the air—"I *wish* you'd *told* me what you were going to do *before you did it.*"

She felt a wave of power that was distinctly like a shrug. "I didn't know I needed to until I was doing it."

"I see," Miranda said. "Well, at least no one can argue that I Enslaved you now. Not after that display."

"Only idiots argued it in the first place," Mellinor said. "But"—she felt a motion that could only be the spirit equivalent of a grin—"you'll like this next part."

Miranda sank into the water, suddenly alarmed. "What do you mean?"

"He means he's the Great Spirit of Gaol now," Eli said beside her. "And everyone knows it."

Miranda looked at him, confused, and he nodded toward the shore. She followed his gaze, and her eyes widened. The city, which had been a knot of controlled chaos, was perfectly still. The lamps were all burning steady, not flashing, and the dark clouds were frozen in the night sky. On the bank across from them, Miranda saw the army of conscripts standing with their torches. The archers drew their bows when they saw the two floating in the water, but even as they notched their arrows, Mellinor gave a warning rumble, and the bows went limp. The soldiers scrambled, but the bows had lost their tension and refused to draw.

"Was that you?" Miranda said in awe.

"Partially." Mellinor sounded extremely pleased with himself. "Most of it is the spirits." He laughed. "Let's just say they didn't particularly like being under the good duke's thumb, and now that I'm here to back them up, they're not feeling particularly charitable toward his forces."

As if to prove him right, at that moment every sword of the enemy army cut through its sheath and clattered to the ground, some of them going straight through the feet of their previous owners. A great cry of fear and surprise went up, and, sensing the chaos, the torches they carried chose that moment to erupt in great geysers of flame. Suddenly, fire was everywhere, and the army broke into a mob. Men in flames screamed and dove into the river, which pulled back at the last moment to let them land in the mud. Others ran away, disappearing down the alleys and leaving the wounded gripping their bleeding feet.

"That's what I call a complete rout," Eli said cheerily. "Though I can't say I've ever seen an army defeated by its own swords before."

Miranda grinned. "Come on," she said, turning to swim for the far shore. "Let's get your swordsman and my dog and we'll finish the duke before he does something drastic."

"Sounds marvelous," Eli said, swimming beside her. "See, we can agree on occasion."

"Don't push it," Miranda said, giving him a sideways look. "Swim faster; you're dragging me down."

"Yes, mistress," Eli quipped, earning himself a baleful glare, which he ignored completely, swimming in long, easy strokes toward the shore.

High overhead, Othril watched the battle of the Great Spirits with a growing sense of terror. This was bad, very bad. He needed to warn the duke before things got completely out of hand. He spun around to start toward the Duke's citadel, but as he turned, something inside him hitched, and he froze motionless in the air. For a moment, panic completely overwhelmed his mind. Had a wizard caught him? Was the duke angry? Then he felt a familiar cold breeze, and he realized what was wrong. He was blowing west.

"Othril."

The voice blew through him, cold and salty and enormous as the western sea. Frozen in place, he could only tremble as he answered.

"All hail the West Wind."

A laugh gusted past, and he felt other winds slide up beside him. Strong, powerful winds, and all blowing from the west.

"Othril," the great voice of the West Wind chuckled. "Did you honestly think that allying yourself with a wizard who coerces Great Spirits would end well?"

"How are you even here?" Othril said with as much authority as he could muster. "Fellbro told you to get out! I don't care how strong you think you are, you can't ignore a direct dismissal. Winds are forbidden by the Shepherdess from interfering in the affairs of other Great Spirits within their own domains!"

"But Fellbro isn't the Great Spirit anymore," the wind said. "You were riding high as the duke's right hand, weren't you? Far more power than a spirit of your level would ever gain in the usual course. I can see how you were tempted, but your days of playing spy and weather-maker for the the duke are over."

Othril began to dispute that, but clawed hands, airy but sharp and cold as iced iron, interrupted him, digging into the core of his spirit.

Panic sent him rigid. Being caught is the greatest fear of all winds, and Othril was no exception. It was how the duke had convinced him to serve in the first place.

A laughing breeze blew over him, but the words it whispered in his ear were as cold as the claws that held him. "It's time to remember your true loyalty, little wind."

Othril struggled one last time, and then he was gone, tumbling off to the west. The other winds watched until his spirit winked out of sight. Then, without a word, they spun up high into the cloud layer and began to carry out their lord's commands.

Slowly, the sky grew dark and heavy with clouds. And then, in long sullen sheets, a night rain began to fall on Gaol for the first time in twenty years.

CHAPTER 20

Duke Edward stood at the top of his citadel. The soft rain fell on him, trickling down his clenched jaw and trembling fists. He was staring at the river, its water shining silver in the night, and the last of his routed soldiers beside it. Behind him, his officers stood uncertainly, waiting for orders, but no orders came. The duke just stood there, staring at the river, growing paler and paler as his rage set in.

It was Hern who dared to speak first, stepping up to stand beside the duke.

"Edward," he said, very softly. "That water spirit is Miranda's. We still have her rings. That's all the leverage we need on a girl like her. We still have control."

"Control?" The duke's voice was low and sharp. "What do you know about control?" His hand shot out, grabbing Hern's collar with alarming strength, dragging the Spiritualist until they were an inch apart.

"I have devoted my entire life to shaping Gaol," he whispered. "Every moment, from the first moment I heard a spirit's voice, I knew that this was my purpose, to turn this ragged hash of spirits into a land of order, discipline, and prosperity. I did not work all those years to lose it now."

"Edward!" Hern gasped against his grip. "I know what you're thinking, but be reasonable. Sometimes controlled retreat is a victory. We still have—"

"There will be no retreat!" the duke roared, tossing Hern to the ground. "I rule Gaol! It is not a matter of that girl controlling the river, but of my spirits disobeying me!" As he spoke, his spirit surged through the words until Hern could barely hear them over its roar. "I rule here," the duke said, turning back toward the river, "and disobedience will not be tolerated."

"Edward!" Hern shouted, but it was too late. A massive wave of Enslavement rolled out of the duke. It hit Hern full force, and he toppled over, dragged down by his rings. The Enslavement surged up the connection he shared with his spirits until he was writhing on the ground. But even as the overwhelming pressure threatened to crack his mind, he reached up and began to pluck his rings one by one from his fingers. With each ring removed, the pressure grew less. He kept taking off rings until he could stand again, and then, using a leather pouch to grab them so the terrified spirits did not touch his skin and reopen the connection, Hern gathered his spirits and fled.

Edward had gone too far. Hern shook his head, making his way quickly down the shaking stairs. He wouldn't help the duke Enslave his country. He was a Spiritualist still, and there were limits to what even he would do. Besides, if word ever got back to Zarin that he'd been involved in this in any way, no amount of politics could save him. So, with that, Hern vanished into the night, running for his tower as the city began to go mad around him.

Miranda pulled herself out of the river, grinning from ear to ear as she bent over to help extract Eli from the glowing water. Gin was waiting for them on the dock, looking as pleased as she was, which didn't seem to be making the elder Monpress more comfortable. Gin's toothy smiles were difficult to appreciate unless you knew him.

"I never thought that would work half as well as it did," he said, lowering his head to help Miranda climb onto the dock. "The city literally leaped at the chance to look for a new master."

"Anything would be better than the old one," Miranda said, pulling herself up by the tough fur on his ruff. "Actually, I don't see how things could have gone better, the duke's control broken, Eli on a chain; all I need now is for Hern to come begging for mercy and I think I'll have just about everything I could want in the world."

"As pleased as I am to be included in such happiness," Eli said, climbing up onto the dock behind her, "I would like to remind you—"

But he never got to finish. At that moment, an ear-splitting howl drowned out all other sound. Miranda, Gin, and Eli all shielded their ears, and even the elder Monpress looked up, startled. The cry went on and on, shaking and changing pitch, like it was being passed from one voice to another, full of terror and wailing and crushing despair.

"Is that Nico?" Miranda shouted. It was certainly desperate enough to be demon panic.

"Nico's panics don't sound like this," Eli shouted back. With a wince, he glanced up at the city, and his face went bone pale. Startled, Miranda looked, too, but even she didn't quite recognize what she was seeing until Gin named it.

"It's an Enslavement," he whimpered. "I've never seen one so large."

Miranda straightened up, forcing herself to ignore the horrible noise and look. Across the river, the city was twisting like a trapped animal. Buildings writhed and screamed, their bricks cracking from the pressure. Fires were breaking out everywhere, shooting up chimneys as their spirits fought the wizard's will. But it was too strong. Even as she watched, the city began to settle down, the buildings crouching low like beaten animals, trembling. Yet for all the flash, Mellinor's captured river seemed unaffected by the crushing force. So did Gin, who was on his feet, teeth bared.

"It's the duke," Eli said beside her, answering her question before she spoke it. "His Enslavement is only for his spirits. He's taking his city back."

"Oh no he's not!" Miranda said, grabbing hold of Gin's fur and pulling herself up. But as she settled on Gin's back, she jerked violently. Her eyes widened, and she doubled over as if she'd been punched in the stomach.

Eli, one arm pulled up beside her anyway from the chain linking them together, caught her as she wobbled. "What's wrong?"

"It's my rings," Miranda whispered, her voice shaking and terrified. "They're gone."

Eli frowned. "I thought that was already established."

"No," Miranda snapped. "I mean they're *gone*. Before they were there, but far away, but just now..." She shrugged helplessly. "It's like a door closed. I can't feel anything."

"Miranda," Gin growled, "calm down. It's way too early for them to flicker out. Get a hold of yourself before you panic Mellinor."

Miranda blanched and glanced over at the river. Sure enough, the water was washing toward her. She waved it away frantically and sat up straight, wiping her eyes with her hands.

"You're right," she said quietly. "But why can't I feel them?"

"Well," Eli said, "who did you say had them?"

"Hern," Miranda said. "He's another Spiritualist. A nasty one."

"Sounds like most Spiritualists," Eli said, nodding sagely. "Present company excluded, of course."

Miranda didn't even bother with the nasty look for that one. Instead, she sat, brow furrowed in furious thought, until all at once she groaned.

"I know what happened," she said, turning to Gin. "Hern sealed himself in his tower. He's too much of a coward to try stopping the duke's Enslavement, so he's separated himself to wait it out. I bet my rings are in there, too, and whatever he's using for a seal is blocking my connection as well."

"Then we have a problem," Gin said. "So long as there's some connection, the spirits can hold out by staying deeply asleep. But if the connection is gone entirely, they'll die within the hour."

"I know, I know," Miranda said frantically. "But I can't just ignore the Enslavement of an entire town!"

"Might I suggest something?" Eli interrupted.

Spiritualist and ghosthound turned to glare at him, but Eli's cool smile didn't falter. "You need to get your rings back before they expire, right? That's part of your oath, isn't it? Protection?"

"Of course it is," Miranda growled.

"But at the same time, you, as a Spiritualist, need to stop this

Enslavement before the entire town is driven mad, or else you violate your oath to protect the Spirit World."

Gin snapped his teeth together. "Get to the point, thief."

"The point should be clear," Eli said. "Even you can't be two places at once, so why don't we split our efforts? You go rescue your rings and I'll take care of the duke."

"Do you think I'm stupid?" Miranda scoffed. "What's to say you won't just turn tail and run? Isn't 'get while the getting is good' one of your rules of thievery?"

"It is," Eli said. "Though not quite in those words. But consider this, dear Miranda"—he rolled up his sleeve—"you're not the only one out for payback tonight."

Miranda gasped. Eli's arms were covered in horrible bruises. Most were red and angry; others were starting to turn a deep purple. She stared at them in disbelief. How had the thief kept up with her? She wouldn't have been able to move with bruises like that, but the whole time that she'd been dragging him along, Eli had given no sign he was injured. Now she felt almost guilty for being so rough with him.

"Anyway," Eli said, letting his sleeve drop again, "it's not just vengeance for me." He glared at the town, which was now almost totally still in submission. "I have no love for bullies and Enslavers."

Miranda believed him on that. From what she'd seen of his tactics, spirit goodwill played an enormous part. He must have been going crazy not being able to talk to the spirits in Gaol. Eli might be a scoundrel and an embarrassment to the dignity of wizardry, but when it came to protecting the well-being of spirits, they were almost always on the same page.

Of course, once she let him go she might never get him back, but at this point surrendering Eli was a small price to pay for not having to choose between the town and her spirits.

"Are you sure you can do it?" she asked, looking him straight in the eye.

"Nearly positive," Eli said. "You already broke Gaol free once. How hard can it be to do it again?"

"Right," Miranda sighed. She was suddenly feeling less confident. "I guess we'll have to break this chain."

"That won't be necessary," Eli said. He held up his wrist and did a quick flipping motion that made her own hands ache to see, and the iron manacle slid neatly off his hand.

"There," Eli said, rubbing his reddened wrist.

Miranda stared at him, deflated. "You could have done that at any time, couldn't you?"

"Of course," Eli said. "But no other escape would have been nearly as enjoyable as seeing your face just now."

Miranda put her head in her hands. "Just go do your part," she said. "I'll be there as soon as I get my rings back. If you can't take the duke, just stall him or something until I arrive."

"As you command," Eli said and bowed.

Miranda gave him one last dirty look. Then, shaking her head, she tapped Gin's sides with her heels. The ghosthound sprung forward, and then they were flying down the dark docks beside the glowing river.

"Think he'll keep his word?" Gin growled.

"I have no idea," Miranda said. "But we've already made our choice; no time for second-guesses."

"Never is," Gin said.

She ducked low on Gin's back as Mellinor parted his waters to let them cross. When they reached the other side, Gin turned north between the silent, trembling buildings and headed toward the tower where, somewhere, her spirits were waiting.

Eli waved until the dog dove into the riverbed, and then sat down with a long, pained sigh to rub his poor, aching wrist.

"There was no need for disjointing," Monpress said, sitting

down beside him. "You could have just borrowed my lock pick."

"What," Eli said, "and ruin the show?"

Monpress sighed. "When will you learn there's more to life than theatrics?"

"About the same time you learn there's more to theft than money," Eli said, slapping the old man across the shoulders.

Monpress grunted at the impact. "We should be going," he said. "Will your companions be along soon?"

Eli looked sideways at him. "The Heart's going strong, and I can hear the demon panic from here, so I think Josef and Nico are a little busy. Even if they weren't, I'm not going anywhere. Weren't you listening? I have a crazed Enslaver duke to bring down."

Monpress gave him a surprised and disappointed look. "You're actually going through with it? Have you forgotten *everything* I taught you?"

"I know, 'the best revenge is a clean getaway,'" Eli said. "But this isn't about revenge, old man, not entirely. It's about principle. Not letting the tyrant win."

Monpress shook his head. "Since when are you a man of principle?"

"Since always," Eli said, getting up. "My principles were just never anything you cared about. Anyway, I didn't volunteer you to come. Isn't it about time for you to make a quiet exit?"

"Past time," Monpress said, standing as well. "But I just lost ten thousand gold standards worth of stolen art trying to save your neck. I'm not about to let you go off and ruin my investment completely."

Eli rolled his eyes. "Thanks for the fatherly concern."

Monpress nodded graciously. "So, I assume you have a plan."

"The beginnings of one," Eli said, scratching his chin. "Can you still throw a clawhook and line two stories?"

"Of course," Monpress said, insulted. "I'm old, not infirm."

"Good," Eli said, starting toward the bridge. "Then this just might work. Come on, I'll explain on the way."

Monpress shrugged and jogged after him, moving silently over the glowing river and toward the cowering city.

CHAPTER 21

Nico crouched, panting. Sted was walking toward her, panting as well, but his sword didn't waver. They'd been going around the room for what felt like hours, neither able to land a finishing blow. Nico was too fast, and Sted was, so far as she could tell, uninjurable. He didn't even defend when she leaped at him, but always went on the offensive, and the maze of long, bleeding cuts running across her body was all she had to show for her efforts.

But it wouldn't last much longer. Already she'd dipped too deep into the demon's power. The blackness was swimming over her vision, and she could feel her eyes burning, which meant they were glowing with the unnatural light. She was getting very close to the edge.

Normally she wouldn't be concerned. She'd gone over the edge and come back before, and it was worth the risk if it meant she could do what needed to be done. But this time was different. This time there was no Josef waiting to bring her back. She slid between the shadows, watching as Sted circled in the dark, racking her brain for a way to finish this quickly, when a voice whispered deep in her ear.

Why not let go?

Nico froze midstep. The words echoed in her mind, but the voice wasn't Sted's. It came from inside her ears, from the dark blotch deep behind her conscious mind.

Embrace what you really are. We could crush him like a bug in one blow, him and that rabid dog sword of his.

Nico began to breathe heavily. The voice was cold and soft and somehow nostalgic, but she couldn't actually remember hearing it before. In answer to that thought, the voice began to chuckle, and Nivel's warning came back to Nico in a cold rush of sudden understanding: Never listen to the voice. Never acknowledge it.

Nico fled the shadows and dropped to the ground behind a crate, slamming a wall down between her mind and the voice. It was happening. She was losing control, just as Nivel had said she would. But Josef was relying on her. She had to hold on, had to beat Sted. Now was not the time to go soft.

As if to prove the point, the boards on the other side of her hiding place began to creak. Sted was moving toward her, dragging his sword along the crates, methodically breaking up every hiding place. Nico crouched in the shadow, examining her options, but any way she came at it, the situation looked hopeless. She'd matched Sted strength for strength, bashed his skull hard enough to crumple it to dust, but even after her best blows, Sted was uninjured. His skin was still whole and without so much as a bruise. Nico bit her lip. He couldn't be unbeatable. No one was unbeatable, but she'd tried everything.

Everything? The voice chuckled. *You haven't begun to try. What are you doing, anyway? Dancing around in circles, trying the same things over and over, like they'll somehow come out differently this time. How stupid.*

Nico slapped her hands over her ears, but unbidden, driven by a force other than herself, her eyes flicked to Sted's shoulder and the narrow sinews bending under his impenetrable skin.

Nico closed her eyes. This was too much. She couldn't fight Sted and the voice. She cracked her eyelids, and her vision snapped back to Sted's shoulder.

The strongest are only as strong as their weakest point, the voice said, smooth as honey. *One hit and you'll have the victory even Josef couldn't manage.*

Nico frowned. For all that she knew she shouldn't listen, it was a good idea. Certainly better than her other options. Knowing she would probably regret this, but seeing no other option, she slid forward. Sted was nearly on top of her, though still clueless. For a League member, he was laughably bad at finding demons. She held her breath, waiting until the very last moment, as his hand was reaching for the lip of the crate that covered her. The moment his fingers wrapped around the splintered wood, she leaped.

She grabbed his sword arm and swung up, moving so quickly he could do nothing but watch as she landed feetfirst on his shoulder. As soon as she had her footing, Nico reached down and grabbed Sted's arm at the elbow with both hands, planting her feet on his shoulder, just like the image the voice had shown her in her mind. Pressing her feet against his straining shoulder right at the joint, she brought his arm up and back with all her strength until, with a sickening pop, she felt his shoulder snap through her boot.

Sted screamed, and there was a great crash as his sword fell to the ground from his limp hand. It was a temporary victory, however. Sted's shoulder was only dislocated, not broken. Before he could recover, she needed to do some permanent damage. So, almost before the sword had hit the ground, she swung sideways, wrapping her legs around his thick neck and, using her motion as torque, threw him sideways. Overbalanced from his huge bulk, Sted slammed to the ground. He tried to catch his fall with his uninjured arm, but Nico was too quick. She kept moving, grabbing his arm and stepping sideways so that he landed on his stomach with her on his back, her foot stamped on his remaining good shoulder and his arm bent backward in her grip.

He was trapped beneath her, unable to move without breaking his own arm. Slowly, pleasurably, Nico bent his arm back over her knee, grinning as the bones groaned under the pressure, ready to snap. But as she bent his arm toward the breaking point, something deep inside her smiled, and her fingers began to move on their own. Her nails stabbed into Sted's arm, digging into the flesh. Panic-blind and terrified, Nico tried to let go, but her limbs weren't listening. Deep in her mind, the voice began to laugh, and, a second later, her fingers broke Sted's iron skin.

Sted's power flooded into her. His thoughts, strength, memories, and experiences flashed through her mind before vanishing into the maw of the dark thing clawing its way up out of the well of her soul. The manacles on her wrists beat against her, the metal glowing white hot, searing her skin. But the pain was far away, overwhelmed by the torrent in her mind. Beneath her feet, she could feel Sted screaming, but she heard nothing. The entire world had shrunk to the power flowing into her and the creature that ate it, leaving no room for Nico at all.

Her mind was being squeezed, her consciousness trampled beneath the demonseed as it devoured Sted. She was slipping away from her own soul, and as she scrambled to stay in her skull, she could hear the demon laughing. The moment the sound touched her, fear turned to anger and, without knowing what she did or how, Nico slammed the full force of her wizard's will down on the connection holding the demon to Sted. The voice cried out in pain, the sound of it threatening to tear her skull apart, and her hand ripped free of Sted's arm, and the connection of power snapped shut.

The enormous man collapsed, and Nico flew off him, thrown by the force of her own command. She landed hard on her back, gasping for air, and in her head, she could almost hear Nivel's voice shouting at her—*never* take the demon's advice.

Never take my advice? the voice said crossly. *My advice brought us closer to victory in five minutes than the last half hour of your jumping around. You were the one who wasted our chance, all because you're too cowardly to embrace your true power.*

But Nico wasn't listening anymore. Slowly, painfully, she sat up. Sted was still on the ground, clutching his bleeding arm. He looked up when he heard her move, his eyes murderous.

"That's it, *monster*," he growled, pushing himself up. He rolled his neck, popping his dislocated shoulder back into place. "No more running. Now you die."

I can finish him for you if you get behind him now, the voice whispered. *Don't be an idiot.*

Nico clenched her fists and held her ground, watching Sted's approach with glowing eyes.

Why keep pretending you have a chance without me? the voice said softly. *Everything that makes you worthwhile, your speed, your toughness, your strength, the ability to move through shadows, it all comes from me. Do you think Josef would keep you around if I wasn't with you? The thief certainly wouldn't. He tolerates you only so long as you're useful. Face it, little girl, I am what makes your life worth living. Without me you're nothing but a stupid, weak, ugly creature. No one likes you. No one cares if you live or die, except me.*

Nico pressed her eyes closed, willing the voice away, but it went on, smooth and dark, seeping into her mind. *You think that by ignoring me you can somehow change things? Do you think you've done any of this on your own? No. I have given you everything, gifts beyond measure, power beyond your deserving. I have saved your life more times than I can count. You've been using my power from the very beginning. Why deny it now? I want to live just as much as you do, so let me help you. All you have to do is let me in, let me control you, take care of you, and you'll never have to be weak again.*

"Shut up!" Nico screamed. The words ripped out of her, and even Sted paused, taken aback.

"This is my body," Nico said. "Since I can remember, all you've done is make everything think I'm a monster. There's no place for you here. So just shut up and go away!"

The warehouse fell silent. Sted was watching her warily, looking for a trap, but Nico couldn't have attacked even if she'd been planning to. Her body was lead beneath her, frozen in place as the dark thing began to crawl back into the well of her soul.

No place, you say? The voice was haughty and cold, sliding like wire through her mind. *After everything I've given you*...It sighed in disgust. *I think it's time for you to learn, little girl, just how worthless you are without me.*

She felt a faint pressure, like a hand on her mind, and then the voice was gone. Suddenly, Nico could move again, and scarcely in time, for Sted was standing over her, his glowing sword washing everything with its blood-red light. Nico flinched and slid sideways to escape into the shadows.

Nothing happened. She blinked in confusion. Jumping through shadows was something she did as easily as breathing. She'd never really thought about how she did it, but now...it was like a door had closed. Even as this realization took root in her head, she felt something else she wasn't accustomed to feeling—pain. Crippling pain shot up her limbs, running in long, burning lines across her chest, her arms, her face as the cuts Sted had landed during their fight, cuts that had healed instantly, reopened. All at once, blood was everywhere. Her head felt heavy and dark, and even the red light of Sted's sword began to dim as her vision darkened, yet she could not escape.

The shadows were closed to her. Her body felt small and weak and beaten, and she knew without testing that her strength was gone as well, along with everything the demonseed had given her.

She had just one moment to look up and watch the shadow of Sted raise his blade before the jagged sword tore into her. Pain exploded through her body, and Nico felt herself flying, carried by the force of the blow. She landed on her back, skidding across the floor until, finally, she hit a crate and lay still. The pain was blinding, overwhelming, and it was all she could do to keep breathing in tiny wheezing gasps. The world was getting darker, colder, and further away.

She gasped, choking on her blood. But even as she desperately fought for breath, the voice spoke in her ear.

It doesn't have to end like this, it whispered, sweet and soft. *All you have to do is surrender. Give yourself over to me, and I will save you. You will have everything you lost and more. You'll never be weak or alone again.*

Nico closed her eyes and focused on her breathing.

The thing in Nico's mind gave a long, deep sigh as Sted's fingers wrapped around her neck. *A failure to the end. This is twice now you've failed me. And to think, you used to be the strongest demon in the world.*

With one final, desperate shove, Nico pushed the voice away. When her eyes met Sted's, they were dark and human again.

"It's over," he hissed.

Nico set her jaw and pinned her hands at her side so her demon couldn't try eating him again. This was it, she knew. After trying so hard, this was it. Still, she'd never give in to the demon, not even to keep living. Tears welled up in her eyes at that thought, and she murmured an apology to Josef. She'd tried to keep going, to cling to life, but the price was just too high. Still, she kept breathing as Sted raised his sword, pressing the sharp tip against her ribs, just below her heart. So long as she was alive, she had hope, even now.

Hope, the demon sneered. *A stupid, human concept.*

"That's the idea," she whispered back.

Her last thought before closing her mind was Josef as she'd first met him, leaning over her on the snowy mountain slope, telling her to breathe. Then the sword came down, and the world vanished.

Josef floated in darkness. He was in pain, horrible pain, but he couldn't see where. His body was missing, lost somewhere in the blackness. It was just him and the pain and the darkness that went on and on and on forever.

"I'm dead," Josef said. It was as much an experiment to see if he could speak as a test to see how that statement felt. The words made no sound, which made sense, considering, but they felt very real when he said them.

Don't be stupid, a voice answered from the darkness. *If you were dead, you wouldn't be in pain.*

Josef flinched. It was the Heart's voice, and if he was hurt enough to hear it, things must be really bad. On the other hand, if the sword was talking, it probably knew what was going on, which meant it was time for some answers.

"If I'm not dead," Josef said, "where am I, and how do I get out?"

You are almost dead, the Heart answered. *I caught your life a moment before it flickered out. I am keeping it alive by holding it next to my own until you decide what you're going to do.*

"What do you mean, 'I decide'?" Josef said. "What's there to decide? I'm not going to die to someone like Sted."

I'm afraid things are no longer that simple, Josef Liechten, the Heart said and sighed. *We were defeated utterly. Struck down. And do you know why?*

Josef felt a twinge of shame. "Because I'm not strong enough."

Correct, the Heart thundered.

Josef choked. The Heart's answer struck him harder than any of Sted's blows.

The Heart sighed. *I've been waiting for a defeat like this to make you understand. You think you know what it means to be strong, but every time a fight pushes you, you wait until the last moment to draw me, then treat my blade as a guaranteed victory, an undefeatable weapon.*

"I have to," Josef said. "You're too strong. You agreed I'm not good enough, but how can I get better if your power blows everything away? You're the greatest awakened sword ever made, but I'm the one bleeding to death on the floor, not Sted. Obviously, the weakness is with me. I have to fix it before I can move forward."

Fights you can win with dull swords are not the ones that make you better, the Heart said. *Every time you fight you handicap yourself, pushing me aside for your dull blades, thinking that doing so will make you stronger. But real strength doesn't come from such cheap tricks. Real strength comes from fighting at the edge of your ability, pushing yourself past the last inch of your resolve with everything you have.*

Rage filled Josef, and he started to answer, but the Heart cut him off.

I chose you as my wielder because I thought you understood this. But from the moment I allowed you to grasp my hilt, you've done nothing but avoid my powers. Not once have you used me to my full potential. You draw me only as a last resort, a final blow.

"But—"

I did not bind myself to you to stay cooped up in a sheath!

Josef flinched at the anger in the sword's voice, but he could not deny what it said.

These last few years we've been together as two parts, the Heart said, *sword and man, without understanding. If you wish to leave this place, if you wish to defeat Sted, this must change. I am not your trump card, not your guaranteed out. I am a sword, your sword. You've come this far on your own, but no farther. If you want to survive, Josef Liechten, then we must emerge from this together, as a swordsman, or not at all.*

"But I don't understand," Josef said. "You want us to work together? How? I hear you only at times like this, when I'm almost dead. Am I going to have to take a mortal wound every time I want to fight, just so we can talk?"

The Heart rumbled. *Do you think you're my first non-wizard wielder? Do you think I would have chosen you to carry me if I thought you were incapable of truly being my swordsman?*

Josef shook his head. "I don't see—"

Do you always need to speak to know why a person fights?

"No," Josef said. "But—"

Do you need words to understand why a sword cuts?

Josef took a deep breath. "No."

Good. He could hear the Heart smile. *You begin to understand. Listen well, Josef Liechten. If we are to fight together, you must see me for what I am, a part of yourself, another facet of your own power. To do that, you must push aside your thinking mind, the mind that requires words, and understand me with what lies deeper.*

Josef clenched his teeth. The Heart was starting to sound like Eli's wizard talk. "You mean like a wizard?"

No, the Heart said in disgust. *I mean like a spirit.*

Josef shook his head. "I still don't understand."

You will, the Heart promised. *Open your eyes.*

"What?" They were open, or he thought they were.

This close to death, even you should be able to see. The Heart's words were an avalanche. *Open your eyes!*

Josef did. The darkness was gone; the pain was gone. He was floating high in a blue sky filled with clouds, and before him, rising like a great wave from the land, was a mountain like none he had ever seen. It was taller than anything in the world, its edges sharp and straight as a blade. Its snowcapped peak cut the sky, slicing clouds as they passed, while its wide base spread for miles and miles in all directions, its roots deeper than humans could comprehend. It stood perfectly sharp, proud and tall, unmovable, unbreakable, and the moment Josef saw it, he understood.

The mountain vanished, and he felt something in his hand. He looked down and saw he was holding the Heart of War. The black sword looked the same as ever, and yet different. When he looked at the blade, the memory of the mountain flashed across his mind.

You have seen my true nature. The Heart's voice was deep and warm. *Do you still need words, Josef Liechten?*

"No," Josef said, tightening his grip on the sword.

The Heart of War laughed, a deep, rumbling sound, and Josef woke.

He was alone, and in a different place from where he'd fallen. Crates were stacked high around him and his wound had been bound, though the bloodstains told him how useful that would have been if the Heart had not intervened. He looked down at the sword in his hand for a long moment, like he was seeing it for the first time.

The path to true strength is not easily walked. The Heart's voice was more like a memory than a sound now. *Now that we've started, there's no going back. I hope you're prepared to bet your life on this.*

"I always have," Josef whispered. "Every single time."

A great feeling of laughter welled up in his head, and the sword's hilt settled hard in Josef's hand. He gripped it with a grin and, using the sword as a prop, began the long, painful process of sitting up. When he was about halfway there, he heard a crash. He froze, listening. It was the sound of something hitting the floor, something small and human. He was on his feet at once, creeping up the pile of crates just in time to see Sted panting over something on the floor. It was dark, but he would know that shape anywhere, the slender back, the long, thin arms lying limp on the floor, the pale, pale skin.

Rage filled him to boiling, painting the room in a wash of

angry color. Rage at Sted, at himself for letting this happen, at Nico for not running from a fight she couldn't win. Hadn't he taught her anything? But the sword weighed heavy in his grip, bringing him down, telling him what must be done.

Even so, Josef wasn't the kind of man to fall on an opponent from behind with no warning.

"Sted!"

The cry echoed through the warehouse, and the enormous swordsman looked up just in time to see Josef leap, the Heart of War held high over his head. The sword felt heavy in his hands, yet Josef could swing it with ease, even more so than before. The blade answered his every movement like it was part of his hand rather than something clasped inside it, and Josef felt a rush like never before as the Heart's triumphant cackle rolled through him.

For a moment Sted just stood there, staring, and then he started to raise his sword to defend. But this time he was too slow. Josef was already on top of him, swinging the Heart with all his rage. The black blade hit Sted in the side with the weight of a mountain. There was a great iron *gong*, and Sted flew backward, slamming into the front wall of the warehouse with a crash that cracked the wooden supports.

Panting from the force of the blow and keeping one eye on Sted's slumped body, Josef limped over to Nico. He'd seen plenty of violence in his time, but she was still hard to look at. An enormous wound ran down her chest, as though Sted had been trying to gut her. Still, he told himself, this was Nico. She was about as killable as a rock wall.

Josef knelt down to check her breathing. Sure enough, he could feel it, a faint breeze on his fingers, and he let out the breath he didn't realize he'd been holding. She was alive. He let himself savor the realization before forcing it down again, turning to face

Sted's twitching body. She was alive, and it was his job now to make sure she stayed that way.

Across the warehouse, Sted groaned and retched, coughing up a streak of bright blood. He stared at it in shock before turning his hateful glare on Josef. Keeping a hand to his side, he stood slowly, pushing himself up by painful inches.

"I'm impressed," he gasped, spitting out another mouthful of blood as he got to his feet at last. "You broke a rib. How long has it been since someone did that? Not for years now." He bared his bloody teeth at Josef. "You'll pay for that."

"If we're paying blood for blood," Josef said, "I think you owe us far more."

Sted grabbed his sword again. "What does it take to kill you?" he grumbled. "This time I'll cut off your cursed head!"

His threat turned into a scream as he began to charge. Instinctively, Josef turned to jump out of the way, but the Heart would not move. For one panicked moment, he stared at the blade. Then he quieted, and understood. Josef planted his feet firmly, in the position shield troops call Bracing the Mountain, and held the Heart in front of him, broad side out, like a shield. There, firm as bedrock, he met Sted's charge.

The swords clashed in a scream of twisting metal and flashing sparks. Sted was snarling, his sword red as fresh blood, pushing with all his strength. The blood rage crashed into Josef, but the swordsman did not break his stance, and he did not move an inch.

Realizing his assault was useless, Sted began to swing wildly, using his superior height and reach to try and get around Josef's iron guard. But everywhere Sted swung, the Heart was there. The great black sword and the man carrying it moved together, flicking from one position to the next with a speed unlike anything they'd shown earlier. Sted struck harder and harder, faster and faster, but Josef and the Heart met him blow for blow, each block flowing seamlessly into the next, and try as he might, Sted could not break the sword's wall.

Finally, desperately, Sted lashed out with his entire body, throwing all his weight into his attack. This time, when the jagged sword met the Heart's dented surface, the glowing blade snapped. It broke with a squeal of metal that made Josef's ears ache, and Sted stumbled back. He held up his sword, now just a foot of toothy metal above the absurdly large hilt, and stared at it like a bewildered child. Then, with a cry of despair, hatred, and utter, devouring rage, he threw himself at Josef.

It was a wild charge. Sted thundered toward him, flailing with the broken sword as though it were still whole, running with his whole body to crush Josef beneath his weight.

It was then, in the madness, that Josef struck. He turned the Heart deftly in his hand, sliding the enormous blade around to meet Sted's flailing arm. He didn't look at the man's bared teeth or his twitching muscles. He didn't look at his own footwork, or how Sted was poised to crush him without the Heart as a barrier. Instead, he focused on the image the Heart had shown him, of the mountain's peak cutting the clouds. He held it in his mind until the picture was burned into his vision, until the need to cut, the way of cutting, not as a sword cuts, but as a mountain cuts, was all he could feel. Only then did he swing his sword, *his* sword truly, for the first time, catching Sted in the left arm, just above his elbow.

The black, blunt blade of the Heart met Sted's impenetrable skin, met and sliced it clean. The Heart cut straight through the flesh, through the bone, with no more resistance than a razor through spider webs. Then it met the air again, and Sted was falling, his arm cut clean off.

The enormous man collapsed on the floor, clutching the space where his arm had been. Josef spun around, taking up his guard again, but he didn't need to. Sted was curled in a fetal position, clutching his broken sword with the only arm he had left while blood poured out of his wound onto the floor. Josef lowered his guard, resting the Heart's tip on the floor, and Sted's head whipped around to face him, his eyes burning with pure, horrible hatred.

"No," he panted. "We're not finished." He forced himself up with his one remaining arm and grabbed the top of his broken sword, clutching the pieces together against his chest. "It's not over."

"No," Josef answered. "It is. You are defeated, Berek Sted."

Sted laughed, a horrible, wheezing sound. "You, you couldn't defeat me in a hundred years," he muttered. "You were lucky, that's all. My sword broke. There's no way you could have defeated me otherwise."

"Luck had nothing to do with it," Josef said. "Get out or bleed to death on the floor, your choice." He swung the Heart over his shoulder and started toward Nico. "I'm finished with you."

"I decide when we're finished!" Sted roared. "Your name, swordsman of the Heart of War. Tell me your name!"

Josef stopped, looking back over his shoulder with a cold, dull glare. "Josef Liechten."

Sted pushed himself to his knees. "See you soon, then, Josef Liechten."

He gave Josef a final, bloody grin, and then said something Josef heard but could not understand. Suddenly, the light twisted around Sted, and a cut opened in the air. It was as though someone had taken a knife to the fabric of the world and cut a hole to another place, somewhere dark and lined with black stones. Sted fell backward, letting the tear in the world devour him, and then he was gone. No sound, no smoke—he simply was not there anymore.

Josef stared for a full minute at the bloody place where the swordsman had been. Even his cut-off arm was still on the ground, but the man was gone. He would have stared longer, but the Heart was heavy in his hand, pulling him toward Nico. Taking the hint, Josef decided to just ask Eli about it later, and he walked over to where Nico had fallen.

He had expected her to be sitting up by now. Nico's ability to heal herself was something he took as a truth of the world. Yet Nico had not moved from where he'd left her, and even in the dark, he could see a darker stain on the floor around her. Fear began to grow inside him, and his walk turned into a run.

The first thing he checked was her breath again, which, though faint, was still there. His relief at that vanished when he looked at her chest. The wound from Sted's sword was still open and bleeding. For some reason, her healing didn't seem to be kicking in. He looked around frantically, searching for anything to use as a bandage to stop the bleeding when he felt something grasp his wrist.

He looked down to see Nico's hand clutching his. Her eyes were open, dark and pleading as they looked at him, and her lips moved in a whisper he couldn't understand.

"Say it again," he said, leaning so that his ear was against her lips.

"My coat," she whispered. "Find my coat."

Josef nodded and glanced around. Her coat was piled on the floor not far from where she lay, and Josef grabbed it. He handed it to her, but the moment the black cloth touched her hand, it began to move on its own. The coat flowed around Nico's body, wrapping itself across her like a cocoon, binding her wound and stanching the bleeding. In the space of a breath, she was completely bound, and Nico gave a long, relieved sigh.

"It protects me," she whispered, looking at Josef again. "Just like Slorn said."

Josef clutched her shoulders. "Nico, what's happening?"

The girl looked away. "I'll tell you"—she breathed—"later."

And then she was out, and the coat slithered over her head, wrapping her completely, leaving Josef alone and confused.

"Powers," he muttered. This was getting worse and worse. Nico was a bundle, he had no idea what was going on, and he had completely missed his part of old Monpress's plan, which, if the growing sounds of chaos outside were any indication, was going very badly.

Nothing for it, he thought, standing up. He had to find Eli. If anyone could tell him what was wrong with Nico and get them out, it was the thief. Mission firmly in mind, Josef set to work. Using a length of fine table linen from one of the shattered crates, he wiped Sted's blood off the Heart and tied it across his back. After settling the sword in place, he took a deep breath, bracing for the rush of exhaustion that always followed. But even when his hand let go of the hilt, he felt the same. Tired, beaten up, but no worse than he had when he was still holding the blade. On his back, the sword settled smugly into place, and Josef arched his eyebrows. Whatever had happened in that black place, it had done more than just bring him closer to his sword. Their partnership had changed; he was sure of it, though understanding the exact extent of the changes would have to wait until he had more time.

Next, because he knew he'd never hear the end of it if he forgot, he grabbed the Fenzetti blade from the corner where it had landed and hefted it on his shoulders. Finally, he gently lifted the black bundle that was Nico and held her against his chest. Going slowly so he wouldn't jostle her too much, Josef walked to the door of the warehouse, which, miraculously, was whole and untouched. He opened it with a swift kick that took it off its hinges and stepped into the night. Clutching Nico carefully, he ran across the one remaining bridge over the now inexplicably glowing river. Soft, cold rain splattered on his shoulders, and he could hear people far away yelling, but the streets he could see were dark and empty. Ordinarily, this would have put him on his guard, but Josef was in too much of a hurry to worry about threats he couldn't see. Instead, he picked up the pace, moving toward the citadel, Eli's most likely location.

He only hoped the thief was alive to get them out of this.

CHAPTER 22

Gin ran through the silent, rain-soaked streets of Gaol with Miranda crouched low on his back. The city cowered around them, crushed under the duke's will. It made Miranda ill just passing by, but she ignored it as best she could. Her duty right now was to get her rings back, then she could help Monpress put the duke in his place... assuming he even intended to carry out his end of things.

She looked back over her shoulder at the river, and Gin growled. "Don't even think about it," he said, picking up the pace. "We've got our plan and we're sticking to it. If we start second-guessing things now, we won't save the town or your spirits."

Miranda nodded and let him run. Hern's tower was on the northern edge of the city, an ornate stone spire surrounded by wealthy houses. Or at least that's how it had looked that afternoon. What met them now as they came to a stop at the end of the charming little street leading up to Hern's private domain was not an elegant tower but an enormous spike of rough stone. Gin slid to a stop and Miranda jumped off for a better look. Hern's tower looked like a boulder had fallen on it. Miranda walked up and put a hand against the stone and then snatched it away again with a grimace.

"It's Hern's stone spirit," she said, shaking her hand where the stone had bitten it. "He's wrapped it around the tower like a shell to shield himself and his other spirits from the Enslavement."

"He has a spirit powerful enough to stand up to the duke?" Gin snorted.

"Normally I'd say no," Miranda said. "But he's got the same advantage we have right now, namely that the duke is stomping on his own spirits, which leaves the Enslavement too thinly spread to press down much on Spiritualist servants."

Gin crouched down, nosing the spot where the rough stone met the cobbled street. "Does it go all the way down?"

"It would have to," Miranda said, tapping the stone with her fingers. "I hate to say break it, but I don't see any other way we're getting in. Of course"—she opened her spirit a fraction, putting a warning edge of power into her voice—"I'm not feeling particularly charitable toward spirits who willingly help Hern stamp out mine."

The stone shuddered, and high above them in the tower, something made a low grinding noise. A second later, the smooth rock face in front of them cracked, and a gap just wide enough for Miranda to slip through opened up.

Miranda and Gin exchanged a look, and the ghosthound sat down firmly.

"No," he said. "That might as well have 'trap' written out in glowing letters. You're not going in. Especially not without me."

Miranda put her hands on her hips. "Who was it who just said we're sticking to our plan?"

"That plan didn't include you facing Hern alone on his own turf," Gin growled. "You might as well hand him the knife to stab in your back."

Miranda glanced at the opening. Inside was pitch blackness, but for the first time since that moment by the river, she could feel the wisps of her spirits through their connection again. Very faint, but there, and that made her decision for her.

"Keep watch, Gin," she said, turning toward the tower. "If you hear anything strange coming from the keep, go and help Eli."

Gin reached out and slapped his paw down on the hem of her skirt, pinning her to the pavement. "What part of 'you're not going in' didn't you understand?"

Miranda took a deep breath and turned to face the hound. This wasn't a card she played often, but sometimes Gin was too protective for his own good.

"Gin," she said stiffly. "They're my spirits, just as you are. Let me go."

It was an order, not a request, and Gin, despite not being a formally bound spirit, had to obey. Slowly, begrudgingly, he lifted his paw, and Miranda walked toward the cleft in the tower.

When she reached the entrance, she stopped and looked over her shoulder. "I'll make it up to you, mutt," she said. "Promise."

"*If* you ever come out of there," Gin growled, looking away, "I will hold you to that."

Miranda smiled, then turned and vanished into the cleft of stone. The rock face sealed instantly behind her.

Hern's tower reminded Miranda more of a wealthy townhouse than a Spiritualist's working office. The inside was all polished hardwood and stone hung with tasteful, expensive tapestries, oil paintings, and fine porcelain. Small oil lamps burned in the dark, giving just enough light to make the elegant hall feel claustrophobic. The lamps were lit in a line leading her toward the stairs, painting an obvious path to Hern. Any other turning was blocked with heavy doors Miranda didn't bother trying. She was already in the trap; she might as well follow it through. In any case, her rings were upstairs. She could feel them strongly now, and they were pulling her toward the spiral stair to the tower's high second floor.

When she reached the foot of the stairs, she spotted something that made her stop. Nestled in the space beneath the stairs was a small pump room. Buckets and clothes were stacked neatly, and below the pump was a large bucket of soapy water probably left by Hern's cleaners, for Miranda couldn't imagine the Spiritualist scrubbing his own floors. Still, it gave her an idea. She stepped sideways, scooping up the sturdy bucket by its wooden handle and holding it carefully behind her back as she began to climb the spiral stairs.

Though they might vary greatly in style according to the individual, all Spiritualist towers were built the same. The first floor was cut into multiple rooms for private living, while the second, connected by a wide spiral stair, was one open room that served as the Spiritualist's office, work floor, meeting room, and library. Hern's tower was no exception. Miranda emerged from the spiral staircase at the center of an enormous room. Dozens of lamps hung from the pointed ceiling, and Miranda had to shield her eyes from the sudden brightness. Even so, it was immediately obvious that Hern's taste for nice things didn't stop at his professional space. This room was every bit as elaborate as the rooms below. Fine silk furniture clung to the rounded walls, arranged in little, inviting clusters perfect for confidences. The wooden floor was smothered in fine rugs and the walls were strewn with paintings, mostly cityscapes of Zarin and lovely lounging women wearing very little.

But what caught her attention the most wasn't the glitz or the opulence, the fine statues or the heavy bookcases filled with leather volumes seemingly arranged by color rather than author or subject. Instead, her focus was instantly drawn to a wooden box sitting on a stone end table just in front of her. It was a simple thing, rough-hewn wood and an iron latch with a heavy lock, but Miranda's heart leaped to see it, or rather to feel what was trapped inside. In answer, something inside the box rattled, a beautiful, tinkling bell sound of gold on gold as her rings clattered together.

"Not another step, if you please," a charming, hated voice sounded from somewhere on her left.

Miranda turned, slowly. There, lounging in a chair beside an opulent liquor cabinet, with a sifter of something golden dangling from his jeweled hands, was Hern himself. The arrangement was so contrived Miranda couldn't help wondering how many setups he'd experimented with before settling on this one. He was dressed in a lounging jacket and soft silk pants, more like a gentleman enjoying an evening at home than a Spiritualist whose land was being Enslaved, and he met her glare with an indulgent smile.

"Now," he said, "don't look like that. You should be happy I didn't just catch you in stone and cart you back to Zarin. I'd be well within my rights, considering the trouble you've caused."

"I don't think you'll have any rights once the Court hears about this," she said. "Having a drink in your tower while your lands are crushed beneath the boot of Enslavement? Have you given up even the pretense of being a responsible Spiritualist, Hern?"

"That is a delicate political situation," Hern said. "Not that you'd understand anything about those, seeing how, yet again, you've barged in and upset a stable and delicate system to satisfy what?" He sneered at her across his glass. "Some childish need for revenge? Or do you just enjoy helping Monpress upset kingdoms?"

Below the edge of the stairwell, out of Hern's line of sight, Miranda clenched her bucket of water. "Enough lies, Hern," she said. "Hide here all you want, but I'm taking my spirits back, and then I'm going to put a stop to this. If you won't do your duty to your lands, I will."

She took a step toward the box containing her rings, but she stopped at the familiar whoosh of flame. Hern was standing now, his outstretched hand wreathed in blue fire.

"You forget yourself, Miranda," he said, grinning from ear to ear. "You are in my tower, on my land. You are powerless, spiritless, and trapped. You are in no position to be making demands."

The flames licked at his fingers in long, threatening waves. It was just what Miranda had been waiting for. In one sweeping motion, she flung the bucket at him. Hern barely had time to understand what had happened before the bucket, and the wave of water flying out of it, struck him straight across the chest. The flames on his hands sputtered out and Hern yelped, leaping back and toppling his heavy chair as he did so.

It was only a momentary interruption, but it was enough. From the second the bucket left her hands, Miranda was running for her rings. By the time Hern had his feet back under him, she had the box in her hands. Roaring with rage, Hern made a throwing motion, and a wave of fire leaped from his hand.

Clutching the box to her chest, Miranda dove behind a long couch upholstered in gold and blue silk. The fire flickered out inches from the couch's surface, and Miranda grinned. She'd known Hern would never risk his nice furniture, not even to get her, and that hesitation would be her victory. She looked at the box in her hands. It was small, about the size of a hat box, and she could feel her rings inside jumping and clattering against the wood, trying to get to her.

Miranda checked the lock, but it was enormous, heavy, and dead asleep. So were the hinges, and the wood itself. Still, she thought, grimacing, there was no point in being subtle anymore.

So with a whispered apology to the sleeping box, Miranda closed her eyes and opened her spirit. Power flowed into her, and she caught it as it surged, sharpening the raw wizard's will to a needle-thin point that she forced through the crack in the box and into her spirits.

The moment the surge of power hit her rings, she felt their power echo back along the connection. The box in her hands burst into a shower of splinters as Durn, her stone spirit, exploded out of his ring. He rose to his full height in the blink of an eye with her rings clutched gently in his enormous stone hands. Almost sobbing with relief, Miranda took her spirits and slid them back onto her fingers, quaking as the connections roared open again as they met her skin. Durn stood guard until she'd fit every last one back on her fingers. Then, her rings awake and flashing like embers on her hands, Miranda stood again and turned to face the man responsible for all of this.

Hern, however, was ready. He stood across the room, his rings blazing like small suns, and a calm, concentrated look on his face.

"So," he said. "It's come to this."

"You were the one who started it," Miranda growled, standing firmly beside Durn's hulking form. "If you're too scared to finish it, then you shouldn't have called that trial in the first place."

"Oh, I'm not worried about the finish," Hern sneered, lifting his hand so Miranda could see not only his rings but the glittering bands of his bracelets set with large, colorful stones, all sparkling with suppressed power. "You might be Banage's protégé, but I'm the older Spiritualist, more experienced, and master of a larger retinue of spirits. No, I know exactly how this will finish. I'm only sad because I'll probably have to kill you, as that seems to be the only way to keep you down." He sighed. "I was so looking forward to parading you in shame before Banage and the Court, but at this point, I'll take what I can get. However"—his face broke into a thin, hateful smile—"with you dead, I can probably blame this whole Enslavement mess on you, seeing as you won't be around to defend yourself, so the situation is not without its silver lining."

"Don't count your victory so easily," Miranda growled, planting her feet and raising her glittering, jeweled hands. "You may have more spirits, but even if I had only one I would count it against all of yours. It's quality and loyalty of spirits that matters, Hern, not quantity, and we have no intention of losing to a man like you."

"Well, then," Hern said, "let's not waste any more time."

He clapped his hands and then thrust them apart, and every stick of furniture in the room suddenly slid back to the tower walls, leaving a large, open space at the center of the room. Hern, the blue fire still flickering on his fingers, took up position on the far end, while Miranda stepped up to stand opposite, Durn hovering over her. They stood for a moment, studying each other, and then, sick of waiting, Miranda attacked.

Durn launched forward on her signal, skidding across the floor in a wave of spiked stone straight for Hern. The Spiritualist flicked his finger, and vines, the same vines that had trapped Miranda earlier, exploded across the rock spirit's surface. Durn's charge ground to a halt as the plants doubled and tripled, trapping him beneath a swirling nest of woody growth. But Miranda was already moving. She crooked her left thumb where Kirik's ruby flashed. At her signal, the stone glowed like a forge and crackling heat poured off of her hands. A moment later, Durn, and the vines tying him down, burst into a pillar of orange flame that blackened the tower's peaked stone roof. The vines fell away instantly, shriveling in a cloud of resinous black smoke and tiny screams before pouring back into the deep green stone on Hern's middle finger. Hern paid them no attention, raising a large blue-green stone on his opposite hand that began to flash blue-silver as he whispered to it.

Miranda jerked Kirik's fire away just in time, as a massive torrent if içy water drenched the place where the pillar of fire had been. The fire poured back into her ring, but Durn, now free from the vine trap, ignored the water that was raising great clouds of steam from his scorched surface and went straight for Hern. Just before the enormous, enraged rock pile reached him, Hern grabbed a heavy crystal hanging from his neck and shouted a name Miranda couldn't make out. As the word left his lips, the entire tower shook, and the stone wall behind Hern burst open, punched open by a great stone fist. Miranda could only stare in amazed horror as she realized what it was. That hand belonged to the stone spirit that was wrapped around Hern's tower. With amazing speed, the enormous stone hand grabbed Durn mid-charge and lifted him in a crushing grip. Durn cried out as the hand tightened and chunks of him began to crumble and fall to the ground.

Miranda thrust out her hand, calling the rock spirit frantically back, but as she moved to help him, Hern made a throwing motion with both hands, and a ring of blue fire roared up around her. Miranda shrank back from the blistering heat and shouted for her wind spirit. Almost before she'd said his name, Eril burst from his pendant and hit the fire full force. He spun in a circle, crushing the flames under a roaring wall of wind so that Miranda could jump out. As she jumped, a cool mist flowed out of the round sapphire on her ring finger. The mist fell like a blanket, smothering the blue fire in an oppressive curtain of water. By the time Miranda landed, the inferno was nothing but a circle of scorch marks on the floor. Panting, she whirled to face Hern, bringing her right hand up. Skarest, her lightning bolt, was already crackling. But as she prepared to launch him, Hern snapped his fingers and a wall of water sprang up in front of him.

Miranda hesitated. Striking water was dangerous for her

lightning. At best, it would be horribly painful for the spirit; at worst, it could diffuse Skarest permanently.

Hern caught her hesitation and seized the opportunity. "Enough!" he said. "With that lightning bolt, you're out of spirits, unless you're going to bring your little moss spirit into the fight. I, on the other hand, am just getting started. I've already shown I can counter everything you throw at me. If we keep going, I'm going to have to start breaking your spirits one by one, beginning with that pile of rocks."

As he spoke, the enormous fist holding Durn tightened, and the rock spirit made a gritty, pained sound. Miranda clenched her teeth, but did not lower her hand or stop the arcs of lightning crackling over it. From behind his wall of water, Hern arched an eyebrow at her.

"Fire at me," he said, "and your little lightning spirit will fizzle before he gets ten paces." He crossed his arms over his chest. "You know that, and so for all your posturing, you won't shoot. I'm calling your bluff, Miranda Lyonette. The day of your trial, you were willing to throw away everything to save your spirits. You wouldn't risk killing one of them now, just to get to me. Lower your hands and I'll let the rock spirit live."

"Don't do it, mistress!" Durn cried, struggling against the larger stone spirit's grip. "You fought for us; we'll fight for you!"

"The rock is right," Skarest crackled. "You came for us like we knew you would. We're not going to be the ones to let you down. Shoot me."

"No," Miranda whispered. "Hern's right; you'll die. We'll find another way."

"We don't need another way," the lightning snapped back. "Look at the water. The spirit he's using as a shield is trembling. For all hitting the water will hurt me, it'll hurt the water twice as much."

Miranda glanced at Hern's water shield. Sure enough, its surface was trembling, warping Hern's smug face behind a lattice of terrified ripples. Her hand crackled. Skarest was gathering power, obliviously intending to shoot whether she gave the order or not, and so Miranda decided to trust him. She focused on her lightning spirit, letting her power flow through their connection until his arcs were painfully bright. Hern must have felt the power building, for his smug expression began to fall, but it was too late. With an enormous burst of blinding light and terrible power, Miranda let Skarest fly.

What happened next was almost too fast to see. Skarest arced toward Hern, flying in a thousand branches of spidering, flashing bolts. Hern raised his hands to brace the water, but then, a moment before the lightning struck his spirit shield, the wall of water vanished. It fell away in a terrified rush, leaving Hern open, unprotected. He had no time to raise another spirit, no time to get out of the way, no time to do anything but stare unbelieving at the white-hot arc before Skarest struck him square in the chest.

There was a tremendous crack, and Hern flew backward, slamming into the stone wall behind him. Deafening thunder clapped a split second after as Skarest returned to Miranda. Now that Hern's power was interrupted, Durn broke away from the great stone hand that held him, smashing the enormous grip to rubble as he fought free and went to stand beside Miranda.

Thus, flanked by her spirits, Miranda stood her ground and watched Hern's slumped body. But the other Spiritualist didn't move. All around them, the tower was shaking as the stone shell fell away, and a stream of sand returned to the crystal around Hern's neck. But still, he did not move.

"Did you kill him?" Miranda whispered, looking down at her lightning bolt.

"No," Skarest sounded very smug. "But he won't be getting up for a while."

Miranda let out a breath and cautiously walked over to Hern. She knelt down beside him and, very gently, turned him over. His chest was burned, but not badly. His hair, however, the long blond tresses he prized so highly, was singed beyond recognition.

Miranda stifled a giggle, covering her nose against the stench of burned hair. "How did you know the water would move?"

"Easy," Skarest crackled. "From the very beginning Hern was a peacock, a liar, and a coward. I knew that a wizard like that couldn't possibly have a bound spirit willing to take a real killing blow from me on his behalf."

"Good guess," Miranda said, standing up.

"Guess nothing," Skarest said. "If I've learned anything from you dragging us to the Spirit Court, it's that bound spirits take after their Spiritualist. If the wizard's good for nothing, the spirits won't be either, doesn't matter how big or how many."

Miranda shook her head. She was endlessly amazed at how her spirits could still surprise her. But before she could start giving orders to secure Hern, there was a horrible clatter from the floor below. Miranda jumped and fell into a defensive position, visions of Hern trapping some sort of vindictive, wild spirit to avenge him if he went down running through her head. He was narcissistic enough to do something like that, she thought, gritting her teeth as she turned to face the top of the stairs, which the whatever-it-was was climbing with astonishing speed. But what popped out of the stairwell wasn't a vindictive spirit, or at least not one of Hern's. It was Gin, and he burst into the room in a flurry of shifting fur and claws.

"Are you all right?" he snapped, looking her over, then looking at Hern. "Oh, good, you did win. I thought you had when the rock barrier went down, but I had to be sure."

"What, so you tore all the way up here?" Miranda winced,

imagining the beautiful, decorated halls smashed to pieces in Gin's frantic wake.

Gin gave her a sharp look. "See if I come to help you again."

Miranda just laughed and shook her head. "Sorry, sorry, I'm very happy to see you. Now"—she shoved her arms under Hern's shoulders—"help me get this idiot secured."

Together they got Hern into one of his chairs and tied him tight with a curtain pull. Once he was secure, Miranda plucked off every bit of his jewelry. It was quite a pile, ten rings, five bracelets, and a half dozen necklaces, all humming with power. These she put in the bucket that she'd thrown at him earlier and gave them to Durn.

"Watch him," she said, giving the rock spirit a firm look. "If he starts to wake up again, club him, but gently; don't crack his skull. Just keep him asleep, away from his rings, and out of trouble."

"Very well, mistress," Durn said. "Where are you going?"

Miranda looked out through the enormous gaping hole in the side of Hern's tower, where the city of Gaol lay dark, silent, and frozen under the Enslavement. "I'm going to make sure that thief keeps his promise."

Durn bowed, and Miranda climbed onto Gin's back. As soon as she was on, he leaped through the hole in the wall, landing neatly on the roof of the house next door. The moment his feet hit the rain-soaked tiles, he was running, jumping along the roofs toward the citadel.

CHAPTER 23

Duke Edward stood soaked and alone on the battlements of his citadel. His guards were gone; so were his servants. He didn't know where and he didn't care. He had larger problems. He stood very still, his eyes closed, his face twitching in a concentration deeper than any he'd ever had to maintain. Below him, spread out in a dark grid, was the city, his city, and every spirit, every speck of stone, cowered in homage to him. Their fear bled through the raging spread of his own spirit, making him feel ill and weak, but he did not loosen his grip. Such unpleasantness was necessary if he was to preserve the perfection he'd worked his whole life to achieve. This was just another test, and though he'd never been pushed to Enslavement before, he'd always been ready to do what he had to do. Perfection was not something that could be achieved through half-measures.

Out on the edge of his control, he could feel the sea spirit that had taken over his river surging. It was gathering water from farther upstream, increasing its size and power. It had doubled since he began the Enslavement, swollen with water until he could no longer feel the Spiritualist girl's hold on it. Maybe she had died, or maybe the water spirit had grown too large for her and broken away. Whatever the case, Hern's idea of catching and forcing her to remove her spirit had never been an efficient option. The river was growing too quickly. In another ten minutes it would have enough water to flood the whole city, an outcome that could break his already tenuous hold on his spirits and ruin his town, neither of which was an option he was willing to consider. No, his path was clear. Reestablishing control meant getting the sea spirit out of his river, and Edward was going to do just that, even if it meant destroying the water.

He reached out, his focus sliding across the cowering city to the warehouses on the northern stretch of the river, where he kept his tanneries. Long ago, when he was just a boy, he'd brought the river to heel by threatening to dump the tannery waste into its waters. Now, forty years later, he made good on that threat. With a great thrust of his spirit, the side of the tannery burst open, and five enormous metal barrels of stinking hide soak, their tops frothy with flies and decay, toppled into the river's newly clear water. He grinned when he felt the Great Spirit's power shudder and cringe as hundreds of gallons of rancid, black-green sludge slithered across its surface.

Still, it wasn't enough. The river surged beneath the layer of poison, denying Edward's control of the area, refusing to retreat. He needed something more drastic, but he was already panting from the effort of controlling spirits so far away. Fortunately, the next step was easy. Even Enslaved, fire needed little encouragement to burn. All he had to do was nudge one of the fallen torches that lay on the docks, dropped by his retreating army, and the flame leaped into the polluted water.

The sludge caught instantly, and the night lit up as hot red fire streaked across the river's surface. The water screamed and churned, raising great waves as it tried to break the surface film of floating sludge and smother the flames, but all it managed was to fan them higher. The duke smiled in triumph, but never let his control waver. Even this might not be enough to drive the invading spirit out.

"My lord?" a small voice whispered beside him. It was plaintive and hoarse, as if it had been calling a long time. He would have ignored it, but if a spirit had gotten up the courage to interrupt him under these circumstances, it was probably important.

"What?" he said, turning only a tiny fraction of his attention from his battle with the river.

The spirit flickered, and he saw it was the castle fire, the single large fire that moved the treasury door and cooked the castle's food and heated the rooms, speaking through the chimney. The fire had remained loyal even when the river had been compromised, which was why he turned to listen more closely.

"The thief, Eli Monpress," it said, its voice crackling. "He's out in the front square."

The duke's patience vanished instantly. "Don't bother me with such rubbish," he said, turning back to the river.

"But sir," the fire said again. "I really think you should look. He's doing something..." It paused, throwing a puff of nervous smoke into the air. "Odd."

"Odd?" The duke looked sideways at the chimney. "Odd how?"

"It looks like he's giving a speech, sir," the fire finished in a rush, its light ducking back down the chimney just in case the duke decided it was wasting his time. But Edward was frowning, considering his decision. The river demanded his attention, but ignoring Eli Monpress was a risk only fools took. He tried it one way, then another, and came to the conclusion there was nothing to be done but to have a look himself. Keeping the back of his mind on the burning river, the duke walked through the small knot of buildings at the top of the citadel to the battlements on the opposite side, which overlooked the square.

The moment he looked down he understood why the fire had called him. There, standing on a pile of barrels and crates he'd scavenged from who knew where, was Eli Monpress. He was standing in plain sight in the middle of the square, and he seemed to be yelling. Very cautiously, the duke shifted a bit of his spirit away from the river and toward the city center. As his spirit moved over the square, he suddenly heard the thief's words loud and clear, and his hands clutched the edge of the battlements in white-knuckled fury.

Eli stood atop his mountain of borrowed barrels like a general in a war monument. Light rain soaked his shirt and plastered his black hair to his scalp, which added nicely to the desired effect. Beleaguered heroes always looked better in the rain.

He threw out his hands dramatically as he spoke, pouring every ounce of every scrap of everything he'd ever learned from a lifetime of unconventional wizardry into his voice. "Spirits of Gaol!" he cried, layering just enough power so that his words flowed smooth and strong over the quivering panic around him. "Look at what's been done to you! Look at the situation you've allowed yourselves to be put in! What has happened in Gaol? Free spirits are beholden to no one save their Great Spirit, and yet here you are, cowering while your river is out there fighting the duke for your freedom!"

"That's not our river!" one of the lamps shouted. "It's that Spiritualist's spirit!"

"All the more reason to be ashamed!" Eli answered, his voice harsh. "That an outsider came and risked their neck to save you, and you won't even help."

A great round of shouts went up at this, calling him wizard thief, and demanding why should we listen to you? Finally, one voice rolled over the rest. It was the door, the great iron door from the treasury, now standing sullenly at the corner of the square, propped up with sandbags.

"What do you know?" it said. "This is all your fault, anyway.

Things were fine until you got here. And now you stand there and tell us to what, rise up? Bah, easy for you! You're a wizard. You never lived with the duke!"

Eli stared at the door, his eyes wide. When he spoke next, there was a tremor in his voice. "You think I don't know the duke's cruelty? You think I just waltzed into Gaol to make empty speeches? Look then!" he shouted, ripping off his coat. "Look for yourselves and then say that I don't know what it's like to cross the Duke of Gaol!"

He unbuttoned his shirt and peeled it back, and a great sound went up from the gathered spirits as his bare shoulders came into view. Eli's skin, always pale, was now a horrid mottle of black and purple bruises. Angry red marks stood out on his lower arms, and his joints were red and swollen until they were painful to look at. All around the courtyard, the spirits who could see the physical world were whispering to those who couldn't. Those in turn whispered to their neighbors, and Eli's injuries got worse with every telling. For his part, Eli stood perfectly still, letting the soft rain splash on his injured skin as the story grew around him.

"So you see," Eli said, gritting his teeth as he gently replaced his shirt, "I, too, have felt what it means to defy the Duke of Gaol."

But the door was not impressed. "Bah," it growled. "What are a few bruises? You're human. You're free from the true horrors. You can't even feel the Enslavement, the duke putting his boot on your mind. If you could feel what we feel, you'd be terrified. You wouldn't last a day living the life we live."

A general murmur of agreement went up at this, but Eli kept his eyes on the door. "And this life," he said calmly. "Do you like it?"

"Of course not," the iron said. "We hate every day, but what can we do? This is our domain; we can't leave it."

"You don't need to leave to be free!" Eli stood up straight, filling his voice with power until it swelled through the entire square. "Listen up, all of you. You're right that, as a human, I can never know the humiliation of Enslavement. But, as a human, and a wizard, let me tell you a secret: *No* wizard, not even the Duke of Gaol, is strong enough to simultaneously Enslave an entire city. The only reason he was able to do it is because you're all afraid of him. It is your own fear that Enslaves you, not the duke! If you want to be free of this life of fear and subservience, then stand up and fight back! His control is already broken, or he wouldn't have had to try an Enslavement in the first place. The only thing standing between you and a free life is yourselves!"

A great murmur went up across the square as the last of Eli's words echoed off the tall buildings. Lamps flickered and houses leaned their eaves together, whispering. Eli remained on his barrels, listening, marking the difference in tone. Fear was being replaced by something else—energy, anticipation, and a raw urge to get out of an intolerable situation. Then, like the tide shifting, the fear came roaring back. In a single instant, the square fell silent. Eli squinted a moment in the dim lamplight, confused, and then he turned around and looked up. Two stories up on the battlements of the square citadel stood the Duke of Gaol.

He looked down over the square in utter contempt, but he didn't say a word. He didn't need to. At that moment, the full weight of his crushing will slammed down on the square. All around Eli, spirits began to squirm frantically, lowering themselves and begging for forgiveness. The duke just sneered, and the Enslavement grew until the weight was unbearable. It was at that moment, when it looked like the spirits would be under that crushing weight forever, that Eli crooked his fingers behind his back. Suddenly, a sound broke the silence. It was a thin, soft whistling noise, as of a rope being spun, and then, out of the dark, something small and black launched from the alley between two houses. Everything in the square turned to look as a stone roofing tile shot through the air, flying in a beautiful, straight arc high over the houses and the cobbled square, straight toward the duke.

What happened next seemed to unfold in slow motion. The duke stared at the tile in disbelief as it whistled toward him. Then, belatedly, he threw up his hands and began to shout a command, but he never got the words out. The tile struck him on the shoulder with a loud, solid *thwack.*

The duke stumbled back with a pained gasp, clutching his shoulder. The tile's impact wasn't a blow to kill him, or even injure him beyond inconvenience. His Enslavement hadn't even wavered, but the change in the square was immediate. All at once, spirits straightened up, gazing in wonder as the duke, the untouchable, terrible, unbeatable Duke of Gaol, lurched from the blow of a single tile.

For a long second, everything was silent, and then, with a great cry, another roofing tile launched itself at the citadel. It fell short, clacking off the stone wall, but the next one whizzed just past the duke's head, forcing him to duck for cover. The moment his head disappeared below the battlements, the square went crazy.

Houses shook, tossing off the drainpipes, shutters, and overhangs that had been their mouthpieces for reporting to the duke's wind. The lamps flared up like tiny, glass-trapped suns, spreading the story of what had just happened down the dark streets in a wave of light. Everywhere, spirits were casting off the duke's order, shouting and carrying on and doing what they wanted. The cobblestones slid out of their perfect geometric alignment to lie comfortably crooked. The tiny flowers in the pristine window boxes sprouted in absurd abundance, spilling leaves and seedpods into the street. Inside the empty houses, whose residents had fled for the walls the moment the conscript army was routed, tables flipped themselves over, chairs fell backward, and neat piles of table linens threw themselves like streamers over everything, creating dancing shapes behind the wobbly glass windows.

It was, in short, beautiful chaos, and Eli could not have been happier. He hopped off his pile of now-jittering barrels and waved at them as they rolled off to wherever they wanted to go. He was sliding his wet jacket back over his sore shoulders when Monpress jogged over from his alley, an anxious look on his usually calm face.

"Excellent job," Eli said with a wide grin, slapping the old man on the back. "Beautiful arc, too. You haven't lost an inch on that throw."

Monpress gave him a sideways look. "Glad to hear you're so happy about it," he said, glancing at a pack of wooden benches as they gallivanted down a side street. "From my point of view, it looks like we just kicked off the end of the world."

"Hardly," Eli said. "We were merely the catalyst for something that had been brewing for years." He smiled up at the empty battlements. "People and spirits aren't all that different in their fundamentals. When the circumstances are primed, all it takes is one act of defiance to set off a revolution."

"I see," Monpress said, frowning as a line of barrels rolled out of a shop on their own accord and emptied themselves into the street, dumping gallons of dark red wine into the gutters. "Remind me never to take you into a country I like."

Eli just grinned and settled back to watch the show.

The Duke of Gaol ran down the spiral stairs of his citadel, taking the broad stone steps two at time. He could hear the chaos through the thick stone walls, and rage like he had never felt burned in his mind, tightening the grip of his enslavement even as more and more of the city's spirits slipped free. Well, he thought as he burst into the great hall of the citadel, not for much longer. He was the Duke of Gaol still. The rebellious spirits would remember who their master was before the sun rose.

The last of his soldiers had already fled, leaving the great hall empty. The duke marched past the scattered benches and to the enormous hearth. The fire was banked for the night, awake and quiet under a blanket of ash. Without hesitation, the duke thrust his hand into the glowing embers, and the fire sprang up with a piteous, crackling roar.

"You're coming with me," the duke growled. "We're putting an end to this."

The fire bowed, shuddering under the Enslavement that roared down the duke's arm. It rose heatless from its bed and settled itself in his hand, flickering across his skin without so much as singeing his white cuffs, too cowed even to burn. Satisfied that this spirit was still loyal, for the moment at least, the duke turned on his heel and walked toward the great racks of weaponry on the far wall. He grabbed an ax with a great, curving moon for a blade. Hefting it in one hand, he mastered the small, stupid spirit with one blast of his will. Thus armed, he marched to the front of his citadel. The great doors flung themselves open as he approached, and he stepped into the chaos that was once his ordered, beautiful, perfect city to face the man responsible.

"Monpress!" he roared, his voice cutting through every other sound.

Across the square, two men looked up, and the duke, one hand wreathed in orange fire, the other gripping his ax, went out to reclaim his authority.

"Eli," Monpress whispered, watching the black figure with the flaming hand and the gleaming ax stalk toward them. "I say this as your teacher. You should run. That man cannot be reasoned with."

"You think?" Eli said quietly. "However, considering the little speech I just made, running doesn't seem like an option."

Monpress sighed. "Do you see the trouble principles get you into? If I'd known you were this eager to throw your life away, I wouldn't have bothered coming here to save you."

"Thanks for the encouragement." Eli sighed, turning to face the duke. "If you don't want to fight, I suggest you leave. This could get ugly."

He expected some sort of protest at this, maybe a dry stab at his supposed inability to do anything without help. But all he got was a hand squeezing his shoulder. "Good luck," Monpress whispered. Then the hand was gone, and so was the feeling of having someone beside him.

Eli gritted his teeth. Couldn't blame the old man, really. He was just living by the rules that had kept him alive through his decades as a thief. The rules he had taught Eli, and which Eli was ignoring right now as he stood at the end of the chaotic square, lounging with his arms crossed as the duke marched toward him.

"I should point out," he said when the duke was ten feet away, "that if you kill me, you'll never know where I stashed all the money I've stolen."

"You've made yourself more trouble than any money could pay down at this point." The duke's voice was an icy knife.

Eli swallowed and took a step back. His back was to the line of houses on the far side of the square, directly across from the citadel. Though the ruckus of rebellion was raging loud and strong around them, the houses facing the duke were silent and crouching. The show of obedience didn't save them. The duke glared up at the wooden structures and raised his left hand, the one wreathed in flame.

"Stop!" Eli cried. "If you burn it, it'll never serve you again."

The duke glared murder at him. "Understand, *thief*," he said. "I'd rather rule a smoking pit than be disobeyed by my city."

He waved his hand in a great, glorious burst of orange sparks, and the house behind Eli exploded in flames.

"Let this be a lesson!" the duke cried, his voice booming through the Enslavement that was, even now, still grabbing at order. "The price for disobedience is death!"

The house screamed and writhed as enormous flames raced across its timber frame, devouring the old hardwood with unnatural speed. But then, as fast as the flames had started, they flickered out. The duke's eyes widened, and he turned to the fire in his hand. It flared up, flickering in terror and pointing wildly at Eli.

Eli was standing at the house's door, one hand gripping the wood of the door frame. He had his back to the duke, and his figure was shimmering with heat. Steam rose from his wet jacket and with it smoke curled from his shoulders in long white wisps, forming a cloud above his head that flashed and sparked. The cloud grew, clinging to him, and by the time the last of the house fires flickered out, Eli's shape was almost invisible behind the thick smoke. A great sound roared up in the sudden darkness, and a giant burst from the sparking smoke. It stood as tall as the house it clung to, glowing and liquid, like flowing fire, in a bulky and almost human shape, complete with a great, grinning face. Little puffs of steam rose from the giant's surface as the soft rain brushed against it, but the fiery monster ignored the water, grinning down at the duke with monstrous glee.

"You see, Edward," Eli said, his voice hoarse with smoke but still mocking, still triumphant as he grinned over his shoulder, "you don't get to set the price anymore."

The duke's eyes narrowed. "So your fire spirit appears at last? I was beginning to think it was a rumor after all when you failed to bring it out during out little talk."

"Come on," Eli said. "You weren't nearly scary enough before for me to bring out my trump cards."

"Really?" The duke scowled. "Well, let's see how many more I can make you play before you die."

"Now," Eli said, turning around, "be reasonable—"

A blast of fire was his only answer. Eli dove sideways as the duke lashed out, sending fire out in great waves, burning anything that would burn. All around them the houses burst into flame, and the wood began to shriek in terror. Eli shouted to Karon. The giant nodded and began moving from house to house, sucking up the fire as he went. But even he wasn't fast enough to stop it all. The duke's enslaved flames leaped with singular purpose, eating up the wet wood like sparks on dry grass, turning the square into a trap of flames.

Grim and grinning, his ax gleaming in the firelight, the duke began to advance on Eli, and Eli, not keen on traps or axes, decided it was time to run. In a burst of speed, he shot past the duke and ran flat-out toward the far side of the square, where the fire had not reached. But hard as he ran, he could hear the duke behind him. The duke moved with amazing speed for a man his age, and just as Eli was about to duck down a fireless alley, the duke gave a shout. There was a flash of light, and a stream of flame leaped over Eli's head, singeing his hair. A moment later, the houses on either side of the alley burst into a hungry fire.

Eli skidded to a stop and turned to find the duke right on top of him, swinging wildly with the ax. The old man held it like a stick of firewood, but with a blade like that, he didn't have to be good. Eli shrieked and jumped out of the way, careful to keep his back to the open square and not the burning buildings.

The duke recovered instantly, hurling a wave of flame, not at the houses, but at Eli himself. The thief was gone before it landed, running along the edge of the square and back toward his lava giant, his last refuge. Before he'd gone a dozen feet, the duke landed a blast of fire on his back, and Eli fell. He rolled across the wet cobbles, smacking the giggling flames with his hands until they were smothered, but while he was putting himself out, the duke had closed the distance, and when Eli looked up again, he saw that he was trapped. They were back where they'd started, at the farthest end of the square from the citadel. Eli jumped to his feet as the duke advanced, ready to run again, but there was nowhere to go. He was right up against the burning doorway of a storefront, with the duke in front of him and everything else in flames.

By the time Eli realized that he was truly trapped, it was too late. The duke's burning hand closed on his shoulder and tossed him to the ground with surprising strength. Eli hit the doorstep hard, crying out as the skin on his shoulder blistered from the duke's burning grip. He started to get up again, but the duke's boot slammed down on his chest, pinning him to the ground. Edward stood above him, a black silhouette against the burning night.

"Go on," the duke whispered. "Call your lava spirit. It won't do you any good. Your head will be off your shoulders before the words leave you."

Eli swallowed, and the duke's boot pressed harder on his chest, crushing the breath out of him.

"I've won, Monpress," the duke said, raising his ax in a shining arc. "I *always* win."

Eli couldn't even think of an answer for that. He could only watch as the ax whistled through the air, flying straight for the exposed area between his collarbone and his neck.

A moment before it struck, something strange happened. The blow, which had been straight and true, turned sideways, landing not in Eli's flesh, but deep in the wooden doorstep beside him. For a moment, both Eli and the duke just stared at the blade. Then Edward ripped it free with a roar of rage and raised the ax again, using both hands this time, the fire from his flame-wreathed fingers scorching the ax's wooden handle. But as he swung again, Eli saw the ax blade flip in the duke's hands. It flipped on its own, and Eli heard a small, terrified voice cry out in defiance, "Death to tyrants!"

With that cry, the metal head of the ax let go of its shaft. It flew into the house behind Eli, burying itself in the burning door. Edward, robbed of the ax's weight, stumbled into his swing. He was still staring at the bladeless hilt in disbelief when another extraordinary thing happened. The wooden shop sign, its painted surface blistered and illegible from the fire's heat, let go of its hinges. Nothing had broken, for the nails were still there, still strong. The wood simply had stopped holding on to them. The sign fell with a fearsome cry of vengeance and struck the duke square in the back.

"Go!" the sign shouted, bearing down on the duke with all its weight.

Eli went. He shot up, kicking the duke out of the way and running past him. But the duke was not done. With tremendous strength, he threw the sign off and made a grab for Eli as he passed, catching the thief's leg and sending them both sprawling on the wet cobbles. Eli kicked, but Edward was too fast. He surged forward, his hands going for Eli's neck, but just before he reached the thief, the ground beneath them began to rumble. At the corner of the square, the iron treasury door launched off its supports with a great, ringing cry. It rolled like a wheel, bouncing over the cobblestones that swiveled to guide it.

"For the cause!" it cried, its iron voice filled with decades of bottled anger. "Death to tyrants!"

The duke had just enough time to look up, his face pale and disbelieving, as the door flipped itself around and, with a final wordless cry of vengeance, fell flat-side down on top of him.

With a great, iron crash, the enslavement over Gaol vanished. The duke's control winked out like a snuffed candle, and all at once spirits were everywhere, piling themselves on top of the door, which was ringing like a gong in triumph. Unfortunately, in their exuberance, they weren't watching for Eli, who was still lying on his back where the duke had tripped him, staring in amazement. When the second hail of roofing tiles nearly took his leg off, he realized he'd better get out.

He rolled over with a groan, moving stiff and slow where the running and the falls had battered his poor bruises, looking for somewhere safe to lie. But everywhere he looked, spirits were rushing forward, trampling him under a wave of pent-up rage. Eli beat them back as best he could, but it was like fighting the tide, and he realized that he was going to be crushed to death under a riot of celebrating barrels, cobblestones, and roofing tile.

He had just enough time to appreciate the inglorious and ironic nature of such an end when a pair of strong arms burst through the jabbering spirits and grabbed him by the shoulders, hauling him up and out in a single motion.

"You all right?" said a blessedly familiar gruff voice, and Eli nearly burst into tears. He'd never been so happy to hear Josef in his life.

"Better than the other guy," he said, but the words turned into a choking cough. Even with the rain, the square was still black with smoke.

"He's fine," Josef said, slapping him on the back.

Somewhere behind them, Eli heard Giuseppe Monpress's familiar sigh. "Glad I found you, then. If he'd died here, he'd have been too burned to turn in for the bounty."

"Thanks for the sympathy," Eli coughed out, slapping his chest to get his lungs clear. He was just thinking about maybe trying to stand on his own when he felt the courtyard rumble and looked up to see Karon coming.

"I've kept the fires confined as best I could," the lava spirit rumbled. "But I think it's time for me to go. The river seems to be taking matters into its own hands."

As if to prove his point, a great crashing sound rose up in the distance, the sound of water washing over things it shouldn't. Eli opened his arms and let Karon's smoke pour into him again, wincing as the pain of the burn on his chest flashed like a fresh wound. But the pain faded quickly, and he pushed off of Josef just before a wave of white water burst into the square. It flooded up the street, surging over the burning houses in absurd, gravity-defying waves. Even the great pile of spirits marking where the duke had fallen was washed under, and everywhere the fire vanished beneath the cool, blue-white surge.

With the water came a stiff wind. It blew from the west, driving the stench of burned wood away. By this point, Eli and the rest had slogged through the water to the steps of the duke's citadel, where they were out of the flood. The wind hit them head-on, chilling their wet clothes and filling the air with the smell of the cold, rocky shore. Then something landed with an enormous splash just around the corner. Eli jumped at the sound, and Josef's hand went to the Heart, but he dropped his grip when the source of the sound came around the corner. It was a little old man, thin as whipcord and with a genteel, scholarly appearance that was only slightly ruined by the way he was wringing the water out of his billowing white robes.

He stopped when he reached the stairs, staring at the huddled group with trepidation as he settled his spectacles on his nose.

"Excuse me," he said, leaning forward inquisitively. "Which of you is Eli Monpress?"

"That would be me," Eli said, stepping forward. "Might I ask who's asking?"

"My name is Lelbon," the man said with a dry, polite smile. "I am a scholar and general errand runner for Illir, the West Wind."

He paused, as if this should mean something to them, but Josef just stared at him, and the elder Monpress leaned back against the doors, keen to see where this would go. Eli, however, broke into a grin.

"The West Wind, you say?" Eli scratched his chin thoughtfully. "And what is the West Wind doing sending representatives here? Gaol certainly doesn't count as the western coast."

"My employer is interested in the well-being of all the lands he blows over," Lelbon said stiffly. "We've been aware of the situation in Gaol for some time, but were unable to interfere due to the local Great Spirit's refusal to allow outside aid. The Spiritualist Lyonette has been investigating for us and, as you can see, has rectified the situation."

"By flooding the whole place," Eli said, laughing. "That's Spiritualists for you."

Lelbon just gave him a sour look. "I was sent to you with a warning. Spiritualist Lyonette is currently speaking with my master, but she will be heading in this direction shortly. I am instructed to relay that it would be wise of you to move on."

"Would it?" Eli said. "And where exactly does your master get off giving me orders?"

"It's only a suggestion," Lelbon said with a shrug. "The great Illir is merely concerned for your welfare. After all, even for as great a spirit as the West Wind, interfering in the affairs of the favorite is politically unadvisable."

"Favorite?" Josef said, looking at Eli. "Favorite what?"

"Forget it," Eli said. "All right, you heard the little old man. Let's get out of here."

"What, just like that?" Josef asked. "We're not going to steal anything?"

"What's left to steal?" Eli said, nodding at the smoldering town and the great empty citadel. "Besides," he said, grinning at Monpress, "according to everyone, *I* already stole the entire treasury from the thief-proof fortress. That's quite enough for one country. We've got the Fenzetti; we're done here."

That's when he noticed that Josef wasn't carrying anything.

"You *do* have the Fenzetti, don't you?" Eli said. "It's with Nico, right? Where is she, anyway?"

"I've got it," Josef said flatly. "Nico's another matter." He turned around and walked into the shadowed doorway of the citadel, coming back with the Heart strapped across his shoulders and two wrapped bundles. One was sword-shaped and wrapped in cloth, the Fenzetti. The other was small and dark and carefully cradled in Josef's arms.

"Wait," Eli said, going very, very pale. "She's not—"

"No," Josef said. "But it isn't exactly good. I'll tell you on the way. Let's go if we're going."

"Right," Eli said quietly, putting his smiling face back so fast Josef didn't even see his expression change. He turned to the elder Monpress, who was still lounging on the dry step. "You're welcome to piggyback on our escape, old man. It makes me feel useful to assist the elderly."

"Your concern is touching," Monpress said, "but I've still a little unfinished business here. Anyway, even your quiet escapes are too flashy for me."

"Suit yourself," Eli said. "See you around."

"Hopefully not," Monpress answered, but Eli and Josef were already splashing across the soggy square. They vanished down a side street headed toward the north gate, where the panicked crowds of people, who had fled to the city border the first time the city went mad, were now surging through the newly opened doors and over the walls, which had shrunk back to their original size and shape on the duke's death.

When the thief and his swordsman had vanished completely

into the dark, Lelbon and Monpress exchanged a polite farewell and went their separate ways, Lelbon down the road toward the river, and Monpress, very quietly, into the citadel. That was the last Gaol saw of either of the Monpress thieves.

CHAPTER 24

Gin raced through the streets and toward the burning square, Miranda clinging to his back, urging him on. Minutes ago, she'd felt the pressure of the duke's Enslavement vanish completely. Since then, everything had been in chaos. The spirits of the city were rioting in their new freedom, and the entire town seemed to be moving as it saw fit. Mellinor's water was everywhere, putting out fires, moving through the streets, but the water's spirit was too large for her to touch now, and their link felt thin and distant. By contrast, her rings felt closer than ever, the connection woven thick and heavy up and down her arms.

A wind rose as she rode, stiff and cold and smelling of the sea, though they were a hundred miles inland. It grew stronger as they went until Miranda could feel it through her clothes, pressing on her skin like a weight. Unbidden, Gin began to slow down, falling from a run to a trot, then a walk, then nothing, standing still on the broad street that opened into the square at the front of the citadel.

"What's wrong?" Miranda whispered. "Keep going."

"I can't," Gin growled. "The wind is blocking the way."

Miranda glanced up, staring at the empty road ahead. The wind was to their back now, buffeting ghosthound and rider from side to side. Then, all at once, the air fell still. High overhead, the clouds peeled back, brushed aside to reveal the moonlit sky, and in the stillness, the air grew lighter. Miranda smelled wet stone, salt, and sea storms, and then, without warning, the West Wind itself was upon them.

Though she couldn't see it, Miranda didn't need to. Playing host to Mellinor had made her an expert at feeling the special nature of the Great Spirits. Still, even if she'd never met one before, she would have known the West Wind for what it was. There was simply nothing else the enormous spirit surrounding her could be. It was the essence of a sea wind, endless, wet, salt laden, and powerful, blowing ever upward. It covered the city, missing nothing, and yet Miranda could feel its attention focus on her as an approving ripple, almost like a chuckle, ran through the enormous, invisible river of power.

"A pleasure to meet you at last, Spiritualist," the West Wind said. "You and Mellinor have undone a great wrong against the spirits of this place. For this, you have our gratitude."

Miranda nodded, dumbstruck. The wind's voice was like a gale in her head. The words ricocheted off the buildings, garbled, and yet there was no mistaking them for anything other than what they were. When she did find her own voice at last, however, she asked a question.

"What of the duke?" she said. "Did Eli succeed?"

"He did," the wind said, "and disappeared shortly thereafter. I am sorry, Spiritualist."

Miranda felt like the wind had punched her in the stomach. She slumped over, letting the crippling feeling of defeat work its way through her. There went her reputation, her ticket back into the Spirit Court. There went her career. *Why* had she let Eli go off on his own?

"Don't look that way," the wind said. "I had Lelbon promise you great rewards for your assistance here, and I keep my word. Already I have sent winds to the Spirit Court Tower in Zarin to speak with the Rector Spiritualis. Banage and I have met before, and I am sure he will listen with an open mind. I have also sent winds to each tower to inform the Keepers of your deeds today, and the great debt I owe you." Miranda felt something in the wind slide, and she could almost imagine that the West Wind was smiling. "Surely, such words of praise will smooth over any remaining rough politics."

Miranda could only nod stupidly. Most Spiritualists had only heard of the West Wind in stories. To actually be directly contacted by such an enormous and powerful spirit would be the experience of a lifetime. They'd forgive just about anything for a chance to curry its good favor.

Seeing her expression, the wind chuckled. "Is it enough, Spiritualist?"

"I suppose," Miranda said, still dumbstruck. "What happens now?"

"Now, I must leave," the wind said. "Winds are not meant to be lords over land. I have received a special dispensation from those who care for this sort of thing to allow Mellinor to remain as temporary Great Spirit for the next few weeks until the river Fellbro's soul can be cleansed and reinstated."

"Fellbro is still here?" Miranda asked. "You mean he's not—"

"What?" the wind said. "Dead? Of course not. It takes more than losing some water to kill a river. Mellinor only pushed it aside for a while. Right now Fellboro's slinking in the mud and sulking. Too long spent living in fear has made his water bitter, but we'll soon have him to rights. In the meanwhile, Mellinor will put the land back in order. Once a Great Spirit, always a Great Spirit. You should stay here as well. I imagine the human side of Gaol also needs fixing."

Miranda looked around at the empty town. "That it does, but I'm not exactly a lady of the manor."

The wind laughed, rippling over her. "I'm sure you'll manage. I'm leaving Lelbon here to help. Try not to be too hard on the little river spirit when it comes back. And Miranda?"

This last bit was whispered, a bare breeze in her ear. "Good luck and thank you. I won't be forgetting your usefulness."

That struck Miranda as an odd way of putting it, but the wind was already blowing past her, rising in a gale and blowing west, clearing the clouds out of the way as the sun began to peek over the horizon.

"Well," Gin said. "Now what?"

"I'm not sure," Miranda said. She was feeling a bit deflated, but happy. If anyone could get her back into the Spirit Court without Eli, it would be a spirit like the West Wind. Still, first things first. "Eril," she said clutching the pearl pendant at her neck. "Go and tell Durn to bring Hern to the citadel so we can lock him up somewhere more comfortable."

The wind tittered at this and left, blowing out in a whistling gust. When it was gone, she nudged Gin forward. He trotted off toward the citadel, tongue hanging out.

"We need to find the second-in-command," Miranda said, running her hands through her hair as her brain scrambled. "Send a runner to the Council and to the King of Argo to find out who's supposed to be taking over, and to explain what happened. I'm not looking forward to that. Plus, there's cleanup, getting the people back in line and back into their homes, rebuilding, so much to do."

"You'll manage," Gin said. "First, let's get some breakfast. I don't think anyone would begrudge me a pig after all that running."

Miranda laughed, and together they picked up the pace, loping past the burned-out buildings and into the great, empty citadel of Gaol.

All in all it took two weeks for the King of Argo to declare the Duke of Gaol's successor. Edward of Gaol had no wife or children, and though his nephew was the obvious choice to inherit, the nature of the duke's death prevented a smooth transition. He'd been murdered, that was certain. Still, the King of Argo couldn't levy charges against a shop sign, roofing tiles, and an iron door. So, after much deliberation, the duke's death was written down as an accident. Once that was out of the way, the nephew showed up almost immediately and proceeded at once to instigate a full inventory of Gaol's wealth and property, a task that left him exceedingly unhappy.

"This is intolerable!" he cried, shoving the account books under Miranda's nose for the fifth time that hour. "Not even counting the water damage done to my priceless treasures, which we're still dredging out of the river, the old goat spent almost forty thousand gold standards on his ridiculous Eli Monpress obsession, ten thousand of which was spent making that brick of a citadel look impressive from the outside! Honestly, it's not even a citadel, just a garrison with overly thick walls and an absurd little mansion stuck on its head."

"Well," Miranda said, "look at it this way: at least Gaol's not in the hole, which is more than I can say for most kingdoms. So why don't you count yourself lucky? You are, after all, one duchy richer than you were last week."

"That's hardly the point!" the nephew cried. "Look here! Here's a check written out to one Phillipe di Monte for 'consultation and advice involving the actions of Eli Monpress.' Written out *the day my uncle died*, no less! It's scandalous!"

"Phillipe di Monte," Miranda said thoughtfully. "Isn't he the villain from Pacso's *The Piteous Fall of Dulain*?"

"I don't care if it was Punchi the puppet!" the nephew shouted back. "I just want to know why *he's* getting almost twenty thousand standards of *my* money when his advice obviously didn't work!"

Miranda didn't have an answer for that. Fortunately, Lelbon appeared at that moment to tell her that Fellbro was almost ready to take his river back.

As it turned out, by the time the duke's nephew contacted Gaol's money changer in Zarin, the gold had already been paid to the mysterious Phillipe di Monte. This sent the poor boy into a rage, and convinced it was Eli himself making a fool of him, the new duke then sent off a letter pledging another twenty thousand to Monpress's bounty, just on general principle.

"That will show the no-good thief!" he said, sealing the letter to the Council Bounty office.

Miranda wisely kept her comments to herself.

Just when she was sure she could take no more, an envoy from the Spirit Court arrived to fetch Hern and Miranda and take them back to Zarin. The wind's words must have had a better effect than even Miranda had anticipated, for the Spiritualists treated her as if she was the Rector Spiritualis himself. This infuriated Hern to no end, which put Miranda in very high spirits as she rode down to the river.

She'd spoken to her sea spirit very little while Mellinor had inhabited the river. He'd simply been too large and too busy to talk with. Now the blue water was gone and the river was back to its usual cloudy green. As Miranda walked out on the dock, Mellinor rose in a pillar of water to greet her, his water cloudy with fatigue.

"I was almost afraid you wouldn't come back," Miranda said. "Not after you'd gotten a taste for being a Great Spirit again."

"Of course I came back," the water said. "I'm a sea, not a river. All this flowing and silt was driving me mad. Besides"—his voice grew wistful—"no river could replace my own seabed. But I'm already resigned to that, and anyway, you're my shore now, Miranda."

She smiled at that, and held out her hands. "Ready to come home, then?"

"More than you know," he said and sighed, sliding back into her with a relieved, sinking feeling.

He sank to the bottom of her spirit and fell asleep almost instantly. When he was completely settled, Miranda turned around and walked back to Gin, who was waiting on the road.

"Come on." She grinned, sliding onto his back. "Let's go home."

"I thought we'd never leave," Gin sighed, loping back toward the citadel where the other Spiritualist waited with Hern, now ringless and bound in chains, to journey with them back to Zarin where, Miranda had the feeling, she'd get a much warmer welcome this time around.

ACKNOWLEDGMENTS

Thank you to Aaron, Matt, Krystina, Steven, Andrea, and everyone who read my books back when they were really terrible. Your feedback got me to where I am today.

VOLUME 3

The Spirit Eater

For Nate, who made it.

PROLOGUE

The great hall of the Shapers had been flung open to let in the wounded. Shaper wizards, their hands still covered in soot from their work, ran out into the blowing snow to help the men who came stumbling onto the frosted terrace through a white-lined hole in the air. Some fell and did not rise again, their long, black coats torn beyond recognition. These the Shapers rolled onto stretchers that, after a sharp order, stood on their own and scrambled off on spindly wooden legs, some toward the waiting doctors, others more slowly toward the cold rooms, their unlucky burdens already silent and stiff.

Alric, Deputy Commander of the League of Storms, lay on the icy floor near the center of the hall, gritting his teeth against the pain as a Shaper physician directed the matched team of six needles sewing his chest back together. His body seized when the needles hit a nerve, and the Shaper grabbed his shoulders, slamming him back against the stone with surprising strength.

"You must not move," she said.

"I'm trying not to," Alric replied through gritted teeth.

The old physician arched an eyebrow and started the needles again with a crooked finger. "You're lucky," she said, holding him still. "I've seen others with those wounds going down to the cold rooms." She nodded at the three long claw marks that ran down his chest from neck to hip. "You must be hard to kill."

"Very," Alric breathed. "It's my gift."

She gave him a strange look, but kept her hands firmly on his shoulders until the needles finished. Once the wounds were closed, the doctor gave him a bandage and left to find her next patient. Alric sat up with a ragged breath, holding his arms out as the bandage rolled around his torso of its own accord and tied itself over his left shoulder. After the gauze had pulled itself tight, Alric sat a moment longer with his eyes closed, mastering the pain. When he was sure he had it under control, he grabbed what was left of his coat, buckled his golden sword to his hip, and got up to find his commander.

The Lord of Storms was standing in the snow beside the great gate he had opened for their retreat. Through the shimmering hole in the world, Alric could see what was left of the valley, the smoking craters rimmed with dead stone, the great gashes in the mountains. But worse than the visible destruction were the low, terrified cries of the mountains. Their weeping went straight to his bones in a way nothing else ever had and, he hoped, nothing ever would again.

The Lord of Storms had his back to Alric. As always, his coat was pristine, his sword clean and sheathed at his side. He alone of all of them bore no sign of what had just occurred, but a glance at the enormous black clouds overhead was all Alric needed to know his commander's mood. Alric took a quiet, calming breath. He would need to handle this delicately.

The moment he stepped into position, the Lord of Storms barked, "Report."

"Twenty-four confirmed casualties," Alric said. "Eighteen wounded, eight still unaccounted for."

"They're dead," the Lord of Storms said. "No one else will be coming through." He jerked his hand down and the gate beside him vanished, cutting off the mountains' cries. Despite himself, Alric sighed in relief.

"Thirty-two dead out of a force of fifty," the Lord of Storms said coldly. "That's a rout by any definition."

"But the objective was achieved," Alric said. "The demon was destroyed."

The Lord of Storms shook his head. "She's not dead."

"Impossible," Alric said. "I saw you take her head off. Nothing could survive that."

The Lord of Storms sneered. "A demon is never defeated until you've got the seed in your hand." He walked to the edge of the high, icy terrace, staring down at the snow-covered peaks below. "We tore her up a bit, diminished her, but she'll be back. Mark me, Alric, this isn't over."

Alric pulled himself straight. "Even if you are right, even if the creature is still alive somewhere, we stopped the Dead Mountain's assault. The Shepherdess can have no—"

"*Do not speak to me about that woman!*" the Lord of Storms roared. His hand shot to the blue-wrapped hilt of his sword, and the smell of ozone crept into the air as little tongues of lightning crackled along his grip. "What we faced tonight should never have been allowed to come about." He looked at Alric from the corner of his eye. "Do you know what we fought in that valley?"

Alric shuddered, remembering the black wings that blotted out the sky, the screaming cry that turned his bones to water and made mountains weep in terror, the hideous, black shape that his brain refused to remember in detail because something that horrible should never be seen more than once. "A demon."

The Lord of Storms laughed. "A demon? A demon is what we get when we neglect a seed too long. A demon can be taken out by a single League member. We kill *demons* every day. What we faced tonight, Alric, was a fully grown seed." The Lord of Storms took a deep breath. "If I hadn't taken its head when I did, we could have witnessed the birth of another Dead Mountain."

"Another..." Alric swallowed against the dryness in his throat. "But the Dead Mountain is under the Lady's own seal. Tiny slivers may escape, but nothing big enough to let the demon actually replicate itself could get through. It's impossible; the whole containment system would be undermined."

"Impossible?" The Lord of Storms shook his head. "You keep telling yourself that. But it is the Lady's will that keeps the seal in place, and when her attention wanders, we're the ones who have to clean up."

The Lord of Storms clenched his sword hilt, and the smell of ozone intensified. Alric held his breath, wondering if he should go for cover. When the Lord of Storms was this angry, nothing was safe. "It's not just a large seed," the commander said at last. "That would be too simple. What we saw tonight was as much a product of the soil as the seed. The Master got his claws in a strong one, this time. Thirty-two League members and a ruined valley are *nothing* compared to what this could end up costing us. We have to find the creature and finish her."

Alric was looking for a way to answer that when the soft sound of a throat clearing saved him the trouble. He turned to see a group of old men and women in fine heavy coats standing in the doorway to the great hall. Alric nodded graciously, but the Lord of Storms just sneered and turned back to the mountains, crossing his arms over his chest. Undeterred by the League commander's rudeness, the figure at the group's head, a tall, stern man with a white beard down to his chest, stepped forward.

"My Lord of Storms," he said, bowing to the enormous man's back. "I am Ferdinand Slorn, Head Shaper and Guildmaster of the Shaper Clans."

"I know who you are," the Lord of Storms said. "We'll be out of here soon enough, old man."

"You are welcome to stay as long as you need," Slorn said, smiling benignly. "However, we sought you out to offer assistance of a different nature."

The Lord of Storms looked over his shoulder. "Speak."

Slorn remained unruffled. "We have heard of your battle with the great demon, as well as its unfortunate escape. As Master of the Shapers, I would like to offer our aid in its capture."

"Guildmaster," Alric said, "you have already helped so much, providing aid and—"

"How do you know about that?" The sudden anger in the Lord of Storms' voice stopped Alric cold.

"These mountains are Shaper lands, my lord," the Guildmaster replied calmly. "You can hardly expect to fight a battle such as you just fought without attracting our attention. Our great teacher, the Shaper Mountain, on whose slopes we now stand, is enraged and grieving. His brother mountains were among those injured by the demon, many beyond repair. As his students, we feel his pain as our own. We cannot bring back what was destroyed, but we do ask that we be allowed to assist in the capture of the one responsible."

"What help could you be to us?" the Lord of Storms scoffed. "Demons are League business. You may be good at slapping spirits together, but what do Shapers know of catching spirit eaters?"

"More than you would think." The old man's eyes narrowed, but his calm tone never broke. "After all, we Shapers live our lives in the shadow of the demon's mountain. You and your ruffians may be good at tracking down the demon's wayward seeds when they escape into the world, but it is my people, and the great mountains we honor, who suffer the demon daily. Tonight, several beautiful, powerful spirits, ancient mountains and allies of my people, were eaten alive. Even for us, who are used to bearing sorrow, this loss is too much. We cannot rest until the one responsible is destroyed."

"That's too bad," the Lord of Storms said, turning to face the old Guildmaster at last. "I'll say this one more time. Demons are League business. So, until I put a black coat on your shoulders, you will stay out of our way."

The Guildmaster stared calmly up at the Lord of Storms. "I can assure you, my dear Lord of Storms, we will avoid your way entirely. All I ask is the opportunity to pursue our own lines of inquiry."

The Lord of Storms leaned forward, bending down until he was inches away from the old man's face. "Listen," he said, very low, "and listen well. We both know that you're going to do what you're going to do, so before you go and do it, take my advice: Do not cross me. If you or your people get in my way on the hunt for the creature, I will roll right over you without looking back. Yours wouldn't be the first city I've razed to kill a demon. Do you understand me, Shaper?"

Slorn narrowed his eyes. "Quite clearly, demon hunter."

The Lord of Storms gave him one final, crackling glare before pushing his way through the small crowd of Shaper elders and stomping back across the frozen terrace toward the brightly lit hall.

Alric thanked the Shaper elders before running after his commander. "Honestly," he said, keeping his voice low, "it would make my life easier if you learned a little tact. They were just trying to help."

"Help?" the Lord of Storms scoffed. "There's nothing someone outside the League could do to help. Let them do whatever they like. It'll end the same. No seed sleeps forever, Alric. Sooner or later, she's going to crack, and when that happens, I'll be there. The next time I corner her, there will be no escape. I don't care if I have to cut through every spirit in the sphere, I won't stop until I have her seed in my hand." He clenched his fists. "Now, get everyone out of here, including corpses. We burn the dead tonight at headquarters. I want nothing of ours left in this mountain."

And with that he vanished, just disappeared into thin air, leaving Alric walking alone through the center of the Shaper hall. Alric skidded to a stop. It was always like this when things were bad, but the only thing to do was obey. Gritting his teeth, he walked over to the best mended of the walking wounded and began giving orders to move out. His words were met with grim stares. Most of the League were too wounded to make a safe portal back to the fortress, but they were soldiers, and they obeyed without grumbling, working quietly under Alric to bring home the dead through the long, bloody night.

Ferdinand Slorn, Head Shaper and Guildmaster of the Shaper Clans, watched the Lord of Storms' exit with heavy-lidded eyes. The other heads of the Shaper disciplines were already dispersing, whispering to one another as they walked into the crowded hall. Only one stayed behind. Etgar, the Master Weaver, youngest of the elders, remained at the edge of the terrace, the embroidered hem of his elegant coat twitching nervously against his shins.

The old Shaper smiled. "Go on, Etgar."

Etgar paled. "Master Shaper," he said, his deep voice strangely timid. "Yours is the voice of all Shapers. I do not oppose your judgment, but—"

"But you do not agree," the Master Shaper finished.

"We're all upset," Etgar said, his words coming in long, angry puffs of white vapor in the cold night. "What happened in that valley is tragedy enough to fill our laments for the next dozen years, but demons are the League's responsibility. Even if we could do something, if the demon is still alive as the League thinks, it's probably gone back to the Dead Mountain by now."

"No," Slorn said. "Once awakened, a seed can never return to the mountain. The seal works both ways, repelling awakened demons from the outside as surely as it pins their Master below the mountain's stone. My son told me that much before he vanished." The old man smiled a long, sad smile and turned his eyes to the snow-covered mountains. "No, Etgar, if the creature is still alive, it's out there, somewhere, and if it wishes to survive the League's wrath long enough to recover its power, it will have to hide. If that is indeed the case, the best place for it is under the only cover the creature has left, its human skin. Demons may be League business, but humans are another matter."

"What difference does that make?" Etgar shook his head in frustration. "Even if she does take a human form to escape the League's justice, what are we to do about it? I want justice served as much as any, but we are crafters, Guildmaster, not bounty hunters. How are we even to search for her?"

"We will not," Slorn said. "We shall allow others to search for us." The Guildmaster reached into his robes and pulled out a small notebook. "She may be a daughter of the Dead Mountain, but so long as she takes refuge in a human form, she will be vulnerable to human greed." He pulled an ink pencil from his shirt pocket and began to write furiously. After a few moments he smiled, ripped the page from his book, and handed it to Etgar. "Take this to the Council of Thrones."

Etgar stared dumbly at the paper. "What is it?"

"A bounty pledge," Slorn said. "The girl, alive, for two hundred thousand gold standards."

Etgar's eyes went wide. "Two hundred thousand gold standards?" he cried, looking at the paper again as though it had suddenly grown fangs. Sure enough, there was the figure, written out in the Guildmaster's nearly illegible hand across the very bottom of the note.

"A small sum compared to what we have lost tonight," Slorn said, his voice cold and terrible. "This world is not so large that we can afford to be placid, Etgar. Too long we Shapers have left these things to the League, and look where it has gotten us. There are more seeds than ever, and now a fully awakened demon slaughters our ancient allies while we do nothing but wring our hands. I don't know what game the Shepherdess is playing letting things get this bad, but we cannot afford to play along anymore. This may all be for nothing, but no matter the outcome, I will not be the Guildmaster who shuts his hall against what he does not wish to see." He reached out, folding the younger man's hands over the paper. "See that that gets to Zarin."

For a moment Etgar just stood there, staring dumbly at the note in his fist. Finally, he bowed. "As you will, Master Shaper."

The old man clapped Etgar on the shoulder and set off for the great hall, the ice on the stones creeping away to make a clear path for him across the wide terrace. Etgar stayed put, looking down at the torn page in his hand, reading it again, just to be sure. Two hundred thousand gold council standards to be paid out on proof of death for the daughter of the Dead Mountain. That was it, no mention of the crime, no personal details, just the amount and a short description of a thin, pale girl with dark hair and dark eyes taken from what one of the wounded League men had been able to get out before he died.

"The Weaver's will be done," Etgar muttered. Frowning, he thrust the bounty request into his pocket and set off across the terrace to find a messenger to take the order to Zarin.

* * *

In the hills at the foot of the mountains, just above the tree line where the snow was still thin, something black fell from the sky. Ice and dirt flew up in an explosion where it hit, leaving a rounded crater on the silent mountainside. Eventually, the dust settled, but inside the crater, nothing moved. The mountain slope returned to its previous stillness, until, when the sky was turning gray with the predawn light, something reached up and clutched the crater's edge. Black and bleeding, it pulled itself up, leaving a trail in the dirt. It climbed over the crater's lip and tumbled down the mountainside, sliding down the slope until it hit the first of the scraggly trees. The creature rasped in pain, clutching itself with long black limbs. It stayed like that for a long while, lying still against the scrubby pines.

As the sky grew lighter, the darkness clinging around the slumped figure burned away, leaving the small, broken body of a girl. She was pale and naked, lying doubled over on her side, clutching her stomach. There was snow on the ground around her, but her body scarcely seemed to feel it. She lay on the frozen ground, never shivering, eyes open wider than any human eyes should, staring up at the mountains above, or, rather, past them, toward something only she could see. Her skeletal body twitched, and she took a shallow, ragged breath.

Why are you still here? The voice was colder than the snow.

The girl on the ground closed her eyes in shame and took another breath.

Stop that, the voice said. *You failed. You lost. What right do you have to go on living? Why do you waste my time?*

The girl shook her head and curled her body tighter. "Please," she whispered, her voice little more than a hoarse vibration in her throat. "Please don't leave me, Master."

The voice made a disgusted sound. *Shut up. You don't get to speak.*

You don't even deserve my attention. Just die in a place that's easy to find so my seed doesn't go to waste.

The girl gave a sobbing cry, but the voice was already gone. Her head throbbed at the sudden emptiness, and she realized she was alone. Truly alone, for the first time since she could remember. She would have wept then, but she had no strength left even to break down. She could only lie there in the shade of the tree, hoping the slope was close enough to fulfill the Master's final request. After losing so completely, it was the least she could do.

It wouldn't be long, at least. Her blood was red again, mixing with the dirt to dye the snow a dull burgundy in a circle around her. Soon, all her failures would be behind her. All her weakness, everything, it would all be gone. She was so focused on this she didn't notice the man coming across the mountain slope toward her until his shadow blotted out the sun in her eyes. She looked up in surprise. He was very tall, dressed like a poor farmer in a ragged wool coat, but his body was that of a fighter, with blades strapped up and down his torso and a monstrous iron sword on his back.

He stood a step away from her, his face shadowed and unreadable with the sun behind him. Then, in one smooth motion, he drew a short sword from the sheath at his hip. This much, at least, she could understand, and the girl closed her eyes, ready for the blow.

It never came. The man simply stood there, staring at her with the blade in his hand. When she opened her eyes again, he spoke.

"Do you want to die?"

The girl nodded.

Overhead, the sword whistled through the cold air, then stopped. The man's voice spoke again. "Look at me and say you want to die."

The girl lifted her head and stared up at him. The morning sun glinted off the sharp blade he held in the air, ready to come down. How easy it would be to let this stranger end it, how simple. And yet, when she tried to tell him to go on, finish what the demon hunters had started, her voice would not come. She tried again, but all she managed was a squeak. The dull red circle on the snow around her was very wide now. Soon, she wouldn't even have a choice. She knew she should take his offer, end it quickly, but her mouth would not move, because it was not true.

She did not want to die. The realization came as a surprise, but the truth of it rang in her, vibrating against the inner corners of herself she'd long forgotten. She had been defeated, abandoned, wounded beyond repair. She owed it to the Master to die, owed it to herself to save the horrible shame of living on when she was not wanted, but still, despite all reason…

"I want to live." The words came out in a croak, and she only recognized the voice as her own from the pain in her dry throat.

Above her, the man nodded and sheathed his sword. "Then take another breath."

She met his eyes and slowly, shuddering with pain, did as he said.

He grinned wide and reached down, grabbing her arms in his hands. He lifted her like she weighed nothing and tossed her over his shoulder. "Come on, then," he said. "I had a long walk up here to see what that crash was, and we've got a long walk back. If you've chosen to live, you'll have to keep your end and keep breathing. Just focus on that and I'll get us back down to camp to see to your wounds. Then we'll see where we go from there. What's your name?"

"Nico," the girl said, wincing against his shoulder. The Master had given her that name.

"Nico, then," the man said, setting off down the mountain. "I'm Josef."

Nico pushed away from his shoulder, trying not to get blood on his shirt, but he just shrugged her back on and kept going. Eventually she gave up, resting her head on his back to focus all of her energy on breathing, letting her breaths fill the emptiness the Master had left inside her. As she focused her mind on the feel of her lungs expanding and contracting, she felt something close at the back of her mind, like a door gently swinging shut. But even as she became aware of the sensation, she realized she could no longer remember how she'd come to be on that mountain slope, or where her wounds came from, and just as quickly, she realized she didn't care. The one thing she could remember was that before the man Josef appeared, she'd been ready to die. Now, clinging to his shoulder, death was her enemy. Something deep had changed, and Nico was content to let it stay that way. Reveling in a strange feeling of freedom, she went limp on Josef's shoulder, focusing only on savoring each gasp of air she caught between jolts as Josef jogged down the steep slope to the valley below.

CHAPTER 1

Two years later.

The house on chicken legs crouched between two steep hills, its claws digging deep into the leaf litter to keep the building from sliding farther down into the small ravine. If Heinricht Slorn had any worries about the precarious position he'd put his walking house in, his face didn't show it. He sat in his workroom, his brown fur glowing in the strong lamplight. His dark, round eyes glittered as they focused on the object taking up most of the large worktable. It was about four feet long, white as a dried bone, and shaped somewhat like a sword, or like a stick a child had carved into a sword. Despite its crude form, Slorn hovered over the object, his enormous hands running over its smooth surface with the painful, meticulous slowness of one master appreciating the work of another.

Pele sat at his elbow, also staring at the white sword. She was trying her best to match her father's focus, but they'd been doing this for two days now and she was getting awful sick of staring and seeing nothing. Sitting in the dark room, her mind began to wander back to the other, more interesting projects she'd been working on before Slorn had put her to work on the Fenzetti blade.

"Pele." Slorn's gruff voice snapped her back to attention. His eyes hadn't left the sword, but that didn't matter. Her father seemed to have a supernatural ability to tell when her attention began to drift. "What is the first thing we determine when examining an unknown spirit?"

"Its nature," Pele answered at once, sitting up on the hard workbench. "A Shaper must know the nature of her materials. Only when a spirit's true nature is known will the Shaper be able to bend it to her purpose."

"Good," Slorn said, reaching out to take her hand and press it against the smooth surface of the Fenzetti. "And what is the nature of this spirit?"

Pele flinched when she touched the sword. It was unnaturally smooth and strangely warm, yet she knew from experience that its surface could not be scratched even by an awakened blade. They'd tried half a dozen blades the morning it had arrived, and none of them had been able to make so much as a nick in the sword's white face.

Slorn was looking at her now, and she shrank under his intense gaze, her brain spinning to come up with an answer. "It's not wood," she said uncertainly. "Not stone either. It could be a metal not yet known, one of a different nature than iron or the mountain metals, perhaps a—"

"Stop," Slorn said. "You're not answering the question. I did not ask what it wasn't."

Pele sighed in frustration. "But—"

"Look again."

Slorn picked up the sword and set it point down on the floor between them. "Look at it as if you'd never seen it before and tell me what you think it is."

Pele bit her lip, looking the sword up and down. "A bone," she said at last.

Slorn grinned wide, showing all his yellow teeth. "All right, let's say, for the moment, it's a bone."

"But that's impossible," Pele said. "Bone metal is ancient. If it was actually bone, it would have rotted away ages ago. And why haven't we found any two pieces together? Surely if it was bone we'd have found a skeleton or…"

She stopped. Slorn was shaking his head.

"You're doing it again," he said. "If you're ever going to be more than a common wizard tinkerer, you need to stop trying to make the spirits fit into your expectations." He returned the blade to the table. "This is the spirits' world, Pele, not ours. We may command them, but they see the nature of things that we cannot. As Shapers, it is our job to fit into the spirits' order, not the other way around. Fenzetti understood this, and that's how he was able to shape what everyone else called unshapable."

He reached out and took the sword, not by its handle but by its point. "A Shaper must remember," he said, wrapping his fingers around the blade, "trust what you see, not what you know. Human knowledge is fragmented, but the spirit always knows its own nature."

With that, he began to tilt his hand up. The table creaked as he pressed against it, the muscles in his arms straining from the pressure. The sword, however, remained unchanged, but then, slowly, subtly, it began to bend. The white point curled with his hand, bending over on itself with a creak unlike anything Pele had heard before. Sweat started to soak through Slorn's shirt, but his face remained calm and determined. His hands were steady, bending the strange metal in a slow roll until, at last, he'd bent it over completely so that the tip of the sword brushed the blade.

He stopped, panting, and slumped over the bench, an enormous grin on his face. Despite the pressure of Slorn's bending, the curve was smooth, like an ox's curved horn. Pele touched it with murmured wonder and then snatched her hand back again. The sword was warm as a living thing.

"It *is* bone," she whispered, eyes wide. "But bone from what?"

"That's a mystery I cannot answer," Slorn said, sitting down on the bench. "But I think it's time we tested the rumor that drove me to send Monpress after it in the first place." Still smiling at the curled tip, he picked up the sword. "Fenzetti wrote that bone metal is indestructible, even by demons. It's the one spirit they can't eat." He paused. "Do you know why I make manacles for your mother?"

Pele shook her head, silent. Slorn never talked about her mother.

"They give the demon something to chew on other than the demonseed herself," he said. "Before she had to be isolated, Nivel and I did many experiments on the subject. She was the one who came up with using restraints. A demon, you see, will always attack spirits outside the demonseed first, since the seed relies on the host's strength until it is ready to awaken. This need to be constantly eating can be exploited by placing a strong-willed material along the host's body. Even though the demon knows better, knows it's a trick, it can't help its nature. It will attack those spirits endlessly, focusing its attention on the manacles instead of the host. This division of attention slows its growth phenomenally. Of course, it's not a perfect solution. Manacles are still spirits, and even the most stubborn awakened steel can only hold out for so long before it gets eaten down. But"—he tapped the bone metal against the table—"let's see how the demon does with a manacle it can chew on forever. If this bone metal is truly inedible by demons, it may slow Nivel's degradation to almost nothing, buying us a few more years to work on a cure."

"But Father," Pele said slowly. "You always say there is no cure."

Slorn's smile faded. "It is good to think that way," he said, laying the bent sword down again. "We must be realists. Still"—he looked at her, and his dark eyes were almost like the human eyes of the father she remembered from her childhood—"your mother has not given up. Not yet. And I would be a poor husband indeed if I let her fight alone."

Pele shook her head, blinking back tears. Slorn put his arm around her shoulders, pulling her to lean against him. "None of that," he whispered.

Pele sniffed and scrubbed her eyes, trying to compose herself. They had work to do. Now was not the time to go crying. But as she tried to pull away, she realized her father had gone stiff. She looked up at him, but he was staring out the window, his round bear ears swiveling.

"Father?" she whispered.

He didn't answer. Then she heard it too. Outside, something thumped in the dark. It was big, and loud, far too loud to be one of the mountain cats, and the bears never came near Slorn's house.

"Pele," Slorn said, "get your knife. We have company."

She did as he told her, grabbing her knife from its hook. While she was belting it on, Slorn whispered something to the wall. She couldn't hear what he said, but the wall's answer was plain.

"I don't know," it said apologetically, timbers creaking. "He's no wizard, and that makes him very hard to keep track of. This one's especially bad. His soul is like a dull spot. He'd never have been able to slip by the Awakened Wood otherwise."

"I am well aware of the wood's weaknesses," Slorn said, giving the wall a pat. "You'd better wake the house."

"Yes, Slorn," the wall whispered, but Slorn was already gone, marching down the narrow hall. He threw open the front door and stepped out onto the rickety stairs. Pele pushed right up behind him, gripping the hilt of her knife as she peeked over his shoulder. There, standing at the edge of the rectangle of yellow light cast from the doorway, clinging to the steep slope with one arm, was a man she never wanted to see again.

Slorn glared down from his steps, crossing his arms over his chest. "Berek Sted."

The man sneered and moved into the light. He looked very different from when Pele had seen him last. His bald head was covered in several weeks' growth of stubbly hair, all except the top, where true baldness had left him bare. His scarred face was overgrown as well and streaked with dirt. His black coat was gone, as was his sash with its grotesque collection of severed hands and broken swords. Instead, his bare chest was wrapped in bandages, most of which were dark with old, dried blood. But the greatest change of all was his left arm. His shoulder and the first half of bicep looked the same as ever, but then, his arm simply stopped. He had no elbow, no hand, just a badly bandaged lump that he kept pressed against his side.

"Found you at last," Sted panted. "Swordsmith."

"What do you want?" Slorn asked, his voice dry.

Sted shifted his weight, pushing off the steep hillside with his one good arm to hurl something straight at them. It landed with a clatter at Slorn's feet, biting into the weather-stained wood. Slorn looked down, arching a furry eye ridge at what was left of Sted's black-toothed awakened blade. The top half of the sword was gone, leaving a ragged, twisted edge, as though the metal had been ripped apart.

"You sold me a faulty sword," Sted said. "I want another, a real one this time. One that won't break when I need it."

Slorn reached down and picked up the broken blade. He turned it over in his hands, and Pele winced. This close, she could hear the metal whimpering.

"Your sword was a quality piece of work," Slorn said. "Even if there was a flaw, the League is the only body entitled to demand my services, and I doubt very much they sent you here looking like that."

"Don't talk to me about the League," Sted growled.

"Ah," Slorn said, his voice cold. "Now I see. You've been drummed out."

"That's none of your business."

"It is indeed my business," Slorn said. "I made that sword for the League, not for you. What was it, Sted? Insubordination? Dereliction of duty?"

"Little of everything," Sted said with a shrug. "To hear that bastard Alric talk, choosing a good fight over a quick demon kill was the end of the world. After all I gave up to join the League, he kicked me out, took away my gifts. But I wouldn't be in this position if your sword had been up to the task, bear man."

Slorn crossed his arms over his aproned chest. "And how did my sword fail you?"

"It was weak!" Sted shouted. "Too weak to take a blow from that blunt bat Liechten uses. I said as much in my defense, but Alric couldn't stand to hear the truth about his precious swordsmith."

Slorn bared his teeth just a fraction. "If that's how you feel, why did you come here?"

"To get what I'm due," Sted said. "After all, it's only fair. You're the one whose failure got me kicked out, so you're the one who's going to have to make it right."

Slorn turned the broken sword over. "I can see from the dents that your sword took several blows from Josef Liechten's 'blunt bat.' An impressive achievement, standing up to the greatest awakened sword in the world. I'd hardly call that deficient." His eyes narrowed. "Though I can't say the same for its wielder."

"Don't blame this on me!" Sted shouted. "I was winning until your sword broke! It's not my fault I lost! I don't lose! Your sword failed me, and now you're going to make up for it. Make me a proper sword, swordsmith! Make me a blade that can take the Heart of War!"

"Impossible," Slorn said, handing the broken blade to Pele. "The Heart of War is the first and greatest awakened blade, forged at the beginning of the world. Even if I could somehow make a blade to rival it, it would be pointless." He glared at Sted. "A blade is only as powerful as the swordsman behind it. I've never seen you fight, but I can tell from how you're acting now that you are no match for Josef Liechten."

Sted sprang forward with astonishing speed and grabbed Slorn by the collar. Slorn was a large man, but Sted towered over him, his face scarlet with rage.

"Mind your snout before I take it off your face!" he roared, jerking Slorn off his feet. "You're going to make me that sword, and then I'm going to kill Liechten and everyone else who's made a fool of me. Starting with you, if you don't watch yourself."

Pele fumbled for her blade, her hands trembling in panic, but Slorn's calm never faltered, even with Sted's screaming mouth an inch from his black nose.

"You will unhand me," he said.

"Or what?" Sted growled.

Slorn smiled, and the fibers of his collar where Sted was holding him suddenly unraveled. Sted was left gripping air as Slorn dropped down. The Shaper landed neatly, and he had just enough time to give Sted a toothy smile before the stair beneath the swordsman's feet snapped like a green branch, launching the larger man into the night. Sted was too surprised to make a sound. He flew through the air, landing with a bone-snapping crack on the opposite slope. He bounced once and then began to slide into the ravine as the leaves that might have stopped his fall skittered away from the source of Slorn's displeasure.

Sted slid all the way to the bottom of the little gorge, landing with a splash in the icy stream. Twenty feet up, Slorn stared down from his stairs, a smirk on his muzzle as his torn collar began to mend itself. "This is my land, Sted," he said calmly. "You don't get to make demands here. Any tacit welcome you had as a League member is now gone, and I suggest you go as well. The forest is unkind to those who threaten me."

As he spoke, a large outcropping of rocks on the slope above Sted began to creak menacingly, but Sted heard none of it. "This isn't over!" he screamed. "You owe me!"

Slorn gave him a final long, disgusted look before turning and marching silently back into the house, pushing Pele ahead of him. The moment the door closed, the house began to move, climbing expertly along the ravine edge on its wooden chicken legs. From the window, Pele could see Sted flailing through the creek after them, but the trees along the water were barring his way, tripping him with their roots and tangling him in their branches. The last thing Pele saw before Sted vanished into the dark was Sted falling into the water, his one arm still reaching out for the retreating house.

"Will he come after us?" she whispered.

"He'll try," Slorn said, easing Sted's broken blade to sleep before tossing it into a barrel full of damaged parts. "The League doesn't take men who give up easily. But don't be afraid; the woods are a dangerous enemy and he's no wizard."

He gave her a yellow-toothed smile and disappeared into his workroom. Pele looked out the window one last time. The dark woods sped by outside as the house crawled north faster than a man could run, farther into the mountains, leaving no footprints behind.

* * *

In the dull light just before morning, Nivel sat as she always sat, straight on her rock with her hands folded across her lap. High overhead, the treetops, flat, black shapes against the gray sky, rocked in the wind, but here in her dry ravine it was silent, except for her manacles. As always, the metal cuffs buzzed against her skin. Their silver outsides were gnawed away in places, revealing the dense steel core. Nivel shifted. The decay was unsettling. Slorn had made the manacles for her just a month ago, but each new set seemed to wear out quicker than the one before. Nivel's lips tightened. She knew what that meant, even if she'd never seen it happen. She knew.

Of course you know. The voice sounded almost bored. *You always knew you would lose in the end.*

Nivel folded her hands tighter.

I don't see why you're putting your family through this, it said. *How selfish, fighting a losing battle on their time. You should just let go, let me have you, and set them free. Do you think your husband likes having a bear's head?*

An image flashed before her eyes, Slorn as he'd looked fifteen years ago when they were first married. But the memory had that strange crispness to it that told her it was the demon's sending, and not her own. It liked to riffle through her mind for weapons, but this was a battle they'd been fighting for a long time now, and Nivel was too wise for these old tricks. She closed her eyes against the image and kept her silence. Speaking to the voice only gave it more power, and she had no more to give.

She was finding something else to think about when a strange shadow appeared at the edge of her ravine. Nivel snapped her head up. It was far too early for Slorn or Pele, and no spirit would come near the warding. It could be a phantom. The demon had been making her see things that weren't there for years. Yet, from the confusion in her head, she felt that this was as much a surprise to it as to her. That terrified Nivel more than any false vision. She couldn't afford surprises.

The figure leaned over the edge of the ravine, peering down, and she saw it was a man. A large man with a bald head and a missing left arm. He had bandages across his torso and scars everywhere else. His skin was filthy and scratched all over, as though he'd been wrestling with a thornbush, and his eyes were the eyes of a madman.

He jumped down without a word, landing in a crouch on the sandy bed of the dead creek. He stayed in that crouch, looking around until he spotted her a few feet in front of him.

"There you are," he said, a crooked grin spreading across his face. "Took me awhile to find this place, but I knew the bear man wouldn't take his house too far from his big secret." He took a step forward, his boots dragging through the dry sand. "They tried to keep it away from us, back at headquarters, but the Lord of Storms has a loud voice and no love for you. To hear him talk, I thought you were some sort of monster, a barely controlled disaster waiting to happen, but you're just a woman."

Nivel glared at him. Her eyes were burning, a sure sign they were glowing, but for once she was glad. The large man didn't look so confident anymore. "Who are you?" she said. "Are you League?" Had her time come at last?

"Berek Sted," the man answered, eyeing her more carefully. "And no, not League. You're a demonseed, aren't you? The one Slorn's been experimenting on, trying to find a cure?"

"We have been experimenting together," Nivel said testily.

The man shrugged. "But you have a demon inside you, right? I want to talk to it."

Nivel recoiled. "Where is Slorn? How did you get here through the trees?"

"Trees can be bashed down like everything else," Sted said.

"As for the bear man, he's not my problem anymore. Are you going to let me talk to the demon, or am I going to have to force it out?" He looked her up and down. "I may not be League anymore, but even I can tell it wouldn't take much. You're so close to the change I'm surprised you can keep a human form."

"Being close to the edge doesn't mean jumping over," Nivel said. "You League types never appreciated the difference, but then, your lot never was any good at subtleties."

"Don't talk to me about the League!" Sted growled, stepping closer. "I'm here on my own. You see, I have a fight to win, and that thing inside you is going to help me." He took another step. "I've seen the kind of power it can give. If it makes a little girl into a monster who can break my arm, how much stronger will it make me?" His hand shot out and grabbed her wrist. "Let me talk to the demon!"

Before she knew what was happening, Nivel lashed out. She kicked him, hard, and Sted flew backward, crashing into the wall of the ravine with enough force to crack the stone. For a moment Nivel just stood there, panting, and then she realized what she'd done.

"No," she whispered, falling to her knees as the demon-given power roared through her. Her wrists, ankles, and neck burned as the last bits of her manacles dissolved. "No no no no."

Yes.

The voice was roaring in her mind, louder even than her terror. But even as it laughed in triumph, Nivel was not beaten. With a wordless cry of rage, she threw open her spirit. For the first time in a decade, power surged through her, filling her until she thought she would burst. Her own soul felt dark and slimy against her mind, polluted by the creature who had lived in it for so long. Even so, she grabbed her power with the intense focus Shaper wizards train for years to master. Grabbed it and turned it inward.

The laughter stopped. *What are you doing?*

"I didn't fight this long to lose now," Nivel whispered around a mouth that was no longer fully human. "I didn't put my family through this to lose to you."

You answered me at last, the voice crowed triumphantly. *Now I really have won. Rest, Nivel, you fought long and hard. Give up; you deserve it.*

Nivel opened her soul wider still, forcing her will stronger and stronger until she almost matched the demon. "No," she said. "Never." Just a little further. Just a little further.

A hand closed on her throat.

Nivel's eyes shot open. Sted was standing over her, his fingers on her neck, bearing down. She began to choke, beating against him with her fists, but her blows were as weak as a child's. Her demon strength was gone.

Of course, dear. Why would I give you anything you so clearly do not want?

Nivel choked again. She couldn't tell if the voice had been in her head or if she had spoken the words herself. The demon drenched her, flooding through her open soul even as it collapsed. All she could see was Sted above her, laughing as he crushed her throat.

I can kill him for you. The words were a whisper in her ear. *All you have to do is let me.*

Nivel's chest began to convulse, and she realized she was laughing.

"You should know by now," she whispered as she dangled from Sted's hand, "I'd rather die to a stranger than give in to you."

Her breath was gone now, and she could feel her body growing heavy. Still, she wasn't afraid. After ten years of fighting, death felt like a release. She could feel the demon's frustration as her consciousness dimmed, feel it struggling to grab final control of her mind and force the awakening. But it was too late. She was dying, but she was dying as a human. Nivel felt her lips curl into a smile.

She may have lost, but so had the demon, and that was as great a victory as she could hope for. Clinging to that final, happy thought, Nivel let the demon, and the last shreds of her life, go. Her last thought was a fuzzy image of her husband, fully human and happy, holding their newborn daughter. She ran to him, arms out and free, as a final, welcome silence fell over her mind.

Sted stood panting in the dark ravine, clutching the neck of the dead demonseed. He could have dropped her at any time, and his muscles begged him to, but Sted ignored them. The bitch was dead—he was sure of it—but she'd died smiling. That was never good. Worse, she was still human. He may have been in the League of Storms for only half a year, but even he'd paid enough attention to know that any demonseed past its first week of gestation should change on death. So why was the thin body hanging from his hand still human?

He was mulling this over when he felt a familiar burning sensation against his fingers. He cursed and jumped back, dropping the body. The woman crumpled to the ground. Then, like a puppet with its strings caught, she jerked. Sted sucked in his breath. The body jerked again, sitting up stiffly. Its back was to Sted, and he briefly considered running before dismissing the idea with a sneer. Men didn't run. So he stood firm in the sand, watching as the corpse turned slowly to look at him.

It was only when he saw its eyes that he was truly afraid. The woman's eyes were enormous, and bright as lanterns. They fixed on him like snake eyes on a mouse, and the creature, for he knew for certain there was nothing human left in the body before him, gave him a small, cold smile. "You wanted to speak with me, yes?"

Sted flinched. The voice coming out of the woman's body was nothing like the voice she had used in life. It was low, strong, masculine, and extremely wrong sounding. Something in it made him want to run, to hide, to cower like a rabbit before a predator. It was a deep, primal need, and for a long moment he had to fight himself to stay still. In the end, however, he stood firm in the sand as the creature in the woman's body examined him.

"You expected something grander," it said bitterly. "So did I. But that woman trapped me at the very end, and if I hadn't taken a bit of you just now, this seed would have died with her." It sighed with a hiss. "Such a waste. This is one of my oldest surviving seeds. If it could have completed the awakening, this cursed trap of a valley would be a very different place right now, and you, dear sheep, would be on your way to the mists."

Sted swallowed. He was barely following this, but the threat in the creature's words was clear enough for a deaf man. Every instinct he had was screaming at him to run, but Sted held fast. After all, he'd come here for a reason, and he wasn't leaving until he got what he wanted.

"You're the demon, then?" he said, standing up straight. "Good, I wanted to talk to you. Seeing how you admitted just now that you wouldn't be here without me, I think you should listen carefully."

The creature chuckled. "Don't think too highly of yourself, Berek Sted. I would have beaten this girl in a few months anyway had you not interfered, *and* had a proper awakening." The woman's head tilted, and the creature's voice grew smooth. "Still, let's not fret on particulars. I know why you came here. I saw it just now"—it tapped its head with one of Nivel's long, pale fingers—"in your mind. You want the power to pay back the Heart of War and its wielder, plus one of my own errant children, for your rather pathetic defeat."

"I wasn't defeated!" Sted shouted. "The League sent me in unprepared with a faulty weapon. If I'd had the power to match that bastard's sword, I would have slaughtered them both! Instead, the coward took my arm, humiliated me, denied me a warrior's death! I won't rest until I pay him back in full!"

The creature gave him a long look. "Under usual circumstances, I'm afraid I wouldn't be able to help you. It takes just the right kind of soul to provide what my seeds need to blossom, souls inevitably belonging to those members of your species who are less deaf than the rest, whom you call wizards. Sadly, you're deafer than most and too old as well, so I cannot give you a seed."

Sted's eyes narrowed. "You're hardly in a position to refuse me, corpse dweller. I may be a one-armed cripple, but I can still bash that body in and reduce your precious seed to a dead nub, so you'd best reconsider."

The creature in the corpse laughed. "Your ignorance is both astounding and refreshing. I can see why they kicked you out. However, while I can't give you a seed, perhaps we can come to an arrangement."

Sted leaned back. "What do you mean?"

The creature gestured at Nivel's chest. "The woman, Nivel, tended her seed for years, far, far longer than any of my others, holding it back through sheer will. A formidable trick, but it had quite the unintended effect. While a seed's awakening can be prevented by the host's will, nothing can stop its growth. Through Nivel's stubborn refusal to give in, she inadvertently created inside herself a seed more powerful than anything I could otherwise get through my formidable prison. Indeed, she has become, almost through accident, the second-most-powerful shard of myself I have ever created." It tapped Nivel's lips. "I am speaking to you through a full-grown seed, steeped in power, yet unawakened. Your meager soul may not be fit to bear a new seed, but it *can* keep this one alive. So, Berek Sted, let me make you a deal. I will give you Nivel's seed and all the power she put into it over ten years of fighting. The seed will give you strength, quickness, and all the gifts I graciously bestow upon my children who do my work in the world. I will set it up so that the Heart of War will come to you.

You will have power, eternal life, so long as you can keep it, and the opportunity to thrash Josef Liechten into the ground. I'll even give you your arm back. Is that not generous?"

Berek Sted swallowed and clutched his bandaged stump. "And what price do you charge for this?"

The creature smiled. "Obedience."

"I'm no one's slave," Sted spat out.

"Who said anything about slaves?" the demon said. "You will be my weapon. An unbeatable weapon, greater even than the Heart of War itself. What do you say, do we have a deal?"

Sted stroked the stub of his arm. He'd sworn never to take another order, but he could not beat Liechten as a cripple. His League powers were gone. His skin was as cuttable and weak as any man's. If he was going to beat the Heart, he needed an edge at any cost.

"And you swear I'll get to fight Liechten?" Sted said. "Man to man, fair and square?"

The demon shrugged. "If fair is what you like, certainly."

Sted nodded. "Then you have your deal."

The creature grinned inhumanly wide, showing a full mouth of teeth and gums. "Welcome to the mountain," it said, its voice a hissing whisper. "Berek Sted."

As the creature spoke his name, the corpse of Nivel jumped forward. It moved impossibly fast, slamming its hands into Sted's bandaged stomach. Sted grunted and fell back as the wounds opened, and he felt something crawl into him. *Crawl* was the only word to describe it. A shadow fell from the dead woman's hands into his stomach, galloping into him on waves of fear, revulsion, and bitter cold. Then, as quickly as it had started, it was over. The woman's corpse flopped to the ground, lifeless again. Sted stood panting, grasping his stomach, but even as he clutched his injured flesh, he felt the skin knitting together under his fingers. Suddenly, the dark shadows of the ravine were clear. The dark was still there, but he could see perfectly. He felt ten years younger, stronger than ever, whole. He had just a moment to revel in this feeling before a crippling pain in his arm sent him to his knees. He turned in horror just in time to see the stump at the end of his shoulder burst open as a hand pushed its way out of his flesh.

Sted cried out in terror. It was no human hand. It was black and shiny, like a bug's shell, and tipped with five long fingers, human looking but wrong. The hand clenched and grasped, pulling itself out of his arm inch by agonizing inch. An eternity of pain later, it stopped, and a new, black arm slightly longer than his own hung from his shoulder, meeting his body in a mash of flesh that hurt to look at.

Sted stumbled back in horror, but the black arm caught him before he could fall. He stopped and stared at the new limb, wiggling each long, sharp claw just as he would his normal fingers. The more he moved the arm, the more he felt its power. The claws were sharp enough to cut bone, and the black skin was as hard as obsidian. He stood there a moment longer, clenching and unclenching his new fist as a smile began to spread over his face.

There, do I not keep my word?

Sted froze in terror. It was the voice from before, but it had not come from the crumpled corpse of the woman on the ground. It had come from inside his head. The creature was in his head.

I told you. He could almost hear it smirking. *You're my weapon now. We're going to be very close, you and I. Now, the bear-headed man is coming. It's time to go home and get your first assignment.*

"Where?" Sted's voice was barely a whisper.

You know where.

And, Sted realized with a creeping horror, he did. Without quite knowing what he was doing, he bent his legs and jumped. The leap sent him flying over the trees, and Sted began to flail as he shot through the morning air.

So much fear, the demon sneered. *Get rid of it. Fear is for spirits, not my creatures. You asked for this, Berek Sted. You came to me seeking power, and power I have given you. Don't tell me you're too weak to grasp it now that it's yours.*

Sted winced. The creature was right. He could feel the power, an incredible force so much greater than his own. His jump just now, the lack of pain from his injuries, even the black arm was starting to feel like part of himself. It was all power, power he'd paid for, power he'd use to pay back his humiliation.

With this firmly in his mind, Sted hit the ground in a shower of leaves and began to run, skipping northward toward the snow-capped mountains through the long morning shadows. He'd show the demon how a real man used power. Already he could feel the fear fading, and the longer he went, the easier it became. Soon, he was grinning at the sheer strength of his motion, the incredible rush of his power.

Deep in his soul, far deeper than Sted's poor, deaf mind could go, the demon began to laugh.

CHAPTER 2

It was early morning in the port city of Mering on the southern coast of the Council Kingdoms. Down in the bay, the fishing boats were preparing to leave the harbor, the fishermen stringing up their nets by lantern light, for the sun was still just a gray ghost below the horizon. High on the bluffs above the docks, the city lay dark and quiet. Weathered board houses clustered in a nest of narrow, sandy streets, their dark windows open to the warm ocean breeze. Toward the rear of town, where the sandy ground was more solid, stood the Fisherman's Rest, Mering's only inn and the only building with an upper story in the entire town, a feature of which its owner, who was also Mering's mayor, was exceedingly proud.

This night was an exceptionally rare event, for all three of the inn's upper rooms were occupied, despite the relatively exorbitant price their prestige and views demanded. But the strange pair of men and the silent girl who followed them had been throwing gold around like chicken feed from the moment they'd walked into town, and so the innkeeper had no qualms about putting them up in the best rooms Mering had to offer, especially since, as outsiders, he could charge them triple. He'd even cracked open his best cask of wine in hopes of getting them drunk for even more money, but all he'd gotten was a rowdy party from his regular customers and terrifying glares from the taller stranger with the arsenal strapped to his chest. By morning, however, everything was quiet, even the seabirds, and it was this strange, chancy silence that saved Eli's life.

He was asleep, sprawled on his stomach on the double bed under the window, snoring quietly. But when one has made his name as the greatest thief in the world, true sleep is a habit you lose quickly, which was the only reason he heard the sound at all. The noise was soft, almost lost in the crash of the distant waves, yet unmistakable to anyone who'd heard it before. A sword snickering in anticipation isn't a sound you forget.

Eli threw himself out of bed as the blade stabbed into the mattress where his bare back had been a split second earlier. He landed on the floor in a tangle of sheets as the man, head to foot in dark clothing, yanked his sword free. Eli didn't waste any more time looking. He turned and bolted for the door.

"Josef!" he shouted, scrambling over the rag rug. "*JOSEF!*"

The assassin caught him on the second yell. The gloved hand closed on Eli's shoulder, pulling him back with an iron grip as the sword, still snickering, flashed overhead. Eli dodged with an undignified yelp, rolling out of the way as the sword whooshed past him to land with a deadly thunk in the floor. The man ripped it free instantly and tried to give Eli a kick in the process, but the thief was already behind him, going for the window. The man whirled around and raised his sword again, grabbing Eli's bare foot in his gloved hand to hold the squirming thief still. But then, just as he was about to bring the sword down on Eli's shoulder, the blade fell from his grasp, and the intruder cried out in pain.

With a lightning-quick motion, Eli caught the falling sword and flipped around, turning the blade on its former master, who was doubled over on the carpet, clutching his sword hand, which now had a throwing knife lodged halfway through its palm. That was all Eli saw before Josef barreled out of the darkness, tackling the man as he went. They landed against the room's wall in a brawling tangle. The man in black was shorter than Josef by a foot, not to mention lighter and injured, but he had a long knife in his unbloodied hand and Josef, for once, was unarmed. For a frantic moment, the man had the advantage. Using the wall for leverage, he pushed the knife toward Josef, going for the swordsman's naked throat. Josef leaned away, but he couldn't get out of reach entirely without letting the man go. When the knife was less than an inch from his throat, Josef had had enough. Faster than Eli could see, Josef ducked inside the man's reach and, with a rolling turn, flipped their positions.

Or he tried to. But rather than turning along the wall, the assassin's shoulder slammed into the unlatched window. With a great bang, the shutters flew open, leaving Josef and the man struggling against thin air. They began to fall, each flailing in the air, reaching in vain for the window frame. Just as they started to tumble out of reach, a thin hand shot out of the darkness and grabbed Josef's wrist.

It was Nico. She was halfway out the window, bracing with both legs against the wide frame, her coat flying around her as she struggled to hold Josef's weight. Struggled and failed. Even braced, Josef's weight was too much, and she was rapidly toppling after him. Just before she lost her footing, Eli's hand grabbed Josef's wrist just below hers, and together they yanked the swordsman back into the room, landing in a heap on the rag carpet.

"Powers," Eli gasped, dropping the assassin's sword, which was no longer snickering. "What about the—"

A sickening crunch finished his sentence for him, and all three of them winced. They sat for a moment in silence before Josef pushed himself up. "I'll check the body," he said, his voice calm, as though he did this every night. "Nico, you're with me. Eli, take the innkeeper."

Eli and Nico nodded and the group split, Josef and Nico slinking down the stairs, quiet as cats, Eli somewhat more loudly, shouting for the innkeeper. Fortunately, the old man was already rushing across the common room in his night cap and dressing gown, a fluttering lamp in his shaking hands.

"Oh, sir!" Eli cried, jumping away from the stairs to cut him off. "Something *dreadful* has just occurred!" And with that Eli launched into a terrible story of robbery, foul play, and tragic ends. By the time he finished, the innkeeper, the night staff, the guests, and every neighbor within earshot was gathered in the inn's common room wearing unified expressions of horror. Eli kept going until he saw Nico wave at him from the front door, signaling that Josef had finished whatever he'd needed to finish. Eli wrapped up his hysterics just as the night watch appeared. Claiming exhaustion, Eli retired to Josef's room, stopping first at his own to retrieve the large stash of coins he'd hidden beneath a loose board. All evidence safely loaded onto his person, he went next door to Josef's somewhat smaller room and locked the door behind him.

"That," he said, "was not how I intended to spend my evening."

Josef didn't even look up from the basin where he was washing his hands. "I think your evening came out better than his, if it makes you feel better."

"It certainly does not," Eli said, flopping down on the bed beside Nico. "Josef, what is going on? We came to this... wherever we are, to get *away* from the hunters for a few days. They're worse than mosquitoes lately. I can count on one hand the number of incident-free days we've had in the last two weeks. Did bounty hunting suddenly become the stylish profession? Have we stumbled into a hunter boom, or do I have a 'Please Ambush' sign on my back that you haven't told me about?"

Josef chuckled, wiping his now clean hands on the towel. "Nothing so complicated. Check out the poster on the table."

Eli glanced over at the end table in surprise, and then reached out to snatch the oversized square of folded parchment, shaking it open as he did so. "It's just my poster," he said, frowning. "Wait, this isn't right." He looked at Josef. "It has to be a joke. Where did you get this?"

"From the inside pocket of our visitor's coat," Josef answered, tossing the towel into the linen bin. "Not that he'll miss it. And it's no joke. That's an official Council bounty notice."

"Impossible," Eli scoffed. "I know my own bounty! Counting what Gaol just threw in, I should be at an even seventy-five thousand, eighty thousand if Miranda would ever do as she promised and combine the Spirit Court's bounty. But even if she accidentally combined it twice over, it wouldn't explain this." He flipped the poster around and held it up. There, below the usual picture of Eli's smiling face, was a number written in tall, blocky strokes: 98,000 gold standards.

"This is a breakdown of government," Eli said. "What's the Council of Thrones coming to if it can't even keep something as important as my bounty straight?"

"Whatever the reason," Josef said, "we may need to lie low for a bit."

"I thought we were lying low," Eli said, still frowning at his poster.

"Lower, then," Josef snapped back. "All this attention is causing problems, like the one that just fell out of your window. That man wasn't your standard thug chasing the Eli lottery. He was a professional. He didn't wake you up or brag or try to take you alive. No, he did it exactly how I would have, clean and quick in the night. If you hadn't woken up when you did, you never would have felt a thing."

Eli gave him a dirty look. "Just how you would have? Have you thought about this before?"

"Only when you're being a jerk," Josef said dryly. "Listen, I don't know why the number is so high, but attacks like this one are only going to happen more often. And once your bounty breaks a hundred thousand, we're going to start seeing armies coming after us. We need our trail to be ice cold when they do."

Eli heaved a defeated sigh. "Fine, fine, where would be low enough for you? And don't say the mountains. I've had more than enough wandering through the wilderness."

Josef leaned against the washstand. "I was thinking we could go home."

Eli froze. That was not the answer he'd expected. Nico, on the other hand, lifted her head. "Home?"

Josef nodded. "It's as low as we get. No one will find us there."

"But home is so boring," Eli said. "Nothing happens."

Josef crossed his arms over his chest. "Nothing's supposed to happen. Do you not understand the concept of lying low?"

"Fine, fine," Eli said, shaking his head. "We'll slip out tomorrow morning before whatever passes as the guard in this boring depression of a town gets too close and decides I look familiar."

"I'm surprised it hasn't happened already," Josef said. "Since you didn't even bother with disguises."

"My disguises are for my jobs," Eli said with a sniff. "I wouldn't waste them on places like this."

Josef just shook his head.

"Anyway," Eli said, lying back on the bed, "if we're going to be cutting out early, let's get some sleep at least. It would be a horrible shame to waste a rare night of sleep in a bed."

"Right," Josef said. "So get out of mine."

Eli looked at him innocently. "But my room still has people poking around in it."

"Too bad," Josef said, glaring. "Floor or hallway, pick one."

After some argument, Eli ended up on the floor with one of Josef's pillows and an extra quilt from the chest. Nico excused herself halfway through the bickering, trailing back to her room with a weary look that stuck with Eli long after Josef put out the light.

"Josef," Eli said in the dark, "what's going on with Nico?"

The swordsman's quiet breathing continued without interruption, but somehow he knew Josef was listening.

"What happened in Gaol?" Eli asked, more quietly this time. "I've seen her lift you over her head like you weighed nothing, so why couldn't she pull you out of the window by herself? There's something going on with her demon, isn't there?"

His question hung in the silence. Then, at last, Josef answered. "Leave it alone."

Eli took a deep breath. "I *have* left it alone. We haven't pulled any thefts since leaving Gaol. I've been waiting to see if she'd snap out of it, or at least say what's happening. But she doesn't tell me anything!" He crossed his arms over his chest. "Everyone's got secrets, but this could get dangerous for us if I can't trust her on a job anymore. Her not telling me she was a wizard was bad enough, but I can get over that. I can understand. This?" He shook his head. "I don't even know anymore."

He heard the bed creak as Josef rolled over. "I don't know what's wrong either," the swordsman said. "And I'm not going to push it. Whatever's going on with Nico, it's a battle she has to fight herself. If she needs us, she'll ask."

Eli frowned. "Are you sure about that?"

Josef's long breaths were his only answer, and Eli knew the conversation was over. He tried to think of a way to bring the topic up again from a different angle, but all he got were more dead ends until, at last, he drifted off to sleep as well, curled up in a ball on the rug in the middle of Josef's floor.

Nico sat on the floor in the dark, her coat wrapped around her, her bony knees clutched to her chest. She sat perfectly still, listening through the wall until Eli's breaths evened out into sleep at last. Only then did she let out the long, shuddering sigh she'd been keeping in. Of all the demon-enhanced senses the seed could have left, why did it have to be hearing?

It's for your own good, the voice whispered, smooth and confident as ever. *I help you hear the truth.*

"Shut up," Nico grumbled, pulling herself toward the narrow bed.

You can't shut the truth out, the voice said. *Ignoring the problem won't change how the thief feels. He's a clever, efficient man. It's only a matter of time before he decides to cut the dead weight. I wouldn't be surprised if he left you here. After all, you're nothing but a weak girl who couldn't even pull Josef through a window. Why would they ever want—*

"SHUT UP."

Nico's words roared through her head, but the voice just chuckled and began to hum a song from Nico's childhood, one of the only things she could remember from before the morning she woke up on the mountain. Unbidden and without reason, tears sprang to her eyes. She wiped them on her coat and bundled herself into a tiny ball in the center of her bed.

You can always come back. The voice's whisper was like a cool wind on her mind. *Why waste your time with people who don't trust you? Come home, Nico. Come home to where you're wanted.*

She took a deep, shuddering breath. "Never listen to the voice." Her words were a harsh whisper, but she could almost hear Nivel speaking them with her. "Never listen. Never listen."

She kept repeating the words until, at last, exhaustion took over and she fell into a deep, dreamless sleep.

And in her mind, the voice waited.

CHAPTER 3

The sun had barely peeked over the ridge above Zarin when Miranda Lyonette, newly reappointed Spiritualist of the Spirit Court, arrived at the gate of the Whitefall Citadel, home of the Council of Thrones. She hopped carefully off the hired buggy and paid the driver, overtipping him just to be sure she had it right. Hired transportation wasn't something she was used to, but she hadn't wanted Gin on this trip. For one, the ghosthound was easily bored, and she had a feeling this visit would be full of waiting. Trips to the Council always were, and a bored ghosthound in the Council of Thrones stables sounded like an invitation for disaster. Second, she hadn't wanted to mess up her outfit riding through the busy streets. She had dressed her best for this, a white silk jacket and matching wide trousers with short-heeled blue slippers instead of her usual boots. She wore her hair bound back in a tight braid that was a bit severe for her face, but she hadn't wanted to take chances with it frizzing on her. After all, it wasn't every day one got a handwritten invitation to the Council from a member of the Whitefall family itself.

The invitation was carefully tucked into her jacket's inside pocket, and though she'd read it through a dozen times since it arrived at the Spirit Court's tower by special courier yesterday, she still wasn't exactly sure why she'd been called to the Council. One thing, however, was certain, the invitation had come from Lord Phillipe Whitefall, Chief Domestic Enforcement Officer to the Council of Thrones and first cousin to Alber Whitefall, the current Merchant Prince of Zarin. There'd been no request for reply, but the letter didn't need one. Miranda had lived in Zarin long enough to know that when a Whitefall asked you to be somewhere, Spiritualist or common townsfolk, you didn't say no.

The guards opened the gate when she gave her name, and as she stepped into the courtyard a white-liveried page appeared seemingly from thin air to escort her into the citadel. Miranda followed the boy across the white-paved yard, under the long shadows of the famous seven towers, and into one of the graceful arching doors. The interior of the citadel was as lovely as the exterior, and positively dripping with wealth. Everything, from the paper-thin porcelain vases nestled in carved nooks between the windows to the thick, golden carpet underfoot, was exquisite, tasteful, and quietly expensive. If Miranda had not been here once before, accompanying Master Banage when she was still his apprentice, she would have gawked openly.

The page led her down half a dozen halls before opening a set of heavy double doors into a long gallery filled with tables. Miranda blinked in surprise. Each table was covered with stacks of paper and tended by a small army of well-dressed men and women. They worked furiously, sorting the piles into smaller piles before passing them along to others who bound the papers and stacked them on the shelves that ran along both sides of the gallery. No one spoke as the page led Miranda between the tables. Indeed, no one seemed to notice her at all. Their focus was entirely on their work, and the only sound in the large room was the rustle of paper. Miranda was still staring when the page stopped suddenly, turning to stand beside a tall door at the end of the gallery.

"Lord Whitefall will see you now," he said, bowing low. "Just through the door, if you please."

"Thank you," Miranda said.

The boy hurried off, walking silently back through the long gallery. Feeling a little abandoned, Miranda turned and opened the door. Like every door in the citadel, it opened silently, and she found herself standing at one end of a large, overfull office.

Overflowing would have been a better description. There was paper everywhere, stacked on tables, rolled up in bins, bursting from the shelves that lined the walls. It was all piled as neatly as possible, but there was simply too much for the room to contain. It clung to every piece of furniture like white blubber, and Miranda had to press herself against the door simply to have room to stand. The only wall of the office not covered with shelves was still covered in paper. Maps of the Council Kingdoms, to be specific, every one of which was blanketed with a forest of colored stickpins.

Directly ahead of her, down the little clear aisle that ran like a valley between the mountains of paper, was a sight that made her pause. At the far end of the room was a large desk covered with the same piled paper that infested the rest of the office, but otherwise it was empty. No one sat in the worn, high-back chair set behind it or on the wooden stool beside it. Still, what caught Miranda's attention was what hung above the desk. There, filling almost the entire back wall of the office, was an enormous piece of corkboard. It ran from just behind the chair all the way up to the room's soaring ceiling, nearly ten feet from start to finish. Miranda had never seen anything like it, but even more amazing was what was pinned to the board—bounty posters, hundreds of them. They were pinned with military precision, marching in a neat grid from the very top of the board to just above the empty chair's headrest.

The collection must have been long going, for the posters at the top were an entirely different color from the ones toward the bottom. Miranda leaned forward, trying to make out the names on the lower line, when a sudden voice made her jump.

"Knocking is customary before entering someone's office, you know."

Miranda stifled an undignified squeal of surprise, composing her features in an instant before turning to face the voice. Standing in a little alcove set just behind the door was a small, balding man with a large gray mustache. He wore a somber but expensive jacket that he somehow managed to make frumpy, and he was carrying a large stack of papers that he had obviously been going through when she had come in.

He gave her a final glare before tossing the papers on the shelf beside him, nearly causing an avalanche in the process.

"Phillipe Whitefall," he said. "I assume you are Spiritualist Lyonette?"

"Yes," Miranda said, dropping a polite bow. "An honor to meet you, sir."

"Quite," Lord Whitefall said, turning to walk briskly to his desk. "Apologies if I don't dawdle on formality, Miss Lyonette. I'm a very busy man." He sat down with a huff that made his mustache bristle. "I've heard much of your exploits from my agents in the field, especially involving Mellinor and this late unpleasantness in the duchy of Gaol. Quite an impressive display for someone so young."

"I was only doing my job as a Spiritualist," Miranda said, smiling despite herself. "The Spirit Court takes all infractions against the spirits very—"

"Yes, yes," Lord Whitefall interrupted. "The Spirit Court's dedication is not what I'm after. I called you here today to talk about your experience with Eli Monpress."

Miranda went stiff. "Well—"

"My primary duty as Chief Domestic Enforcement Officer is the maintenance and enforcement of the Council's bounties," he said, cutting her off again. "I receive the pledges, set the figures, track the criminals, oversee poster production and distribution, so on and so forth. That's how you came to my attention." He reached into the nest of papers on his desk and plucked out a formal letter bearing the Spirit Court's seal. "Several weeks ago, our office received this rather strange request from you, Spiritualist Miranda. You wrote on behalf of your Court asking that I combine the Spirit Court's private bounty with the Council's offering. Is that correct?"

He waved the letter in front of her until she nodded.

"Hardly a common thing," Lord Whitefall went on, tossing the letter back into the piles. "So I did a little digging and discovered some rather interesting facts about your recent exploits." He paused, giving her a long, probing look. "It seems you are something of an expert on Eli Monpress."

"I wouldn't say expert, my lord," Miranda put in quickly. "It's true I've been involved with Eli Monpress on several occasions, but I'm hardly in the position to tell you anything you don't already know. My bounty request was simply a fulfillment of a previous promise to Monpress."

"If you're anxious about your past failures to catch him, don't bother." Lord Whitefall sat back in his chair with a heavy creak of leather. "I'm not here to judge you, my dear. Quite the opposite, in fact. What I'm interested in is your experience."

Lord Whitefall put his feet up on his desk, resting his glossy leather boots on a stack of bound ledgers. "Monpress is a bit of a thorny problem, you see. His fame greatly outstrips his threat, to the point where it's becoming fashionable to be his victim. Why, in the last two weeks I've gotten four separate bounty pledges from kingdoms all across the Council, all for crimes I'm certain Monpress did not commit. Not that it matters to the nobles who placed the bounty." He snorted. "The silver goes missing and they send me a letter screaming Monpress."

"You mean people are placing false bounties?" Miranda said. "But why?"

Lord Whitefall shrugged. "Notoriety. Excitement. The Council has made this a smaller continent. It's no longer enough to be the richest and most fashionable person in your kingdom. You now have to compete on a Council-wide scale. For some, this means being on the fashionable end of everything, even if it's a fashionable theft. It's well known that Monpress only steals the best, so if he robs you, that means you had something worth stealing. The higher Monpress's bounty goes, the worse the problem gets. I have to send officers to investigate every crime, but even if

I find no proof of Monpress whatsoever, even if the object they claim was stolen is still sitting in the middle of their treasury, I can't do anything about the bounty pledge. It's their money. I can't stop them from spending it on stupid things."

"But that's ridiculous!" Miranda said. "If false reports become rampant, how will the Council track Eli's actual crimes?"

"Ah," Lord Whitefall said with a grin. "That's where you come in."

He stood and walked around to the front of his desk, looking Miranda square in the eye. "I'd like to make you an offer, Spiritualist Lyonette. As you are no doubt more aware than most, tracking Monpress is a very difficult prospect. The man moves like smoke, and leaves less of a trace. Reaching the scene of his crimes before what little clues there are have vanished is nearly impossible. Catching him in the act, completely so. But you, you're different. You have observed the thief at his work—even, if the reports are right, worked with him on two separate occasions."

Miranda went pale. "Those were—"

"Highly mitigating circumstances, I know," Lord Whitefall said. "Powers, girl, I don't care about *why* you were there, just that you *were*. Your experience with Eli Monpress is unprecedented. It makes you far too valuable to leave with the Spirit Court, which is why I'm offering you a job."

"Really, sir, I—" Miranda stopped cold. "Wait, what?"

"A job," Lord Whitefall said slowly. "To address your combined bounty request, I'm creating a new position within my department, and I'd like you to fill it. You would be head of the Eli Monpress joint investigation for the Council of Thrones and the Spirit Court. The position comes with full access to Council resources, complete autonomy on all matters involving Monpress, and the ability to call upon the aid of any kingdom in the Council without question. What do you say to that?"

"It's..." Miranda struggled for words. This was far beyond anything she could have dreamed of. "It's a very generous offer, sir. But"—better to get this out now—"why me? I would of course be happy to offer my knowledge and services to assist the Council in bringing Monpress to justice, but investigation head? Surely you have your own people who are vastly more experienced."

"That I do," Lord Whitefall said. "But I'm not about to waste them on Monpress." He ignored Miranda's insulted look and pointed up at the bounty posters on the board behind him. "Monpress is a thief, nothing but a two-bit con man with a flare for the dramatic. He's not a threat to the Council. The only reason his bounty is nearing the hundred-thousand mark is because he steals from people who can afford to put a large price on his head. This, combined with his propensity for grandstanding, has inflated his importance to the point where we at the bounty office can no longer ignore him. But look here."

Lord Whitefall walked over to the corner of his office, beckoning for Miranda to follow. He stopped in front of a second, smaller corkboard decorated with ten bounty posters pinned in two neat rows. Miranda frowned, wondering why these posters were singled out. Then she saw it. Every single poster displayed had a bounty of more than one hundred thousand.

"Look here," Lord Whitefall said. "These are the faces of true threats to the Council. Criminals who earned their bounties with blood, not flamboyance. Take this one"—he tapped a poster toward the bottom with the sketched face of a middle-aged man with a hook nose and an impatient sneer—"Izo, the Bandit King." Lord Whitefall's voice was almost reverent. "Over the last five years, he's banded together all the small bandit groups that prey on the trade routes through the northern kingdoms into his own private military. We had to send an army up last year to keep him from taking over the kingdom of Chessy all together, and we still didn't catch him. The northern kingdoms have always been the poorest in the Council, yet they got together and posted one hundred and fifty thousand gold standards to Izo's capture. And if that's not enough, look here."

He tapped the poster beside it, which had no picture at all, only a number, 200,000, and a name.

"The Daughter of the Dead Mountain," Lord Whitefall read quietly. "The only bounty request we've ever received from the Shaper Wizards. No one knows who she is, or exactly what she did, but if it was bad enough for the Shapers to come to us, I don't think I want to know. She has the second-highest bounty ever offered. As for the first…"

His finger moved to the poster at the far end, the oldest of all the posters. The picture was of a man with slicked-back dark hair and a grin that made Miranda's blood run cold. His face, neck, and shoulders were riddled with scars, and his eyes told why. Even from the crude drawing, the killing gleam in them was undeniably terrifying, as was the number written below.

"Five hundred thousand gold standards," Miranda read in a hushed voice. "What did he do?"

"More than a man should," Lord Whitefall replied. "That's Den the Warlord. He first appeared during the Council's war with the Immortal Empress, selling his services as a soldier for hire. The Council hired him first, and he slaughtered the Empress's forces like a butcher in a pen of lambs. But then she offered him double what we could and Den switched sides, single-handedly wiping out an entire Council legion in one night."

Miranda shook her head. "Surely that's an exaggeration."

"Not enough of one," Lord Whitefall said. "He disappeared after that. Powers grant that he met a bloody end, but we don't know for certain. The Council considers five hundred thousand a fair price to make sure the traitor's dead."

Lord Whitefall sighed. "As you see, my dear, my office has far more serious problems on our hands than a flamboyant thief. But his bounty demands we do something, and so I am giving him to you. Banage assures me you're a competent, clever sort of girl, and your experience with Monpress is certainly unparalleled. That said, I'm completely confident placing the job in your hands. Assuming you take the job, of course."

He looked at her, and Miranda swallowed. "It's a great honor, but I'd have to get permission from the—"

"Oh, I got Banage's blessing this morning," Lord Whitefall said with a flippant wave of his hand. "He's keen on seeing you broaden your horizons. Do you have any other objections?"

"Well, I..." Miranda trailed off. "Not at all. I would be honored, Lord Whitefall."

"Excellent," the balding man said, smiling. "I'll have them set up an office for you in town and move all the Eli files over. Now, since Monpress is a wizard, you won't be reporting to me. You'll be under Sara."

"Sara...?" Miranda prompted, waiting for a last name, or at least a title.

"Yes," Lord Whitefall said, completely missing the cue. "Sara's in charge of everything magical for the Council. She's been bothering me about Monpress since he first popped onto the bounty rolls, so I just let her have him. I've far too much to do handling the real criminals, anyway."

"Yes, my lord," Miranda said, trying not to be insulted. "When do I start work?"

"Tomorrow," Lord Whitefall said. "I'll tell Sara to send someone round to fetch you." He looked down at his papers. "That's all. You can go. The page will show you out."

And just like that, the meeting was over. Lord Whitefall seemed to have shut out her presence entirely, going through the endless papers and muttering to himself. After a few awkward moments, Miranda bowed, excused herself, and made her way as quickly as possible to the door. As Lord Whitefall had promised, a page was waiting for her when she opened it. The boy escorted her back through the opulent hallways to a waiting buggy and, after politely refusing Miranda's tip, left her to go on her way.

Miranda rode in silence all the way to the Spirit Court's tower, wishing more than ever, as the buggy crept through the crowded streets, that she'd brought Gin. She had to talk to Master Banage, had to figure out what it really was she'd just agreed to. But the traffic had no respect for her urgency, and so she sat slumped in the cushioned seat, fuming while the morning sun beat down on the white walls of the Council capital.

CHAPTER 4

Josef, Eli, and Nico settled their bill and left the port of Mering in a bit of a hurry the morning after their unfortunate incident. They took a good chunk of the inn's larder with them, for, as Eli pointed out numerous times, a thief could hardly be expected to pay for *everything.* Thus resupplied, they set off west and a little south along the coastal plain. Eli kept them to the back roads, cutting across the rolling hills on cart tracks that were little more than dents in the grass. Josef grumbled about more walking, but Nico rather liked it. Picking her way over rough roads kept her mind occupied just enough to push the voice back, and the exercise made her feel invigorated and human, a sensation she was learning to cherish. The whole experience was so pleasant, she didn't even notice Eli's strange path until they started seeing signs for the great port at Axley.

"No," Josef said, stopping right below the signpost. "No major cities."

"Relax," Eli said. "We won't have any trouble. I'm just going in for a pickup."

Josef gave him a skeptical look. "A pickup?"

Eli nodded. "You'll see."

And he was right. When they reached the city walls, Eli went in alone, coming out less than an hour later with a cart, a mule, and an extremely smug expression.

"A cart?" Josef said, glaring. "You came here to pick up a cart? We could have gotten that anywhere."

"I highly doubt it," Eli said, beaming down from his perch on the cart's seat. "Come around and have a look."

Nico and Josef walked around to the edge of the cart, Nico hopping up on the little wall that ran along the road so she could see. The cart was covered with a thick oiled sheet, and underneath were large bags, each marked with a tag.

"Mr. Miller?" Nico said, reading one.

Josef just shook his head. "You'd think I'd be used to this by now." He opened one of the bags, revealing a sparkling stack of loose diamonds in a variety of cuts and sizes. "You're as bad as a squirrel, burying stashes all over the continent."

"Ah," Eli said. "But unlike a squirrel, I remember where I leave things. Reliable storage is vital to a thief, and the good merchants of Axley do most of their business with pirates and smugglers, so they're very kind about not asking too many questions. They even threw in the cart for free."

Josef looked sideways at the mule, which was standing perfectly still, glaring at him. "How generous," he mumbled, taking a step back. "Is this it then?"

"Powers, no," Eli said with a laugh. "I haven't been home in a while. We've got three more stops to make. Hop on."

He scooted over to make room, and Josef jumped up onto the seat beside him. Nico climbed into the back, holding her coat close. She kept clear of the mule. Animals were better than most spirits at sniffing out a demonseed.

Of course. They know a predator when they see one.

"Shut up," Nico muttered.

"What?"

Her head shot up. Eli was looking back at her, his face concerned. "What did you say?"

Nico shook her head and scooted down among the bags, biting her tongue. She didn't speak again until it was time to stop for the night.

They made four more pickups, two at smaller towns, one at a crossroads tavern, and one in the middle of an otherwise perfectly normal field. That one had looked like just a rest break to admire the scenery until Eli had a chat with one of the large stones. After a short exchange, the stone rolled away to reveal a small treasury of valuables, including two midsized statues and a large painting wrapped in waxed cloth.

"I don't get it," Josef huffed, lifting one of the statues into their straining cart. "When did you find the time to hide all of this stuff? I never see you do any work after a robbery."

"You should pay more attention," Eli said, carrying a wooden chest fixed with a broken exquisite gold lock. "I'm always working. There." He shoved the chest into the final bit of open space left in the cart. "That should be it."

"Can the mule carry it all?" Josef asked, looking doubtfully at the overloaded cart.

"Of course," Eli said, hopping into the driver's seat. "I asked the cart to help." He winked at Josef. "I told you. I'm always working."

"So I see," Josef grumbled, helping Nico into the back of the overloaded cart before climbing up himself.

Nico settled herself as well as she could on the lumpy bags of treasure, pulling her knees in to avoid bumping them on the painting's sharp edges. "Where now?" she said.

"Homeward bound," Eli answered. He tapped the reins, and the cart lurched forward, down the field and back onto the dirt road, where Eli turned it north and west, toward the plains.

They rode for two days straight. They would have made better time, but Eli insisted on stopping in every village with a bounty board to see if his bounty had taken another spontaneous jump upward. It hadn't, though Eli couldn't figure out if that was because the number had ceased its strange inflation or if the towns they passed through were simply too small to receive timely bounty updates. Either way, he spent most of his spare breath coming up with theories.

"It's probably an impostor," he decided for the second time in as many hours. "Someone banking on my fame."

Josef chuckled. "Don't you mean robbing on your infamy?"

Eli gave him a sour look. "I would write the bounty office myself and ask if I thought I'd get an answer this year. Bunch of paper-pushers, they probably have five approved explanations and they still don't know what's going on."

The farther they went up into the great plains at the heart of the continent, the more desolate the landscape became. Each village they passed was smaller and farther out than the one before until, at last, they gave out all together, leaving only the rolling hills of endless grass. Neither Josef nor Eli seemed concerned by the sudden nothingness, but Nico crouched down in the cart as far as she could get from the enormous empty space that stretched out all around her.

"It has been awhile," Josef said as the mule trudged through the tall, yellow grass. "I can't even make out the road anymore."

"I don't see how you would know," Eli said. "Considering the last time I brought you here, you were unconscious."

Josef grunted and Eli turned to grin at Nico. "This was before we had you to drag him around when he goes down. I had to use a wheelbarrow."

Nico smiled back faintly, but his words drove a sharp barb into her mind, reinforcing how useful she'd been and, in contrast, how useless she was now. She held her breath, waiting for the voice to make a comment, but nothing came. Still, she could feel it, a cold, clammy blackness just behind her conscious mind, watching smugly, letting her draw her own bleak conclusions.

The sun was just beginning to set over the rolling hills when the cart came to a creaking halt. Nico dragged herself up to see why Eli had stopped them and saw the thief standing on the driver's bench.

"There you are," he shouted over the wind as Josef and Nico stood up to look as well. "Home."

They were on the edge of a wide, shallow valley, and below them was a village. At first glance, it looked very much like the other villages they had passed, a small cluster of stone houses arranged in a square around a well. But the more one looked at the village, the stranger it became. For one thing, each of the stone houses was at least two stories, well kept, and prosperous looking.

There was glass in every window, all the shutters were painted in bright colors, and every door sported a cheery lamp with a colored-glass shade. The square between the houses, which in the other towns had invariably been little more than a stretch of hard-packed dirt, was a carpet of bright green grass. Little fields, just as green as the grass in the square, dotted the slopes all around the village. There were gardens behind the houses as well, each boasting an amazing variety of plants, from common plains wheat to tropical fruit trees. Large herds of fat cattle, fluffy sheep, and dancing goats grazed on the hills above the fields, tended by woolly dogs and boys on horseback. The whole picture was, in short, beautiful, pastoral, prosperous, and amazingly out of place on the empty, rolling plains.

"Come on," Eli said, jumping out to lead the mule down the hill. "We should be in time for dinner."

A crowd had gathered by the time they reached the edge of town. Villagers flowed out of houses, some young, many old, but all plump, well dressed, and healthy looking. They gathered around the well, and a cheer rose up as Eli walked the cart into the square.

"Welcome back, Mr. Mayor!" A great man with a bushy red beard pushed his way through the crowd to grab Eli's hand, shaking it fiercely. "It's been too long."

"Good to be home, Derrik," Eli said and grinned back. He turned and grabbed Nico, pulling her forward. "You all met my swordsman on my last visit. Now I've added another hand to the game. This is Nico. Make her feel welcome."

Another round of applause went up. Nico tried to pull back, away from the attention, but Eli's hand on her shoulder held her firm, and she could only look down at her feet as the people began to chatter.

With a final squeeze, Eli left her to mingle with the crowd, all of whom seemed to be falling over themselves to shake his hand. Josef stepped up to take Eli's place beside her, and they watched in silent fascination.

"What is this place?" Nico whispered as the people began to fawn over Eli. "They're as bad as spirits around him."

"Of course," Josef replied quietly, shifting the enormous sword on his back. "Eli owns this town."

Nico frowned. "Owns it? Even the people?"

"Especially the people," Josef said, stepping away from the cart as a horde of people swarmed over it, opening bags and sorting through the various priceless treasures inside.

Nico didn't follow him. She stood where she was, watching with a mixture of horror and amazement as the townsfolk ravaged the cart. They opened bags and spilled the treasures out onto the grass, sorting the coins, gems, rings, bracelets, crowns, and so forth into piles. Each villager gathered up a collection, and then went to the man with the red beard who made a note in his ledger of what each person had taken. Once it had been accounted for, the people carried their armfuls of treasure, Eli's treasure, things Nico had helped him steal, into their houses, and all with Eli not five feet away, still chatting and shaking hands while Josef stood solemnly beside him, neither of them doing anything about it.

All across town, doors were being thrown open so the people could move the goods into their houses, and what Nico saw inside made her eyes go wide. Every house in the square was absolutely full of treasure. There were tables set with golden plates and gem-encrusted cutlery, ready for dinner. Famous paintings that belonged in king's halls hung over stone fireplaces, protected from the soot by makeshift wooden mantels. She saw young children sitting on silk carpets playing with rubies the size of their fists. One house even had a lamp inlaid with gold coins instead of mirrored reflectors nailed to its front entry, the round coins turning the light butter yellow. Everywhere she looked, the wealth of nations had been reduced to simple home furnishings, and Nico, who didn't say much under the best of circumstances, was at a complete loss for words.

"Amazing, isn't it?" said a soft female voice beside her. Nico whirled around to find a woman not much taller than herself standing beside her. She was very pretty, in a demure sort of way, with dark blond hair and delicate features. She smiled at Nico and gestured toward the cart, which was almost empty.

"I had the same reaction you did when I first saw it," she said. "But that's how the mayor likes it, and so that's what we do." She turned and held out her hand. "I'm Angeline. I run the school here. Derrik is my husband." She nodded at the man with the red beard who was still taking inventory from a line of people with armfuls of treasure. "He's the deputy here. He keeps Home running when the mayor is out."

"The mayor?" Nico said, taking her offered hand shyly. She wasn't offered handshakes much. "You mean Eli?"

Angeline put a slender finger to her lips. "Don't use that name here. It's bad luck. Even in the middle of the plains surrounded by friends, we don't want to take any chances."

"I don't understand," Nico said, lowering her voice. "What is this place?"

"It's Home," Angeline said simply. When it was obvious this explanation didn't make things any clearer for Nico, Angeline took a breath and tried again. "You saw how there was no road into town, right?"

Nico nodded.

"Well," Angeline continued, "there used to be a dirt trade track going across the plains, and that was what supported this village. Then, eighteen years ago, the Council of Thrones completed the Great Road, its first large building project. The Great

Road connected the southern kingdoms with the northern half of the Council, becoming the world's longest trade highway and, in turn, completely eliminating the need for the little dirt track that ran by the village.

"The village deteriorated. The land here is hard, and with no money from traders, the young people left. Eventually, there were only a handful of families still living here, and it looked like the village would vanish altogether, like so many others on the plains. But then a miracle happened." Angeline's face grew wistful. "One day, or so my husband tells it, the mayor walked in from the plains. Just appeared from nowhere, leading a cart almost exactly like the one he brought today. The mayor brought everyone together in the square and made the village an offer. He would buy everything, our houses, our land, our well, everything. He wanted to buy the town."

Nico nodded. It sounded exactly like something Eli would do.

"Several of the people were angry, of course. It was all family land. Where would they live if this stranger bought it? The mayor answered that he would buy them too. Everyone in the village, old, young, whole, or crippled, was to be put on his payroll. In return for his money, all he wanted was our secrecy, a safe place to rest every time he was in town, and the pledge that we would keep all outsiders away. Of course, this just made people more skeptical than ever, but that's when he unveiled the gold." Angeline chuckled. "After that, there were no more objections. He was voted mayor that night, and he renamed the town Home. We've flourished ever since, and not just with money. Our fields have produced with hardly any work on our part, doubly so after one of the mayor's visits. The well stays full even in drought, and we don't have trouble with storms or wild animals. We live a blessed life here, and it's all because of the mayor."

Nico squinched her eyebrows together. "And how often does he—"

"He brings in a cart like this once, maybe twice, a year," Angeline finished for her. "Until two years ago, he was always alone. But then the swordsman joined, and now you." She gave Nico a very serious look. "I know you're one of his trusted companions. Please know that everyone in this village would die before betraying the mayor. No one wants to go back to how things were, or risk our great fortune. We spend only the coined gold, and only far away. We never trade any of the unique treasures. We follow his orders to the letter, always, so don't worry, you're all safe and welcome here."

Nico wanted to tell the woman that she hadn't been worried, but Angeline seemed so concerned that Nico think well of them, she had no choice but to smile and nod. Satisfied, Angeline gave Nico's hand a final squeeze and walked over to her husband, handing him a fresh ledger just as his was about to be filled up. The cart was almost empty at this point, and Eli, having shaken hands at least four times with every one of the two dozen villagers, wandered over to stand beside Nico again.

"Well," he said, "what do you think?"

She gave him a sideways look. "It's quite an extravagant setup."

"I would settle for nothing less," Eli answered, and then he sighed. "I'm only sad the Duke of Gaol is dead and can't see this. He would have turned purple."

Nico didn't understand that statement at all. She was trying to think of something to say when her stomach gurgled loudly.

Eli laughed. "Hungry already? Josef's rubbing off on you. Come, let's go ask about dinner."

He grabbed Nico by the shoulder and walked her toward the red-bearded man with the ledger who was deep in conversation with Josef. Angeline was nowhere to be seen, and both men looked very grim.

"Ah, Mr. Mayor," the deputy said. "I'm afraid—"

"We've got a problem," Josef finished for him. "Seems last night a stranger came into town asking for Eli Monpress."

Eli's smile faded. "A stranger? *Here?* What kind of stranger?"

"A girl, Mr. Mayor," the deputy said. "None of us had seen her before. We took her into custody at once. I must assure you that Home is as safe and secret as—"

"It's all right, Derrik," Eli said. "I'm sure everyone here has been playing by the rules. Did this girl say where she was from or why she was here?"

"No, Mr. Mayor," the deputy said, shaking his head. "She wouldn't say anything, other than that her name was Pele."

Eli's smile faded instantly. "Powers," he hissed under his breath. "All right, where is she?"

Derrik motioned for them to follow him. "This way, sir. I've got her at my house."

He led them across the grass and toward a large house at the far end of the square. Nico expected him to stop at the steps, but he walked past the front door and around to the back of the house, where a pair of double doors was set into the ground.

"You've got her in the cellar?" Eli said. "You haven't been treating her badly, I hope."

"Of course not," Derrik said, unbolting the large lock. "I've got a nice little room down here I use for storing grain. It's dry and comfortable, but this door's the only way out. I thought it would be best, considering...Anyway, she hasn't complained, just sits and waits for you."

Eli nodded and, as soon as the doors were open, started down the stairs. "Wait here," he said when the deputy began to follow him. "We won't be long."

Looking a little taken aback, the man nodded and stepped aside, letting Eli, Josef, and Nico climb down into the cellar.

It was just as the man had said, a small, dry room in the cellar with a lamp and a bed and a stack of books that had obviously been brought down from the house above. Sitting on the edge of the bed was a familiar girl in hunter's leathers with a long, lovely knife at her hip and dark circles under her eyes, as though she'd been crying.

Eli stopped at the foot of the stairs and gave her a long, serious look. "Hello, Pele."

The girl nodded. "Eli."

Eli grabbed a stool from the corner and set it down beside her. "You chose a difficult way of getting in touch, you know," he said, sitting down with a long sigh. "Why not just get your father to reach me? Slorn has more tricks than any three bears put together."

"If I could do that, I wouldn't need you in the first place," Pele said, her voice going a bit ragged. "My father's…Slorn's gone missing."

There was a long silence.

"Missing?" Eli said at last. "Men like Slorn don't just go missing." He leaned forward and grasped Pele's hand. "What happened?"

Pele didn't try to take her hand back. Instead, she leaned forward, blinking back tears, and began to tell her story.

By the time she finished, Eli was looking grim indeed, and Pele was sobbing openly.

"After what Sted did to my mother, Father was inconsolable," she said, her voice quivering. "He locked himself in his workroom and wouldn't come out for two days no matter how I beat on the door. Then, on the third morning, he came out dressed in traveling gear and said he was going after Sted." Pele took a deep breath. "I wanted to go with him, but he said someone had to stay and take care of the house. He said he had to go, that he'd made a promise to the League of Storms to keep the seed secret and safe.

That it was the only reason the League had let him keep Mother alive in the first place. So he left and I stayed behind. He said he'd contact me when he knew something, but that was three weeks ago. Since then, I've heard nothing. Please." She gripped Eli's hand. "Please, Eli, you're one of his oldest friends. You have to help me find him."

Eli calmly began extricating his fingers from her grasp. "Pele," he said gently. "I'm a thief, all right? This isn't really my area of expertise. Surely there's someone else—"

Pele refused to let go. "But you go everywhere. You know all sorts of things. And there is no one else. Father took all his contacts with him. I only knew where you were because this village is listed as your delivery address in our records."

"You're panicking," Eli said, his voice calm. "It's been only three weeks. He probably hasn't even found where he's going. Slorn's a powerful wizard. He can take care of himself."

"But he's not a fighter!" Pele said fiercely. She turned to Josef. "I know you beat Sted in Gaol. That was why he came to us, to get a new sword that could beat yours. He took my mother's seed when we wouldn't give him a sword. Please, I don't know what else to do. The man is a monster. I can't let my father face him alone. If you won't help me, then tell me where to go, or tell me where to find Sted and I'll help my father myself, just—"

She cut off when Eli stood up suddenly. "All right," he said, running his hands through his hair. "I'll help you. Just calm down."

Pele's eyes lit up. "Thank you!"

Eli waved his hand. For all her gratitude, he didn't look happy at all. "Come up and have some dinner, and we'll see about moving you into a real room."

Pele shot up from the bed, grabbing Eli and hugging him tightly. "Thank you, thank you!"

"Yes," Eli said, extricating himself from her grip. "Let's go on up. We've been on the road all day and we're tired. Let us get some food and rest and then we'll see what's to be done about our missing bear, all right?"

Pele nodded and, after embracing him one last time, ran up the stairs with a smile on her face. Eli followed more slowly, his smile quickly fading to a grimace. Nico and Josef exchanged a look as they followed Pele and the thief out of the cellar and into the deputy's house, where he and Angeline were just getting supper on the table.

Dinner was a grand spread. There was pork and braised potatoes; some sort of pea soup, which was green, creamy, and delicious; roasted squash; and a large basket of fresh biscuits, golden and flaky and dripping with honeyed butter. Everyone ate with gusto, even Nico. Normally she despised eating. It felt too much like what the demon did, but her stomach was growling and she dove into the very human pleasure of stuffing herself full of delicious food.

Pele was stuffing herself too. The second Eli had agreed to help her she'd started to look better and was now eating her dark circles and pale cheeks away with a vigor only teenagers can achieve. Josef ate as he always did, efficiently and enormously, much to Angeline's delight. The only person who wasn't stuffing himself was Eli. He ate and made conversation, letting the deputy fill him in on what he'd missed being away from Home. Still, to Nico, who spent much of her time watching, it was clear Eli's mind was somewhere else. He ate his food perfunctorily, not with the energy he usually showed toward a good meal after days of living off hardtack and whatever animal was unlucky enough to get caught in Josef's traps. Though Eli appeared to be actively engaged in the deputy's reports, Nico could see the slight glaze in his expression that meant he was really thinking of something else entirely, and whatever it was, he wasn't happy about it.

After dinner, Pele wanted to discuss plans to rescue Slorn, but Eli gently turned her around and sent her to bed. She put up a fight, but not much of one. It was obvious she'd been sleeping even worse than she'd been eating. Angeline took her off to a bed that wasn't in the basement while Eli said his good-nights to the deputy. Then, motioning for Josef and Nico to follow, he slipped out the door and into the night.

"Come on," Josef said, standing up from his chair with a long-suffering sigh. "He's planning something. Let's find out what before he just goes and does it."

Nico nodded and followed the swordsman out the door. They walked across the grassy square, following the dark outline of Eli's gangly figure away from the bright houses and up toward the hills. When they reached the edge of the valley, he stopped suddenly and flopped down in the scruffy grass. Now that they were away from the town lights, the full moon was brighter than ever. Even without her demon-enhanced vision, Nico had no problem finding a flat spot of ground near Eli. Josef flopped down on the other side, dropping the Heart on the ground with a dull thunk.

Almost before they were seated, Eli began to speak.

"Well," he said, his voice dripping with bile. "Some trip Home this has been. Can't I even relax for one day without something coming up?"

"Don't whine," Josef said. "You could have said no."

"Easy for you to say," Eli snapped. "You don't have a compassionate bone in your body. I've known the girl since she was ten, Josef. What was I supposed to say? 'Sorry about your dad, but I'm on holiday. Good luck, chop chop'?" He flopped back on the grass with a disgusted sigh. "So much for lying low."

For a while, no one said anything. Then, at last, Eli sat up again with a frustrated groan. "Anyway, this is all beside the point. Even if Pele hadn't asked me, I'd have to go investigate. No matter how insufferable he can get, Slorn's an old, old friend. We have to help him. He'll never make us toys again if we don't." Eli tilted his head skyward, staring at the bright moon hanging alone in the black sky. "I only wish Slorn'd asked me himself. Then I could have at least gotten a huge favor out of the deal, maybe even free work. Now I'm stuck doing a sob job pro bono."

"Can't make money all the time," Josef said with a shrug.

Eli's only answer to that was a loud harrumph.

"Well," Eli said after a long silence, "done is done. First thing now is to find Slorn."

"Considering we're talking about a man with a bear's head, I don't think it'll be too hard," Josef said. "It's not like he can just blend in."

"Don't underestimate him," Eli said, lying back on the grass again. "If it were that easy, Pele wouldn't have come here. Slorn's surprisingly skilled at not being noticed."

"What about a broker?" Josef said. "Could we just pay one of them to find him like you did with the Fenzetti blade?"

Eli shook his head. "Brokers are great for finding inanimate objects but lousy at finding people. Also, we're trying to stay low, remember? The last thing I need is a broker getting suspicious. Goin was way out on the borderlands, so it was worth the chance, but we're in the middle of the Council Kingdoms. Any broker we could visit would probably have my poster on the wall. The moment I walked in I'd become a new commodity to sell."

"So, what?" Josef said. "Do we start asking in the usual channels? Spreading money around?"

"No, no, no," Eli said. "Far too risky, and I'm not spending cash on a job with no payout. Also, this is *Slorn* we're talking about. If the usual tactics worked, the Shapers would have gotten him years ago. What we need is a new angle." Eli began to grin. "Remember, we're not just looking for a *man*. We're also looking for a *bear*, and fortunately I know just who to ask when it comes to bears."

Josef looked skeptical. "You never struck me as the bear hunter type."

"I'm not," Eli said, standing up with an extremely self-pleased smile. "And I didn't say anything about hunters. Trust me, this is much better, and the best part is I won't even have to use a favor. I'll just cash in one of Slorn's. It's only fair that he should pay for his own rescue."

"You seem awful confident," Josef said, staring up at him. "Are you sure this is going to work?"

"Of course it will work," Eli scoffed. "My plans always work." His voice shifted at Josef's oh-come-on look. "Well, perhaps not always as I'd first intended, but they *do* work. Anyway, it's the only plan we've got." Nico jumped as Eli's hand settled on her hooded head. "I'm sure I don't need to remind you of the consequences of letting the only man in the world capable of creating coats and manacles that can hold a demon captive vanish into the night."

Josef gave him a dirty look. "Don't use her to make your points."

"Ah," Eli said. "But the point has been made." He gave Nico's head one last pat before turning back toward town. "Come on, we need to get packed. We've got a long trip ahead of us."

Josef didn't move. He sat glaring at Eli's back as the thief trotted down the hill. Finally, when Eli's long shadow disappeared inside the house, Josef pushed himself off the ground with a sigh.

"He can be a real ass sometimes," he grumbled, offering his hand to Nico.

"He is doing this for me," Nico said. "At least partially."

"Don't be fooled," Josef growled, pulling her up. "He's doing it for himself. He lives for favor swapping as much as fame and thievery. This is just another move in whatever game he plays. Don't let him trick you into thinking otherwise."

"I know," Nico said, but her words didn't sound convincing, even to her. Josef could label and dismiss Eli's reasons, but Nico couldn't. After all, that whole business with the Fenzetti had been for her, same with the trip up to Slorn's in the first place. It hadn't bothered her then because she'd been a participating, worthwhile member of the team, doing her share and helping as she had been helped. Now…

Now you're deadweight.

Nico closed her eyes.

Worse. The voice was low and laughing. *You're a liability without payoff, a bad piece of meat. The thief is no idiot. How long until he leaves you somewhere? He only uses you to keep the swordsman in tow, but even a muscle-brained lug like Josef will realize what a bad deal you've become sooner or later. What happens then, little Nico? What will you do?*

Nico didn't reply, though she wasn't sure if that was because she knew better than to talk to the voice or because she didn't have an answer.

Come, little girl. The voice was honey dripping down her throat. *You already know how to help, don't you?*

But I don't know. Nico winced and slammed her lips tight; the answering thought had been automatic.

Yes, you do. Think, if you can. Who is Slorn after?

This time Nico refused to let her mind go forward. It did her no good. The voice rolled right over her wall of silence.

He's after Sted, the man who killed his wife and took the subject of their life's work, Nivel's precious seed. Sted is in my realm now, and you should know better than any that I always keep an eye on what belongs to me.

The memory overwhelmed her as the voice faded. She was standing in a room underground. She was older, powerful, standing beside a figure made out of darkness that meant more to her than any life. The figure took her hand, the long, cold fingers sliding across her palm, and a rush of loyalty, security, power, and safety sent her to her knees. The figure, the source of all her fealty, did not help her up. Instead, the cold hands reached and took her head, turning it toward the far end of the room. There, cut into the stone, was a map. A great map showing all the world, from the Council Kingdoms to the Immortal Empress's lands and the great frozen country far to the north. It was carved in relief, the mountains standing up from the stone as sharp and cold as the real thing, and crouched on this tiny, perfect model were little black creatures with wispy beetle legs.

The figure made a small, beautiful gesture, and she understood. The black creatures were markers for something greater, their slow, crawling movements reflections of a larger scale.

My seeds, the figure's voice hummed in her bones, masculine and resonant with a dark beauty that filled her with a terrible longing for home. *Every single one of them, all across the world.*

Nico swallowed.

Just ask. The cold hand reached up to stroke her cheek. *Ask and all shall be given to you, my dearest daughter, seed of my own heart.*

She clutched the long, cold fingers, tears flowing down her cheeks. "Yes, Master."

"Nico!"

Her eyes shot open. She was sitting on the grassy slope by Eli's town. Josef was leaning over her, his concerned face inches from her own. This close, she could see the pale scars running below his stubble. Nico flinched away, squeezing her eyes shut before he could see the tears in them.

"Are you all right?" He ran his hands over her limbs. "You fell down. What happened?"

"Nothing," she said, ashamed at the dreamy lilt in her voice. The haze of the memory still clung to her mind, fogging her thoughts with overwhelming loss for the safety she'd felt standing beside the figure. Her body grew heavy as the memory of power faded, leaving her small and helpless as a blind grub on the grass. She wasn't even sure if what she'd just seen was her own memory or a sent one, but the wetness on her face was real, and she wondered, not for the first time, if she was losing her mind.

You can't lose what isn't yours, the voice whispered. *Every bit of you belongs to me, willingly given. Why do you hold back now?*

"Leave me alone," Nico whispered.

"What?" Josef leaned closer. "Did you say something?"

Tell him, the voice said. *Just speak the truth. Tell him you can ask me to find Sted at any time, and through him, Slorn. Make them happy, or lie here and be a burden. Your choice, dearest.*

Nico sat up, her coat twitching over her hands as she scrubbed her face. "I'm sorry," she whispered. "I'm just tired."

"Understandably," Josef said, helping her up. "Let's get to bed before Eli decides he needs to leave tonight."

Nico nodded and started down the hill again, this time with Josef walking beside her, watching. His face was blank, but she knew him well enough to know he was worried. Well, she decided as she straightened up, he didn't need to be. She wouldn't lose, and she wouldn't let them down. She'd find a way to be useful without the demon. She'd do everything she could to make sure Eli's plan worked. She didn't know what that was, but she'd do it. She didn't need the voice.

But even as the thought spun through her head, she could feel the weakness coming back, the feeling of being lessened, of being lost, and with it, the echoing memory of the power she'd had in the memory. The power and security she could have again, if she would only ask. That feeling was the only answer the voice made, but it was an answer for which she had no retort. Tiny and beaten, she followed Josef into the house and shut the door on the night.

CHAPTER 5

The mist was still thick on the plains when three figures slipped out of the deputy's house and into the sleeping town of Home. There was no one in the square to see them creep out through the window, or to see the large bag of foodstuffs they helped themselves to from the baker's larder. Once they had shoved as much as they could carry into a flour sack, also pilfered, they vanished into the ghostly fog, slipping silently into the hills without a sound.

Across the grassy square, a young man slid down from his window and stretched the hours of waiting out of his joints. Finally, the thief had made his move. Shaking with excitement, he crept across his bedroom to the ostentatious writing desk his father had made for him out of a pair of matched thrones the mayor had brought in last year. He reached behind the desk's left leg and felt around until his trembling fingers found the bit of extravagant carving he was looking for. Grinning, he pressed down, hard. There was a little *clack* of a latch, and a small, wooden compartment popped out by the desk's foot, just above what had been the larger throne's clawed armrest. His hands went greedily for the tiny compartment. He'd discovered it by accident a few months ago, and even his father didn't know about it. He'd always wondered what a king would store in that secret place. Poison maybe, or state secrets. Whatever it had been, surely not even the secret stash of a king had ever held a treasure like this.

He raised his hand, bringing up a marble-sized sky-blue globe of crystal bound by silver wires to a silver chain. Gentle as a new father, he rolled the globe in a circle around his palm as he had been told. As it moved, the blue globe began to change color, shifting from clear, calm sky to the deeper, turbulent blue of the north sea. As the color shifted, something inside the globe began to move as well, showing the sphere was ready. After looking over his shoulder one last time, the young man crouched and cupped the globe to his mouth. Then, as softly as he could, he whispered, "Sara."

The response was immediate. The globe flashed between his fingers, and a woman's voice, cross, clipped, and vaguely scratchy, answered. "Has he moved?"

"Yes," the boy whispered. "All three of them left at dawn. They took a bunch of food with them."

"A long trip then." The woman's voice paused, and he heard her let out a long breath. "What about the stranger girl?"

"The mayor met with her." The young man was whispering quickly now, for the dawn was beginning to slip through his window, a sure sign that his mother would come looking for him soon. "Turns out he did know her. She's staying at the deputy's house now. Only name I could get for her was Pele."

"Pele?" The woman's voice was sharp as razors. "You're *sure* it was Pele?"

"Yes," the boy said, grinning. When she cut in like that, it meant she was pleased. "Pele, tall girl, very upset. She had this crazy knife on her, never seen one like it before."

There was a pause from the other end, and then, "All right, good work." He heard the scratching of a pen. "Thank you. Keep me posted if the mayor reappears or the girl tries to leave."

"And my reward?" the boy said quickly.

The woman made an irritated sound. "Your reward is the same

as ever. Three years of service, and then I will bring you to Zarin. All you have to do is keep reporting and not blow your cover and it's a done deal. That is, unless you keep bothering me about it."

"Yes, Sara," the boy whispered, his voice shaking. "I'm sorry."

"Just keep me informed," she said. "And don't do anything stupid. Remember, idiocy is its own cure in time."

"Yes, Sara," he said again, but the globe in his palm was already fading back to light blue, a sure sign that she was already gone.

He sneered at the globe. The woman might be his only chance at getting out of this nowhere backwater, but Powers, was she high-handed. One day, when he was in Zarin living like a lord with followers and women and a big city house, he'd make her swallow that sharp tongue.

A clatter from downstairs disrupted that happy line of thought, and the boy lunged toward the desk, dumping the orb on the chain back into the secret compartment just as his mother's footsteps sounded on the stairs. He dove for his bed, still made up from the night before, and jumped between the sheets right as his mother banged on the door, yelling for him to get up and come do his chores before breakfast. He made a noncommittal sound and waited under the covers as she climbed back down. Only when her footsteps vanished did he let out his breath.

In the town of Home, betraying the mayor was an unthinkable crime. Sometimes even he couldn't believe what he was doing, but he had to do it. It was his only way out of this tiny, isolated, prison of a town. Keeping that thought front and center in his mind, the young man threw open his door and clattered down the stairs. Under his window, hidden in the dark of the secret compartment of a wronged king, the orb lay quiet and still, listening.

"You have a spy in Monpress's town?" Alric, Deputy Commander of the League of Storms, smiled thinly as the blue orb in the woman's hands faded from stormy sea to calm blue. "Why am I not surprised, Sara?"

The woman sitting at the cluttered desk beside him leaned back in her leather chair and took a draw from her long-handled pipe. "Because you are a man incapable of surprise, Alric," she said, blowing a line of smoke in his direction. "Though you seem to delight in surprising others. Now, did you stop by just to eavesdrop on my private correspondence, or do you have a matter you actually came to discuss? If so, you'd better get on with it. I'm very busy right now."

With any other member of the Council of Thrones, Alric would have called that a bluff, but with Sara it was the absolute truth. Despite the Council's supposed indifference to magic, the office of its chief official on the subject was a hive of activity at all hours of the day. Actually, he didn't know when Sara slept. He'd never seen her leave her labyrinthine compound deep below the Council keep. Even so, he took his time answering. Busy she might be, but her implied threat was an empty one. She would never kick him out before learning why he'd come. No reason he couldn't use that edge to get a few answers of his own.

"Even the League isn't exactly sure where Monpress goes to lick his wounds," Alric said, taking a seat on the worn couch beside her desk. "Yet here you are, not only with knowledge of the village's location but with a spy already set up inside. Very impressive; how did you do it?"

"Quite simple," Sara said, putting her booted feet up on the desk in front of her and obviously trying not to look like she was bragging. "When Eli's stolen goods failed to show up for resale, we knew he was hoarding them somewhere. With his flair for the dramatic, I was sure he wasn't stuffing his treasures under some rock. That left stashing the property, probably in a town. So I put out a general search with the Council tax bureau for any unexpected prosperity, and sure enough I found an interesting report of a little town in the middle of nowhere that, mysteriously, despite losing its place on the central trade route thanks to the Council's completion of the Great Road, has continued to pay its annual taxes every year, even while all the towns around it were defaulting."

"You found him through tax fraud?" Alric was impressed despite himself.

"Just the opposite," Sara said. "Eli's a clever boy, far cleverer than those idiots at the bounty office give him credit for. He knew there's no faster way to get the Council's attention than to skip on your taxes. Unfortunately, in his anxiety to slip under the audits, he neglected to take into account that the only thing more suspicious than defaulting on your taxes is to be the one town in a failing area that doesn't." She paused, giving Alric a smoke-wreathed glare. "But you didn't appear in my office unannounced to talk about Eli. Why are you here, Alric?"

Alric leaned forward. "You are a great friend of Heinricht Slorn, are you not?"

Sara's mouth twitched. "Heinricht is a colleague of mine. There's no greater mind for Spirit Theory on the continent. We often work on problems together. But I don't know why you're coming to me. He's *your* pet Shaper."

"He is indeed very important to our interests," Alric said benignly, refusing to rise to the bait. "However, a short while ago, he vanished. I had hoped that, as his friend, you would have some clue to his whereabouts. We're very concerned, you see."

"Yes, I'm sure you are," Sara said, smiling as she cast a pointed look at the golden sword at Alric's hip. "Swordsmith slipped the leash, did he?"

"Call it what you like," Alric said, casually adjusting his coat to cover his sword's hilt. "I'm only asking if he's contacted you. Slorn is a proud man, but he's in a desperate situation. Desperate enough that I wouldn't be surprised if he's tried to reach you through his own relay point." His eyes flicked to the blue orb on its silver chain, still lying on Sara's desk where she'd put it down. "The information and resources at your disposal are quite considerable, and Slorn's not a man to pass up opportunities."

"What makes you think I gave Slorn a relay link?" Sara said, quietly picking up the blue orb and dropping it into the strongbox on her desk, where it landed on top of a dozen other orbs just like it. "Each link is a monument of wizardry, the product of months of work by myself and my team." She snapped the strongbox lid shut. "They are for Council use only."

"Really?" Alric said. "How interesting, then, that you planted something so valuable in the hands of a boy spy just to keep an eye on Monpress."

"Not at all," Sara said. "Eli is of great interest to the Council."

"Really?" Alric's smile sharpened. "If that's the case, then it's even more interesting that you don't share your information, or the town's location, with the Council Bounty Office."

"If you're here to talk Council politics, Alric, I suggest you move on," Sara said crossly. "I have quite enough of it without your nosing about. Now, the answer to your question is no. I have received no communication from Slorn for weeks. Is there anything else I can do for the League?"

"Just let us know if anything comes up," Alric said, pushing himself off the couch. "The League's interests rarely overlap with those of the Council, but we've worked together enough for you to know that our word is good. You can believe me when I say that we will not forget your cooperation in this matter."

"Quite," Sara said. "You don't need me to see you out, I'm sure."

"No, thank you." Alric held his hand out in front of him and closed his eyes, concentrating on his office back at League headquarters. His neat desk, the dark stone, the heavy book piled with paperwork that had undoubtedly multiplied in his absence. It took less than a second before the air shimmered in front of him, opening a long, narrow slit that glowed bright white at the edges. Through it was his office just as he had envisioned it. It was a very neat opening: no sound, no flash, just a slight breeze, but then, Alric had been a League member for a very long time.

He put one foot through, stepping down on the cold stone of the League fortress, then he paused, standing halfway between two places, and looked over his shoulder. "Oh, Sara," he said, almost as an afterthought. "The girl who appeared in Eli's town, your spy said her name was Pele, correct?"

"You heard it as well as I did," Sara said stiffly, looking at him around a plume of pipe smoke.

"Slorn has a daughter with the same name," Alric said. "Isn't that interesting?"

"Does he?" Sara said. "I don't keep up with his family."

"A pity," Alric said, smiling. "Good day, Sara, and don't forget to keep me informed. The League is a good friend to those who help us."

"And a bitter enemy to those who don't," Sarah finished. "Point made, now get out."

Alric gave her one final, gracious smile before stepping completely into his office, the cut in reality vanishing with a dim flicker behind him.

Sara sat in her office for a while after he was gone, smoking furiously. Then, with a long sigh, she reached over and yanked the bell pull in the corner. It made no sound when she pulled it, but a second later, a lovely, long-haired man in a garish red coat, green britches, and a tall pair of polished black boots entered her office with a flourish.

"Forget our discussion this morning," Sara said as soon as he closed the door behind him. "We're going bear hunting after all."

"Oh?" The man arched one perfectly manicured eyebrow. "Why the change of heart?"

"It's the stakes that have changed," Sara said. "Not the heart. We might have a very rare opportunity to catch two wayward talents in one swoop, but we're going to need a strong grip."

"So send Tesset," the man said. "He's the strongest grip we've got. And I'll go along to make sure he doesn't have one of his fits of morality."

Sara shook her head. "No, for this we need the biggest hammer we can get, Sparrow." She leaned back in her chair. "I want you to get me Mellinor."

For the first time since he'd entered, Sparrow's smug expression faltered. "Banage's girl? But she's the head of the Monpress investigation. The particulars of our deal with the Spirit Court involving her employment with the Council are very strict."

"As I said," Sara said, grinning, "the stakes have changed. If Slorn sent his daughter to Eli, then we can only assume the thief is in this race as well. Banage's pet has a strange connection with Monpress, and that's exactly the kind of leverage we're going to need to pull this off. I must have her. No one else will do."

Sparrow ran a long hand through his glossy hair. "Banage won't like it."

"Hang Banage," Sara said, blowing a ring of smoke at him. "Just go find the girl and convince her to come along. That's what I pay you for."

"As you wish," Sparrow said, turning back toward the door.

"Have her here tomorrow morning," Sara called as he left. "First appointment."

The door closed without an answer, but she knew Sparrow had

heard. Even if he hadn't, she didn't care. There were larger games afoot. Sara turned back to her desk and reached under the piles of drafting parchment scribbled with designs and notes. After a little fumbling, she pulled out the long, narrow slip of paper she'd hidden when Alric had stepped unannounced into her room, right before the badly timed call from her spy in Eli's village had come in. It rankled her that Alric had been there to yank that bit of information, but she pushed her annoyance aside. He was the sort of man who it was better to assume knew everything already anyway. That way you were never caught off-guard.

She smoothed the strip of paper between her fingers. It had arrived this morning, dropped through her window by a large bird she didn't recognize. That much wasn't unusual. She often received messages that way, but the contents of this paper were something else entirely. It was a short letter, barely more than a paragraph, asking for assistance in a chase. The letter was not signed, but there was no need for a name. It was a hand she knew well. After years spent poring over whatever of his documents she could get her hands on, Slorn's writing was as familiar as her own.

"Well, well, Heinricht," she murmured, feeding the note into the little furnace in her office. "Looks like you'll get your help after all."

She smiled as the paper curled into ash. As it burned, she looked up at the wall above her desk. There, pasted to the metal, were two rows of nearly identical wanted posters. They were arranged chronologically, each bearing the same name above a portrait of the same smiling, boyish face. The only differences between them were the list of crimes, which grew longer and denser with each printing, and the number below the portrait. It was the number that was truly impressive, climbing exponentially from its start on the first poster at three hundred standards to the newest entry, a freshly printed sheet at the end bearing a number large enough to be a national budget: ninety-eight thousand gold standards.

Sara reached up to touch the closest poster, tracing her finger along the boy's intricately shaded jawline. "High stakes indeed," she whispered, her face breaking into a smile. "Let's see whom luck favors this time around, my little Eliton."

On the wall, the poster's unchanging face smiled back, just as it always did.

CHAPTER 6

Miranda Lyonette squinted at the tiny script of the report in her hands, wishing, for the hundredth time that hour, that the Council had decided to save money in some way other than teaching its scribes to write in microscopic strokes. It would also help if the investigators could somehow manage to be thorough *and* interesting in their reports. It might be asking a bit much, but how anyone could make Eli Monpress's theft of the Queen of Verdun's diamond crown and his subsequent getaway through the burning canals *boring* was beyond her comprehension.

Miranda threw the report on the table and leaned back in her chair, rubbing her tired eyes. It had been three weeks since Lord Whitefall had made her head of the joint Spirit Court and Council of Thrones Monpress investigation. True to his word, he'd arranged an office for her the next day, and Miranda found herself operating out of a Council warehouse by the river that was uncomfortably warm during the day and damp at night. This was tolerable, however, for the space was large enough for Gin with plenty of room left for the enormous stacks of filing shelves Lord Whitefall had sent over from the main Council offices. She had also been provided with a staff, consisting of a runner, a scribe, and a file clerk. This had struck her as odd at first. She'd thought she'd be getting a Council investigator, or at least someone familiar with Monpress, but that was before she'd discovered exactly how much paperwork was involved in her new position.

One week into her new job and she understood why Lord Whitefall's office looked the way it did. The Council produced paper at a spectacular rate. Every afternoon a cart brought boxes of reports, observations, and strategies from the central office. Each was copied in triplicate, one for her to sign and send back as proof that she had read it, one for her active use, and one for her records. Worse, nearly all of it was useless—commentary on past crimes and idiotic suggestions from Council members who seemed to get all their information on Monpress from the gossip sheets, where he was a regular and much followed figure, even when he hadn't pulled a crime in over a month.

"Especially when he hasn't pulled a crime in over a month," Miranda muttered, looking balefully over at the other stack of papers on her desk. Shorter than the Council reports but still an impressive pile, these were great sheets of cheap yellow paper folded in half and printed with enormous lettering. The top one proclaimed MONPRESS STILL AT LARGE!!! above a dramatized engraving of a jaunty Monpress carrying a fat man with a crown, presumably the king of Mellinor, over his shoulder while a tall man with rings on his fingers and another figure in the white uniform of the Council guards looked around cluelessly in the background.

Miranda rubbed her throbbing temples. If the Council reports were dull and overresearched, the gossip sheets were the exact opposite. Below the picture were paragraphs full of exclamations and bold claims with the important points underlined for maximum impact. Where was Monpress now? Why hadn't he been active? Was it a cover-up? Why wasn't the Spirit Court doing anything? Where are the bounty hunters?

The speculations ran all the way to the fold, which was a bit long even for cheap sensationalism. Still, with Eli gone to ground, the public was hungry for more coverage, even when it was a simple rehashing of known information. Miranda reached out and flipped the paper open, grimacing as the cheap ink smudged onto her fingers. The feature on Monpress continued below the fold, ending with an editorial piece from an anonymous Concerned Council Member titled OUR GREATEST THREAT.

"Who is the greatest threat to our security today? Besides the ever-present threat of the Immortal Empress from across the sea, a look down the Council's bounty list provides a feast of villainy. Yet ask the man on the street, the farmer in the field, and the answer is always the same: wizards. We all know of the events in Mellinor, where a wizard nearly took control of a kingdom single-handedly through force of his magic. The so-called Spirit Court has told us this was the doing of Eli Monpress, but if that's so, then why does Monpress go uncaught? How does an organization that can talk to the wind itself fail to capture a man so notorious? The answer is simple enough for a child: Because they are in allegiance with the thief! How many more disasters will we allow the wizards to blame on Monpress, their 'supposed' rogue? How much higher must Monpress's bounty get before we wake up and realize that our anger should be focused not on the thief, but on his masters, the so-called Spirit Court and its king, Etmon Banage!"

There was more, but Miranda didn't bother to read it. She balled up the paper and threw it as hard as she could across the room. It landed beside Gin, who woke with a snort, glaring at the paper before turning his orange eyes on his mistress. "I told you not to waste your time with that trash."

"It gets worse every day!" Miranda shouted, slamming her hands on the table.

"It's always been like this," Gin said. "It just seems worse because you're paying attention to it now."

"Look." She grabbed a fistfull of yellow sheets from the stack and shook them at the hound. "Every one of these sorry excuses for print sings the same tune: 'The Spirit Court is a bunch of bungling idiots who can't catch a thief,' 'Eli Monpress is working for the wizards!' And it's *always* us. You never see one of these anonymous letters criticizing the Council."

"That's because the Council outsources all its catching to bounty hunters rather than sending its own people," Gin said, yawning. "Easier to blame someone when you know their name."

"That's not it and you know it." Miranda glared at him. "It's just what Master Banage said would happen. That thief is ruining the reputation of the Spirit Court! Master Banage's name, *all* our names are being dragged through the mud on the front page of the Zarin gossip sheets and it's *all Monpress's fault*!"

"So why are we sitting around here?" Gin said, standing up. "You're head of the Eli investigation. Let's go catch him."

"Catch him doing *what*?" Miranda cried, gesturing at the snowdrift of paper on her desk. "Eli hasn't robbed so much as a roadside charity box in a *month*."

"At least we'd be out there doing something," Gin snapped back. "Better than being in here, pushing paper and getting angry at gossip sheets. Who ever heard of catching a thief by reading reports?"

"No," Miranda said fiercely, shoving her reports into order.

"This is where I need to be. The Council has the best information network on the continent. If Eli pulls anything, I'll be the first to know. And this time it won't be like Mellinor or Gaol. This time I'll have the full backing of the Council. No more going after him alone, no more playing up to local officials. We'll come down on that thief with the combined forces of the Council of Thrones and the Spirit Court. Bam!" She slammed her hands on the table. "I'd like to see him wiggle out of that."

Gin flicked his ears back at the crash. "Why are you getting so worked up? I thought we kind of liked Eli now."

Miranda stuck her nose in the air. "Thinking he's not evil isn't the same as liking him. He's a scoundrel and a lawbreaker and a thief, not to mention a liar, and though I will admit he's not a bad sort of guy underneath all that, it hardly makes up for the rest." She clenched her fists. "I'm going to catch that thief, Gin. I'll bring him trussed up like a hog before Master Banage and clear the Spirit Court's name once and for all. And then I'm going to use the bounty money to put these *liars*"—she swatted the stack of gossip sheets—"out of business for good."

"Don't waste your gold," said a lilting, unfamiliar voice. "More would just spring up."

Miranda and Gin both jumped and whirled around to face the sound. There, five steps inside the locked and bolted door, was a man. He was very tall and dressed extremely oddly. He wore red snakeskin boots with pointed toes, black trousers that were far too tight and were embellished with lemon-yellow thread, and a green velvet jacket the color of new grass over a bright pink shirt and a maroon vest. His long hair was ice blond shot with black (an obvious dye job, though she couldn't say which, if either, had been his original color), and his head was crowned with a large red hat trimmed with gold that he wore swooped down over his eyes.

"Anyway," he continued, traipsing into the room as if he'd been invited. "There's no point in getting angry at the gossips. If it wasn't the Court, they'd be after someone else."

"Who are you?" Miranda shouted, jumping up, her rings flashing as her chair toppled over behind her. But Gin was even faster. By the time the words were out of her mouth, he had launched himself off the floor and pounced on the man, pinning him to the ground.

"How did you sneak in here?" Gin snarled, his orange eyes blinking rapidly, as though he was having trouble focusing. "How do you make no sound? Why do you flicker like that?"

The man smiled up at the large, sharp teeth hovering inches above his head. "Easy, doggie," he said, his eyes darting toward Miranda. "I'm afraid I'm not a wizard. So if your guard dog is addressing me, he's wasting his rather terrible-smelling breath. If you wouldn't mind?" He wiggled helplessly.

Miranda made no move to call Gin off. Instead, she walked across the room to stand over the man as well. "You haven't answered my question," she said. "And I'll add Gin's to it, since you can't hear. Who are you? How did you get in here? What are you doing?"

"You left out the part about the flickering," Gin growled, leaning harder on the stranger's shoulders until the man's face turned pasty against the garish backdrop of his hat. "Can't you see it?"

Miranda shook her head. Other than questionable color choices, the man looked normal to her.

The stranger wiggled one hand into his pocket and flipped out a card, which he tossed toward Miranda's feet.

"The name's Sparrow," he said as she picked it up. "I got in through the door, and I do almost anything. Tonight, I'm an errand boy. I've been sent by our mutual employer to request your presence at a meeting tomorrow morning."

"Employer?" Miranda said, holding the card by its edges. "Lord Whitefall?"

"That windbag?" The man laughed. "No, dear, I'm no paper-pusher. I'm talking about Sara, the lady running the show."

Miranda looked at the card in her hand. It was surprisingly plain, considering the man it belonged to, just a white rectangle on heavy stock with a small engraving of a sparrow in flight in the lower left-hand corner. She flipped it over. The back was as blank as the front, save for a small notation written in slanting script: *8:40.*

"Eight forty?" Miranda read, brows furrowed.

"Yes, and don't be late," Sparrow said. "Sara keeps an extremely tight schedule. She'll be intolerable if you throw it off."

She gave him a suspicious look. "Where am I going?"

"The Council citadel, of course," Sparrow said, tilting his head sideways so that he wasn't directly under Gin's bared teeth. "Just show up and I'll bring you down. I play doorman as well as messenger."

Miranda slipped the card into her pocket. "Is that all you have to tell me?"

"Yes," Sparrow said. "Can you get this dog off of me? I'm having trouble feeling my legs."

Miranda looked at Gin and jerked her head to the side. With a final growl, Gin pulled back, circling around to stand beside Miranda as Sparrow sat up and wiped his face with an orange handkerchief.

"I can see you'll be a delightful addition to our team," he said, standing up stiffly. "I'll see you tomorrow, yes?"

"Eight forty." Miranda nodded. "I'll be early, and your Sara had better have a good explanation."

"Oh, she has dozens," Sparrow said. "Getting one out of her is the challenge." He straightened his coat and turned to face her, tipping his extravagant hat politely. "Until tomorrow, Miss Miranda."

He flashed her a wide smile and then, spinning on his tall heel, walked out the previously locked door. Gin watched him intently, ears swiveling, but Sparrow made a perfectly normal amount of noise as he left, and the dog seemed disappointed. He stared at the door as it swung shut, growling low in his throat. "I don't trust that man."

Miranda could only laugh at that. "What was your first clue?"

"No," Gin said sharply. "There's something really wrong about him."

Miranda stopped laughing. "What do you mean?"

"He flickers," the dog said. "He's hard to look at, like he's there but not."

"Flickers how?"

Gin made a frustrated sound. "I can't explain it. It's just wrong. I had to look at him with my eyes to see him clearly. I've never had to do that before." He looked at her intently. "You should be careful tomorrow."

"I always am," Miranda said. "Still, I don't care what's wrong with the man. There's something going on and I want to know what. Whitefall said this Sara person was in charge of wizard affairs for the Council. If she's calling me in, it could mean she has some information about Eli. Anyway, whatever this meeting is about, it has to be better than paperwork."

Gin gave her a firm look. "I'm going with you."

Miranda shook her head, reaching out to scratch his long nose. "I wouldn't have it any other way."

Gin leaned into the scratch, but he stayed put as Miranda gathered her things and closed up the office for the night. Only when she blew out the lamp did he rise and pad through the doorway, going ahead of her into the rowdy Zarin night.

* * *

The next morning, thirty minutes after the eight o'clock bell, Miranda and Gin trotted up to the front of the Council fortress. As the Council's offices didn't open for formal business until ten (since no Court official worth his silks would be up before then), the gates were still closed, but Miranda was able to get past the guards with her official title and a well-placed growl from her ghosthound.

The growl was, perhaps, a little harsher than it needed to be. Gin was in a foul mood this morning. He'd spent the whole ride over trying to convince her to turn around, but Miranda would hear none of it. Truth be told, Sparrow's sudden appearance last night was the most exciting thing that had happened since Lord Whitefall's letter arrived, and she wasn't about to waste her chance, even if Gin's hunches had a bad habit of being right.

They waited in the courtyard, out of the way of the few carriages that came and went. Miranda spent the time checking her rings. She woke each spirit, soothing and nudging it until each ring glowed with its own light. Mellinor was already awake and waiting at the base of her soul, his cool presence dark and cautious.

After about ten minutes (ten minutes exactly, Miranda would wager), Sparrow appeared from a small door on the far side of the yard. He was dressed this morning in a long fuchsia coat that dropped to his knees with gold buttons and cream lace spilling out of the cuffs. His pants were orange and covered with some sort of black beadwork that clacked as he walked. They were wide-legged, and their ends were stuffed into the tops of his low black boots, which boasted silver heels and toes. He wore no hat, and his hair was all blond now, but a different shade from last night, more honey than white blond, and tousled in a way that suggested he'd spent an hour arranging it to fall just so.

Miranda winced at the clashing colors and leaned in close to Gin. "Is he still flickering?"

"Worse than ever," Gin growled.

"It's more like he's fading," Mellinor put in. "I don't like it."

"No one seems to," Miranda muttered. "Keep watch; let me know if it changes."

"Why?" Gin said. "You won't be able to see it."

"That's why you're the ones watching," Miranda hissed, and then smiled graciously as Sparrow stopped before her.

Sparrow dropped a flourished bow. "Miranda," he said. "Right on schedule. I'll take you in directly." He paused. "Will you be bringing your pet as well?"

Gin snarled at that, and Miranda put her hand on his nose in a warning gesture. "Gin goes where I do," she said.

Sparrow shrugged. "We'll have to take the back way, then. Follow me."

He led them through an arched breezeway and out onto a side path that had been cleverly hidden behind the ornamental trees. It was narrow going. They were walking down an alley with the outer wall of the Council fortress towering over them on one side and the side of the fortress itself going up on the other. There was room for the three of them to walk single file comfortably enough, but Miranda couldn't help feeling trapped as the road circled downward and the walls grew higher and higher around them.

At last, when the morning sky was a thin strip far overhead, the steep road stopped at an enormous pair of double doors set deep in the citadel's base.

"Apologies for taking you in through the service entrance," Sparrow said, fishing a ring of keys out of his monstrosity of a coat. "But I doubt your puppy would fit down the tunnels."

"This is fine," Miranda said over Gin's growling. "I had more than enough of Council finery on my previous visit to last me awhile."

Sparrow unlocked the door and held it open for her, motioning for Miranda to go first. Miranda stepped inside with a curt nod of thanks, then stopped again, her mouth dropping open. She was standing inside the largest room she'd ever seen. It was twice the size of the throne room in Mellinor and easily half again as tall as the Spirit Court's hearing chamber. Or that's what she guessed, since she couldn't actually see the ceiling. The chamber was huge and hollow, with pillars sprouting from the stone floor at regular intervals, climbing up into the darkness. Between the pillars, set in rows like the giant, gray eggs of some enormous insect, stood tall, fat, cylindrical towers. The towers stretched off forever in all directions, a forest of identical gray metal ovals suspended on an iron framework that kept their ends off the floor. Miranda was still gawking at the sheer number and size of...whatever they were when Sparrow shut the door behind them and locked it again.

"This way," he said, starting off into the darkness.

Miranda followed, craning her neck as they walked between the metal cylinders and up a set of wooden stairs that had been built into the framework. Gin followed more slowly, delicately picking his way along the narrow path. The stairs led to a wide wooden scaffolding that ran like a suspended road between the strange metal cylinders. Tiny glass lanterns lined the metal railing that separated the walkway from the straight drop down to the stone floor, their collective soft glow casting large, ominous shadows behind the iron towers.

"What are they?" Miranda whispered as they walked down the scaffold, gawking at the endless forest of metal silos just out of arm's reach.

"Tanks," Sparrow said, picking up the pace. "This is the Relay Room. Don't touch anything, please."

Miranda's eyes widened. "You mean the Ollor Relay?"

"You know any other relay the Council cares about?" Sparrow said. "Watch your step; we're turning."

Miranda followed him blindly. Her mind was entirely on the metal cylinders around him, the tanks. The Ollor Relay was the backbone of the Council of Thrones. The precise way it worked was a closely guarded secret, but it had something to do with water, which explained the tanks. She wasn't exactly sure how it was used, but common knowledge was that a person with a Relay point could speak to a person at the base Relay from any distance, and the person at the base could speak back, or pass the message on to another Relay point somewhere else entirely. It was this ability to communicate instantly across the kingdoms that had allowed the Council armies, which had included only a handful of countries at the time, to beat back the much larger invading army of the Immortal Empress twenty-five years ago. That impossible victory had sealed the Council of Thrones as the foremost power on the continent, an achievement Merchant Prince Whitefall had leveraged to form the greatest coalition of nations in the world.

The Council would have grown even faster if access to the Relay had been more widespread, but Relay points were famously rare. However, looking out over the endless rows of tanks, Miranda suddenly had a hard time believing the Relay was as small as people claimed. True, she had no idea how it worked, but there must be hundreds of tanks down here. How could such a huge infrastructure support only a tiny number of Relay points?

She was puzzling over this when Sparrow's rapid pace suddenly slowed. They were approaching a brightly lit crossroads of several scaffoldings, the center of which seemed to be a single, enormous tank. As they got closer, however, Miranda realized the giant thing in the center wasn't a tank at all. It was a building. A great, metal building inside the larger room, complete with a rounded roof and a half dozen little chimneys spewing steam. The building was several stories tall, but the main story seemed to be the one level with the scaffolding. The building was at an intersection of walkways, and the suspended scaffolding joined together to form a wide platform. On the platform, men and women in plain white jackets and trousers clustered around long tables, their work lit by enormous hanging lanterns that burned steady and bright. Metal doors opened and closed without sound as workers entered and left the metal building, which looked to have more workstations inside.

The workers shuffled out of the way as Sparrow, Miranda, and Gin stepped onto the ring of wooden scaffolding. Sparrow ignored them completely and walked straight across the wooden boards toward the building's largest door. He pushed it with a grunt, and the heavy metal slab swung inward, revealing a dimly lit room.

"Go on," Sparrow said, standing aside. "It's a bit cramped, but Sara wanted to see you in her office so this visit wouldn't interrupt her work too much. You understand, of course."

"What work does she do?" Miranda said, stepping inside.

"Everything that matters," a brisk voice answered.

Miranda's head snapped up, and she found herself looking into the blue eyes of a small, formidable woman. She was sitting on a leather chair set directly between three large desks covered with... Miranda wasn't quite sure. The farthest was swamped in Council papers, which Miranda could recognize too well these days. Most of these were dusty and untouched, however. The other two desks were far neater. One supported a large, bright lamp and a stunning variety of jars filled with various amounts of a clear liquid and a small book open to a page filled with neat, tight handwriting. The other desk was covered in what looked to be pages of lists and drawings, all laid out neatly, with arrows drawn across the edges connecting one page to another.

The large office was otherwise sparse. There was a bookcase filled with leather notebooks and a threadbare couch set against one wall, but otherwise, nothing. None of the niceties Miranda would have expected from a Council member with such obvious authority. Her walls, however, were far from bare. The metal was covered with notes and drawings on all sides, including diagrams of the tanks outside covered in the same tight, neat handwriting as the papers on the desk.

But all of these were to be expected in an office at the heart of the Relay. What caught Miranda off-guard were the posters papering the space above the largest desk. There, laid out in a neat grid, was a complete collection of Eli Monpress bounty posters. They started when his bounty had been a mere three hundred and went up all the way to the current ninety-eight thousand with a good bit of room at the bottom for new additions. Seen all together, the effect was quite impressive, and Miranda couldn't help smiling at the thought of how Eli would react if he saw it. Probably insufferably.

The woman herself was dressed in the same plain white coat and trousers as the other workers, but any plainness ended there. Her hair was pale ginger streaked with gray, tied up in a coil of braids at the top of her head. Her face was lined, especially between her eyebrows where she scowled, but otherwise she didn't look very old. She mostly looked serious, harried, and already out of patience. A long pipe dangled from her lips, which accounted for the spicy reek of smoke that permeated the room, and a pair of spectacles hung on a gold chain around her neck. Otherwise she wore no decoration, not even rings. However, from the way Miranda's spirits were buzzing, she knew without a doubt that this woman was a wizard, and powerful one.

The woman looked Miranda over, starting with the feet and working her way up. Next, she switched her gaze to Gin, who had somehow managed to squeeze himself through the door and was now sitting nearly doubled over behind Miranda, his eyes narrow and sharp despite the indignity of his cramped position, and ended on Sparrow, who was pushing Gin's tail out of the way in an attempt to shut the door.

"You must be Miranda Lyonette," she said when she'd finished her inspection. "You're not as pretty as I'd thought you'd be, considering your family. Nice hair, though, and strong spirits. I can see why Banage made you his favorite."

Miranda bristled. "I assure you, madam," she said through gritted teeth, "neither my looks nor my family has anything to do with my position."

Sara rolled her eyes. "Don't get your hackles up, girl. I was only making an observation." She took a drag off her pipe and blew a long line of smoke into the air. "This is why I don't usually work with Spiritualists. You're all so prickly and bound in. Terrible waste of wizards. Though I suppose the world must have you."

Miranda's rage must have been clear on her face for Sara laughed. "Feel free to disagree all you like. I welcome constructive argument. But if you're just going to be miffish, you'd better get over it quickly. Those who can't take an honest opinion don't last long down here. Right, Sparrow?"

Sparrow, who'd given up on Gin's tail and taken a seat on the couch, merely smiled. "No one lasts long with you, Sara."

"Not so," Sara said curtly. "You've been with me five years."

"That's because I care more for your money than my ego," Sparrow said. "Get to the point before the Spiritualist girl becomes terminally insulted and my trip becomes a waste."

Sara turned to Miranda. "Right. Then let's see it."

Miranda stared at her. "See what?"

"Your Great Spirit," Sara said, giving her a look that said this should have been obvious. "If you're going to be working for me, I have to see what I'm dealing with."

Miranda started to object, but stopped. It wasn't actually an unreasonable request. Swallowing her temper, she closed her eyes and gave Mellinor a little mental nudge. A nudge was all it took. With that curious, skin-crawling feeling of being a faucet, the water spirit poured out of her. When Miranda opened her eyes again, Mellinor was floating beside her, a ball of pure, blue, strangely smug-looking water, spinning slowly before Sara's obviously rapt attention.

"A Great Spirit," she whispered, stepping forward, smiling and as bright eyed as a child. "I've met several, but I've never seen one come out of a person."

"Nor will you," Mellinor said. "So far as I know, my circumstances are unique."

Sara reached out, tracing her fingers across the water's surface. "Absolutely marvelous."

Mellinor puffed up a little at that, and Miranda covertly rolled her eyes. Her sea could be as bad as her dog sometimes.

Sara didn't notice. She was busy walking around Mellinor, stepping high over Gin's paws where there wasn't room. "Do you still have tides?" she asked. "Currents? What about your salinity?"

"No tides," Mellinor said. "Not enough water. My currents were always my own. I changed my salinity to match Miranda's blood. It seemed the easiest thing to do, and I don't care for much salt, anyway."

There was something dark in his voice as he spoke that last bit, but Sara just nodded and jotted several notes on a pad that she fished from her pocket. Miranda, however, was busy staring at her water spirit. She'd never even thought to ask questions like that, and she was starting to feel ashamed. Mellinor was her spirit. She should know all there was to know about him, not leave it to some stranger.

Sara looked as though she had more questions, but a whistle outside made her put away her pad.

"Well," she said, "if the sea's on your side, the tide may wait, but time never will." She gestured at Miranda as she went back to her chair. "You can pull him back now. You've made the team."

"Team?" Miranda said, stretching out her arm. "What do you mean?"

Mellinor took his time coming back, obviously appreciating the attention from Sara. Miranda resisted the urge to nudge him along.

"I'm the Head Wizard for the Council of Thrones," Sara said, sitting back down at her desk. "Officially, I'm in charge of all wizards working for the Council, though I don't bother with most of them. They're dull dropouts from the Spirit Court mostly, with no will to speak of. They're better left in the copy rooms ordering ink spirits around. But you," she said, grinning. "You, Miranda, with your shining sea and your dog and whatever else you've got on your fingers, are different. I thought you would be. That's why I had Phillipe Whitefall send you that letter."

Miranda frowned. "I thought I was appointed as head of the Eli Monpress investigation on account of my experience with the thief."

"Yes, well, that was the reason I fed the bounty office." Sara took a long splinter from a box on her desk and held it near her lamp. At once, a spark jumped from the lamp flame to the splinter's end. "Only way I could get you away from Banage, really. He doesn't have much patience for me," she said, touching the burning splinter to her pipe. "It wasn't hard. Phillipe jumped at the chance to make the thief someone else's problem. Of course," she said between puffs, "it would be wonderful if you *could* catch Eli for me. I'm even more keen to meet him than I was to meet you. I'm very interested in the way this world works, you see, the different aspects of wizardry and spirits and how they interact. Things like how a Great Spirit could shrink himself down small enough to fit into a human while maintaining his essence as a Great Spirit. These are the curiosities I love to surround myself with. It keeps the mind young. But Eli's the greatest mystery of them all. A wizard whom every spirit obeys." Her voice grew almost wistful. "Now *that* is something I'd love to examine for myself."

"You'd have to get in line," Miranda said, crossing her arms over her chest. "There are a lot of people who want a piece of Eli Monpress." Sara gave her a sharp look, and Miranda glared right back. "Perhaps I haven't made this clear, but I am a Spiritualist first, foremost, and forever. I agreed to work for the Council to get support and information in my hunt for Monpress. With all due respect, Lady Sara, that doesn't include being one of your 'curiosities.' If I'm only here so you could have a look at Mellinor, I'll be on my way."

Sara gave her a smoky smile. "Direct," she said. "I like that. Very well, Spiritualist Lyonette, I will answer in kind. I pulled the strings to bring you here because we have a delicate matter on our hands. One of my dear friends, a Shaper and a great scholar of wizardry, has vanished. Though he's not formally involved with the Council, it would be a great loss for all of us if Heinricht Slorn were to remain missing. Therefore, I am putting a group together to find him and bring him safely back to Zarin under the Council's protection."

"Slorn?" Miranda frowned. The name was desperately familiar, but it wasn't the one she'd been waiting for. "I'm sorry to hear about your missing friend," she said. "But I don't have time to—"

"Slorn has many friends from all walks of life." Sara's voice rolled right over her. "Including a certain thief."

She paused, and Miranda had to swallow her words, motioning for the woman to get on with it. Sara did no such thing. She merely sat there and smoked, watching Miranda squirm. Finally, when she obviously felt Miranda had stewed enough, Sara continued.

"We have a good tip that Slorn has asked for Eli's help as well as mine. However, Eli doesn't know where Slorn is." Sara smiled. "I do."

Miranda's eyes widened as Sara's implications hit her. The idea of getting somewhere before Eli did was almost intoxicating. "Where?"

Sara arched her eyebrows at Miranda's abandoned aloofness. "You'll go on the mission then?"

Miranda stopped cold. Powers, she'd stepped right into that one. She took a moment to think, keeping her eyes away from Sara's cool, sure expression. If she left Zarin and Sara was wrong about Eli going after Slorn, she could miss his next theft altogether. Besides, one look at Sara and the company she kept was enough to set off a whole tower full of warning bells. Miranda's eyes slid over to the couch where Sparrow was sitting with his legs crossed, watching her. Just being in the same room with him put her on edge. But if Sara was right…

She felt a warmth against her back as Gin leaned in behind her. "You should take it," he growled low in his throat. "Even if Eli robbed Lord Whitefall's mansion tomorrow, we'd still be eating his dust. A trap is always better than a chase."

Miranda nodded. You could always trust a predator about these things. Still, she decided as she glanced at Sara, no need for the old lady to know her intentions just yet.

"If I went," she said slowly, "where would I be going?"

"No, no, no," Sara said, shaking her head. "That's not how this works. You don't get confidential information for free. I asked you, are you joining us? Answer, yes or no, and I'll decide what to tell you after."

Miranda took an angry breath and nearly marched out right then and there. It was her need to catch Eli that kept her in place. Could she really throw her chance at catching him away over rankled pride? After all, she had no other leads, and just the thought of going back to paperwork nearly made her ill. Miranda grimaced and looked over her shoulder at Gin, who flicked his ears as if to say it was her choice. Miranda bit her lip. Well, she'd already come this far. She might as well go in all the way.

"All right," she said, looking Sara directly in the eyes. "I'm in."

Sara grinned in triumph. "Are you familiar with Izo the Bandit King?"

Miranda nodded.

Sara waved her pipe in a grand gesture. "That's your answer."

Miranda stared at her. "What?"

"Be here tomorrow at dawn, packed for a long journey," Sara said, sticking her pipe back in her mouth. "I'll give you the rest when I explain the plan to everyone."

"Everyone?" Miranda said.

"Yes," Sara said, looking at her as though she were stupid. "Dawn tomorrow, don't be late."

And that was all the answer Miranda could get.

Hours later, Sara was still in her office. She sat at her least cluttered desk, reading through the day's stack of observations while distractedly eating a bowl of fish soup that one of her assistants had brought down hours ago. The soup was congealed and cold, but Sara didn't seem to notice, shoving a spoonful around her pipe and into her mouth whenever the thought of eating could get past the dozen other issues demanding her attention. She was just scraping the bottom of the bowl when the door to her office slammed open.

She dropped her spoon with a frustrated huff. "If this is about tank seven," she said, spinning around in her chair, "I already know. There's no reason..."

Her words trailed to a stop as she got a look at the man who'd barged into her room. He stood in the doorway, tall and impossibly imposing in his severe red robes. His black hair was touched with gray at the temples while his clenched fingers, wrists, and neck were laden with enough gems to make a king jealous. He looked angry enough to spit nails, and his blue eyes were flashing murder, but Sara couldn't help smiling as she leaned back to take him in.

"Hello, Etmon," she said, blowing a thin line of blue pipe smoke into the air between them. "It's been too long."

If possible, his fists clenched tighter still. "Not long enough."

Sara's smile widened. The sight of him was nostalgic enough, but the sound of Etmon Banage's furious voice made her feel twenty years younger. "This seems to be my week for unexpected visitors," she said. "To what do I owe the pleasure?"

"You never change, do you?" Banage said. "Still asking questions you already know the answers to just to make me say it. I'm here to tell you that my apprentice will not be accompanying your goons on whatever scheme you're plotting. I lent her to the Council at the request of Lord Whitefall to assist in the capture of Eli Monpress, not so that you could use her as spiritual muscle whenever you had a problem your undertrained, impotent Council wizards couldn't handle."

Sara bit down on her pipe. "Don't get angry, Etmon. It's bad enough seeing you in those ridiculous red bed-sheets your little social club requires without your face changing to match. And for your information," she added quickly, cutting off Banage's furious retort, "I am doing nothing improper. Your little Miranda is going to help my people set a trap for the thief, among other things."

"It's the 'other things' that concern me," Banage said through gritted teeth. "I knew I was taking a risk letting Miranda get anywhere near the Council, but Whitefall assured me you would keep your claws out of her affairs. Miranda is a strong wizard and a fine Spiritualist who's been through a great deal in the last year. I won't have you abusing her sense of duty to trick her into doing your dirty work."

"As if I could," Sara snapped, her anger rising to meet his. "She's as moral and dutiful and closed-minded as any of your flock. You don't have to worry about her."

"Don't tell me what to do with my own people!" Banage roared. "You're sending her to the edge of the Council to make some kind of deal with Izo the Bandit King. Have you finally lost what little grip on reality you ever possessed?"

"You're one to talk about reality," Sara said. "Seeing as you live in some black-and-white fantasy where we catch thieves without dealing with the underworld."

Banage sneered, and Sara blew out a long huff of bitter smoke. "Anyway," she said, "the deal is done. The girl already agreed to go, and as a servant of the Council, she's legally obligated to see the job through. So if that was the only reason you had for honoring me with your presence this evening, I'm afraid you're out of luck, old man. Run on home to your tower and let me get back to my work. You know, the stuff that's actually important."

"Oh, yes," Banage scoffed. "I forgot. Your work is more important than anything else." He thrust a jeweled finger at her. "I'm taking this to Merchant Prince Whitefall."

"Go ahead," Sara said. "He'll just side with me. Council matters are my playground, Etmon. Go back to your tower and your fawning, self-righteous Spiritualists. Tell you what, when we catch Eli, I'll bring him by and you can preach him to death."

Banage whirled around, his fists clenching in rage, and Sara heaved a frustrated sigh.

"Why did you even come?" she muttered. "You knew it would be like this."

Banage didn't look at her. "Because," he said quietly. "Fool that I am, I still believe that, someday, you will remember your oaths."

"What, to the Spirit Court?" Sara's eyes narrowed. "Or to you?"

Banage didn't answer. He walked out of her office without another word, slamming the door behind him with a crash that made Sara wince. She glared at the closed door for a long time, furiously puffing on her pipe until the bowl was nothing but dead ash. Shaking her head at the wasted time, she emptied her pipe into the dregs of her cold soup and got back to work.

CHAPTER 7

Nico gasped at the thin, cold air and pulled her coat tighter across her shoulders. She walked with her face down, her boots crunching over the crust of ice on the rocky slope. They were far north, beyond the Council Borders, farther even than Slorn's Awakened Wood, on the cold, high slopes of the Sleeping Mountains. An impressive distance, considering it had been only three weeks since Eli had driven them out of Home before dawn. That much wasn't unusual. Eli was always in a rush when he had a job in mind, but this time keeping up had been much harder.

It doesn't have to be.

Nico grimaced. The farther north they went, the stronger the voice became.

Why do you do this to yourself? The voice echoed loud and clear through her head, as though the speaker were standing behind her eyeballs. *All I ask is honesty, Nico. Embrace what you are and you can have everything back, your strength, your senses, everything.*

Nico stomped her aching legs down and focused on the sound of frozen pine needles as they crunched under her boots. "How much farther?"

"Not far," Eli said. He was well ahead of her, walking lightly between the scrubby evergreens like he didn't know what tiredness was.

"So you keep saying," Josef grumbled, keeping pace with Nico. "Is this another of your moving houses?"

"No," Eli said. "Or I don't think so. I've never actually been here before."

Josef stopped and stared at him. "Then how do you know where we're going?"

"I don't," Eli said cheerfully. "Not many do, past this point. It's not exactly on a map."

Josef sneered up at the mountains surrounding them. "Fantastic. Three weeks on a death march just to get lost in the mountains."

"I'm not lost," Eli said sharply, turning around to face them. "We are exactly where we should be. And if the stories I've heard are correct, we shouldn't be able to go much farther before our hosts find us."

Josef opened his mouth to ask another question, but stopped

midbreath. He dropped to a crouch, his hand flying to the hilt of the massive sword on his back. A second later, Nico heard it too, the faint crunch of something moving in the woods. Something large. She dropped to a crouch beside Josef, ignoring the protests of her aching legs. Looking around, she could see nothing but trees and stones and empty country, the same as she had seen for the past two days. But she knew something was there, a darker shadow beneath the shaggy pines, watching them. Beside her, she heard Josef draw the Heart. Off to her left, something growled.

"Ah," Eli said brightly. "That would be them now."

Nico watched wide-eyed as Eli trotted back down the hill and stopped with a grand bow, flourishing his hands dramatically. "Greetings, ancient guardians of the heights! I am Eli Monpress, and—"

"We know who you are," a voice rumbled. "Get out. This is no place for humans."

Nico swallowed as several more growls went up in agreement. She felt Josef shift, his muscles clenching. He might not be able to hear the voice, but the obvious threat in the rumbling sound from the shadows required no interpretation.

"Don't be so hasty," Eli said, putting up his hands. "I'm here on behalf of a mutual acquaintance, Heinricht Slorn." A great round of growls went up at this, and Nico winced at the sound of claws scraping on frozen ground. Eli didn't even blink. "I ask an audience with Gredit."

For a moment, nothing happened, and then the trees around them began to rustle, and Nico pulled back as the source of the growls stepped into view. All around them, stepping out of trees and from behind stones, were enormous mountain bears. They moved in, yellow teeth bared and ready, shaking the snow off brown, furry shoulders that stood taller than Nico's head. The bears stopped at the edge of the trees, growling and pawing the ground. Only one bear came closer, striding across the frozen stones until he was a few feet from Eli. When he was close enough to reach out and bat Eli across the face with his massive paw, the bear stopped and, far more gracefully than Nico could have imagined, stood up on his hind legs. Nico swallowed. The bear was ten feet tall at least, and from the way he glared down his silver-streaked muzzle at the thief, she didn't doubt for a moment that he could crush Eli like a ripe berry if he wanted, and they all, especially the bears, knew it.

"You have a lot of nerve coming up here and saying that name," the bear growled, brown eyes darting between Eli and Josef. "Tell the deaf one to put up his weapon."

"It won't matter if I tell him," Eli said. "Josef does what he wants. However"—he leaned forward conspiratorially—"maybe if you weren't giving him such reason to use it, he might put it up on his own."

The large bear glared at Eli and then jerked his head. All around the circle, the bears backed away. Josef, well used to one-sided conversations, got the point and slowly slid the Heart back into its sheath.

Eli smiled at the bears. "Now," he said, "about that audience?"

The lead bear dropped back on all fours. "If you want to talk with Gredit, we'll take you there, but don't expect to like what you hear. He doesn't care much for your kind."

"So I've heard," Eli said. "But one takes the chances one must. Lead on."

The bear gave him a final poison look and turned around, trotting off into the trees. As the other bears did the same, Eli turned to Josef and Nico. "Stay close," he whispered.

"Right," Josef said, easing his daggers in and out of his sleeves. "Close to the pack of enormous bears."

"Never a boring moment," Eli said with a grin before turning and jogging after the bear. Shaking his head, Josef followed. Nico stayed close behind, holding her coat tighter than ever.

The bears followed no path. They trundled straight across the mountainside, hopping easily over rocks and fallen trees. Nico had the suspicion that they did this on purpose, to make it hard for their human followers, but they had another thing coming if they thought they could slow down people who traveled with Eli Monpress with a little hazardous countryside. Nico, Josef, and Eli kept the pace, following the bears along the mountain ridge until they reached a narrow valley ringed on all sides by old, dark firs.

The bears slowed, picking their way down to the narrow, swift stream at the valley's base. The air here was different than the slopes. It clung in the throat, wet and thick with the wild smell of pine and fur. The damp cold went straight through Nico's coat, making her movements slow and clumsy. Fortunately, the bears stopped when they reached the water and turned upstream.

"There," the largest bear said, looking over his shoulder at Eli.

They didn't have to ask what he meant. Down by the water they could see what had been hidden by trees from above. Ten feet up the slope, nestled back in the gray stone of the mountain face, was a cave, and all around the cave were bears. Even Eli pulled back when he saw them. The bears were all different sizes and colors. Some were enormous and black, while others were smaller and honey brown. They sat in clusters, watching the intruders with cold, dark eyes.

"I didn't bring you here to stare," their guide rumbled. "Go and be done, or leave now."

Eli gave the bear a smile, but even Nico could tell it wasn't one of his best. The bear just turned away with a huff. Thoroughly dismissed, Eli started up the hill, Josef and Nico close behind him. The bears at the cave mouth didn't move. They just watched as the humans scrambled up the muddy slope toward the cavern's entrance. It was a large opening, three times Josef's height and wide enough for four carts to drive abreast with space to spare, but the musty smell that drifted out of the dark, a potent mix of wild animal and old blood, was enough to give even Eli pause.

The moment they stopped, all the bears began to growl. Eli jumped at the sound and gave himself a shake. Then, with a dazzling smile at the rumbling bears, he marched into the cave as though he were entering a banquet where he was the guest of honor. Nico and Josef followed more cautiously. Once they were inside, the gray light faded. The cave only seemed to get bigger the deeper they went, and in the shadows Nico could make out more bears watching them as they stumbled across the uneven floor in the dark.

Fifty feet from its entrance, the cave ended abruptly in a slope of broken rocks, and sitting on the rocks like a king on his throne was the largest bear Nico had ever seen. He towered in the dark, lounging with his back against the broken stone. Even lying back, the bear was nearly fifteen feet tall, and almost as broad. His enormous paws, each large enough to crush Nico's head like a walnut, rested on his monstrous stomach, the black claws moving slowly back and forth through his black, coarse fur.

As her eyes adjusted to the dark, Nico realized that the bear's fur was actually more gray than black. His pelt was crisscrossed with thin patches where scars interrupted the growth of his coat, and one of his black eyes was silver with cataracts. But any illusion of age and weakness was dispelled when he bared his massive jaw full of yellow teeth in an expression that could have been a grin had it been less terrifying.

Undaunted, Eli stopped at the foot of the great bear's slope and dropped a deep, formal bow. "Greetings, Gredit, eldest of all bears," he said solemnly. "I am Eli Monpress, and I come before you to beg a boon for one of your—"

"I know who you are."

Nico winced at the bear's voice. It was deep enough to shake the stone below her feet, and full of anger.

Eli glanced up from his bow, and the bear gave him a nasty sneer.

"So," Gredit rumbled. "The white bitch's favorite has come to ask a boon from me. This is quite the turn."

"Not for myself," Eli said quickly. "I would never dream of troubling you for my own benefit. I'm here on behalf of our dear, mutual friend, Heinricht Slorn."

The bear's eyes, black and cloudy silver, narrowed. "And what would Slorn want of a lapdog like you?"

"He hasn't had the chance to tell me," Eli said, straightening up. "He's gone missing."

The bear made a horrible sound, like a growling cough, and it took Nico a terrifying moment to realize he was laughing.

"Now it comes together," the bear said, still chuckling. "You want me to tell you where he is."

"You are the Great Spirit of the northern bears," Eli said simply. "It *is* within your power."

"And what would a human know of my power?" the bear said. "We bears have been here as long as the mountains themselves, as long as the winds in the sky. What would you know of that?"

"Nothing at all," Eli said. "But I'm not here for history. I'm here to learn what I need to know to save a friend. A *mutual* friend, unless I am sadly mistaken."

Gredit gave him a long look. "We honor Slorn. Of all your kind, he was the only one who used your unnatural power over spirits to help us. But"—the bear growled at Eli's growing smile—"that gratitude does not extend to you, little favorite." The bear leaned back on his throne of crumbled boulders. "If you want our help, you'll first have to prove what you are."

"But you already know me," Eli said. "You interrupted me to make that much clear."

"Oh, I know you," the bear said. "I'm no blind fool like your lot. But I want to see the proof for myself." Gredit bared his teeth. "Show me her mark, or get out."

Eli took a deep, frustrated breath. "Surely there's another—"

A chorus of deep growls from all over the cave cut him off. Eli looked around with a grimace. "All right," he said, shaking his head. "Get a good look. I'm only doing this once."

Eli closed his eyes, and Nico gasped as a tremendous pressure swept over her, making every hair on her body stand on end. She wasn't alone. All around them, the bears began to shuffle, grumbling and keening. The thief, however, stood perfectly still, feet spread, eyes closed, his face calm and untroubled as the pressure mounted. After a few seconds Nico could barely move, and yet, for some reason, she wasn't afraid. There was something comforting about the pressure, something warm and familiar. And then she realized what was happening. Eli had opened his spirit. The pressure, the hot feel of familiarity pressing on her skin; it was Eli's soul flung wide. Now that she knew what it was, she could almost feel its shape in the air. Eli's soul filled the room, spreading in all directions, and everywhere it touched, spirits woke.

Even Josef saw it. He stood beside her, blades in hand, watching in amazement as the bears trembled. Trembled, and began to bow. And it wasn't just the bears. All around them, the world was paying homage. The breeze from the mouth of the cave stilled. The stones rearranged themselves, tilting down and whispering obedience. Everything, from the lichen on the cave roof to the dirt on the floor, bowed down when Eli's spirit touched it, and though Nico did not understand why, she could feel it too. Deep inside, deeper even than the demonseed, something called for her to show obedience. The urge was so strong that she found her eyes had lowered without her knowing, and try as she might, she could not raise them again.

Of every spirit in the room, only the great bear seemed unaffected. He watched from his throne, his massive head rested on one oversized paw, perfectly still, even as the stone he sat on fought to bow down. Just before the force became unbearable, he raised his head. "Enough."

Eli's eyes opened and the pressure vanished. All around the cave, bears pushed back to their feet. A few began to growl, but most stayed silent, their dark eyes fixed on Eli, their haunches lowered reverently.

Up on his seat, the great bear sighed. "I see the mark of the favorite is as powerful as ever. The Shepherdess's touch is laid strong on you. How strange, then, that she would let such a bright treasure run around loose."

"I'm no treasure," Eli said. "I am myself and no other. Now"—he folded his arms over his chest—"I've done as you asked. Tell me where Slorn is."

The bear laughed. "Your display may have awed my children. They are too young to see past the Shepherdess's glamors. I, however, am too old to be much impressed with such theatrics. I have seen many favorites, after all."

"Then why did you make me do it?" Eli's voice was angrier than Nico had heard it in a long time.

"To get her attention," the bear answered, growling so low the stone vibrated under their feet. "She may let you run wild through her creation, but I'd bet my fur she's always got an eye on you. After that display, I know for certain she's watching very closely. Good. I want her to hear what I have to say."

He eyed Eli hungrily. "I am the lord of bears, favorite. It is my purpose to protect my children. I feel every creature of my blood as though they were my own flesh, and I protect them with tooth and claw. So it has always been since before the Powers were born. Before the Shepherdess or the Weaver or the Hunter. Yet, look at me." He ran his paw across his silvered coat. "For the first time since the beginning of creation, I grow old and weak. My sight dims and my claws grow dull. I fear I am dying." The bear drew a deep breath. "I do not expect a human to understand. Your kind die like flies. But I am no mere flesh creature. Of all Great Spirits, I am one of the oldest. I was created by the Creator to be the guardian of all bears. So long as they thrive, I thrive. Yet here I am, old and weak. What does this mean for my children?"

Eli started to say something, but the bear kept going. "Every year my bears grow smaller, stupider, and weaker," he growled. "The mountains, our neighbors and friends since time began, sleep and do not wake while the dark hunger they were assigned to guard sends its seeds into the world unhindered and unchecked."

Nico swallowed and pulled herself deeper than ever into her coat.

"But I am a Great Spirit," the bear went on. "I do my duty. All of this I brought to the Lady's attention again and again, but I never heard a word back from her. For years this went on, and not knowing what to do, we kept living as we always had. Then the darkness took one of my greatest sons."

All around the room, the bears bowed their heads in sadness. "Gredeth," they rumbled.

"Yes, Gredeth." The great bear's voice was thick with loss. "Greatest bear of his generation. It was Gredeth who found the human wandering in our woods, its soul already half eaten by a seed of the thing that lives below the Dead Mountain." The bear made a disgusted sound. "Blindness and power are a reckless combination, and putting them together in one creature was the Shepherdess's greatest folly. The blind human, infected and mad, wandered into our territory, and brave Gredeth did what needed to be done. He fought the monster and won, devouring it so the black seed would not destroy our lands. But his bravery was his undoing. The seed survived the devouring and took root in Gredeth himself."

The great bear's good eye grew sad and distant. "I could do nothing," he rumbled. "I tried. I sent word to the Shepherdess. I threw away my pride. I *begged*, human. Begged her for aid as I have never done before, and received *nothing.* Gredeth continued to decline. The seed ate him until he was only a shell. That was when Slorn appeared. He was wise for a human, and very knowledgeable about the ways of the demon. We put our trust in him, but Gredeth was too far gone, and in the end, all Slorn managed was to slow the seed's growth."

The bear heaved a great sigh. "I was grateful that the human had tried and bade him go with my thanks. But Slorn had not given up. He proposed a radical plan. He would take what was left of Gredeth into himself. Just as he mixed metals, he would meld human and bear spirits into a new soul. I would have forbade it, but Gredeth asked me to change my mind. He wanted to live, proud bear, not die to the hungry dark. With no answer still from the White Lady, I did what I deemed best. I helped Slorn take Gredeth's soul and body into his own. The result was neither man nor bear, but he was Gredeth just as much as he was Slorn, and my dear son still to this day."

The bear's voice faded to a low rumble as the story ended, and the cave fell silent. In the stillness, Eli stepped forward. "If that's how you feel," he said softly, "help me help him. Tell me where he is."

The great bear's glare grew cold as iced stone. "I will help you on one condition. You, the favorite, must call Benehime down. The great Shepherdess was deaf to my begging. Now let's see if her deafness extends to you. Call her and ask, favorite, why, if she is guardian of all spirits, does she not kill the thing under the mountain? Why does she allow her world to stagnate unattended while she wastes her time with favorites? Why did she create humans and give them power over every true spirit, yet make them so blind they can do nothing but fight and enslave the world around them?"

With a great creaking of bones, the lord of bears stood up, towering over them. "Bring her down to finally answer for her negligence!" he roared. "I will not cower before her as all the others do! Call her down, favorite! Bring her before me and I will make her answer!"

His booming voice rang through the cave, and all the bears began to cower. Nico felt like cowering as well. She could feel the ancient Great Spirit's anger in her bones. Yet Eli did not step back. He just stood there, looking the raging bear straight in the face as he spoke one word.

"No."

The great bear's snarl shook the stone, but Eli did not move.

"I am no one's dog," Eli said. "I'm the greatest thief in the world. Benehime may call me her favorite, but that was her choice. My life is my own, not hers, and not yours. I sympathize with your plight, I really do, and I hope you get the chance to call her out for every spirit she's ignored. But you'll have to find someone else to tempt her down because I won't ask her for anything ever again."

The bear sat down again with a great crash. "Then find Slorn yourself."

"Come on," Eli said, a little more desperately. "You just said Slorn was like your son. How—"

"He is my son, as much as any bear," Gredit growled. "If he wished for my help, he would have asked for it, not sent you. But no message have I received, no cry for aid. You are the one asking, not Slorn, so you must pay the price." He tilted his enormous head. "I will tell you that Slorn is far from here. If he's in as much danger as you seem to think, he will certainly die before you can find him on your own. I'm your only chance."

"Surely we can come to some other arrangement," Eli said. "I have many other talents besides being the favorite."

The great bear tossed his head. "This is not a negotiation, human. The only reason you are still alive right now is because you are the favorite."

Eli took another step forward. "But—"

"Call down the White Lady or get out."

Nico shrank back at the menace in Gredit's voice. All through the cave, bears were growling through clenched teeth. The open menace was clear enough that even spirit-deaf Josef went for his sword, but Eli's hand stopped him before he could draw.

"It seems we are at an impasse," Eli said, stepping back again. "Thank you for your hospitality, Lord Bear, but your price is too rich for my blood. We'll find Slorn on our own."

"So you say." The great bear was grinning now. "But you'll be back. I'm your only path to saving Slorn, and you don't seem like a human who takes failure on the chin." The other bears laughed at that, which only made Gredit grin wider. "See you soon, favorite of the Shepherdess."

Eli gave him a polite smile and a half bow before turning on his heel and marching toward the cave mouth. Josef and Nico fell in behind him, keeping right on his heels as the sound of laughing bears followed them out into the sunlight.

Eli marched down the valley, fists clenched. When he reached the bottom, he jumped over the stream and started up the other side, climbing with a singleness of focus that was hard to keep up with. Nico was covered in sweat by the time they cleared the valley's edge, and even Josef was breathing hard. Eli took no notice. He simply flung himself down on a sunny bit of crumbled stone and glared as hard as he could down the valley at the cave now hidden by thick trees.

"Stupid, presumptuous, stubborn bears."

Josef crossed his arms over his chest. "You want to translate all that growling for me so I know what you're talking about?"

"Oh"—Eli flung his hands out in frustration—"spirit politics. He knows where Slorn is, but he won't tell me unless I do something I swore never to do again."

"Uh-huh." Josef scowled down at him. "And what is that?"

"Something I'm not going to talk about," Eli said. "My plan didn't work out, all right? Let's just leave it at that."

"No," Josef said, and Nico cowered at the anger in his voice. "Don't treat me like an idiot just because I could only hear half the conversation. The bear wanted something and you wouldn't give it. Why? What's more important than finding Slorn?"

"You care a lot about Slorn all of a sudden," Eli said, glaring at the swordsman.

"Don't change the subject," Josef snarled, leaning menacingly forward. "Besides the fact that he's always been a stand-up sort of guy by us, Slorn is the only man who can make Nico the tools she needs to fight off the seed inside her. If that bear knows where he is, then we need to give that bear what he wants."

"You think it's that simple?" Eli yelled. "How long have we been working together, Josef? Two years? Three? And how many times in those years have I passed up an opportunity to do things the easy way?"

"Every time," Josef said.

"Never," Eli snapped back. "If I could just give the bear what he wants and walk off happy, I would, but I *can't.* Not this time. So let's just move on."

"No," Josef said again, louder than before. "How can I trust you to do the right thing when you won't even tell me why? For all

I know this *is* the easy way out for you. You tried to find Slorn, it didn't work out, oh well, back to thievery." He stared at Eli's suddenly downcast eyes. "That's it, isn't it? You're just going to let him go, aren't you?"

"What else am I supposed to do?" Eli shouted. "The bears won't help me. I can't find Slorn on my own, and in any case, Heinricht didn't even directly ask for my help. For all I know Pele's overreacting and Slorn has the situation well in hand. I tried my best, all right? We've spent three muddy, profitless, fameless weeks on this nonsense. I think even Slorn would agree we gave it our best shot. But it's over. We lost. Slorn could be anywhere. He could be on the other side of the world and we wouldn't know. We'd have a better chance of convincing the Spirit Court to give me Spiritualist of the Year than of finding our bear man at this point."

Eli was flailing his arms by the end, but Josef didn't even flinch. "That's still not an answer," he said. "As I see it, you're the one making this difficult. Why won't you give them what they want?"

"What part of 'I can't' don't you understand?" Eli shouted.

Josef crossed his arms. "Maybe it would be easier to understand if you told me what it was?"

"So that's it," Eli scoffed. "You don't trust me."

"Oh, I trust you," Josef said. "I trust you to be a con man, a liar, and a thief. That's why I put up with you, because you're the best at what you do. But that same stellar reputation makes it hard to take what you say at face value."

Eli gave him a nasty look. "Do I ever ask you about your past, Josef? Do I ever pry? No, I respect and trust you to handle your affairs and do your job." He whirled to face Nico, and she shrank back farther still. "Do I ever ask you how you got your seed? Have I pressed you at all about what happened in Gaol, or why you've suddenly become the weak little girl you always appeared to be?"

"That's out of line!" Josef shouted, stepping between Nico and Eli.

"Is it?" Eli shouted back. "She's just as much a part of this as either of us. Despite your mother-hen routine, she can speak for herself. We're all thieves together in this."

"This isn't a heist, Eli!" Josef roared. "If Slorn dies because of your pride or whatever idiocy keeps you from going back in that cave and finding out what we need to know, we're not losing some gold or risking imprisonment. If we can't get Slorn, Nico's the one who's going to lose." Josef reached out and grabbed Nico's arm, dragging her between him and Eli. "Coats wear out," he said, pulling her coat back to reveal her wrist, where the silver cuff danced against her thin arm. "So do manacles. If there's no one there to replace them, then you're sending her into battle naked. How could you do that to someone you claim to trust as one of your own?"

Eli glared at him around Nico's upthrust hand. "I won't call Benehime," he said, his voice so quiet the words were more breath than sound.

Josef's glare was cold and sharp. "So you won't do what it takes to save Slorn?" he said. "You'll break your trust with Nico, your trust with me, and you won't even tell us why."

"No," Eli whispered. "But I will tell you this." He leaned in until his cheek brushed Nico's arm. "I will break every oath I have before I give up my freedom."

Josef's muscles tensed, and Nico could feel his fist closing, his fingers tightening on her arm. Eli went stiff as well, his blue eyes cold and guarded. Nico could barely breathe from the tension in the air. She'd seen them fight many times, but never like this. Never seriously.

And it's all your fault. The voice in her head was closer than ever, barbed and laughing. *Josef wouldn't even care about the bear if it wasn't for you. Now you're about to break up one of the most enduring friendships of our age, and all because you're too weak to live without props from your little missing Shaper bear.*

A terrible chill went through Nico's body. Eli and Josef were the only people who mattered to her, and they were fighting, destroying years of trust, all because of *her.* She had to stop it, but how?

You know how. An image filled Nico's mind, a great black mountain where snow never fell and wind never blew. It was there for only an instant, but the old terror at seeing it nearly made her brain go numb.

You know how to find Sted, the voice said as the image faded. *I showed you before. Find Sted and you find Slorn. This is your chance to be the solution instead of the problem. All you have to do is stop being a coward. But do it quickly, while you still have people left to worry about.*

Another image flashed across her mind. It was there less than a second, but it was sharp enough to burn into her brain. Eli walking one way, Josef walking another, both of them looking over their shoulders at her in accusing hatred as they left her behind. Alone.

"Stop!" Nico shouted.

Her voice echoed across the valley, and both men jumped. Nico stared at them, horribly aware of the tears rolling down her face. She could still see the hatred in their eyes.

"Stop," she said again, quietly now. Josef, alarmed and looking a bit surprised, carefully released her wrist and stepped back. Eli did as well.

"I know how to find Slorn," she said, the words tumbling over one another in her rush to get them out. "All we have to do is find Sted. He's the one Slorn's after."

"Find Sted?" Eli said, mulling it over. "How?"

Nico took a deep breath. After this, there was no turning back. "Sted has Nivel's demonseed inside him. We can find it easily if we go to the place where all demonseed are connected."

Josef gave her a guarded look. "Where?"

"The Dead Mountain."

Josef sucked in a breath, but Eli's eyes flashed at the possibility.

"Step into the demon hive itself," he said thoughtfully. "Find the bear by finding the bait." His eyebrows arched. "Sounds brilliant."

"Sounds dangerous," Josef said, staring at Nico. "Can you even go there?"

"No," Nico said, her voice thick and halting. It had never been spoken, but she knew deep in her soul that if she ever set foot on that black slope, she would never leave it again. "But I can take you to the edge."

"And we can take it from there," Eli said, grinning. "I've always wanted to know what was on the demon's mountain. If even a tenth of the stories are true, it's bound to be a macabre wonder of the world. And let's not forget the thrill of breaking into a place even the League won't go."

"That had better not be what this is about," Josef growled.

"Of course not!" Eli looked hurt. "But you can't fault me for seeing the many side benefits of Nico's delightful plan, which solves our problem at no cost to ourselves."

"Don't be so sure," Josef said. "I don't know much about these things, but I don't think the Dead Mountain is a place you just walk into."

"Neither was the fortress of Gaol," Eli said with a smile. "That's the whole point of walking in."

The swordsman gave him a dirty look. "Don't turn this into one of your stunts. You're still not off the hook."

Eli's face grew deathly serious. "I didn't imagine I would be. Are you in on this, or are you going to be difficult?"

Josef put a hand on the Heart of War's hilt. "That depends on her," he said, and turned his stony glare to Nico. "If you want to do this, Nico, I'm behind you, but only if you really want to. Don't let Eli make this about him."

Eli harrumphed at that. Nico and Josef ignored him. "I want to help," Nico said. "I owe Slorn a greater debt than any of us."

Josef nodded. "Then lead on."

Nico closed her eyes, opening her soul to the nagging pull in her bones she'd been ignoring all the way north. Her feet turned of their own accord, and when she opened her eyes again, she was facing north and west. Though she could not see it yet, and wouldn't for a long time, she knew she was pointed directly at the Dead Mountain.

As she stepped forward, she tried to marshal the feeling that she was doing the right thing. That she was helping Eli and Josef instead of being a burden for once. But every step left an ashy taste on her tongue and a dull pain in her legs. Deep inside her mind, scraping the bottom of her thoughts, she could feel the voice smiling. That alone chilled her more than the cold wind, and no matter how tight she pulled her coat, she could not get warm again.

CHAPTER 8

They climbed for three days, moving ever higher into the sharp, gray mountains. The trees vanished on the second day, replaced by thorny shrubs, and then nothing, just endless slopes of bare stone and snow. At night, great gusts blew in icy sheets across their meager campsite, leaving tracks of frost on the path that Josef had to break up with his boots before they could move on. Still, despite none of them being dressed for mountain weather, they made good time, mostly thanks to Karon, Eli's lava spirit.

As soon as the cold became uncomfortable, Eli had opened his shirt and had a nice long chat with the burn on his chest. Karon was happy to help them stick it to the ice and wind spirits, and he cheerfully kept the air around Eli as warm and dry as a smokehouse.

"I only wish it didn't reek of sulfur," Josef said, pressing up the mountainside. "I'd almost rather deal with the cold."

"Well, don't let me stop you," Eli huffed, though even he looked a little green. "Who am I to stand between a man and his frostbite?"

Nico would have chuckled at that, but even a smile felt out of place on the gray slopes. They were getting close. Though she kept her hood down and her eyes on the path, it did little good. She could see the mountain all the time now, even when she closed her eyes, which she did as little as possible. It only made her more aware that she was never alone. The voice sat like a lump in her mind, rarely speaking but ever present, a constant weight that could not be removed or ignored.

"Nico?"

She jumped at her name and looked to see Eli staring at her.

"You stopped. Are you all right?"

Nico swallowed. She didn't remember stopping. "I'm fine," she said softly.

Eli gave her a look of superb disbelief, and she hurried forward, scurrying up the mountain until she was at the edge of Karon's warmth.

If you embraced what you were there would be no need for these charades, the voice tsked. *If the thief and the swordsman are so important to you, why bother fighting this fight we both know you're going to lose? What do you hope to gain? Admit it, everyone would be so much happier if you just accepted your fate.*

Nico clenched her jaw and focused on pulling herself up the slope. Eli followed behind her, watching her back with a cautious, closed expression.

Josef reached the top of the slope first. He'd taken to pushing forward, plowing through the snow to make a path for the others before falling back to the circle of Karon's heat to warm up again. This time he waited for them, standing impatiently at the peak while Nico and Eli trudged the last fifty icy feet. The top of the slope was not the top of the mountain, however. Instead, they came out in a short, narrow pass between two peaks. It was a forbidding place, a wide alley of stone paved with sharp, icy rocks and crusted snow, but it was sheltered from the wind and that was enough to make it feel almost homey.

"At last," Eli said. "I thought we'd be climbing forever."

"We may not be done yet," Josef answered, picking his way down the pass. "Don't get too cozy."

Eli's mouth twitched, but he said nothing. Though they were speaking mostly as usual, Nico was keenly aware that Josef and Eli still weren't looking directly at each other. It made sense, of course. No matter how close the friendship, the things they'd said outside the bear's cave couldn't be forgotten as easily as that. Still, Nico couldn't even look at them together without feeling a horrible pang of guilt. She had to find Slorn as soon as possible, she thought, hurrying down the pass after Josef. The sooner the pressure was lifted and the problem was resolved, the sooner they could all go back to how they were before.

She caught up to Josef quickly, not because she was moving so quickly but because the swordsman had stopped. He was standing at the other end of the sheltered pass, staring out at the white landscape beyond with a hard look on his face. She didn't have to ask him what he saw; she could feel it waiting out there, beyond the snow.

"We're here, aren't we?" Josef said softly.

Nico could only nod, forcing her foot to take the last, terrified step to stand beside him and look out on their final destination.

The pass between the mountains let out on a steep, snow-covered slope that plunged down into a little valley. Snow blew in sheets across it, hiding everything else behind a blanket of pure white, but here and there the wall of snow thinned, allowing a fleeting glimpse of the mountain at the other end of the valley. It towered above the other peaks, twice as high as any of the lesser mountains that ringed it, its cold, black stone showing through the blowing snow like dark water under ice.

"There's no snow on its slopes," Josef said, squinting against the white storm.

"No," Eli said, stepping up to join them and bringing the welcome sphere of warmth with him. "No snow, no water, just dry, dusty stone, and the cold, of course." He glanced at Nico. "Or so I've heard."

Nico looked away. She didn't know how to answer that. All the way here she'd been probing her mind, trying to dig up memories about her time on the mountain. The closer they came, the more familiar things had felt, but a black haze hung over her mind, drawing a curtain between the morning Josef found her from everything before it. Nico frowned. Perhaps the demon ate her memories as well as her soul. Perhaps she really was starting to lose her mind.

You can't blame everything on me, the voice purred. *You locked those memories away yourself. Pity, you were so much stronger then. It sickens me when I think of what you threw away.*

Nico firmly turned her attention toward the valley floor. She did not want to hear it.

"All right," Eli said, dropping his bag on the ice at his feet. "Since you can't go to the mountain, Nico, Josef and I will sneak in ourselves and find that map you mentioned. We'll have to take Karon with us. Will you be all right without heat?"

Nico considered. "I should be. I'm sheltered here, and I've got my coat. I'll be good until nightfall."

"Plenty of time," Eli said, glancing at Josef. "Let's go."

Josef nodded, and the pair of them started down the steep slope toward the black mountain. Eli skidded a little on icy snow and half ran, half slid down the first slope. Josef, however, took one step and stopped cold.

Nico thought he was testing the ground, but the seconds ticked by and still he didn't move. Eli recovered his footing and, realizing he was alone, glanced up at his swordsman.

"Are you all right?" he called.

Josef didn't answer. He had a look on his face Nico had never seen on him before. On anyone else, she would have called it bewilderment. For a long minute he just stood there, the wind blowing snow into his short blond hair. Then, very slowly, as though he were pushing against enormous pressure, Josef lifted his arm, raised his hand to his shoulder, and, with a flip of the buckle, undid the strap that held the Heart of War to his back. The sword fell to the ground with a crash that echoed off the mountain walls, sending the snow sliding down the slopes. The second he was free, Josef staggered forward, panting and red-faced like he'd just run a mile in full armor.

Eli looked from sword to swordsman. "What just happened?"

"I don't know," Josef said, struggling to stand upright. He turned to face his fallen sword, which was lying on the ice just inside the ravine. Scowling, he leaned forward and grabbed the handle with both hands, pulling as hard as he could.

The sword did not move.

Josef braced his legs and pulled again, but the sword stuck to the icy stone as though it had grown there, and nothing Josef did could move it. After the third pull, he fell backward into the snow. Josef sat up again with a flurry of thrown snow, gasping and glaring at his sword. But the Heart just sat there, black and silent as ever.

Eli climbed back up the slope and leaned over the sword until his nose was almost level with the leather-wrapped hilt, staring intently. When he had examined it from every angle, he stood up with a shrug. "I guess it doesn't want to go to the Dead Mountain either."

"That's too bad," Josef said, breathing hard. "Because I'm not going in there without it, so it'll just have to come along."

He grabbed the hilt to pull again, but this time he stopped, his face going ghostly pale.

"What?" Eli said.

Josef shook his head, like he was trying to clear it. "It can't go," he said.

Eli stared at him. "*What?*"

"The Heart just told me it can't go to the Dead Mountain," Josef said again.

"Since when do you talk to your sword?" Eli scoffed.

Josef gave him a murderous look. "It's more like a feeling, but I know what it said. It told me it has to stay here."

Eli sighed. "Well, did it give a reason?"

Josef crossed his arms. "Sure, it explained all its motivations to me in great detail. And then we sat down and had tea."

"Okay, okay," Eli said, putting his hands up. "The Heart stays. But if it's not going, then you shouldn't either."

Josef arched an eyebrow, and Eli shook his head. "I'm not saying anything about your fighting prowess, but if you can't bring your big weapon I'd probably have an easier time sneaking in alone."

"How does that make sense?" Josef growled.

"It's the first rule of thievery," Eli said with a shrug. "One person makes less noise than two. And I'd much rather you be here with Nico and the Heart than stuck on some mountain with just me and your pot-metal normal blades."

Josef's hands flicked to the blades on his hip, as though he was about to show Eli just how dangerous those pot-metal blades could be, but Eli was already walking over to the cranny where he'd dropped his bag.

"If I go solo then I can do things I can't do with you two," he said, pulling a folded bundle of black clothing out of his sack. "Anyway"—he began to take off his jacket—"it's not like I'm planning on fighting. I'll have a much easier time giving trouble the slip if I don't have to worry about you and your bash-happy ways."

Josef frowned but didn't argue the point. Satisfied, Eli leaned on the wall and began pulling off his boots. He placed them carefully beside his pack, followed by his jacket. Then, standing in the snow in his shirtsleeves and socks, Eli shook out the folded black cloth and started to pull it over his head. It was a tight fit. The fabric was obviously meant to go over the skin, not other clothes, but Nico didn't blame Eli for layering. Even with Karon there to keep him warm, the cold was bitter. When the black cloth was wrapped all the way down to his feet, Eli slid on a pair of padded black boots, completing the ensemble. When he straightened up, he was dressed toe to chin in a black catsuit not unlike the one Giuseppe Monpress had worn back in Gaol.

"Don't ever tell the old man I actually wore this," Eli said, pulling the last bit, the black mask, over his head. "I'd never hear the end. Of course"—he grinned behind the thin cloth—"mine has improvements."

"I hope they make you demonproof," Josef said. "You've got four hours before dark; don't dawdle."

"Yes, Mother."

Josef snorted indignantly. Eli gave them a final wave and started down the slope, half walking, half sliding over the ice-crusted snow. Despite being a black dot on a field of white, he vanished almost instantly. Still, Nico and Josef watched for several minutes more, just in case.

Finally, Josef turned around. "Come on," he said. "Let's see if we can find something that will burn before I turn blue."

Nico nodded and hurried after him. For the next half hour they scoured the ravine and the slope they'd come from, eventually gathering enough burnables to make a fire. It was a small, pathetic thing, but at least it was bright and warm, and they huddled together beside it.

Now that it was clear they weren't going to the Dead Mountain, the Heart let Josef pick it up again. He sat with the black blade in his lap, idly running his fingers across its pitted surface. This close, Nico could smell the bite of cold iron and the fearsome, bloody scent of the sword itself. Even so, it was a comforting, familiar smell, and for the first time since they'd seen the bears, she began to think things might turn out all right.

That was when the sunlight began to fade.

"Powers," Josef grumbled, looking up at the fast-moving clouds. "A storm. As if we didn't have enough to deal with."

He lowered his head and crouched tighter over his sword, but Nico could only stare wide-eyed as the swift, gray clouds were pushed aside by black, angry thunderheads moving against the wind. "Josef," she whispered. "I don't think that's a normal storm."

He looked at her, and then looked up again. By this point, the storm clouds blotted out every inch of sky. They tumbled overhead, enormous and midnight black, lit up from the inside by flashes of blue lightning. Thunder crashed, drowning out even the howling of the wind outside the pass. Josef muttered a curse and stood up, the Heart of War in his hand. It was as dark as night in the ravine now, their pathetic little fire the only sputter of light.

All at once the world flashed bright blue as lightning struck, and in the lightning, a tall man appeared before them. His long black hair fell over the shoulders of a long black coat edged with silver. A long sword with a blue-wrapped hilt sat on his hip, and his long, ageless face was transformed by a triumphant smile.

The lightning faded, but the image of the man was burned into Nico's eyes. In the second before the thunder crashed, a harsh, laughing voice spoke over the howling wind.

"Alone at last."

Nico went cold as the stone behind her. She knew that voice. It came roaring from the memories she'd locked away, from the place in her mind she could never go. Instinctively, she dropped into a fighting stance, feeling stupid even as she lifted her tiny fists. But she didn't back down. So long as Josef stood beside her, she could not ever run away.

As her eyes adjusted to the returned darkness, she saw that the man in the black coat was looking at her. His blue-silver eyes flashed like the lightning in the sky, and his victorious smile grew even colder as he opened his mouth to speak.

"Don't move."

The command fell on her like an avalanche, slamming Nico to the icy rock. Her breath flew out of her lungs as she crashed into the stone, and she felt a sharp pain as her arm, caught beneath her by the sudden fall, snapped like a twig. Gasping, she tried to roll over, to save her injured arm from her weight, but she could not move. She couldn't even twitch. It was just like what Sted had done in Gaol, only a thousand times stronger, a million times. That time at least she had been able to shift a little; now it took every ounce of her will just to take another breath.

Not for much longer. The voice filled her mind, louder than even the blood pounding in her ears. *You know who this is, Nico. You know how he works. He's letting you breathe, playing with you, savoring his victory. Soon, when he decides or when the pain becomes too much, you'll suffocate under the weight of the spirit's hatred for our kind. But there's no need to suffer. No need to be weak. After all, you've broken his hold before.*

Nico took a desperate breath and closed her eyes, but something inside her head reached out and pried them open again, forcing her to look as Josef stepped forward, his mouth moving in words she could not hear over the pain.

Tears running from eyes she could no longer close, Nico watched Josef reach back and draw the Heart of War. A moment later, the horrid man in the black coat drew his own blade. Her breaths were coming in shallow little gasps now as the swordsmen faced each other, and though she would have gladly broken her own neck to do it, she could not look away.

Watch closely. This time the voice was a bare whisper over her mind. *Everything that's about to happen is your fault.* The voice grew fainter with every word. *When you're ready to do what's necessary, when you're ready to fight again, I'll be here.*

With that, the voice trailed off, leaving Nico to gasp in the sudden, enormous silence of her own head.

Less than five feet from her crumpled body, the two swordsmen lunged.

Out of the corner of his eye Josef saw Nico crumple, but he put it out of his mind before she hit the ground. Nico could take care of herself. She was a survivor, and she'd keep surviving, so long as he protected her chance to fight. To do that, he needed all his attention on his opponent. Across the stone ravine, the man in the coat smiled and drew his sword with a blue-silver flash. The blade shone in the heartbeat of light, long and gently curved, cutting the air with a thin whistle. The man in the coat took a step toward

Nico and Josef matched him, sidestepping to block his path, the cold, dull blade of the Heart of War ready in his hands.

The man stopped and stared, his pale face almost amused. "Do not try me, human," he said. "Step aside. This is none of your concern."

"Nico and I are comrades," Josef said simply. "Her concerns are my concerns."

"Is that so?" The man arched a thin eyebrow. "Are you so eager to die, then, comrade of a demon?"

"Death comes when it comes," Josef said. "I won't step aside for it."

The tall man's eyes narrowed. "Have it your way, Josef Liechten, Master of the Heart of War."

"That's unfair," Josef said. "You know our names, but we don't know yours."

The tall man swung his sword up, resting the flat against his shoulder. "I am called the Lord of Storms. So I was named when I was pulled from the sky and given my purpose, the eradication of the creature who stands behind you and all others of her kind. I cannot be killed and I do not give up. Now do you understand the position you are in?"

"More than before," Josef said, tightening his grip on the Heart. From the moment he saw the clouds overhead, the Heart had been almost vibrating in anticipation. He could feel its excitement even now, and it made his own pulse quicken. The only thing that roused the sword was the possibility of a good fight. Josef smiled, remembering that night in Gaol. From the way the Lord of Storms was talking, a fight seemed inevitable, and this time, Josef was determined to honor his sword. This time, he wouldn't hold back.

"I've found that men of purpose are the best fighters," Josef said, looking the taller man straight in the eye. "Tell me, Lord of

Storms"—Josef's face broke into a wide smile—"are you a good swordsman?"

"What does it matter?" The Lord of Storms gave him a bored look. "I told you, I can't be killed. No matter what you do, the end will be the same. I will kill the demon. You can either die with it, or step aside."

Josef didn't move. "It may be you can't be killed," he said. "But never did you say you couldn't be defeated." He reached up and undid the buckle on the belt of knives across his chest. The heavy belt of blades fell to the ground with a thud, followed by the swords at his waist. Piece by piece, Josef shed his weapons. When he dropped the last knife from his boot, he stepped toward the Lord of Storms, completely unencumbered. "I'll ask you again. Are you a good swordsman?"

"I am the first swordsman," the Lord of Storms answered. "And the best."

"Then I will not move," Josef said, pointing the Heart's dull, dark blade at the Lord of Storms' chest. "I am Josef Liechten, and I will become the greatest swordsman in the world. So come and fight me, Lord of Storms. Give me a challenge worth dying for."

The Lord of Storms looked at him for a long time. "I won't spare you once I begin," he said. "If you step down this path, there's no turning back."

Josef braced his feet on the icy rock, the Heart sure and heavy in his hands. "I've never needed a path I could turn back from."

The Lord of Storms laughed. "You are bold to the point of stupidity," he said, swinging his sword so that it matched tip to tip with the Heart. "I find that refreshing. Very well, Josef Liechten, your life has bought you a lesson in the difference in power between you and me. It will be quick, so learn it well."

Josef's answer was to lunge, swinging the Heart of War with both hands. The black blade whistled through the air, carrying the weight of a mountain as it swung under the Lord of Storms' sword and up toward his unprotected chest. What happened next happened too fast for Josef to see. One second the Lord of Storms' guard was broken, the next, the long, blue-white sword was in front of him, poised to meet the Heart's charge. The two swords met in a blinding clash, and the Heart stopped cold.

Josef grunted as the breath slammed out of his lungs. Hitting the Lord of Storms' parry was like running into a stone wall at full speed. He bore down with a roar, pushing with all his strength. The Lord of Storms stood before him, a bored look on his sharp face, holding the blue-silver sword against the Heart of War's straining blade with one, bored hand. The will of the Heart pounded through Josef's muscles, clearing his vision and sharpening his senses to a level he'd reached only once before, and it was only thanks to that painful clarity that he perceived what was about to happen.

He caught the gleam in the taller man's eyes just in time before the blue-white blade swung, cutting through the air where Josef's head had been a split second earlier. Josef danced back, panting, bringing the Heart up again. But the Lord of Storms lowered his blade, looking at Josef as though he were seeing him for the first time.

"If you're good enough to dodge my attack, then you're too good to die like a dog here," the Lord of Storms said calmly. "The Heart chooses its wielders with great care. It must see great potential in you. Don't waste its time on a battle you can never win."

The Heart of War quivered in Josef's hands, rejecting the idea, and the Lord of Storms looked surprised.

"You always did love lost causes," he said, shaking his head. "But facing me with a deaf boy for a wielder is foolish even for you. The Lady will not be happy when she hears how you're using the freedom she gave you."

The Heart burned against Josef's hands, and a surge of strength flowed up his arms, urging him forward. Josef didn't need to be told twice. He charged, but this time he was watching for the Lord of Storms' lightning-fast block. Sure enough, it moved into position with a silver flash, but with the Heart's rage singing through him, Josef moved even faster. He dropped and rolled under the Lord of Storms' sword, coming up inside the taller man's guard with a triumphant cry as the Heart of War's black blade bit into the Lord of Storms' unprotected ribs.

The Heart slid into the Lord of Storms' side, cutting flesh for a split second before a flash of lightning blinded Josef, and the Lord of Storms vanished. Josef reeled as the resistance disappeared, flying through the air on the force of his blow, which was now lodged in thin air. He was still trying to make sense of what had happened when something hard and impossibly sharp struck his back directly between his shoulder blades. Josef slammed into the ground, gasping and choking on the blood that was suddenly everywhere. The Heart of War clattered from his hand, but Josef couldn't see where it had landed. Flashing spots danced across his eyes, but as he struggled to push himself up, something cold and dull slammed into his ribs, flipping him over onto his back.

The Lord of Storms towered over him, taller and darker than before, his long black hair dancing in a wind that blew only for him. His lightning-colored sword was dark with blood, but what caught Josef's eye was the man's left side, where the Heart of War had stuck. There, where the wound should have been, black clouds were billowing. There was no blood, no bone, just black thunderheads swirling in and out of the gap in the Lord of Storms' black coat. Josef blinked in disbelief as lightning arced across the wound, and the hole in the man's side began to shrink. The clouds pulled together until there was only the smooth fabric of the Lord of Storms' coat, leaving no sign that he had been breached at all.

Josef's horror must have been plain, for the Lord of Storms' face broke into a wide grin.

"Ah," he said and chuckled. "The arrogant boy begins to understand his situation." He held out his sword, pressing the flat against Josef's cheek. "And I was so impressed. To think, someone as spirit deaf as you was able to feel the Heart's will. I haven't seen such a thing in centuries, yet here you are, on your back like all the others, not even realizing you're dead."

Josef tried to answer, but his retort turned into a hacking cough. He spat out the hot blood in his mouth and tried to focus, but his back was burning against the freezing stone, and he could feel the slick, hot blood melting the ice below him. It hurt to breathe. It hurt to move. Above him, the Lord of Storms was blurring, becoming just another shape in the red dark, and Josef realized with a start that he was dying. Truly dying, from a single blow.

The Lord of Storms watched sadly as Josef struggled to breathe, and then he turned in a swift motion.

"I am not without honor," he said, walking to the far end of the narrow pass. "You fought well for what you are, so I shall give you a warrior's death." He turned again when he reached his destination, sword held delicately in his long hands. "Stand up," he called, fixing his eyes on Josef's. "Stand and die as the swordsman of the Heart of War should."

The pass fell silent. Even the endless winds outside ceased their blowing, leaving the narrow space between the cliffs dark and still, save for Josef's ragged breathing. With a low groan, Josef's hand reached out from his chest and began to feel for his sword. He found it at once, the rough-wrapped hilt jumping into his grip. He expected the Heart to say something. He was certainly gone enough to hear it, but the black blade stayed silent.

A great, clear sound rang out between the mountains as Josef plunged the Heart of War into the stone. He took a long, shuddering breath and, using the Heart as a crutch, pulled himself up. The moment he was no longer horizontal, blood began to rush down his back. The pain between his shoulders grew so intense he had to stop a moment, halfway between sitting and standing, just to bear it. But a second later he was moving again, uncurling inch by inch until he was standing straight, facing the Lord of Storms with his sword clasped in both hands. He would not die. He would not fail Nico. He would not fail Eli. He would not fail his sword. He hadn't thrown everything away to die like this. He would stand and meet the monster, the man whose body was made of storms, and he would not go down.

The Heart of War radiated its approval, and he felt its strength flowing back into him, clearing his vision, dimming his pain. This was it, the final blow, and they would make it together. But as he stepped into the ready position, a piercing cry stopped him cold. It was high and keening, and it came from behind him. Even the Lord of Storms looked startled, and they both turned to find the source of the sound. What Josef saw next turned his blood to ice water.

"Powers," he whispered. "Not now."

CHAPTER 9

Eli climbed down the snow-covered slope until the pass hiding Josef and Nico from the wind was itself hidden by the blowing snow. This turned out to be a shorter distance than he'd anticipated, thanks to the rather spectacular blizzard howling on this side of the peak. The flurries were so thick he could barely see his own feet as he picked his way down the cliff, but the white storm did little to hide the mountain rising across the valley ahead, enormous and sharp against the endless snow.

Eli let out a low whistle. The mountain was an inkblot on the white landscape. Impossibly tall, it towered over the surrounding peaks, its black slopes rocky and bare without a flake of snow or twig for cover. Eli stared in wonder at the mountain a moment longer before he sat down in the snow to wake up his suit. Sneaking into castles and treasuries was one thing. To sneak into the home of the demonseeds, he was going to need all his tricks.

"Eli." Karon's whisper was like smoke in his ear. "Are you sure about this?"

"Getting cold feet?" Eli asked, laughing as he rubbed his hands on his sleeves. "I didn't think it was possible in a lava spirit."

The burn in his chest began to tingle, a sign that the lava spirit was not in a joking mood.

"I'm positive," Eli said, his voice steady and certain. "This is our best chance of helping Slorn, and the *only* chance to get around Josef's stubbornness." He heaved an annoyed sigh. "The man is thick as his sword, sometimes. If I hadn't taken Nico's offer I might have ended up on the wrong end of that iron pigsticker. A famous death to be sure, but not the kind I want."

"Josef wouldn't raise his hand against you," Karon said. "It's not his way. As for Slorn, he's a better friend to you than most, but to go willingly onto forbidden ground? The very home of the demon? That's too much, even for him. So why are we here? For real, this time."

Eli closed his eyes. "Nothing gets by you, does it?"

The lava spirit chuckled. "I've lived in your chest for four years now. If I can't call your bluffs, then your tongue really will have turned to silver."

"Fair enough," Eli said. "I am here to find information on Slorn, but also because Nico suggested it. I always suspected she knew more than she was letting on, and now's a good time to show I trust her advice."

"Do you?" Karon sounded surprised.

"Well, I certainly want her to think so," Eli said. "I don't know what's going on with that girl most of the time. If she feels I trust her, maybe she'll open up a little more, especially about her powers, or the lack thereof. But"—he lowered his voice to a whisper—"that's just extra, sugar on the pie. Really, I'm here because it is forbidden." Eli leaned back and stared up at the shadow of the mountain. "It's the only place in creation Benehime forbade me to go."

"Naturally," Karon said. "You're her darling. She didn't want you to become a bed for a demonseed."

"No, I don't think that's it," Eli said. "Not all of it, anyway." He squinted through the snow. "Living with her, I always felt like I was a doll in her perfect white doll-house. Nothing there existed unless she willed it, even me. Everything I did, I did because she wanted me to do it. So while she always said I had everything I wanted, what I really had was everything *she* wanted. But I always knew, even then, that somewhere beyond the white world there had to be places she didn't control. Places where the spirits didn't fall all over themselves to answer her every beck and call. I think the Dead Mountain may be one of them."

"But it was the Shepherdess who trapped the demon under the mountain," Karon whispered. "Her will that keeps it pinned." A tremor ran through Eli's chest, and he realized the lava spirit was terrified. "This isn't something we want to mess with, Eli."

"Maybe so," the thief said, grinning. "But we're already here.

We need to find Slorn, and there's no harm in just taking a look. Besides, last time I checked, even demons weren't omniscient. If we play our cards right, they'll never know we were here."

The burn tingled again, painfully this time, and Eli gave his chest a pat. "We'll leave at the first sign of trouble," he promised. "Fast as we can, trust me."

"First sign, don't forget."

"I swear," Eli said.

The burning sensation faded, and Eli rubbed his chest with a long, painful breath. Now, to business. He looked down at his suit. It was a simple cat burglar suit, all muted grays and blacks tied close to keep his limbs limber. This particular suit was a little worn. It had been given to him by the original Monpress, back when the old man still thought his adopted son would make a respectable cat burglar one day. He'd learned better, of course, but Eli had kept the suit. Not for sentimental reasons, but because he'd remade it with some improvements.

Eli moved his long fingers over his padded shoes, drying them out with Karon's heat and talking constantly about what he needed them to do in the low, excited voice that smaller spirits found irresistible. They woke easily, the woven fibers turning like snakes under his fingers. Once his feet were awake, he moved up his legs to his chest, then his arms, talking constantly in that same low voice. He did his mask last, unwrapping and holding it up between his hands as he gave an extremely energized pep talk about what they were all about to do together.

Altogether the process took about fifteen minutes. Of course, if his suit had been made from Shaper cloth it would always be awake and he wouldn't have to go through this every time, but Shapers were nosy, and Eli preferred to keep the true nature of his thieving clothes a secret. If the old Monpress had taught Eli anything, it was that you never showed all your cards. Besides, Shaper cloth was horridly expensive.

Now that it was properly awake, Eli's cat burglar suit began to show its true value. Every thread had seven colors, a spectacular bit of dye work that had taken Eli five tries and one very angry cloth merchant to get right. Once awakened, these threads had one job: turn in unison so that the color on the suit's surface best matched the color of whatever Eli was hiding against. Now that every piece was awake, the effect was instant. The moment Eli tied his mask back around his face, his suit went dapple gray-white, a perfect match for the snow he crouched in.

Eli grinned behind his mask. It wasn't perfect, of course. Even when he could blend them together by alternating threads, seven colors was hardly enough to camouflage him from someone who was really looking. Someday, when he had favors to burn, he'd have Slorn make him a suit with a hundred different colors. Assuming, he thought bleakly, they found the bear in time. For now, though, he was satisfied to creep through the snow, keeping Karon's heat just at his body as he made his way across the valley until, at last, he stood at the foot of the mountain where piled snow met bare stone in a razor-sharp line.

Eli stopped, staring at the division between the normal world and the forbidden. Finally, he took a deep breath and, bracing himself one last time, lifted his foot out of the snow and placed it carefully on the mountain's dry slope.

Nothing happened. Eli blinked, confused. He'd always imagined that setting foot on the Dead Mountain would feel different, forbidden, or at least dangerous. But standing there, with one foot on the stone and one in the snow, he didn't feel anything special. In fact, he felt absolutely nothing. It was like stepping into a void. He could hear the wind screaming behind him, the wet of the snow pressing against his back, but ahead there was nothing but cold, empty silence. Even so, it took him a solid minute to put his other foot on the slope. It was the emptiness. Stepping into something that silent, that bare, made him feel tiny and weak, like a rabbit stepping into an open field when there were hawks overhead. Eli swallowed. He wasn't used to feeling like prey.

His suit dutifully switched from dapple white to dull black as he began his creep up the mountain. It was rough going. Other than being coal black and completely bare of snow, it was much like any of the other mountains in the range, only taller and sharper, unshaped by wind for who knew how long. The air on the slope was still and heavy, yet even as he took great gasps of it, there wasn't enough. He felt light-headed and weak, and it only got worse the farther up he went. He clung to the slope, a tiny black spot moving up the great black spike of the mountain's peak, until, at last, he reached a ledge.

Eli threw himself onto the flat surface with a relieved gasp and lay there on his back for several minutes, catching what breath he could from the strange, heavy air. When he felt somewhat himself again he lifted his head and looked around. He was lying on the lip of a long, level rise tucked between the sharp cliffs of the mountain's face, cutting between the impossible slopes almost like a path. But that wasn't all. Eli tilted his head, staring at the ground beside him. The ledge was covered in fine black dust, proof that, even separated from the elements, the Dead Mountain was decaying. Well, Eli thought, no surprise there. No physical body, not even a mountain, could keep itself together without its spirit. But it was what he saw in the dust that caught his eye. There, not an inch from his head, was a small scuff in the blanket of powdered stone, a long depression in the unmistakable shape of a human foot.

Eli sat up, careful not to touch the footprint. There was another one not far from it, and another by the cliff's edge, following the slope of the ledge behind the cliffs and up the mountain.

"Well, well," Eli said, standing. "Not so lifeless after all."

Karon's only answer was a deep, terrified shudder as Eli dusted himself off, turned his suit a duller black with a wave of his hand, and began to follow the footprints up the mountain. The path, for it was unmistakably a path now, wound up the mountainside, cutting back and forth to avoid the steep drops between the cliffs. Eli climbed it slowly, partly because he was being careful and partly because he couldn't go any faster. The air was nearly unbreathable now, thin and dank and icy cold. Every breath burned his lungs, yet he couldn't stop gasping. He sucked in the air as best he could, moving at a slow shamble until the path he was following suddenly and unceremoniously ended at the lip of a little hidden valley. Eli cursed and dropped, pressing himself against the ground as he stared wide-eyed over the valley's edge.

"I don't believe it," he whispered.

Just below him, nestled in a hidden valley on the Dead Mountain, was a town. It was a small town, two dozen stone shacks arranged in a semicircle around a stone cistern half filled with greasy water. Still, that was two dozen more shacks than Eli had expected to find on the forbidden mountain. All around the shacks, people in threadbare black robes moved with their heads down, carrying boxes from a horseless wagon into a small cave at the other end of the valley under the supervision of two large men in matching black leather armor.

"Who sets up shop on the Dead Mountain?" Eli whispered. When Karon didn't reply, Eli answered his own question. "They must be cult members. I remember hearing the League saying something about the cult of the Dead Mountain, misguided idiots who actually want a demonseed inside them."

"How can they live here?" Karon said, trembling. "Can't they see it?"

"Of course not," Eli said, waving his hand in front of his face. "Blind, remember?" He paused. "Out of curiosity, what does it look like?"

"Like something that should never be seen," Karon whispered. "We should leave."

"Not before we get what we came for," Eli said, scooting forward. "Nico described a map room, but I bet we won't find one in those shacks. My money is on that." He pointed at the low cave entrance across the little village where the people in the robes were carrying the boxes down into the mountain itself.

Karon grumbled, but Eli ignored it. He pushed himself up into a crouch and began to inch his way down into the valley. The mountain was silent around him, the dead silence of a land without spirits, and every movement he made sounded like a crash in his ears. But the people down in the valley didn't seem to notice him at all. They just kept hurrying back and forth, their faces as blank as corpses' as they ferried the boxes from the cart to the cave. Eli reached the outermost shack without incident, and he stayed there, back pressed against the loose stone, until the cart was empty.

Once the last box had been unloaded, one of the armored guards reached down behind the wagon seat and pulled out a small bundle. The bundle struggled as the guard set it on the ground, and Eli realized with a horrified shock that it was a child. A little boy, no older than four, wrapped in a dirty cloth and tied with ragged ropes, his smudged face downcast and streaked with dried tears. The boy's thin neck was angry and red, as though something had rubbed it raw, and Eli clenched his jaw. He'd seen those injuries on children before, down in the southern islands where Council law was thin. He couldn't see from where he was, but he would bet the boy had similar marks on his wrists, ankles, and waist. Slavers liked to keep their merchandise secure.

One of the pale, robed figures came forward to take the boy, grabbing him by the shoulders. The child tried to struggle, but it was clear he had no more strength to fight. The robed figure led him away, pulling him to a stone hut that was set off from the others. The cultist opened the gray door with one hand, and Eli shrank back at what he saw inside. There, tied in the dirt like animals, were five more children, boys and girls. They were all tiny, skeletal things. None of them looked up when the newcomer was shoved inside. The boy fell with a sad, light thud as the cultist slammed the door behind him, plunging the children back into the dark.

"They're all wizards," Karon whispered.

"I'd guessed that already," Eli whispered back.

"Don't you see? Those are the beds of future demonseeds." Karon's voice shook with rage. "Aren't we going to do something?"

"What can we do?" Eli said, taking a deep breath. "We're here for information, not to play hero. Even if I wanted to, we've got no backup. First rule of thievery, if you must fight, only fight the fights you can win."

Back at the center of town, the cultists were bowing before the cart guards, bending to scrape their heads against the stone. The two large men sneered in unison at the display and turned away, each grabbing one pole of the cart's empty harness. Then, with a sickening and familiar twisting of shadows, they vanished, taking the cart with them.

Eli rolled his eyes. "Of course this place would be crawling with demonseeds."

"We should move while they're gone," Karon said. "Before anything worse shows up."

Eli nodded and crept between the shacks toward the cave,

keeping an eye on the local inhabitants. He might as well not have bothered. Now that the demonseeds were gone, the people slumped to the ground, exhausted. They didn't speak, didn't touch one another. They just sat there, staring at the ground, their frail hands clutching the dusty stone. Just looking at them gave Eli the creeps, and he shuffled faster than he should have toward the cave.

The moment he stepped inside, the sunlight winked out. It was as though the cave's mouth was a line the sunlight could not cross. Eli blinked in the dark, letting his eyes adjust. Slowly, he saw that the cave was piled with boxes, all made of the same gray, flimsy wood, and all of them unmarked. There was one right by Eli's feet, and he nudged it experimentally. Whatever was in the box, it was horribly heavy, for the crate didn't even budge, but the wood on the outside fell away in flakes, completely dead. Eli would have investigated further, but Karon was burning in his chest, reminding him to keep moving.

Careful not to touch the fragile boxes, Eli edged his way past the stacks and started deeper into the cave. He walked for some time, stumbling in the thick, heavy dark. The cave floor was uneven and tilted upward, climbing toward the mountain's peak. Eli crept low in the dark, keeping as silent as he could, but they didn't see anyone, or anything, until suddenly, after nearly an hour of climbing, the cave opened up again. Eli blinked in the sudden brightness. The cave let out onto a cliff high above where they'd entered. He'd crossed the mountain as well, and as best as Eli could tell he was now on the opposite face from where he had entered, looking north. The view was spectacular. He could look down for miles on the peaks of the lesser mountains, snowcapped and silent in the afternoon sunshine. It was actually quite pretty, and Eli stood a moment, enjoying the scenery, until Karon made a little, terrified noise. Eli whirled around, arms up, ready to take on whatever demonseed or cult thrall was surely about to jump them. But there was no one. Just another view.

Eli stood and stared, trying to make sense of what he was seeing. He was looking down on a valley, a long, straight stretch between mountains just like the approach he'd taken to the Dead Mountain, only this valley obviously should not have been there. No natural formation of stone could have made a valley that straight. It ran like a road from the foot of the Dead Mountain due northwest, and wherever a mountain got in its way, that mountain was sundered, ripped apart in long, terrible gouges until only sheer cliffs remained.

"What happened here?" Eli's voice was barely a whisper.

"I don't want to know," Karon whispered back. "But one thing is certain. Something ate those mountains."

"Ate?" Eli said. "What do you mean, 'ate'?"

"Look at the valley floor."

Eli looked, squinting to make sense of the tumbled impressions beneath the drifts of snow. Slowly, the random shapes came together to form enormous craters. He could see the great ripped-up places where mountains had been, but now nothing was left except piles of boulders, their faces as black and dead as the slope Eli stood on.

Eli swallowed. "What eats a mountain?"

"I already said I don't want to know," Karon rumbled, pulling farther back inside Eli's body. "It's like the demon of the mountain itself escaped and made a run for it, eating everything in its path."

"Come on," Eli said. "If that had happened we'd all be dead. But you're right; something came out." He crept closer to the cliff edge, his eyes following the trail of destruction north and west toward the horizon. "I wonder where it was going. The only thing north of here is the Shaper Mountain." He frowned, contemplating. "*And* I wonder what stopped it, and why I haven't heard about it. I would like to think I'd know about something that eats mountains."

Karon's burn began to singe. "Let's just go."

Eli tore his eyes away from the destruction and set back to the task at hand. The path between the two cliffs was steep, narrow, and open. Had there been wind, the crossing would have been impossible, but this being the Dead Mountain, Eli was able to pick his way along the narrow going with little trouble. After a hundred feet, the path began to jackknife, taking them steeply upward toward the Dead Mountain's knife-sharp peak. They saw no one as they went, not a guard, not a cultist, not a seed, nothing but dead stone and air. They walked so long Eli began to wonder if he'd missed something, for they were quickly running out of mountain. But just as he was about to suggest they turn around, the path ended abruptly at the mouth of a cave.

Eli stopped in his tracks. This was not like the cave they'd come in through. That at least had been somewhat normal, just an opening in the stone. This was like looking into a pool of ink. No light penetrated past the stone's edge. Instead, the cave's darkness seemed to press outward like a living thing, moving subtly just beyond what Eli could see. He stared into the blackness, waiting for Karon to say something, but the lava spirit was silent. For a moment, Eli seriously considered turning back, but the idea of having to explain to Josef that he'd chickened out gave Eli the burst of courage he needed. With a final breath of the cold, thin air, Eli lurched forward and stepped into the dark.

The blackness swallowed him as soon as he moved. All light vanished, and for a moment Eli stood there groping like a blind man. He was on the edge of turning back around when he realized that, despite this, he could still see. The dark was total, and yet it did not obscure his surroundings. He was standing at the apex of a large, circular cave. Perfectly circular, he realized, as though it had been cut into the stone with inhuman precision. The floor was smooth underfoot, the black stone polished to a slick edge except for the pattern cut deep into its surface. Eli followed the grooves with his eyes through the strange not-dark, biting his lip as the familiar symbol came into focus. It was Benehime's mark.

Eli swallowed. Now that he knew what he was looking at, what he saw directly ahead of him suddenly became much more terrifying. At the center of the room, standing at the place where the lines of the Lady's mark came together, was a man. He was dressed in the same dark robes as the cultists of the valley below, but unlike them, this man was not stooped or downtrodden. He stood straight and haughty, his arms crossed over his chest in a way that only emphasized how skeletally thin he was, and his eyes glowed with a cold light that illuminated nothing.

For a long, long moment, no one spoke. Eli stood frozen at the edge of the circle, his boots just touching its outer border. Karon's mad fear was burning through him, mixing with his own until the urge to run was so strong it was physically painful to remain still. But Eli did not move. He stood his ground, clamping down as hard as he could on the terror while Slorn's voice played over and over again through his head.

Demons feed on fear.

After almost a minute of silence, the man at the center of the circle began to chuckle. "Very brave, little favorite."

Eli winced. There was something horribly wrong with the man's voice. It was far too deep for his thin frame, and there was something wrong with the tone. It was like an inner harmonic was missing, leaving only the shell of a voice. But even the strangeness could not mask the power that reverberated through it.

"You did an excellent job getting past my servants," the man said. "Of course, since I knew weeks ago that you were coming, you needn't have bothered. They had orders to escort you up."

"How hospitable," Eli said slowly. "And who are you?"

"Come, now," the man said, laughing. "You know who I am. Your little lava spirit certainly does."

Eli crossed his arms over Karon's burn, shielding the terrified spirit. "Humor me."

"My kind do not indulge in the conceit of names," the man said, walking forward. "But my children call me the Master of the Dead Mountain."

There was something horribly wrong with the way the man walked. It was jerky, unnatural, like there was something inside his skin moving just a hair faster than his flesh.

"Of course," the man said, stopping a bare inch from the edge of the circle, so close Eli could smell his flesh rotting. "Your mistress gave me another name."

"Yes," Eli said, making sure he was firmly outside the circle of the Shepherdess's seal. "Demon."

"There." The strange, horrible voice hummed with satisfaction. "Was that so hard?"

The demon smiled at Eli's sour look and turned on his heel, marching back across the seal with that horrible jerky walk until he was at the opposite side of the cavern. "As I said, I knew you were coming, and I know why you're here." The demon put out his hand, brushing the wall where it touched the circle's edge. All at once, the stone began to change. It sank away from his touch in places and rose to meet it at others, forming an intricate carving of tiny mountains, valleys, and seabeds across the curve of the wall. Eli watched in amazement as a perfect map of the world emerged from the dark stone, and not just the Council Kingdoms, but the Frozen Lands of the far north and the great realm of the Immortal Empress herself, far across the Barrier Sea. As the land took shape, other things appeared as well. Small, black shapes seeped from the black stone. Round, multilegged buglike things with shells like liquid tar. They rose from the stone and crouched on the continents, tiny antennae quivering whenever the demon's hand passed near.

"Here," the demon said, stretching up to point at one particularly large black beetle crawling far to the east of the great black point marking the Dead Mountain, somewhere in the coastal foothills of the Sleeping Mountains. "This is where you'll find Sted. If you hurry, you might even catch him before that bear-headed friend of yours does." He looked at Eli, his face all concern. "And I would hurry. Between the two of us, Slorn doesn't stand a chance."

Eli just stared at him, utterly speechless for once in his life. This encounter had taken a sharp turn from horrifying to bizarre. "Wait," he said. "Wait, wait, wait, what are you doing?"

The demon looked hurt. "I'm helping you."

"Yes," Eli said. "Why?" He pointed at the map, so confused he almost stretched his arms over the seal before he caught himself. "Why show me this? Why tell me where Sted is? You know I can't possibly trust you."

"You came here specifically to see this map," the demon said, dropping his arms. "If you can't trust me, why did you even bother?"

Eli snapped his jaw shut. He couldn't tell the demon that spying on the map would have made the information much more trustworthy than having the thing presented to him. But what was really getting under his skin was how much the creature knew. How did the demon know they were after Slorn? How had it known he was coming? It was a powerful, powerful creature with a wide network of spies, so he was willing to accept a certain amount of omniscience, but this was getting downright uncomfortable.

"Come now, Eli," the demon said when the thief's silence had stretched on too long. "You and I both know I'm your last shot. Old Gredit won't tell you anything without payment. I'm giving you this for free. You can either take it and save your friend or go back to stealing kings and stocking that charming little museum of a town you keep as a monument to your own audacity."

"How do you know all this?" Eli shouted. He regretted the words as soon as they were out. If there was anything he knew about demons, it was that you never showed them a weakness. But if all his secrets were hanging in the open air, he had to know *how*.

Across the blackness, the creature inside the puppet suit of flesh grinned wide. "My dear thief," he said. "A father sees everything through the eyes of his children, and my children are very, very watchful."

Eli's stomach dropped to his feet as everything fell into place. "Nico."

The creature smiled wider still. "First rule of thievery," he quoted. "The last place a man looks is under his own feet."

Eli took a step back. "I'm going now," he said, keeping his voice carefully flat. "You'll forgive me if I don't thank you for your help."

"I never expected you to," the demon said with a toothy smile. "Good-bye, Eli Monpress. I'll be watching."

Eli's mouth twitched, but he kept his face blank. He walked backward, his eyes locked on the demon's glowing gaze until, at last, he reached the cave mouth. The afternoon sunlight hit him like a hammer, and Eli stumbled, blinking in the brightness. As soon as he could see again, he was off, sprinting down the mountain as fast as his legs could carry him with no care at all for how much noise he made.

"I don't believe it," he hissed. "She's been playing us for fools this whole time. How could I have been so stupid? Awakening and going back? Skipping through shadows like it's nothing? She's been his little creature this whole time, and I ate it up. I believed that *drivel* about fighting for her humanity. She's nothing but a little *spy*."

"Eli," Karon said in a warning tone. "Remember that the demon is a trickster. You can't trust anything he says."

"Trust has nothing to do with it," Eli snarled. "He made his case clear enough."

Karon's heat flickered under his skin. "What are you going to do?"

"First, I'm getting off this mountain," Eli said, slowing down to navigate the thin strip of path between the cliffs where he'd stopped before to gawk at the horrible destruction left by the thing that ate mountains. "Then, I don't know. Nothing at first. Josef is going to be the linchpin in all of this. I'll have to break it to him slowly."

"I still don't understand *why*," Karon said. "Why would the demon put all this energy into spying on you?"

"Because I'm the favorite," Eli said bitterly. "Because I'm the greatest thief in the world. Because spirits listen to me whether I want them to or not. Because I'm the key to Benehime, who locked him up in the first place."

"Then why would he let you know he was watching?"

"I don't know!" Eli shouted. "There are so many angles going on, I don't know which way is up anymore. But trust me, I'm going to find out."

"Just watch out you don't break your team when you do," Karon muttered.

Eli had no answer to that. He plunged ahead, racing for the tunnel he'd taken up here from the cultists' encampment. He was so intent on getting off the demon's land, he didn't even notice the enormous storm clouds on the other side of the mountain, blackening the entire mountain range where he'd left Josef and Nico.

CHAPTER 10

When the Lord of Storms' sword cut into Josef's back, Nico lost control. She raged against the pressure holding her down, muscles burning as she fought to stand and attack the smug man made of storms who stood over Josef. She wanted to rip him open, to eat him whole, to punch that smug look off his face.

All she managed was to lift her head a fraction off the stone before the Lord of Storms' command slammed it down again.

She turned her cheek against the ground with a frustrated sob. She was so worthless. Across the ravine there was a soft, wet thump as the Lord of Storms turned Josef's body over with his boot. She heard the hateful sound of his haughty voice, followed by Josef's hacking cough. Nico began to shake. She couldn't even lift her head to see him, but she knew, completely and instantly, that Josef was dying. He was dying, and she couldn't save him. Couldn't do *anything.*

She stopped, holding her breath. This was where the voice would speak, offer her power. But her head was silent. The waiting stretched on. She could hear the Lord of Storms telling Josef to stand. Stand and face his death. She heard Josef moving, the great ringing sound of the Heart as he thrust it into the stone to pull himself up. The horrible shallowness of his breath as his life bled out of him.

And still, the voice stayed silent. All she could hear was the pathetic, doomed sound of Josef's breathing as he stood to face his death. A death she couldn't even turn her head to see.

Suddenly and without warning, a rage like she'd never felt ripped through her. If this was how it ended, why was she holding out? What did any of her sacrifices mean if Josef died? The Lord of Storms would kill her as soon as he finished Josef. Why was she even trying?

A good question.

Nico gritted her teeth. Fine. She didn't care anymore.

"You win," she whispered against the stone. "Give it back."

The words hung in the air, heavy and irretrievable. Slowly, languidly, the voice answered.

No.

Nico choked. "But you said—"

You want power? Power to save your swordsman?

She nodded.

Then prove it. Beg.

Something inside Nico began to tremble. "What?"

Beg for Josef's life. The voice spoke each word slowly, pointedly. *My gifts are for obedient children. You've been quite the pain in my side, little lost seed. If you want my help, beg for my forgiveness.*

Nico's breath came in shallow, tiny gasps. Across the silent pass, she could hear the crackle of the Lord of Storms as he raised his sword, hear the soft drip of Josef's blood as it hit the stone. She had no more time.

She squeezed her eyes shut with a sob and pressed her forehead into the ground.

"Please," she whispered, dragging the word out like a vital organ. "Give my power back. Let me save him."

Deep in her soul, she felt the voice smile. *Say it.*

"Please," Nico whispered again. "Master."

Pain and power hit her like a wall, and the world went black.

Nico screamed as her body wrenched itself from the stone, a high, keening sound that grew less and less human with each passing second. Inside her, the seed rose like bile, clawing its way to the front of her mind as deep, triumphant laughter filled her ears.

The Master's voice wiped out all other sound. *Welcome home, little slave.*

The last thing Nico saw was Josef's face, pale and horrified, before the blackness ate everything.

Nico's scream echoed off the icy walls, repeating over and over in the frozen silence. For a long moment the three of them, Josef, Nico, and the Lord of Storms, stood frozen, and then Nico began to change. Her shaking stopped. She grew taller, her skeletal body rounding out, muscles forming under skin that was no longer pale but growing dusky and hard. With a horrible crack, her broken bone reset itself as her arms stretched out, her fingers lengthening and sharpening until they barely looked human at all. But the worst by far was her eyes. It nearly made Josef sick to watch. Her eyes were stretched wider than any human's should be, the dark irises fading behind an eerie yellow glow.

She fell to a crouch, her arms and legs spread out around her like a spider about to spring. When she opened her mouth, now horribly stretched to accommodate a growing set of jagged, razor teeth, the sound that came out wasn't human at all.

"You came to catch a demon, Lord of Storms," the creature hissed. "Not butcher a man. I am your opponent now."

As she spoke, something else rode beneath the words, spreading through the canyon in an invisible wave. It struck Josef's mind like a night terror, a primal fear that went to his core. He was not alone. Above him, the mountains began to shake, the stone squirming and sliding over itself in terror. Josef stumbled as the ground beneath his feet turned to jelly, and it was only with the

Heart's help that he saved his back from another slam as he went down. The whole pass was shaking now, forcing Josef to scramble for cover as boulders began to slide down from the cliffs. Within seconds, the whole ravine was thrashing in terror, all except for the place where Nico stood.

The ground below Nico was no longer dull gray stone streaked with ice, but coal black and bone dry. Even in the dark it stood out from the surrounding, panicking stone. It was a blot, a circle of dead, quiet nothing spreading from her feet, and as it grew, so did Nico.

She's eating the mountain. The Heart's voice boomed in Josef's head. *You have to stop her.*

Josef flinched at the edge on the Heart's voice. If he hadn't known better, he would have said the sword was afraid. He started to ask how he was supposed to do that when another voice crashed through his mind, crushing every other sound.

Don't move.

The ravine froze. The mountains froze. Nico froze. Even Josef went perfectly still. Stones hung frozen in midfall and dust stood suspended in the air. Nothing dared to move. On the opposite edge of the pass, the Lord of Storms lowered his hands with a grim smile. His body was going fuzzy at the edges, little bits of his clothes fading back and forth from cloud to flesh while his sword flickered in his hand, the blade flashing between metal and a curved bolt of lightning.

Josef's eyes widened. He tried frantically to get his sword up, but he could no more move than he could hear the spirits' voices. However, the Lord of Storms seemed to have forgotten him entirely. His attention was only for Nico.

"You," he said, his voice thick with something very close to joy. "It is you, isn't it? I always knew. I *always knew* you weren't dead. I had no proof, but I knew." He threw out his empty hand and another sword, a perfect twin of the blade he grasped in his right, flashed into existence. "Now"—his face broke into a monstrous grin—"now we finish what we started." He raised his swords for the charge. "Daughter of the Dead Mountain!"

Across the frozen pass Nico screamed, a horrible sound of loss and mad anger woven through hundreds of voices, and vanished. She exploded from the shadows behind the Lord of Storms an instant later, her claws going for his back, just as he had struck Josef. The Lord of Storms turned without moving. One second his back was to her, and then his body flickered and he was facing her, meeting her blow with both blades, his face mad with joy as they crashed in a shower of sparks.

The Lord of Storms swept his swords with a roar, cutting a great gash in the mountainside. Nico dodged easily, flitting up through the shadows to the cliff top before launching herself down again, claws going straight for his unguarded head. She laughed as she flew, reveling in the intoxicating freedom of her power. Everything was so easy, so fast. Strength pounded through her limbs, banishing the pain, the fear, the constant worry. With all the power flowing through her there was simply no room for thought, no time for it. All that existed was her, the power, and the threat who must be killed. What did it matter if she couldn't stop to remember why?

She landed on the Lord of Storms with a gleeful scream, rending him from shoulder to ankle before he managed to flash away. For an intoxicating moment she could taste him on her fingers, a sharp mix of electricity and compressed power. Oh, what she could do with that power if only she could get more.

"You'll find me hard to chew, monster." The Lord of Storms' voice echoed through the ravine, and Nico turned just in time to see him blink back into existence, whole and uninjured as always.

Nico frowned. Had she spoken out loud? Well, no matter. He'd chosen a bad place to reform; his back was full to the shadows. She grinned wide and prepared for another jump.

The Lord of Storms lowered his swords. "How much longer will this farce go on?"

Nico shifted, unsure at this new ruse.

"The years you spent in starvation with the thief must have damaged you," he said, thrusting his sword at her. "This is barely worth my time. Look at you, nearly human, too weak to even damage my human shade. Any of my League could cut you down as you are now."

Nico answered by slipping through the shadows behind him, leaping at his open back. He spun and met her halfway, lightning swords cutting deep into her wrists. She screamed in pain and danced back while the Lord of Storms looked on with disgust.

"I have seen you hover in the sky on impossible wings," he sneered. "Blacker than night and larger than the mountain that spawned you. I have seen you eat Great Spirits like a wolf eats rabbits. Do not insult me by pretending at this *weakness*!"

He vanished only to reappear behind Nico, his long swords pressed against her throat. "Let go," he hissed in her ear. "Let go and we shall fight as never before. I have been hobbled and bored these past years, a slave to that woman's fancies. Give me something to feel alive again or I will kill you here."

Really, my Lord of Storms? You would sacrifice the lives of innocent spirits for a good fight?

"Really, my Lord of Storms?" Nico whispered, her throat fluttering against the swords as she breathed. "You would sacrifice the lives of innocent spirits for a good fight?"

The blades at her neck drew closer. "Spirits are sheep," he said bitterly. "Stupid, panicky creatures. I am the Shepherdess's dog, sworn to keep predators from the flock. If a few sheep are killed in the wolf catching, what does it matter? So long as the wolf is killed, the dog is free to do what it likes. And it's been so long since I had a real challenge." The blades drew closer still.

Nico flitted away, emerging from the shadows at the other end of the ravine clutching her bleeding throat. Deep in her mind, a feeling of wrongness nagged at her. She shouldn't be doing this, but why? It was so hard to concentrate.

Forget it. The Master's voice flooded her mind, cold and dark and reassuringly strong. *You're home, Nico. You don't have to think anymore. You don't have to try. Go to sleep. Put yourself in my hands and I will awaken you to your full potential. Then we'll see if our dear Lord of Storms stays so cocky.*

Nico almost cried as the relief washed over her. She'd been fighting for so long, what or how she couldn't remember, but she felt the tiredness in her bones. But everything was different now. The Master was with her. She could give in. Already she was relaxing into the welcome dark. As she sank, she could hear a girl's voice screaming, crying. It sounded so familiar, but Nico couldn't be bothered to turn and see. She was so tired.

There's a good girl.

Just as the last bits of her mind began to sink into the dark at the heart of her soul, something extraordinary happened. All at once, the mountain silence was broken by a deep, ringing gong. The sound of it shook the ground below her feet and forced her eyes open. Across the ravine, the Lord of Storms stood against the cliff, a surprised expression on his face and the great iron length of the Heart of War sticking out of his chest, pinning him to the stone like a butterfly on a board. For a second, all was still, and then, with a great rumbling roar, the Heart's spirit burst open, and the weight of a mountain slammed down.

Nico went down flat on her back, pinned to the icy stone, unable to move. Even the Lord of Storms was still, crushed by the mountain's weight. A few feet from her, at the edge of the ravine, a man pushed himself to his knees, then to his feet. She watched him get up, amazed that he was moving, for he was covered in blood. He stood a moment, steadying his large frame on his shaky feet, and started to hobble toward her, his scarred face terrifying in its determination.

"Nico." His voice was as bloody as the rest of him. "You told me you would never give up."

Nico hissed and struggled, but the mountain's weight held her flat. The man didn't seem hindered at all. He limped over and fell to his knees beside her. "What you're doing isn't fighting," he said softly. "It isn't moving forward. It isn't making anyone stronger. So long as you want to keep trying, keep fighting, I'll fight beside you. But if you've truly given up, then I'll save the Lord of Storms the trouble and kill you myself." He sat back and met her eyes with a calm, serious gaze. "Are you still with us, Nico?"

Somewhere inside her, deeper than the dark she longed to escape into, deeper than the Master's iron, undefeatable power, a tiny, sobbing voice answered, "Yes."

"Then take another breath," said Josef. "And come back."

Don't listen, the Master said. *He's sabotaging you. He doesn't want you to be stronger than him.*

Nico pushed the voice down with a firm mental hand. "No," she said.

She spoke with her own voice now, the small, pathetic thing crawling up from the depths it had been pushed into, and all at once, her spirit poured open. She ripped the darkness that had claimed her mind, shredding it to nothing, pushing free. Her body convulsed against her, clinging to the strength, the power, but she threw the demon gifts away. The second she cast them aside, the pain flooded back, and she screamed in agony as her body withered back to its true, bony shape. Her vision went dark as the nightsight left her, and her eyes burned as the demon light faded. But even as she transformed from powerful being to shuddering wreck, Nico began to sob with relief. Despite all odds, despite the terrible pain, she had not lost herself. She was still human.

Well, mostly.

When she could open her eyes again, she looked down at her once broken left arm, squinting in the dark. What she saw didn't surprise her, but knowing made it no less terrifying. There, growing out of her shoulder where her left arm should have been, was a demon claw. Its skin was as black as the Dead Mountain, and the curled hand had claws instead of fingers. The limb was awkward and ugly, far too long for her small body. Experimentally, she tried moving it, and the pain that followed sent spots dancing over her vision. When she could breathe again she clutched the arm to her side as best she could under the Heart's enormous pressure, belatedly trying to hide the hideous thing from Josef.

But Josef just looked at her with dry interest. "Can't change it back?"

Nico shook her head.

A reminder—the Master's voice was hard and cutting—*of what you threw away. When will you learn, idiot girl? You can't stop being what you are just because you say so. You're mine. You've always been mine, and I will have you in the end.*

"Not if I can help it," Nico grumbled, less sure than she would have liked.

We'll see. The Master's voice sweetened. *Just remember, I didn't force this on you. You begged to have your power back. It's only a matter of time before you beg again. When that happens, Nico, there will be no turning back.*

To make the point, her demon arm began to burn. Nico clutched it to her side, closing her eyes against the sudden tears of pain. Josef stayed on his knees beside her, waiting patiently until she opened them again.

"I'm sorry I can't let you up yet," he said, his voice straining. "The Heart's the only thing keeping the Lord of Storms from ripping us both apart."

Nico nodded, glad that she had an excuse to stay on her back. "What are we going to do?"

"I haven't decided yet," Josef said, grabbing her coat and tossing it over her.

The coat began trying to wrap itself around her as soon as it landed, but Nico paid no attention. "We have to treat your wounds," she said, eyeing the blood on the ground with growing fear.

"I'm fine for now," Josef said. "The Heart is helping me. It's been carrying me this whole time."

Nico shook her head. "Still, you have to do something before—"

Josef raised his hand sharply and she snapped her mouth shut, confused. Then she felt it as well. Deep below the crushing weight that held her down, something was pushing back. Overhead, the dark clouds churned in a great vortex, flashing with lightning as a howling wind blew ice in horizontal sheets across the ravine's top. The stone cliffs began to groan as the Heart fought back, but the storm was quickly growing into a hurricane, and the Heart, powerful as it was, was still just a sword.

With a scrape of metal, the black blade slid out of the stone, landing with a resounding clang at the Lord of Storms' feet. As it fell, the mountainous weight vanished, and the Lord of Storms stepped forward, his face pale as lightning and contorted with rage. He walked toward them, growing larger with every step as entire pieces of his body swirled between solid flesh and looming storm. His swords were no longer even a semblance of mundane weapons, but two controlled bolts of hissing blue lightning clutched in his hands.

"I'm through playing," he said, his voice true rumbling thunder as he raised the lightning in his hands. "This ends now."

Nico could only stare at the bright death coming toward them, but beside her, she felt Josef start to stand. *Of course,* she thought, *he would never sit for his death.* Jaw clenching, Nico started to stand as well, clutching her useless black arm as she struggled to her feet.

The Lord of Storms began to charge, raising his lightning swords with a shout of pure rage as he barreled toward them. Standing beside Josef, Nico squeezed her eyes shut, ready for the strike.

But the blow never came.

She waited, confused, before slowly opening her eyes. Then she blinked them again, not sure of what they showed her.

Eli stood between them and the Lord of Storms. He was still in his black thief suit, and he was standing with his arms out, perfectly still. The Lord of Storms was still as well, his lightning blades a scarce half inch from Eli's forehead.

At first Nico didn't understand why the Lord of Storms had stopped, or *how* he could have stopped a blow with such momentum. Then she saw it. Just above Eli's head, sticking out through a white line in reality, was a pure white hand. It reached through the air, the long, shapely fingers clutched around the Lord of Storms' lightning swords. The ravine was deathly silent. Nothing made a sound. Even the Lord of Storms was still, a horrified expression on his white face. In the stillness, a second line appeared beside the Lord of Storms, and another white hand shot out to grab him around the throat. The Lord of Storms made a frantic, choking sound, and then, in the space it took to blink, he was gone. The Lord of Storms had simply vanished. The white hands were gone too; so were the dark clouds overhead and the howling wind, leaving them alone in the now silent ravine.

Eli turned around, taking off his mask. "You all right, Josef?"

Josef looked at him a second and started to say something, but before he could get out a sound his eyes rolled back in his head and he toppled over, landing on the stone with a horrible, folding crunch.

"Josef!" Nico and Eli cried together, dropping to their knees beside the swordsman.

"Powers," Eli muttered, looking around. "I didn't know he had this much blood in him." He reached down and grabbed Josef's shoulder, grunting with effort as he lifted the swordsman to get a look at the wound on his back. When he saw it, his face went white.

"His back is filleted," he said, turning to Nico. "How long did he fight like this?"

"I—" Nico stopped, shuddering as she remembered the dark haze that had consumed her mind for part of the fight. "I'm not sure. Things happened quickly."

Eli looked at her, but not like he usually did. Not slyly or openly or with one of his too congenial smiles. No, he looked at her like he was seeing her for the first time, and Nico felt something clench inside her.

He knew.

He knows everything, the voice whispered.

At her side, the black, monstrous arm began to burn, and Nico clenched it closer under the drape of her coat, glad that this at least was hidden from Eli's piercing glare.

Finally, Eli turned his eyes back to Josef. "We need to get him medical attention," he said softly. "And we're not going to find that here. Let's start with getting him to the Heart. Where is it?"

Nico pointed across the ravine to the great crater in the wall where the Lord of Storms had been pinned. It was so dark now she couldn't even see the Heart's shape on the ground, but she could feel it, a large, angry presence in the dark.

Eli nodded and slid his arms under Josef's. "Help me. He's a lug, but we've a better chance of moving him than the Heart."

Nico nodded and moved to Josef's feet, grabbing one with her good arm and one with her demon claw through her coat. If Eli noticed the strange arrangement, he gave no sign. Together, grunting with effort, they lifted Josef off the ground and shuffled him over to his sword. They nearly dropped him when they reached it, but found the final bit of strength to put the swordsman down gently before flopping on the ground beside him, panting.

"I like the muscles more when he's the one carrying them," Eli groaned, leaning back against the shattered cliff face. He reached out and wrapped Josef's hand around the Heart's hilt. The unconscious grimace on the swordsman's face eased at the contact, and his breathing grew less shallow, but he still looked deathly pale.

"We have to get him to help," Nico said.

"I know that," Eli snapped, whipping his head to look at her. "Where are your manacles?"

Nico flinched. "Over there. I had to—"

Eli waved his hand dismissively. "If you're still human it couldn't have gone that badly. Get them; we're leaving in just a moment."

Nico nodded and hurried across the bloody stone with a horrible sinking feeling in her stomach. Eli had never been this sharp toward her.

He's using you because he can't move the swordsman alone, the Master said calmly. *How practical.*

Nico closed her mind to the sound and walked over to where her manacles were lying in the center of the black circle of stone. She hesitated. She could feel the absence of the stone's spirit here like a hot brand across her body. With a deep breath, she closed her eyes and grabbed her manacles, slapping them on as fast as she could. They began to buzz like insects the moment they touched her, and she felt some of the pressure ease from her mind. When they were all in place, two on her wrists, two on her ankles, and the large ring around her neck, she put her coat on properly, keeping the demon arm inside beside her rather than chance putting it through the sleeve. Throwing her hood up so her face was hidden, she turned away from the circle of dead stone and ran to where Josef had dropped his weapons. These she picked up lovingly, gathering the bandoliers of throwing knives, the sheathed swords, and the long-handled daggers he wore in his boots into her arms before hurrying back to Eli.

The thief nodded when she approached, but he didn't look at her. He was staring down the ravine they'd climbed to get here, his face invisible in the dark.

"There's no chance we can get him down that, is there?"

Nico looked down at the steep mountainside they'd scrambled up only hours ago, before everything went wrong. "No."

Eli sighed. "Desperate times, desperate measures, and all that." He stopped and looked at her, eyes flashing in the dark. "What I'm about to do, you will tell no one." His voice was quiet and deadly serious. "Swear to me on Josef himself you won't."

Nico stepped back. "What are you going to do?"

"Just swear," Eli said.

"I swear," Nico answered quickly. If it would save Josef, she didn't care if Eli turned into the Master of the Dead Mountain himself.

"Right." Eli turned away. "I'd say don't look, but there's really no point anymore. Just don't say anything. I haven't done this in a while."

Nico nodded, but Eli wasn't paying attention to her anymore. He walked to stand at Josef's feet and, after a deep breath, closed his eyes. Nico leaned forward, expecting to feel the hot rush of his open spirit crash over her like it had before, back with the bears, but she felt nothing but the cold wind. So far as she could tell, Eli was just standing there. Then, without warning, the air rippled in the dark in front of him, and a thin, white line appeared. It grew as Nico watched, cutting soundlessly through the empty space until it was as tall as Eli himself. When it reached the ground, it turned slightly, and a hole opened. Nico blinked in amazement. Hanging in the air in front of them was a door in the world. Through it she could see what looked like the inside of a small cabin, complete with a cold stone fireplace and green trees dancing outside the tiny window. She stared unbelieving even as a warm breeze floated through to brush her skin. Nico breathed it in, smelling pine and the musty scent of unused furniture. It was real, but where it was Nico had no idea.

Eli nodded and turned to grab Josef's arms again. His movement snapped Nico out of her gawking, and she scrambled to get the swordsman's legs. Using Josef's arm to move the Heart, for there was no other way to move it, they placed the black blade on his chest. Then, grunting with effort, they lifted sword and swordsman and carried them through the hole in the air.

Nico gasped as she stepped through. The biting cold of the pass vanished instantly, replaced with crisp air that felt almost balmy by comparison. Their boots clomped on the wooden floorboards, tracking in dirty snow that melted quickly as they lugged Josef through the gap in the world. The second Eli was through, the opening vanished, fading into the air with only the lingering smell of ice and stone to prove that it had ever been.

They were standing at the center of a large, well-appointed cabin filled with evening sunlight. Paintings of rustic scenes hung on the rough timber walls above dusty racks of wine bottles and sheet-covered furniture. There were even gold candlestick holders on the mantel above the large stone fireplace.

"Stop gawking and help me get him on the bed," Eli gasped, pulling Josef's shoulders toward a narrow bed in the corner. Nico scrambled to help, and together they set the swordsman down on the heavy blankets.

"We have to stop his bleeding," Eli said, pushing past Nico toward a chest at the other end of the room. He dug into it, pulling out a jug of clear liquor, bandages, and a surgeon's thread and needle. "You'll have to sew him up," he said. "Help me turn him over."

"No," said Josef's breathy, pained voice.

Eli and Nico were at his side in an instant.

"Don't be stupid," Eli said. "And don't talk. We're going to get you patched up."

"No," Josef said again, shaking his head. "The Heart is telling me it's going to handle things."

"What?" Eli cried. "Is the pain making you delusional? You can't even hear spirits and you're telling me your sword is promising to un-fillet your back?"

"Something like that," Josef whispered. "The Heart also says that it has a lot more experience in keeping swordsmen alive than you do, and that you should mind your own business."

Eli jerked back. "And does it have anything else to add?"

"Yes." Josef's voice began to slur and fade. "Don't move me for two days."

"Two days?" Eli shouted. "We're supposed to sit here and watch you bleed for two days?"

But Josef didn't answer. He lay on the bed, eyes closed, his chest moving in long, shallow breaths beneath the Heart of War, which lay across his chest from chin to knees with his white-knuckled hands still clutching the hilt. With a long, angry sigh, Eli pushed away from the bed and began shoving the first-aid supplies back into the trunk. Nico watched, biting her lip as Eli walked over to the dusty wine stand, grabbed a bottle at random, and flopped down on the floor.

When it was clear he was more interested in digging the old cork out with one of Josef's throwing knives than giving her vital information, Nico asked the burning question. "Where are we?"

"Safe," Eli said, popping the cork at last. "Well, safer. We're still in the Sleeping Mountains, though not as far north as we were, and much farther east, about fifty miles from the coast. This is one of Giuseppe Monpress's many hideouts. The old fox set them up years ago as refuges of last resort in case things got too hot, which explains the extravagant furnishings." He cast a disapproving eye at the richly appointed wine rack. "He could never stand to be without his luxuries. We're still technically inside Council lands, but no patrols come up here."

Something about the way he said that made Nico distinctly uncomfortable. "Why not?"

Eli took a long drink from the bottle. "Because this is bandit land," he said, wiping his mouth on his sleeve. "The Council can claim it all they want, but without influence in the area, it's all talk. Izo is the real power here." He took another swig. "Bastard has a bounty higher than mine."

"Will he be a problem?" Nico said.

"Shouldn't be," Eli answered, leaning back against the cabin wall. "Not unless we make trouble for him, which we might have to." A strange expression passed over his face. "I didn't just choose this place because it was safe and far away. This is also the closest spot I knew to where Sted is."

Nico's eyes widened. "It worked then! You learned where Sted is!" She couldn't believe it. Her plan had worked! But Eli didn't look happy.

"Yes," he said slowly. "Among other things."

Nico flinched at the bitterness in his voice. The black arm began to ache beneath her coat, and Nico clutched it as subtly as she could. It didn't matter, though. Eli was staring into his bottle with a focus so intense, she got the feeling he was not looking at the wine so much as avoiding looking at her. A cold, heavy feeling settled at the base of Nico's stomach, and she scooted closer to Josef, tilting her head down so she didn't have to watch Eli staring anywhere but her.

You always knew he would turn on you. The Master's voice was soft and coy. *It was only a matter of time.*

Nico put her head on her knees. Outside, the sun sank lower. It was going to be a long two days.

Benehime stood in her white nothing, a furious scowl on her perfect white face as she stared at the man hanging suspended by his thumbs in the air before her.

You presume too much! she hissed, her voice like cut glass as she paced back and forth in front of the Lord of Storms' dangling body. *I told you to stay away. I told you to let it be. And still you disobey!*

On her last word, she slapped him across the face. Wherever she touched him, his body broke apart into black, flashing clouds. The Lord of Storms cried out, his voice more gale than scream.

You are my creation! she roared. *Mine to do with as I see fit! To use in what work I choose! A tool does not act without its master, or have you forgotten what you are?*

She lowered her hand, and the Lord of Storms slowly pulled himself back together. But when his face reformed from the thunderheads, his murderous expression was even harsher than hers.

"It is you who has forgotten, Shepherdess," he growled through gritted teeth. "You knew the Daughter of the Dead Mountain was still alive. You knew, and you let her wander free, all because of your shameful intoxication with that thief! Have you forgotten what happened the last time she awoke? Have you forgotten your duty?"

I forget nothing! Benehime began to stalk back and forth in front of him. *Do you think I fear the demon? The little worm trapped under a rock he can never lift? In the five thousand years since I tore the spirit from the mountain and flung the dead stone on top of him, the creature has never managed to get so much as a tendril over the edge of my seal. The seeds he sends out are a nuisance, nothing more. And even if he succeeded, even if a seed managed to grow large enough to be a real threat, I would just trap the new demon as I trapped its father.*

"And at what cost?" the Lord of Storms yelled, straining against the unbreakable force of the Lady's will that held him in place. "I don't know if you've taken time from your little one-sided love affair to notice, but this world isn't what it was, Shepherdess! This isn't some nuisance seed grown too big. If the Daughter of the Dead Mountain were to fully awaken and start feeding in earnest, we would need another great mountain to keep her down, and we both know you no longer have one to spare. Have you forgotten what's at *stake*?"

He jerked against his bonds like he was trying to throw his arms out, but all he managed was to set himself swinging slightly in her hold. Still, from the way her eyes narrowed, it was clear Benehime didn't need the gesture to know what he meant.

All around them, at the edges of her white world where she did not look, something was moving. Everything was still perfect, still flawless white, but beyond the white perfection, something pressed against the walls of her world. Long claws scraped at the barrier like knives against a sheet stretched taut, probing and searching for weakness. The movements were small, faint, gray shadows, but they were everywhere, pressing in on every inch of the Shepherdess's domain.

"They never get tired, do they?" the Lord of Storms whispered. "That is the fate that awaits all of us if you forget your duty."

I forget nothing, the Lady said, layering cold power into the words until he writhed beneath her voice, his body flashing between flesh and storm. But even her displeasure was not enough to keep the Lord of Storms from raising his head to met her eyes again.

"Everything I do." He spat the words at her. "Everything I've ever done has been in your service. If you will not let me do my job, then dissolve me back into wind and water right now, because I won't stop until all demonseeds, all threats to your domain, are crushed, even those who hide in your favorite's shadow."

Enough! The Lady's voice echoed through the white nothing, and the Lord of Storm's body dissolved into cloud, his cry of pain becoming a low rumble of thunder.

You would be so lucky if I dissolved you, she said, glaring at the thunderhead floating where the Lord of Storms' suspended body had been only a second before. *But you belong to me, and I have no desire to toss you aside just yet. I have been too soft with you for too long. Go and blow out your anger over the sea. We'll see if some time as a mindless storm will help you remember the obedience you owe me.*

She waved her hand and the thunderhead vanished. Baring her teeth at the place where he had been, the Lady whirled around and stalked back to her sphere.

In all her white world, the sphere alone was vibrant and colorful. Inside that perfect bubble, the world, her world, hung in suspended beauty. Continents floated on a flat, glassy sea, their wrinkled faces covered with tiny forests, golden deserts, and rolling plains dotted with tiny grazing creatures. White-capped mountains rose from the forested hills, their snow-covered peaks cutting through the clouds like islands on a second, sky-bound sea. Deep beneath the oceans, sea trenches scored the heavy layers of stone that filled the lower half of the sphere, cutting down to the glittering red flow of the magma that pooled at the sphere's lowest point.

Benehime's eyes flicked past all this with the contempt born of long familiarity, darting past the mountains and the glittering rivers to a wild stretch of sea. The moment she focused on the sea, the Lord of Storms appeared above it. In his true form, he was the size of a small continent and utterly mad, a roving war of wind and water. As she watched, the storm spun in circles, eating the lesser clouds, whipping the sea into a froth. Storm surges forty feet high began to wash over the southern tip of the eastern continent, soaking the desert beneath a brine of terrified water. Benehime watched as a medium-sized city was washed under, and then she turned away in disgust.

Who was he to think he could tell her things she did not already know? She was the Shepherdess, had been the Shepherdess since the beginning. Everything within the sphere was hers alone to direct, to control. In the balance of power between her and her brothers, this was her domain. She turned back to the sphere, looking not at the growing storm, but north to the wooded foothills of the white-capped mountains.

She laid her hands lovingly along the curve of the sky. Angry as she was, there was opportunity here. The Lord of Storms had disobeyed her, raised his sword to her favorite, but he had also forced Eli to use the power she'd given him to travel her sphere freely for the first time in years. He'd shown he was willing to use gifts he'd sworn to her face he would never touch again in order to save his swordsman. What other slips might he be willing to make if pressed hard enough?

A smile spread across her white lips. Now that her darling had decided to play with things she'd warned him against, life was going to be a great deal more difficult for him. Usually, this would be the point where she stepped in to help, but not this time. This time, the Lady decided, she would make Eli come to her. This time, she'd let him stay on the hook, let things get as bad as they could get. Only when he was broken and defeated would he realize what he had thrown away. That, when he begged for her help, was when she would save him and bring him home at last to her side.

Benehime sank down beside her sphere, watching the northern forest where, somewhere, her favorite was sleeping. Behind her, ignored, the claws continued to slide over the edge of her white world while far, far away, too distant for any ears except her own, something screamed in endless hunger. Benehime turned her head and leaned forward farther still, deftly focusing her attention on the tiny world inside the sphere until it was all she knew.

CHAPTER 11

Gin was growling deep in his throat. Miranda reached down and pinched him, hard, but that only sent the growl deeper into the dog's chest and did nothing at all for the predatory glare the ghosthound fixed on the overdressed man riding in front of them. She pinched him one more time, then gave up, flopping forward against the prickly fur of the dog's neck. The growling had been going on for nearly two weeks, but she couldn't really blame Gin. She would growl at Sparrow too if she had the throat for it. Traveling with the man was insufferable.

"He's too slow," Gin mumbled through his long, clenched teeth. "He packs like an idiot, can barely set up a camp, wakes up too late, and he eats too much."

"Why are you still complaining?" Miranda said. "It didn't help yesterday; it didn't help two weeks ago. What makes you think it'll help now?"

"We'd have been there last week if that fool didn't take two hours every morning getting his clothes right." Gin's fur bristled. "We're in the middle of nowhere and that idiot acts like he's going to a party every night. And he won't stop *flickering*." The dog shook himself. "If looking at him didn't make me feel ill I'd eat him just to make it stop."

Miranda rolled her eyes. That again. She'd stopped pressing the dog for an explanation of Sparrow's "flickering" days ago, but getting him to stop complaining about it was like asking him to stop growling—impossible. She sat up again, looking over Gin's ears at the path they'd been following since yesterday. Sparrow was well ahead of them, guiding his nervous horse between the thick trees like a Zarin dandy leading a shy partner through a new and intricate dance. He was certainly dressed the part. His plumed hat, orange silk coat, and chocolate-brown trousers tucked into gold-tooled boots would have been at home in any Zarin ballroom. Here in the ragged woods of the mountain foothills he looked like a misplaced tropical bird.

Gin shook his head, and the growling was back, stronger than ever. "Tell me again why we can't just leave him in the woods."

"Because as Sara's second, he's the highest-ranking Council official we've got," Miranda said. "And he has all the papers we need to bribe Izo. Trust me, I would have left him at the Zarin gate if I'd thought we could get away with it."

"Sara would have done better to send more like the other man," Gin said. "Save us all some time."

Miranda agreed. The morning they left Zarin Miranda had been met at the gate by Sparrow and another, a man who called himself Tesset. She had no idea if that was his last name or his first, maybe neither. Sara's goons seemed to be one-name-only kind of people. Unlike Sparrow, however, Tesset had shown up in sturdy travel clothes, a long, brown coat and worn-in boots, and carrying a small pack. She'd been a little concerned that he had arrived with no horse, but she'd found out quickly that the lack of a mount didn't hinder him. The man could run forever, and Sparrow's pace wasn't exactly breathtaking.

Right now, however, he was nowhere to be seen. That wasn't unusual. Tesset tended to disappear for hours, running ahead to scout the area and keep them on track. Miranda appreciated his skill, but his excursions meant she was alone with Sparrow and the inane conversations he started every few hours. If Tesset didn't vanish without a word every morning, Miranda would have insisted on scouting with him just for a break.

Gin's growling hitched, and Miranda looked up to see that Sparrow had stopped. A moment later, she saw why. Tesset was standing beside him, his dull, brown clothes and short, brown hair blending in with the undergrowth. Miranda smiled and nudged Gin forward. She didn't care if he'd come back to report they were about to be eaten by cannibals; any break in the monotony was welcome.

The two men stopped talking as she approached, and Sparrow's horse began its terrified dancing that always occurred whenever Gin was closer than ten feet.

"Ah, Miranda," Sparrow said, getting his horse under control with some difficulty. "Splendid timing. Tesset here was just informing me that we're closing in on our destination."

"Two miles straight ahead," Tesset said, reaching out with a calm, strong hand to grab Sparrow's horse before it threw him. "We've been passing his watchposts for the last two days, so we should be getting a welcome soon."

"Two days?" Miranda said, glancing around at the deep woods. "I haven't seen anything."

"You wouldn't," Tesset said. "Unless you knew where to look."

"Spoken like a true expert," Sparrow said, leaning over his now subdued horse's neck. "Tesset here is the closest legal thing you'll find to a guide for this area."

Miranda gave Tesset a curious look, and he shrugged his broad shoulders. "I grew up around here," he said simply. "Of course, that was back when these hills were nothing but a patchwork of ragged gangs, before Izo pulled them all together. In a strange way, Izo's made it easier for us. If things were still the way they were in the old days, we would have had to bribe half a dozen petty bandit lords by now."

"The benefits of unified government are myriad for all walks of life," Sparrow said with a sigh.

Miranda ignored him. "How did Izo do it?" she asked. "Pull the gangs together, I mean. Have there been other bandit kings?"

"None like Izo," Tesset said, shaking his head. "There've been a few leaders whose gangs got pretty big, but nothing on Izo's level. Right from the start, Izo was smart as well as strong, very charismatic, and, most important, ruthless. He raided other bandits as much as he raided the Council, and eventually there was no one left strong enough to stand up to him. No one knows exactly how many men he controls, but considering the reports from the border towns, I'd say at least five thousand fighting troops, maybe more. Anyway"—he turned and started walking again—"we'll see for ourselves in a moment. He's already sent a welcoming party."

Miranda scowled. "How do you—"

"He's right," Gin said, pricking his ears up. "Men and horses approaching from the north." He gave Tesset a respectful look. "That man must have ghosthound ears to hear that."

"Or advanced knowledge," Miranda murmured. "Keep on guard."

Gin nodded and they began to follow Tesset, who was still dragging Sparrow's horse by the reins, down the path. Miranda sat high on Gin's neck, straining to catch the jingle of approaching horses, but all she heard were birdcalls and the wind in the trees overhead. After several hundred feet, Tesset stopped again and stood in the center of the path, waiting. Gin's ears were swiveling madly, but to Miranda the forest was achingly silent. She was about to lean down and ask the hound what he heard when the men stepped out from behind the trees.

There were too many to count. The forest was suddenly full of men dressed in drab colors, sitting on their horses like they'd been waiting. Though no glint of metal showed at their hips or boots or anywhere else knives were generally kept, Miranda was sure they were armed to the teeth and would show it well enough if provoked, and she kept a firm hand on Gin's fur. Tesset and Sparrow, however, looked perfectly calm, even a little bored by the men's sudden appearance. They waited patiently until the oldest of the bandits, a tall, lanky man with prematurely gray hair, nudged his horse forward.

"Welcome, strangers," the man said, his voice thick with a coarse, mountain accent that turned words into gravel. "What brings you so bold into King Izo's trees?"

"Diplomacy, good sir," Sparrow said, his words dripping with politeness. "We seek an audience with your master, and his trees seemed a good place to start."

"Audience, eh?" The bandit scratched his scarred chin. "And what does a peacock like you want from the king of bandits? We already got a fool."

This raised a huge laugh from the men, but Sparrow's smile only deepened. "It's Sparrow, actually, and I come on behalf of the Council of Thrones to make your master a very generous offer."

"Generous?" The bandit's eyebrows shot up. "Now I know you're lying. The Council don't know the meaning of the word, not without a hook wrapped inside. Why don't you save our time and your skin and just tell us the catch now, before we string you up for the crows?"

"Nothing would delight me more," Sparrow said. "But my offer is for Izo's ears alone."

The bandit gave him a long, hard look, then shrugged. "Your death wish, pretty bird. Follow us."

The bandits turned and started into the woods, falling into a loose circle around Miranda, Sparrow, and Tesset. Their formation was ragged, and Miranda got the feeling they were used to riding much closer around prisoners, but several of the horses were already wide-eyed being so close to Gin, and the bandits weren't taking any chances. As they rode, Miranda could see how the bandits had snuck up on them. Every bit of their tack, from the bridles to the stirrups and even their horses' hooves, was wrapped in wool cloth to make no sound. They rode in absolute silence, communicating through hand movements when they talked at all. In answer, Gin began to creep as well, matching their silence as though it were a competition. Tesset was also silent, his boots soundless on the leaf-strewn ground. By contrast, Sparrow was garishly noisy, his heavy bags and flashy tack creaking and jingling like a circus cart.

They made their way through the woods and onto a well-maintained road leading up a hill between two cliffs. Though she saw no one, Miranda could hear the creak of bowstrings on the rocks overhead. Their guide whistled, and the creaking bowstrings fell silent. Grinning wide, the bandits started up the hill again, motioning for their guests to follow. The narrow path forced them to walk single file, and Miranda was cursing her luck at being forced to stay behind Sparrow yet again, especially since he kept stopping. But a few steps later, she understood why. There, just beyond the pass, lay what Miranda could only describe as a bandit capital.

It was a box canyon cut out between two rocky hills and ringed with large conifers that hid it from the surrounding woods. Inside the canyon, wooden buildings of all sizes, from one-room log huts to enormous timber halls, covered every inch of the sandy ground. Wooden lookout towers sprouted like weeds from every other rooftop, often connected to other towers by rickety rope bridges, and every one of them flew the same red banner: a crudely painted black fist floating in the air above a mountain, ready to slam down.

People came out to watch as the bandits escorted their guests into the city, and Miranda was shocked to see women and young children peering down from curtained windows. The roads between the houses were hard-packed dirt, but there were torches at every intersection, each stocked and ready for the evening lighting as in any civilized city. There were shops with their doors open to the fine weather, restaurants with the day's offerings drawn in chalk on wooden boards, and even glass windows in a few of the larger buildings. Looking down the roads as they passed, she saw a mule-driven mill beside a bursting grain silo. Another road led to a slaughterhouse with a pen full of pigs and chickens and a sign advertising fresh meat, and somewhere just beyond that she could hear a smithy working, the banging hammers accompanied by the acid smell of steelworking.

Miranda gripped Gin's fur. Steel usually meant swords, good

ones. As they rode toward the center of the canyon town, she saw more and more men openly wearing weapons. Their swords were not the mismatched collection of stolen goods she would have expected, but standardized blades from the same smithy. Likewise, the drab clothes the men wore weren't actually ragtag, but uniform sets cut from the same cloth. Subtly, her fingers crept over her rings, gently waking her spirits. What kind of a bandit camp was this?

At the center of the canyon the buildings opened up, and they entered what looked like a town square. Only here, the square was more like a great, sandy lot, and at its center, rather than the fountains or wells or community halls generally found at the heart of towns, an enormous pit had been dug down into the floor of the canyon. The pit was about eight feet deep and circular, braced along the edges with wooden beams to keep the soil from sliding. At one end, a raised platform stuck out over the pit's edge, forming a small stage. The other was dominated by a large tower with a covered pavilion at the top. Red and black banners hung from every available ledge, surrounding the pit in a blaze of crimson. Miranda stared out the corner of her eye as they rode by, trying to figure out the pit's purpose. They had almost reached the other side of the square before she realized it was an arena.

She'd heard about places where men fought to the death for the crowd's entertainment, but seeing one in person made her feel ill. Of course, she shouldn't have been surprised. This was Izo's city. What more could one expect from a man who called himself the Bandit King? She'd let the town's unexpected civility lure her into a sense of false security, but the large, brown stains on the pit's sandy floor were enough to cure her of any further delusion. Miranda shuddered at the barbarity.

As they left the central square, the buildings changed. If this were a normal town, she would have said they were entering the government district. The construction was more stone than wood now, the buildings taller and wider, with red banners spilling from their windows like bloody waterfalls. Several buildings had their doors flung open to let in daylight, and Miranda could see the front rooms of barracks, training halls, tack stores, and weapon stocks, all well supplied. A block away, acrid forge smoke belched from a set of tall chimneys. These were matched by another set farther down the road, and Miranda began to wonder just how many forges this city had.

That thought was put out of her mind when their guide led them around a blind corner and stopped at the entrance of the most intimidating building Miranda had ever seen. Unlike the others, it was all stone and iron, built directly into the cliff face. There were no windows, only doors that led out onto archer galleries with red banners the size of Gin hanging from their ramparts. The fortress was fronted by a great gatehouse with a barbed portcullis raised halfway so that its jagged spikes hung over the entry like hideous teeth ready to snap. Inside the gatehouse, the tiny paved yard was full of armed men sharpening their swords, obviously bored. They did not look up as the new arrivals filed past, but Miranda could feel their eyes on her as their bandit guide led them through the yard to the iron-bound doors of the hall itself.

Here they dismounted, the bandits holding Sparrow's horse as he jumped down. No one offered to hold Gin, and that made Miranda smile. Outnumbered and surrounded as they were, it was comforting to remember she still had power on her side.

The citadel doors were thrown open to let in the afternoon light, revealing what was clearly not so much a room as a natural cave improved for human habitation. The stone floor had been chiseled flat and the walls braced with wooden beams to keep the stone from collapsing. It was quite dark, and the sparse torches seemed to make it only darker. From where she stood in the sunlight, Miranda could see only about twenty feet inside to where the hall had been split in half by a wrought-metal gate marked with the same fist and mountain as the banners outside.

Sparrow squinted into the dark hall. "Very impressive," he said, sounding decidedly unimpressed. "But we didn't come all this way to see a cave. Where is Izo?"

The bandit grinned and pointed at the gate. "Through there. You can leave your horse with the boys. They'll take care of your things."

"Which is why I'm taking them with me," Sparrow said, unhitching his bags and flinging them over his shoulder with surprising ease.

The bandits laughed at that, and their guide gave Sparrow a knowing wink before waving for them to follow him into the dark hall. The iron gate opened before they reached it, and a man stepped forward to greet them. The moment she saw him, Miranda began to shiver. She didn't know how she knew, but she knew all the way to her core that something was terribly wrong with the man in front of her. He wore no weapon she could see, and he was skeletally thin. His face was pale and hollow, and though his clothes were fine, they hung strangely limp on his body, like rags on a scarecrow. Behind her, Gin began to growl deep in his throat.

Even their bandit guide seemed a little put off by the man. He went through the gate without looking at him, motioning for his guests to follow. The strange man just watched them pass, his eyes eerily bright in the dark as he shut the gate behind them.

On the other side of the iron gate was a smaller but far grander chamber. Fat torches hung on the walls, their smoky light painting everything in flickering reds and oranges. Rich rugs lined the stone floor and gold glittered from the ornate wooden cabinets that lined both walls. But all of it—the silks, the rare metals, the chandelier of antlers hanging from the high cave ceiling—was just a guide for the eyes, leading them toward the back of the cave. There, on a raised stage lined with an impressive display of weaponry, below a great red banner marked with the same icon of the closed fist and mountain she'd seen all through the city, was an enormous iron chair covered with furs, and seated on the furs was a man.

Miranda blinked. For all the buildup, he was not particularly impressive. Though he was sitting, it was clear he was not remarkably tall, his shoulders not particularly broad. His black hair was streaked with white, and his face, though perhaps handsome once, was now old before his time, worn by years of hard living and bad food. His eyes, however, were sharp as daggers as they watched the newcomers enter his hall. His gaze jumped from one to the next without even a raised eyebrow for Gin. He wore no jewels, no weapons, but plain as he looked, Miranda would have known who he was even without the throne. She'd seen his picture on Whitefall's wall. This was Izo the Bandit King, the third-most-wanted criminal in Council history.

"Well, well, Garret," Izo said in a deep, rich voice as the skeletally thin man climbed up to stand beside him. "What do you bring?"

Their bandit guide bowed. "Messengers, my king. They say they're from the Council."

Izo began to chuckle. "Well, well, fifteen years of getting the cold shoulder from Zarin, and here you are. To what do I owe the honor?"

Sparrow stepped forward with a flourish, his voice booming theatrically through the cave. "Greetings, great Izo, lord of bandits. My name is Sparrow, assistant to Sara, Head Wizard of the Council. This"—he gestured toward Miranda—"is Miranda Lyonette of the Spirit Court, and"—his hand shifted again—"Tesset, our guard and guide. We have been sent here by the Council of Thrones to make you an offer."

"An offer?" Izo grinned at his bandit. "If the Council wants me to stop raiding their borders, you're a pretty sorry showing, little bird."

"Please," Sparrow said. "Such matters are between you and the northern kingdoms. We are here to find a missing wizard, a man named Heinricht Slorn, who we believe has come to your lands."

"Ah," Izo said. "I see. You want to know if I have him."

"Or the freedom to search for him in your woods without having to worry about waking up with a slit throat," Sparrow said.

"The woods are fraught with danger," Izo said with a shrug. "I'm not a charity house, Mr. Sparrow, but I could perhaps see my way toward helping you, if the price was fair."

"I have been given the authority to be very fair in this matter," Sparrow assured him.

"Is that so?" Izo sat back, stroking the stubble on his chin. "Give me an example."

"Well," Sparrow said. "Take your latest incursion into Council lands. Your men burned and pillaged the city of West Clef, and Markel of Sorran, the rightful lord of West Clef, is understandably upset. He's been pushing the Council to formally declare war on your little operation for years. Now he's got a few hundred dead tradesmen and a burned Council tax office to add to his complaint. He may be a small border lord, but his words are falling on very sympathetic ears at the moment. I wouldn't be surprised if the Council voted to take action within the year. However"—Sparrow raised a long finger—"should your help guide us to our man, alive and well, I can promise you that no declaration of aggression will ever get past committee. A great promise indeed for such a small inconvenience on your part, don't you agree?"

The thin man leaned over and whispered something in Izo's ear. The bandit nodded and began to smile.

"Great indeed," he said, sitting forward. "But why are you

wasting my time with talk of missing wizards? Why not get straight to why you're really here?"

For a moment, Sparrow looked surprised, but the expression was gone so quickly Miranda thought she'd imagined it. Izo, however, missed nothing.

"I'm no backward mountain horse thief," he said slowly, shifting his eyes to Miranda. "I make it my business to know everything I can about what goes on in the Council Kingdoms, but even if I were ignorant as you seem to think me, I would know the name Miranda Lyonette, the poor Spiritualist who keeps bungling the capture of Eli Monpress."

Miranda stepped forward, red-faced, but stopped when she felt a hard grip on her wrist. She looked over to see Tesset shaking his head.

"Did you think you could just slip her past me?" Izo scoffed. "Did you think I would not know? You said yourself, this is my land. I know everything that happens here, and I would never miss something as splendidly convenient as the three of you just happening to show up in my town the day after Monpress himself mysteriously appears inside my borders."

This time even Sparrow looked shocked, and Izo grinned so wide Miranda could count his gold-capped teeth.

"Oh, I knew," he said. "I was thinking of how to catch him myself. Ninety-eight thousand gold standards will catch any man's attention. Though, now that you're here, things are more interesting than simple money." He turned his smile to Sparrow. "I may be a bandit, messenger bird, but I'm not stupid. I know what kind of power your mistress Sara can throw around in the Council when her mind is set."

Sparrow made a good show of looking abashed. "I would never imply—"

Izo waved his hand. "Save the flowery talk. Truth be told, I don't really care why you came into my lands, be it hunting missing wizards or thief catching. But if you want to do whatever it is you came here to do, then here are my terms." He leaned forward on his throne. "First, I want all charges and bounties against me dropped. Second, I want full recognition of my sovereign right to the northlands, from the Sorran border to the mountain peaks and from the edge of the Shaper lands all the way to the eastern sea."

He sat back when he was finished, enjoying the stunned silence.

It was Miranda who recovered first. "Impossible!" she cried. "Sorran to the peaks? From the Shaper lands to the sea? That would make you the largest kingdom in the Council! It's never going to happen. You're a bandit and a murderer, not a king. You have no sovereign right to anything."

Izo gave her a hard look. "Is this the Council's answer?"

"Not at all," Sparrow said, cutting in front of Miranda before she could say anything else. "*If* you help us find Heinricht Slorn, and get us Monpress alive, *and* we are able to bring both safely back to Zarin, Sara will see to it that you become a king in full."

"Done!" Izo said, standing up. He marched down from his throne and took Sparrow's hand, shaking it hard. "Garret, make our guests comfortable. Tonight, we plan a trap even the famous Monpress can't weasel out of."

Their bandit guide saluted and waved for them to follow. Miranda was still trying to get a word in edgewise, but Sparrow's sharp heel was digging into her foot. She gave him a murderous glare as the bandit led them out through the iron gate and back into the hall. They walked in silence down the steps and under the gatehouse. When they reached the main road, their guide ducked almost immediately into a small alley, stopping at a wooden guest-house right beside the keep. Garret left them with promises they'd be called when Izo wanted to see them again, and Sparrow tipped their guide well before dumping his bags on the largest of the soft beds downstairs.

"Well," he said. "I don't see how that could have gone better."

"Really?" Miranda said. "Because I don't see how it could have gone worse. Izo? A king? You just sold a crown to the most violent criminal in Council history."

"It's not like he's getting his crown on the cheap," Sparrow said. "He *is* sacrificing a ninety-eight-thousand gold-standard bounty."

"Men like Izo don't deserve crowns," she grumbled. "Do you honestly think Sara will be all right with this?"

"Sara will be delighted." Sparrow's voice grew very dry. "Remember, sweetheart, I've worked with her far longer than you, and I've seen her make men kings for less. Monpress is something special to her, more than Slorn, and far more than you or I. If letting some bandit play king is all it takes, she'll consider him cheaply bought."

"But it's not right," Miranda said.

"Who cares?" Sparrow answered. "If you get a chance to nab Eli and clean off the dirt he kicked all over your shiny white tower, what do you care about how he was caught? So a bad man gets away with his crimes, so what? It happens every day. That's how the real world works, sweetheart. Bad people doing bad things and getting rich off it. Powers, girl, for all we know, this may be the best thing that could happen to this situation. At least if Izo's a king under the Council of Thrones, he can't go raiding his neighbors anymore. Did you think about that?"

Miranda bit her lip.

"Didn't think so," Sparrow said. "We need you here, Miranda. You're the one who knows Eli. Don't get all moral on us about things you can't change. Focus on the good. Catch Eli, go home a hero, and let us deal with Izo. Okay?"

"Okay," Miranda said, stomping up the stairs toward the loft bedroom.

There was no way Gin could fit into the small house. So the

moment she got upstairs, Miranda threw open the window only to find the ghosthound had anticipated her, jumping up and making himself comfortable on the roof of the neighboring building, much to the alarm of the current inhabitants. He crawled over when he saw her open the shutters and stuck his head in.

"I hate to say it," he growled, "but the bird boy has a point."

"I know," Miranda snapped, flopping down on the bed. "I don't want to talk about it. I'm done with Council politics. Let's catch the thief and go home."

Gin rested his jaw on the windowsill. "How are you going to catch him?"

"I've got a plan," Miranda said, burying her face in the pillow. "This time, he'll be the one who's surprised."

Gin gave her a suspicious look before pulling his head out again and setting about the serious business of cleaning the road grime off his silver, shifting coat.

Izo sat on his throne for a long time after his guests left, taking in the feeling. After so many years of scrabbling at the edges, fighting like dogs with other bandits over every inch of backward woodland, he was almost there. He would be Izo the King.

"Just as the Master promised."

Izo flinched at the cold voice and turned to find Sezri standing over him, a skeletal horror draped in a mockery of flesh, his dark eyes glowing in the sunken shadows of his sockets. Izo turned away. He had no intention of tainting his moment of triumph with the thin man's creepiness.

"The Master is with us always," Sezri continued. "Watching, listening; nothing is hidden from him. Truly, you could ask for no better ally."

"Aye," Izo said, standing up. "And I've paid for it. Your 'Master' had first pick of every captive we've taken over the last three years, not to mention all our wizard children. There's not a soul in this camp who can hear the winds anymore, thanks to you. Your master said he'd make me king."

"And you're well on your way to being one."

"By a lucky guess, and none of your doing," Izo sneered, walking over to his weapon wall. "This Monpress tip was just a lucky break for you. How could you know he'd be up here? Or that the Council dogs would be on his trail? I was the one who put two and two together and made the deal, so don't act like I should be falling down on my knees to your boss. I pay my tribute and I'll reap my reward, but don't think you can lord a lucky strike over me and call it a plan."

Sezri stared at him, his too-wide eyes brighter than ever. "You should be more careful with your assumptions," he said slowly. "The Master has hands everywhere, and he plays a game on a higher stratum than any of us can comprehend. The arrival of Sara's monsters, the appearance of Monpress, your own position at the nexus, it was all laid out by the Master, and it will all fall apart without his continued goodwill. You would do well to remember that."

Izo sneered. "We'll see."

Sezri just smiled, a strange baring of teeth that was more unsettling than his glare. "That reminds me," he said. "In order to make sure the capture of Monpress goes smoothly, our Master has sent another of his children to help us."

He made a beckoning motion with his skeletal hand, and Izo's guard went up. Sure enough, though his room was ordered empty and locked at all times, a figure stepped out of the shadows beside the wrought-iron door. Izo gritted his teeth. He hated how they could do that, slip through shadows like fish through water.

Izo felt even less happy about this new arrival when the man stepped into the torchlight. He wasn't sure what he'd been expecting, another skeleton like Sezri, perhaps. Whatever it was, this man was not it. He stomped out of the shadows, a giant, taller than Izo's best bruisers and built like a bull. Scars ran across his body, some pale and ancient, others red and angry, crisscrossing his muscles like deep-dug canals. His clothes were filthy and they hung from him with the same shapeless weight as Sezri's dark rags. He stood crooked, with his left shoulder higher than his right, as though his left arm pained him. Izo understood that any man with scars like those could be expected to carry a serious injury, but whatever was wrong with the man's arm was hidden by the long, dirty cape he wore flung over one shoulder.

Sezri waited until the man was fully in the light before continuing. "Izo," he said, "may I introduce Berek Sted."

Izo's eyes went wide, and he began to grin in spite of himself. "Berek Sted?" he said, all anger forgotten. "*The* Berek Sted? The famous pit fighter? Powers, man, you're a legend!" He grabbed Sted's uncovered hand and shook it hard. "The boys here love you. I tried to find you to invite you to join us a year ago, but you'd disappeared." His voice trailed off. A foot and a half above him, Sted was glaring down, his eyes shining with the same unsettling light as Sezri's.

Izo dropped his hand and stepped back. "I guess I know why, now," he muttered. "Still, it's an honor to have a legendary fighter in my camp."

"I didn't come here to put on a show for bandits," Sted growled, his scarred face pulling up in a sneer. "I came because this is where Josef Liechten will come."

Izo paused. "Josef Liechten?"

"Monpress's pet swordsman," Sezri said. "Sted is here to deal with him. With Josef out of the way, Monpress's party should be no trouble at all." He smiled wider, forcing Izo to look away from the hideous sight of a human face pulled in ways it was never meant to go. "Is not the Master thoughtful?"

"Very," Izo muttered.

"You will call the Council dogs tonight," Sezri went on as though Izo had not spoken. "Let them take the thief and the girl he keeps with him while Sted handles Liechten. Monpress is fickle, so we may not have long to act. Set it up quickly and you will be king before the month is out."

Izo couldn't help grinning at that thought. "There, at least, we agree," he said, stomping down the stairs from his throne. "I'm going to make the rounds. We meet at sundown. I want both of you there."

Neither of the men answered, but Izo just kept walking. He was king here, not them, and he would not stoop so low as to look back to see if they would follow. Instead, he pushed his way through the iron gate and stomped into the yard, yelling for his guard. Tonight, everything needed to be perfect, for tomorrow he was going to make himself king.

Sted watched the iron gate swing closed with a deafening clang. "He's older than I expected," he said when the sound of Izo's shouting had faded. "Shorter, too."

"Izo has been the Master's servant for many years," Sezri said. "Our numbers are greatly increased by his ambitions."

"Who cares about your numbers?" Sted snorted, shifting his arm beneath his cape. "When do I get to face Liechten?"

"That depends on you." Sezri's voice was decidedly colder this time. "Follow the plan and you will have everything you desire. Be an idiot and I'll rip the seed right out of you and give it to someone more worthy."

Sted gave the skeletal man a sneering smile. "Is that what the voice tells you to do?"

Sezri's eyes glowed brighter than ever. "He doesn't have to," he said, his voice carrying a hint of the strange double harmonic Sted had come to associate with well-entrenched seeds. "Unlike you, or the girl who had that seed before you, I am an obedient servant of the Mountain. In the end, the Master's desires will be fulfilled. I suggest you make sure you're on the right side."

"I've only got one side," Sted said, shifting his arm below the cloak again. "Mine."

"So I've heard," Sezri said. "You should watch yourself, Sted."

"I do," Sted said, turning away. "Better than anyone." He stepped sideways, slipping into the shadows. "See you at the briefing."

He gave the thin demonseed one last smirk before vanishing into the shadows. Sezri glared a moment at the empty space where he had been, and then vanished as well, disappearing like a puff of smoke on the wind, leaving the great hall empty and dark as the sun began to set behind the mountains.

CHAPTER 12

Josef woke up to horrible, blinding pain. His back felt like someone had removed his spine and replaced it with a hot iron rod, and the rest of him didn't feel much better. On the off chance his lungs worked, he took an experimental breath. It hurt. Powers, did it hurt, but not more than anything else. That gave him hope, and, very slowly, he opened his eyes.

He was lying in a bed in a cabin. Dappled sunlight streamed in through the open window, bringing with it the smell of mountains and trees. Josef frowned. He dimly remembered Eli and Nico moving him. After that, things went blank. He could tell from the light that they were no longer high in the mountains, but where?

Taking another deep breath in an attempt to clear his foggy mind, Josef began the serious business of finding his sword. He unclenched his aching hands and began to feel along the bed frame, careful not to make a sound.

"It's on top of you," said a familiar voice.

Josef's head shot up, sending waves of pain down his back, and he cursed loudly as Eli's smug face appeared in the air above him.

"Good morning, sunshine," Eli said. "Glad to see you up."

Josef glared murder at the thief and moved his hands to his chest. Sure enough, the Heart was resting directly on top of him. At least that explained the feeling of having a boulder on his ribs. He relaxed down into the bed with a long breath. "How long have I been out?"

"About three days," Eli answered, pulling his chair closer to the bed. "And I've got the crick in my neck to prove it. You've been hogging the only bed. I've had to make do with a spare cushion on the floor."

Josef was not sympathetic. "What about Nico? Where is she?"

"Who knows," Eli said. "Out."

Josef was startled by the hostility in his voice. "What happened?"

Eli shrugged. "The usual. You went down, Nico went crazy, I got us out. We thought you were going to die on us for a while, but the Heart did an excellent job patching you up. You look like you usually do after one of your fights now, which is miles better than the bloody mess you were when we laid you down."

"And what about Nico?"

"Powers, Josef!" Eli cried. "Can you think about something besides the girl for two seconds? I go out on a limb, not even a limb, a *twig*, to save your hide, and when you wake up all I hear is Nico this, Nico that. I don't even get a thank-you."

"Thank you," Josef said. "Don't get angry about it. You can take care of yourself, but Nico has a hard time with that right now. So when you say she's 'out,' like you don't even care—"

"Maybe I don't," Eli snapped. "Maybe you shouldn't either."

Josef stared at his friend. In the four years he'd known Eli, he'd never seen the thief this upset.

Eli looked away and took a deep breath. "Josef," he said, more quietly. "When you found Nico, did you ever wonder why she was out there naked on the mountain?"

"Of course," Josef answered. "But I figured she would tell me when I needed to know. I'm not concerned with people's pasts, Eli."

"Maybe you should be," Eli said, running his hands through his dark hair, which was getting long and scruffy. "You know how oddly she's been acting, right?"

Josef nodded.

"When I was in the mountain, I heard things," Eli said. "I'm not someone to trust everything I hear, but this made too much sense to ignore. You've heard of the Daughter of the Dead Mountain?"

"I've seen the posters."

"Who hasn't?" Eli said with a shrug. "Two hundred thousand gold standards, the second-highest bounty ever posted. It's twice as high as *mine*." Eli scowled. "I think that's what bothers me most. All this time, and she didn't even have the courtesy to—"

"Stop," Josef said. "Just stop. I know where you're going. Nico is the Daughter of the Dead Mountain. So what? The Lord of Storms told me as much, but you can't hold it against her. She lost her memory, remember? Maybe she didn't even know."

Eli rolled his eyes. "Come on, Josef. You're stubborn, not stupid. Do you really believe all that garbage? Memory loss," Eli said and snorted. "She remembered well enough how to get back to the mountain."

"Yes," Josef said. "To help us."

"She lied to us."

"She kept a secret," Josef corrected. "You're hardly in a position to blame others for keeping secrets, Monpress."

Eli said sullenly, "This is too big. She should have told us."

"And what would you have done?" Josef said.

"Not what I did," Eli said. "She *lied* to us, Josef. We let her take off her manacles. I took her to Slorn's *house*, to *Nivel*. Do you know what she could have *done*?"

"I never heard of her doing anything," Josef said. "And I never heard her lie. I never heard her say anything about the Daughter of the Dead Mountain, that is, when she could say anything at all without you taking up all the breathable air." He glared at Eli. "Whoever she is, whatever name you give her, it doesn't change the last year. She's still the same Nico who put her life on the line dozens of times for your stupid thefts, who risked exposing her past to help you find your bear-headed friend, which was more than you did, I could add. So if you have something to say about that Nico, unless it's how you're going to go find her and tell her I'm all right, then I don't want to hear it."

Eli looked away. "It's not like that," he grumbled.

"Then don't make it like that," Josef snapped back. "I don't ask about your past, I don't ask about Nico's, and I haven't told you about mine because the past doesn't matter, Eli. What we did and who we were are just dregs compared to who we are now and how we act when the sword is coming down. Think about that while you go out to find Nico."

Eli started to say something, but then he snapped his mouth shut and stood up, sweeping the chair back with a clatter. He grabbed his blue coat from the peg on the wall and stomped out the door, letting it slam shut behind him. Josef listened until the thief's angry footsteps faded into the forest, then lay back with a long sigh.

"He's gone," he said. "You can come in now."

Something rustled below the window, and Nico quietly climbed into the cabin. Her hood was down, but it did little to hide her puffy eyes and wet cheeks. Josef held out his arm and she ran to him, burying her face in his hand.

"He hates me now." Josef felt the words more than heard them.

"He may," Josef said. "Eli doesn't like surprises, but he'll get over this. He can be a selfish idiot on occasion, but he's rarely deliberately unfair. He'll come around soon enough and things will move on. We're all survivors. We'll be all right."

Nico didn't move, but her breathing was slowing. Josef cupped her cheek gently. They sat like that for a while, Nico on her knees beside the bed, her head in Josef's hand. Then, without warning, Josef went stiff.

Nico looked up immediately, but Josef put his finger to his lips, listening. Gently but firmly, he pushed her aside and sat up. Pain shot through him, but Josef stayed silent. The Heart was ready when he reached for it, the hilt almost jumping into his hand. With another burst of pain, he stood, and after a few wobbly moments, found his feet again. When he was sure he would not fall down, he crept toward the cabin door and pressed his eye against the crack.

"Oh, no," he groaned. "Not again."

"Liechten!" A horribly familiar voice cut through the thin cabin walls. "Master of the Heart of War! Come and fight!"

Josef steeled his shoulders and opened the door, leaning on the frame for support as he stared at the crowd waiting in the little clearing around the cabin. They were bandits, that much was obvious. A bit better equipped than what he was used to, but Josef dismissed them as soon as he noted their sloppy stances and turned his attention to the real threat, the enormous man standing at the head of the group.

Josef heaved an enormous sigh. "Hello, Sted."

Eli tromped through the woods, kicking the leaves and fallen sticks and whatever else got in his way. This caused the trees around him to rustle uncomfortably, but for once Eli didn't care. He should have known better than to bring this up with Josef. They'd been together on and off almost since the beginning, back when his bounty didn't even warrant its own poster, and though their arrangement had always been one of mutual benefit—he got a swordsman and Josef got to fight as much as he pleased—he'd *thought* they were friends.

Eli gave the rotten stump in front of him a particularly hard kick. Even he knew that was unfair. Josef had stayed with him even when there were no good fights to be had. He might be a stubborn idiot sometimes, but he was a loyal one. But why did the swordsman always have to take Nico's side?

He didn't understand, Eli decided. He wasn't a wizard, he didn't talk to spirits, he didn't really know how horrible demons could be. Of course, Eli thought with a sigh, he was just as bad, letting himself get caught up in Nico's power, forgetting what she really was. Well, the monster on the mountain had cured him of *that* delusion. The demon had made it very clear that the Nico they knew, the Nico Josef defended, she was just a shell. A cracking one, he realized with a shudder. It wasn't a question of whether she would change, but when. When she'd been a normal seed, it had been easy to sweep that little unpleasantness under the table.

Now that he knew what she really was, the stakes were different, and the game was getting too rich for his blood.

Eli stared at the woods in front of him, the rolling hills of dappled shade and fragrant evergreens. Thinking about it rationally, he should keep walking. He'd been a thief long enough to know when it was time to cut your losses and get out, but...

Eli stopped in his tracks. First rule of thievery, the *actual* first rule the old Monpress had drilled into him, was never risk what you couldn't afford to lose. He couldn't lose his team, not if he wanted to get his bounty to one million. Over the last year, he'd pushed higher and further than ever, and Nico had been a part of that as much as Josef. Even knowing what he was messing with, he couldn't give that up. Not yet.

He was still standing there, sucking his lip as his better judgment warred with his ambition, when a loud noise, a whistle followed by a thunk, sounded right beside his ear. Eli jumped on instinct, throwing himself sideways into the leaves. He rolled into a crouch, then stopped and looked up. An arrow was quivering in the trunk of the tree he'd been standing beside. Eli stared at it dumbly for a second and then craned his neck, frantically looking for the bowman.

Another arrow slammed into the ground beside him before he even got his head up. Realizing he was still an open target, Eli scrambled to the other side of the tree, madly beating on the trunk as he went.

The tree rustled grumpily. "What do you want?"

"I need to know where that came from," Eli whispered, pointing at the arrow.

"What are you talking about?" the tree said. "I don't feel..." It stopped. "Why is there an arrow in me?"

"That's what I'm asking," Eli said.

"How should I know?" The tree was starting to panic.

"Ask the arrow," Eli said, giving the bark a push. "Quickly, please, if you don't mind."

"Good idea," the tree said, and lapsed into mad rustling.

Eli kept as close to the tree as he could, trying to look everywhere at once. He would have asked the arrow himself, but the tree could get it to talk faster than even he could, short of opening his spirit. But as the seconds stretched on and on, the tree just kept rustling until its leaves were raining down.

"Well?" Eli said.

"Nothing," it answered. "That arrow's dead asleep."

"So wake it up."

"What do you think I was trying to do?" The tree snapped its branches. "Someone put it to sleep."

Eli cursed his luck. "Well, can you see anyone who might have shot it? Another human?"

"I don't see anything that's not always here," the tree said, more confused than ever. "Other than you and the arrow."

Eli was about to offer to pull the arrow out and have a go at it himself when he heard the telltale whistle of fletching, this time from his right. He ducked just in time as another arrow landed in the tree and the wood cried out in surprise and pain.

"Did you see that one?" Eli said, scrambling to get to the other side.

"No!" the tree shouted. "I don't see anything!"

Another whistle screamed through the forest as an arrow struck the ground right beside Eli's foot. This was when he decided to forget finding the archer and just run.

He sprang forward, dashing through the trees. Arrows whistled behind him, each bolt striking his footprint a second after his boot made it. He ran as fast as he could, lungs slamming for air while his brain spun even faster, trying to come up with a plan. The trees were sparse and open, offering little cover. He saw a rocky defile to his left and tried to turn, but the arrows struck the ground in front of him, landing deep in the soil where he would have been if he'd moved a second faster. With an undignified squeak, Eli turned on his heel and kept running, trying the turn again a few dozen feet later only to have the arrows cut him off again. The third time it happened, Eli knew he was being driven. Every time he tried to dodge left or right, the arrows pushed him straight again, forcing him east down a slope toward a wide mountain stream.

It was a trap for sure, Eli realized grimly, but he couldn't stop. Already his feet were sliding on the slippery leaves, forcing him to run even faster or risk going down the hill on his back. He skidded down the bank and landed in the creek with a splash. The mossy rocks slipped under his boots, sending him sprawling face-first into the icy water. He was up instantly, sputtering as he scrambled back to his feet only to slip again. He fell cursing back into the water, flailing around to make himself a harder target. But as he scrambled to get his legs back under him, he realized that the arrows had stopped. He paused, listening, but the forest was silent except for the soft trickle of the water.

Carefully this time, Eli stood up. Maybe he'd gotten out of range of the archer? If that was the case, whoever it was would be coming down after him. He looked over his shoulder, eyeing places on the opposite bank where he could hide and see who had been shooting at him. He spotted a good vantage point and began to quickly, but carefully, pick his way across the slick rocks. He'd made it halfway across the streambed when the water suddenly stopped.

Eli tripped and pitched forward, arms flying out to catch himself, but there was no need. The water, which had been running against his legs, was now hard as baked clay, and he was baked in as well, trapped from the knees down in crystal clear, freezing cold, perfectly still water.

After several moments of desperate tugging proved this wasn't something he could just yank his legs out of, Eli calmed down and took stock of the situation. The water had stopped moving for as far as he could see up and down the creek. Except for the wind overhead, the stream valley was perfectly silent. Experimentally, he tried to wiggle his toes, but even they were trapped, entombed in the water that had flowed into his boots before the freeze. No, freeze was the wrong idea. The water wasn't ice. It was just stopped. Stopped and not talking about it, which meant there was a wizard around.

The moment that realization crossed his mind, he knew who it was. He turned slowly, and there was no shock on his face when he saw a woman with red hair stepping out from behind a tree with an enormous grin on her face.

"Miranda Lyonette," Eli said. "A pleasure, as always."

If possible, the Spiritualist's grin grew even wider. "For once, we agree."

There was a rustle of branches from across the valley, and Eli turned to see her dog loping down the far bank with a grin that matched his mistress's.

"You've outdone yourself," Eli said as Gin joined her. "Caught me flat-footed and unprepared. The arrows were especially nice. Brava, my dear. So what now? Is there a contingent of Spiritualists coming to clap me in irons?"

Miranda shook her head. "No. You showed me how effective irons were back in Gaol. This time I'm using something you can't wiggle out of."

Eli smiled politely. "Which is?"

Miranda stepped into the stream, and Eli swallowed when he saw the still water slide back to make a dry path for her. She walked forward over dry stones, stopping just out of Eli's reach, her smile wider than ever.

"Eli Monpress," she said, her voice deep and joyful, "you are under arrest for crimes against the Spirit Court and the Council of Thrones."

"That's a pretty broad accusation," Eli said. "Can't you be more specific? This *is* my arrest. It would be a shame to gloss over my impressive record."

"Oh, don't worry," Miranda said. "I'm certain they'll read the whole list at your trial." She leaned forward and, to Eli's enormous surprise, gave him a long, slow wink. "See you on the other side, Eli Monpress."

As she spoke, the stopped water started moving again, but not down the creekbed. It flowed up Eli's body, covering his chest, his shoulders, and finally his head. He struggled and thrashed, but the water simply pushed back, rendering his blows meaningless. He took a deep breath just before the water went over his head, and the last thing he saw was Miranda's face grinning triumphantly before everything went black.

Miranda was almost giggling as she watched Mellinor swallow Eli's head. A trickle of icy water rushed over her feet as Mellinor released control of the creek back to the local spirit, but she wouldn't have cared if she'd been on fire at this point. She'd done it. She'd *actually* caught Eli Monpress.

"Don't smile too hard," Gin said, splashing through the water to join her. "He's not in Zarin yet. I won't feel safe until he's sitting in Banage's office."

"Even Eli Monpress will have a hard time escaping if he's unconscious," Miranda said. "How's he doing?"

"Out cold," Mellinor answered. The pillar of water was floating completely separate from the creek now, with Eli's slumped body cocooned at its center.

Miranda sighed happily. "It's a beautiful sight. How long can you keep him like that?"

"Long enough," Mellinor answered. "Just keep me near a source of water and I should be able to hold him like this all the way to Zarin."

Miranda motioned Gin over. The dog came sullenly, wincing as Mellinor slumped the water-bound thief across his back.

"He's cold," he grumbled, ears back. "And wet."

"It's just for a little bit," Miranda said, adjusting Eli to lie across Gin's haunches. "Buck up."

"We should move," Mellinor said. "The creek is returning."

Miranda looked down. Sure enough, the water was up to her ankles now, and blisteringly cold. She shivered and made her way to the opposite bank as fast as she could. Gin padded along beside her, careful of his precious cargo. The water rose as she went, and by the time they were safely on the other side, her tall boots were soaked.

Miranda looked down with a shrug. Nothing could ruin her mood right now.

"Mission successful, I see," said a voice behind her.

Gin jumped and began to growl deep in his throat. Miranda put a warning hand on his muzzle. Well, she thought, turning around, *almost* nothing. Sparrow stood behind her, leaning against a tree with his bow resting on one shoulder. His gaudy clothes were gone, replaced by a drab brown suit that seemed to shift in and out of the tree shadow, but his smile was smug as ever.

Sparrow glanced at Eli's unconscious, water-bound body, though he was clever enough to stay clear of Gin himself. "I'll hand it to Sara," he said. "She knows how to pick the right person for the job. Well done, Spiritualist. Shall we go back to see how the others are faring?"

"You can go," Miranda said. "I'm still not convinced Izo's fighter can beat Josef Liechten or Nico. I want Eli as secure as possible, as quickly as possible, just in case."

"Caution does you credit," Sparrow said, turning on his heel. "I'll meet you back at the camp."

Miranda watched as the man walked into the trees without a sound, vanishing into the hills far quicker than any human should.

"I hate how he does that," Gin growled.

"Me too." Miranda sighed.

Gin shook his head in frustration. "No, you don't understand. Before at least he was flickering. Now it's like he's not even there."

Miranda frowned. "What do you mean, 'not even there'?"

"Forget it," Gin said. "I can't even explain it to myself, so I'm not going to bother trying to explain it to you."

Miranda flushed and started to say that she was perfectly capable of understanding if only the dog would take the time to describe things properly, but she shut her mouth at the last moment. Sparrow wasn't worth antagonizing Gin any further. She'd just have to get him to elaborate later. She followed the ghosthound up the bank, watching as Eli bounced on his back. That made her smile. One look at the captured thief was enough to renew the good mood Sparrow had dampened. "Come on," she said, picking up the pace. "Let's get our guest situated."

Gin grumbled, but he matched her speed, and they trotted together up the valley toward where their bandit escort was waiting to bring them back to Izo's hidden city.

CHAPTER 13

Using the Heart as a crutch, Josef limped out of the cabin, keeping his eyes on Sted. The man was even larger than Josef remembered, towering a good foot over the tallest of the ragtag bandits that followed him. He had no black coat this time, and no red sash of trophies. There was no sword at his hip either, no weapon at all from what Josef could see, unless he was hiding something under the ratty black cape that covered his chest, shoulders, and arms.

Sted met Josef's gaze, baring his teeth like a dog. "What is this?" he said. "Are you a cripple now? Stand and fight, if you can."

"I am standing," Josef said flatly. "But even if I couldn't, I could still beat you. After all"—the swordsman smirked—"I've done it before, with worse injuries than these. By the way, how's your arm?"

Sted's eyes flashed with anger. "You'll see soon enough," he growled. He turned to the man beside him, the only one of the group of bruisers who didn't look like he smashed rocks with his face for a living. "This one's mine. Get the girl."

Behind him, Josef felt Nico cower.

"Nico," he said, his voice low. "Run."

"No," she whispered, shaking her head furiously.

"Do it." Josef's voice strained as he lifted his weight off the Heart.

"No," Nico said again.

Josef glared over his shoulder. "Don't be an idiot. I saw what happened up by the mountain. I've seen your arm. If you fight to win here like you are, you could lose everything we've worked for. Run, I'll find you. I promise."

Nico stared at him, clutching the arm she hid beneath her coat, her dark eyes wide. Then, without another word, she turned and ran.

She tore around the cabin, sprinting wildly through the trees. Josef watched her until she vanished over the closest rise, and then he turned back to Sted. As he did so, he noticed that the man Sted had spoken to, the one who didn't look like a bandit, was already gone.

Coldly, slowly, Josef put it out of his mind. He'd done what he could for Nico. If he was going to survive to keep his promise, he'd need all his concentration for the fight ahead.

Sted waved his arm, and the bandits fell back, taking cover in the ring of trees around the cabin. Josef stayed put, conserving his energy. His sword felt heavy as lead in his hands, a sure sign he was at his limit, even with the Heart's help. His only hope was to beat Sted in one blow. His eyes flicked to Sted's covered shoulders. Unless all League men could reform their bodies like the Lord of Storms, that cape was probably there to hide Sted's missing arm. That is, if Sted was even a League man anymore. Without a coat or a sword, Josef wasn't sure. But he could feel the Heart warning him through the warm metal not to be cocky. League or not, whole or not, Sted was no one to take lightly. He gripped his sword tighter. He'd done this before. One good blow, that was all he needed.

The clearing fell silent as Sted, still seemingly unarmed, took his position. Warily, Josef matched him, keeping the Heart close. Overhead, the treetops danced in the wind. Leather creaked as the bandits eased their weapons into their sheaths, but Sted did not move. Josef's hands grew sweaty against the Heart's hilt. He turned them slowly, keeping his blade even with Sted's chest and his eyes on Sted's feet. The blow would come from Sted's right hand, whipping out from under the cape. He could see it already. All he needed was a hint to when it was coming and this fight would be over. The ground crunched as Sted's heavy boots dug into the dirt. Josef sucked in a breath. This was it.

He stepped forward, bracing the Heart for the blow just as Sted's feet vanished. Josef stumbled, eyes darting frantically. There was no way Sted was that fast, but the man was no longer in front of him. Even as his brain was finishing the thought, the Heart tugged hard in his hands. Josef spun on instinct, raising his sword just in time as the enormous man lunged out of the cabin's shadow.

The Heart met Sted's attack in a horrible squeal of metal, and Josef's knees buckled under the onslaught. His instincts were screaming at him to dodge back, get a better position, but Josef couldn't move. He just stood there, staring, trying to make sense of what his eyes saw.

Sted towered over him, taller than ever. His cape was gone and he was bearing down on the Heart with his arm, his *left* arm, the arm that should not be there. He had no sword, no weapon. He'd stopped the Heart's blade with his *hand.* No, Josef couldn't even call it a hand. It was a claw. An enormous black claw clutching the Heart's cutting edge with five talons curved in a mockery of fingers. Even as Josef realized what he was looking at, the Heart began to buck in his hands.

It was a signal that needed no interpretation. At once, Josef jumped back, wrenching his sword out of Sted's black grip. He danced across the clearing, keeping the Heart close to his chest until he was out of Sted's reach. Only then did he look down.

There, on the blade's cutting edge where Sted's hand had touched it, were five shallow notches in the exact shape of Sted's talons. The metal wasn't dented or broken. It was simply gone.

Back by the cabin, Sted straightened up. "What do you think?" he said, spreading his arms wide. "Still feeling cocky?"

It took all of Josef's determination not to look away. There was something incredibly wrong, something vastly inhuman about the black thing growing out of Sted's left shoulder. It hung crooked from his frame, a foot longer than his still-human right arm and twice as large, bulging with muscles that twitched and spasmed. But most horrible of all was the spot where the black arm connected. Just below his shoulder, Sted's pale skin and the black abomination met in a twist of red, raw flesh.

At once, everything came together. The fast movement, jumping through shadows, the arm... Slorn may have thought it was impossible for a nonwizard to become a demonseed, but Josef knew those signs well enough. He looked down at his injured sword. They needed a different strategy.

Straightening up, Josef flipped the Heart in his hands and plunged it point first into the ground. He could feel the metal clinging to his skin, warning him not to do this, but there was nothing else to be done. If Sted was a demon, then fighting him with the Heart would only make him stronger and the Heart weaker. There would be no winning that way, and so Josef let the Heart go. The moment his fingers left the wrapped hilt, he felt his wounds seize up. A tide of pain and dizziness swept over him, and he nearly fell. He planted his feet at the last moment, steadying himself in a fighter's stance, and thrust his hand toward the bandits standing at the edge of the circle.

"Sword. Now."

He heard the bandits shuffle, but he kept his eyes on Sted. The enormous man looked skeptical for a moment, then he nodded, and Josef heard the familiar sound of a blade sliding from a sheath followed by the thunk of metal on the dirt beside him. Without looking, he ducked down, hand sliding across the leaf litter until his fingers found the hilt, and brought his new sword up with a flourish.

Sted's face broke into a cruel smile. "You're going to fight me with that?"

Josef glanced at the sword in his hand. It was pathetically short, more like a long knife than a sword, and dull gray with tarnish.

"It's a blade," Josef said. "That's all a swordsman needs."

"Really?" Sted grinned wide. "Show me."

The words had barely reached Josef's ears before Sted was on top of him. Josef caught Sted's open claws a second before they landed in his head, digging his feet into the dirt as his poor, dull sword fought to hold the parry inches from Josef's face. Above him, Sted's eyes began to glow like embers, and the dull metal of the sword started to hiss as Sted's claws bit into it. Hiss, and then vanish.

Josef ducked and rolled, breaking the parry and dragging his sword to safety, but Sted didn't let him go. He lashed out, claws digging through Josef's shirt and into the flesh beneath. Josef gasped and rolled away, but it was mostly instinct. His head was getting fuzzy as he scrambled in the dirt, wiggling out of Sted's grip just in time to catch the next swipe on what was left of his sword. But even as he raised his arm, he felt his muscles going slack. The damage from the Lord of Storms that the Heart had been holding back for him was building up again. His vision was dimming until he could barely see Sted break his parry with a sideways swipe. The sword tumbled from his fingers, breaking into pieces as it hit the ground, and Josef would have followed if Sted had not grabbed what was left of his shirt.

"What is this?" Sted's voice roared in his ear. Josef felt his feet leave the ground as Sted lifted him by his collar. "What happened to your back? You're so bloody you can barely stand. Is this how you face me? Is this the best you can offer?"

Josef tried to point out that Sted had been the one bellowing at his door, not the other way around, but all he managed was a choked gurgle. It was very hard to breathe with Sted holding him up by his neck.

Sted dropped him with a disgusted grunt. Josef landed hard on his side, and for a moment all he could think of was the pain. When his mind at last cleared enough to focus on things outside his body, he found he was being lifted up by several of the bandits while Sted's booming voice shouted out orders.

"Get him to his sword. It's the only thing keeping his carcass alive. We'll take them both back to camp."

Someone said something Josef couldn't hear, and Sted roared in anger.

"No, we're not going to kill him! No one is to touch him without my permission! Josef Liechten is *my fight*, and I will have it proper and on my terms if I have to kill every one of you sorry bandit dogs! Now get his sword in his hand! You'll never lift it otherwise."

Josef felt someone take his hand and thrust it clumsily forward. A wave of relief washed over him as his fingers met the Heart's hilt, and he was even able to wrap his hand around it.

"Good," Sted said. "Take him back to town and get him to the medics, and don't let him drop that blade. Remember, he is my fight. Keep everyone else away from him, especially those Council pigs. Anyone who touches him will answer to me. Go!"

Josef felt the world sway as the bandits hurried to do Sted's bidding. They carried him strung between two men like he was a hunting trophy with the Heart dragging behind them, its hilt tied to Josef's hand with a long strip of cloth. Sted walked beside him the whole time, enormous and terrible, shoving his cape back over his monstrous arm. When he saw Josef looking, he grinned wide.

"Don't worry," he said. "I'll kill you soon enough, but on my terms. I didn't sell my soul to slap your beaten carcass around. Rest and enjoy what little life you have left, Josef Liechten. When you're ready to give me the victory I deserve, we'll face off again. That time, Master of the Heart of War, I won't stop until I have your heart in my hand."

Sted began to laugh at that, a horrible, mad sound. Josef felt himself jerk as the bandits carrying him began to move faster, desperate to put some space between themselves and the mad monster. Josef stayed awake as long as he could, but soon even Sted's laughter faded behind the rush of blood in his ears, and he slipped into unconsciousness.

Nico ran. She shot through the forest, scrambling gracelessly over fallen logs and gnarled roots with little thought to where she was going. All that mattered was speed, getting away, so she ran until her legs burned and her lungs felt like they were going to burst.

You're such a coward, the Master whispered. *Running to save yourself while the swordsman goes to his death. He can't fight in his condition.*

Nico gritted her teeth and ran harder.

You're not even making progress. Look, all that work and you've barely moved.

Nico glanced over her shoulder before she could stop herself. The Master was right. She could still see the thin plume of smoke from the cabin's chimney through the trees. She also saw no sign of pursuit. Nico slowed down, sucking cold, precious air into her burning lungs as she eyed the forest, straining to hear above the thundering of her heart. But the forest was still and empty around her, the sunlight moving in dapples across the leaf litter as the wind tossed the treetops high overhead. Under her coat, clutched against her chest, her transformed arm began to ache.

Pity you didn't take me up on my offer, the Master said. *If your hearing was anything like what it used to be, you would never have stopped.*

Even before the words had faded from her mind, a pair of hard, strong hands grabbed her shoulders from behind.

Nico shrieked and kicked backward, landing a solid strike on whoever was behind her. But the hands on her shoulders didn't even flinch. She scrambled desperately, panic clouding her mind, and all at once, her coat reacted. She felt the black fabric clench around the hands on her shoulder, the stiff cloth growing sharp as needles as it dug into the skin.

The person holding her grunted in pain, and the grip on her shoulders vanished. Nico tumbled to the ground and was up again in an instant, clutching her coat with a whisper of thanks. As soon as her feet hit the ground she was running, pounding flat out into the woods, only to come skidding to a stop a second later.

She hadn't seen anything move, hadn't heard steps on the leaves, yet, somehow, a man in a long brown coat, his hands bleeding from where her coat had stabbed him, was already in front of her, watching her with calm, brown eyes.

"Amazing coat you have there," he said softly, holding up his injured hand. "That wasn't in the briefing. You caught me by surprise, but don't count on doing it again."

As he spoke, the wounds on his hands closed before Nico's eyes. She blinked, then blinked again, but the wounds were still gone, leaving his skin whole and smooth. She'd never seen anything like it outside of demonseeds, but, while she wasn't sure who or what this man was, she knew he wasn't a seed. His skin was too swarthy, his build healthy and whole. She watched, dumbstruck, as the man quietly wiped away what blood was left on a handkerchief. Nico swallowed. Whatever he was, one thing was certain: he was faster than her. Running was out of the question. If she wanted to get away, she'd have to fight.

She planted her feet in a defensive position, keeping her transformed arm close to her chest. It twitched beneath her coat, itching for the chance to lash out, but Nico locked it in place. She might be weak like this, but she didn't need demon strength to take down a larger opponent. Josef had taught her well. All she needed was a lucky break, an open jab at his throat, and she could knock his wind out and get away.

The man watched her take her position with a blank, calm expression, hands in his pockets like he had all the time in the world. Then, faster than Nico's eyes could track, he struck.

A fist hit her hard in the gut. Nico gasped, but before her brain had registered the pain, the man's leg swept around to knock her own out from under her. She reeled and would have fallen, but at the last moment her transformed arm shot out to catch her. Nico stared at the black claw clutching the ground below her, unsure if the arm had moved by her reflexes or on its own. Whichever it was, she didn't have time to worry about it. The man was right in front of her, his fist coming up to catch her jaw. Nico scrambled back, bringing up both arms in defense as the man's fist missed her face by a fraction, leaving his guard open. Seeing her chance, Nico struck, her hand flying for his now unguarded throat.

It was only when her jab entered her field of vision that she realized her mistake. The hand flying for the man's throat was not her pale, white fist, but the black, transformed claw. It struck before she could think to stop it, digging deep into the flesh of the man's neck. Desperately, frantically, she tried to pull back, but it was far too late. Dark, delighted laughter rippled over her mind as the man's spirit roared up inside her, and the demon arm began to eat.

Nico shook uncontrollably as the man flowed through her, past her, and into the thing buried deep inside her. She could feel his soul as it slid by, warm and alive and pulsing with controlled strength, but she could do nothing to stop its flow as the demon ate and ate until the blackness was drowning out her conscious mind.

Then, without warning, it stopped.

The thing inside her roared in frustration, sucking and pulling at the connection through the black arm, but its efforts changed nothing. The flow of the man's spirit had dried up. All at once, the dark weight on her mind began to recede, and Nico cracked her eyes open. She knew already what she would see. She had eaten men before. She would see his body falling from her hand, gray and lifeless, turning into ash as it hit the ground, too empty to even hold its form.

But when she looked up she saw the man, still alive and standing in front of her. Her black claw was still lodged in the flesh of his throat, but though she could feel the demon pulling, trying desperately to get at the life just under the man's skin, nothing was happening. Somehow, the demon could not eat him.

"How?" She didn't know she had spoken until the word was out.

The man pried the black arm from his neck, and Nico saw the gouges from the claws already beginning to close. "I am king of myself," he said simply. "My body is mine alone. Nothing can happen to it that I do not allow."

He dropped his grip on her black wrist and raised his arm. Nico saw the blow coming, but she was too amazed to even move out of the way as his hand came down hard on the back of her neck. The last thing she felt were the man's arms as he caught her, and then everything was gone.

CHAPTER 14

The water over his head parted, and Eli sucked in an enormous breath. He sat there a moment, reveling in the joy of breathing, before Miranda's face dipped down to fill his vision. She grabbed his head, checking his eyes and throat.

"You're right," she said. "He's fine."

Eli thought she was talking to him until he heard the water at his throat bubble in answer.

"Of course I'm right," Mellinor said. "It's my water."

Miranda's mouth twitched in a smile before returning to a stern line as she looked down at Eli.

"Turn him around," she said haughtily. "I'm going to change out of these wet clothes and then we'll see what the plan is."

"Shouldn't you include me in this conversation?" Eli said. "This is my neck you're talking—"

His words cut off with a choke as Mellinor heaved sideways, spinning him dizzily in his watery prison. Eli thrashed, but the water was like cement around him, and all he managed was to get a giant mouthful of cold, salty water down his windpipe as the sea spirit turned him completely around. He coughed loudly and spat out the water on the wall that was now five inches from his nose, filling his vision.

"There's no cause for violence," he said, still hacking.

"If you want to keep enjoying the air, you'll keep your mouth shut," Miranda said, her voice floating from the room behind him. "One more word and I'll let Mellinor put you back underwater. Gin! Do you see Sparrow anywhere around?"

"No." The ghosthound's growl was muffled, and Eli realized he must be outside the small building they were in. Of course, there was no way the hound could fit *inside.*

"Stop him if you see him," Miranda said, her voice dampened by the clothes she must have been pulling over her head. "I want him to ask Izo's men to move us to a better location. I'll need more room to properly contain the thief for tonight."

Eli craned his neck, looking around at the small wooden hut with its low, easily scalable windows looking out onto quiet, sheltered back alleys. "This place looks fine to me."

"Shut up," Miranda and Gin said in unison.

Eli turned sullenly back to the wall.

"I'll send Sparrow your way if I see him," Gin said. "Hurry up, it's already getting dark."

Miranda made an annoyed sound and the room lapsed into silence, broken only by the soft shuffle of clothing.

Eli stared at the wall, listening with interest. From what he could hear, Miranda was six, maybe seven feet away. Far too short for a break even in the small room, assuming, of course, he could get out of the water spirit, which he couldn't. Karon would be no use. The lava spirit's burn was waterlogged, and Mellinor was the bigger spirit anyway. The sea would win for sure if it came to a fight.

Eli tried a few experimental movements, then stopped. The water was like a vise, pressing into him so hard he couldn't even wiggle his fingers. He struggled a bit more, just on principle, before flopping down against the water to wait it out.

He'd been like that for only a few moments when he felt something brush his cheek. Eli jumped, lashing his head back in surprise. Or he tried to. All he managed was to wrench his neck into an awful crick. Eli winced and turned to see what had touched him. His eyes widened in surprise. There, standing right next to Mellinor's water, was a man. He was dressed in dull brown with a bow over his shoulder and a quiver of very familiar arrows.

The man put a finger to his lips. "Don't say anything," he whispered. "My name is Sparrow, and I have an offer for the great Eli Monpress."

Eli stared at the man, curious now. He wasn't a Spiritualist, or even a wizard, Eli would wager. Even Great Spirits perked up when a wizard spoke, no matter how used they were to having them around, but Mellinor had remained perfectly still. Still, there was something very odd going on. For one thing, the man had to be standing right behind Miranda, but the soft sounds of her changing hadn't even paused. The Spiritualist could be a little blind at times, but it wasn't like she would just miss something like this. Even stranger, Gin hadn't made a sound either. That made Eli very cautious. Unless there were two men named Sparrow here, this was the one Miranda had asked the hound to look for, and any person who could sneak past an alert ghosthound was someone to be treated with respect.

Sparrow smiled as he watched Eli's thought process and deftly flicked a card out of his front pocket. "Before you ask," he said softly, slipping the card down Eli's shirt collar, "no, they don't know I'm here." He leaned casually against the wall. "I'm something of an oddity, you see. I've been told I'm the opposite of a wizard, something completely beneath the world's notice, or some such. I don't fully understand it myself, but it's dreadfully useful, especially when sneaking around a girl who relies on spirits to do her watching." He glanced sideways beyond Eli's line of vision to where Miranda was getting ready. "Unless I'm wearing something with some life and color to it, spirits can't see me at all, so I thought I'd take advantage of my current drab attire to have a little chat with you. Of course"—he frowned—"the moment you speak, the jig is up, so things are going to be a little one-sided, I'm afraid. But I'm sure I can count on a man known for his curiosity to keep his mouth shut until he gets an explanation."

Eli gave him a sour look, but nodded.

"Good," Sparrow said. "You should know first that I'm not Spirit Court, and I'm not after your bounty either. I work for the Council of Thrones. Specifically, I work for the Council's Head Wizard, and she's very interested in you."

Eli's eyes went wide as coins, and he mouthed one word.

Sara.

"Who else?" Sparrow said. "I'm afraid things are about to be very difficult for you, Mr. Monpress. Miranda's on the warpath. I wouldn't be surprised if you were standing trial before Banage within the month. However, it doesn't have to be that way." Sparrow leaned a little closer. "Sara has asked me to assure you that you will always be welcome in her department."

Eli glowered and said nothing. Sparrow shrugged and gave Eli's head a wet pat. "The offer's there, when you're ready," he said, moving silently back toward the open window. "Just remember, the Council's been planning your hanging since your bounty hit twenty thousand. It promises to be quite the event, but even this could be quietly forgotten if Sara wanted it to be. Think on that a bit. I'll be in touch, should you need me." He gave Eli one final smile before slipping quietly through the window, vanishing without a sound into the alley beyond.

Eli was still staring when Mellinor jerked beneath him, whirling him around to face Miranda, who was dressed in one of her standard riding suits, a deep blue one this time, with her red curls pulled up in a severe ponytail and a deep scowl on her face.

She folded her arms over her chest as Eli smiled at her. "What were you looking at just now?"

"Absolutely nothing of consequence," Eli said.

Miranda's look told clearly how much she believed that, but before she could say anything, Gin poked his head in the front door. "Sparrow's headed toward Izo's."

Miranda shook her head and grabbed a handful of Mellinor's water.

"Where are we going now?" Eli said, but Miranda didn't answer. She just dragged him, water and all, out the door and into the dirt street beyond.

Miranda marched into Izo's hall, leaving a wet trail on the grimy stone as she dragged a water-bound Eli behind her. Sparrow was already waiting for her. His drab clothes were gone, replaced by his usual finery, now a green silk coat covered with a short blue cape that set off his eyes in a way that was obviously planned. He looked impossibly smug, as always, but his expression was somewhat tempered by the sight of their prize being flung around like a wet towel. Miranda paid him no attention. She stopped when she reached the middle of the hall, slamming Eli down on his knees before Izo's empty throne.

Sparrow leaned over. "Miranda, dearest," he whispered. "Perhaps it is not the best idea to bring the object of a negotiation to the negotiation."

"The only spirit I trust him with is Mellinor," Miranda said through gritted teeth. "He's not leaving my sight. And don't call me dearest."

"She can get very touchy," Eli said, his voice somewhat burbled by the watery prison sloshing at his chin.

Sparrow gave him a dashing smile. "The greatest thief in the world. It is quite the honor to meet you, Mr. Monpress."

Eli grinned back. Miranda glowered and snapped her fingers, giving Mellinor a nudge that sent Eli's head back underwater.

"Don't encourage him," she said pointedly.

She let Eli bubble a bit before bringing him up again. "I told you," she said quietly, glaring down at the thief. "You're here because I can't leave you alone, not because we like your company, so keep your big mouth closed." She straightened up, pushing a stray curl out of her face. "Honestly, what part of 'prisoner' don't you understand?"

"Oh, I understand," Eli said with a wet grin. "I've just never been in agreement with the concept."

Miranda rolled her eyes, but before she could retort, or stick him underwater again, the iron gate rattled as Izo entered the room. He was dressed far finer than before, with a scarlet silk jacket over polished chain mail and a black cape edged extravagantly in gold thread. Miranda grimaced. He looked like every tacky minor lord in the Council district of Zarin, which was probably his intent. He was grinning like a cat as he stalked over to his chair, flanked on one side by the thin man in black, Sezri, and on the other by the enormous brawler with the ever-present cape over his shoulders, the man called Sted.

"Well," Izo said, settling down into his throne. "Well, well, well. Let it not be said that Izo doesn't deliver. Monpress kneels before me while his pet swordsman lies unconscious in my infirmary. I hope you understand now, friends, the power of the Bandit King. I have given you the uncatchable thief on a platter, as promised. Now we'll discuss the details of how you mean to hold up your end of the bargain."

Miranda started to point out how they had been the ones doing the actual catching, but Sparrow cut her off.

"Of course," he said, "we could not have asked for a better outcome, and the Council always keeps its bargains. We will leave for Zarin first thing tomorrow, and I will return personally to hand you your invitation to the Council within the month, *King* Izo."

Sparrow looked up, obviously expecting a smile at this new title, but Izo wasn't smiling. He lounged back on his throne, his eyes lidded and dark as he looked Sparrow over.

"No, no, pretty messenger bird," Izo said slowly. "That's not how this works. I may be king, but I'll always be a bandit, and bandits don't get to be kings by blindly trusting the word of Council dogs. No member of the Monpress party leaves my camp until I have the writ from the Council acknowledging my kingship in my hand."

"My lord," Sparrow said, his voice buttery and soft. "That's simply not possible. It would take two weeks at least for me to return to Zarin. Without Monpress, it could take months to convince the Council to act, even for someone as connected as Sara."

"Then I will keep him for months," Izo said. "But he's not going anywhere until I get my price."

"That's unacceptable," Miranda said. "Every moment the thief spends outside of the Spirit Court's full security is a chance for him to escape. This isn't some cat burglar you can just lock in a cell. This is Eli Monpress we're talking about, the man who broke into, and escaped from, the great citadel of Gaol. Even if I stayed in your camp to guard him, I couldn't promise I could keep him safely bound for months. If he doesn't leave for Zarin immediately, we could all lose."

"Miranda," Eli said gently, "I'm touched. Praise from you is praise indeed."

Miranda waved her hand, and Mellinor's water went over Eli's head again. She held it there until his face was blue. "Shut up," she muttered, keeping her eyes on Izo. The Bandit King was leaning on his throne, scratching his scarred chin thoughtfully.

"I understand your complaint, Spiritualist," he said. "But my terms stand. Monpress goes nowhere until he is paid for. If you want to get him back to Zarin, I suggest you convince your Council to move quickly."

Sparrow smiled. "May I have a moment to discuss this with my colleague?"

Izo shrugged and waved his hand. Sparrow bowed in thanks before grabbing Miranda's arm and dragging her back to the gate.

"I told you to keep your mouth shut," he whispered harshly, though the calm smile never left his face.

"But we have to get Eli out of here," Miranda whispered back.

"Yes," Sparrow said. "And now he knows that. Never give information away, Miranda. Fortunately, the deal he just offered isn't bad. Eli is still only one half of this operation. If you stay to make sure he remains caught, there's a good chance you'll come into contact with Slorn at some point. I'm going to take his deal to Zarin. You and Tesset will stay here. With Tesset doing the hunting, Slorn should be in hand by the time I get back, and then we can all leave together with our missions complete."

"No," Miranda said. "You're not listening. If we wait, Eli *will* escape. I've caught him twice before, Sparrow. He's slipperier than Zarin's bookkeeping. I've put aside too much and worked too hard to accept a risk like this."

"This is a negotiation, Miranda," Sparrow said, and though his pleasant expression never changed, his voice was starting to sound annoyed. "You don't get to just make demands. Sted has most of the cards. We have to compromise. Stay here, keep the thief underwater, look for Slorn, and I'll be back in a month. Everything else is details."

Miranda glared at the floor. He didn't understand that this whole situation was going to fall apart if it depended on keeping Eli caught. But before she could think of another way to explain things, Eli spoke up, his voice ringing loud and clear through the throne room.

"What about my swordsman?"

Eli smiled smugly as everyone turned to look at him. "My head may be worth more than some kings see in a lifetime," he said, "but Josef carries the Heart of War. The Head Wizard of the Council is a collector of oddities, isn't she? She would never forgive you if you let the greatest awakened blade ever created go without a fight."

Sted lurched forward, but Izo's voice stopped him.

"The sword is already spoken for."

Eli's eyebrows shot up in surprise. "Is that so? King Izo, you're a cleverer bargainer than I gave you credit for, keeping the best prize safely off the table."

"Will you *shut up*?" Miranda hissed, knocking Eli down with a wave of water.

"That's because it's not Izo's to give!" Sted roared. "Liechten and the Heart were promised to me!"

"Sted!" Now it was Izo's turn to shout. He glared down from his throne at the enormous man, red-faced with rage. "Everything in my domain is mine to give if I please! I am king here!" He whirled to face Sparrow. "I'll make you another deal. You need the thief out quickly? Fine, I'd rather not wait to be king. I know you have a Relay link on you that allows you to talk directly to your mistress in Zarin. Tell her that she can have everything—Monpress, the Heart of whatever, freedom to hunt down your rogue wizard, *everything*, if Merchant Prince Whitefall himself comes up to welcome me as an equal to the Council by the next full moon."

"Merchant Prince Whitefall?" Miranda almost laughed out loud. "You want the Head of the Council of Thrones, the Grand Marshal of Zarin, to come *here*? Have you lost your little bandit mind?"

"No," Izo said coldly. "But you will lose your Spiritualist tongue if you speak to me that way again."

Miranda bristled, but snapped her mouth shut when Sparrow's hand grabbed and nearly crushed her arm.

"Forgive my companion," Sparrow said, his voice honeyed and dripping with sincerity. "She is a Spiritualist and a native of Zarin, and as such suffers from an overinflated sense of importance." Miranda shot him a sharp look, and the grip on her arm tightened until she could no longer feel her fingers before he let go.

"It's late," Sparrow said. "Minds are tired and tempers are running short. I will bring your offer to my mistress and have an answer for you by morning. Thank you so much for your generous hospitality, King Izo."

He bowed genteelly and turned on his heel, marching out of the hall. Miranda followed a second later, dragging Eli behind her. The thief went with a bemused grin on his face and a little wink at Sted, who was in the corner turning purple with rage while Sezri held him back. Gin joined them when they reached the keep stairs and fell in behind Eli, glaring straight at the thief with his teeth bared. Now that Gin was looking after their prisoner, Miranda was free to turn on Sparrow.

"We were just getting into negotiations," she whispered. "Why did you make us leave?"

"Because it was time to leave," Sparrow said. "Or didn't you see the murder in the big one's eyes?"

Miranda looked over her shoulder. Sure enough, she could see Sted through the iron gate shouting something at Izo, who was rising from his throne in red-faced fury as he answered.

"Stop looking," Sparrow said sharply.

Miranda turned back to the torch-lit road. "Whatever you say; one night won't make a difference," she grumbled. "There's no way you're getting Whitefall up here."

Sparrow's grin vanished, and he looked sideways at her with a condescending sneer. "You assume too much, *darling.* There are two pillars that prop up the Council of Thrones. The first is Merchant Prince Whitefall; the second is Sara. If push came to shove she could have the entire Whitefall family up here tomorrow, and for a combination of Slorn, Eli Monpress, and the Heart of War, she just might. She's been talking about that sword for years, but has never been able to find it." His voice softened, and he tilted his head thoughtfully. "Who would have thought its current wielder would be traveling with the thief? Though it makes sense, considering the spectacular feats his group has pulled off."

Eli burst out laughing at that, though the sound turned into a squeak when Gin bit him. Sparrow blithely ignored the entire affair.

"I'm going to check on Tesset," he said. "Then I'll drop by the infirmary to see this Heart of War for myself. You go back to the house and lock the thief down for the night. Tomorrow, I'll answer Izo's demands. You can come along if you promise to keep your mouth shut this time."

"No promises," Miranda said, halting at the door of the house they shared.

Sparrow didn't even stop, he just waved his hand as he walked down the dirt street toward the barracks where the infirmary was set up. Miranda watched him go for a moment and then turned on her heel and stomped off the other way, looking for one of Izo's men to bully into giving her her own building to stay in. Gin stayed close behind her, his eyes pinned on the water-bound Eli as he bumped along behind in his liquid prison.

Back in Izo's hall the air was growing violently tense. Sted stood at the base of the stairs to Izo's seat, held back only by Sezri's slender hand across his chest. "You have no right!" he roared. "Liechten is mine!"

"I have every right!" Izo shouted back, standing before his

throne with his hand on his sword. "Everything in this land is mine to do with as I please, and I will not have my rights disputed in front of my guests by one of my own men!"

"I'm none of yours!" Sted bellowed. "I'm no one's servant! I am Berek Sted! I came back from death for this, and I *will* have my rematch with Josef Liechten even if I have to do it on your corpse!"

"Sted!" The demonseed's thin fingers dug into the larger man's cape-covered chest.

"No, Sezri." Izo sneered. "Let the ox bellow. Your Master has been a good ally to me, but I will not be told how to handle my affairs. I rule this land, make no mistake, and I will use its prisoners as I see fit." He sat back down on his throne, drawing his sword and laying it across his lap as he glared at Sted. "Leave. I grow tired of your tantrums. Tomorrow, I'll decide what's to be done with the swordsman. Beg your Master that I don't also decide what's to be done with you."

For a moment, Sted's eyes went wild. He pressed against Sezri until the smaller man began to tilt and it looked like Sted would fall on Izo like a tiger. But then, like a curtain falling over a lamp, the furious light went out. Sted stepped back, turned on his heel, and marched out of the hall, slamming the iron gate as he left. Sezri watched him leave, never moving until Sted's enormous shadow vanished into the night.

"That," he said, turning to look at Izo, "was a very foolish game to play."

Izo waved dismissively. "I've been leading bandits for fifteen years. You think I don't know how to handle men like Sted?"

"Sted isn't one of your thugs." Sezri's voice was sharp with disgust. "Have you forgotten whom he serves?"

"Men like that don't serve anyone but themselves," Izo said, laughing. "Your Master is kidding himself if he thinks otherwise."

"My Master sees all things," Sezri said quietly. "It is by his goodwill alone that you have risen as far as you have. You would do well to keep that in mind."

"He helped," Izo said. "He gave me monsters like you, but I was the one who planned the raids, who beat the other bosses. I was the one who took every two-bit gang from here to the coast and turned them into an army capable of taking on Council cities. True, it would have taken me much longer without your Master's aid, but he has received good payment for what he's given. I've kept my end of the deal. Slaves flow from my camps to the Dead Mountain every day. Now it's his turn. He promised to make me a king of the Council, and I will hold him to his debt."

"And you shall be king," Sezri said. "Offering them the swordsman was nothing but foolish arrogance and impatience."

"Call it what you will," Izo said. "I did what I had to do to make the Council move. If that upsets your Master's deal with Sted, that's not my problem. I'm not about to sit back and give up what I'm owed so your Master can pay another."

Sezri clenched his fist. Izo's arrogance was going too far. Inside him, he could feel the strength of the seed building, ready to lash out, to show this pathetic little man the true power of the Master. But before he could even think the command, the beloved voice filled his head.

Enough, Sezri.

The demonseed closed his eyes, nearly crying as the Master's voice rolled across his mind.

Let the human do as he likes. All will be answered. Now, go and find a spirit you can devour without raising alarm. Your strength will be needed soon.

"Yes, Master," Sezri whispered, bowing his head. "All will be as you command."

The voice chuckled, sliding over his soul like a hand stroking a cat. *Such a good child.*

"What was that?" Izo's voice snapped Sezri from his euphoria, and the demonseed glared in disgust at the tiny, human spirit on his makeshift throne.

"Do as you like," Sezri said, turning on his heel. "King Izo."

There was a scrape behind him as Izo stood up. "I hope you're going to check on Sted."

Sezri didn't answer. He simply stepped into a shadow and vanished, sliding through the dark until all he could feel was the seed inside him and the fading power of the Master's voice on his soul. He stopped when he reached the forest just beyond the city. There, in the dark shadow of the trees, he began to hunt for a spirit that would suit the Master's purpose, unaware of the pair of animal eyes watching him from branches above.

Nico sat in the dark in the corner of the small house, her coat draped over her head like a funeral shroud. Directly across from her, the tall man in the brown coat sat on a bench by the fire, staring at her. Outside, bandits were laughing and drinking; inside, the room was silent except for the low hissing of the coals. They hadn't spoken a word to each other since the woods.

None of this would have happened if you'd just accept my gifts. The swordsman's dead and it's all your fault. You know that, don't you?

Nico closed her eyes and buried her head in her knees.

Across the tiny room, the door opened, letting in a swirl of cold, smoky air before shutting again. Nico glanced up. A man wearing a green silk coat, green ballooning pants tucked into tall, polished boots, and a short blue cape with silver lining was standing in the entrance. He looked startlingly out of place, but the man sitting by the fire nodded a familiar greeting.

"Sparrow."

"Tesset," the foppish man replied as he bolted the door behind him.

The man in the brown coat, Tesset, waited until Sparrow was finished before asking, "How did it go?"

"The usual way," Sparrow said, unhooking his cape with a shrug. "Wonderfully, then horribly, and finally stopping somewhere just short of acceptable. Izo's no idiot, but he's not subtle enough for politics. He played his hand straight and strong. Unfortunately, though not surprisingly, the Spiritualist and Monpress mucked things up. I had to make some large concessions, but I think we ended up with the better deal in the end."

"What kind of concessions?"

"He wants his welcome to the Council issued by Whitefall himself," Sparrow said, flopping down into a chair beside the fire. "Here, by the end of the month."

Tesset winced. "That's a tall order. Sara will have your skin."

"I don't think she'll care one jot when she hears what she'll be getting in exchange," Sparrow said, grinning wide. "Not just the thief, but the Heart of War. Plus freedom to search for Slorn and all the other little things we'll wring out once Izo's prancing around in his crown like a little girl playing princess."

Nico's head shot up, and she wasn't alone. Even Tesset's eyes went wide.

"The Heart of War?" Tesset said. "You mean the great awakened sword?"

"You know of anything else with such a pretentious name?" Sparrow yawned. "I just got back from having a look for myself. No wonder no one recognizes it. It looks like a piece of junk. Great big dented black metal monstrosity, almost as bad as those Fenzettis Sara made us hunt down last year. It didn't even glow. Even the cheap awakened swords glow, but I didn't see a thing."

"How do you know it's real, then?" Tesset said. "Sara won't be happy if you make her pull strings for a bluff."

"Who do you take me for?" Sparrow scoffed. "I tried to pick it up, but I couldn't even move the hilt. Couldn't even wiggle it. That sword has the weight of a mountain, just like Sara said. Fortunately, its wielder is still breathing or we'd be in real trouble, paying through the nose for a sword we can't move."

"Josef's alive?"

Both men turned to glare at her, but Nico didn't care. Her relief was like a crushing weight on her chest, grinding every other concern into dust. "Is he all right?"

Sparrow considered a moment before answering. "He's alive for now, and less bloody than I'd expect. But seeing as he's under the questionable care of Izo's surgeons, all of whom seem to be bandits no more intelligent or sober than the common rabble, that's all I can say for now."

Nico took a deep breath, and Sparrow chuckled.

"This must be what they call 'loyalty among thieves,'" he said. "Your concern is truly touching, but I suggest you worry less about the swordsman and more about yourself, darling. Of every piece of this expedition, yours is the most expendable. The only reason you're alive right now is because of Slorn."

Nico shrank back into her coat. "Slorn?"

"You're something of a consolation prize," Sparrow said, taking off his boots. "Slorn's research on demonseeds and the corresponding nature of the spirits they inhabit is priceless. However, with the death of his current experimental specimen, my mistress is worried he'll drift out of the field. That's why we're giving him you. Sara has long known of Slorn and Eli's friendship and the coats he makes to hide your... condition. Your job will be to keep Slorn happy, give him something to study once we bring him back to Zarin. Assuming, of course, we can find him at all." Sparrow frowned in annoyance. "He's being very difficult at the moment. But don't fret, darling. If nothing else, we'll trade you in to the League. Sara just loves having Alric owe her favors."

He spoke so fast his words made Nico dizzy. He reminded her of Eli when the thief was making a particular effort to be as difficult as possible. Still, his point was clear enough. She was a payoff, either to Slorn or to the League. That alone gave her leverage, and if Eli had taught her anything, it was that leverage was never something to waste.

"If I cooperate," Nico said slowly, "will you make sure Josef gets what he needs to heal?"

"Of course," Sparrow said. "Considering we need his carcass to haul the Heart of War, he's safer than you. Though don't go getting any ideas. This can be as pleasant as you choose to make it. Sit in your corner like a good girl, don't give Tesset any excuse to do what we pay him to do, and everything will be nice and smooth." He reached into his waist pocket and pulled out something that looked like a blue glass ball on a leather thong, which he proceeded to roll between his fingers. "I've got to report in and get Sara to agree to all this, and then I'm going to bed. Tesset, since you never seem to sleep anyway, you've got night watch."

Tesset nodded, never taking his eyes off Nico as Sparrow stood and climbed the ladderlike stairs into the house's upper loft. There was some commotion as he settled into bed, and then a blue glow flashed in the dark. It shimmered for a moment, cold and watery on the cabin's pointed ceiling, before vanishing as he threw his covers over it. If she strained her ears, Nico could just make out Sparrow's hushed voice speaking as though he were having a conversation. No matter how hard she listened, however, she couldn't make out the words. Eventually, she sat back against the wall and turned her attention to Tesset, who hadn't moved an inch from his seat by the fire.

Unbidden, her eyes went to the smooth, unmarred skin of his throat, and the black arm she kept buried against her chest began to itch and tremble. How had he done it? She'd felt the connection open, felt the demon as it started to eat him. How had he pushed it back?

Across the room, Tesset's eyes flicked from the fire to meet hers again. "You're wondering how I stopped you?"

Nico froze. Could he read minds as well?

"Go on," he said. "Ask. The first step toward knowledge is a question."

Nico bit her lip. This could be a bluff, a trick to get her to reveal a weakness. But the man across from her didn't seem like the tricky type, and Sparrow had made it perfectly clear she meant little to them. Underneath her coat, her arm was itching more than ever, and she decided to risk it.

"How did you do it?"

"I've already told you," Tesset answered. "Back in the woods. You could not eat me because I did not will it."

"I don't understand," Nico said. "Will stops spirits, not demons."

"And what are you?" Tesset said.

Nico looked down at the floor. "A demonseed."

"Wrong," Tesset snapped. "The demonseed is what's inside you. But you are a human, the greatest spirit of all. The spirit with will, who can control all others."

"That's not true," Nico said. "A wizard can't control another human."

Tesset stood up, pulling his bench closer to Nico's corner until he was almost on top of her. "We have a long night ahead," he said, sitting down. "Let me tell you a story."

"What kind of story?" Nico said, pressing her back to the wall. This close, it took all of her strength to keep her arm from lashing out again. She kept it pinned behind her, the long demon claws scraping at the back of her coat.

"The best kind," Tesset said, settling in with no care for the danger of being so close to a demonseed. "A true one."

He gave her a knowing smile and began.

"I was born in these mountains, and like all male children born here, I joined a bandit gang as soon as I was old enough to follow orders. I was a hotheaded boy with a small, closed mind and a knack for getting in fights. A good bandit, in other words. I was also a wizard, someone who could listen to the winds and trees passably well. A powerful combination, and one that landed me a nice position in Mel's Red Fist, the largest and most fearsome of the bandit gangs at that time. I loved being in the Red Fist. This was thirty years ago, before the Council of Thrones was around to give bandits a hard time. Pickings were fat, and we were the richest, scariest guys around. That's a heady thing for a kid, and I was deadly loyal to Mel, the man who'd brought it all together and the greatest fighter I'd ever seen.

"The day after I turned seventeen, we returned to our camp to find a man waiting for us. This wasn't unusual. We often had vagabonds and deserters from other bandit gangs show up begging to join the Red Fist, but this man was different. He was the largest man I'd ever seen. He had no weapon, and he was dressed in rags and cast-off furs, but the way he carried himself made other fighters look like bumbling toddlers. He just stood there in the center of camp as we rode in, making our usual ruckus, and when we were quiet, he asked which of us was the boss.

"After a good laugh at the stranger's expense, Mel rode forward and announced that he was the leader of the Red Fist. As soon as he said this, the stranger challenged him to a fight. He'd heard Mel was the strongest of the bandit leaders, having the biggest, strongest gang and a nasty reputation as a dirty fighter, and he wanted to see for himself. Mel said this was all true and accepted the challenge. While Mel got his ax, we stood around laughing and arguing over who would get stuck digging a grave for this idiot who was stupid enough to challenge our boss. The stranger, however, was still unarmed. Mel told the man to draw a weapon, and the stranger replied that he would if he needed one. This made Mel furious, and he charged, meaning to cut the stranger's head off. The next moment, Mel was on the ground in a pool of his own blood and the stranger was walking away."

Tesset shook his head. "None of us saw a thing. One second Mel was charging, the next he was down. He died a few minutes later. Of our entire gang, I was the first to recover, and the first thing I did was run after the stranger. I'd never seen a fight like that. Mel had always been my idol, the ceiling of how far a man could rise. Then this stranger appears and in one blow shows me that the top is further than I could ever imagine. So I caught up with him. He was moving slowly, like he was disappointed. When I reached him, he grabbed me around the throat and asked if I wanted to avenge my boss. I didn't even see his hand move. I told him that I'd never seen a man move like him. Could he teach me, or at least tell me his name?"

"And did he?" Nico asked.

Tesset chuckled. "No. He dropped me on the ground and told me to go home. But Mel was gone, and I had no home to go to. So I kept following him. The man walked day and night, but somehow I stuck to his trail. Every time I caught up, I would ask him to teach me. Looking back, I was desperate. I'd based my whole life around being strong, and in one motion this man had blown away my entire idea of strength. I couldn't let him just walk away. So I made a nuisance of myself and, finally, after a month of eating his dust, the man turned and asked me my name. I told him, and he shook his head. 'That's a weak name,' he said. 'From today, your name is Tesset. If you want to learn from me, I'll give you six months. Anything you learn during that time is yours to keep. After that, we're enemies, and if I ever see you again, I'll kill you.'"

Tesset began to laugh. "I was terrified of course, but I didn't want to look weak. I agreed, calling the man Master. He told me no man was master over anyone but himself, and that I was to call him by his name, Den."

Nico's eyes went wide. "Den the Warlord," she whispered. "The man from the bounty posters?"

Tesset nodded. "Of course, this was before the war, before he betrayed the Council. But he kept his word to me, and for six months he taught me one thing."

"One thing?" Nico said.

"Yes," Tesset said. "It was something I'd always known, what all wizards know, but most will never understand." Tesset placed his hand on his chest. "As a human, a wizard has will. This will is what gives him control over all the world save only the spirits of other humans. However, there is one human spirit a wizard does control." Tesset thumped his hand on his chest. "His own. My body and my soul are subject to my will. Just as an enslaver can make a mountain rise up and walk to the sea if his spirit is strong enough, so can I make my body do impossible things by conquering my soul with my will. Once a man has mastered himself, he has no king, no conqueror, no predator but himself, and that, demonseed, is the answer to your question."

Nico could not believe what she was hearing. "It can't be that simple," she whispered.

"It's not," Tesset said. "But that doesn't make it untrue." Faster than she could react, he lunged forward and grabbed her arm, the demon arm she'd been keeping pressed behind her. She pulled back frantically, but he was stronger than her, stronger than anyone she'd ever fought, and his grip didn't even shake as he pulled her black, clawed hand into his own. The demon hand clawed at Tesset's skin like a hungry beast scenting food, and Nico squeezed her eyes shut, waiting for eating to begin. But nothing happened. There was no roaring connection, no feeling of another spirit pouring into her. Nico cracked her eyes a fraction and then opened them in wonder at the sight of her clawed hand clutched between Tesset's palms, his tan skin whole and sound.

Tesset's dark eyes met hers, and when he spoke, his voice was an iron bell. "There is nothing you or your demon can do to me if I do not will it," he said. "I am master of myself, and nothing can happen to me unless I allow it. Do you understand now?"

Nico stared at their clasped hands. "No," she whispered. "Teach me."

Tesset smiled and released her. "I have already taught you."

Nico gaped at him. "No," she said, grabbing his hand again. "You have to teach me how to do it."

Tesset gripped her fingers so hard they ached. "I taught you as Den taught me," he said. "It is so simple, yet it has taken me over thirty years to get to where I am now. But it is not a matter of strength or training or anything else won by hard work. It is a matter of understanding. A child could master it in one day if only their mind were free enough. To truly become master of yourself, you must be willing to throw everything else away. Fear, anger, doubt; these things undermine your authority. You must become as an enslaver to your own soul. Once you have achieved that, nothing can control or limit you ever again."

Nico stared at him, bewildered. But Tesset just smiled, releasing her hand.

"It helps to find a goal," he said, his gruff voice almost wistful as he leaned back to stare at the fire. "Mastering your soul becomes easier when you're chasing something greater than yourself. Mine is to meet Den one more time before I die and finally fight him as an equal."

"But," Nico said, "he's had that enormous bounty on his head for twenty-five years now with no news. How do you even know he's still alive?"

"He's alive," Tesset said fiercely. "Wherever he is, I know he's alive. Men like Den don't die without the world knowing. One day I will find him, and then I will show him how much I have learned."

Nico looked at Tesset as though she were seeing him for the first time, his brown hair touched with gray, his brown skin warm and dark in the firelight, his hawk-nosed face set with absolute determination, and she believed him. She licked her dry lips, thinking of what she would ask him next about how she could begin down the road to understanding what he'd told her. But before she could get the words out, she was cut off by the unmistakable sound of a door being kicked down, followed immediately by the sound of a dog snarling and a woman's surprised scream.

CHAPTER 15

"There," Miranda said, straightening up. "That should do it."

The house she'd been moved to was smaller than the one she'd shared with Tesset and Sparrow, but far better suited to her purposes. It had been a storage building, and as such it was one large room with a high roof and a pair of double doors wide enough for Gin to squeeze through. He was now lying stretched out against the wall with his head resting on his paws by the front door and his haunches hanging out the back. Next to him, a small wood-burning stove with a roaring fire far larger than it was meant to contain kept out any chill the open back door might have let in. Other than the stove, the building had no furniture. Miranda had made the bandits move it all out to make room for her custom prison.

Everywhere Gin wasn't, a bed of soft, springy moss covered the plank floor in a thick green carpet. At the center of the moss was what could only be described as a stone barrel. The barrel was filled to the brim with impossibly blue water, and sitting in the water up to his chin was Eli, looking extremely nonplussed.

"I'm getting a cramp," he announced, shifting in the water, or trying to. "It's unhealthy to stay still this long. And the water is cold."

"You'll live," Miranda said, leaning against Gin with a smug expression. Eli gave her a pathetic look, and Miranda, after a dramatic eye rolling, waved her hand. All of her rings were glowing like embers, but it was the cloudy emerald taking up the bottom joint of her left thumb that flashed the brightest. A moment later the stone barrel creaked and widened a few inches, giving Eli room to fold his legs.

"Much better," the thief sighed. "Thank you, Durn."

The stone spirit rumbled a warning before settling down into his new shape.

Eli arched his eyebrows and leaned forward. Or he tried to, but the water stopped him before he'd gotten more than an inch. He made himself comfortable as best he could, grinning at Miranda as though this half-forward trapped position was what he had intended all along.

"I've been in a lot of prisons," he said. "But this has to be the most elaborate. How long do you intend to keep this up?"

"As long as I have to," Miranda said. "It's clear we're not getting out of here anytime soon, and I know better than to leave you alone. So until I get you to Zarin and hand you over to Banage himself, I'm not taking my eyes off you."

"What, you're just going to sit there and stare at me?" Eli said. "I'm flattered, don't misunderstand, but aren't you being a bit unreasonable? I mean, I'm just sitting here enjoying the soak while you're keeping every spirit you have on full burn. That's got to take it out of you. How long do you honestly think you can keep it up?"

"I'll worry about that," Miranda said.

There was no reason to tell the thief, but she'd planned out a schedule. Right now, Kirik, her fire spirit in the stove, and Alliana, her moss, were on guard. When they got tired, she'd bring out Eril, her wind spirit, and Allinu, her mountain mist, to take their place. Durn, being stone, could watch forever, and she knew better than to question Mellinor's resolve. Keeping up all these spirits was difficult, but it wasn't like she had anything more important to do. When she did need to sleep or empty her bladder, Gin could keep an eye on things. It wasn't a perfect solution, but since Sparrow was dragging his feet, it would have to do. One thing, however, was certain: She was not going to give the thief a moment of leeway. Not an inch of freedom. She had won; she had him. All she had to do to secure her victory forever was get him back to Zarin. This time, she would make sure that happened, no matter the cost. This time, Eli would not escape.

"Being at the center of so much attention, I feel like I should be more entertaining," the thief said with a grin. "How about this? Free my hands and I'll show you a card trick."

Miranda gave him a stony glare and said nothing.

When he realized this approach wasn't going to work, Eli let out a long sigh and slumped back against Mellinor's restraining water.

"You know, I'm actually very impressed," he said, his voice surprisingly sincere. "That was a neat little trap you pulled off back in the river. Of all the people who've chased me over the years, you're the closest thing I've ever had to a real rival. There've been so many bounty hunters who've come after me, so many traps, and yet no one has come quite as close quite as many times as you, Miranda. Back when I first started this whole million-gold-standard bounty thing, I always envisioned a great rival, some famous bounty hunter who would track me all across the Council Kingdoms and give me a real run for my money. But I never in my life thought it would be a Spiritualist."

Miranda frowned, not sure how to answer. Fortunately, she didn't need to, for Eli kept going.

"I just don't see what you're getting from all this effort," he said. "You've already achieved more than most Spiritualists do in a lifetime. You've got nearly two full hands of rings, position, power, a Great Spirit at your beck and call. You don't seem to care about money or fame, and you're not the type who enjoys the chase for its own sake, so far as I can tell. I keep waiting for you to give up, go home, get a Tower, write some long-winded treatise on spiritual ethics, but you never do. You keep coming after me. Why is that?"

"Is that a trick question?" Miranda asked, keeping her voice carefully flat.

"No," Eli said slowly. "It's a sincere one."

Miranda leaned back, resting her head on Gin's ribs. "Because it is my duty."

"Nonsense," Eli said. "It's the Council's job to catch thieves."

She gave him a long look. "That may be, but the Spirit Court cannot ignore your actions. You go around using spirits to steal kings without even trying to hide it. Every job you pull is a production, a grand sensation to build your reputation as Eli Monpress, the wizard thief. The Spirit Court exists to promote two goals: the ethical treatment of spirits and building the public's faith in wizardry. In case you've forgotten, wizards used to be seen as tyrants, hated by spirits and people alike for abusing their power. For the last four centuries, the Spirit Court has worked to change that by taking down those who abuse spirits and by holding all wizards accountable to a moral code, whether they want to be held accountable or not."

"You can't force your morals on the whole world," Eli said.

"We don't," Miranda said. "We force them on other wizards, because if we didn't, the bad times would return faster than you could imagine. Spiritualists swear to uphold the Spirit Court's code of ethics precisely so that we never go back to those dark days. That is why, when you decided to abandon those morals, to use your power as a wizard to flout the law for personal gain, it became my duty to stop you. Your actions throw a black shadow on all of us and undo the hard work of a great many good people. It's so much easier to tear down a reputation than to build it, to inspire fear and suspicion rather than trust. That's why I have to stop you, to protect the work of all the Spiritualists who went before me and save the trust they built, which you now take advantage of."

Eli heaved a long, hard sigh. "You remind me very much of someone I used to know when you lecture like that," he said quietly. "How is it Spiritualists can turn anything into a matter of duty?"

"It's called having principles," Miranda said, crossing her arms over her chest. "Some of us don't have morals as flexible as yours."

"Well, no one could ever accuse you of flexibility," Eli said dryly. "Unfortunately, I fear we will never come to an agreement. Your world is far too black-and-white for me."

"There's no agreement to come to," Miranda said fiercely. "Don't forget who's up to his neck in water."

Eli smirked and started to answer, but he never got a chance. At that moment, the door exploded.

Miranda screamed in surprise, throwing up her arms to shield her face as bits of wood shot across the room. She fell to the ground as Gin slid out from under her, leaping to his feet with a snarl, his patterns swirling madly as he turned to face the door, ears flat back against his skull. For a moment, she couldn't even see what he was growling at through the dust and debris. Then the man stepped into the room, and Miranda felt her skin grow cold.

Sted stood in the doorway. He was shirtless, and his cape was gone. For a moment, Miranda could only stare in horror at the hideous thing growing out of his shoulder. The black skin, as hard and polished as scorched glass, was so alien, so beyond what she expected, that Sted had walked almost all the way to where Eli was trapped in the water before she realized it was his arm. With that realization, everything else fell into place, and she flung out her hand. At once, Durn threw himself back, sliding along Allinora's mossy bed to rest beside Miranda, Eli safely squeezed between the layers of rock and water. The thief started to protest, but Mellinor's water covered his head before he could speak. Never taking her eyes off the intruder, Miranda nodded in thanks. Now was not the time for distractions.

"I knew something was wrong with you," she said, stepping between Sted and Eli, who was bubbling furiously under Mellinor's water. "But I never thought Izo'd actually be stupid enough to employ a demonseed. It must be an idiocy common within the criminal element."

Behind her, Eli made a sound that was half burble, half scoff, and she flicked Durn's ring. There was a loud scrape as the rock closed over Eli's head, trapping him inside a cocoon of stone as well as water. Miranda nodded. Mellinor could give him enough oxygen to keep him from drowning for ten minutes at least, and she was taking no chances.

Sted stood where Durn had been, glaring at her with eyes that were far too bright for the dim room. "I serve no man but myself," he sneered. "I'm here for the thief. Hand him over."

"Never," Miranda said, pulling Allinora's moss back into her ring, away from the monster at the door. "Eli Monpress is under arrest by the authority of the Spirit Court and the Council of Thrones."

"Really?" Sted's voice was slow and sharp, like a knife working through frozen flesh. "And are you ready to die to keep him?"

Gin snarled beside her, and Miranda couldn't help baring her teeth as well. "I couldn't do my duty if I wasn't," she said. "Leave now or I'll call the whole deal off and Izo will never be king."

Sted threw back his head and laughed, a horrible, hollow sound that rattled up from deep in his chest. "Izo?" he cried. "Who cares about Izo? Weren't you listening, girl? I'm here for the thief, preferably alive, but I'll take what I can get. Your fate I'm far less picky about. Move." He took a menacing step forward, heavy boots creaking on the bare plank floor. "*Now.*"

Miranda held her ground, hands clenched in sweaty fists around her rings. Spiritualists didn't fight demonseeds; it was too risky. But she could not back down. Not now, not when she had Eli. Her resolve was set, and Gin must have felt it, for before she could open her mouth to answer Sted's threat, the ghosthound lunged forward.

It was a tight jump. The little room wasn't large enough for Gin to turn around in let alone get any momentum for a flying attack, but Miranda would never have known it. Gin sprang from a standstill, a shifting blur of claws and teeth aimed straight for Sted's neck. Sted had nowhere to dodge and no time to duck before the dog's teeth sank into his neck and shoulders.

They fell backward, Sted stumbling into the splintered remains of the door with Gin on top of him, the ghosthound's teeth lodged in his torso. Miranda felt like cheering. Gin knew as well as she did that the only way to win this was to take Sted down in one blow, before he could eat them or terrify her spirits into submission. From where she stood, it looked like the hound had done just that. Even demonseeds went down when you ripped them in half. But then, just when it looked like Sted was done for, Gin yelped and jumped back, slamming against the rear wall of the house in a scramble of legs and wild shifting fur.

"Bastard!" the dog roared.

Gin's muzzle was slick with blood, which wasn't surprising, considering he'd just bitten a man through to the ribs, but this was too much. Gin coughed, bringing up more blood as he circled to face Sted again, his head low and cautious, as though he were the one who'd just taken a blow instead of dealt one. Across the room, Sted stood up, a superior grin on his face. Gin's bite draped across his neck and shoulders like a bloody shawl, but the holes were closing as Miranda watched.

"Not fast enough?" she asked quietly.

"No, I got him," Gin snarled, sending blood across the floor. "Bastard let me get him. Let me get in good before he started to eat."

He coughed again, adding more blood to the pool on the floor. "I don't get it," he panted. "I could feel him eating me. It was just like before, with Monpress's girl. But there's no fear."

Gin was right, she realized. Other than her spirits, the room was calm. There was no panic, no overwhelming fear like she'd felt in Mellinor. If Sted wasn't standing there with his monstrous arm, healing right in front of her, she wouldn't have even known he was a demonseed.

Gin growled. Sted was coming forward, a feral grin on his scarred face.

"Is that all?" His voice was thick with laughter. "Is that all you have to throw against me? A pet dog?"

"Miranda," Gin said softly, never taking his orange eyes off Sted. "Take the thief out the back. I'll hold this bastard here while—"

A whoosh of flame cut off his words. The fire in the stove blazed up to the ceiling, and Sted burst into flames. He screamed in pain and began to flail wildly. Gin turned to look at Miranda, who was lowering her hand, Kirik's enormous ruby burning like a bonfire on her thumb.

"No playing hero tonight, mutt," she said, pressing her fingers against the pendant on her chest. A great wind rose up, and the fire on Sted grew white-hot as Eril, her wind spirit, blasted it like a forge bellow. Sted screamed again, beating the flames, but Kirik clung tight. The blast of heat was enough to blister Miranda's skin, but she didn't step back. Triumph surged up Kirik's connection, and the ring on Miranda's thumb began to almost vibrate with the fire's victorious joy as Sted sank to his knees.

Then, in the space between breaths, the tide turned. The flames were still blazing bright, the smell of burned flesh thick in the air, but Miranda could feel something pulling on the connection that tied her to Kirik. It felt as though the fire spirit was going further and further away from her, fading into the distance. The feeling was so alien that, for a moment, she could only stand dumbly. Then, like a splash of cold water, she realized what was happening.

"Kirik!" Her voice throbbed with power. "Come back now!"

"No!" the fire roared. "I've almost got him!"

"Kirik!" she cried again. She could feel it clearly now, vibrating up their connection. Sted was eating the fire even as it burned him, devouring the spirit's soul. Through the flames, she could see his charred skin mending, growing whole again as he sucked in the fire's essence. But Kirik wasn't stopping. He burned brighter than ever, the heat roaring until the wooden roof began to smoke, but Sted was standing up, his black, clawed hand clutching the fire, drawing it in, and Miranda decided enough was enough.

With a wrench of her spirit she'd never had to use before, she grabbed Kirik and pulled him back. It hurt. The fire burned her control, fighting her, screaming that he had almost won, but Miranda slammed her will down like a forge hammer. Roaring with defeat, the fire fled back to its ring and the ruby's light went out. Dumbstruck by what had just happened, Miranda stared at her ring, her vision wavering as her heart thudded in fear. The red stone was now the color of charred coal, and she could barely feel Kirik at all.

A gust of wind hit her as Eril returned to his pendant, and Miranda forced her attention back to the fight. Sted was on his feet again, standing in a circle of black char. Smoke filled the air, but most of it came from what was left of the roof and the floor. Sted's clothes had been reduced to blackened rags, but his skin was nearly untouched, and what bits of it were still charred were healing before Miranda's eyes.

She cursed under her breath as he turned to face her, his teeth bared in a hateful smile. "Anything else?"

Miranda clenched her fists. All her rings except Kirik's were trembling against her fingers, not with fear, but with anger. They wanted to kill the monster, to stamp Sted out of existence, but Miranda held them back. She raised her hand and gave a silent order. It took a moment for Durn to comply, but eventually the rock spirit opened his stone cocoon, revealing Eli, now unconscious, curled up like a baby in Mellinor's blue globe. The next order was the hardest she'd ever had to give. She reached out to the thick cord connecting her to Mellinor, and the globe of water collapsed. Steam hissed as the cold water ran over the charred wood, washing Eli up in a little heap at Sted's feet.

Sted bent over, scooping the thief up with one arm. "That was the smart choice," he said. "But then, who could expect a woman to give a good fight?"

Miranda shook with rage, but when she spoke, her voice was as cold as Mellinor's water. "If I back down, it is only because I value my spirits more than any prize or pride that thief could bring me. Take him and go, but be warned, Sted." She spat his name. "When we meet again, I'll make you suffer for what you've done."

"Is that so?" Sted said, slinging Eli over his shoulder. "In that case, I'll make a point to eat every one of your little spirits. That is, if I can be bothered to remember."

Gin snarled, but Sted just turned, laughing, and started toward the door. Before his foot hit the ground, he was gone, vanishing into the long shadows. For a moment Miranda just stood there, almost too angry to breathe, then she knelt down beside Gin. "How is it?"

"I'll live," the hound grumbled, licking the blood from his muzzle. He caught her look, and his enormous orange eyes narrowed. "If you're thinking what I think you are, the answer is yes."

"Are you sure?" Miranda said, suddenly hesitant.

"I wouldn't have said anything if I wasn't sure," Gin growled. "If you think for one second I'm going to let that bastard get away with our prize, then you can find yourself another ghosthound. Get on."

Miranda didn't ask again. She pulled Mellinor back into her body and vaulted onto Gin's back. The second she was on they were running, smashing through what was left of the shattered door into the torch-lit street. She caught a glimpse of Sparrow's shocked face, Tesset and Nico standing behind him, but she put them out of her mind. This had gone far beyond Council games and power plays. It was between her and Sted now. Gin thundered through the streets, sending bandits flying when they got in his way. He cleared the last row of buildings in one leap and stopped on the edge of the box canyon that hid Izo's city from the world. He raised his head, holding his nose up to the night air, and took several large sniffs.

"This way," he said, turning north so hard Miranda's neck snapped. She grimaced and bent low on the hound's back, clinging to his fur as they raced through the dark woods, chasing the shadow of Eli's scent on the cold mountain air.

"I don't know how we're getting out of this." Sparrow's voice held none of its usual charm as they stomped through the torch-lit streets toward Izo's fortress. "And that's not a turn of phrase. I really, honestly, do not know how we are going to make this situation into anything other than an unmitigated disaster."

Behind him, Tesset stayed silent, matching Sparrow's frantic pace with his long, ground-eating steps. As the shortest, Nico had to run to keep up or be dragged by the rope Tesset had affixed to her wrists. It was an awkward setup, but Sparrow had refused to see Izo alone and Tesset couldn't leave Nico unguarded, so they had no choice but to face the fallout together.

When they reached the hall, the guards told Sparrow that Izo was waiting for them at the infirmary, though they wouldn't tell him why.

"Probably just wants to save time," Sparrow muttered bitterly.

"If that were the case, he'd have asked us to meet him at the burial pit," Tesset pointed out.

Sparrow shot him a dirty look and kept going, winding his way through the maze of barracks and training grounds until they reached the long, low building that served as Izo's infirmary.

"Looks like they took a pigsty and replaced the pigs with bandits who could tie a bandage," Sparrow muttered, nodding to the boy who opened the door for them. "Remember, let me do the talking."

"That's why you're here," Tesset said calmly.

Sparrow shook his head and walked faster.

The infirmary was a long hall lined with beds. Most were empty, the stained sheets dumped in piles at their feet. Izo was waiting for them at the very end with several men in drab surgeon's smocks. They were all standing around a bed, and Izo was shouting something, his words so slurred together by rage that Nico could barely make them out.

"I don't care if you have to stab him again!" the Bandit King roared. "Wake him up! Now! And where is that Council peacock?"

One of the doctors pointed nervously over Izo's shoulder, and the Bandit King turned, his face going even redder when he caught sight of Sparrow.

"You!" he shouted, grabbing Sparrow by the arm. "You'd better have something to tell me. Where's the wizard girl?"

"I couldn't say for sure," Sparrow said, his voice pinched with pain. "Probably off after your bruiser. You know, the one who stole our thief?"

Izo bared his teeth and jerked Sparrow up until the smaller man was within kissing distance. "You'd better watch that fancy tongue of yours, boy. I'm in no mood to humor Council dogs who can't even keep their downed prey."

He spat in Sparrow's face, then dropped him. Tesset caught him before he could fall, and Sparrow nodded his thanks, pulling an orange silk handkerchief from his pocket to wipe his face with a disgusted grimace. Point made, Izo turned back to the bed.

This time, Nico was close enough to see who was in it, and her heart clenched. There, lying beneath the surgeon's hands, was Josef. His stern face was pale and calm, his eyes closed in sleep. His clothes had been cut away and his wounds rebound, with the exception of the center of his chest. That was where the Heart lay, and from the way Josef's clothing had been cut, it was clear none of the surgeons had tried to move it, not even to get at his wounds. They probably couldn't move it, Nico realized. The Heart never moved unless it wanted to. That thought, along with the steady rise and fall of Josef's chest, made her feel better than she had since she'd first opened her mouth to tell Eli about the Dead Mountain.

After another minute of failed attempts to wake the swordsman, Izo sent the doctors away. They fled as Izo leaned over Josef's sleeping form. He watched the swordsman for a moment and then reached out his hand and slapped Josef hard across the face. Nico lunged forward before she knew what she was doing, catching herself painfully on Tesset's leash, but Izo didn't seem to notice her at all. He lifted his hand and slapped Josef again, but as he pulled back for a third blow, there was a flash of movement from the bed. Whatever it was happened too fast for Nico to see, but one moment Izo was standing over Josef, his hand coming down on the swordsman's cheek, and the next he was on the floor cursing, with Josef's hand locked around the Bandit King's newly broken wrist.

The swordsman opened his eyes and gave Izo a lazy, deadly glare. "Don't ever do that again."

Izo wrenched his hand free with a pained gasp and jumped to his feet—though, to his credit, he paid no attention to his injury. All of his rage was focused on the man lying in front of him.

"You're Josef Liechten?"

"Powers," Josef sighed, slumping back into bed. "If you wanted to know that, there was no reason to wake me up. You could have asked her." His eyes flicked over to Nico. "Are you all right, Nico?"

Nico started to answer, but Izo stepped between them.

"I'm asking the questions," he snarled. "You're the one Sted has this big grudge with, correct?"

"I beat him, if that's what you mean," Josef said. "He's a bad loser."

"That much is obvious," Izo said. "Tell me then what you make of this."

He produced a scrap of paper from his pocket and flung it at Josef. The swordsman caught the paper deftly and studied it with a scowl.

"It's from Sted," Izo said. "He left it on my doorstep sometime after midnight. He's taken Monpress hostage and says he'll bring him back unharmed only if you will answer his challenge. A one-on-one duel in three days' time."

"Well, I'm glad you told me," Josef said, handing the letter back. "Because I could barely make anything out of his writing. I've seen better penmanship from five-year-olds."

"Who cares about his writing?" Izo shouted. "Monpress is worth a kingdom to me! I want him back."

"As he loves to remind people, Eli is worth several kingdoms," Josef said flatly. "What do you want me to do about it?"

"Isn't that obvious?" Izo said. "You're going to give Sted the fight he wants or I'm going to kill you here and now. That clear enough for you?"

Josef looked the bandit up and down. "Ordinarily, I'd say you're welcome to try, but if you just want me to fight Sted, then we have no quarrel. I was going to do that anyway."

"Oh." Izo deflated a bit; he'd obviously been pumping himself up for a fight. "Good then. Makes things easier."

"However," Josef continued, "if I'm going to get Sted to give up Eli, there are a few things you'll need to provide me with."

Izo crossed his arms. "Like what?"

"To start, a place to fight," Josef said, pushing himself up into a semisitting position. "Preferably somewhere people can see him. This is a pride fight, so people need to be there to see him or his pride will not be avenged. Sted doesn't care about Eli. He'll give the thief up easily when he sees he's getting what he wants."

"You can use the arena," Izo said. "That's what I built it for, and Sted was an arena fighter."

"That will work," Josef said, nodding. "I'll also need a few supplies. How many blacksmiths do you keep in your camp?"

Izo frowned. "What kind of a question is that?"

"How many?" Josef said again.

Izo ran a hand through his thinning hair. "Twenty-two, not counting apprentices."

Josef arched his eyebrows, impressed. "Good. Tell them all to start making swords. I'm going to need a hundred at least, preferably more, made from the blackest, cheapest metal you can give me."

"What game is this?" Izo said. "You've got the greatest awakened sword in the world right there on your chest. Why should I waste my men and resources making you pot-metal blades?"

Josef lay back again. "Those are my terms," he said. "If you don't like them, find someone else to fight Sted."

Izo looked down with a snarl. "All right, a hundred blades. Anything else?"

"Yes," Josef said. "I'm still healing. If you want me in any condition to fight in three days, you'll keep yourself and your doctors away. The only person I want staying with me is Nico. Everyone else will have to leave."

"Done," Izo said, turning to face Tesset. "You don't have a problem leaving the girl here?"

Sparrow opened his mouth to protest, but Tesset was faster. "Not if I am allowed to stay with her as her guard."

Josef looked at Nico, who gave him the thinnest hint of a nod.

"I'm fine with that," Josef said, making himself comfortable again. "Remember, don't touch me for three days or I won't be fit to fight an old man like you, much less a monster like Sted."

Izo seethed with rage, but turned away without a retort. "You," he said, glaring at Tesset. "Keep an eye on both of them. Nothing is to disturb his sleep. If the Council messes this up for me, I'll hang all of you by your own guts, just see if I don't. And you"—he turned to Sparrow—"I hope you talked with your Sara, because the plan is going ahead as agreed."

"Assuming, of course, you hold up your end," Sparrow said.

Izo bared his teeth. "You'll have Monpress, make no mistake. No one steals from Izo."

He made a rude gesture, just for good measure, and then stomped out of the infirmary, shouting for his guards. Sparrow frowned and started speaking with Tesset in a low, hushed voice, but Nico didn't bother to listen. She walked to Josef's bedside, her feet silent on the wooden floor, and sat down on the stool beside him.

She'd thought he was already asleep again, but Josef opened his eyes when she sat down, giving her a weak smile. "Glad you made it," he said softly. "Everything all right?"

"We're prisoners," Nico answered. "And Sted's got Eli."

Josef thought about this for a moment and then gave a tiny, pained shrug. "We've gotten out of worse."

Nico tried to share his certainty, but the angry wounds on his chest made it hard. "Can the Heart really heal you in three days?"

"Oh, I could fight now," Josef said. "The Heart of War is exceptionally experienced at keeping its swordsmen standing. So long as I didn't let go of the Heart, I'd be well enough. But I'm not going to have the Heart, so I need some extra time."

"How will you beat Sted without the Heart?" Nico felt like a traitor even saying the words, but she couldn't imagine how he could win without his sword.

"You'll see when it happens," Josef said, his voice growing soft and sleepy. "Trust me."

Nico nodded and Josef closed his eyes again, sinking almost instantly into a deep sleep. A minute later, Nico heard Sparrow leaving and what sounded like Tesset pulling up his own stool behind hers, but she didn't turn to see for certain. She just sat there, watching Josef, standing guard beside his bed as the sun began to peek over the mountains.

CHAPTER 16

Eli woke with a start. He was lying on his side, curled in a ball on a cold stone floor with his face pressed against a stone wall. He lifted his head away from the wall and gave his limbs an experimental wiggle. Tied, of course, ankles, legs, arms, and hands. He sighed and flopped his head back down on the stone. This captured thing was becoming depressingly frequent. Still, he wasn't wet anymore, which meant he wasn't with Miranda, and that greatly improved his chances of escape. Spiritualist spirits were so stingy. Of course, if he wasn't with Miranda, where was he?

Slowly, painfully, Eli wiggled against his bindings, turning by fractions until he was on his back. Unfortunately, this only made him more confused. He was in a cave, a high one from the little scrap of sky he could see through the distant opening. A thin, cold breeze blew across him, carrying the smell of snow. He sniffed again, searching for woodsmoke or pine, but he caught nothing but wet stone and frozen water. Wherever he was, he was far away from Izo's camp, far away from anywhere, and that, much more than the ropes, posed a problem.

Eli started wiggling again, turning until his back was to the wall. First rule of thievery, always know what's around you. The cave was quite small, barely six feet across and twice as deep, with a ceiling low enough to make a child claustrophobic. Still, despite the cave's tiny dimensions, it took three look-overs for Eli to realize he wasn't alone.

Sted's enormous shape took up the entire back of the cave, his dull clothes blending perfectly into the dark stone. He was hunched over with his eyes closed, his right arm resting on his knees and his head touching the cave's ceiling even sitting down. His other arm he held cradled against his chest, the black claws twitching. Even in the dark, what little Eli could see of the claw was enough to make him ill. It was simply too alien, too inhuman, the way the black, hard shell met Sted's flesh in that sickening melding at the shoulder…

Eli shuddered and looked away before he really was sick. But as he lay there waiting for his stomach to calm down, he realized something else. With the exception of the place where his hideous arm connected to his body, Sted had been uninjured. Frowning, Eli snuck another glance, just to be sure. It was true. Sted's clothes were blackened in places, ripped in others, but his flesh was whole and uninjured.

Eli bit his lip. Sted was a demonseed, that much was obvious, but even Nico didn't heal instantly. This left two possibilities: Either he'd been out longer than he thought, or Miranda had gone down very quickly. Neither was a possibility he liked to consider.

Sted's eyes were closed, but Eli was sure he wasn't asleep. Never one to lie in silence, Eli took the opportunity to speak first.

"Congratulations!" he said, lifting his head to grin at Sted. "You've caught—"

"Shut up." Sted's voice was flat and annoyed. He opened his eyes a fraction, revealing the eerie, unnatural glow beneath the heavy lids. "Prisoners who talk too much end up dead."

"That would be some very expensive silence," Eli tsked. "I'm worth much more alive."

"You think I care about money?"

Eli considered. "No. No, I don't think you do."

Sted nodded and lapsed back into silence. After about three minutes, Eli couldn't bear it any longer.

"At the risk of the aforementioned premature death," Eli said in his most charming voice, "would you mind if I ask why you took me from the Spiritualist? Doesn't seem your style, quite frankly."

Sted said nothing. As the minutes stretched on, Eli resigned himself to curiosity. But then, suddenly, Sted answered.

"I took you to force Izo's hand," he said. "That idiot was going to give Josef Liechten to the Council, but now that I have you, all that's changed. Izo will have no choice but to give me my fight."

"Hold on," Eli said, wiggling along the stone floor until he could look at Sted straight on. "You stole me, Eli Monpress, greatest thief in the world, a ninety-eight-thousand gold-standard bounty, just so you could fight Josef?" If his hands hadn't been tied, he would have thrown them up in the air. "*Powers*, man, he'd fight you for free. Just take me back. I'm sure he'll oblige."

"I will," Sted said. "In three days."

Eli frowned. "What happens in three days?"

"I'm letting him heal," Sted said simply. "My victory over the Heart of War and its wielder is not something I want polluted by a handicap. I will fight Leichten when he's at full strength or not at all. You're here to ensure I am not rushed or dictated by the petty ego of that bandit thug. Once I've defeated Josef, I'll set you free."

"Set me free?" Eli said. "Just like that?"

"Or kill you," Sted said, tilting his head. "Depends on how generous I'm feeling and how much trouble you make for me. Whatever happens, you won't be going back to Izo. That bastard deserves nothing, trading away what he'd already promised."

"Well," Eli said, "he *is* a bandit."

Sted gave him a murderous look, and Eli snapped his jaw shut.

When he was sure the thief would stay silent, Sted continued. "In three days, we head back down the mountain. Until then, you're going to sit there and not talk. And don't even think about escaping. I don't sleep much these days, and your dead carcass will still buy me my fight. Am I being clear?"

"Decidedly," Eli said. "But can I ask you one last question?"

Sted frowned. "You can ask."

"You used to be League, or that's what Josef told me after your fight," Eli said. "So why did you kill Nivel? When Pele said you took Nivel's seed, I assumed it was some internal League struggle. But now it's clear that you took Nivel's seed for yourself, even though Josef said you were spirit deaf. So, why? How did it happen? Why did you switch?"

"To fight Josef Liechten," Sted said simply. "I made a deal. A bad one on both sides, as it turned out, but I won't give up until Josef Liechten is lying dead at my feet. He's the only man who ever truly bested me, and if I'm going to die, I'll die undefeated."

Eli's eyebrows shot up. "But—"

He swallowed his words at Sted's glare. Clearly, that was all the answer he'd be getting. Turning away from Sted's uncomfortable, glowing gaze, Eli rolled back toward the wall. He wiggled a bit, trying to find the most comfortable angle, but it was hopeless. Finally, he gave up and flopped on his back, staring up at the low stone ceiling.

It was going to be a very long three days.

Gin crashed through the forest, panting as he jumped over fallen logs and scrambled up slopes slick with fallen leaves. Miranda hunched low on his back, doing her best to avoid looking at the lightening sky or thinking about the fact that they'd already passed that rock formation twice before. But even as she tried to keep hope alive, the ghosthound padded to a stop at the edge of a creek.

"It's no good," he panted. "They're gone. Sted was too fast. I don't even know if we're in the right part of the mountains anymore."

"Just a little farther," Miranda said, clenching her hands in his fur. "We just need a hint of his scent."

"He's gone." Gin snapped the words, then shook his head and lowered his tongue to the swift water, drinking deeply. "I lost him hours ago," he said when he was finished. "We need a different plan."

"Like what?" Miranda said, gritting her teeth. "Go back to the bandits? Wait?"

"We're not going to find him by wandering around," Gin snarled.

His tone stopped her cold, and Miranda leaned back. He'd been running all night; of course he was tired. They were both tired, but the idea of going back to that camp empty-handed, of letting Eli slip through her hands *again*...

She leaned forward, resting her forehead against Gin's neck. She couldn't do it. She couldn't lose again, not like this. But what else was there to do? Saying he couldn't find Eli wasn't something Gin would admit unless he was truly out of options. The forest was huge, and they didn't even know if Sted had continued north or changed direction entirely. No, finding him in the woods would require more luck than she had. She needed to reconsider her options.

Miranda took a deep breath and forced herself to think clearly. There were only two reasons Sted would have taken Eli: the bounty or as a bargaining chip against Izo. That meant he would eventually be headed either toward Zarin or back to Izo's camp.

She discarded the bounty idea immediately. If Sted was going to Zarin, then he was already so far ahead of her there was little point in giving chase, and Eli would end up in custody whether she caught him or not. Also, whatever Sted was, he certainly didn't seem like the type to walk into Lord Whitefall's office and ask for a voucher. And there was that display last night. No, Sted was after Izo. She was sure of it, and that meant he'd be heading back to the camp.

Miranda grimaced. As much as the idea of going back to Sparrow empty-handed grated, she had to admit it was the best choice. Also, Josef and Nico were still at the camp. If Eli escaped from Sted, that's where he'd go, and if Sted wanted something from Izo, that's where he'd take the thief.

"All right, mutt," she muttered into Gin's fur. "Take us back to Izo's."

But the ghosthound didn't answer. He was standing still as a statue below her, staring down the stream bank.

Miranda looked around. "What?"

"We're being watched," Gin growled low in his throat, ears going flat against his head.

Miranda pressed herself against his back, mentally nudging her rings awake. She winced when she was forced to skip over Kirik's smoldering ember, but she couldn't think about that now. "Is it Sted?" she whispered, slightly hopeful.

"No." Gin was growling full tilt now. "It's a wizard."

Miranda was about to ask how he could be so sure when a man appeared on the bank a dozen feet downstream. Miranda didn't see where he had come from—he seemed to just appear from the woods—but once she saw him, she could look at nothing else. There, walking toward her, was a large man with a bear's head. She thought it was a mask until she saw the eyes staring at her, intelligent and dark above the sharp-toothed muzzle. Miranda swallowed and began to call her spirits. But even as she reached for the threads of power that tied her to her rings, the bear-headed man stopped and put up his hands.

"I mean no harm, Spiritualist." The voice that came from the bear's mouth was deep and gruff, but undeniably human. "You seem to be lost and in need of some assistance."

"We need no assistance," Miranda said carefully.

"No?" The bear face looked skeptical. "Do you always keep your fire spirit on the brink of flickering out, then?"

Miranda paled, and the bear-headed man smiled. "I thought not," he said. "Miranda Lyonette would never put her spirits in such danger unless things were very grave."

"How do you know my name?"

The bear-headed man laughed, a deep, rumbling sound. "There aren't many Spiritualists who ride ghosthounds and carry great seas inside their bodies. For those of us who study spirits, you're quite the oddity. I would know, being somewhat of an oddity myself." He touched his muzzle with his hand. "Come," he said, turning. "Let's get your fire stoked before it flickers out. I can hardly bear to look at it."

Gin did not budge an inch, and Miranda made no move to force him. "Who are you?"

The bear-headed man kept walking down the bank. "I'm Heinricht Slorn. Now come."

For a long moment, Gin and Miranda could only stare at his retreating back. Then Miranda looked down at Kirik's dark ruby, and they followed.

The bear-headed man led them up the creek bank to a row of tall bushes, the deep green, waxy-leafed kind that thrive on steep mountain slopes. He pushed the branches gently aside and turned to motion Miranda forward like a well-mannered host inviting guests into his estate. Miranda dismounted stiffly and ducked under the branches. Gin eyed the tiny space with scorn and lay down on the bank. Slorn waited a moment more, and then he turned and followed Miranda into the canopy, letting the branches fall quietly behind him.

Miranda had not gone more than a few steps into the bushes before she stopped, staring in amazement. Parked at the heart of the little grove was a large wagon. No, that wasn't right. Wagons had wheels. This was shaped like a wooden traveler's wagon, complete with a rounded wooden roof, shuttered windows, a chimney pipe, and a set of folding steps going up to a painted door. But down at the bottom, in the spots where the wheels should have been, were six long, splayed legs. Each leg stuck out from the wagon's body at a right angle and cornered sharply at a knobby joint before reaching the ground on a wide, flat foot with five splayed toes, like a lizard's. Each leg appeared to be newly carved from green wood, bright yellow-white and smelling of sawdust, and they sprang from the cart as though they had grown there. There were no joints, no nails, just the fresh wood of the legs lying flush against the older, stained wood of the wagon's body, molded together as though they'd always been that way. She was still trying to make sense of it when she saw something even stranger. The legs shuffled, adjusting their weight, each one flexing and adjusting its splayed foot so that the cart sat slightly closer to the ground as Slorn came up and flipped down the little stair.

"There," he said, smiling as the red-painted door opened for him of its own accord. "Come in and we'll have a look at your ring."

"How did you do that?" Miranda said, and then bit her tongue. She hadn't meant to blurt it out like a child gawking at a street magician's trick, but Slorn didn't bat an eye.

"I'm a Shaper," he said as he stepped inside, as though that explained everything.

Well, Miranda thought, in a way it did. Even Master Banage

wasn't exactly sure how the Shapers did what they did. One thing was certain, though, the bear-headed man wasn't abusing his spirits. She could practically hear the wood beaming as she gawked at it, the legs shifting to show the cart at its best. That pride made her feel more comfortable than any assurance Slorn could have given, and she hurried up the folding stair after him.

The covered wagon was much more spacious than she would have guessed from the outside. One wall was lined with hinged bins, all neatly latched and labeled. The other was taken up by a folding cot, now stowed away, and a little table that bolted to the floor. Slorn was already sitting on one of the folding seats, his large hands fussing with the small iron stove just large enough to heat a kettle that was built into the wall just above the table.

Slorn unlatched the cold grate and placed a few sticks of wood into the stove's tiny iron belly. "There," he said, leaning back. "Put your ring in."

"Are you sure?" Miranda said, unfolding the chair opposite him and sitting down. "Kirik's a bonfire spirit. I don't want to risk your wagon."

Slorn's bear eyes widened, and he looked at the stove. "What do you think?"

The stove made a scornful sound. "I've never met a fire I couldn't contain," it said, opening its grate wider. "Give him to me."

Miranda blinked in surprise, first that the grate was awake, and second that it was so confident. She slipped Kirik's ring from her finger and placed it with the wood in the stove's belly. The second her hand was clear, the stove snapped shut and a blast of hot air hit her face as the fire crackled to life. A surge of relief radiated up Kirik's connection, and Miranda felt like sobbing with relief herself.

Across the table, Slorn's eyes glowed with pleasure. "My stove is very good with fires," he said. "An hour and your Kirik should be good as new." He reached overhead, taking a shiny copper kettle from a hook on the ceiling. "It would be a shame to waste the heat; may I offer you some tea?"

"Yes, please," Miranda said, still shaking.

Slorn got up and walked over to the water barrel, holding the kettle crooked as the water arced up the spout of its own accord. Impressed as she would have been, Miranda saw none of it. Her eyes were locked on the roaring blaze behind the stove's grate as a great lump of guilt rose up in her throat. She hadn't realized how close she'd come to losing Kirik. Her thoughts went to Gin outside; Gin, who'd run all night for her. Her mind flashed back to the night before, to Gin retreating, blood dripping from his muzzle as he glared at Sted. Was he really all right, or had she been too blind in her pursuit to see? What had she been thinking, fighting a demonseed? She should have tossed Monpress at his head rather than risk her spirits. Miranda clenched her fists. She was becoming as obsessed with him as everyone else seemed to be. What must Slorn think of her, a Spiritualist who nearly killed her fire for a thief? What would Master Banage say?

She jumped as Slorn placed two steaming mugs on the table and looked up to find him staring at her, his dark eyes almost human in the glow from the stove.

"Don't be too hard on yourself," he said. "It's a strong spirit's deepest nature to fight a demon and save the weaker ones from the panic. That you were able to pull the fire back before it was devoured is a sign of the deep bond of trust between you."

Miranda gaped at him. "How did you know?"

"What?" Slorn said. "About the demonseed? What else could do that to a spirit? Also, I've been keeping an eye on Izo's camp for some time." His voice deepened into a growl. "There's a man there I have unfinished business with."

Miranda swallowed, suddenly very aware of Slorn's massive

jaw full of sharp, yellow teeth. "Is that why you wrote to Sara for help?"

"At the simplest level, yes," Slorn said, his voice suddenly calm and smooth again. "But Sara and I have been professional colleagues long enough that I knew a simple letter wouldn't be enough to get her to act, at least not in the immediate, large-scale way I needed her to. That's why I made sure my daughter knew how to find Monpress, and that Sara would find out."

"Wait," Miranda said. "You mean that wasn't a leak?"

"Of course not," Slorn said. "At this point, I can afford to leave nothing to chance. I tracked Sted alone as long as I could, but as soon as it became clear he was entering Izo's service, I knew I needed a larger pressure than I could provide myself. I needed the Council, which meant I needed Sara, and if anyone can get that woman to play her cards, it's Eli Monpress."

"Hold on. You're after *Sted*?" Miranda knew she was just repeating things now, but she really could not believe what she was hearing. "*Why?* Demonseeds are League business. Why waste time fussing around with Sara and Eli? Five League members could clear out Izo's entire camp in an hour. You seem to have more connections than Lord Whitefall himself, so I can't believe you don't have a way to contact the League."

Slorn leaned back, his inhuman face suddenly distant, and Miranda snapped her mouth shut. She'd said too much. She gripped the handle of her mug, waiting for a rebuke, but when the bear-headed man spoke, his voice was gruff and low.

"Can I tell you a story?"

Confused, Miranda nodded.

Slorn took a deep breath. "Ten years ago, my wife, Nivel, disappeared. We were both Shapers then, wizards of the Shaper Mountain. Up there, in the snow, we are always in the shadow of the

Dead Mountain. When a wizard disappears, like Nivel did, it usually means only one thing. They were taken by the mountain."

Slorn stopped here, and Miranda watched nervously, unsure if she should offer comfort or simply wait for him to continue. Fortunately, Slorn made the choice for her.

"Because of this, to protect ourselves and our mountain, the Shapers have a law. Any wizard who vanishes is considered dead. Should they be seen again alive, they are to be given to the League as a demonseed. When Nivel vanished, I was prepared to mourn her. But then, suddenly, she came back."

Slorn looked up, dark eyes flashing. "Do you know what it is like, Spiritualist? To see the dead walk again? I expected a monster, but she was the same Nivel I married, my best friend, the mother of my daughter."

"She wasn't taken by the mountain?" Miranda said.

Slorn shook his head. "No," he said darkly. "You misunderstand me. She was what we feared, she was a demonseed. But what I had never been told, what I never prepared for, was that the person would remain unchanged. Nivel had always been strong, always forceful and determined. None of that had changed. She knew what had happened to her. She could feel the seed, but she did not want to give up, and I could not let them take her. So we did the only thing we could do: we ran. We fled the Shapers with our child, and for the last ten years we dedicated our lives to studying demonseeds, how to hide them, how to control them, and, ultimately, how to defeat them. *Ten years*, Spiritualist. Most seeds survive for one if they're quiet, but through constant deals with the League, constant concessions, we held on. And we were making progress, learning so much. But then, a month ago, all of that was ruined. Sted, then just a defeated swordsman, snuck into the valley where my wife was hidden. She was deep in the seed's trance and she could not fight back. He killed her and took her seed into his own body, becoming what before this I would have named impossible, a nonwizard demonseed." Slorn stood up, walking over to gaze out the wagon's tiny window. "I have been tracking him ever since."

"I see," Miranda said softly as his words faded. "You want revenge for your wife. But still, surely the League could help. That's their job, isn't it?"

Slorn began to chuckle, the sound horrible and out of place in his menacing mouth. "Again," he said, turning to look at her, "you misunderstand me. If it was only revenge I desired, I could have had that long ago. I could have called the Lord of Storms down that very day, but it's more complicated than that. Do you know what the League does with demonseeds?"

Miranda shook her head.

"First," Slorn said, "the host body is killed. Demon-possessed spirits are fearsome combatants, which is why all League members must be excellent fighters, but after the fight is when the League's true function becomes clear. When the host body has been defeated, the League member splits it open. Carves it straight down the middle, like a hunter gutting a deer, and takes the seed. Depending on how long the seed was active and how many spirits it ate, the seed can be anywhere from one inch to a foot in length.

"Demonseeds are the product of a seed being placed in a host," Slorn continued. "The host can be killed, but the seeds themselves are not from our sphere and cannot be destroyed by any known method. The best the League can do is lock them away. They have a great vault in their headquarters, a storehouse of every seed they've ever purged. Once a seed enters their possession, it never comes out again."

Slorn looked her straight in the eyes. "Nivel and I both knew it would end eventually," he said. "Maybe not as it did, but still, no one can fight forever. However, the final stage of our research requires the seed itself. There is so much more it can tell us, so many questions to answer. If I let the League get ahold of Sted, then the seed inside him, Nivel's seed, disappears forever into their vault, and ten years of the work my wife suffered for with it. That, Spiritualist, is why I needed Sara, why I needed you and Monpress and this whole farce. I'm fairly certain Sted, being spirit deaf, will never muster enough power to awaken the seed by himself. Already, not being a wizard, he can't generate the kind of fear usually associated with demonseeds, so the League is searching blindly. That gives me a good chance, especially now that he's stolen Monpress."

Miranda started. "How did you know about that?"

Slorn gave her a look. "I told you, I've been watching everything. How else do you think I found you out here?"

Miranda knew she looked petulant, but she couldn't help it. Lately, it seemed she was always the last to know anything.

"Don't worry about your thief," Slorn said, resting his elbows on the table. "Sted is a blunt man who lives only to beat the wielder of the Heart. He cares nothing for Eli's bounty or his true power. He only took the thief to get a hand up on Izo. Now that the prize everybody's after is safely in his possession, Sted is free to demand what he really wants, a rematch with Josef Liechten."

"How can you sound so pleased about it?" Miranda said. "I know Josef has the Heart, but this is a demonseed." Her mind flitted back to the ruined throne room in Mellinor, to Nico crouching in the dark, her eyes glowing like lanterns while the world screamed around her, and she shivered. If that was a controlled demonseed in a little girl's body, she'd hate to see what a brute like Sted could become.

"I wouldn't worry overmuch about Liechten," Slorn said. "Sted may be a demonseed, but he's a mediocre swordsman. The Heart, on the other hand, doesn't let just anyone swing it around."

Miranda frowned, sipping her tea. She was still turning things over in her mind when a metallic clank nearly startled her out of her seat. Across the table, the oven popped open, spilling out a geyser of blisteringly hot air.

"Ah," Slorn said. "Good work."

Without tongs or mitts, he reached his hand into the roaring stove. Miranda was about to shout a warning when she saw the fire peeling back for him. When he took his hand out again, Kirik's ring was sitting in his open palm, the ruby glowing like a red lamp. Miranda took the ring from his hand. The gold was warm to the touch, but nowhere near as hot as it should have been. Inside, she could feel Kirik sleeping, happy and content and fully himself with no sign of his previous injury.

"I don't know how to thank you," she said, sliding the ring lovingly onto her thumb.

"No need," Slorn said. "I would be a poor wizard indeed if I saw a spirit like that and did nothing."

Miranda sat turning her ring on her finger as Slorn cleaned the embers from the stove and restowed the kettle on its hook. By the time he'd finished tidying up, she'd come to a decision.

"Slorn," she said, sitting up. "Take me with you."

The bear-headed man turned to look at her, curious, and Miranda continued. "I owe Sted a thing or two myself. Let me help you take him down. If I go back to Izo's now, I won't be able to do anything except go along with everyone else's plans. You seem to know everything, but you may not know that Sparrow has orders from Sara to make sure you come back to Zarin with us, whether you want to or not. Take me with you and I'll keep him back long enough for you to get out with the seed."

"A generous offer," Slorn said, scratching his muzzle. "And in return, I suppose, I look the other way while you capture Monpress."

Miranda winced. She wasn't used to people seeing straight through her like this. "I know he's your friend," she started. "But—"

"You misunderstand me again," Slorn said. "I'll gladly take your help. Monpress reaps what he sows, but he knew that when he decided to become a thief. Besides, I imagine he rather likes having someone as dedicated as yourself on his trail. He would be cross with me if I tried to protect him."

Miranda chuckled. Slorn's words made sense in the twisted, Eli-logic sort of way.

"Well," Slorn said, "if we're going to be working together, the first thing I'll ask is that you get some sleep. You've been riding all night, and I can't have that sort of a liability on my hands. I'm going outside to check up on a few things. You can use my bunk in the meanwhile."

Miranda tried to protest, but Slorn was pulling the folding bed down, its crisp, white sheets already tucked into place. He grabbed a pillow and a blanket from a cabinet beside the door and tossed them on the bed.

"Sleep well," he said. "We'll discuss strategy in a few hours when your mind is awake."

He gave her a polite nod and vanished down the stairs, the red-painted door falling quietly shut behind him. Miranda stood there a minute more before she gave in, flopping down with a loud sigh on the surprisingly soft trundle bed. She had barely kicked her boots off before she was asleep, her head pillowed on the pile of blankets Slorn had left for her.

Slorn heard the growling before he'd reached the wagon's bottom step. He turned to see the Spiritualist's ghosthound lying at the entrance to the dense bushes, his enormous orange eyes watching Slorn in a way that was far too predatory for comfort.

Slorn stared right back. "She's asleep."

"I can tell that," the ghosthound said. "I presume we're throwing our lot in with you, then?"

"For the time being," Slorn said, nodding. "Is there something you'd like to add?"

"If that's what Miranda says, then that's what we're doing," the ghosthound said with a yawn. "I just wanted to make sure I didn't need to rip your throat out before going to sleep."

Slorn heard the wagon hiss, and he put his hand on the wood, sending out a calming tendril of his spirit. The hound yawned again, showing an impressive line of teeth, and then, almost in the same instant, he was asleep, curled in a ball with his long nose buried in his tail.

Slorn waited until he was sure the ghosthound wasn't bluffing before letting out a long, low sigh. He had no doubt the dog would have killed him if he'd threatened the girl, no questions asked. Slorn shook his head, marveling. Shapers could blend spirits together in ways no other wizard could, but he'd never seen anyone who could match a good Spiritualist for spirit loyalty.

He whispered to the bushes, and they stretched out their branches to cover the dog's sleeping form. It would be awhile before Sted moved again. There was plenty of time to let his guests sleep a bit before moving on. Meanwhile, he would gather more information.

Slorn turned and walked out of his hidden camp, climbing farther up the slope until he reached the crest. They were high up, higher than his own Turning Wood, and the air was cold and swift. Squinting, Slorn looked up and north, following the line of the cliffs until he spotted his wind riding high and bright over the sleeping mountain spirits. He raised his hands, sending a flash toward the wind. It danced a moment longer and then dropped down, spiraling through the trees until it ruffled the fur on his face, making his eyes water.

"The swordsman has agreed to the fight," it whispered. "It was very hard to make out, I hope you know. The spirit deaf are so difficult to focus on."

"I appreciate your efforts," Slorn said. "What about Sted?"

The wind shivered when he said the name. "In the mountains, I think. He's even harder to follow than the others. I can't make out exactly what he is, but I don't like him at all."

Slorn wisely stayed silent on that. "Thank you very much for your help. I won't forget it."

"Don't tell *me* you're happy. Tell the West Wind," the spirit said. "Why else do you think I'm doing this?"

"Of course." Slorn nodded. Even after all these years, spirit politics baffled him, especially winds. "Would you mind going back to the camp?"

"If you like," the wind sighed. "Staying in one place too long makes me ache."

"It won't be for long," Slorn said. "I'll join you there this evening. And I'll be sure to inform the West Wind of the great pains you've taken to help us."

This seemed to please the wind immensely, and it took off with a great whoosh, shaking the thin trees as it flew skyward and turned south, back toward Izo's camp. Slorn watched it go, staring up at the blue dome of the sky until his wind was long gone and replaced by other winds, all moving like great currents through the sky.

He was about to turn back when a flash of movement caught his eye.

As always, something inside him, inside the deep animalistic instincts he'd inherited when he let the bear into his soul, told him to look away, but the stronger part, the curious, purely human side of him, tilted his head upward. There, above the snowy mountaintops, above the winds, something was moving on the dome of the sky itself. It was a subtle motion, one he couldn't have seen at all if he hadn't been looking for it. He'd first noticed it years ago by chance. Now, against his better judgment, he looked whenever he caught a glimpse. High overhead, pressing against the arc of the sky itself like a weight pressed on a taut cloth, was the faint outline of a long, bony, clawed hand. As he watched, the hand scraped slowly downward, running long, sharp grooves in the sky that vanished the moment it passed, only to be replaced by another hand, sometimes smaller, sometimes larger, pressing down again.

Fear like no fear he'd ever felt before began to well up inside him, and a great need stronger than any instinct screamed at him to look away. Even so, he locked his eyes a moment longer, watching the hands scrape across the dome of the sky.

"Slorn?"

He jumped at the voice, whirling around to see the wind waiting, circling him in worried little circles.

"Yes," he said, struggling to keep his voice normal.

"I just came back to let you know the West Wind told me to tell you to be kind to the Spiritualist girl. Who knows why. Spiritualists are busybodies, but Illir's word is law."

"I'll look after her, don't worry," Slorn said, managing a weak smile.

The wind spun again. "Slorn." Its voice was not nearly so certain this time. "What were you looking at?"

"Nothing," Slorn lied. "Nothing at all."

The wind made a frightened wheezing sound. "It's not good to stare at the sky."

"It's nothing," Slorn said again. "Off with you."

The wind held on a moment longer and then whipped away, flying hard and fast between the trees. Slorn waited until it was completely gone before wiping the cold sweat from where the fur met his neck. When his breathing was steady again, he walked down the slope back toward the bushes. He did not look at the sky again.

CHAPTER 17

When the sun rose on the third day, Josef Liechten woke up, took the Heart of War from his chest, and stomped off to his fight. Nico trailed him like a shadow, pulling Tesset behind her so that they made a strange sort of line pushing their way across Izo's camp. The city was packed. Bandits wearing the Bandit King's red and black had come from all across the mountains, abandoning their small camps and outposts for a day of glory.

"What are all these idiots doing here?" Josef growled, glaring as a gaggle of young men, some barely into their teens, made themselves comfortable on a rooftop with a good view of the arena. "This is a duel, not a circus."

"For the men up here, the two are the same," Tesset said. "Sted may have forced Izo to play host, but you're kidding yourself if you think Izo isn't going to get something out of it. The Council's been cracking down and troop morale is low. How better to boost it than a spectacular fight to the death? It's a clever use of a bad situation, but Izo's famous for turning things to his favor. He didn't become king of the bandits for his nobility, you know."

Josef shook his head in disgust. "I just hope he remembered his end of our deal."

"He did," Nico said softly. "They've been hammering for days."

Josef didn't need to ask what she meant by that, for a moment later the arena itself came into view. Lying on the hard-packed sand was a jagged heap of newly forged swords. Some blades were almost black with imperfections, others were actually crooked, lying sideways across the blades beneath them. Still, hundreds of swords in all. Josef grinned and clapped his hands together.

"Perfect."

Izo was standing at the arena's edge with his retinue and the foppish man from the Council, whose finery was looking a little wilted today. They both turned as Josef approached, and Izo brightened visibly, grinning so wide Josef could count his gold crowns.

"The sleeper wakes," he said, laughing. The Bandit King was dressed in silks like a lord and obviously in a fine mood as he stretched out his hand toward the pile of swords. "See, it is all here, as promised. You asked for a spectacle and I delivered."

"The crowd is too much," Josef said. "But Sted will probably like it, so let them stay. Neither of us will be holding back, though, so I can't vouch for your men's safety."

"What bandit looks for safety?" Izo scoffed.

Josef shrugged and stared down at the circular pit of the arena, measuring the wood-braced walls with his eyes. "In that case, get some of your men started putting the swords on the walls. The blades are no good to me piled like that. I need every one of them on a hook, hilt up. I'm guessing that's your seat?" Josef nodded toward the short tower at the edge of the arena topped with a crimson-covered box that held benches, a throne, and a balcony.

"Who else's?" Izo said.

Josef ignored his boastful grin. "I'll need a pillar about the same height directly across from it. There." He pointed. "Just a simple post will do, so long as it's at least a foot thick."

"Easily done," Izo said. "But why?"

"I need a safe place for this." Josef reached over his shoulder and grabbed the Heart's hilt. In one motion, he brought the enormous black blade over his shoulder and plunged it into the ground. The blade sank a foot into the hard dirt before it stopped.

Izo cocked an eyebrow. "As you like, swordsman. But better make it two feet."

He snapped his fingers, and his men ran forward to get their orders. Moments later a small army swarmed into the pit, moving swords and getting the ground ready for the post Josef had requested. While they worked, Josef sat down on the arena's edge, staring at the sandy circle until the men were shadows and all he could see was the field of battle. Behind him, he could feel the Heart's power waiting, but he kept himself apart. As he'd slept, the Heart had been with him, fighting the fight against the Lord of Storms over and over again. Through it all, the sword never spoke, but the underlying message behind the endless fight was as strong and solid as bedrock. In their fight with Sted, Josef and the Heart had taken the first real step toward becoming a swordsman. They had achieved the unspoken understanding between sword and man. But that wasn't enough, not for a fight like the Lord of Storms. To beat a man like that—no, not a man—to beat a force of nature like the Lord of Storms would take the greatest swordsman in the world wielding the greatest awakened sword. He had one part of the equation. Now it was time to work on the other. He crunched his knuckles together. Sted may have demanded this fight, but Josef was going to use it to his fullest advantage.

He heard a soft rustle and turned to see Nico sitting down beside him, the rope taut across her wrists. Tesset stood a good five feet away, talking urgently with the foppish man. It was the farthest Josef had seen him stray.

"They're talking about Miranda," Nico said. "She chased off after Eli and hasn't come back yet."

"Then we know the thief isn't caught," Josef said. "The Spiritualist girl is a better soldier than most wizards. If she had caught him, she'd have brought him back to the chain of command, and for now that seems to be the peacock man."

"Sparrow?" Nico said, wrinkling her nose. "I don't think she likes him."

"Like has nothing to do with duty," Josef said. "I just hope Sted doesn't do something stupid. He's never been someone you could count on for sense."

Nico stayed silent at that, and Josef looked over, taking note of the haunted look in her eyes, which now seemed permanently too bright for whatever light they were in.

"I'll beat Sted," he said.

"I know you will," Nico answered. "That's not it." She paused for a moment, sinking deeper into the dark folds of her coat. "Sted's a demonseed now. I don't know for sure how, but if he killed Nivel, then I can guess. He's not a wizard, but he has powers like I used to have."

"I know," Josef said. "I fought him a little back at the hut. He's got speed, shadow jumping, incredible strength, but I've sparred with you, remember? I know what seeds are capable of, and Sted's on a different plain entirely, a lower one. He may be more dangerous now than he was in Gaol, thanks to that arm of his, but it's a brittle kind of strength. He made a bad bargain when he left the League."

Nico pulled herself in tighter, and Josef looked over to see she was clutching her arm under her coat. "Don't underestimate how dangerous he is, Josef," she said quietly.

"I don't," Josef answered. "But I also refuse to underestimate my own abilities. Even the crooked metal pokers down there will strike true if the swordsman wills them to. I know I will beat Sted, Nico. My only worry about this whole business is what happens when I do." He heaved a frustrated sigh. "That part of things was always Eli's job. I'm just here to fight."

Nico looked worried. "I don't think he has a plan this time."

"Don't be so sure," Josef said, leaning back. "Eli's sleeves have more tricks up them than mine have knives. Well"—he shook his empty sleeve—"usually. But I've been with the thief a long time. If there's anything he can pull off, it's an escape. Trust him."

Nico lowered her eyes, leaving a lump of things unsaid in the air. Josef ran a frustrated hand through his short hair. He understood the silence even better than if she'd spoken. She trusted Eli to run, just not to take her with him. Josef gritted his teeth. He didn't blame her for thinking that. It couldn't be easy to trust the thief after the things Eli had said back in the cabin. But as he'd said, he'd known Eli for a long time, and for all his flaws, the thief had never left a companion in the lurch. It took him awhile sometimes, but he always came around. All Josef could do was put it out of his mind, focus on winning, and trust that today wouldn't be the first exception to the rule.

They sat the next half hour in silence, watching as the bandits hung every last one of the shoddy, pot-metal swords on the arena walls. It took a team of ten men to raise the giant log Izo had selected to hold the Heart. When it was fully upright, the log's top was four feet above the arena's edge, but a dozen from the sandy floor, too high for either Sted or Josef to reach. Josef kicked it a few times to make sure it was secure before plunging the Heart deep into the wood. The sword slid in easily, poking out the top of the pole like a trophy in a tournament. Satisfied, Josef returned to his seat beside Nico to wait. Tesset joined them this time, his face neutral as ever, despite his heated discussion with Sparrow.

Neither Josef nor Nico asked him any questions, and he did not volunteer any information. Sparrow, however, had stomped off and was now sitting in Izo's box, swinging a blue jewel on a leather thong and apparently talking to himself. Josef watched him awhile, and then put the fop out of his mind. Even if they were officially prisoners of the Council of Thrones, he had larger problems than Council business. Instead, he jumped down into the arena, circling and getting a feel for the sand, picking out some of the least warped swords to wear at his hips for the opening blows. Overhead, the sun climbed higher into the sky and the bandits began to settle into whatever seats they could find with a good view of the arena. Izo himself was up in his box, talking with the strange, thin man in black who seemed to be constantly at his side, while a bandit poured wine from a barrel into tall glasses. By noon, a hush had fallen over Izo's bandit city. Though no time had been agreed on, everyone was waiting, craning their heads to be the first to catch a glimpse of Berek Sted when he entered the arena.

"I don't understand it," Miranda grumbled, pressing her eye against Slorn's leather-bound glass telescope and shifting her weight so that the root she was lying on would stop digging into her ribs. "And I don't like it."

"What's to understand?" Gin yawned beside her. "It's an arena fight. You humans can be remarkably savage, considering your diet is mostly plants."

"Who lines an arena with swords?" Miranda said. "And *my* diet is mostly plants. I know people who could put your carnivorous ways to shame." She shifted her position again, switching the scope to her other eye. "What's Liechten playing at? There's no way he'll be able to reach the Heart from the arena floor if he leaves it up there."

"The man is a good hunter," Gin said, his voice deep and approving. "If it's up there, he has a reason."

"I just hope Sted doesn't take too much longer," Miranda said, getting up. "I'm going back to report to Slorn. Keep an eye on things."

Gin laid his head on his paws, patterns swirling lazily over his muzzle. "If anything exciting happens, I'll let you know."

Miranda shook her head and started creeping through the undergrowth. They'd arrived early yesterday morning, setting up camp on the highest part of the rim of the stone canyon that shielded Izo's camp from the outside world. It had been a breathless run. The legs on Slorn's wagon weren't there for show. The thing had scampered through the forest as fast as Gin could run, and Miranda still wasn't sure who had been slowing down for whom. They'd cleared the distance from the mountains back to Izo's in record time, slowing only when they reached the ring of patrols and towers that guarded Izo's home base. There, creeping past lookouts, Slorn had led her to a place on a rocky outcropping both high and out of the way with a good view of Izo's land. From the multiple flattened weeds in the hideout, it was clear he'd camped here before, but what had really shocked Miranda was what he'd left waiting for his return.

It was so out of place up here among the scraggly bushes, she hadn't even noticed it at first. Now it was always the first thing she saw whenever she came back to camp. Behind the bushes where Slorn's wagon crouched was a large...something. It was squat and lumpy, about as tall as she was, and covered in a drab cloth. A line of empty barrels made a sort of makeshift fence around it, keeping her from getting a good look at its shape, but it moved sometimes, and she could just make out the sharp wooden ends of what looked like carved spider legs poking out from the edge of the cloth. Slorn hadn't even mentioned it when they arrived, but something in the bear's eyes kept her from asking, and she'd never found the chance to peek. She did wonder, though.

As usual, Slorn was sitting on the stairs of his wagon, working something in his hands. It was roughly a foot long, round at one end and pointed at the other, vaguely off-white and soapy looking. At first, she'd thought it was the beginning of some Shaper project, an uncarved block he'd turn into something beautiful, but she never heard its voice and its shape never seemed to change. Slorn just kept turning it over in his hands, staring at it like it was the most interesting thing in the world.

He didn't look up from the thing as she entered the clearing, creeping low even though she was well out of sight of the city. "How's it looking?" he asked in his usual gruff voice.

"No sign of Sted yet," Miranda answered, straightening up. "Josef's acting stranger than ever. He's got them lining the arena with swords, really awful-looking ones. I'm no metalworking expert, but I can see the warping from here. Plus, he just put the Heart of War up on a stand like a trophy." She stopped. "You don't think he's wagered it, do you?"

"No," Slorn said. "Josef knows better than anyone it's not his to wager. Still"—he raised a hand to his muzzle, scratching it thoughtfully—"putting down the Heart is a clever plan. I wonder who thought of it, Eli or Josef?"

Miranda gave him a funny look. "How is putting your best weapon out of reach for a hard fight clever?"

"Think, Miranda," Slorn said. "What good is the world's

greatest awakened blade when you're fighting a demonseed who cares nothing for what it eats?"

Miranda opened her mouth, and then snapped it closed. "Of course, that explains the awful swords. Metal with so many impurities is bound to have tiny, sleepy spirits, providing no meal for the seed even if he eats dozens of them. He's set up the fight to protect his sword and keep Sted from getting stronger." She nearly grinned at the simple cleverness of it. Why hadn't she thought of that?

"Actually, Miranda," Slorn said, looking up at last. "I've been meaning to ask you a favor. How strong is your sea spirit?"

Miranda gave him a funny look. "Mellinor's pretty strong. Depends on how much water is around."

"I see," Slorn said, nodding over her shoulder. "And do you think Mellinor could fill those?"

Miranda turned, following his gaze to the line of empty barrels around the cloth-draped shape. "Easily," she said, turning back. "Why?"

"I'm going to need some water," Slorn said. "I'd been meaning to talk to a local stream about it, but I've run out of time. I was hoping your Mellinor could oblige me."

"Sure," Miranda said, grinning. "What do you need us to do?"

Slorn opened his mouth, but he was cut off by a low growl from the trees.

"There's Gin," Miranda whispered, dropping her voice even though there was no chance of being overheard.

Slorn nodded and stood up, carefully placing the white lump of whatever it was on the wagon steps before coming over to join her. They crept back through the woods together, sliding in beside Gin, who was nearly over the cliff edge in his excitement. One look and Miranda could see why. The crowd of bandits, who'd been thick as flies over the city for the last day, were pulling away from a cloaked figure walking in from the north end of town. Even at this range, she could see Sted clearly, a head taller than anyone else, and behind him, stumbling through the dust on a rope leash like a petulant puppy, was a figure she knew even better.

"Eli Monpress," she said, frowning. "He doesn't look good."

"He's fine," Gin growled. "Just making life hard for Sted, which is the most sensible thing I've seen him do."

Miranda nodded and looked over her shoulder for Slorn, but the bear-headed man was staying back, keeping to the trees, his animal eyes large and sharp as he watched Sted drag the thief into the center of town. Down in the valley, a ragged cheer went up.

Josef stood on the arena's edge, eyes squinting against the noonday sun as Sted strutted into the center of town. Bandits scrambled out of his way, whistling and shouting. Josef ignored them, focusing instead on the figure stumbling in Sted's wake. Eli looked tired and disoriented, but unharmed. That was good enough for him, and Josef turned his attention to Sted. The enormous man came to a stop at the opposite side of the arena and grinned a wide, violent grin at Josef like he was the only man in the world.

"Well, Sted," Izo's voice boomed down from his box, "you showed up. Hand over the thief, and the swordsman will fight you on whatever terms you like."

Izo's words hung in the air, but Sted didn't even seem to hear them. He stepped out onto the arena's edge before tossing Eli's rope in the dirt. The thief scampered away as Sted reached up and ripped the threadbare cloak from his shoulders. A great gasp went up from the crowd, and even Josef's breath hitched. Sted's black arm was there, same as ever, but it looked almost natural compared to his chest. The black rot no longer stopped at the shoulder, where the arm connected. It had spread down, spidering across the enormous man's chest in long, inky tendrils. The blackness poured into his scars like tainted water, eating its way across the remnants of his tattoos.

Quick as a flash, Sparrow stepped out from behind Izo's booth to grab Eli's rope, jerking the thief off his feet. He twisted the rope around his hand several times before leading the thief over to the far edge of the arena where Tesset was holding Nico. Sted didn't even seem to notice what happened to his prisoner. He stood on the arena edge, drinking in the fear and revulsion as it rolled off the crowd, grinning at Josef like a wolf that's finally cornered the running stag.

But Josef was too distracted to be intimidated. "Powers, man," he said in a low voice. "What have you done to yourself?"

Sted's smile faltered a moment before it was replaced by a sneer. "Nothing like what I'm going to do to you."

He leaped off the edge, landing on the arena's sandy floor with a thud Josef felt through his boots. Josef cast one last look at Nico and Eli before jumping down as well. Realizing they were about to get the blood they'd come for, the bandits began to cheer, but the sound was very far away. Here in the arena, Sted took up every scrap of Josef's attention, leaving none to spare for roaring crowds.

"I see you're able to stand again," Sted said, walking across the arena. "Finally found your courage, eh?"

Josef's answer was to draw the swords at his hips, swinging the warped blades in a whistling circle before settling into a fighting stance. Sted stared at him, his eager expression turning to one of disbelief.

"What is this?" he roared. "What are those, fire pokers? Is this some kind of a *joke*?" He looked around, spotting the Heart high on its post. "I didn't call this fight so we could dance, Liechten," he growled, thrusting his clawed arm into the air, curved fingers pointing at the Heart's hilt. "Take your sword and fight me like a man!"

"Why should I?" Josef answered, looking pointedly at Sted's transformed hand. "After all, you could hardly be called a man anymore."

Sted's eyes narrowed. "I'm going to butcher you like a pig for that."

Josef raised his swords, a feral grin coming over his face. "Try it."

Sted clenched his fists with a roar, and then he was gone. Josef waited for the step from the shadows and whirled to his left, catching Sted's clawed hand in his blades.

"I'm not like your coward girl," Sted whispered as his claws began to eat through the steel of Josef's swords. "I don't hold anything back. Take the Heart and fight for real or I'll kill everyone here, starting with you."

Josef glared at him through the quickly vanishing cross of his blades. "You might have always been a monster," he said. "But you were an indifferent brawler and even less of a swordsman. I don't need the Heart to beat you."

"Have it your way," Sted hissed, and brought his demon arm down, ripping Josef's swords in two.

But Josef had dropped the swords before Sted had finished speaking. He jumped nimbly back, hands going out to grab two fresh swords from the arena wall. The crude hilts slid into his hands and he brought the new pair forward just in time. Sted charged with an enraged scream, slamming them both into the arena wall hard enough to knock Josef's breath out, but not hard enough to break his guard. For all its power, it was a sloppy hold, and Josef ducked under Sted's arms with a quick step, his swords flashing in the sun as they raked under the larger man's right shoulder.

Josef turned as soon as he finished the follow-through and was greeted by the beautiful sight of fresh, red blood running from two large gashes across Sted's ribs. Even with his ears ringing from being bashed against the arena wall, he could feel the crowd's roar through the sand. Had he been younger, stupider, he might have raised his arms in triumph, but he settled for a smile as Sted whirled around, hands going to stanch the flow of blood from his wound.

"No more iron skin, I see," Josef said, flicking the blood from his blades onto the sand. "You'll have to be better than that if you don't want me to carve you up, Sted."

He paused, waiting for a comeback, but Sted just smiled, his eyes unsettlingly bright, and removed his hand. Josef blinked. The blood was still there, slick and red against his skin, but the wounds were already gone.

"Yes." Sted chuckled as Josef's eyes widened. "Now you see. If you mean to carve me up, you'll have to hit much harder than that."

Josef started to answer, but Sted was on him before he could open his mouth, claws going for Josef's throat. Josef blocked wildly, losing half his left sword in the process. He blocked again on the broken shard, but Sted was faster than ever. He flitted through the air, feet barely touching the ground thanks to the demon-gifted speed. Josef had no time to square his defense before Sted's right fist, his human fist, slammed into Josef's side. Josef coughed and staggered, but his remaining blade held true, keeping Sted's claws away from him even as they sliced through the discolored metal of the sword. Sted roared and punched again, but this time he hit only air as Josef spun away, abandoning his sword, now skewered on Sted's claws, and lunged for the wall.

The first sword he grabbed came apart in his hands, the hilt sliding off the blade as soon as he touched it. Josef swore and grabbed the next one, spinning just in time to keep from getting pinned against the wall. The second he moved, Sted switched up.

Midcharge he turned and kicked off the wall with his legs, launching himself at Josef.

It happened so quickly there was no time to dodge, no time to block, so Josef did the only thing he could. Holding the warped sword with both hands in front of him like a spear, he dug in his heels and met Sted head-on. This time it was Sted who didn't have time to defend. He slammed into Josef, sending them both crashing to the ground. Josef felt his shirt rip, followed by the skin of his shoulders as he skidded across the sand. Sted's weight bore down on him, and he could feel the man's monstrous claw tearing at the ground beside them, trying to stop the momentum and get control back, but Josef's eyes saw only his own hands gripping the now-broken hilt of his sword, the warped, discolored blade of which was now lodged deep in the bloody mess that was Sted's human shoulder.

Ten feet from where they'd started, the slide stopped, and the moment he could raise his arms again, Josef dropped the hilt, clasped his hands in a double fist, and brought them down hard on the broken blade lodged in Sted's shoulder. It worked even better than he'd planned. The sword had landed not in Sted's shoulder blade, but inside the arm socket. Josef's fists hit the sword like a hammer against a wedge, and Sted roared in pain as the blade lurched sideways, disjointing his shoulder with a sickening crack.

Using both boots, Josef kicked himself free, scrambling across the sand before Sted could grab him again. The moment his feet were under him, he was running for the wall. He grabbed two more swords from the endless line and spun to face Sted again, but the enormous man was still on the ground clutching his shoulder. Overhead, the bandits were screaming, a great roaring ocean of throats that drowned out even the pounding blood in Josef's ears. With a deep breath, Josef took a step forward, his eyes narrowing until Sted was all he could see.

It was a sickening, pathetic sight. Sted was thrashing on the ground, struggling to get his clawed arm up to his shoulder to pull out the blade while his human arm dragged on the sand beside him, useless. He finally got it, dragging the blade out with a pained roar. He tossed the broken shard away, glaring at Josef with eyes both too large and too bright.

"Don't look…so cocky," he panted, clutching his mangled shoulder. "Our duel isn't anywhere near over."

"Our duel never started," Josef said. "Duels are tests of strength and skill between two equal combatants. This"—he swung his sword, taking in the bloody sand, Sted's limp arm, the roaring crowd pressing in along the arena's edge—"this isn't a duel. This isn't even a fight; it's a slaughter. You're not even a swordsman anymore. You're an animal, an enraged bull wallowing in the dirt." He flipped the flimsy swords in his hands. "I'm glad I couldn't use the Heart on you now," he said. "It would be a disgrace to the blade to waste it on blood like yours."

Sted's face went scarlet, and he began to pant, squeezing his butchered arm until the flesh bulged beneath his grip. "I'll show you a fight," he spat. "You'll eat those words with your blood before the day is through."

As he spoke, a horrible sound spread through the arena. It was an unnatural cracking noise, like hollow bones snapping, underlaid with the wet, sucking sound of something being drawn in. Josef stared at Sted, horrified, as the black stain from his demon arm began to grow. It leached across his chest, sliding under his skin, pouring into the rivulets of his scars like a black, hungry tide. As it spread, the horrible sound grew louder, and Sted's shoulder began to pull together. Muscles sprouted out, bridging the gap between shoulder and arm. Bones pulled together, joints snapping into place as dark skin grew to cover the wound. It happened with blinding speed. One moment his right arm hung limp and useless;

the next, Sted was pushing himself up with it, the gaping wound now no more than a patch of discolored flesh over his healthy, functional shoulder.

Sted grinned a horrid, feral grin and raised his fist to thump his chest, which was now completely covered with the black stain. "Slaughter, you said?" His voice had a strange double resonance to it that made Josef's blood run cold. "How do you intend to slaughter a man you can't even wound?"

"The same way you take apart any animal," Josef said slowly. "One limb at a time."

Rage flashed over Sted's face, and he leaped forward with a roar. Josef sidestepped the mad charge in one neat movement, bringing his swords down across Sted's open back. They struck in a clean slice, but Sted didn't even flinch. He dug his feet into the sand and spun around, his clawed arm angled to smash into Josef's face. But again, Josef was too quick. He jumped back, bringing his swords up for another swing. However, just before he struck, Josef stopped, staring at his swords in amazement. The blades were unbroken, but where the cutting edge should have been was a new curve in the exact shape of Sted's back. The edges of the metal were still hissing, as though the blades had melted on contact. For a moment Josef just stared, trying to understand what had happened, and then he heard the hated, hollow sound of Sted's laughter.

"Surprised?" Sted said. He was laughing like a jackal, showing all his teeth as he tilted his shoulders, showing Josef his back.

The moment he turned, Josef understood. Sted's back was the same as his chest, covered in the horrible blackness, including the skin where Josef's strike had landed. The wounds were still there, still open and puckered and smoking slightly, but no blood leaked from the inky flesh, and the muscles flexed beneath it with no sign of pain.

"You see now, don't you?" Sted laughed. "You're right when you say I'm not a swordsman anymore. I'm so much more than that. So much greater than you or any pathetic human could ever be."

"You say that," Josef said, tossing the ruined swords aside. "But what happens when that black stain covers all of you?"

Sted shrugged. "Who knows? You'll be dead long before that happens. After that, I don't care." He dropped into a crouch. "Come then, Josef Liechten. I'll break your little swords until you're forced to use the Heart, and then we'll have a real rematch. Then we'll have the fight I sold my soul for. Come," he said and beckoned. "Give me my victory."

Josef didn't answer. They stood for a moment, sizing each other up. Then, in the same moment, they both moved, Josef dashing for the wall as Sted dashed for him. Josef got to his objective first, grabbing a fresh sword. Sted knocked the blade aside, his claws going through the metal like paper. He struck again and Josef ducked, scrambling out of the larger man's reach. He'd dropped the ruined sword the moment Sted touched it, but he had another in his hand at once. He sprinted for distance, then turned and lobbed the sword with all his strength. The flimsy blade wobbled through the air, horribly off-balance, but it didn't have to fly far. It caught Sted in the thigh, ripping into the flesh. For a moment Sted stumbled, then he was charging again, ignoring the sword in his leg even as Josef saw the black mark spreading beneath the rips in his trousers to surround the wound.

The moment he took to watch nearly cost Josef his head. Sted's figure wavered in the air, and then the larger man was on top of him, raking his claw across Josef's chest. Swordless, Josef did the only thing he could. He kicked Sted hard on his injured thigh, bashing the closing wound with his boot heel again and again. On the second kick the sword fell out, completely dissolved by the black mark that was spreading down Sted's legs. Sted didn't even seem to notice. He clung to Josef like a mad dog, biting and clawing, dragging the swordsman down under his weight. Josef's legs began to buckle. Despite the flurry of clawing, Sted had yet to land a clean hit on him, but Josef could feel the sting from a dozen smaller wounds. Already his shirt was growing warm and damp as the blood trickled down. He had to get out, fast.

Josef dropped to the ground, going totally slack just as his old arms instructor had taught him in the earliest days of his training. It worked perfectly. He slid out of Sted's grip like an eel, touching the sand with his hands for just a moment before ducking between the larger man's legs, leaving Sted stumbling forward under his own weight. As he went down, Josef reached out, grabbed one of the discarded, ruined swords from the sand, and sliced the jagged, broken blade across the still-human skin of Sted's lower back.

Sted bellowed and fell, landing hard in the sand. This time Josef didn't wait for him to get up. He ran straight for the wall, grabbing for the next sword. But as he reached the edge of the arena, he felt a cold claw grab his ankle. He stumbled, slamming against the arena wall just as Sted's fist slammed into his back. Grunting in pain, Josef fumbled for a sword. His fingers closed around the first hilt he found, but he was too slow. The hand on his ankle jerked up, and Josef felt himself lifted into the air. Sted rose from his crouch, holding Josef upside down by his leg, and then, with a great roar, he sent the swordsman flying.

Josef sailed through the air, tucking his feet instinctively toward where he thought the ground was. The world was a blur of sky and sand and the yelling crowd. Then he crashed into the dirt, and everything went black. For a second, Josef thought he was out. Then his breath came thundering back and he retched, coughing the gritty sand out of his mouth. He forced his eyes open, blinking against the enormous black spots that danced over his vision.

Across the arena he could see Sted walking forward, kicking broken swords out of his path.

With a gasp that was half sand, half air, Josef forced himself up. His hands raced over the arena floor, searching for his sword. After what felt like a year, his fingers found the warped hilt, and he brought the blade up, holding it between him and Sted as he forced himself to his feet. Overhead, he could see the bandits cheering, see Izo sitting on the edge of his balcony with a worried look on his face, but he couldn't hear anything. The blow had left him temporarily deaf. He took another breath and forced himself to focus, to tighten his vision until there was no more crowd, no more sting from the cuts on his arms, no more tickle of blood dripping down his chest. There was only him, Sted, and the swords. When he had his center again, Josef held the warped blade steady as Sted began to charge.

"Powers," Eli muttered. "Sted's going to carve him into little slices if this keeps up much longer."

"It is a difficult fight," Tesset said. He was standing at the arena's edge just like Nico and Eli, watching the fight with keen interest. "Liechten is the superior combatant, but so long as Sted keeps regenerating, he has the upper hand. Your swordsman will have to land a finishing blow soon or Sted will simply outlast him."

Nico clenched her fists, her eyes glued on Josef as the combatants went around again. Tesset was right; Josef was bleeding freely from a dozen small cuts. His movements were still lightning fast, but Nico had been watching Josef closely since the moment she woke up on the mountain, and she could see the telltale signs of exhaustion creeping in: the way his eyes narrowed even in shadow, the sloping set of his shoulders as he swung his swords, the slight hesitation when he jumped. The two men had been going full tilt for almost twenty minutes at this point, and while Sted seemed as ready as ever, Josef was pushing his limits.

"Let's hope they finish it soon in any case," Sparrow said, swinging Eli's leash from side to side. "Fantastically entertaining as it is to watch two grown men try to kill each other, we've got a schedule to keep. What do you think you're doing?"

This last bit was a shout as Eli suddenly dropped to his knees and reached down into the arena.

"Helping," Eli said, grabbing the shoddy sword on the wall below him. "He'll lose unless he can get a blade that will actually be able to finish Sted, and no one benefits if Josef loses."

"Put that down!" Sparrow shouted, jerking Eli's leash. But the rope unraveled in his hands, slipping off Eli's neck with a snicker.

Eli looked over his shoulder and gave Sparrow a wide grin. "Don't ever forget who you're dealing with, bird boy. Next time, you should listen to Miranda."

"Tesset!" Sparrow shouted. "Grab him!"

"No point," Tesset said. "He'll just get out again. Besides, if he was going to run, he wouldn't have slipped the rope here where he's cornered."

"Excellent observation," Eli said, nodding sagely as he sat down on the arena's edge.

Sparrow had no answer. He just stood there, sputtering, as Eli placed the warped sword in his lap. Nico leaned in to watch as Eli began knocking on the blade with his fist.

"You'd better wake up," he shouted. "You're missing everything!"

For a moment nothing happened. The sword, its uneven surface a mottled mix of gray and black, just lay there. Eli kept knocking, harder now, and shouted again. "You're missing the chance of a lifetime!"

The sword rattled in his hand, and then, very slowly, a tiny voice said, "What?"

"At last," Eli said. "I was beginning to worry you'd sleep right through it."

"Right through what?" the sword said, sounding more alarmed.

"The fight of your life," Eli said. "Look down in that arena. You're going to be in the hands of the greatest swordsman in the world, the Master of the Heart of War itself!"

The sword's anxiety began to wane. "The what?"

Eli rolled his eyes. "The greatest awakened blade ever created. Do you have any idea what an honor you've been selected for?"

He waited for an answer, but the sword remained silent. A second later, Nico realized it had fallen back asleep.

"Damn small spirits," Eli grumbled, whacking the blade against the arena wall. "Come on, wake up."

"What?" the sword said again.

Eli shook his head and tried a different approach.

"Are you ready?" he said, his voice brimming with excitement.

"Ready for what?"

"To fight," Eli said. "You're a sword. It's your purpose."

"I'm a sword?" The sword rolled back and forth in his hand. "Since when?"

"Doesn't matter," Eli said, grabbing the sword by the hilt. "Now, I want you to go out there and give it your all."

"Powers!" The sword rocked itself toward the arena. "Do you see what's happening down there? Look at all those broken swords!"

"Failures," Eli said. "Listen, everything depends on this. Don't fail me. And don't go back to sleep. You stay together, no matter what it takes, do you hear me?"

"I'm not going down there!" the sword shouted.

"Forget those other swords," Eli shouted back. "They were weak. You're different. You're going to win!"

"I don't want to win!" The sword was vibrating madly in Eli's hand. "Get me out of here! I never asked to be a sword!"

"You have to fight," Nico said. "That man is a demonseed."

Eli and the sword both turned to stare at her. Nico shrank back, unsure if she'd overstepped her boundaries, but Josef was dying down there. She had to go on.

The sword wobbled uncertainly. "He doesn't look like a demonseed to me."

"He's a special kind of seed," she said, taking the sword from Eli, careful to keep her coat draped over her hands. "One made to hide from spirits and eat them when they're not looking. That's why the League can't find him, and that's why you have to stop it."

"Me?" the sword said. "No, no, no. I don't want to be eaten."

"You'll have a strong ally," Nico said, pointing at Josef. "The greatest swordsman in the world. But he needs a sword. You have to stand up to that demon. You have to fight!"

The sword didn't answer. It sat there, trembling in her hand. Then, all at once, the trembling stopped. "Do it," the sword said, its tiny voice suddenly calm and collected.

Nico stood, shouting Josef's name as she rose. Across the arena, Josef looked up from his struggle against Sted's hold. The moment he did, Nico threw the sword at him. It flew through the air in an unnaturally straight arc, screaming vengeance and death to the demon as it went. Josef caught the blade one-handed and dragged it across Sted's human arm.

The sword cut like a razor, going straight and deep into Sted's elbow. Sted screamed and lost his hold on Josef's shoulder just long enough for the swordsman to spin away. Nico cheered, and beside her, Eli gawked, amazed.

"How did you know that would do it?"

Nico looked at him. "All spirits hate demons," she said quietly.

"Normally, the fear keeps all but the strongest of them from fighting. But Sted isn't a wizard. He can't open his spirit, and so the fear isn't broadcast. Without the crippling fear, even small spirits are free to be heroes."

Eli pursed his lips. "That's actually quite brilliant."

"Thank you," Nico said, surprised, but all the good feelings from the compliment faded when she looked back at Josef, who was bracing for Sted's next charge. "It won't be enough, though. Even awake and trying its best, that sword can't become something it's not. It's still pot metal, and Sted is still a demon."

"Then we'll just have to overwhelm him," Eli said, reaching down to grab two more swords from the arena wall. "I'll wake them up; you get them going."

Nico grinned wide. "Right."

They worked quickly. Some swords didn't want to fight, and Nico set them aside. Others, though, were ready from the moment Nico told them Sted was a demonseed. These she tossed to Josef. He caught each one, sticking it point down in the sand beside him. The first sword they'd thrown him was already whittled down to a sliver, but it was still fighting, slashing Sted like a blade five times its sharpness.

Sted ignored the swords at first, attacking Josef with single-minded purpose. But as the blades began to build up, and the blade in Josef's hands refused to break like all the others, his focus began to shift.

"What?" he shouted, swiping at Josef's head. "You think it matters that your swords aren't snapping like rotten wood anymore?" He thrust his arm into the air, proudly displaying the gash that Josef had made earlier, which was now little more than a red line on his skin. "You can't beat what you can't kill, Liechten! Not without real power. Give up! You don't have a hope without the Heart."

But Josef just smiled, dodging his swipe neatly while catching the next sword Nico threw with one hand. He swung his swords, one fresh, one eaten to nothing but still holding on, and announced in a voice loud enough for everyone to hear, "The day I need the Heart to beat an amateur like you is the day I give up swordsmanship."

Furious, Sted launched into a mad charge, and that was when Josef struck. He jumped out of the way and spun, bringing his swords down on the back of Sted's neck so hard the larger man lurched forward, landing in the sand with a grunt. As soon as he was down, Josef was on top of him, ramming sword after sword into his back. Sted bellowed in pain, but Josef only moved faster. He filled Sted up like a pincushion, using every sword Nico and Eli had woken for him. Nico could hear the blades all the way at the edge of the arena. They screamed at the demon, pressing down with all their might, turning to widen the wounds even as they pinned Sted to the sand.

Plunging the last sword down into Sted's spine, Josef stepped back. He was panting, sweat and blood running down his sides, but his face was triumphant. Sted thrashed on the ground like a speared bull in front of him, the sand turning black as his blood ran down the swords. The blades hissed as he devoured them, but this was too much even for his healing abilities. His struggles grew weaker and weaker, and then, at last, they stopped.

The arena fell silent. The crowd stood still, staring in wonder at what had just happened. Down in the arena, Josef took a careful step forward, nudging Sted's leg with his foot. The demonseed did not move, and a grin spread over Josef's face.

"It's finished," he said, turning to Nico and Eli with his hands raised in victory.

A great cheer went up. Up in the wooden stands and the rooftops, the bandit crowds were falling over one another in their excitement. Money changed hands frantically as wagers were called in, and everyone was smiling, especially Nico. She stood on the edge of the arena, grinning like mad as Josef started toward them. But then, just as she moved to jump down and congratulate him, the Master spoke.

Nothing is over until I say it is.

As the words echoed in her head, a piercing scream shot through the air, and Sted ripped himself up. Josef whirled around and stopped cold, staring in horror as Sted pushed himself to his feet. Blood dripped from his body, sliding in red rivers over skin that was now totally black. He stumbled forward, his head up, his eyes too wide and bright as lanterns. When he opened his mouth, the sound that came out was no longer human at all.

"Not yet," he said. "I will not lose."

Even as the words tumbled from his black lips, Sted began to run. He lurched across the arena, leaving a trail of blood behind him. Despite his wounds, he ran faster with every step until he reached his goal. Sted slammed into the post that held the Heart of War. The wood groaned and crumpled under the demonseed's pressure, and the Heart tumbled down, landing with a great crash on the sand below. Even before it hit, Josef was running toward his blade, but he was too late. Grinning around teeth that were suddenly too large and too sharp for any human mouth, Sted laid his hands, now both transformed into claws, on the blade, and the Heart of War began to scream.

CHAPTER 18

The Heart's scream reverberated through the air. Nico fell to her knees, slamming her hands over her ears as it hit her. Eli was down as well. She could see his lips moving as he shouted something, but she couldn't hear anything except the enormous roar of the Heart of War as Sted's claws dug into the black metal. Then, as quickly as it started, the sound stopped.

Nico looked up just in time to catch Sted's surprised expression before the Heart of War erupted in a blinding flash of light. The blade did not change. It was still the same black, dented metal, and yet it shone like noon sun on fresh snow. Even as she saw the light, Nico heard another sound, like a whip snapping, and Sted flew backward. He rocketed through the air, blown backward by the Heart's will, and landed with a bone-cracking crunch on the edge of the arena. The Heart was blown backward as well. It flipped through the air, whistling gracefully, its light fading to a warm glow as it landed perfectly in Josef's outstretched hand.

The second the Heart was in his grip, Josef rushed at Sted, who was still lying stunned at the arena's edge. He moved so fast Nico's eyes could barely keep pace, but when he struck, Sted was no longer there. Josef stopped his blow and whirled around just as Sted crawled out of the shadows on the other side of the arena. Nico held her breath. She couldn't even call the thing on the ground Sted anymore. Sted had been human, at least in form. This was something that did not belong in the world. Its skin was pure black, but deeper. Looking at the thing was like staring into a void, like the shape on the ground was a hole in the world rather than the remnants of a man. What had been human arms were now sickeningly long, thin as beanpoles, and triple jointed, bending to completely circle Sted's body. Its legs were long and powerful, tipped with claws that had sliced through what was left of Sted's boots. But worst of all was his face. His face was a black nothing, too black to look at. The only thing Nico could make out were the rows of sharp, uneven teeth, and the eyes. Sted's eyes floated in the void that was left of his face, enormous and golden yellow. Shapes moved behind them, horrible clawed shadows that made Nico's skin crawl, but she could not look away. She could only watch as the creature opened its mouth in sickening slow motion, its long, black tongue sliding hungrily across its jagged, black teeth.

The demon panic hit her like a stone wall. She felt Eli seize up beside her, and even Tesset stumbled. For a moment they sat there, paralyzed, and then the world went crazy. All around them, spirits began to panic. The ground was shrieking, the sand was shrieking, the wooden arena walls were shrieking, even the blunt swords were shrieking in terrified horror. Behind them, Nico could hear the wooden buildings weeping in fear, followed by the surprised shouts of bandits as the rooftops and balconies began to twist and pull against their supports in a desperate attempt to flee. This started a human panic, and the arena crowd dissolved into pure chaos in a matter of seconds. Bandits were pouring out of collapsing buildings, crying in terror as the ground under their feet tried to run with them. Nico could hear Izo shouting from his box, but his orders were drowned out in the panic. None of the bandits so much as looked at him as they fought and clawed their way down the packed-dirt street toward the gates.

But even as the screaming bandits jostled past her, Nico didn't look away from the arena. Despite the fear, Josef was still advancing, the Heart rock-solid and steady in his hands. The demon hissed and sank to the sand, its triple-jointed arms reaching out, claws spread, ready to strike. Josef turned the Heart to a defensive position, but the blow never came. Instead, the demon just grinned, a sickening spread of teeth, and plunged its clawed hands down into the arena sand.

The ground lurched with a horrific scream that soared above all the others. Each tiny grain of sand cried in mortal terror before snuffing out in a silence that was even more horrible as a black circle began to grow from the demon's claws.

"Josef!" Nico screamed, lurching forward until she was almost falling into the arena. "It's eating the spirits! You have to strike now!"

But she never knew if he heard her, for at that moment the ground erupted. Nico's coat seized around her shoulders, yanking her back just in time as enormous stone spikes stabbed up from the arena floor. Great swords of stone charged upward with a vengeful scream, scattering sand everywhere as the awoken, angry, deep spirits of the bedrock lurched forward to crush the demon.

The creature dodged effortlessly. It slipped through the shadows faster than even Nico had once been able to, snickering as the stone spikes crashed and broke when they tried to give chase. But Nico wasn't even watching the demon anymore. Her eyes were glued to the tiny figure flying through the air, launched upward when the ground exploded below his feet.

"*JOSEF!*"

Josef tumbled as he flew, his body going slack. Nico sucked in a breath as the Heart left his hand. He landed with a crash in a building two blocks away from the arena. The roof shattered when he hit, sending wood raining down through the hole he left behind. The Heart landed in the next building over, crashing through a shuttered window like a sledgehammer through paper.

The crash rang out over the din of the panicked spirits, and Nico shot up before she knew what she was doing. But as she started to run to Josef, she was yanked off her feet. Her breath slammed out of her as she landed on her back. She coughed and retched, staring hatefully at Tesset, who was standing over her, holding the rope that was tied to the manacle at her neck.

She bared her teeth at him like an animal. "Let me go!"

Tesset gave her a dry look and opened his mouth. But whatever he was going to say, he never got it out, for at that moment something extraordinary happened. All around the arena, white lines began to appear. They cut down through empty space, first five, then ten, then twenty, all shining the same brilliant white. The lines hung in the air, shimmering for a split second, and then men in black coats began to step through.

They came out with swords drawn, surrounding the arena in a loose circle. The moment their feet were on the ground, half of them opened their spirits, pressing the panicking landscape into submission. The other half kept their focus on Sted, who was clinging to the edge of one of the stone spikes with his claws. The demon hissed and dug its claws into the screaming stone, ready to pounce, when another white line opened in the air not a foot from Nico's head. Nico scrambled sideways just before a man stepped through. He was dressed in the same black coat as all the others, but he had an undeniable air of competence and command. He had a thin, intelligent face and a slender, golden-hilted sword that, unlike the others, was still sheathed. Though he'd nearly stepped on her, he didn't even look at Nico. He simply walked to the edge of the arena and held out his hand, his long fingers pointing directly at Sted.

Don't move.

The words slammed down like a boulder. Nico could feel the weight of them pressing on every inch of skin that wasn't protected by her coat, but for Sted, things were much worse. The moment the man spoke, the demon howled and fell. It toppled from the stone spikes and slammed into what was left of the arena floor below, shrieking in that horrible dual-tone voice as it fought against the weight.

Nodding, the man lowered his arm and glanced over his shoulder, looking straight at Nico. She shrank into her coat, clutching her transformed arm against her chest. But the man said nothing. After several awkward seconds, Sparrow broke the silence.

"Hello, Alric," he said, dusting himself off. "Fantastic timing."

Alric gave him a blistering look. "Shut up, Sparrow. I don't have time for whatever games your mistress is playing." He reached down and grabbed Nico's rope, dragging her to her feet. Once she was up, he turned and grabbed Eli before the thief could object, nearly throwing him into Sparrow. "I have no idea how you caught Eli Monpress," he said. "Frankly, I don't care. If he's stupid enough to get himself caught, then that's none of my affair, but I want these two out of here now."

Sparrow arched an eyebrow. "But you seem to have the situation well—"

He was cut off by an enormous roar as Sted began to thrash. Several League members threw out their hands, shouting commands to the spirits as the demon fought to get to its feet.

"*Go!*" Alric shouted, his hand going for his sword as he jumped down into the arena.

"You heard the man," Sparrow said, grabbing Eli.

Eli pried Sparrow's hands off him. "Now wait just a—"

His words cut off as Sparrow grabbed the length of rope Eli had slipped out of earlier and flung it around the thief's neck. "Let's go," he said, yanking the rope so tight Eli's face began to turn red.

Tesset nodded. He reached down and scooped Nico up, tossing her over his shoulder like an oat sack.

"No!" Nico screamed, writhing against his grasp. "We can't leave Josef! He'll die without the Heart!"

But the two men kept going, Tesset carrying her, Sparrow dragging Eli, who was digging in his heels as best he could with a rope crushing his windpipe. They ran through the collapsing city. Bandits were good at running away, and the dirt streets were nearly empty now, save for a few stragglers and those unfortunate enough to have been trampled in the panic. The buildings groaned and twitched around them, collapsing as they watched, and Sparrow began to push them faster, cursing loudly as he fought to drag a still-struggling Eli behind him.

"Want me to knock him out?" Tesset said, looking over his shoulder.

"No," Sparrow grunted, yanking the rope tighter. "Sara would kill us if we injured him. What is it about this damn thief, anyway? First Sara goes crazy for him, and now the great Alric himself stoops to giving me the time of day just to tell me to get him out of town?"

Tesset shrugged and got a tighter hold on Nico, who was trying to claw his face while kicking him in the chest as hard as she could. It did no good, of course. Hitting Tesset was like trying to beat a rock into submission. But she kept trying. Dumped over his shoulder as she was, she could see the great cloud of dust rising from the arena as Sted's roar echoed through the box canyon. Nico bared her teeth and fought harder. She couldn't even see the roof Josef had crashed through anymore, but she was certain he wasn't up yet, not without the Heart. He was defenseless, unconscious, and alone. If the panicked spirits didn't kill Josef on accident, Sted would for sure. She had to get to him.

"Stop it," Tesset said, thwacking her across the back. "You're slowing us down."

"Then leave me!" she shouted.

"Calm down," he said softly. "You can't win. Don't make me hurt you."

"No!" Nico shrieked. She bent her neck back as far as it would go, staring him in the eyes. "If he dies, I can never repay him. He gave me my life as I know it. He taught me everything. If that story you told me was true, then you know what it's like to owe your rebirth to someone. I can't just let him die. *You have to let me go!*"

"Don't be stupid," Sparrow said. "That's the League back there, sweetheart. Have you forgotten what you are? I don't know why Alric spared you, but I wouldn't count on him to do it again. You go back, and they'll have two seeds to bring home to Papa Storm instead of one. You're much better off going home to Sara and seeing what she can make of you. I'm sure she'd like a demonseed of her own."

Nico beat her human fist uselessly against Tesset's back as the arena fell farther and farther behind. Hot, frustrated tears streamed down her cheeks. Josef was dying, and she could do nothing. She'd never felt so useless in her entire life.

That's because you are useless. The Master's voice was nearly cackling with laughter. *Sted didn't even have a proper transformation, the deaf idiot, and he's got nearly twenty League men fighting tooth and nail just to contain him. You can't even beat one man to save your precious swordsman's life.*

"No." Nico sobbed.

Yes, the Master said. *And you have no one to blame but yourself, you miserable, pathetic failure.*

Nico slumped against Tesset's shoulder. The Master was right; he was always right. It didn't matter how hard she tried or how much she fought, she was weak. Weak and pathetic and worthless and untrustworthy and a failure and—

Her thoughts stopped as something brushed against her cheek. She looked up in alarm before she saw it was her coat. The black fabric had wrapped itself up nearly to her head, coiling itself like a snake ready to strike. It knew she was upset, she realized, and it was reacting to her, trying to protect her just as Slorn had told it to. Suddenly, she had an idea.

She bent her head down and pressed her lips into the fabric. In all her life, even the parts she couldn't remember, she was sure she'd never tried what she was about to do, but at this point, she didn't care.

I wouldn't try it, the Master said sadly. *It won't work. Failures like you shouldn't waste other people's time on wild shots.*

So what, she thought fiercely. *It's not like I have anything left to lose.*

The voice laughed and said something back, but Nico didn't hear it. All she could hear was the memory of Josef's voice in her ears telling her that even if she failed, she could not stop trying. You were only a failure once you stopped trying.

Holding his voice in her mind, she took a deep breath, and, for the first time in her life, began to talk to the spirit of her coat not as a seed, but as a wizard.

Tesset stopped running, slamming his feet into the hard-packed dirt. Sparrow skidded to a stop a second later, turning just in time to see Tesset whip Nico off his shoulder and hold her out in front of him like an ill-behaved child.

"What are you doing?" he said. "You've been muttering for nearly a minute now."

Nico just stared at him, her lips drawn tight.

"Powers, Tesset!" Sparrow said, bracing himself against Eli, who was now blue, but still kicking. "You stopped us for some muttering? Knock her out and let's go."

Sparrow reached to bash Nico across the back of her head, but his hand hit nothing but air. At that moment, Nico's coat unraveled, and she dropped out of Tesset's hands.

Tesset grabbed for her as she fell, but the threads of the coat wrapped around his arms, spoiling his aim. Nico landed on her feet and rolled away, coming up just out of reach with her arms out, ready to block whatever came next.

But nothing came. Tesset just stood there, watching her as he calmly tested the massive tangle of black thread that tied his arms together. He was alone in his calm, however. Beside him, Eli and Sparrow were staring at her like she'd grown another head.

"Powers, child," Sparrow said. "What happened to your arm?"

Nico lowered her eyes, carefully avoiding Eli's horrified stare. "None of your business. Give me the thief."

Sparrow started to laugh. "Are you joking? If you're going to run, then run. I'm sick of your trouble, but the thief stays. There is no way I'm leaving this bollixed-up pit empty-handed."

Nico shifted her stance. Without her coat, she could feel the spirits around her, already awake and on the verge of panic, start to lose control. The voice in her head was silent, but she could feel him waiting, watching in anticipation. "Give Eli to me, or else," she said.

"Or else what?" Sparrow rolled his eyes. "This is taking too long. Tesset, let's go."

Tesset looked at him. "You sure? Alric said to get her to safety."

"Hang Alric!" Sparrow said, pulling Eli's rope taut. "Since when are we League? There isn't enough cash in the world to make me put up with this."

As he spoke, Nico flexed her demon claw. She couldn't take Tesset, but Sparrow was another story. She tried one last time. "Let him go."

Sparrow sneered and started to turn away. Nico raised her claw with a snarl, but just as she launched herself forward, an enormous whistling scream cut through the air as something shot overhead. It exploded through the buildings, including the one right next to them, and landed with an enormous crash in the arena behind them.

For one long second, everything seemed to stop. Tesset's mouth opened, shouting a warning that he never quite got out. Beside him, Sparrow was staring up as the enormous wall of the building above them, broken by whatever it was that had crashed through the town, broke free of its supports and began to fall forward. Even Eli had stopped struggling. He was also watching the wall as it fell toward them, his bound hands coming up to cover his head. And in that long, slow moment, Nico decided what she would do.

She spun in midair, turning the demon arm away from Sparrow. The creature inside her snarled in frustration, but Nico ignored it, focusing all of her attention on her other fist, her striking fist, just as Josef had taught her. Sparrow was wide open as Nico's human fist slammed into his jaw, knocking him back. He stumbled in surprise, and his hands let go of the rope around Eli's neck just as Nico caught the thief's shoulder. The moment she had him, Nico changed directions, kicking off the ground and throwing herself toward the collapsing wall. She glanced up and found what she was looking for, a glass window. She stepped into position and forced Eli down, covering him with her body as the wall crashed around them.

The glass broke over her shoulders, and Nico grunted in pain as the shards sliced her skin. The ground shook under her feet as the wall landed, and then, quickly as it had happened, it was over. Nico cracked her eyes open. She was standing perfectly in the center of the window, surrounded by broken glass. Eli was choking and panting beneath her, grabbing his throat, which was bright red where the rope had cut in. Right beside his knee, buried by the broken glass, she could see Tesset's hand, still wrapped in the threads of her coat. The rest of him was lost beneath the collapsed wooden beams.

She reached down and helped Eli to his feet. "Are you all right?"

"No." Eli coughed. "I'm bruised, beaten, and bloody…and alive, thanks to you."

Nico smiled and bent over, reaching down for the thread of her coat. It woke when she brushed it, sliding up her arm like a snake. She winced when she touched Tesset's skin. His hand was still warm, and she felt a twinge of guilt. For all that he'd been her captor, he'd been a good man. Too good to die like this. But she couldn't think about that now. She kept her arm down, letting her coat reweave itself across her body until she was completely covered again.

"Let's go get Josef," she said, standing up.

"Right," Eli said, rubbing his neck as he looked around at the wreckage. "I don't suppose you know what that was just now."

"No," Nico said, picking her way quickly through the debris. "And I don't care. All I want to do is get to Josef."

"Fair enough," Eli muttered, starting after her.

Their building wasn't the only one that had collapsed. The dirt roads were now more like tunnels through great piles of broken timber, and they had to change direction several times when the way was blocked. The air was filled with horrible sounds, mostly the demon's horrible screaming mixed with explosions and the sound of buildings collapsing, though at this point Nico was surprised there was anything still left to collapse. But despite the horrible noises, she pressed on, letting the sounds lead her toward the center of town, where Josef was.

They were almost there when Eli broke the silence.

"Nico," he said, quickening his pace until he was walking beside her. "Why did you do that?"

His voice was soft, but Nico flinched anyway. "What?"

"Save me."

She took a deep breath, pushing a fallen beam out of the way. "Because Josef would have saved you. And because we're a team." She stopped to look at him. "Comrades don't leave each other in the lurch. Aren't those your words?"

Eli nodded, but his face was closed and expressionless, just as it had been during those awful three days in the cabin. Nico looked away, blinking back tears.

Did you really expect anything to change?

Nico shook her head. But then, just as she reached out to knock a broken beam out of the way, Eli grabbed her human hand. She froze, but he didn't let her go.

"Thank you," he said, squeezing her hand in his.

Nico looked up in surprise.

He gave her a wide, genuine smile before letting her go. Nico didn't move. She just stood there, staring as Eli walked past her and started pulling at a fallen window frame that blocked their way.

"Are you coming?" he said, looking over his shoulder.

Grinning wide, Nico ran to help Eli tear down the last bits of debris between them and the building where Josef had landed.

The outer edges of Izo's bandit town were completely destroyed. Great piles of wood and broken glass lay over the once orderly streets, and those buildings that were standing were little more than skeletons teetering on supports that still occasionally twitched in terror. But down on what had been the road to the canyon's southern exit, the rubble was stirring.

Glass slid crashing to the ground as Tesset pushed himself up with a groan, tossing the splintered wood beams aside with one hand. His other hand was still on the ground, fingers dug into the dirt where he'd braced himself to make a shelter of his own body for Sparrow, who was curled in a ball on the ground, coughing and clutching his bleeding nose.

"Do you see them?" he choked out.

"No," Tesset said, surveying the wreckage.

Sparrow began to curse loudly, tearing off his ruined coat and using the silk lining to wipe the layer of dust from his face. "This is just bleeding brilliant. No thief, no demonseed, no legendary sword, and no missing Shaper wizard. Let's just quit now, before Sara sticks us on file duty for the rest of our lives, how about?"

"No need for that quite yet," Tesset said. "We know where they're going."

"The swordsman?" Sparrow said. He wiggled his tongue around before spitting the dirt out of his mouth. "There's no way we can beat them there, and I'm not sure I want to. Just listen."

He hardly needed to point it out. The demon's scream was everywhere. It reverberated through the air, horrible and unnatural. Despite his years of training to master such a basic human weakness as fear, Tesset couldn't help the cold shudder that ran down his spine. Still, his face was bored and impassive as he stared down at Sparrow. "Do you want to be the one who explains to Sara why we're coming back empty-handed?"

Sparrow heaved an enormous sigh and held out his hands. Tesset yanked him up, and they began to clear their way toward the arena, now hidden behind the toppled buildings.

Benehime crouched by her sphere, a wild look in her white eyes as she watched her darling boy run through the panicked city.

Just one word, she murmured, clenching her fingers against the pulse of demon-born fear reverberating through the world. *Just one plea.* She smiled as she saw Eli trip. *Things will only get worse, darling. How much farther can you go on your own? How much more can you suffer for your pride?* She pressed her lips against her orb. *All you have to do is say you need me. Submit, and all the world will be yours, darling star.*

But as she watched him, something blurred her vision. She

blinked several times, but it was no use. A great wind was circling at the top of her sphere, deliberately obscuring her view. Scowling, Benehime crooked her little finger. The wind vanished instantly, reappearing in the nothingness beside her.

Illir, she said coldly. *You had better have a good reason for making a nuisance of yourself.*

The West Wind bowed deeply before her. "All apologies, Shepherdess. I knew of no other way to get your attention."

Benehime frowned. *And why does a wind need my attention?*

"With all respect, White Lady," Illir said, his enormous voice shrunk to a shaking whisper, "my winds are in a demon-driven panic. I would never presume to question your judgment, Lady, but it is hard to quiet them while you keep our protector, the Lord of Storms, blowing on the southern coasts."

Benehime's eyes flicked to the tropical sea where the Lord of Storms was still raging, just as she'd left him.

He disobeyed me, she said. *I will not interrupt his punishment for something as small as this. Tell your winds the League will handle it.*

"The winds see much, Lady," Illir said, trembling. "It is hard to put them at ease when Alric and the spirits who have come to his aid are so clearly in over their heads."

The Shepherdess's hand shot out, grabbing the wind at its center. Illir screamed and began to thrash, but she held the wind tight, pulling him close until his breeze ruffled her white hair.

You are the Great Wind, she said slowly. *Find a way to keep your subordinates in line, or I will find another wind who can. Understand?*

"Yes, Lady," Illir panted.

Good. Her grip tightened. *Any other complaints?*

"Yes, actually," Illir said.

Benehime's eyes widened. *This had better be important.*

"It is the most important question I've ever asked," Illir said. "Several days ago, an old, old friend and one of your strongest spirits, the great bear, Gredit, vanished. I ordered my winds to look everywhere, but they found no trace of him, not even his body. You would be within your rights to kill me for this impertinence, Lady, but if my years of loyal service have ever pleased you, answer my question before you do. What happened to my friend?"

A slow smile spread across the Lady's white face. She opened her hand, and the wind fell from her fingers, shuddering with relief.

You are very bold, Illir, she said. *I like that. You are also loyal, and I like that even more. If you want to know, I will tell you. Gredit was an old spirit, far past his prime, given to fits of hysteria and insubordination. Even so, he was one of my flock, and so I tolerated his behavior. But then, in his delusions, he threatened one of my stars, my own favorite.* Benehime grew very grave. *This I could not forgive. I am a lenient mistress. I set very few rules. However, there is no place in my sphere for spirits who disobey. Am I making myself clear, West Wind?*

"Very, my Lady," Illir said. "I will go and calm my winds now. I apologize for wasting your time."

Benehime nodded and went back to her sphere, sending the wind away with a flick of her finger. *Don't let it happen again.*

The wind vanished, spinning back down to the world below. She watched for a moment, and then smiled when she saw him fall back down to reassure the lower winds. Illir was a smart spirit. He knew the limits of his place, unlike the bear. Still, she had not known they were friends, and she made a note to keep a closer eye on the wind. Satisfied, she went back to watching Eli crawl across the ruined city. She'd let things go very far this time, but it would be worth it. This time for sure, he would call her. He would fall crying into her arms, pleading for rescue, and then everything would be as she wished. She need only be patient and wait for him to beg.

Benehime smiled at this, running her white fingers gently across her sphere. Behind her, the claws began to press more fiercely on the walls of her world while, down on the ground, the demon grew larger.

CHAPTER 19

Sir!" one of the League men shouted, grabbing Alric by the sleeve. "It's no good, sir. We can't hold him down."

Alric didn't need to be told. He had his will on the demon as well, and he could feel for himself just how useless it was. The ability to command the spirits to hold down a demon regardless of their own safety was a power the Shepherdess herself granted to the League, but its weakness was that the command was only as strong as the spirits who obeyed it. Here, even with the bedrock spirits helping, it wasn't enough, not for this demon.

Down in the spike pit that had been the arena, the demon roared and batted at the League men who sliced at it. Whenever it touched their swords, large chunks disappeared from the blades, and the demon grew larger. Already, the monster was close to twelve feet tall and showed no sign of stopping. Alric sighed in frustration, shoving his own sword back into its sheath.

"Stop attacking!" he shouted. "It's no good. We're only wasting our swords."

The League stopped its attack at once, forming a loose circle around the demon, who, now that it was no longer being attacked, turned and began to eat the bedrock spikes.

"Sir!" One of his lieutenants ran over. "We have to do something. If it keeps eating like this, the demon will soon be too large to contain."

"It's already too large to contain," Alric said, watching the stone writhe as the monster bit into it. Rage washed over him. He'd faced hundreds of awakened seeds in his long years with the League, but this one was different. Different and familiar.

"This isn't a normal takedown," Alric said. "This is the seed that was in Slorn's wife. I'd know it anywhere."

His lieutenant grimaced. "I thought Slorn's wife was contained."

"Apparently even the world's greatest Shaper couldn't contain a demon indefinitely," Alric said dryly. "What I want to know is what it's doing *here*, and why it's in Sted's body."

"Sted?" His lieutenant recoiled. "Berek Sted?"

"Who else?" Alric said. "Stop panicking and you can feel his soul clear as day, what's left of it anyway."

"But Sted was spirit deaf. How—"

"I don't know," Alric snapped. "But it's thanks to his not being a wizard that this situation isn't any worse than it is. Though his being here with Nivel's seed nicely explains what happened to our missing swordsmith." He sincerely hoped Slorn wasn't dead. Artisans like him were impossible to replace.

"All right," Alric said. "We're dealing with a seed that spent ten years germinating inside the body of a powerful wizard, but is now trapped inside a spirit-deaf shell. That is our only advantage. The devouring force is already too strong for awakened blades or spirit commands, and because the seed is lodged in a human, directly commanding the host spirit is out of the question." *As always*, he thought with a sigh.

"We need the Lord of Storms," his lieutenant muttered, his face pale as he watched the demon finish the stone pillar and leap to the next one. "Where in blazes is he?"

Alric wanted to know the same thing. The Lord of Storms had left in a hurry a week ago and hadn't been heard from since. This happened sometimes, but never for this long, and never without a message. Still, Alric kept his mouth shut. Things were bad enough without panicking his men.

"We can handle this," he said, clapping his lieutenant on the shoulder. "We are the chosen protectors of the world, blessed by the Shepherdess herself. She would not have given us our gifts if we were not able to handle whatever situation arose."

"Yes, sir," the man said, gripping his sword with renewed determination.

Alric smiled and released his grip, hoping he hadn't just told the biggest lie of his career.

"Spread out," he ordered. "We're going to take the creature down in one strike, before it can eat our swords. I will deal the cutting blow to the chest that frees the seed. The rest of you focus on its joints. Try to take off the limbs, just like in drill."

"Yes, sir!" the men shouted, fanning out in a circle.

Alric positioned himself at point, directly in front of the demon, who was still feeding with little attention to its attackers.

Alric drew his sword with a crisp metallic scrape. It lay heavy and perfect in his hands, impossibly long and slender, the cutting edge glowing with its own golden light. He looked at it sadly. His beautiful Dunelle, Last Sunlight, his partner and treasure. If this strike succeeded, it would probably be her last. From the way the hilt pressed into his palm, she knew it. But she shone as brightly as ever, urging him to strike the blow. Alric tightened his grip. She had been his best sword; he owed her a valorous death.

Sensing danger, the demon stopped eating. It coiled itself

on what was left of the sandy arena floor, enormous claws flexed and ready, its jaw open and drooling around its horrible, ragged teeth.

"On my mark," Alric said, raising his glowing blade. "Three. Two. One—"

As the word left his mouth, a whistling scream drowned out his voice. He threw his head back just in time to see something white crashing through the buildings behind him. It flew screeching over his head and into the arena, striking the demon square in the chest.

The demon's scream ripped through Alric's mind as the ground rocked under his feet. The shock wave hit him a second later, knocking him over. Alric's hands went instinctively to cover his face as he landed hard on his side, buried instantly by the wave of dirt, rocks, and broken swords that flew out from the impact. For a moment, he lay there, stunned, and then he began to thrash, kicking himself to his feet and scrubbing the dirt from his eyes just in time to see something enormous, white, and sharp-toothed running across the ruined city toward him.

"Alric, isn't it?" said a familiar, female voice. "Are you all right?"

Alric looked up to see a ghosthound staring down at him, and on its back was a redheaded woman with a concerned expression on her face.

"Miranda Lyonette," he said, coughing. "What are you doing here?"

"Saving your neck, League man," the ghosthound growled, nodding toward the center of the arena.

Alric turned to look. The place where the demon had been crouching seconds earlier was now nothing but an enormous crater. He stared at it for a second, not quite believing what he saw.

"What did that?"

Miranda grinned and pointed behind him. Slowly, Alric turned around and his eyes went wide. Standing on the rim of the canyon that surrounded the bandit city was Heinricht Slorn. He was crouched on one knee, holding something on his shoulder that Alric didn't have a name for. Nearly as long as Slorn was tall, it was metal and hollow, like a tube. It had two legs in front that dug into the ground at Slorn's feet to brace its weight, but its back was a nest of piping that hooked to an enormous wagon, which was absolutely covered with water. Even at this distance, Alric could see the blue water arcing in and out of a dozen different containers, moving against gravity and glowing with its own watery light.

Alric shook his head and sheathed his sword. Of course Slorn was here. He should have known it would all come together. At the canyon's edge, Slorn lowered the metal tube from his shoulder and hopped into the water-filled cart. The cart began to move as soon as he was in, climbing down into the valley on spindly spider legs. It picked its way over the wreckage and came to a stop at the arena's edge. The cart knelt and Slorn climbed down, landing stiffly beside Miranda.

"Well," the Shaper said, staring at the crater. "That worked rather well."

"Quite," Alric said. "Mind telling me what you did?"

Slorn reached into the bag slung across his chest and took out a white object. It was the size of a small melon, slightly longer than it was round, and sharpened to a rough point at one end. Its surface was smooth, like carved soap, and from the way Slorn held it, Alric could tell it must be very heavy indeed.

"What is it?"

"Bone metal," Slorn said. "Rather amazing stuff, really."

"And inedible by demons," Alric finished. "Very clever. But how did you do that?" He pointed at the destroyed buildings.

Slorn gave him an astonished look. "Water pressure," he said, like it should be obvious. "Spiritualist Lyonette was kind enough to lend me the use of her sea."

Alric glanced at the blue water that was still flowing in great arcs from barrel to barrel and smiled. "You made a bone-metal shot for a water cannon powered by a sea?"

"Can you think of a better way to take down a demon as powerful as Sted?" Slorn said.

"Yes," Alric said. "But in the absence of the Lord of Storms, I'll take your solution. In the future, though, Heinricht, I'd appreciate it if you left League business to the League, or at least told us what you meant to do before you did it."

Slorn had the good grace to look abashed at that, and Alric stood up to survey the damage. The other League men were getting up as well, many slowly, some clutching broken bones. But they obeyed instantly when Alric motioned for them to form a perimeter around the crater. Once his men were in position, Alric moved forward, keeping his hand on his sword as he crawled up the crater's edge to peek into the hole Slorn's cannon had left.

The demon lay sprawled at the bottom of the crater, motionless. Its long, unnatural arms were flung spread-eagle, the left one shattered below the second elbow. The demon's head was bent backward at a hideous angle and surrounded by broken teeth while its chest was caved in completely, the shell-like skin shattered around the bone-metal slug, which had passed straight through the ribs to lodge in the creature's spine.

Alric was still studying the damage when he heard a scrape on the dirt. He turned to see Miranda lying next to him, staring wide-eyed into the crater.

"Is it dead?" she whispered.

"A demon is never dead until you take its seed, Spiritualist," Alric said. "You can watch if you like, but do not interfere."

He could see her starting to ask what he meant, but Alric gave her no chance. He stood up and signaled to his men. They nodded, and the League members began to move slowly down into the crater. When they were in arm's reach of the demon, Alric drew his sword. He could see the seed's edge through the demon's shattered chest, a black, wet, oblong shape just below the heart, wrapped in bloody tissue. Alric cursed under his breath. Most seeds were a few inches long, never more than six. If his eyes weren't deceiving him, this seed was over a foot. No wonder the demon had given them so much trouble. He didn't even want to think about what would have happened if this seed had awakened in a wizard instead of a spirit-deaf lug like Sted. Seeing the reality of the situation, Alric began to regret all the times he'd championed Slorn's research. If he'd known that something like this was living inside Nivel, he would have killed the woman himself.

He held his sword out, slipping the point deftly inside the demon's shattered chest. But just as he was about to press his blade against the sinew connecting the seed to the host body, he heard the faint sound of a sucked-in breath.

Alric threw himself back, snatching his sword out just in time to block the enormous black claw before it landed in his head. The demon launched itself up with a earth-shaking roar, its shattered arm flopping helpless at its side as its good claw pulled on Alric's blade. Alric tried to yank his sword free, but the creature slid its claws down the blade to grab Alric's arm. The claws dug into his flesh, and the monster lifted him clean off the ground. He barely had time to kick before it threw him as hard as it could.

Alric tucked and rolled, landing on his feet at the edge of the crater. But even as he caught his balance, he heard a hideous crunching as the demon grabbed one of his men and shoved him, sword and all, into its mouth. The other League members cried out and charged, hacking at the demon with their screaming swords. The demon ignored them. It simply kept eating, pushing Alric's lieutenant between its broken teeth as it devoured the man whole.

"The head!" Alric shouted, charging back down the crater. "Take off the head!"

But it was too late. The moment the lieutenant vanished down the monster's throat, its wounds began to heal. Its broken arm snapped itself back together with a hideous cracking of bones, and the gaping hole in its chest began to knit together. The League men were still attacking, but the sword wounds closed as soon as they were made, and each new strike injured the sword more than the monster it struck.

"Fall back!" Alric shouted, grabbing the nearest soldier.

His men scrambled back, and the demon rolled to its feet, screaming as a fresh wave of demon panic washed out of the crater.

"Alric!" Slorn shouted.

Alric whirled around to see Slorn back atop his wagon with the long metal cannon on his shoulder again, and this time, Miranda was beside him.

"Hold it down!" the bear-headed man bellowed.

He didn't need to say anything else. Alric threw out his hand and opened his spirit until the entire panicking world was roaring in his ears. He grabbed everything, every weeping spirit, every terrified spec of dust he could touch, and forced them all into one command.

DON'T MOVE.

The world froze, and the demon fell to its knees. It threw its head backward, roaring in defiance as it fought the command, but Alric held it firm. It took everything he had. He could feel the sweat pouring down his face, feel everything in the town fighting his hold in the panic to escape the demon, but he did not let go. With every second that passed, he fought to hold it just a second more, hoping it would be enough.

"Do it!" he shouted. "Do it now!"

On the edge of his vision, he saw Slorn slam the bone-metal slug into his cannon. Behind him, Miranda raised her arms. The spider-legged wagon began to shake as the impossibly blue water raced across it, picking up speed as it flowed from barrel to barrel in an endless loop. Slorn mouthed a command, and the cannon's metal legs uncurled, anchoring the Shaper on the wagon's top just as the Spiritualist thrust her hands forward. The second her hands moved, the water followed, blasting itself into the piping at the cannon's back. There was an enormous crack as the water hit the bone metal, and then the sea's triumphant roar. The bone-metal slug shot out of the cannon faster than Alric could see, nearly turning the wagon over with its force. It split the air with a whistling scream, flying right past Alric's ear to land square in the demon's neck.

The shock wave blasted Alric into the air. He landed on his back in the dirt, but was on his feet in an instant, waving his hands in a desperate attempt to see what had happened. The crater was thick with blown-out dirt. He could hear Slorn's wagon scrambling behind him, probably trying to right itself after the cannon's kick, but he couldn't see anything but yellow, billowing dust.

He'd taken two blind steps when the demon's claws lashed out of the dust cloud and hit him hard in the shoulder. Alric went down with a shout, raising his sword instinctively to block the next blow. But the claws went right over him, thrashing wildly through the air.

Alric rolled clear, gripping his bleeding shoulder as the dust began to settle. The first thing he noticed was that several of his men were down, knocked over by the blast wave or taken out by the demon, he didn't know. The cratered arena they'd been fighting in was now twice as deep, and he could see the outline of the demon at its center, still madly lashing out. Alric wiped the dust from his eyes with a bloody hand. How could it still be standing? Had the shot missed? But as his vision cleared, he saw the truth. The demon's head was gone, blasted clean off, but the body was still fighting. It struck blindly, the claws stabbing out. As he watched, one of the random blows landed in the back of one of his downed men.

Alric shouted, but it was too late. The man screamed as the claw skewered him, and the demon stopped thrashing to lunge at its kill, dragging the man toward its ruined body as its claws began to eat his flesh right then and there, drinking in his power to heal its wounds.

"Shoot it again!" Alric shouted, scrambling up the edge of the crater. "Damn it, Slorn, shoot it again! Now!"

Miranda jumped down from the scrambling wagon, landing on her waiting ghosthound. The water followed her, sliding over her shoulders like a mantle as the hound cleared the distance to Alric in one jump.

"There aren't any more shots," she said as Gin slid to a stop. "We only had two."

Alric gritted his teeth. "Then we do this the hard way."

Miranda jumped down. "What do you mean the har—Wait!"

But Alric was already gone. He charged through the dust cloud, picking up speed as he ran down the crater toward the demon, who was still eating its victim.

He launched himself off the slope, drawing his sword in a golden flash. Hungry and blind, the demon didn't raise a claw to defend itself. Alric's blow sliced into its back, his golden blade peeling through the demon's shell and into its spine. The creature screamed, and the demon panic hammered Alric's mind. But he was further than fear could reach. He pressed the blow, cutting down through the demon's torso. It dropped the soldier and reached backward, clawing wildly at Alric, but it was too late. With a shout of triumph, Alric turned his sword and sliced up through the tissue that connected the seed to its host.

The demon howled. Claws ripped into Alric's back and threw

him down. He landed under the demon's clawed feet. There was no time to dodge; the thrashing demon's claws landed right on top of him. He closed his eyes, bracing for the explosion of pain as the demon's foot ripped into his chest, but he felt nothing. He opened them again, staring up in amazement. The demon's foot was on his chest, but there was no weight to it. The monster was still thrashing, but with every movement, bits of it were breaking away. The demon was crumbling like ash, breaking apart and floating away. Already, the fear was receding as the demon crumpled in on itself. By the time Alric managed to sit up, it was nothing more than a pile of black dust around a long, black seed.

Alric took a deep, pained breath. It was over. The demon was dead. He looked around, doing a quick count of his men. Two dead for certain, three more lying motionless, but the rest were pushing themselves up. Not bad considering what they'd faced without the Lord of Storms' backup. But there was one loss he felt more than the others.

Alric looked down at the sword in his hands. The long, slender blade still glowed faintly with its own golden light, but the cutting edge was ravaged. Enormous chunks were missing, leaving great gaps all the way to the core of the blade.

"Dunelle," he whispered. "My Last Sunlight. I'm sorry. I'm so sorry."

"You did what had to be done." His sword's ringing voice was warped and muffled with pain, but the pride in the words stood bold and clear. "It has been an honor to serve you, sir."

The golden light grew dimmer as it spoke, and Alric felt tears in his eyes for the first time in a century. "The honor has been mine," he whispered, laying the destroyed blade across his knees.

He heard the crunch of boots behind him, but he did not take his eyes from the blade until the last of the golden light faded out completely.

"A noble sword," Slorn said, his voice soft by Alric's ear. "One of the finest I ever made."

Alric nodded, but said nothing. Slorn knelt down beside him. "I know it will be no replacement, but I can make you another blade."

"I don't need another blade," Alric said, sliding his ravaged sword back into its sheath.

Slorn left it at that. "You should see to your wounds."

"What," Alric said, "and leave the seed to you?"

Slorn stiffened. "That is not what I meant, but it is Nivel's seed." He turned his bear head, staring at the long, black shape lying in the demon's dusty remains. "It is all I have left of our work together, of our lives. If I was ever kind to you, Alric, if our work ever opened a door of thought in your mind, you will let me study it a moment before you lock it away."

Alric heaved a deep sigh and waved him on. Slorn stood with a murmur of thanks and walked over to kneel by the seed, staring at it with an intensity Alric had never seen.

"You really should do something about that shoulder," said a voice behind him. "You're bleeding everywhere."

He looked back to see Miranda hovering at the edge of the crater.

"Thank you for your concern, Spiritualist," he said, pushing himself up. "But your worry is wasted. I am very hard to kill. It is my gift."

Miranda frowned. "Your gift?"

Alric smiled. It was refreshing to meet someone who didn't know all the secrets for once. "The League requires great sacrifices of its members. To counterbalance this, the Lord of Storms bestows gifts upon us. Some men choose power, others choose invulnerability. I chose eternal life."

"You mean you can't be killed?" Miranda said, impressed.

Alric frowned. "There is a wide difference between eternal life and invulnerability to death. I can be killed just like any other man, given enough damage, but over the years I've gotten fairly good at staying alive. Don't worry, it will take more than this to kill me."

He left her pondering that and walked off to gather what was left of his men. There was much to clean up before the day was done.

"Eternal life," Miranda said, shaking her head. "No wonder he's always so smug. I'd be smug too if I knew I was going to survive almost anything."

"Well, I don't like it," Mellinor said. "The only defense most spirits have against humans is your short lives. No matter how bad it gets, we can always outlast you. An immortal wizard sounds like a disaster to me. Thank goodness he's working for the League and not trying to rule some spirit domain somewhere."

Miranda was slightly insulted by that train of logic, but she held her tongue, turning instead to see how Gin was faring.

"Find anything?"

"I've got Eli's scent," Gin said, running his nose along the ground. "No trail yet, though." A little dust cloud rose up as he spoke, and Gin sneezed several times. "This is a horrible place to be looking," he snorted. "The dirt's so jumpy it's flinging itself up my nose. We'll have to wait until the League calms things down before I can get a good fix."

Miranda sighed in frustration. "The trail will be stone cold by then."

"Even I can't work miracles," Gin said, lashing his tail.

"Sorry, sorry," Miranda grumbled. "It's just that every single time I get close to catching Eli, something horrendous happens, and it's getting really old."

"Don't worry, we'll catch him," Gin said. "Sparrow had him last, remember? Much as I can't stand him, the bird boy is just as sly as the thief. It'll all work itself out."

"I hope so," Miranda said. "Because if I have to go back to Zarin empty-handed one more time, I think I'll cry."

Gin whimpered sympathetically and went back to sniffing. Miranda strolled along beside him, searching the destroyed town for a clue, any clue, the thief might have left behind.

CHAPTER 20

Nico and Eli found Josef buried beneath a collapsed house. He was unconscious and bleeding badly, but miraculously unbroken.

"Probably because he was out before he hit," Eli said, grabbing the swordsman by his arms. "Going limp saves your bones, though I can't vouch for the rest of him."

Nico nodded, pushing a beam off the Heart, which was lying in a crater of its own about ten feet away. When she had the path clear, she grabbed Josef's feet and they hauled him over to his sword.

"There," Eli said, folding Josef's fingers around the hilt. "Now let's get out of here."

Nico couldn't agree more. They couldn't see the fighting from where they were, but the sounds coming from the crater that had been the arena were horrible enough that she didn't want to. Using Josef's arm for leverage, they got the Heart on his chest, and Eli tied it down using a strip of Josef's shredded shirt. When the swordsman was secure, Eli grabbed his shoulders while Nico got his legs and together they carried him out of the wreckage to the road.

It was slow going. Josef was amazingly heavy and the road was constantly blocked by toppled buildings, forcing them to retrace their steps and go around. They kept to the side streets as much as possible, but even when they had to use the large main roads, they saw no one. Except for the League men at the arena, the city was empty. The bandits were long gone, and Nico didn't blame them one bit. She would have run too if she could have.

Yes, you're very good at running.

Nico closed her mind and focused on keeping up with Eli's grueling pace.

By the time they reached the canyon wall that separated the bandit city from the surrounding forest, her knees were ready to buckle. Josef's body seemed to grow heavier with every step. Her arms ached with the strain of holding him. Sweat dripped into her eyes, making them burn, but worst of all was her transformed hand. Though she'd wrapped her demon claw in her coat as best she could, she could still feel Josef's flesh through the cloth, feel the life in him calling out. The claws twitched in anticipation. The raw hunger she felt every time her transformed fingers brushed Josef's skin made her ill, but she could not let him go.

You're only having this problem because you refuse to accept yourself, the Master said with a sigh. *How many times have you carried the swordsman's unconscious carcass? Fifty? A hundred? More? You never had problems helping him then. Now look at you, ready to fall over after a quarter mile.*

Nico tightened her grip. Unfortunately, it only made her hand itch worse as she pressed it into the flesh of Josef's calf.

If you would only accept reality, everything would be so much simpler. For the first time that she could remember, the Master's voice sounded earnest. *I can help you control the hunger. I can even help you remember what you've forgotten. I can make you a god among insects, Nico. A power Eli Monpress would treasure above all others and a companion Josef Liechten would never abandon. I can make you everything you want to become. All you have to do is stop being stubborn. You are my child, my dearest daughter. I know more than anyone what it is like to be outcast. You don't have to struggle on alone. Let me help you.*

The words were so sweet, so sincere, that for a stumbling moment, Nico almost gave in. But then Nivel's words, words, she realized with a stab of sadness, she would never hear her speak again, sounded loud and clear in her mind.

Never trust the voice.

What? The voice was sneering now, all sincerity gone. *You're still listening to that woman? That pathetic creature? Did you know she died without lifting a finger to save herself? Defeated by Sted, the one-armed, spirit-deaf, League reject? She died like a dog, whimpering and crying for her precious bear-headed freak of a husband. Is that the kind of strength you want?*

The voice began to laugh, but Nico cut it off.

"You said she died without a fight," she whispered fiercely. "But you said nothing about her giving in. She didn't, did she? She died with her soul intact."

I ate her soul and gave her seed to Sted, the Master said.

"No," Nico said, eyes wide as the revelations tumbled through her mind, snapping into place one by one. "That would make her less powerful. You would never accept a weaker servant when you could have a stronger one. She beat you, didn't she? Nivel died human. That's why you had to give Sted her seed." She stopped midstep, causing Eli to stumble.

"Nico?" Eli said, looking back. "What's wrong? What are you muttering about?"

"She was the master of herself," Nico said, her voice trembling with wonder. "You couldn't take her."

Eli gave her a nervous look. "Take who where?"

Don't get cocky, the Master snarled. *I've been very, very patient with you, Nico, but this is your last chance.* An image invaded her mind, a long-fingered hand outstretched in the dark. *Take it. Take it now and I promise you'll never feel pain again.*

Nico stared at the outstretched palm and, slowly and deliberately, spoke one word.

"No."

The image vanished.

That is the last mistake you'll ever make.

"Nico?" Eli put Josef's shoulders down and hurried to her side. "What in the world are you—"

Before he could get the last word out, a figure stepped out of the shadows behind him and clubbed Eli across the back of his head. It happened so quickly Nico didn't even have time to drop Josef's legs before Eli was knocked sprawling onto the leaf-covered ground.

"Eli!" Nico rushed to his side, but before she'd taken two steps, the figure from the shadows grabbed her arms and wrenched them behind her. She screamed in pain and twisted her neck back to see a tall man with pale skin holding her down, his eyes glowing with that horrible light.

"Excellent work, Sezri."

Nico turned to see Izo, his lordly silks torn and filthy, step out of the trees. The Bandit King didn't even look at her. He walked over to where Eli was groaning on the ground and jerked the thief to his feet.

"Do you mind?" Eli said. "I'm getting pretty tired of being dragged around like a prize at the fair."

"Too bad," Izo said, sliding a long knife against Eli's throat.

"That's what you are. What you made yourself when you decided to court your bounty rather than mitigate it like any sensible criminal. But you shouldn't complain. It's precisely because you're the prize everyone wants that you're still alive. Though how long you'll stay that way is entirely up to you. The posters do say 'Dead or Alive.'"

Eli leaned nonchalantly against the knife's edge. "I'm worth more alive."

"That may be, but the extra gold is offset by the trouble you cause. Corpses are far less of a liability." Izo lowered his knife. "Don't forget that."

Eli's smile faltered just a hair. "Consider it remembered. So, what now? Are you going to chop me into bits and mail me to the Council?"

"Not yet," Izo said. "First, I regroup my army, administer some needed discipline, and then I'm going to hold the Council to its bargain."

"Oh, yes," Eli said. "Me for a throne. It's a bad deal, you know. I'm worth more than—"

The knife returned to his throat, cutting Eli off midsentence.

"That's better," Izo said. He gave the thief a push, and they began walking northward, into the woods, away from Nico and Sezri.

"You know, Monpress," Izo said, "I can see now why my bounty is higher than yours. You're nothing but a fraud, a little thief with a pathological need for attention. You don't know what it means to have real ambition."

Eli gave him a nasty look, but kept his mouth shut. Izo just smiled and looked back over his shoulder. "Sezri," he said, "now that we've found the thief, we've no need for the girl. Kill her, and the swordsman. I don't want any more liabilities."

Nico's eyes went wide, and Eli started to protest, but Sezri didn't move. He just stood there, holding Nico's arms in a lock against her back, staring into the distance like he was listening to something.

"Sezri!" Izo shouted, shutting Eli up with another jerk of his knife.

The demonseed ignored him. He tilted his head down to stare at Nico, his free hand moving up to grip her jaw.

"Did you think you could run?" he whispered. "The Master always knows where his children are." The hand on her jaw tightened. "You don't deserve this," Sezri hissed. "He gave you everything and you threw it in his face. But I serve the Master in life and death with all my soul. I will show you what it means to be a child of the Mountain."

"Sezri!" Izo roared, but the name was lost in Nico's scream. With incredible strength, the demonseed forced her jaw open and pressed his mouth to hers. Nico's eyes went wide as the connection exploded open, and Sezri began to pour into her. She writhed against him, beating him with her fists while her mind recoiled from the wrongness of the man's flowing into her. This couldn't be happening. Demonseeds couldn't eat other seeds.

No. The Master's voice was hard as iron. *But you're not eating him. He's feeding you every spirit I told him to eat into you.* The Master chuckled. *Such a good, obedient child.*

A look of bliss spread over Sezri's face as the Master praised him, and the flow of devoured spirits sped up. Nico choked and gasped, trying to pull away, but her transformed arm shot up of its own accord, ripping into Sezri's chest to gorge on the spirits inside him. The flow of spirits doubled, and blackness washed over her mind. Nico felt her control slipping as the tide of power poured into her. She fought to hold on, to close her mind, but it was too late. The blackness was everywhere, eating her thoughts, her fear, her control until there was nothing left to hold on to.

I told you, the Master said, *I always win.*

And then even his voice vanished as Nico fell into the dark.

A piercing scream ripped through the air above Izo's destroyed city, followed by a pulse of fear that sent Miranda to her knees. She gasped for breath, clutching her rings as her spirits began to panic. Gin was on the ground beside her, whimpering, and even Mellinor was shaking. One by one, she got control again, calming her spirits with an iron will. When they were as steady as she could hope to make them, Miranda looked around. She was clearly not the only one who'd been caught off-guard. The League men had stopped in their tracks, and even Slorn was on his feet, staring into the distance. Alric stood beside him, his calm, severe face distorted in a look very close to sheer terror.

"No," Alric said. "Not now."

Realizing she would probably regret it, Miranda turned to look as well. There, past the northern edge of the bandit city, something horrible and black was rising above the trees. As she saw it, Miranda felt her spirits start to panic again. She wanted to join them. The thing was like nothing she'd ever seen, awake or asleep. As she watched, two more enormous black things rose beside the first, unfolding in hideous slow motion. After a terrible moment, she realized they were wings. Enormous wings, taller than the trees, reaching up with their hideous clawed talons toward the sky.

The thing jerked, and the scream sounded again, bringing with it a blast of fear even stronger than the first that turned her bones to jelly. When Miranda could move again, she looked frantically for Alric. Whatever that thing was, it was surely a demon. That meant the League could make it stop. But Alric wasn't there anymore. The spot where he'd been standing seconds before was now empty, save for the telltale glimmer of a cut in the air as it vanished.

"He abandoned us!" Gin howled.

Miranda didn't think that was the case, but she couldn't even get the words out. All she could do was hang on as the waves of fear broke over her.

Izo had dropped his hold on Eli when Nico's transformed arm had ripped through Sezri's chest, but neither the thief nor the bandit had moved. They just stood there, frozen, unable to look away.

For a few seconds, the two demonseeds stood as close as lovers, and then Nico pushed him away. The thin man fell like a tree. His body shattered when it hit the ground, and he turned to black dust that seemed to vanish even as Eli watched. When it was finished, all that was left of Sezri was a small, black seed, about the size of Eli's middle finger, that fell to the ground like a stone.

Nico, however, stayed perfectly still. Eli began to fidget. The way she was standing, he couldn't see her face, but it couldn't be good. He took a hesitant step forward.

"Nico—"

Nico threw back her head, and a scream like he had never heard blasted through the air. Eli slammed his hands over his ears, but it was no use. The scream went straight to his soul. But worse, far worse, was the wave of fear that followed. For a moment, Eli was drowning in pure, abject terror before he got his mind back under control. Behind him he heard Izo screaming, and then a loud crash as the Bandit King fell, but he didn't turn to see where or why. His eyes were trapped by what was happening in front of him.

Still screaming, Nico threw out her arms, human and demon claw. The manacles on her wrists were going mad, beating themselves against her skin. With a horrible wrenching of flesh, toothed mouths appeared on Nico's arms. They gnashed their horrible, spiny teeth and bit deep into the manacles. The metal screamed and shattered, wailing as the demon mouths ate the pieces. The same thing happened to the collar at her neck and the shackles on her ankles.

When the last shred of metal vanished into the hideous mouths, Nico's coat, which had clung faithfully to her the entire time, tore down the middle. The cloth cried as it ripped, the threads still reaching out for one another even as they snapped, but it wasn't enough. The coat fell in a shredded pile at Nico's feet. Without the coat, Eli could see that her skin was now the same horrible black shell as Sted's, but even as he wrapped his brain around what that meant, the shell began to crack. Liquid black oozed from the lesions, and Nico began to grow.

At that moment, all trace of humanity vanished. Blackness ripped from Nico's body, forming long, clawed arms reaching out from a shape that was like nothing he'd ever seen. It was long and spindly and full of sharp angles, or that was the impression he got. He couldn't look at it for very long before the terror overwhelmed his mind. He caught glimpses of eyes in the blackness, great glowing yellow orbs, and not just two. There were hundreds scattered across the unspeakable expanse of the demon's body. They clustered on the demon's long head, gathering at the edges of its great, fanged jaw, which opened slowly, dripping black bile as it screamed again. Its black body convulsed as a pair of wings, black as coal and as sharp as knives, burst from its back. The creature stumbled forward at the impact, and the new wings flapped awkwardly, stretching for the sky with clawed talons. Its enormous, clawed feet ripped into the forest floor for balance, tearing up great mounds of roots and stone in the process. These turned to black dust as Eli watched, their souls devoured by the creature's touch.

Unable to tear his eyes away, Eli would have watched until he too was eaten. But then, just before Nico's deadly skin reached him, a rough hand grabbed him by the collar and tugged him sideways. Eli felt the strange whooshing sensation that came with traveling through a cut in the world before landing on his face on the ground twenty feet from where he'd been standing. Izo was there too, still staring dumbly into the distance, but that was all Eli could make out before the hand on his collar dragged him up until he was inches from Alric's enraged face. Even so, it took Eli a few seconds to realize that the vibrations coming from Alric's frantically moving mouth were words.

"I said you have to do something!" Alric shouted, shaking Eli until the thief saw spots. "The Lord of Storms is missing and I can't contact the Shepherdess on my own. She'll listen to you. You have to make her do something or our world will be devoured!"

Eli's poor brain had a hard time keeping up with that. "What do you mean?"

Alric's grip on his collar tightened until Eli thought he was going to choke. "Look at it!" the League man shouted, forcing Eli's head until the thief had no choice but to look where Alric wanted. "This isn't some errant seed grown out of control. It's the *Daughter of the Dead Mountain*!"

The demon was nearly twenty feet tall now. It reached out, dragging its hands along the ground, leaving great, blackened rents in the forest wherever it touched. Its enormous mouth devoured the trees whole, and the air was full of the screams of dying spirits.

"I can't stop it," Alric said. "The whole League can't stop it, not without the Lord of Storms. Even then, he took its head off last time and it still didn't die."

"What do you want me to do?" Eli shouted. "The Shepherdess is the guardian of all spirits. If she won't leave her little white world for *this*"—he pointed at the demon—"what's my opinion matter?"

Alric jerked him. "Oh, come off it! You're her favorite little pet. She'll do anything you want, even her *job*."

Eli started trying to pry Alric's fingers off his collar. "That's a low blow," he muttered. "Even for you."

Alric's eyes narrowed. "I do what I have to, favorite. Now, will you do it, or do I have to kill you to get her attention?" He dropped Eli and drew his sword, pressing the ruined edge against Eli's chest.

Eli swallowed, eyes flicking from sword to swordsman. He did not doubt for a moment that the League man would do it. Alric had never been the idle-threat type. But...

"Forget it," Eli said, crossing his arms over his chest. "Groveling to Benehime for help is on the same level as dying, so far as I'm concerned. You'll have to think up a better threat."

Alric stared at him for a moment, and then he drew his fist back and punched Eli square across the jaw. Eli fell backward, flailing to catch himself, but Alric was there first, grabbing him around the throat.

"*Do you think this is a game?*" Alric's fingers pressed tighter on Eli's windpipe with every word. "Do you have *any* idea *what is at stake*?"

"More than you do," Eli choked out. He wrenched himself from Alric's grasp, rubbing his bruised throat. "You think the Shepherdess isn't watching this right now? She could fix everything with a single word, but she won't. Not while there's a chance of forcing me to ask for it. That's what she's like. It's all a game to her. She's trying to corner me, to make me act how she wants me to act. But I'm no one's dog, Alric. Not hers, and not yours."

Alric screamed his answer, but the words were lost as the ground began to erupt. Great shards of stone shot from the ground as the great sleeping spirits of the mountains woke and began trying to fight the threat. Eli, Alric, and the still-staring Izo fell as the ground rolled like a bucking bull beneath them. Alric was back on his feet at once, bracing his legs against the moving ground like a sailor on a storm-pitched ship. Eli stood more slowly, gripping a screaming tree for support, watching wide-eyed as the valley began to tear itself apart.

The spirit's fight was over as soon as it had begun. The demon ate the stone spikes even as they struck home, absorbing the screaming spirits into its growing body until there was nothing left but black dust falling down on the valley like snow. Even so, blind and desperate with panic, the spirits kept attacking. With nothing left to lose, the ground tore itself open beneath the demon's feet, screaming vengeance as great stone hands reached out to pull it down and crush it beneath the bedrock. The creature stumbled, grabbing hold of the fissure with its long claws. Scenting victory, another fissure opened in the other direction, trying to spoil the demon's hold. The creature screamed and began kicking with its claws, cracking the fissures and collapsing them in on themselves even as it ate the stone. Eli watched in horrified silence, unable to speak until he saw something horribly familiar on the edge of the collapsing cliff. After everything he'd just seen, it took him a few seconds to realize he was looking at Josef's unconscious body, still lying where they'd left it when Alric had pulled them to safety.

"Josef!" Eli shouted. But it was too late. The ground collapsed beneath the swordsman, sending him falling into the abyss.

"*Josef!*"

As Eli screamed Josef's name, the demon moved. With horrifying speed, it caught the falling swordsman between its claws. The demon climbed out of the collapsing fissure, carrying Josef and the Heart, which Josef still held clutched against his chest, in its palm. When it reached a stretch of unbroken ground, the demon gently laid the swordsman down. It hovered over him a moment, staring at him with its hundreds of yellow, glowing eyes. Then, with a horrible scream, it turned and began to attack the forest more violently than ever.

Eli ran to Josef and pressed his fingers against the swordsman's neck. He heaved a huge sigh of relief when he felt his friend's strong, steady heartbeat. Despite what the demon had done to everything else it touched, Josef was unharmed.

"She's still in there," he said, looking up at the rampaging demon with a sort of wonder.

His thoughts were interrupted by Alric as the League man yanked him around.

"Now do you get it?" Alric shouted, shaking him. "There's nothing we can do, humans or spirits, to stop that thing. We need the Shepherdess, and you're going to get her." He swung his ruined sword up, the broken gold glinting in the dusty sunlight. "Last chance, favorite. I'm ready to die to do what I have to do, and I have absolutely no qualms about taking you with me. Call her down or die for your pride. Either way, this ends now."

Eli flinched away, his brain madly trying to think of a way out. But before he could even open his mouth, a deep, deep voice he'd never heard before spoke over the roar.

"Leave him, League man. Even if she does come down, we will suffer for it."

Alric and Eli both turned. On Josef's chest, the battered blade of the Heart of War began to glow.

"If you call down the Shepherdess, she will deal with this one as she did the last," the Heart said. "She will bury it under a mountain, and we will have twice the problems we have now."

"No," Alric said. "The Daughter of the Dead Mountain is still not a hundredth the size of the original. All we need is—"

"Demonseeds are shards of the great demon," the Heart said. "Fractures small enough to escape its prison and move freely through the world. Yet each tiny piece has the same attributes of the whole. Think. The League, the Shepherdess's arm in this world, can't even destroy those small seeds, only cut them off from their human hosts and store them in starvation. What, then, can the Shepherdess do with a demon this size except what she did with the original? Mark me, Alric, she will do what she did before. She will seal it beneath a mountain. But this time there is only one remaining mountain spirit strong enough to hold a shard of the demon that large in check, and I very much doubt the Shaper Mountain would be willing to spend the rest of eternity as a sword."

"Wait," Eli said. "You mean you..."

"Yes," the Heart answered. "At the beginning of this world, I willingly gave my body as a prison for the demon. In return, the Shepherdess let me choose my new form. I chose to be a sword. It has been a hard, lonely journey, but I have never regretted my choice. However, I will not let another be forced to it, least of all my brother, who has dedicated his life to guiding his Shapers."

"Wait," Eli said. "The Shaper Mountain is your brother?"

"All mountains are my brothers," the Heart said. "But the Shaper Mountain, Durain, is my twin. We two were birthed from the will of the Creator at the dawn of the world to stand as guard and guide to the lesser mountains. We were the greatest of the Great Spirits of stone, and we can never be replaced. The Shepherdess is not the Creator. She can only guide and order the spirits, not form new ones. When the demon first came, I gave up my body to serve as a prison because I knew my brother would watch in my stead. But now, history repeats itself. My brother is the only mountain strong enough to hold the creature Nico has become. If you call the Shepherdess down now, she will have no choice but to use the only tool she has left, and the last of the great mountains will be gone."

"That's a fine sentiment," Alric said through gritted teeth. "But we have no choice. I cannot sit here and watch that thing eat the world."

"But we do have a choice," the Heart said. "The thief saw it himself. Inside that monster is one of our own."

"The girl is gone," Alric said. "Don't kid yourself. Human spirits are the first consumed on awakening."

"Then why did it save Josef?" Eli asked.

Alric's eyes narrowed. "How should I know?"

"Nico is still alive," the Heart said. "She is a survivor. I had my doubts as well at first. Since the morning Josef took her naked from the crater, I have come close to killing her myself on several occasions. Every time, I thought the demon had won, but every time she fought back. I think that this time will be no different. That thing may not look like Nico, but it is still her body. So long as there is some shred of her soul left, so long as she still has will, she is still a wizard. So long as she has will, she has the weight of a mountain, and there is still hope."

Alric shook his head, but Eli stared past him, watching the demon with an uncharacteristically serious expression on his face.

"Alric," he said quietly, "I'll make you a deal."

Alric sneered. "This isn't the time for tricks."

"No," Eli said. "No tricks, just a clean proposition. We may not have always gotten along, but Nico is still my companion. I take only the best into my line of work, and she's no exception. The sword is right. The demon never beat her before, and I'm willing to bet my life and my pride that it hasn't beaten her now." He held up his hand, fingers splayed wide. "Five minutes. If she doesn't beat her seed in five minutes, then I'll do anything you want. I'll call Benehime down here to dance with you, if you like. Do we have a deal?"

Alric considered for a moment, and then released his death grip on Eli's shirt. "You do realize that in five minutes there may not be anything left to save." He looked at the demon, then at the Heart, and then at Eli. "All right," he said, sheathing his sword. "Five minutes."

Eli nodded and stepped over Josef's splayed body. He ran to the edge of the ruined fissure, parts of which were still collapsing and, cupping his hands to his mouth, shouted as loud as he could.

"Nico!" he cried, layering just enough power into the words to make sure they would cut through everything else. "Listen! Me, Josef, the Heart of War, we're betting it all on you! You've got five minutes to turn this around before Alric and the League get their way, but I think you can do it. I'm sorry about before. I was stupid. I admit it. Come back to us, Nico, and everything will be like it was, only better. Just you, me, Josef, and anything in the world we want to steal. All you have to do is kick that demon out and come home. Five minutes. We'll be here waiting for you."

His voice echoed through the hills, and the spirit panic dimmed to listen. On the other side of the fissure, the demon paused its eating. It stood there, listening for one long moment. Then, with an angry scream, it began to eat again.

Panting, Eli sat down on the crumbling stone, rubbing his hands over his dusty face and hoping on whatever luck he still had that he'd made the right choice.

CHAPTER 21

Nico raised her head. She could have sworn she'd heard someone calling her, but now, no matter how she strained her ears, all she heard was silence. She was alone, sitting on a cold floor of smooth black stone. It went on forever in all directions, an endless, endless darkness of the kind she'd seen only once before.

"Yes," a deep, smooth voice whispered behind her. "When you were with me."

Nico spun around, sliding back on the stone. A man was standing behind her where there had been no one a second before. He was tall and broad shouldered, dressed in a simple black shirt and dark trousers tucked into tall boots, just like Josef's. He looked a lot like Josef too, and a little bit like Eli, but the cruel look in his golden eyes belonged to only one person.

"Master." Her whisper was little more than a breath.

"At last you remember." The man smiled.

Nico did remember. She remembered the slave pens. How she'd been taken from them. How the cult members had held her down, their dead white faces leering beneath their cowls. She remembered the hideous feeling of the seed, then barely larger than a grape pit, being shoved down her choking throat. But more than that, she remembered the unadulterated joy of the Master's good opinion. The absolute pleasure that came from being a good child who pleased her father. The warmth, the understanding, the acceptance that no one outside could give her.

The Master opened his arms, and she ran to him, flinging herself against his chest with a sob. Joy and belonging like she'd never felt washed over her, but even as she savored the feelings, there was something wrong about them. Something alien, almost sticky in her mind. Slowly, painfully, she released her grip and stepped back.

"You're making me feel this, aren't you?" she whispered.

"Of course," the Master said, stroking her hair. "You're home now. It's only right you should share in my happiness." He ran his hand under her chin, tilting her head up until their eyes met. "You are mine again, every bit of you. My greatest weapon is back in my command, and she'll never escape again. Is that not cause for joy?"

Nico ducked out of his grasp, or tried to, but her body would not move. The Master just smiled and kept petting her, stroking her hair like a huntsman petting his prize hound.

"Now, now," he tsked. "You lost, Nico. You don't get to play keep-away anymore. It's over; take it gracefully. If this works out the way I expect, a new Dead Mountain will be born. I'll be twice as powerful as I am now, and it's all thanks to you. That's why I'm being so generous, despite everything you've done. If you were any other seed, I would have crushed you and left you to die the moment you disobeyed me, but I didn't. I stayed with you, despite your defiance. I never abandoned you."

He slid his hand up to cup her cheek before stepping back.

"You should be grateful," he said. "I have given you everything. Made you the ground for my greatest creation. Yet even now you stand there staring at me like you're some kind of victim." His smile grew impossibly cruel. "I have done nothing to you that you did not deserve. It is I who have suffered the most, suffered as you denied me over and over again, despite everything I've done for you. Have you nothing to say?"

"No, Master." Nico lowered her head. "I am sorry, Master."

The Master's arms slid around her shoulders, pulling her against him as the sticky, alien joy flooded her mind. "There, there," he said. "I forgive you. It's over now. You've lost. You don't have to think anymore. You don't have to try. I'll take care of everything. Just let it go. There's a good girl."

Nico let herself slump into his arms. She couldn't even remember why she'd been fighting, only that she'd been trying so hard for so long. But the Master was here now, and he would take care of everything. All she had to do was be good, do as he said, and nothing would ever hurt again.

But as that thought circled round and round in her mind, a tiny, lingering doubt nagged at her. She felt like she was forgetting something terribly important.

"Wait," she said. "Where's Josef?"

"Gone," the Master said. "Abandoned you, along with that no-account thief. Everyone has abandoned you, except me. They see you as a monster. They're probably trying to kill you right now."

"No!" Nico said, looking up at him. "Josef would never abandon me."

The Master slapped her hard across the face. Nico stumbled and fell without a cry, landing hard on the cold stone floor.

"Never speak back to me," he said, his voice colder than the stone. He walked to where she had fallen, his steps fading off into the endless nothing. Nico gasped as he grabbed her hair, yanking her up until her feet were a foot off the ground. He grabbed her chin with his other hand, pressing so hard she thought her jaw would break as he turned her face to his.

"Your body is my body now," he said slowly. "Your soul, your power, everything. It is all mine. You are only here because I wish it." He dropped her, and she crumpled. The moment she was down, he kicked her in the ribs, sending her tumbling across the floor. She slid to a stop several feet away, panting against the cold stone. When she looked up again, the Master was standing over her, looking down on her like she was a piece of trash in his way.

"Never defy me again," he said. "I am your Master. You live by my generosity alone. Never, ever forget that."

Nico pressed her head down onto the stone. Desperate, sobbing apologies and promises of obedience filled her mind. She wanted to shout that she would never disobey again, that she had no master but him, but for some reason her mouth would not open. She could not speak the words.

Pain exploded through her as the Master kicked her again, and she flew across the endless chamber, landing so hard she saw spots.

"Do you think you're too good for this?" he shouted. "Or do you not understand the very simple words I am speaking? Has being a weak, pathetic, stupid creature for so long also made you mute?"

Nico began to hyperventilate. She moved her mouth desperately, but no sound came out. She could hear the Master coming toward her, and her body seized up in preparation for the kick she knew was coming. Why couldn't she say it? Why couldn't she swear that his will was the only will she knew?

Because it's not true.

Nico stopped cold. The voice spoke in her head like the Master's had so many times, but it was not his. It sounded like Nivel, like Eli, like Josef, like Miranda, like Tesset. Like everyone who'd ever said, in one way or another, what the voice said next.

The only human soul a wizard can control is their own.

At last, her lips parted, but the whispered word that slipped out was not what she had meant to say.

"Why?"

The answer came a heartbeat later. *Because a wizard has no master but herself.*

As the last word faded, Nico recognized the voice. It was her own. All at once, she understood. She understood everything, and she knew what she had to do.

She caught the Master's kick right before it landed in her side. He stumbled and nearly fell. He caught his balance at once and stomped down as hard as he could on her fingers, but Nico did not let go.

"I know what you're doing," she said, turning her bruised face to stare at him. "You're trying to intimidate me. To get me to surrender."

"Get you to..." The Master thew back his head and laughed. "Why would I waste my time on someone so stupid? You need power to surrender. You have nothing."

"No," Nico said. "You forced me to awaken, but you didn't beat me. I never surrendered my will. This is still my body."

"So what?" the Master sneered. "You're too far gone to go back now. You've eaten thousands of spirits. You nearly ate Josef and that horrible sword of his. Everyone's seen what you are. There's nothing for you out there. You belong here, with me. You've always belonged here. That life out there was a joke, a dream. Even if I'd done nothing, the end would have been the same."

"No," Nico said again. "Only if I'd let it. This is still my body, my soul." Her crushed fingers tightened on the Master's boot. "I am king here."

She stood up in a fluid motion, throwing the Master back. He flickered in the air, landing perfectly several feet away, but the look on his face, the mix of rage and disbelief, was as good as if he'd stumbled. Nico pushed herself up, wincing as her muscles protested. She ran her hands over her body, wishing she had enough light to see the damage.

The moment she wished it, light appeared. A beautiful shaft of yellow sunlight shot down from the air above her head, creating a wide circle around her. Nico looked at herself in the sudden brightness, examining her broken fingers and the bruises on her ribs and knees. She closed her eyes. When she opened them again, the bruises were gone. Her fingers were straight again, and the pain had vanished. She realized with a shock that it had never really been there to begin with. This was her soul, her world; everything that happened here, including pain, only happened because she allowed it.

She looked up at the Master. No, she scowled. Not Master, not anymore. The demon was looking at her cautiously now, circling just on the edge of the sunlight. Now that she had light on her side, she could see the thing behind his human form. A great, black shape lurking in the dark with a mouthful of jagged, glistening teeth.

Fear began to creep in and Nico tore her eyes away from the demon's true self, forcing herself to focus on his human face as she said the two words she'd wanted to say her whole life.

"Get out."

"Ah." The demon chuckled. "You think that now that you've had a little revelation about the nature of the soul you can do the impossible? Sorry, princess, it doesn't go that way. This might be your soul, but you're still a demonseed. So long as there's a piece of me in your body, you can't kick me out."

Nico narrowed her eyes. "You always lie. Why should I trust you now?"

The demon crossed his arms and gave her a sly smile. "If it were that easy, Nivel would have been free of me her first year. She was much smarter than you, and more determined. She had something to go home to. What have you got? Eli? Josef? You think they'll take you back after what you did?"

"I don't know," Nico said. "But I'm going to let them decide that. You don't get to say anything anymore."

"Don't I?" the demon said with a smirk. "Just because you know the rules of the fight doesn't mean it gets any easier. You're still the Daughter of the Dead Mountain. My mountain, my daughter. Your powers are my powers, and the more you use them, the stronger my presence becomes. You may have retaken control today, but you will never, ever be free of me."

"Then I'll have to live with you in a way I can handle," Nico said.

She closed her eyes and pictured what she wanted. When she opened them, everything was just as she'd imagined. She was standing in a wide-open field, like the ones around Home. Noon sunlight blasted down from the clear blue sky, banishing every shadow, except for one. In front of her, the demon stood in a pit. The pit alone was still black, shaded from the sun by the boulder balanced on its end above it.

The demon stood at the edge of the light, staring up at her with a smug smile. "You can't lock me away forever, Nico. The moment you are weak, the moment your control wavers, I'll be back. And you will be weak. The longer we fight, the stronger I'll become, while your power will only diminish. No matter how hard you struggle or for how long, the end will be the same. After all, you're just a human. I, on the other hand, have all the time in the world. Sooner or later, you'll be just like Nivel, alone and helpless in the dark. When that happens, I'll be there, and you will crawl on your knees begging for what you just threw away."

"That may be," Nico said. "But Nivel died with her soul intact." She reached out and put her hand on the boulder. "And so will I."

With that, she gave the boulder a push. It rolled sideways with a slow scrape and fell into the pit. The demon kept eye contact the entire time, smiling even as the boulder came down.

See you soon.

Then the boulder landed with a solid thunk, cutting him off completely.

Nico closed her eyes, feeling the warm sunlight on her skin, the wind against her bare shoulders, listening to the perfect silence of her world without the demon. She stood like that for a long moment, drinking it in. Then, with a deep breath, she turned her back on the boulder and began to walk across the plains, back toward the real world and the people who were waiting there for her, for good or ill.

CHAPTER 22

Time's almost up," Alric said.

Eli nodded, but didn't say anything. It had been four minutes since he'd shouted at the demon, and about two minutes since it had suddenly stopped moving. Now it was just standing there, staring stupidly at the sky with its hundreds of horrible eyes while its wings flapped slowly. Eli wasn't sure if this was a good development or a bad one in the long term, but at least it wasn't screaming anymore.

"Time," Alric said. "All right, Monpress, do it. Call the Shepherdess."

"No need," the Heart rumbled. "Look."

Eli and Alric both stepped backward as the demon, now grown twice as tall as even the tallest tree, began to dissolve. The hideous body broke apart, collapsing like a dried-out sandcastle to the destroyed forest floor. The darkness became simple black as the glowing eyes winked out one by one. Once it began to fall apart, the demon was gone in less than a minute, and everywhere it had touched, the valley began to grow back. A great torrent of dirt filled the sundered ground. Broken rocks repaired themselves, and though the toppled trees could not be righted again, new growth instantly began to spring up from the felled trunks.

The last to dissolve was the demon's head. It fell with a shudder, the jagged teeth breaking free before dissolving like everything else until only one part remained. Nico landed gently on the new grass where the demon had been standing only moments before. She was naked, but something moved to cover her as Eli watched, snaking over her body so quickly his eyes could barely keep up. It had covered half of her before he realized it was her coat stitching itself back together.

He started to laugh and ran to her, dropping to the ground just as she opened her eyes, which were no longer even slightly yellow, but a deep, deep brown.

She stared at him, confused. "Is Josef okay?"

"Yes," Eli said, grabbing her hand. "Are you okay?"

"Yes," Nico answered, smiling. "More than okay."

"So I see," Eli said. "You'll have to tell us how you did it later. Right now, it's time to collect. You just won a very nice bet for me."

Nico frowned. "I did?"

Eli just grinned and stood up, turning to Alric, who was still walking over.

"Well," Eli said, "I believe I just saved your bacon."

"What?" Alric stopped and crossed his arms. "You put all of our lives on the line for a long shot and I'm supposed to fall over myself thanking you?"

"I never said anything about a thank-you," Eli said. "I'm a thief, remember? I can't use thank-yous. No, we made a deal, Alric, Mr. Deputy Commander. I held up my end, but we never set down what you would pay if I won."

Alric gave him a dirty look. "And an uneaten world is not payment enough?"

"Of course not," Eli said. "Who do you think you're talking to?"

"Look," Alric said. "I don't think—"

Eli rolled over him. "There's also the little matter of you threatening to kill me earlier. Considering you're not even supposed to go near me, I think you should be more open to bargaining."

Alric started to say something, then he looked away. "What do you want?"

"Oh," Eli said, "just a tiny favor. Itsy-bitsy, won't take but ten minutes of your time."

"What?" Alric said, glowering.

Eli grinned from ear to ear and began to lay out his plan. By the time he was finished, Alric was ready to revisit the option of killing him.

Miranda sat on the edge of a broken building with Gin's head in her lap. She kept her mind perfectly blank, letting her calm be an anchor for her terrified spirits. The demon had stopped screaming ten minutes ago, but it took longer than that to bring her spirits out of their panic after something like this. Deep inside, however, Miranda couldn't help shuddering. She could still see the thing in her mind's eye, the hideous wings reaching up to claw the sky. If that's what it had looked like to her blind human eyes, she dreaded to think what her spirits had seen.

She had heard horrible stories of demons all her life, but not even in the most terrifying had there been anything like what she'd seen today. How could something like that even exist? Wasn't the League supposed to keep this sort of thing from happening?

When her spirits were finally calm again, Miranda opened her eyes. The League men were moving around her, putting things back together, just as they had in Mellinor. They worked in pairs, walking down the destroyed streets putting buildings back together with a few hushed words and a wave of their hands. Slorn was still down in the crater working on Nivel's seed with a pair of League men standing guard over him. Alric, however, was conspicuously absent. That bothered Miranda, but the League men didn't seem worried. Maybe he was still dealing with the other demon? She bit her lip. That seemed like a lot for one man to handle. She looked north, studying the trees where the enormous creature had been scarcely an hour ago. The forest was deathly still now, but she could still see the monster's shape above the trees, an aftervision burned into her eyes even when she closed them. Miranda sighed. She'd just have to deal with it for now. Things like this took time to fade away.

Anxious to be moving, Miranda left Gin where he was and walked over toward Slorn. The bear-headed man was handing the seed to the League men, who took it with gloved hands. One of them made one of their cuts in reality while the other put the seed in a black sack. When it was secure, they stepped through the portal, vanishing instantly. Slorn watched the space where they had been, his face distant as Miranda walked up to him.

"Did they make you give it up?" she asked.

"They would have," Slorn answered. "But I handed the seed over of my own volition. I had learned all I could hope to learn from it." He looked up, staring off at the snowcapped mountains. "That thing was never a part of my wife," he said quietly. "Nivel's soul has already been reborn. All I can do now is work to make this world a place that is worthy of her."

He reached into his pocket and pulled out a sealed letter. It was quite fat, several pages, and sealed with a large smear of wax. Slorn hefted it in his hand, and then tossed it high into the air. It spun a few times, and then took off like a bird, soaring through the air south and a little east.

Miranda whistled, impressed. "What was that?"

"A letter for my daughter," Slorn said. "Explaining where I went and why I'm not coming home. I'm not sure where she is, but the letter will find her sooner or later. Preferably later. I don't want her trying to follow me."

Miranda frowned. "You're not going home?"

"No," Slorn said, walking past her toward his wagon. "I stayed in isolation for Nivel. Now that she's gone, there is much for me to do. The world is changing, Spiritualist, and not for the better. A great demon eats an entire forest and the Shepherdess doesn't even send the Lord of Storms to deal with it." Slorn snorted as he pushed his spent cannon under the now dry and empty barrels. "I've dedicated ten years of my life to studying demonseeds, and yet the League has never asked for my findings, nor welcomed them when I forced the subject. Their Shepherdess has no interest in how to make things better. She only cares to keep things as they are, even as her world crumbles around her. So I'm taking my work to someone who will care."

"Who?" Miranda said.

"The Shaper Mountain," Slorn said, climbing into the wagon seat.

Miranda's eyes widened. She'd heard stories about the awakened mountain, but she'd never been there. No one had, except Shaper wizards. It was rumored they knew more about spirits than anyone, and if Slorn was an example, she believed it.

"Take me with you," she said.

He looked down at her, confused. "Why do you want to go?"

"Because I hate working for the Council with jerks like Sparrow," she said. "Because I'm sick of going back to Zarin empty-handed, and because I'm sworn to protect the Spirit World." She looked north again, tracing the outline of the demon that was still burned into her eyes. "After this afternoon, catching Eli Monpress to save the Spirit Court's pride feels almost petty." She turned back to Slorn. "Let's just say my priorities have taken a pretty significant shift in the right direction. If you're taking your knowledge of demonseeds to the Shapers to make sure things like that don't happen again, then I'm going with you."

Slorn leaned back. "And what of your orders? What about Sara and the Council?"

Miranda rolled her eyes. "The Council can choke on its paperwork for all I care, and Sara can go back to her menagerie. The only command I follow is Master Banage's, and he would tell me to go."

Slorn smiled, showing his sharp, yellow teeth. "Yes, I believe he would. Very well, you can come if you like. I warn you, we'll be moving quickly over hard terrain. I hope you're ready."

"Travel we can do," Miranda said. "Just say the word."

Slorn's spider-legged wagon stood up with a creak, and he turned it back toward the cliff where his other wagon waited. Gin was already up by the time Miranda reached him, his long body pulled in a great bowing stretch.

"So we're tossing our lot in with the bear," he said. "Good. I like him much better than the idiot bird."

"Glad you feel that way," Miranda said, jumping onto his back. "Because we're in deep now."

"Like we ever do anything halfway." Gin snorted.

Miranda gave him a friendly kick, and he bounded forward, hopping over the destroyed city after Slorn.

"There they go," Tesset said, watching the ghosthound through a hole in the wreckage.

"You see?" Sparrow said. "I told you she would turn traitor."

Tesset looked over his shoulder, but Sparrow wasn't talking to him. He was talking to the ball of blue glowing glass in his palm.

"She *is* Banage's little pet." Sara's voice pulsed through the orb. "I'd hardly expect her to do otherwise."

"Well, what do you want us to do about it?" Sparrow said. "Eli's gone, the Heart is gone, and now Slorn's off to who knows where. Even if the Spiritualist hadn't run off, this whole bloody mission would still be a disaster. I say we cut our losses and head back to Zarin before Izo finds us and sends our skins to Whitefall's office as a warning."

There was a huff over the orb that Tesset recognized as Sara blowing a stream of smoke into the air. "There's no call for such drama," she said. "And there's no call for scrapping the mission. Honestly, you just got up there. Coming back now would be a waste. I want to know what Slorn is up to and what kind of mission he found to inspire Banage's girl wonder. Follow them."

"Sara!" Sparrow cried.

"Do it," she snapped. "I'm cutting off now. Whitefall just sent a page. I have to go to some sort of emergency meeting in ten minutes and it will take me at least that long to get up to the hearing room. I'll check in tomorrow to see how you're doing, and I don't want to hear any complaints, Sparrow. Don't forget, there's still a nice-sized bounty on your head I could turn in to Whitefall any time I like, and they don't hand out prison sentences for what you've done."

"How could I forget," Sparrow grumbled, but the orb had already gone dim. He glared at it for a moment more and then shoved the Relay into the pocket of his ruined silk jacket. "Well, isn't this just lovely?"

"It is," Tesset said. "It's been awhile since I had a good old-fashioned hunt."

Sparrow harrumphed and ran his fingers through his dusty hair.

Tesset watched him, frowning. "Why didn't you tell her about the demons?"

"Because I'm trying to get out of here, remember?" Sparrow said. "If I'd told her, she would have asked us to investigate that as well, and I'd rather her hand me to the bounty office on a platter than go anywhere near that place."

"She'll find out," Tesset said. "And she's going to be mad."

"We'll worry about that when it comes," Sparrow said, giving up on trying to tame the dusty mess on his head. "Come on, let's get this over with."

Tesset nodded and followed him out of the maze of broken buildings. He was grinning. A hunt, and a fine quarry too. Just what he needed to combat the city softness he'd been sinking into. He needed something to push him forward, because he wasn't getting any younger. Somewhere out there, Den was waiting for him. When they met again, Tesset knew he would have only one chance to show his master that his lesson had been well learned. He had to be ready.

Clenching his fists, Tesset started jogging toward where they'd last seen the ghosthound. Sparrow stumbled along behind him, sending a stream of curses into the late-afternoon breeze.

Sara marched up the stairs of the fourth and largest of the Council Citadel's seven towers. Servants in flawless white pressed themselves against the walls as she passed, peeking at her curiously from under their lowered lashes. She bit her pipe and kept walking.

The meeting room was already full when she got there. Council officials milled beside the catering table, enjoying the array of little sandwiches, cheese plates, and brandy aperitifs that the Council demanded even for its emergency meetings. Sara pushed right past them, going straight for a tall man with close-cropped silver hair holding court by the picture windows, the only person in the room who actually mattered.

"Whitefall," she said, nodding as the crowd parted to let her through. "I'm extremely busy. What's this all about?"

Merchant Prince Alber Whitefall, Lord Protector and Grand Marshal of Zarin, gave her a politician's bright smile. "I was hoping you could tell me, Sara dear." He touched her shoulder, guiding her in beside him. "I received an urgent message from the League of Storms. Normally, they fall under your jurisdiction, but this time the message was addressed specifically to me. Very odd. Haven't I asked you not to smoke in here?"

Sara took a pointedly long draw from her pipe. "What does the League want with you?"

"I don't know, the reasons were quite vague, but the letter specifically said that I was to call a meeting with you, Phillipe, and all the upper Council. And since you've always stressed that the League of Storms is never to be ignored, I did."

"Phillipe?" Sara gave him a skeptical look. "The bounty office windbag? What does the League want with him?"

"I'm sure I don't know," Whitefall said. "But that's my cousin you're talking about. Only I get to call him a windbag." He waved and smiled. Across the room, the topic of their conversation jumped, and then hesitantly waved back before returning to his plate of sandwiches.

Sara rolled her eyes. "Well, since we're all here, can we get this mystery meeting under way? I have work to do."

"Not quite yet," Whitefall said, adjusting the lapels of his black dinner suit. "We're still missing the representative from the Spirit Court. And, of course, whomever the League is sending to enlighten us."

"Spirit Court?" Sara said as the doors opened. She looked over her shoulder just in time to see Etmon Banage himself sweep into the room.

"Powers," she muttered, smoking furiously.

Etmon saw her as well, but to his credit the only change was a slight hardening of his eyes as he approached to pay his respects to the Merchant Prince.

"Lord Whitefall," he said with a nod. "What is the emergency?"

"I think we're about to find out," Whitefall said, glancing toward the far wall. Sara and Banage both turned to see a thin white line dropping down through the air. When it reached the floor, a man stepped through. Sara winced. Alric looked furious. He also looked worse for wear. His face was badly bruised, and he walked with a limp. Of course, in his line of work, that wasn't unusual. What was unusual was the man he was dragging behind him.

By the time the white doorway closed, the room was silent. Everyone was watching the Deputy Commander of the League of Storms and the man dragging on the floor behind him. When he was sure he had everyone's attention, Alric tossed the man forward. He fell sprawling, leaving thick smears of dirt on the silk carpet.

"Ladies and gentlemen of the Council of Thrones," Alric said through gritted teeth. "I bring you Izo Barns, also known as Izo the Bandit King, wanted by the Council for one hundred and fifty thousand gold standards."

The man on the floor curled into a ball, moaning softly to himself with his eyes wide open like a horrified child. Alric just stood there with his arms crossed over his chest.

It was Sara who recovered first. "What's wrong with him?"

"Nothing," Alric said. "He's just had a bit of a fright. But it doesn't matter. His bounty is good whether he's dead or alive, correct?"

This question was directed at Phillipe Whitefall, though it took a few moments for the bounty office director to realize that.

"Yes," he said, his voice trembling as he bent over for a closer look at Izo's terror-stricken face. "Izo, scourge of the north, wanted dead or alive for one hundred and fifty thousand. But how did you catch him?"

Alric closed his eyes and took a deep, calming breath. "I didn't. Izo the Bandit King was captured by Eli Monpress. I'm only here to deliver him."

There was a collective gasp around the room, and then everyone started talking at once.

"Hold on!" Banage's voice rose over all others. "What right does a wanted criminal and enemy of the Council have to a bounty?"

"Well," Phillipe Whitefall said, wiping his brow with his handkerchief. "There's no rule about who can turn in bounties. Keeping them open to lawbreakers actually encourages derision within the criminal element."

"That's all well and good," Sara said. "But how does Eli intend to claim his hundred and fifty thousand? Is he coming to Zarin to collect it himself?"

"Of course not," Alric said with a long-suffering sneer. "Monpress wishes for the reward to be added to his own bounty."

This time the room went silent.

Merchant Prince Whitefall stepped forward. "You want us to add a hundred fifty thousand to Monpress's bounty? But that would bring it to..." He looked at his cousin.

"Two hundred and forty-eight thousand, your grace," Phillipe answered.

"Two hundred and forty-eight thousand," Whitefall said, jabbing his drink at Alric. "A number like that is on the level of nations. We can't pin that sort of power on a thief. What kind of fools do you take us for?"

"I am only the messenger," Alric said. "Will you combine the bounties or not?"

"It's not like we have much of a choice," Whitefall said. "If we deny him, we break our own laws. I'm not about to set a nonpayment precedent that will jeopardize our highly successful bounty system."

"I take no more joy than you in this," Alric said. "Monpress will be watching for his new posters. If they do not show up within the month, the world will know that the Council does not pay its debts."

"No need for threats," Whitefall said, sipping his drink. "The bounty will be adjusted, may the Powers save us all."

Alric nodded and turned around. The white slit in the air opened immediately, and he stepped through into what looked like a destroyed town. Sara got a glimpse of shattered buildings and mountains in the distance before it closed again. She frowned and made a note to check with Sparrow to see if he'd heard anything about demons in the north.

By this point, guards had been called in to apprehend the man on the carpet, but it was hardly necessary. Izo was limp as a rag doll, his face still frozen in a mask of fear. Sara watched as the guards dragged him away, then turned to find Whitefall deep in conversation with Phillipe and half a dozen representatives from the major Council Kingdoms. It wasn't worth the political capital to butt in, so Sara turned, walked to the window, and looked out over Zarin as the white buildings turned golden under the setting sun.

"Can you believe this?" a familiar, angry voice said behind her.

She turned as Etmon Banage stepped in beside her, his sharp face scowling as he stared at the city below.

"What?" she said. "Our being forced to see each other more than once a year?"

Banage's glare could have melted the glass. "That's not what I meant, and you know it."

Sara took a long draw off her pipe before answering his question properly. "I thought it was a fairly clever plan."

Banage bristled. "It's a disgrace to the Council and the entire bounty system."

"Good thing you don't care about the Council, then."

"The Council speaks for us all," Banage growled. "I'm in it whether I want to be or not. What I don't understand is how the boy did it. I can't even get the League of Storms to give my Spirit Court the time of day, and here's Eli with Alric himself on a string."

Sara smiled. "Impressive, isn't it?"

Banage stared at her. "How can you think that?"

"How can you not?" Sara snapped. "He's your son too, Etmon."

She whirled around and stomped toward the door, sending

officials scrambling to get out of her way. Banage stared after her, shocked beyond retort. When he came to enough to realize he was being stared at, he turned back to the window and glowered out over the city as the lamp-lighters began their rounds.

Benehime sat in her white nothing, staring, as always, at her orb when a man appeared in front of her. There was no opening portal, no door in the air. One moment there was nothing, and the next he was standing there, glaring down at her.

Shepherdess.

Benehime's white eyes narrowed, and she pushed her orb aside. The man's white face was that of an old but active man with a pure-white beard that fell to his knees. His hair was the same, a snowy cascade that hung around him like a robe. His white hands were folded in front of him, the white fingers long and skilled, and his eyes were the same white as her own.

Weaver, she said. *You're out of your element.*

You left me no choice. The Weaver's deep voice filled the air. *Not when you take such risks.* He looked at the orb. Benehime followed his gaze to the ruined valley where the demon had woken.

I had everything under control.

Did you? The Weaver's beard did nothing to hide his frown. *It didn't look that way from where I stood.*

It is not your place to be looking at all, Benehime said fiercely. *Your place is to tend the shell. The sphere and everything inside is my domain.*

So it is, the Weaver said. *But when your risks threaten the shell, they become mine as well. What were you thinking, letting a demonseed grow that large? You put everything in danger, and not for the first time, I hear. Your spirits have been complaining to me. They say you ignore your duty, that you play favorites to the point of exclusion. Have you forgotten why you are here?*

I forget nothing! Benehime shouted. *It is you who has forgotten his place, Benehin! Now get out. You have no right to order me around.*

And you have no power to make me leave, the Weaver said. *We three, Shepherdess, Weaver, and Hunter, are the children of the Creator, equals in all things. There is no power you can wield that I cannot counter. You may force your spirits to grovel at your feet, but you cannot touch so much as a hair on my beard.*

Benehime stood up, eye to white eye with the Weaver. *This is still my sphere. It is by my will alone that you can exist at all in this place, and I am done listening to the hysterical ravings of a cowardly old man. Leave, now, before I force you out.*

The Weaver stayed perfectly still.

Eyes still locked with hers, he stretched out his white hand and laid it against the edge of her domain. As if in answer, the dim shapes of clawed hands began to gather, their edges pressing hard against the wall, scraping at the fabric that separated her world from theirs. Far in the distance, the screaming grew louder.

The shell is a delicate thing, the Weaver said, stroking the thin barrier as the claws scraped against his hand. *I can maintain it against assault from without, but not from within as well.* He glared hard at her. *Remember, sister, the Hunter's day of rest comes soon. When that happens, it will be two against one. I suggest you think very carefully about what happened today, Benehime. We have served together for a long, long time. I would hate to lose you over something as petty as a favorite, sister.*

I forget nothing, Benehime whispered. *Get out.*

As silently and suddenly as he had appeared, the Weaver vanished. Benehime stared at the place where he had been for a long time. Eventually, her white eyes drifted past it, to the edge of her domain and the long, clawed hands still clustering where the Weaver's hand had rested. With a furious snarl, she turned back to her sphere and buried herself in her world.

ACKNOWLEDGMENTS

Thank you to Peggy, Steve, Judith, and Rob. This book would not exist without everything you do.

extras

meet the author

Alyssa Alig

RACHEL AARON was born in Atlanta, GA. After a lovely, geeky childhood full of books and public television, and then an adolescence spent feeling awkward about it, she went to the University of Georgia to pursue English literature with an eye toward getting her PhD. Upper division coursework cured her of this delusion, and she graduated in 2004 with a BA and a job, which was enough to make her mother happy. She currently lives in a '70s house-of-the-future in Athens, GA, with her loving husband, overgrown library, and small, brown dog. Find out more about the author at www.rachelaaron.net.

introducing

If you enjoyed
THE LEGEND OF ELI MONPRESS,
look out for

THE SPIRIT WAR
The Legend of Eli Monpress

by Rachel Aaron

The old swordsman was kneeling in the dirt, blowing on the embers of last night's fire when he saw the boy approaching. He paused, keeping low to the dusty ground as he watched the boy start up the hill towards his campsite. The boy was a tall one, skinny and fair but with the large shoulders and wide ribs that spoke of the large man he'd become once he finished growing into them. The swordsman pegged him at seventeen, maybe a little younger, but he wore the two short swords at his hips like he knew how to use them.

The swordsman sat back with long sigh and glanced at the great, black sword stabbed in the sand beside him.

"They never give up, do they?"

"No," the sword answered. "Thank the Powers. I think we'd both die of boredom if they stopped coming."

The swordsman sighed. "Speak for yourself."

The sword didn't answer, but the ground creaked as it settled itself deeper. The old swordsman shook his head and sat back to wait.

It took the boy the better part of an hour to climb to the top of the old swordsman's hill. At last, he pulled himself over the final boulders and stepped panting into the circle of dusty brush outside the cave where the swordsman made his home. He caught his breath and straightened up, fixing his eyes on the swordsman with a challenging glare.

"I'm looking for Milo Burch," he announced. "You him?"

The old swordsman frowned. "Why would a boy like you be looking for an old has been like Burch?"

The boy stepped forward, planting his feet in first position. "I've heard he's the greatest swordsman in the world, wielder of the legendary Heart of War. I've come to challenge him."

"Really?" The old man rubbed his graying beard. "How did you get here?"

The boy paused, thrown for a second. "I walked."

The swordsman looked at him, and then looked out over the scrubby, flat desert that stretched as far as he could see in all directions. "You walked?" He said. "Alone?"

"Yes, alone." The boy's voice was growing frustrated. "Are you Milo Burch or not? I was told he lived out here. If you're not him, then I'll be going."

"Let's say I am," the swordsman said. "Who would be asking?"

The boy straightened up. "I am Josef Liechten, and I demand a duel for the title of greatest swordsman."

The swordsman started to laugh. "You demand it, do you?"

He choked out at last, wiping his eyes. "I'm afraid you'll be a little disappointed. 'Greatest Swordsman''s not a hat you can pass around, and it's not like there's anyone out here to see your victory over an old man." The wind blew as he spoke, its lonely whistle a sharp reminder of the vast emptiness around them.

The boy set his jaw stubbornly. "Doesn't matter," he said. "Are you going to fight or not? I didn't walk all the way out here to stand around talking."

The old swordsman stood with a deep sigh and walked over to the scrabbly tree that grew just beside the little space he used as his fire pit. "You certainly sound determined, Josef Liechten," he said, reaching up to break a dry branch. "I'm too old to go tumbling around with kids, but I can see that trying to talk you out of this duel nonsense would be nothing but a waste of breath."

The boy, Josef, nodded.

The swordsman turned, holding up the branch he'd just taken from the tree. "How about we make a deal? If you can break this, I'll fight you."

Josef stared at the stick in the old man's hand. It was a sad thing, knobby and dead, its ends already cracking under the force of the old man's grip.

"I think it would be a greater challenge not to break it," he said, his voice turning cautious. "Is this some kind of trick?"

"If it was, I certainly wouldn't tell you," the old man said, his tanned, leathery face breaking into a grin. "Then again, the greatest swordsman in the world would hardly have to resort to tricks, don't you think?"

Josef glowered and shifted his feet. "All I have to do is break the stick," he said slowly. "Just break it, and you'll fight me for real?"

The old swordsman nodded. "That's it."

Josef scowled, and then he drew his swords. They were good work, the old man noticed. Well balanced and a good size for Josef's reach. It seemed the boy knew something. That was good. He was too old to waste energy on idiots.

"Come at me whenever you're ready," he said, lifting his stick.

With one final, annoyed look, Josef charged.

It was a good assault, a straight on rush and then, three steps in, a feint to the left. Milo Burch stayed still just long enough to let the boy think he'd fallen for it and then quietly ducked out of the way. The boy charged past him and stopped, boots skidding on the lose dirt. He turned around, panting. Mile smiled at him, resting the stick on his shoulder.

"That was good," he said. "Perhaps you should try—"

Josef was running before he could finish, cutting around to Milo's left. Again, Milo let him get just close enough to commit to the blow before ducking down. Josef's sword whistle over his head, and the boy stumbled past him. Josef cursed loudly, and Milo stepped right to avoid the second sword that thrust from below. He spun around as Josef carried the thrust through, bopping the boy on the head with the stick as he passed.

Josef yelped in surprise and stumbled, falling to the ground. Milo sighed.

"If I'd taken your duel, that would have been the end, you know," he said, swinging his stick. "I won't think less of you if you want to give up."

He'd barely finished when Josef dropped the sword in his left hand. The knife came a second later. Milo opened his hand, letting the stick drop in his grip just before the knife sliced through the air where it had been. As soon as the knife was past, he side stepped again as Josef followed through with a lunge at his legs.

"Again, not bad," Milo said, grinning. "Why don't you—"

"Shut up!" Josef shouted, grabbing for the stick with his now empty left hand.

Milo stepped neatly out of his reach, making Josef stumble as he over balanced. The boy was panting now, his face red from the sun and slick with sweat.

"You're not a bad fighter, you know," Milo said gently. "Surely you're good enough to see the difference between us. You know you can't win, there's no point in pushing yourself."

Josef scowled at him, breathing hard, and then flicked another knife right at Milo's hand.

This went on all afternoon. Josef would attack and Milo would step out of the way. Josef never attacked the same way twice, but the end result never changed. As day wore into evening, Josef's lunges grew slower, but he did not stop until finally, as the sun sank below the horizon, he tripped and fell and did not get up again.

Milo leaned on his stick. "Are we done?"

Josef didn't answer. He just lay in the dirt, panting. Milo sighed and set the stick on the ground beside the fire. He walked over and, shoved his hands under Josef's arms, began dragging him toward the cave.

"What are you doing?" Josef gasped.

"Keeping you from dying of dehydration," Milo said. "I also imagine you would like some food."

Josef stared at him. "But I'm your enemy," he said, the words wheezing.

"You're the only one who said that," Milo said. "I was sitting here minding my own business." He dumped Josef unceremoniously on the floor of the cave. "Do you want some water or not?"

"Yes, please," Josef said, lying flat on his back. "Thank you."

"Polite," Milo said, handing him the water skin. "I like that."

Josef was too focused on drinking to answer.

He drank the entire water skin and half of another, and then ate the five loaves of bread that were meant to keep Milo the next week. He was still chewing when he fell asleep. When he was sure the boy was out, Milo tossed his blanket over the boy and walked out to sit beside the great black sword that was still staked beside the fire.

"What do you think?"

"He is stubborn as a rock," the sword said. "He's slow, his movements lack subtly, and he has no grace."

Milo arched a white eyebrow. "Since when do you care about grace?"

"A minimum is required," the sword grumbled. "Still, he lasted five hours. That's the best yet."

"It is, isn't it," Milo said, rubbing his aching arms. Dodging all day was harder than it used to be. "He's spirit deaf, you know."

He felt the sword's ambivalence brush over him like a shrug. "I've had many deaf wielders. Hearing isn't what matters. It's everything else."

"Well, you'll have to stop being so picky," Milo said quietly. "We don't have much time left."

"I have all the time in the world," the sword answered. "Still, we'll see. Tomorrow, maybe."

"Tomorrow," Milo nodded, lying back to watch the moon rising over the desert.

Josef woke with the sun in his eyes and the old man standing over him, poking him in the shoulder with the hated stick.

"Morning," Milo said, grinning.

Josef smiled back, and then, fast as he could, rolled to grab the stick. For a second it was in his grasp before the old man snatched it away.

"Nice try." He sounded genuinely impressed. "Shall we begin?"

Josef pushed himself up, wincing as every muscle in his body protested, and reached for his swords.

"Ready."

They fought all morning with nothing to show. Everything Josef tried, the old man countered. The desert sun was brutal, burning Josef's skin through his shirt. Sweat soaked everything he owned, but he did not let himself stop. The old man had yet to admit it, but there was no more question in Josef's mind. He was fighting Milo Burch, the greatest swordsman in the world, famous across all the Council Kingdoms. It had to be him, no one else could be this fast. This was the reason he'd traveled all the way to the desert, why he'd walked through the heat and the burning sand for two days. It didn't matter if Burch was toying with him, he could not lose now. Not when he was this close.

Noon came and Josef kept going. His movements were jerky, and he could scarcely see through the burning sweat in his eyes. His limbs were so tired he actually dropped his sword a few times, but he pushed on until, at last, there was simply nothing left to push.

He didn't realize he'd fallen until he saw Milo standing over him, pressing a water skin to his cracked, dry lips.

"You know," he said softly. "There's a fine line between being determined and being an idiot. If you keep this up I won't have to lift a sword to kill you. You'll kill yourself."

Josef choked on the water. He tried to sit up, but he had no strength left in his back. In the end, he settled for lying back and letting the water trickle down his throat.

"Josef," Milo said. "Give up, would you? When you're old as I am, you've seen enough of the world to recognize its patterns. You think you're unique, but I've seen you dozens of times. Let me guess, you were the best swordsman in your village or wherever you came from. Swordwork came as easy to you as breathing, and soon there was no one who could give you a challenge. You took to wandering, fighting whoever was strong enough to teach you something. You've probably defeated a hundred men, haven't you?"

"More," Josef croaked.

Milo shrugged. "Your problem is you're young. Impatient. You're think that by beating me you can somehow jump to the top, but you can't. You can't beat me, and you can't jump ahead. The sword must be earned, Josef. Strength that comes easily is no strength at all."

Josef opened his eyes, squinting in the bright light. "I know that," he whispered. "But I'm not fighting for strength."

The old man's face was too far away for him to focus on, but Josef felt him frown. "What are you fighting for?"

"I hurt a lot of people when I decided to be a swordsman," Josef wheezed. "Let a lot of people down. That's why I have to be the strongest."

"Do these people care if you're the strongest?" Milo said quietly.

Josef shook his head. "But they will," he said. "I have to show them—"

His words broke into coughs as he choked on the water again. It didn't matter, though. Milo finished for him.

"You have to be the strongest to give meaning to their suffering," he said, tilting his head.

Josef nodded, breathing deep as the coughing subsided. "I was the one who left. If I'm not the best, then I hurt her for no reason."

"That's a dangerous way to think," Milo said quietly. "There's a good chance you will never be the best. That you will die alone and forgotten, remembered only as a disappointment."

"I don't believe in chance," Josef whispered. He looked at

Milo and raised his sword. His hand shook as he lifted it, the sword sliding in his weakening grip. Josef forced himself to be calm, to be strong one last moment. The shaking slowed, and then, for one breath, stopped. That was when Josef moved.

He tossed his sword into the air, over Milo's head. The old man's eye went wide, but Josef grabbed the old man's wrist where he was holding the water bottle, pinning him in place. Trapped, the old swordsman could only watch as Josef's short sword flew through the air, spinning in wobbly arcs, and landed behind him, on top of the stick he'd laid aside when he knelt to help Josef. The blade landed sideways, bouncing away the moment it stuck, but the branch was old and brittle, and it was enough. The stick cracked with a soft pop, breaking into two ragged halves.

For a moment, all Milo could do was sit there, watching the broken remains of his stick rocking in the hot desert wind. Then he turned and looked at Josef with a strange, bemused expression on his weather worn face. Josef grinned back.

"I never stop fighting," he said. "I'm holding you to your word, Milo Burch."

"And I never go back on my word," Milo said with a sigh. "Tomorrow, then. At dawn."

Josef nodded and released the old man's hand. He grabbed the water skin and drank until he drained it. When he was finished, he crawled across the baked ground and collapsed on blanket just inside the cave, falling asleep instantly.

Milo picked up the broken pieces of his stick. When he had them both, he sat down with his back against the broad slab of scarred black metal that stood rooted in the sand and began feeding the pieces into the fire.

When Josef woke the next morning, the cave was empty. He took a long drink from the water barrel and helped himself to a breakfast of bread and dried apples from the swordsman's supplies. When he finished, he grabbed his sword from where he'd dropped it and walked out onto the hilltop.

Milo Burch was already there, sitting beside the now cold fire pit with his back against the massive, black metal shape that dominated the open space. As Josef stepped into the sandy ring around the fire, Milo held out the sword Josef had thrown to break the stick. Josef took it, sheathing it opposite its brother on his hip. When they were both ready, he took his stance and waited for Milo to begin.

The old swordsman stood with a sigh, rubbing the small of his back as he straightened. But his hands were empty as he turned to face Josef.

"Wait," Josef cried. "Where's your sword? I'm here to fight the master of the Heart of War. Let's see it."

Milo shook his head and laid his hand on the wrapped handle of the great metal monster in the ground beside him. Josef's eyes widened. The black slab was enormous, he couldn't even think of what it must weigh. A man Milo's size shouldn't even have had the muscle to lift something that heavy, and yet the old swordsman pulled it up easy as a farmer pulling a weed out of new tilled dirt.

"I thought we agreed, no more games," Josef said. "What is that thing? Where's your sword? Where's the Heart of War?"

"This is the Heart of War," Milo said, swinging the black blade in front of him.

Josef almost laughed out loud. "*That* is the Heart of War? That, that *iron post* is the greatest awakened blade ever made? You're kidding. It doesn't even have a sharp edge. It couldn't cut paper."

Milo smiled. "A sword cuts whatever its swordsman wants it to cut. The Heart is no different."

Josef scowled. "We'll see."

They took their positions on either side of the dead fire. Josef readied his blades, keeping the man's movements from their earlier fights clear in his mind. He almost thought the old man should have stuck to the stick. There was no way he could move fast enough carrying that enormous weight. There had to be a trick or something. Maybe the sword was hollow? Something that large couldn't be solid metal, not if a human was meant to lift it. Still, the few awakened blades he'd beaten had all had their own oddities. He'd just have to push and see what happened.

"You know," Milo said. "You don't have to go through with this. I meant it when I said you were a good swordsman. Give you a few years and you could very well become the best, but not yet. The Heart won't let me hold back. You should stop now, while you still can."

"I told you before," Josef said. "I never stop. I can't stop." He raised his sword. "Guard yourself."

The words had barely left his mouth when he lunged. He pushed forward, slamming his feet down faster than he ever had before. He would only get once chance. He'd learned the first day that he couldn't beat the old man in speed, but yesterday he'd proven he could still trick him. He'd seen the strain in Milo as he stood up. The days of fighting had taken their toll on his old body. Now, weighed down with that enormous sword, especially after so long fighting with a stick that weighed nothing, there would be a hesitation in his first strike as his body got used to the weight difference. That was when Josef had to strike.

He rushed forward, boots pounding on the sand, watching the old man's arm for the moment he lifted the sword to parry. He had to parry. What else could you do with a sword that big?

But the old man didn't move. He just stood there, watching as Josef came closer and closer. When he was one step away, Josef realized he might have been wrong. The old man might be too slow to catch him. There might be no need to wait for the hesitation in the parry. Already his swords were racing for the man's torso, one high, one low, and for one shining moment, Josef thought he might actually land the blow before Milo could move.

One moment, that's all it was. And in that moment, Milo Burch attacked.

It happened so fast Josef couldn't see the blows, but he felt them. There were three in the space of a second. The first shattered his left sword, the second broke his right, and the third hit him dead across the chest. That last blow knocked the breath from his lungs and sent him flying backwards. He hit the side of the hill like a stone hurled from a catapult. For a moment all he could feel was the rough ground on his back and the strange feeling of air against his chest through his sundered shirt, and then pain like he'd never felt before slammed down, and he hit the ground with a sound that would have been a scream had he still had breath.

He floundered in the dirt, his whole body convulsing. Somehow, he ended up on his back again. That was when he saw it, though it took him several moments to realize that the bloody mess he was looking at was his own chest.

A deep, perfect cut ran from his left shoulder to his right hip. It was perfectly straight, as though he'd been cut by a razor, but so deep he had to look away. When he turned his head, he saw Milo crouching beside him, leaning on the Heart of War as he bent down to whisper in Josef's ear.

"Worst pain you've ever felt, isn't it?"

Gasping, Josef could only nod.

"This is the pain of defeat," the old swordsman said. "You are dying. I have defeated you utterly. Even if I were to bind your wound right now, there's no saving your life. This is the end. So now I'll ask you, was it worth it?"

Josef looked at him and wheezed, "Yes."

Milo paused. "And if you'd known this was how it ended, would you still have broken the stick?"

"Yes," Josef said, his voice little more than a grating of breath. "I would rather die trying than ever give up."

"Is that so?" Milo said. "Then prove it. Take another breath."

Josef grimaced and looked down at his sundered chest. He tried to talk, but he had no air for the words.

"I can't," he mouthed.

"If you can't, then all your struggles to this point, all the pain you've caused, it's all for nothing," Milo said, his voice taunt. "Take another breath, Josef Liechten."

Josef closed his eyes and focused on his lungs. For an eternity, nothing happened. His body was going stiff. Nothing would obey him. He concentrated, pouring every speck of his consciousness into that one action. The pain was so intense now he could barely think, but he felt his chest rise and fall, and suddenly he had air again.

His eyes popped open just in time to see Milo's face break into a grand smile. The old man held out his hand, offering something. Josef blinked, it was dark and heavy and, he could see now, larger than it looked.

"If you walk the path of the swordsman, you will feel this pain hundreds of times," Milo said. "You will never know a moment's peace, even if you move to a hill in the middle of the desert. Your life will be brutish, violent, and most likely short, but it will also be glorious. This is what it means to live your life on the sword. You said you would rather die trying than give up. Now you must try living, or die. If you want to live, Josef Liechten, then reach out as far as you can and take your sword. Rise a swordsman, the master of the Heart of War, or do not rise at all."

His words fluttered against Josef's ears. The world felt very far away now. Even the pain was going now, but Josef could still see the black shape of the sword hovering high above him. With the last of his will, he lifted his arm. He saw his hand moving above him, his fingers stretching up to clutch the wrapped handle. The moment his fingers made contact, a voice deeper and broader than any voice he'd ever heard spoke through him.

Welcome to your rebirth, swordsman. The words were more vibration than sound, but they were clear as carvings in his mind. *As you gave your life to become a swordsman, so did I give my life to become a sword. We are the same, you and I. Will you fight with me?*

Josef could not speak, but the answer echoed in his mind.

I will.

It is done, the voice said. *Welcome to your mountain, master of the Heart of War.*

As the voice faded from his mind, so did the pain. Strength like Josef had never felt flowed into his body. All at once he could breath again, his eyes were clear and open to the world. His arms moved without pain, and he was able to stand enough to let Milo guide him back to the cave and wrap him in the blankets, all the while dragging the massive black blade behind him.

He fell asleep the moment Milo lay him flat, the Heart of War clutched to his chest. How long he slept, Josef never knew, but when he woke it was night and Milo Burch was gone. The cave was empty except for the bloody blankets Josef lay on, the water barrel, and a large supply of food. A loaf of bread and a water skin lay on the ground beside his head, and Josef ate